Threads of Chaos

Book of the South

J. Michael Gorday

For:
Dave, Dan, Shannon, Steve, Ken, and Dale.
For Melissa for all the years.
And for Kimberly, who helped me remember what happiness
feels like.

Author's Note

When I began this journey many years ago, I envisioned a story that had many parts to it. Once I had written my final draft, I had over a thousand pages of text. Due to publishing restraints, the original manuscript had to be split into two separate books. Which worked out fairly well, in the end.

This book, subtitled, The Book of the South runs concurrent with the second book which will be called The Book of the North (obviously) and will follow different characters as they move through the Threads of Chaos timeline.

My hope is that they will not create confusion in this format (although, given the idea, might be advantageous.) and that both story lines will flow together as they were intended when originally written.

Please enjoy this story as I have in its creation.

Arquilon

Vistan

Calif

The Wound

New Sea

Margain

Hestaff

The Rift

White Rock Mountains

Tergaard

Nur

Scandin

Oth
Salar

Tippon Ya

Leera

The Broken Lands

The Broken Lands

Prologue

Death Moon Risen

Year 2557; Hedrican Calendar

The two moons, Sun'arr and Cos'arr, conjoined now, one behind the other in a yearly phenomenon that marked the height of winter, blocked the disc that was the sun, casting the land in a dusky twilight as the sword thrust forward. As one, those hundreds of women skilled in the Powers of the World, Earthmothers, themselves spread thinly through the lands, pitched forward grasping their chests in pain that only hinted of the agony to come.

Crimson sprayed from around the blade of the murderer, its supernatural heat ruining the metal's temper and scalding the rock where it splattered. The Threadbearer slid from the melting sword, a smile across old features, eyes quickly losing their glitter. As he fell, the very earth upon which his blood spilt reached up to cradle him in a loving embrace while the robed killer stared and the first of the world's shivers caused the sand beneath their feet to jump like raindrops in a puddle.

Blue arcs danced among the grit, snapping and popping. Above, the conjoined moons, Cos'arr, in front, which meant 'death' in the old tongue, the only witness to the murderer's greatest achievement. Looking from directly overhead, it was a black eye wreathed in flame. In no time, the body of the dying Guardian disappeared forever into the rock as if it were sinking into water.

The edges of the remaining hole began to flow and twist, shaping itself with undulating ripples. Then, liquid cracks snaked out in all directions. The air hummed with the charge of thousands of lightning bolts, while above, dark wisps of cloud crawled, forming a slow vortex centered on the dark face of the moons. Finally, the murderer moved sluggishly away from the shifting grave in which the Threadbearer disappeared. Deep down, far down below the mountain, the Earth groaned.

The weakest of Earthmothers died with screams in their throats. Those standing atop the Steps of Ellynthryll amidst the armies of the North where the Owl was finally Revealed while the vast hordes of Gelron the Deadlord crashed upon them like the surf, turned away from the carnage and looked westward with visages of fear and agony. By the time the first faint shivers reached them, Gelron's armies began falling away like wheat before the scythe, the Deadlord having been struck down as foretold; his power lost to the coming rage.

The Earth groaned again, sending tendrils of rock writhing into the air, forcing the killer to backpedal quickly, only to trip on the long robes he wore and start tumbling down the path which brought him there. The first of the Earth's Blood burst from the growing wound, like an overfull bladder, splattering molten rock much as the wound of the Threadbearer had. A great blob landed onto the back of the killer and ate into him quickly, making him shriek and squirm, blotting out the yammering in his head; his master's persistent questions. He scrabbled against the rock, full awareness of his impending doom shunting the pain away enough to get his feet under him. Another grinding moan shook the mountain and the rock skin around the thrashing gash waved outward, bowling the robed assassin forward onto the path.

The air sizzled with blue-white lightning, globes and forks that formed in the dimness and bobbed and flashed. He scrambled behind a huge stone to hide but quickly changed his mind when the boulder began sinking into the mountain. A gout of red flame shot up from the growing pit, throwing a black cloud of smoke billowing upward toward the churning vortex. He dove away, a squeal of terror flying from beneath his hood when he found his foot caught by the liquid earth. The rock's grip was terrible and slow in releasing his boot. Heat rolled down the disintegrating path and radiated up from below, sucking the air from lungs and shriveling eyes.

Crowlin, the Thread Cutter, servant of the being called Blackskull, ran blindly down the incline, as much to get away from the laughter in his head as to escape the growing maelstrom. Behind him, the wound continued to thrash, drawing more deeply the groans of the world below. Several times lightning sizzled around Crowlin, searing him, burning his robes, making him stumble and cry out. When the mountain fell in upon itself with a terrible thunder, Crowlin gave a last shriek before being swallowed by grinding rock.

Suddenly, relative silence overtook the mountains, only the whisking noise of millions of tons of dust and rock reigned, sweeping across the lands, uprooting trees and laying them flat, scouring the grass from the soil, choking all life.

Yet it was only a pause, an inhale before the final scream.

Beginning with a deep churning rumble that lasted only seconds, a great explosion blasted what was left of the mountain walls around the Threadbearer's grave. Rock melted, slagged, and ran in rivers. White hot flame gouted high, scorching the air, seemingly pulled by the black eye of Cos'arr into a towering, power filled column that reached into the heavens. The languidly crawling dark clouds swirled into the pillar becoming a true vortex that spun itself outward in a great sheet of blackness shot through with red tears. The screams and cries of the dying were silent against the roaring of the Wound.

For three days the World cried out in agony. Mountains crumbled and plains ripped. Cities were buried under waves of loam and the roiling seas flooded the places laid low. The skies opened up and vomited fire and acid. Tornadoes of flame tore across the surface followed by twisters of ice. Those closely connected to the Earth, not just the Earthmothers, suffered in terrible agony, coiling and twisting and shrieking while millions of other creatures were snuffed out or terribly altered. Of the Earthmothers, all but five were not to survive. In some places grass bloomed and died within minutes, while in others it lay completely untouched under a peaceful blanket of snow. Soil boiled, water turned to stone.

The sun remained hidden those three days behind the double moons which would no longer move across the sky, becoming a single, circular, white tombstone above the place where Crowlin became the Thread Cutter; above the grave of the Threadbearer. The fury of the Wound would eventually subside, but not stop, leaving a spreading blanket of black and red anchored to it by a massive column of fire and power. Months would pass before the dust finally settled, and years would crawl by before the weather stopped behaving oddly.

Somewhere in the depths of the world, in places dark for time immemorial, eyes flickered open.

Chapter 1

Five Years Later . . . .

*D*arkness.

Thick and comforting, like floating in warm water without the distress of drowning. Not night, but something more complete. Deep. Abstract. A place where Time did not exist; a place very near the ideal of peace.

Yet . . . .

. . . 'e dead? . . . .

Turbulence in the quiet blackness, resisting the completeness of peace that seemed so close. There was a desperation to it that could not be ignored.

. . . Yea. . . .

The calmness retreated as the disturbance grew. Faint windows of consciousness appeared; not an awakening, but more of an awareness of sensation beyond the curtain of pitch. The small swirls of movement coalesced, forming spears of perception that pierced the darkness like slow bolts of lightning.

. . . Check. . . money!. . . .

Great waves suddenly washed by, threatening to break the link to the comfort of the darkness. But it abated as quickly as it had come.

. . . Nea, none!. . .'bout sword?. . . .

. . . No!. . . bad luck!. . . leave 'im!. . . .

As awareness slipped away again, the drifting comfort moved nearer. The nagging sensation subsisted though, forming a barrier against the completeness promised by the blackness. A thread that connected this existence with another, different one, even while descending further into the thickness of the darkness. When even that nearly thinned away, a shockwave of sensation blasted through the black once again. The wave began to subside when another one washed past.

Then another.

And another.

The ever-elusive comfort fled farther away at every shuddering wave, each coming more and more frequently and with greater intensity. A faint diffusion of light invaded the darkness; a great pressure building with it as the shockwaves blew past. The lightening grew rapidly like the dawn, until there was no longer any darkness, but a bright, painful redness. The expanding pressure neared the point of explosion. Trailers of thought flittered about like gnats.

The shockwaves intensified until, all at once, the sensation translated into a piercing flash of pain that radiated out from a point of impact, gradually subsided until the next burst. The tension became a burning singe. As did the glaring redness. The completeness of peace was lost in the tumultuous mixture of the three sensations warring against one another. The suffering became unbearable. . . . the struggling and panic of drowning, trying to reach the surface, but caught on something.

A great gasp exploded, filling lungs with air, expanding to take in as much of it as could be held, even though a blaze of fire swept through the neglected tissue. A flapping sound followed, receding rapidly. The exhale was forced and quickly replaced by another great, desperate sucking in.

The cycle repeated several times before breathing became more relaxed and rhythmic. The burning slowly diminished until it was nothing more than a dull throb at each intake.

Consciousness returned, and with it, an awareness of surroundings. The smell of loam and vegetable rot filled nostrils with each breath. Warmth sank into skin from somewhere above, and a damp chill crawled up from below. Pain pulsed lower on a body not fully awake, keeping rhythm with a heartbeat that thudded loudly somewhere. A gritty substance lined the inside of an otherwise dry mouth and something cool caked one side of a face still tingling with newfound life.

A ragged cough dislodged more of the rough stuff into the mouth and incited several spasms of liquid agony to course through the body. Once the pain ebbed, another small cough flung the gritty substance out onto a quivering chin. A grasping mind, sluggish only moments earlier, raced now; trying furiously to organize disjointed thoughts and feelings; trying to identify the sensations now assaulting the awakened consciousness. Panic began to spiral through a body newly risen like a gale, when a sudden feeling of recognition slipped through the chaos. There was a pause, a holding of the breath as unspoken directions to relax spilled from the reasoning part of the mind.

The breath was let go, pulled back, let go again, slowly.
Mud!

The thought broke from the quieting maelstrom of the mind and hung there like a beacon. Instantly, thoughts aligned with consciousness.

It was mud that coated his face and mouth and was the origin of the cold dampness on which he lay. It was sunlight that warmed him and caused the redness he saw through his still closed eyelids. It was soil and decaying leaves he smelled.

He breathed in another breath and held it, savoring the scent, then expanded his awareness externally as the hold on the souring air was released. Chirping and twittering reached in. A breeze rustled and whispered through the leaves of trees around and above. Water bubbled and gurgled somewhere not far. There was grass tickling his neck.

Face and chest were turned up toward the sky, but his lower body lay twisted so that his right knee and foot were still embedded downward in the mud. One leg splayed out to the side, the knee hovering above the ground because of the awkward position. Right arm lay under his back, pinned against something hard and unyielding that dug into his lower spine. Left hand lay on a heaving chest.

Slowly, an eye opened, the other clogged shut by drying mud. Light lanced into the seeking orb, pure and bright, forcing it closed amidst a sting. Only after blinking for several seconds was he able to open it wide against the day.

A large blur obstructed one side of his view, a testament of how thickly the mud was built up on that side of the face, but above was a pristine blue sky interrupted by several tall trees pointing towards a single spot far distant. Leaves danced in the breeze, casting off different shades of green. A wet quality to the trunks seemed to sharpen their characteristics.

The man moved, lifted his shoulder from the muck to relieve the discomfort of his leg and whatever was digging into his back. A shocking bolt of pain shot up his body from his thigh, causing an instant jerk back, a hiss escaping from clenched teeth. After a panting moment, he slowly twisted and straightened until he was lying in a more natural position, gritting his jaw all the while against the stabbing sensation the movement brought. He slid his free hand down his body, bending at the waist to keep from moving his leg. Midway down the outside of his thigh, fingers encountered torn clothing and a hypersensitivity that caused him to suck at the back of his teeth. The area was wet with warm, sticky fluid.

After a moment, he began a light circular inspection of the area, tracing around the region of least sensitivity and working inward slowly, stopping several times when he pressed too hard against exposed nerves and had to catch his breath. After that, maneuvering slightly, biting back the pain, he looked at the damage.

A ragged wound about the size of his open palm darkened his outer thigh, close to his knee. It was not a slash or cut, but seemed to be several small radiating punctures where flesh had been ripped out. A dark red intermingled with the white of sinew and bone showed near the center of it. The blood had already stopped flowing and it prickled like the stabs of hundreds of needles. He didn't know where he had received such a wound, it was odd, as if . . . .

Suddenly, the memory of the strange flapping noise he heard just as he had taken his first breath flashed back. He scanned the trees as best as he could, stopping when his gaze fell across a large, dark shape perched on a branch not far. A fat raven preened its glistening feathers between uncomfortably long glances in his direction.

The sudden clenching of his innards echoed his mind.

It's eating me.

The creeping horror that followed sank deep, stirred up the silt of his most primal instincts and boiled up into an empty retch; body spasmed painfully, trying to purge a knotted stomach. After the episode, he lay back, breath coming in quick spurts. Whatever he was laying on dug into his back again, yet, for long moments he ignored it, his eye closed, as he took mental stock of himself.

How long have I been here?

No answer came as to why he was lying in the muck, wounded, feeding the birds. Nor did an answer come from the trailing thought of, *who am I?* But that realization was just an afterthought overshadowed by the situation as his mind scrambled to find answers to his immediate concerns. Rapidly, questions filled him, over and over. Why did his body ache all over? How did he come to be in the mud, twisted over to look at a sky while the damp chill seeped into his back? Why had he suddenly attracted the attention of an enterprising carrion bird? What was he laying on? He asked himself repeatedly, silently urging his brain to give up the answers he knew must be there.

Slowly, fleetingly, small glimpses of memory flickered to life and died. Something in the woods. Something unnatural. Ripping. Tearing.

Pain.

He tensed against the flashing remembrances, though, a knowing welled up inside that the danger had passed. Whatever had attacked was lying dead somewhere close. As his body relaxed, another sensation welled up.

Thirst.

Even as he noticed it, the thirst became all encompassing. It raked at the insides of his stomach, clawed at throat, and chewed on the back of teeth. His tongue seemed to expand to fill a suddenly dry mouth. Abating it was all that mattered, but as he tried to sit up, groaning with the effort, he found that he was in worse shape yet, and had to lie back down. Many beats of his heart passed as he gathered what little strength he had, then rolled to his side and pushed himself up with his arms, bringing his quaking legs under him with some effort. Now in a sitting position, he relaxed, caught at fleeting breath, and waited for vision to clear. There was a moment of consideration about lying back down but the thirst had become desperate. A few minutes more of concentrated effort and he began the struggle to stand. With another groan, he rocked back onto his feet and pushed up, slowly achieving his goal through popping tendons and crying muscles. The wound on his thigh blazed at the movement and fresh blood oozed from its itching surface, but the man was able to grind through it.

Then he was bent over, holding a clenching stomach and gagging as a wave of dizziness and nausea assaulted him. The earth he was standing on seemed to sway like a ship in a storm; and he scrambled to stay on his feet, but his stomach clenched with agonizing force again, dropping him to his knees. The heaving of his guts left him exhausted, trying to calm ragged breaths. Head hung listless, even as he tried to spit the acid taste from his dry mouth. The thirst doubled, becoming a nest of fire ants in his stomach. Slowly, he reopened his eye and simply stared at the ground, not bothering to lift his head yet.

The impression his body had made in the mud slowly came into focus. Fine folds and lines, the texture of his clothes, imprinted the dark substance. Laying half-buried across the middle was a sword, itself leaving its own impression of its crisp edges. The hilt and guard lay within the boundary of the body-print. He probably had a large bruise on his back where it had been digging into it.

Many minutes passed in staring, not so much in interest as much as a focal point to help gather strength enough to try again to stand. Still, he noted that the sword was very well crafted and bore some engraving on the guard, hilt and a portion of the blade not covered in grime. A faint glimmer of recognition crossed his mind but was quickly put out by the surging of his thirst.

He reached out, mechanically, grabbed the hilt, and worked the blade from the mud. The metal rang as it left the muck. Levering it up took some effort, but the tip was finally pushed into the ground. Taking a few deep breaths, he pulled himself up using the guard. The blade sank further, but soon found more solid purchase, allowing him to put most of his weight on it as he stood. Stomach lurched and dark mist filled his head again, its intensity waning against his preparedness.

He waited, swaying slightly, until the wave passed, then looked around. Several yards to his left, a small creek burbled across the open area. This was where his thirst was directing him.

Using the sword as a cane, he took a tentative step towards the water, nearly fell as the weakness still battled to overwhelm him. He concentrated, took another step with similar results. His vision was blurring again; and the ants in his guts were swarming, but the thirst could not be denied. It was a living thing that had taken control of his being. A brutal master, it forced him to take another step, and another, leaning heavily on the sword. Soon, a stumbling rhythm developed.

Only a few feet from the siren song of the bubbling water, he fell, tangling the sword blade in his legs. The keen edge bit into his shin, near his knee, drawing a cry from him. He landed hard, face down, the air exploding from lungs. Vision darkened around the edges; breath came in forced inhalations and ragged exhalations. The ants in his belly bit and chewed, leaving white-hot trails on his insides, and the pain from his newest wound shot through him at every beat his heart made. Yet, the thirst was worse, a clawing, terrible need; irresistible. *I'm dying*, said a quiet, small part of his mind, but the need for that water overrode the desire to let it happen.

Leaving the sword sticking oddly up from the grass, he dragged himself the last few feet with desperate urgency and plunged his face into the water.

The icy chill startled him awake enough to feel the caked on mud dissolving and washing away. He drank deeply, heeding only the call of the thirst, scarcely remembering to pause for a gasp of air. But it was not to be quenched. With a straining effort of will, he brought his head up out of the frosty waters and rolled over onto his back. *If I'm going to die, then, at least, I'll do it looking up into the blue of the sky.*

Breathing was shallow and hard, even after resting. The wounds on his leg were itching madly. The agony in his gut was not gone but seemed, at least, tamped down by the drink, though the accompanying thirst still raged. His vision, cleared by the refreshing bath in the cold water, began to gray around the edges once again.

Death comes!

That notion was tickling some area of recognition in his brain, too. He mentally poked at it, but nothing would surface.

Suddenly, his stomach gripped him harshly, squeezing from a faraway mouth, a groan, and coiled his body into a ball. The ants swarmed anew, becoming white hot terrors within seconds. His body continued constricting. Fire consumed him from within as an unearthly coldness froze him without. The blaze finally reached fingers into his mind, searing and scorching his nerve endings with such relentless rage that he was soon writhing on the ground by the stream. Some nether portion of his mind, yet untouched by the flames, realized he was screaming, even as the darkness overtook him.

Chapter 2

Five Servants

"*H*e fell here," came the croaking reply to the question. Looking down from his emaciated mount, Crowlin studied the disturbed earth and flattened grass. It did indeed look as if something heavy fell there. And thrashed.

He smiled at that, but it quickly turned to a frown when he remembered their quarry was not there.

Crowlin looked back at Reegan. The other was stooped over, the thick, voluminous dark robes he wore—as they all did—hiding his grotesque figure from view. Gnarled, clawed fingers traced patterns in the pressed mud as he peered around the area.

"Well?" Crowlin rasped. Reegan was looking past the stream, toward the thick forest on the other side.

"He was carried away. By *Ffolk*, from the looks of it," he answered, pointing in the direction of the trees.

Crowlin turned and looked behind him, past the other three cloaked, bent figures that made up the group, at the path they had just traversed. Back there lay the remains of the creature their prey was ravaged by. The creature in which the Master put so much trust and was now disappointed. He then looked toward the forest where Reegan had pointed, and continued to scan the tree-line until his gaze came to rest northward. His knees pressed slightly into the bony sides of his horse, causing it to jerk forward with a snort. All it would take would be a swift kick to its flanks and he could be gone.

Crowlin grunted, much like the wasting horse. It was a desperate thought; a feeble attempt at kidding himself.

Something jarred his attention and he turned back to look at Reegan, who was gazing at him expectantly. Crowlin realized he had said something.

"What?"

"He was moved only a few days ago," Reegan answered, then hobbled to his mount, his dragging twisted foot carving a furrow across the scene, and pulled himself up onto the beast. Reegan's horse, too, was near its end; its skin sagged against bone, bare in several places where the dull hair had given up and fallen out. A thick carpet of dry, flaking flesh coated its haunches and rump. These would not make it another few days, especially considering their quarry might be a few days ahead of them.

"We need to find new mounts," Crowlin said, more to himself.

"But what of Pendragon?" Reegan asked, nudging his horse closer.

"He won't be far, especially after the torture he received back in that glade." He pointed back the way they had come, where the nightmare creation sent before them was slowly dissolving into the soil. "He needs rest and healing. We have time. We will go south. Find more mounts. We need to feed too."

He pulled the reigns over his dying horse's neck and nudged the beast into sluggish action. Reegan stared after them as they passed, then brought up the rear as the party followed the stream southward.

Chapter 3

Awakenings

*E*yes sprang open to view nothing but darkness. Trickles of sweat coursed down a face that felt disembodied, catching the air and chilling it. He lay on something soft and a heaviness covered him, but it was not the grass near the creek. It was somewhere different, somewhere enclosed from the elements. That, he could sense without his eyes; though, several times he blinked in an effort to see. *Where am I?* kept knocking on the front of his head. He swallowed. His throat ached, but the thirst was gone. *Thank the Heavens.*

Then he heard it. The soft whisper of cloth upon cloth very near to him.

He sat up quickly, grabbing at a hip for a weapon that should have been there, but, instead, hands tangled in the sheets and blankets which lay on him. The thumping of his heart beat loudly in his ears, drowning out any other noise he might hear. Something moved close by, its form an inky blur to his right. He struggled furiously to untangle arms from the linens, a grunt of frustration forcing its way past clenched teeth. The inkiness reached out and touched his shoulder.

It was soft and warm against his bare flesh and a calming, tingling feeling radiated out from it, warming his body instantly and influencing a cease in the struggle.

"Shh!" the form intoned. The voice was soft, too, and comforting. He relaxed enough to let the hand gently, but firmly, press him back down into the bed. As the sheets were drawn up on his chest again, a distinctly female voice spoke softly.

"Lie back. You must rest. You are well but still very weak."

He started to speak, but found he could not. Indeed, the sudden flurry of motion left him almost gasping for breath. The mysterious woman's hand moved from his shoulder to his forehead, leaving a tingling imprint on his skin where it left off and again on the sweat coated skin of his head.

"Sleep," she whispered. A commanding tone lie beneath its soft one that his body reacted immediately to. A sudden drowsiness overtook him and his eyes drooped. Breathing relaxed and the comfort of the bed-sheets was too difficult to resist. Consciousness again closed in about him.

Chapter 4

Misgivings and Concerns

*S*andoren paced methodically, eyeing the area enclosed by the vines of empathic *valeurith*. There were three others in the small space: an Elder, the Healer and a guard. He was aware of their scowls when they looked his way, which added to his nervousness, but attempted to keep it from bothering him too much. Just being in this village was nerve-wracking enough. The strange spirit pull of the Faellyn's Summoning Song coming from Oth Salar, tickling deep in his chest, only complicated the matter. The wish that they were on their way was a thought that battled with his concern for his companion.

Alex had already been in the adjacent area separated by the vines for hours now, not even taking a break. *How long did it take to heal one of these wretched people?* By pure chance they visited, tired and hungry, and for what? She had hardly been given greeting when she was being ushered into the *valeurith* hut to heal someone whom their own Healer was unable to help.

He looked toward the seated pair, his lip curling slightly. They merely looked outside, conversing with each other in their native tongue as if he was not even present.

Damn, arrogant Traelynn.

Hardly anyone spoke to him since their arrival, but he had received enough stares as he followed the troupe to the hut. They all but fawned over Alex, their respect gleaming in their purple eyes as they asked the Earthmother questions, while giving him less courtesy than a common vagrant. Such was the way of the exalted ones. For the umpteenth time, Sandoren wished a plague on them.

His nervousness and frustration were reaching its peak when Sandoren caught himself and tried to calm down. He looked to the outer entrance, the vines still hanging open, and gazed out into the night enshrouded village. The guard standing near gave a suspicious stare, unconsciously fingering the hilt of the slim long sword that dangled from his belt. Sandoren fought to ignore the gesture.

He strode purposefully toward the egress, feeling the weight of his own weapon as it tapped against his thigh. The guard, momentarily surprised by his sudden movement, tensed and wrapped slim fingers around the hilt. The two older Greyffolk stopped talking, similarly jolted by his action.

"Relax!" Sandoren said, his voice louder than he wanted. "I'm just getting some fresh air."

"Don't wander too far, *Faellyn*," the guard spat back at him. He was shaken, but trying to not appear so. "We wouldn't want anything to happen to you. Unless, of course, you are going to heed the call of that nerve rattling Song."

Sandoren glared at him and considered belting him across the face, but that thought passed quickly. "I'm not Faellyn, Gray. I'm Narene," he said, trying to hide the contempt in his voice. Sandoren didn't like being here, and he more than didn't like these *Traelynn*, but he was more interested in leaving once their business was finished.

"Faelymarr is just as bad," the guard said. "Or maybe worse." Sandoren's fingers twitched, but he held onto himself. Instead, he pulled his gaze away and stepped out.

He had passed the threshold when he heard the whisper of the *valeurith* open from the room in which Alex had disappeared hours ago. Sandoren turned quickly and looked at the figure leaning against the tree buttressing the vines, startling the guard so much that the man had his sword half drawn before realizing he was not being attacked.

Alexandra's normally full face was pasty and thinned. Large dark hollows hung beneath half-lidded, slightly feverish eyes. Her long hair was dull and unkempt, hanging around her shoulders like drought riddled ivy.

"Alex!" he exclaimed as he rushed to her, nearly knocking over the two elders as they stood. She fell heavily against him, a grateful sigh escaping her mouth.

"All you alright, *Qaela?*" the older of the two asked.

"Yes, I'm fine," she rasped. "Your visitor is well, but still very weak." She was already out of breath from speaking. Sandoren led her to one of the naturally formed benches the old ones had been using, and tenderly sat her down, sitting next to her to continue his support.

The elders and even the guard wore worried faces as they watched the woman.

"Is there something I can do for you, *Qaela?*" the other old one asked. "You look far worse than you say you are."

"No, Korin," she answered, voice trembling. "There is nothing you can do for me. He will probably sleep for a few days," she indicated the area from which she had emerged with a feeble flick of her hand. "But he will be fine."

"What was it?" Korin asked. "I thought it was poison, but it would respond to none of my treatment."

"It was poison, *Faethe,*" she said around several shallow breaths. "It was a dark, unnatural poison. I am surprised he survived as long as he did. He must have an extraordinary constitution."

"Yes, so we gathered," Korin said.

"If you please, Elders," she said, still fighting for breath. "Would you excuse Sandoren and me for a moment? I must speak with him privately." Contemptuous eyes shifted over him.

"Yes, *Qaela*, as you wish," the older one finally said. "Take as long as you need. In the meantime, we will prepare lodging for you and your. . .companion."

"Thank you, Prime-elder, but we will not be staying," Alex said, drawing surprised looks from all in the room, even Sandoren. "We have pressing matters to attend to south of here."

"But, Earthmother, you are tired. You need rest," said the Prime-elder.

"No. I am grateful for your offer, but this requires some urgency."

The Prime-elder, brows knitted in concern, nodded, daring not to argue any further. "Then accept my gracious thanks for your assistance this day."

"You are welcome, Prime-elder."

He smiled, a half smile that did not cover his disappointment or his worry, and gestured to the two others who then followed him out into the night. The *valeurith* vines dropped closed behind them.

"Alex, are you crazy!" Sandoren exploded before the vines finished swaying. "You are near unconsciousness with fatigue! You cannot do any more traveling this night."

She lifted a hand and placed her fingers against his lips. They were hot. Not only was she tired, she was feverish. He put his hand against her face, drawing in a harsh breath as he felt her burning skin. Sandoren drew back from her to look her directly in the face. Her skin was sunken, worse than when she had come out. She looked back at him, the struggle to remain conscious evident in her eyes.

"You are ill, Alex?" he said. "W-why didn't you accept that healer's offer for help? W-why-"

"There was nothing he could do, just as there was nothing he could do for the man in that room." She smiled, feebly, glancing at the vines separating them from her patient.

"What does he have to do with this?" he was struggling for solid ground, he knew. Alex's face was growing ashen, her eyes were beginning to cloud, and he was beginning to panic. " I-I, what—."

She reached out and grabbed him by the shoulders, forcing him to focus on her face. Alex then closed her eyes, visibly gathered her strength.

"Listen to me and don't interrupt." Her voice was low but carried a commanding tone. It stopped Sandoren cold, bringing his state of being to that utter calmness one falls into the moment before a battle starts; that state of clarity before death is either delivered or met. He stared at her as she slowly opened her eyes. They were clear once again, deep pools of green. "The poison is in my body. It is a dark and evil substance. The only way to save the man in there was to draw it from him and put it into a viable receptacle. Me."

"But-"

"Sandy, listen!" she cried, bringing him back from the brink of panic he nearly went over. He focused on her again. A shiver of cold worked through his body as he realized that the clarity in her eyes was fear. "You must get me someplace secluded where I cannot be disturbed so I can leech the poison out. Someplace with water."

"Give it to me!" Sandoren spouted. His mouth was dry, his body shivering. A wan smile crept to her lips.

"It would destroy you before we got ten paces outside the village."

"Do it anyway!" he nearly yelled, desperation overcoming him.

"Dammit! Listen!" she flared "I can carry the poison for a while, but you have to get me to a water source where I can disperse it. I sense a stream a few miles south of here. Now stop being chivalric and get me out of here, or I will be dead before the sun rises!"

He stared, an idiotic expression slackening his face for several moments while her words sank into his precariously clutching mind. Then, with sudden alacrity, he stood and picked her up. She was light in his arms.

"Sandy?" she said softly. She was fading rapidly.

"Yes, Alex?"

"Sandy? That man is one of the one's we've been looking for."

Her statement caused him to pause, momentarily, only the surface implications reaching his frantic brain. She sighed, putting him in motion once again. He kicked at the vines before they could respond to his need and carried his burden into the lightening morning.

Chapter 5

Discovery

$\mathcal{F}$iltered sunlight streamed into the room from above. For several minutes the man with no name watched dust motes dance within the thin beams before taking a look around the small area he lay in, first taking in the woven thatch of the ceiling resting on thick oaken limbs spreading out above him. The bed he lay in seemed to be left of center of a roundish vine hut supported by a huge tree, though only the branches were visible. The curving wall was several shades of gray and green defined, seemingly, by tightly interwoven branches of small thin trees or vines. He saw no supporting beams on the inside of the wall so presumed there were several sheets woven together on either side of a framework. He squinted. It appeared that this wall had recently been built or patched for he could barely make out fresh leaves within the weave.

"The *valeurith* stands by itself. It lives," came a voice from the other side of the room. He quickly turned, the sudden motion causing a spell of dizziness that blurred his vision. Someone was sitting at a small table looking at him. The blur in his eyes was slow to recede, so he was only able to stare at the figure while it sharpened; until it became more than a blotch of color. After many moments, he looked on the person with clarity. Soft, lavender colored eyes looked back at him.

"You are still weak, but the Earthmother said it will pass soon." A thin smile etched a thin face. "I am Solarin, Prime Elder of this village."

"Y-you're. . . " the man's voice was course from disuse, so he cleared it a couple of times. "You're. . Highffolk?"

"Not quite." Distaste pulled at the corners of Solarin's nose, slight though it was. "I am *Traelynn*. My people are distantly related to the *Faellyn*, the Highffolk, as you call them. How do you feel?"

"Like I've been gnawed by a dragon" he said as he sat up. "What happened to me?"

"I should like to ask the same of you. But first, tell me your name so we can be properly acquainted." The Prime Elder leaned forward, placing his elbows on the table. Cupped in his hands, he held something that appeared to be a necklace, the cord coiled out from a charm or amulet of some sort to the surface of the table. His fingers absentmindedly traced the designs on it.

"My name? . . . I . . ." *What is my name?* His mind searched frantically until finally a thought, a small voice, slipped into his questing mind. "I am known as Marc Pendragon."

At this, the Elder's fingers stopped exploring the medallion and his eyes briefly grew wider. He stared at Marc for a hard minute, making him a bit uncomfortable. Then he relaxed, the thin half smile creasing his face again. "Greetings, Marc Pendragon. Long has it been since I have heard that name. So, the mystery grows."

"Mystery?"

Solarin sat back, again that piercing gaze fell upon Marc. "You were found by a stream, apparently dead, a few days ago by a patrol of our warriors. They could find no wounds. Only torn and ripped clothing." He paused, somewhat expectantly, then continued when no questions were forthcoming. "Upon being disturbed, you put up a stiff fight. The patrol leader swore you were dead until moved. They brought you here, struggling all the way. Our healer tended you, though he too could find only fresh scars when you took a rest from your thrashing. He suspected you had been poisoned, but by what was beyond him. He could neither cure you. It was expected, as marvelous as it was that you had survived thus far, that you would soon be dead. Luckily, an Earthmother arrived the day after we brought you. She worked long into the night drawing the poison from your body until it no longer plagued you. She tells me that, by all accounts, the poison that ravaged you should have destroyed you long before you were found."

Marc watched as the Elder spoke and hazily remembered the soft hand on his head. "I'd like to thank her, as I thank you, for your kind treatment?"

"Unfortunately, she had pressing matters elsewhere and left soon after making sure you were well, much to our disappointment." Indeed he did look disappointed, if only fleetingly. "Near your body was found a sword." He gestured to a chair near him upon which a sword belt dangled. A gleaming hilt emerged from a long, wide scabbard. He recognized it as his cane, but little else. "It is a remarkable weapon, an ancient weapon of the type carried once by the High Knights of Ellynthryll. It has a name. . . . Anduin." He paused for some recognition from Marc. It didn't come. "One of the only other belongings that was found, or shall I say found us, as you were brought here, was a magnificent horse that followed the band at a distance. Of course, I can only assume it belongs to you. The animal is near here. He is being well taken care of."

Solarin was still looking at him with that questing, piercing gaze, but Marc did not know why. He hardly knew his own name, much less remembered a horse or the sword.

"I don't understand, Elder, what are you asking?"

"To my knowledge, all the High Knights were wiped out several millennia ago, during the Knight Wars. Yet, here, in my presence, is a man possessing a sword from that era, a very conspicuous one at that, owning a loyal great stallion and bearing the name of Pendragon, a prominent, legendary, family within that Order." Again that almost unnerving pause; that unswerving gaze.

"Are you, Marc Pendragon, a High Knight of that old Order?"

Marc almost choked. He looked down to the packed earthen floor, trying to force his mind to remember. Anything. He could not, so looked up again, a small sad smile spreading onto his face. "No. I don't remember a whole lot right now, but I'm fairly sure that I am not a High Knight." *He was sure, wasn't he?* "Besides, didn't you say they were all wiped out?"

The Elder's eyes suddenly dimmed , almost imperceptibly, and he exhaled in a slow, silent sigh. As an afterthought, he looked down into his hands where his fingers had once again begun tracing patterns over the medallion he held. That spark of hope flared again.

"Can you explain this, then?" he asked, tossed the necklace at Marc, who, clumsily, caught it by the leather cord. The medallion spun about and rapped him smartly on the knuckle. He grabbed the large metal disc with his free hand and simultaneously messaged the throbbing area briefly before inspecting it.

The disc fit snugly in his palm and had a weightiness that reminded him of lead, though the metal was nondescript, neither polished nor tarnished, just dull. It seemed to be bronze. Embedded in the center was a red gemstone, smooth, without facets, that caught the light and held it deep inside where it burned like a star. Radiating out from the jewel were eight raised lines, four long and four short arranged in the manner of the compass points; the four long lines forming a cross with the smaller lines in an 'X' fashion intersecting the middle areas defined by the longer lines. He flipped it over. On the other side was a similar symbol, only the long radiating lines curved to the left while the smaller, middle lines curved to the right. Aside from the stone, he guessed it was worthless, though he had never seen a facet-less gemstone, either, for that matter. At least to his knowledge.

"It's just a bauble. A good luck charm or other such token." Marc said, tossing the necklace onto the table-top. It thudded dull on the thick wood. The Elder looked at him, his countenance suddenly saddened and, yet again, the spark went out of his lavender eyes.

The Prime Elder sighed, this time audibly and looked down at the surface of the table. The necklace caught his eye and he reached out and picked it up, stared intently at the dull metal for a few moments, then carefully wrapped the cord around it and set it back down near the center.

"Things are not always as they seem," he murmured then forced a smile and stood. "Rest now. If you have any needs, just place your hand on that table, there by the bed, and someone will be summoned. Once you are well enough, feel free to wander about the village. You are by no means restricted to this room."

"Thank you again for your hospitality, and I apologize if I have bothered you with my candor. There are many things that I still cannot recall from my memory. I am not entirely sure that my name is Marc. If I have offended you in any manner, I hope you will forgive me this."

The Prime Elder held up his hand in negation. "You have offended no-one. Indeed, I do hope, sir, that your memory loss is only temporary. There are many questions and strange circumstance surrounding your appearance and I have much hope that those questions will be answered." He paused, momentarily looking down at the table top, then again at Marc. "We all do. For now, though, I have taken too much of your time and will take my leave. I will look in on you again, *Qaela*. Rest well."

He turned and walked out between vines that separated of their own volition, leaving Marc to his own thoughts.

Marc stared after him for a long time, pondering all that the Elder had said to him during his brief visit but got only a headache in answer. He finally placed his face in his hands, rubbed his eyes, then his temples. It seemed that the Elder was putting much too much emphasis on his name and possessions. He was quite sure he was not what had been implied. Face lifted, eyes itching slightly from being rubbed, looked at his hands. They were rough; calloused from hard labor. Or fighting. On the back of his right hand was a dark discoloration that coiled up his forearm a few inches. It resembled a dragon. A tattoo, perhaps, or maybe just an odd birthmark. His muscles, too, were toned, rippling beneath sun-darkened skin when he flexed them. His body was used to strenuous work, though he did not know whether it was from swinging the sword dangling from the chair or from farming. Indeed, even he could draw the same conclusions: a sword, a horse. Yet, it all hinged on his memory. If he could not remember, then, was it true?

Instead of fighting with his obstinate brain about his identity, he continued to investigate his tiny haven. It was small and sparse, but comfortable. The table seemed to be carved from walnut or chestnut and was finely polished yet unstained. The craftsmanship was superb, he could not even discern seams or pegs, but the lighting was not actually bright enough to detect fine detail. The smaller table Solarin indicated was similarly made. Upon it rested some clothing, neatly folded. He still could not see any pegs or such, but, again, the light was still not bright enough to tell.

Suddenly, the room did brighten. He looked around and found he could see through the vines, out into a forest bathed in midmorning sunlight. "Interesting," He mumbled. A moment later, the vines closed themselves, knitting together with a whisper that shut out the light of the day. He concentrated again. The vines opened. "Very interesting." He remembered the Elder saying the wall lived but this was bordering on the incredible. Did he mean that the walls were sentient? Could they read his mind? If the walls could read his mind, could they also communicate that message to another? What an ingenious way to gather information; in such a way that the person being read had no knowledge of it; passive questioning. Well, if that were so, then they were still at a dead end, because he still had no memory to look into. His only thoughts were of the present.

He resumed his study of the larger table. Even in the bright shine of sunlight, he could not see a peg, or seam. *Seam.* He smiled. 'Things are not what they seem' the Elder had said. *What an apt statement.* Besides the table, the chair on which the sword belt hung and the chair on which the Elder had sat, the only other piece of furniture in this side of the room was a pedestal which held a large wooden bowl. A washbasin, no doubt. All made from the same dark wood. The floor was tightly packed earth. The bed on which he sat felt like down and the sheets and blankets were made of a smooth, silky cloth, quite comfortable and warm.

Slowly, his eyes were again drawn to the hilt of the sword sticking out from its sheath. The pommel and cross-guard were crafted of silvery blue steel; the design simple, elegant, but functional. Etching was evident on the teardrop shaped pommel. Fine, black leather wound the grip in tight, neat spirals and bore no sign of wear. He reached out, paused, then grasped the hilt. It was warm and comfortable, the grip was solid. He slid the blade from the scabbard, half expecting it to catch on grit and sand that had surely been in the sheath, but it came out smoothly with a small metallic hiss.

It was a double edged bastard sword, exquisitely balanced and lighter than he imagined it would be. Etching rode up the flat of the blade from the cross-piece to about the center where the flat turned into a fuller groove which then extended to nearly the tip of the four and a half foot blade. It, too, shone with a silvery blue sheen, and the cutting edges were as keen as if it had been forged yesterday.

He held it up and looked closely at the etching on the blade. It was some sort of ancient writing, but it was not a language he knew. Or remembered at any rate. He looked past the writing into the mirror finish and saw two iron gray eyes peering back at him. He suddenly had a notion and slid the marvelous weapon into its housing, then gently rolled to the other side of the bed.

The Elder had said to lay his hand on the small table if he needed anything. He did so, and instantly found a warmth concentrated around his open palm. The table began to hum, then, soon, it emanated a low, deep resonating tone.

Within seconds, the vines through which the Prime Elder exited parted and a young ffolk woman stepped into the room and stopped. Her characteristically lavender-colored eyes were accentuated by high, delicate cheek bones and slim nose. Silvery tinged tresses framed a face of soft alabaster. She was dressed in a loose fitting satiny gown of forest hue that very subtly displayed the curves of her body.

"Is there something you require, *Qaela*?" she asked respectfully, her eyes not quite meeting his. In embarrassment, he realized that he was completely nude and quickly covered himself with the sheets, but she did not seem to notice.

"Y-yes," he said, formulating thoughts faster than words. "Do you have a mirror I could look at, please?"

"Yes, *Qaela*, I shall return with one in a moment. Is there anything else you require? Maybe food? Or drink?"

He wasn't hungry, but thought it may be wise to try and get something down. "Yes, some bread if you have it," he said, then added as an afterthought, "And water, too, please."

"I will return promptly," she said, nodding once and backing out.

He sat a second longer, thought to take advantage of the girl's absence and do something about his nudity. He quickly grabbed his clothes, separated them, then struggled into his breeches. As he did so, he noticed they had been cleaned and mended. There no longer was a ragged, gaping hole in the left leg of the pants. He stopped for a closer look. They did not even appear to have been stitched or sewn. These *Traelynn* seemed to be a people of high caliber craftsmanship. Absently, he rubbed the flesh of his thigh where the bird had gouged it. The skin was smooth and whole. Terrific healers, too, it seemed. He marveled for only a minute more before he finished tugging on the pants. The weakness remained, but renewed strength was slowly coursing into his body. The dizziness and blurred vision from sudden movements was only slight, and, though he was a bit winded from the simple exertion of pulling on his clothing, he was not exhausted.

He was drawing his tunic over his head when he heard the whisk of vines as the girl entered. She waited quietly in the door while he finished pulling the garment down and buttoned the top few buttons. He then stood, using the bed frame for support. He waited, but the unyielding dizziness and nausea did not assail him. However, his legs were still weak and barely held under his weight, even buttressed against the bed. Yes, it would still be awhile before he was fully recovered. Slowly, he began shuffling around the bed toward the girl. He heard her suck in her breath nervously.

"*Qaela*, you should not be trying to walk so soon after your ordeal, especially without aid. Please sit while I get you someone to help support your weight," She exclaimed.

"No. . . need," he said, trying not to gasp. "I'm . . .almost. . .finished." He worked his way to the side of the bed facing the door and sat down heavily. Noting the distraught look of concern on the girl's face, he said, "I'm. . .okay. . .Why. . .do you keep. . .addressing me. . .with that. . .name?"

"*Qaela*?" she asked. Marc nodded a couple of times, still trying to catch his breath.

"It means 'honored guest'," she explained.

"Please, my name is Marc. Address me by that."

She deferred, shaking her head rapidly. "Oh, no sir. It would not be proper of me to address you otherwise.".

"That's fine," he said, her quick refusal causing him to acquiesce. "May I see that mirror now?"

She moved to the table and set down the tray she held. On it lie a small loaf of bread, a knife, napkin, goblet, and a polished silver mirror. She picked the mirror up and brought it to him, only a soft whisper of sound preceding her.

"Thank you," he said softly as he took the item. His fingers brushed hers and she reacted as if shocked, pulling her hand back quickly. Her eyes widened, but only momentarily, then she began to back rapidly towards the door. "Please, stay," Marc said quickly, then waved to the open chair. "Sit. I may need help picking up the pieces."

An unconscious smile came to her lips, lighting her eyes, and she sat where he had indicated. He smiled back at her, nodded, then closed his eyes and took a calming breath, nerving himself to look into the polished metal. After a moment and some trepidation, he opened his eyes.

A rugged man looked back at him from the surface of the mirror. The face was somewhat pale, but still tanned and weathered by the outdoors. A strong, muscled jaw-line, lean, angular cheekbones and a chiseled brow dominated the visage. Iron gray eyes looked at him, cold, depthless, ageless. Thick hair, once a dark chestnut, almost black, was now frosted with large brushstrokes of gray at the temples. He was cleanly shaven. It was the face of a man who had seen thirty-five, forty summers.

Is this me? Marc thought. His free hand came up and touched his cheek experimentally, pulling at his skin. The man in the mirror did the same. *I guess it is.* He studied his face for a long time, getting lost in the process, as it was like seeing it for the first time. He still did not remember anything. He knew the face was his, but there was no familiarity about it at all. It could be the face of a stranger, for all he knew. The face of someone met in passing, forgotten once past.

The whisper of cloth broke him from his intense deliberation. He looked up to find the woman halfway to the door. "Wait!" he exclaimed. "I'm sorry."

"No need to apologize, *Qaela*," she answered without turning to look at him. "This is a private matter. I should not be here."

"Please, don't go. I have questions."

"As you wish," she said softly, turning to him. Moisture rimmed her eyes. *Why*? He asked himself. She again sat down, but avoided looking directly at him.

"What is your name?" Marc asked, trying to change the subject.

"I am Maelyrin. I am the Faethe's apprentice."

"The Faethe? Who. . ."

"The Healer. I am the Healer's apprentice."

Oh. That would explain her not being bothered by his nudity. She seemed very uncomfortable now, though, and still refused to look directly at him. She wrung her hands together in her lap several times.

"Are you okay?" he asked, cautiously. "I don't wish to make you nervous."

She looked down at her hands and attempted to say something, but her throat hitched up. It was her turn to take a couple of deep breaths. Forcing herself to relax, she finally looked up, yet would still not make direct eye contact.

"It is forbidden for me to stay too long," she stated, gulped, then: "It is not proper and generally not allowed. But, the Faethe. I am his apprentice, so-"

"So you have certain duties that require you to set aside propriety to get the job done?" he finished for her. She nodded, relief and embarrassment rising into her cheeks.

"I mustn't stay too long. . . ." she said, leaving the thought unfinished.

He looked at her silently as a crystal tear began rolling down her cheek. It was quickly wiped away with a brush of a finger, but she had already lost her struggle for self-control.

"I'm sorry. I didn't know. Please go. I will not ask you to put yourself in a compromising position again." She stood hastily, smoothing her dress nervously. "Before you leave, though, could you answer me a quick question?"

"Certainly."

"Could you tell me the nature of these walls. They seem to be reading my mind and doing things before I can." She smiled despite her fluster.

"The walls are *valeurith*. The vines have an empathic nature. They can sense your needs as far as temperature, lighting, and passage is concerned."

"Temperature?"

"Yes. If you need it to be cooler, the vines will expand the mesh to allow air to flow through more readily. If you need warmth, the mesh will contract, trapping the heat."

"Thank you," Marc said, relieved, to some degree, to know the vines were not reading his mind.

"Is there anything else you require, *Qaela*?"

"No. Thank you, Maelyrin, I am fine for the moment. I apologize for putting you in an awkward position."

"Thank you," she said, quietly, almost inaudibly she added: "Marc."

Maelyrin quickly gathered herself and whisked out of the room. Marc's gaze followed her until the vines closed off his view. He sighed, still not knowing where he was, who he was, how he came to be here. At least he knew what his face looked like. That was a start. He hoped his memory loss wasn't permanent, the thought echoing the concern of the Elder. There was, nevertheless, a nagging familiarity about his situation. Not necessarily the *Traelynn* or the room, but something about the memory loss. It almost seemed he could reach in his head and pluck it out of his mind, but, try as he might, he could not force an answer.

He moved himself heavily to the chair from which the sword dangled, and sliced a thin piece of bread. Behind the loaf, he found a small dish of some sweet smelling substance. He dipped the end of the knife in it and brought it to his tongue. It was some type of crushed fruit, very tasty and not too sweet. He spread some of the stuff on his slice of bread and began eating, slowly, while pondering his dilemma. After taking the first few bites, he realized how hungry he really was and made short order of the entire loaf.

Marc soon became sleepy again and moved back to the bed. He wondered briefly how long he had been here in this village, but that thought only fluttered through his drifting consciousness. He considered undressing, but decided it would take too much effort. Instead, he slid under the sheets and was, in moments, fast asleep.

Chapter 6

Musing on Reality

*T*he ants entered and exited the hole almost randomly. Those going in carried bits of leaves and seeds. Those going out fanned out onto several different paths and trails that worked their ways into the grass surrounding the mound. The shadow cast across it seemed not to bother the small creatures, nor did the large, dirt encrusted feet that encroached on their territory. Indeed, several ants placidly crawled around and over them before continuing on one of the trails leading through the lush grass.

The owner of the overlarge feet did not notice the crawling of ants on his flesh as he squatted beside the mound. Large, round, dull eyes stared passively at the hole, wholly considering the mound, grass, and moving ants. He never moved, seemingly a statue of flesh, as he gazed. His shadow crawled, like the ants, away from the mound of carefully placed grains.

Something large and heavy spattered the sand near where the shadow's head marked the ground, gouging out a small crater in which it lay. Ants boiled from the hole, random chaos assuming their previous behavior. The watcher's eyes slowly moved to take in the foreign object that had so disturbed the creatures, regarding it with the same dullness. The squatter seemed not to recognize the large rock.

Moments later, another shadow fell across the watcher and the ant hill, merging with his and eclipsing the warmth of the sun that had been beating down on the bronzed flesh of his wide, naked back. His gaze crawled away from the rock and turned up toward the caster of the shadow, which was, too, a dark form around which a halo of sunlight shone. A slack, wide grin formed on a round tanned face.

"So here you are, Stupid," said the dark form. A rhythmic, slapping noise played background to the low voice. A sound that tickled something in the squatter's head, causing his large eyes to blink reluctantly. Beyond the interloper, another, higher pitched voice asked, "What's 'e doin', Colin?"

"Same as usual, Bren," answered the shadow. "Not working on his chores." The slap became a pop. The slack smile began turning into a knowing grimace.

"C-colin?" asked the squatter. Lightning cracked into the side of his face, exploding across the flesh of his cheek, throwing his head back, dropping his body to the ground. Thunder followed it in the form of a booming voice. "Shut up, Dummy! No one gave you permission to speak!"

Slowly, the squatter picked his face from the ground and looked up. Several ants raced across the flaccid round mask of dirt. The side of his face that had been struck throbbed terribly and something hot and slick ran down his cheek. A large hand came away from the pain with red liquid on fingertips regarded dully before the eyes moved to the shadow. A blunt *thwap, thwap,* drew his attention, his gaze resting on the shadow's hand. A thick fear worked onto the squatter's face.

Colin held the whipping stick.

"Wha'd ya' wanna do, Colin?" asked Bren, still obscured by the shadow's larger form. The squatter did not look away from the thick stick banging against Colin's thigh, so did not see the grin ooze onto the older youth's blocky face. "What we always do when Mudswine misbehaves," Colin said.

The vicious tone was lost on the squatter, but not the meaning. He began a slow scramble away from Colin. Something heavy thudded into his belly, expelling all the air in his body and filling him with rumbling pain. His arms and legs suddenly became jelly and, again, he fell over into the grass. A moan escaped him. "Where're you goin, freak?" cried Bren.

"Look at that, Stupid! You dirtied my foot," said Colin slowly, holding out his mud encrusted bare foot under the dull eyes of the squatter. "I guess we are going to have to double your punishment, eh, Bren?"

"Yea!" Bren answered, giggling, advancing enough so that his shadow joined that of the holder of the whipping stick. He was smaller than Colin, slimmer, making them both together almost as large as the squatter, but fear shown only in the eyes of the downed boy. The other two pairs gleamed with a dark light, even though Bren twitched spasmodically as if nervous.

The squatter sucked in a deep breath and tried to roll over on his hands and knees, but suddenly, the two shadows blurred into motion. Blows began raining down upon him, from foot, hand, and stick. Pain blasted through him, eliciting grunts and cries of pain and fear. Laughter drifted down through the haze, along with other, more sinister, epithets. In a frenzy, he rolled away and, by miracle, was able to scramble his legs underneath him. With a strength born of his fear, he launched forward, away from his assailants, into a long stumbling run. Pain hindered him and blood ran freely from a dozen wounds, but he quickly outdistanced the two punishing shadows. Blindly, he ran toward the edge of the forest that bordered the grassland that contained the buildings in which he lived. A hard, sharp object thudded into his back. Something dark and round fell from the sky before him, landing in front of him and tumbled and bounced along with him. His breath came in long, slow, measured rhythms despite his pain.

He was nearly to the edge of the woods when something heavy pummeled the back of his head. Light flared behind his eyes; legs faltered. Clouds rimmed his mind. Barely aware of his situation, he plunged into the thick undergrowth; twigs and branches slapped against his face. Vines and creepers clutched at his stumbling feet. With a groan, he tripped and fell down a slope into a large hollow, coming to rest against the exposed roots of a large tree, where he lay still, eyes closed, breath irregular. Had he been conscious, he may have seen the large ground viper slithering toward him, though he may not have understood what it was.

Chapter 7

Bitter Realization

*A*lex rolled over, a low groan punctuating it. Nearby, Sandoren leaned against a large oak tree, studying her sleeping form; the harsh look of concern quickly softening as he began to realize that she seemed to be getting well. The soft yellow of dawn was beginning to bathe the glade, but the sun had not yet crested the mountains to the east. The sharp chill of predawn still hung in the air, pinching his extremities, and the tinkling pull of the *Faellyn* Song grabbed at his heart. He hardly noticed.

Their flight here had become a fuzzy dreamlike image, but the ensuing hours were burned into his brain right behind his eyes and would not leave him for a great time to come. He should have listened when she had told him to go into the forest and not watch as she 'cleansed' herself. He had gone into the woods, but not far. And watched. It would have been better for him had he not. Better for his sanity. *One day, your worry will put you in a position you don't want to be in.* She told him that often.

This time it was true. He had sensed that even before he watched her writhing on the carpet of grass in agony, her arm thrust rigidly into the iciness of the stream. As she had called out in pain, he had realized there would have been nothing he could have done. Standing in helpless suffering as well, wanting to turn and run, but not able, he had been trapped;

forced to watch her cycle through moaning discomfort to twisting, wailing torment and could do nothing. He could neither run to her. He was frozen with horror, watching the inkiness flow from her fingertips and turn the cold, clear water blacker than any night; destroying all growth of natural things inches from the bank. Shame filled him when he realized his relief that his former act of bravado had not been accepted. He knew, without a doubt, that he could not have survived even a portion of what she had gone through and he was glad that corruption had not afflicted his body. He was ashamed and sickened all the more.

Alex moaned again and pulled her knees up to her chest. He could see color in her face. Warm color that replaced the pallid corpse-like skin sagging from it earlier. She seemed more relaxed, as well, having rid herself of the rictus that had contorted her body unnaturally, looking more an overgrown sleeping child now than a powerful Earthmother who had just undergone one of the largest trials of her life. He noticed, also with relief, that the black water was no more. Of course, the foulness of its passing was still evident.

He dropped a heavy sigh and tried to look to more pleasant thoughts. The horrible images were not so easily banished, however. They continued to plague him, taunting him with what had been revealed about himself. His thoughts whispered to him. *Coward*, they said. *Selfish coward. . . .*

Alexandra Moonglow's eyes flickered open, watering against the light. A metallic dry taste coated the inside of her mouth and throat. Her body still ached in several places and she could feel the weakness throughout. But she was alive, and she could see the glorious morning light sparkling amongst the dew washed grass and leaves. She was alive. She had been lucky this time.

Alex let the view soak into her mind for a few more minutes then lifted her head slightly, stifling a groan that was trying to escape. Sandy was not far, leaning against a tree and staring into the forest, a darkly intense look creasing his face. She knew without having to ask that he had watched her. *Stubborn ass*! He had to be questioning himself; degrading himself. *Why does he never fully listen to me*?

"Sandy?" Her voice was dry and cracked. He apparently did not hear her.

Sandy? It echoed through his brain. It meant something. *Sandy*? He found himself staring aimlessly into the forest. The sun had risen considerably. It was fully visible through the tops of the trees. He had locked himself into his brooding and lost track of time. *Alex! Something must be wrong. . . .*

Her bright, clear green eyes were gazing at him. Concern quickly changed to soft mirth as she regarded him. "Good morning," she said hoarsely.

"Alex?" He came away from the tree. "Are you well?" She waved him back and he relaxed, reluctantly.

"Of course I am. Isn't it evident." Weak smile. "Yourself?"

He grunted in frustration, a thin line of ire creasing his brow. "I'll never understand you, Alex! You nearly died this morning! And for what! An ungrateful Greyffolk! And then—"

"Human," she spoke evenly, a twitch of a grin tugging at her mouth.

"Human? What?"

"He was a human."

"Oh. Whatever he was, you risked your life—a human in a Greyffolk village?" The confusion exploded onto his features, toppling his train of thought. *What was a human doing in a Greyffolk village*? "I—wha—"

Alex suddenly laughed, filling the glade with mirthful music. Joy and relief washed through him, taking his brooding with it. She was alright. She was vibrantly alive. That still didn't explain about the human. "Explain," he said, trying to sound deadly.

"He is one of the one's we are looking for. Don't you remember the charge given to me by Gyssel?"

He thought a moment. "Yes. You said it right before you passed—"

"Sandy. I am well. You needn't blame yourself for my pain. You saved me. So, put it behind you!"

Easier said. He thought. "Okay."

She pushed herself into a sitting position, breathing hard and shaking. Sweat was already trickling down her forehead. He tensed; began to rush to her, then constrained himself. She was, after all, safe. The weakness would pass. "I'm starving," she said, smiling.

Chapter 8

Release

*M*aelyrin's tears blurred her vision such that she could not see the small hut across the glade, so she put her face in her hands and wept into them. Neither did she see the looks of concern cast in her direction by passersby, even as they maintained a respectful distance. She didn't need to see the stares, she felt them. But she did not care at the moment. Her position, unique as it was, commanded a separation that she had not acclimatized to yet. It was a separation of awe, respect, and, mostly, fear. Had she been bleeding from a wound, she could scarcely believe those passersby would breach the circle of 'respect' that constantly surrounded her. Here, in her own village, among her own people, she was, unconsciously, a pariah. She was alone. However, this was not why she cried bitterly into her slim hands. She was weeping for her village, for her people, not her position or its ramifications. She also wept for the man who now slept in the hut across the glade, though she knew as little about him as he, himself, did. She cried long into the night.

Chapter 9

Dreams of Pain

*M*arc was standing on a hilltop. It was midday; the sun bright and warm on his face. Looking down, he saw that he wore ancient, but well-kept armor. Beside stood a beautiful woman. She was as tall as he, graceful, supple. Sunlight sparkled from her golden hair; wearing a white gown and holding his arm. He could feel her touch even through the mail he wore. There was murmuring behind them, as of several people. Marc did not need to look to see how many. A man in long robes, priestly robes, approached them.

The ceremony was short, and within minutes the tall graceful woman was now his wife. He kissed her, a long, simple sweet-tasting kiss that was happily returned. Applause surrounded them. It was time to celebrate. They began turning, to present themselves to their guests as one.

Someone screamed. Then chaos.

Marc turned swiftly, moving in front of his wife and drawing the sword at his belt with practiced ease. Several creatures were tearing into the group gathered there. They looked like men, but somehow disproportioned. They were obsidian and wore no clothing. Nor did they seem to have any features, facial or otherwise. They ripped through the fleeing guests as easily as running through a garden, striking them down with quick slashes with long sharp claws. Two of the inky creatures broke from the crowd and rushed him and his wife. He took a step forward, meeting their charge with a wide sweep of the sword. There was little resistance, which surprised him, and he found them writhing in pain on the ground before him. They had made no sound, though, as they died.

He had little time to think about it before he was surrounded and had to fight off more. The creatures died easily but they were many and pressing in mercilessly. He was starting to tire. Then, his wife screamed. With renewed strength, he slashed about him, dispatching the remaining creatures and turned to find the source of the scream.

She was not far, still standing near the crown of the small hill, backing slowly away from two of the creatures. Her dress was torn at one shoulder and three thin lines of blood ran down her cheek. The two men-things seemed to be taunting her. The body of the priest lay in a heap nearby. A rage unlike any ever experienced before overcame him.

He charged the two things, which, upon hearing his screech of anger, turned towards him. The first fell quickly to a backhanded slash with the sword. He followed with a thrust at the midsection of the second which twisted, trying to avoid the blow. His sword bit deeply. For the first time since seeing the creatures did he look straight into one's face. It was featureless, only small bumps and ridges that defined the underlying bone structure. Although there was no mouth, it seemed to be smiling at him; the skin creased into a crescent shape on the lower half of its face. Then, it merely stepped away, and walked down the hill. His wife was there, staring dully at him. He looked down, following the blade of his sword until it reached its terminus in bright red splashed against pristine white.

He screamed.

There was only darkness to look out into. A cold sweat bathed him, drying quickly from a breeze which blew through the room. His breath heaved and tears streamed down his face. Marc sat absolutely still, trying to calm himself, let his eyes adjust to the darkness. The room was empty this time. He, thankfully, relaxed.

"It was just a dream," he whispered *Was it*? His voice was hoarse. He cried silently for a few minutes, letting his hot tears stream unchecked down his face. Yet, he did not know why. It was a dream, it had to have been. But, there was something familiar, and painful, about that, too.

He hit the bed beside him, growling in frustration. There were too many things that seemed familiar to him, but he could not grasp them. Was it a dream or a window to his past? He did not know. The images had been dreamlike, but there was something indescribably real about it also. The pain he felt at that moment was certainly, entirely real.

He sighed, then wiped away the moisture from his eyes. Forced his body under control, breathing deeply to calm a thrumming heart. Marc lay back, clasping his hands on his chest, and stared at the ceiling. He could barely make out the branches and thatch, seeming just as ethereal as the dream images. He closed his eyes and once again attempted to remember something further back than the last few days. Try as he might, no memory would surface. There was only a blankness. Even the dream began fading rapidly, the details fuzzing together until it was a mass of thought; unfocused images, until they, at last, faded. No pain, no tears. There was only a memory of having woken from a bad dream.

Marc shifted his attention to the slight breeze blowing through the room. It carried the scent of pine and evening dew with it. Listening to it became his focus as it flowed through the thatch of *valeurith*, every so often slowing, then switching directions slightly, bringing him the hoot of an owl or call of a night bird. It bathed his skin in coolness and playfully tousled his hair. It seductively lulled him towards slumber. As the last of his resistance faded, the direction changed again. He drifted into sleep to the muffled sound of a woman sobbing.

Chapter 10

Comfort and Doom

"*W*hat is it child?" the voice came softly, but startled her with such force it seemed a yell. She flinched her gaze toward the speaker, a gasp exploding from her. Her tear blurred vision just made out the Prime Elder staring at her, but his presence did not comfort her. A beam of moonlight slanted through the trees and bathed him in silver light. Dark shadows bled in several places on his aging face. How terribly sad he seemed to her just then, not the stern pillar of stone the entire village leaned upon.

"Nothing, *Saerleanne*." She quickly wiped her eyes. "Just tired I guess." He glided towards her, leaving the pool of light behind him and casting his features into darkness. He settled down beside her on the natural bench, moving with the slowness of the elderly, but the gracefulness of a leader.

"Nothing, child?" he said offhandedly. He gazed into the village as she bowed her head. "This man means much, doesn't he?"

"Yes, *Saerleanne*."

"Then, you have *Read* him?" She closed her eyes, knowing this question was coming but wanting to avoid it as long as possible. He had said it with as much carelessness as he could yet still could not conceal the underlying tone of fear and awe. She stared at the ground before them.

"Child," his voice became soft, tender like that of a parent. "you are gifted. A gift that only comes once a generation. It is something not understood by any who don't have it. Yes, it frightens us. All of us. But your gift is most important to us. It will one day help us to find the Tears and return us to the days before they were lost. Yet, that is not its only purpose. Please, child, tell me what you saw."

His words were little comfort. It did not banish the realities she faced every day. She continued staring downward, not wanting to speak; not wanting to reveal an answer he already knew.

"I could not *See* him, *Saerleanne*," she said softly, forcing the words out, frightened, herself, of their meaning.

"What?" he asked, as surprised at her comment as she was scared. "I thought that your Sight was. . ."

"Infallible?" she stated. *That is why everyone is frightened.* She thought viciously. *Nothing hides from me.* "It is, *Saerleanne*. Usually."

"I don't understand." It was a prompt, not a confession. No one understood her.

"He is like a shadow when I *Look* upon him. A curtain I cannot *See* through."

The Prime Elder leaned back against the huge old oak the bench surrounded and gazed up into the dark canopy above. Nothing but the whispering leaves disturbed the evening for many minutes, and she did not bother to hasten him. He was deep in thought, which meant he was deeply frightened. She didn't need a 'gift' to understand that mannerism. The Prime-elder was rarely at a loss for words.

Maelyrin listened intently to the world around her while letting her eyes wander through the night-enshrouded village. The distant chirruping of crickets, the call of night birds, the trees whispering quietly to each other. The sounds soothed her as they often did when she sat here this late. But not as well as usual. Inevitably, her eyes fell upon the hut the stranger slept in and lingered there.

"What does this mean?" the Prime Elder finally said. She turned to look at him and found he was watching her intently. Something very few did, and she realized he had been doing it for some time. Deep pain and sadness etched his soul behind his large eyes, adding to the weight of responsibility for his people that he carried alone. A large portion was given over to remarkable kindness but that was walled away. Kept from the majority of the villagers; kept from the majority of himself. Very few knew him like that. He allowed few to know. With her, it had not been a choice. With her, nothing was hidden. She watched his joys, fears, loves, everything the Prime-elder was, for several moments.

"I don't know what it means, *Saerleanne*," she said cautiously. "But he brings death with him. And life. This, I can see; though I wish I could not." She silently cried out in anguish, in fury.

"Tell me, child. I must know," he prodded her, his voice grave.

Tears welled, then flowed freely down Maelyrin's cheeks, the sobs building in strength. She didn't want this responsibility; this curse. More than at any time before, she craved ignorance. She craved the innocence that had been taken from her long ago. But it was not to be. She was too far down the path; knew far too much. Had been raped by knowledge, and forever would remain scarred.

"I don't know when. I don't know how. I don't even know why. But. . .This man brings doom like a carrier of plague wherever he goes. Because he is here, our village has been sacrificed. We have been sacrificed. . . "

"Are you certain?" Solarin asked, a calm iciness to his voice.

Her sobs were starting to bubble and froth, threatening the iron control she was attempting. "I am certain. Though I cannot *See* him, I can *See* 'around' him. I . . . I am certain." She could control herself no longer. Maelyrin fell against the Prime-elder and let her soul bleed into his comforting shoulder.

Chapter 11

Findings

*A*lexandra stepped lightly from the bole of the huge oak, glancing around at the heavily forested area ahead of her. She moved to the side, allowing Sandoren an egress from the ephemeral tunnel stretching far back through the center of the ancient tree. Hand on sword hilt, he advanced out from under the canopy of branches, casting coldly efficient looks into the undergrowth. Alexandra turned and placed her hands against the rough bark, gazing into the long corridor. Slowly, the tunnel closed, the walls weaving together until there was not even a seam in the old facing. For several seconds, she leaned against the huge oak, feeling the coarseness of its exterior, the beat of its own life-force, against her cheek and palms as she regained her strength. Her ordeal with the poison still left her weak, despite the rest and food, and manipulating the Elemental Powers further drained her. "Thank you," she whispered and, with a deep breath, pushed away from the tree before Sandoren noticed and began worrying over her like a nursemaid. Swaying slightly, Alex turned to the task at hand. The pulling sensation had been growing in her since she awoke. It was stronger now.

The way ahead was choked with shrubs and creepers and smaller trees. Beams of sparse sunlight slanted down through the canopy of the huge spreading arms of many oaks and white-woods, illuminating dancing dust motes and buzzing insects. Sandoren was no longer visible, no doubt scouting the perimeter. She smiled. Sometimes he was overprotective, but, on more than one occasion, that protectiveness had saved their lives. He appeared to her left, opposite of where he disappeared. Though he made not a sound, she knew where he would materialize. Proof of all the years spent together. She smiled again.

"All clear," he said in a near whisper. She nodded. "Where are we going?" he asked after a moment, still keeping his voice low.

"That way," she said, pointing directly away from the trunk of the tree, toward the southwest. "There is a creek nearby and I am thirsty again." She waved his sudden concerned look away. "The poison took more than itself, Sandy. It will be a few days before my body balances itself out physically. I will need all the nourishment I can get." She smiled, even though Sandoren's eyes were clouded. "I'm already hungry, too." A moment later, he gave a hesitant nod, then turned and headed in the direction she pointed.

Alex watched him steal ahead, graceful as a feline and as quiet, and sighed. *He carries more responsibilities on his shoulders than he needs to.* Came the thought. *One day, he will burden himself far too much.* She shook her head, then, and just as silently, followed him into the choking undergrowth, unhindered as if there was a path five feet wide.

It was midday, but the temperature was comfortable, cool in some places, the sunshine being soaked up by the upper leaves of the canopy. Alex allowed the scent of loam to fill her nostrils in deep, long breaths as she studied the woods around her. This area was yet untouched by the Unbalance and Taint that threatened from the far northwest. It was largely pristine and complete, the ecosystem entirely in Balance. The thrum of Power was strong here, and it touched her deeply, filling her with a joy that could never be explained or described. She half believed she could simply stop here and live out her life. She wanted to believe in the possibility, anyway. It saddened her that she knew that this would not last. That this place, too, would eventually end up a wasteland of blighted, dying vegetation. Or worse.

Alex paused a moment and shook her head briskly to try and clear her mind of those thoughts before they had time to lodge themselves deep within her soul, before they could corrupt and destroy her determination and hope. *It will not happen!* She told herself. *It will not!* Angrily, she continued to stride after Sandoren.

Soon, they came to a small stream of crystal water, where she eagerly threw herself down on her belly and began scooping up handfuls into her mouth. It was cold and clean and sweet. She savored it, held it before swallowing. Sandoren stood over her, watching the brush all around them while she drank. Once Alex had finished, he knelt and took a couple of handfuls for himself as she dusted off the front of her clothes. "What is it we are looking for?" he asked before taking another drink.

"We are looking for the other," Alex said absently. Her gaze flowed along the creek and swept up into the trees. She listened intently to the sounds around them. The babble of the creek, the breeze through the leaves, the lazy buzzing of insects, and the calls of birds all mixing in a soft orchestra. The smell of earth was strong here, by the brook. She breathed in deeply once again and smiled slightly.

"Who would that be?" he asked.

"I don't know."

"Alex?" he was looking down at the shimmering water and nervously fingering the hilt of his sword. "Why? Why you? Why not one of the others?"

Alexandra stood up and gently laid a hand on his arm. "You know why, Sandoren," she said quietly, willing him to look at her, though he would not. "I'm the only one strong enough. There is no other."

"I fear that you seek your death, Alex!" he snapped, jerking his arm away and stepping from her.

"Sandoren al' Reaydon!" she retorted. "After all the years we've faced dangers together, all the travails and journeys, why in the world are you now concerned about Death?"

"Because this time, I cannot help!" he hissed, slamming a fist against his thigh. "I can do nothing but stand by and watch! Like that wretched poison! This. . ." he quickly unbuckled his sword belt and held the scabbarded blade and leather belt up. "This is useless against what we face!" he threw the sword and strap to the ground. "Your connection to the Earth is useless! I was with you when we tried to enter that blasted land, remember? I saw how weak and drained you were and we were not even within 50 miles of the Wound! To what end will you go? To what lengths will you take?" He was huffing, his face red, and hands clenched at his sides.

Alexandra stared at him, storms raging behind her emerald eyes. "I will do what I must!" she spat. "And so will you, you sanctimonious ass!" He blinked in surprise. "We are too old to be thinking like irresponsible brats. The world is in Chaos. Things Unnatural walk its lands. Whatever is spewing forth from that place is growing. In the span of only five years, since it opened, the Taint that comes from it has already spread throughout the Starlight Mountains, destroying, twisting! There are no more Living Trees remaining there. There are dark things crawling from there. And while it is only a small portion of the things going on in the world, if left unchecked, it will eventually cover all the lands and seas, perverting the Natural, severing the Connections that hold it together. If my death will slow it even a bit, it is worth it. All that I stand for, here and now; all that I am, is nothing. Nothing! If I stand by and watch! You of all people should understand why! How is it that you can ask me these things?"

Under her tirade, Sandoren shrank from the angry stance of the righteous to the slumped form of the penitent. Eyes downcast and head bowed, he shuffled from foot to foot. "I—I'm sorry!" he whispered hoarsely. "All these years of fighting, working to keep the Balance. It seems so hopeless now. There seems no rest until death. Within the last few years, things have changed so much. These Shattered Lands. These creatures. These wars and this Emperor in the North. This Chaos. It seems we fight in vain. It seems the more we fight, the quicker the Balance shifts against us. I grow tired, Alex, as I know you do. And the more tired I become, the more I question." He finally looked up at her, meeting her green eyes with his crystalline blue. "I did not mean to upset you."

"I know." She sighed, stepping forward and taking one of his hands in her own. "I know. I am tired as well. I question myself as well. This Age is coming to a close, events are occurring much more quickly the closer to that terminus. What we do may be in vain, but we must go on. No matter how many prophecies exist; no matter how many omens and portents speak, the future is not written until it is the present. To not even try to write ourselves into that future, no matter what it may be, is truly in vain. Our chance to halt this Taint lies with these two people and me. I do not know how or why, I simply know that they do. And I intend to make our future brighter than what it now seems, even if only a little." She smiled warmly and patted his cheek. "My closest friend, someday we will be able to rest, the both of us."

"Your only friend," he said with a half smirk, causing her musical laughter to burst forth. Sandoren withdrew from her touch and stooped to pick up his sword belt. "I will be there with you," he said as he strapped the weapon back around his waist.

"You always have," she retorted, laughter fading.

"So," he said, looking around. "Where do we go from here?"

Alex looked around with him, though the object of their search was pulling at her from the southwest. Just as she was about to answer, a distant, muted yell drifted to them from that direction. Sandoren spun smoothly to look, his sword seemingly sliding from its scabbard on its own volition. She nodded. "That way."

"They are just younglings looking for trouble," Sandoren whispered minutes later as they stood behind a large oak looking out into a sun drenched glade. A tall human boy, maybe sixteen years of age, slapped at tall weeds with a stout stick, while a smaller boy about the same age whined about going home. Neither was blessed with handsomeness and both wore ragged woolen breaches and dirty, holed shirts. "Farmers," he said with just a tinged of distaste.

"Let us go then," Alex said. "before you decide to scare them off." He shot her a falsely fierce look, then nodded in ascent. The pair faded away from the two youths and the glade, Alex leading. When they were far out of earshot, she pointed and said, "That way." She led the way back around the glade, giving enough berth to avoid the questing children, and headed back into the deeper undergrowth. Soon, they came to the edge of a large sunken hollow, where she stopped and pointed. Sandoren followed the gesture, but saw nothing but a large patch of lush undergrowth beneath a wide reaching oak.

"What?" he asked.

"There is the object of our search," she said, still pointing at the base of the tree.

"Where?"

"Within that undergrowth," Alex whispered. "Look at how lush and vibrant," she added, to herself more than to Sandoren. Long thick blades of grass grew densely where too much shade existed; blades longer and more luxuriant than the surrounding turf. The tree under which the patch rested was more healthy than its neighbors, its leaves wider, more deeply colored. She could feel a focal point of Elemental Power pulsing within the enfolding vegetation in slow rhythmic waves. The focal point was strong. Stronger than she ever felt before. Alex thought it odd that she hadn't felt it before she did. The way the energy rolled over her, she could probably feel it on the other side of the world.

Without warning, she scrambled down the slope toward the patch, leaving Sandoren to stare confusedly at her destination.

"I thought we were looking for a person?" he muttered darkly. Sandoren turned and surveyed the woods behind them, cocked his head and listened intently. The distant tramp of the two boys reached his ears. It appeared that they were headed toward them, albeit, in a random manner. "Noisy brats," he said. There could be all types of wild beasts lurking around, just waiting for that kind of commotion. He shook his head then followed after Alexandra. "We should hurry," he said as he caught up to her. "Those kids are libel to attract more attention than an army moving through a field of copper chamber pots."

Alex arched an eyebrow at him before turning to the patch. Before her, the lush grass parted, revealing a figure laying in the center. A large human drawn into a fetal position, dirt and dried blood encrusting the naked flesh of the person's upper torso. Sandoren stared, but could not see the rise and fall of his chest. "He's dead," he stated.

"No," she answered, sounding distant. "He's still alive, though his heart beats very, very slowly."

"How--?" he did not know quite what to say.

"He is in a deep hibernation, his body all but shut down." She took a deep breath. "He's healing. The wounds are many. He was badly beaten."

Sandoren stepped forward and kneeled at the figure's side. "Who would—" he stopped himself. He had seen worse in his long years. He reached out and gently grabbed the person's meaty shoulder and rolled him over on his back. "He's just a boy," he said tightly as he looked into the round, young, striped face.

A loud hiss split the quiet and a piercing pain lanced into his thigh. Sandoren's dagger was out in a flash, but it dropped to the forest floor as his fingers suddenly became slack. Dumbly, he stared at his hand, a shocking numbness turning his body to jelly. His mind worked furiously, but a clouding fog was working its way through his head. Nerveless, Sandoren toppled over the body of the boy, the last thing he saw, the head of a large serpent withdrawing back into its coil.

Chapter 12

Sojourn, Small as It Is

A large plate of fruit and bread awaited Marc on the table as he awoke to the sound of the village already in full activity. He listened for several minutes while allowing his eyes to adjust fully to being opened. Outside, villagers passed by, speaking to each other in musical tones. Marc could not understand them, but their meanings carried an underlying edge of anxiousness. Still, the bustle was vastly unlike human villages. Here, things were quiet, soft, even when they spoke to each other as opposed to the clang and rattle of pots, hammering of lumber, noisy gossip. He found he enjoyed this atmosphere. It rendered a peacefulness to his mind. Perhaps he should join a monastery and live out the rest of his life in silent perusal of day to day life.

An inkling of thought told him he was being absurd.

He stretched, feeling the strength of his muscles sustaining themselves. He was ready to leave. Marc straightened his clothing in a leisurely manner, pausing occasionally to eat pieces of the succulent fruit. He was basking in the range of motion he could get from his muscles and joints. After polishing off the bread and drinking down a cool cup of water, he sat down on his bed and pulled his boots on, then headed for the door. The *valeurith* parted for him, revealing a small room beyond filled with morning's light.

Marc saw the lithe figure of one of the ffolk exiting hastily, casting a quick shadow from the parted vines. "Wait!" he said hesitantly, but the ffolk disappeared, either not hearing him or ignoring him. He stopped, considered for a moment, yawned and stretched, then strode to the opening. The freshness of woodland air mixing with the rich loam of the earth breathed into him a joy and calmness he somehow knew to be rare.

Dew bejeweled leaves and grass greeted him as he looked out into a large glade surrounded by massive oaks. *Valeurith* twined and hung about them like draperies, bestowing upon the area a close, but not choked, feel. He sensed that the vines somehow complimented the huge trees instead of competing with them or strangling them. Dispersed throughout the tree line and beyond, some hugging the massive trunks, some free standing beneath the far reaching arches of the branches, were larger clusters of the vine, which, upon concentrating, emerged as small huts and other buildings. Several shrubs and bushes rose from the forest floor in strategically placed areas which alternately lent an aesthetic quality to the composition and added to its camouflage.

Indeed, he realized that had he not known to consciously look for a village he knew to be here, he might have walked right through the middle, thinking the area was just a wonderfully wild thicket of growth. Marc also realized his mouth hung slack while gazing into the village, like an idiot pleased with a puppet show, or a thief gazing at the rarest of jewels. He composed himself, feeling the stirrings of embarrassment start to flush his cheeks.

Marc stepped from the doorway onto the soft bed of grass and looked around the glade. Several ffolk moved through the tree line, walking lightly, almost gliding, with a grace few humans achieved. Most wore clothes in varying shades of greens and browns, some of purples or crimsons, but all deep, rich colors of a satin-soft material. Styles, too, varied, but whether skirt, or dress, or robe, or trouser and shirt, all were practical and functional. Many of the women had their silvery hair tied back in braids, while others let their long tresses cascade freely down their slender backs. The men were more uniform, wearing their hair shoulder length and free. The children were typical, running, playing; hair mussed and clothes dirty, calling to each other joyously.

As a whole, he had to admit that these were a beautiful people and was touched anew each time he saw a member of this delicately-sculpted, violet-eyed, musically-toned race. Underneath it was strength of spirit evident, subtly, in the way they carried themselves, the way they spoke, and even in the thin long swords some of the men wore on their hips. Woe to any that mistook their beauty for weakness. Marc almost felt ashamed of being the rugged human that he was and was slightly envious. They seemed at peace with their surroundings and with themselves; seemed to have reached a perfection of form, of attitude that eluded all other races, including other ffolk.

Yet, there was a deep undercurrent of sorrow in each and every one of them. He could see it in their eyes, hear it when they spoke. Something so strongly embedded within their spirits that it could almost be felt without the benefit of vision or hearing. And it was impervious to the prying of others.

It was well known that the Greyffolk collectively were searching for something called the Rains, or Tears, or some such. He couldn't quite remember. But, it was rumored, that this was the cause of their sadness. It was also well known that no-one, not even the Greyffolk themselves, knew what exactly they were searching for. Regardless, they searched, but would not, possibly could not, elaborate on it.

A large grin broke out over his mouth and he chuckled. Marc's former thoughts were forgotten as he realized what had just occurred. He was remembering! Small abstract memories maybe, but he knew them to be his and was tremendously pleased. Marc urged his mind toward something more specific, but it clamped down and refused to give anymore. It was a start though, and, hopefully, it would be soon when his memory broke free of its shackles. Very soon. He was already starting to think of it as his other self.

"Well, you are looking quite well," a familiar voice said from his far right. Upon turning, he saw the Prime Elder walking towards him, hands outstretched; a thin smile creasing his elderly face. Slightly behind him and to his right was another of the ffolk, aged, but not as much as the Prime Elder, and a deep penetrating quality to his otherwise kind eyes. Behind them, trailing a couple of yards, head slightly bowed, was Maelyrin.

"Yes. I am feeling much better, thank you." He gave a smile that was half token in response to the quickness with which he had company. The Prime Elder strode up and placed his hands on Marc's wide shoulders. "Excellent," he replied.

"Are you still experiencing memory loss?" the other ffolk asked. His tone was unhurried, yet demanding like a city official at census time. Marc squinted back. The Prime Elder, noting this exchange, sidled around Marc, holding his hand out toward the stranger.

"Ah, I'm sorry, you haven't formally been introduced. *Qaela*, this is Korin, our Faethe. Korin, this is Sir Marc Pendragon." The Faethe's brow arched at the name, but there was no movement within his eyes. "A pleasure," he said after some moments.

"Greetings, Faethe. I am told you worked long to help me. I am grateful," Marc said. "I haven't regained the important memories, but others slip in once in a while." He watched Marc with the same piercing gaze the Prime Elder had when they had had their first conversation. "I am sure your memories will return in time."

His gaze left Marc and fell upon the Prime Elder "*Mythesal, helas thon sunmar qoala zym.*"

"*Varlesthyll,*" the Prime Elder answered. Korin glanced back at Marc. "I am glad that you are well and hope you enjoy your stay with us."

"Thank you," Marc replied. He was mulling over the interchange between the two elder ffolk, finding the strange, musical language somewhat familiar, when the Faethe turned and walked around the hut. He saw Maelyrin's eyes follow him until he disappeared and a slight change of, possibly, relief come over her.

"Korin is busier than usual today," the Prime Elder stated, sounding more excuse than observation. "Is there anything we can do for you, *Qaela*?" He returned his gaze to Marc and smiled again, but revealing only the deep sadness within his violet eyes. Marc pretended not to notice.

"Yes. I would like to walk around a bit, get a little exercise. And I am very interested in seeing more of your beautiful village before I leave."

The Prime Elder blinked and the corners of his mouth twitched downward, but only for a second. "You are leaving?" he asked. "Do you think that is wise?"

"Yes," Marc said. "I am well enough to travel and have taken up too much of your hospitality. Aside from the obvious, I feel a drive to do so."

"Are you not happy with the treatment you have received?"

"No," Marc said quickly, holding up his hands. "No. Not at all. I am quite happy with your kindness, but I must go. It is unexplainable, but undeniable. Though I promise I will not do so until I have taken in the beauty of your village."

"Ah, good," the Prime Elder said slowly. The reticence in his voice echoed in his eyes, but he smiled warmly. "I am glad you enjoy your surroundings. It is not often we have visitors, so it is a pleasure for us that you see as much as you wish. I suspected you would probably like some company. Maelyrin will show you around. Take as long as you like. I have some duties to attend to so will not delay you any longer. Enjoy." He, too, exited quickly, somewhat nervously. His reply also seemed insincere, giving Marc a pause. Maelyrin was watching him as intently until he hove out of sight. When she looked up and found Marc gazing questionably at her, she began to blush.

"Did I miss something?" he asked.

"Miss something?" a small grin began to curve along her slim face.

"They seemed rather in quite of a hurry to divest themselves of my company."

"Oh please do not take offense, *Qaela*." She said. "If you require someone else to accompany you, I can arrange it."

His hand came up and a smile broke on his face. "No. No, that's not what I meant. I would prefer your company over theirs anytime, but they seemed nervous. And I wouldn't want to place you in an uncomfortable position."

"Oh. Do not worry about me," she said, a taste of grimness lacing her comment. "The Faethe is a little upset because his talents were unable to benefit you, and you confuse him. The Prime Elder? He tries to please everyone, so gets flustered when there is not harmony around him."

"How do I confuse him?" She wasn't being wholly sincere, either.

"He thought you would not be healthy enough to move around for another two or three weeks."

"Two or three weeks?"

"Yes. That is what he told the Prime Elder. That you should still be too weak to move. He said you heal too fast."

"Did he? Maybe he doesn't know much about humans."

"The Faethe spent many of his young years in the company of humans. He knows much about your kind." The rebuke was sharp, but there was no anger in her voice or her eyes, only pain.

"I'm sorry," he said softly. "I meant no disrespect. Will you forgive me?" She looked at him a long time. The pain in her eyes seemed to intensify, and, at one point, he felt she was looking through him, then they cleared of all emotion and she nodded. He sighed inwardly. Still, he sensed she wasn't quite telling the truth, and something in the back of his mind told him that wasn't quite what was said to the Prime Elder. He decided, however, to drop it. "I understand a horse followed the men that rescued me. Could you take me to him?"

She smiled. "Yes. A magnificent animal." She took his arm at the elbow and led him toward a small path that exited the glade. For several minutes they wound through barely discernible paths through the village. Marc noticed several times the intense glances they received. They were quick, furtive looks full of curiosity and, even, outright fear. He realized that most of the fearful looks were directed towards his guide. Maelyrin, on the surface, seemed not to notice, but he could see the tenseness in her petite frame as she walked and the carefully constructed veneer of outer calm on her face. He idly wondered if his presence was causing the stirrings, but quickly banished that notion because of her behavior. She had much practice in her appearance of unconcern. Those looks of fear were old and had been long directed at her.

Marc walked quietly as she led, showing him points of interest within the village, but his interest was only half genuine as his mind tumbled over thoughts and observations of his guide and the villagers' reactions. It was by pure reflex that he did not run into her when she stopped.

They were at the edge of a large clearing, the village behind no longer in sight. Maelyrin, now more relaxed, smiled up at him and pointed into the glade. "He is there," she said.

Following her outstretched arm, he found himself looking at a large white stallion grazing near the opposite edge. She had been right when she had said 'magnificent'. The beast had to be at least seventeen hands high and was heavily muscled under the coat of ivory. Marc's brain went into a frenzy of recognition, but whatever was trying to push to the fore was being tangled in a mass of fog. He noticed Maelyrin gazing at him with that faraway look. Marc stared at the stallion, trying so hard to remember that beads of sweat broke out on his forehead, but those thoughts still wouldn't rise. The horse, clipping several bites of lush grass and chewing contentedly, looked up and over at the two watchers. His ears twitched.

"Whitesteel," he mumbled as their eyes met. The beast heaved forward and began to trot toward them, muscles rippling. "I can see why," said Maelyrin, the slight twang of awe echoing her thoughts.

"What?" Marc replied, giving her a sidelong glance. She looked up with sparkling violet eyes and smiled. "His name. I can see why his name is 'Whitesteel'." The stallion drew closer, digging great clods of earth from his passing, then slowed to a walk. He snorted then nuzzled Marc in the chest nearly throwing him from his feet.

"Hello, old friend," Marc said tenderly, scratching the great beast behind the ears and hugging the hot neck. "It has been some time, hasn't it?" The reply was a strong nudging from Whitesteel's head and a soft whinny.

Maelyrin moved silently away and seated herself on a low hanging branch of a nearby tree and watched Marc and the stallion become re-acquainted. Marc patted and scratched the beast while talking in a low tone while the horse responded with nudges, snorts and nickers. She tried once again to *Read* him, but still could not. There was something her Sight just could not penetrate. A small smile curled on her lips. She could not *See* him. It was both frustrating and exhilarating at the same time. The curse that separated her so distantly from her own people did not work against this human. The thought that maybe all humans were immune to her Sight drifted up. It was a consideration that gave her comfort. Maelyrin broke from her thoughts to find Marc gazing at her, a smirk of sorts gracing his features. Whitesteel was trotting back into the glade.

"I told him to go back and play," Marc said, following her gaze at the great animal. "Are you okay?"

"Yes," she said lightly, still watching the beauty of the galloping stallion. "I was just thinking of something."

Marc walked over and sat on the branch near her, causing it to sway. Maelyrin suddenly became unbalanced from the movement and nearly pitched backward, but Marc shot out a hand and steadied her. She looked down to the large callused hand on her arm, the heat that flowed from his touch seemed nearly to burn her. Something else welled up in her; a hot feeling she had never experienced before. Surprised at her reaction, she looked up, finding Marc gazing intently at her with those iron gray eyes.

"Is something wrong?" he said, breaking the spell that had begun to entrance her. Maelyrin blinked, realized her mouth hung slightly open, then turned her face away to hide the flush rising into her cheeks.

"I'm fine. . ." she answered. "Y-you just. . . startled me." Marc's hand relaxed and withdrew. She held her breath, still feeling the sensation his touch had left, and quietly attempted to calm her rapid heart.

"Maelyrin? The Prime Elder said there was some other equipment with Whitesteel." He waited for her nod, then, "Do you know where it is kept?"

"Yes. It is in the hut you have been using."

"Really?" he looked a little confused. "Where?"

She grinned at his naïveté "There is more to the *valeurith* than what you have seen."

"It appears that there is quite a bit that I haven't yet realized about your village and people," he replied. Maelyrin shifted and looked away quickly. Concern and embarrassment washed over her face, but she took rapid control over it and masked it with her neutral expression. Marc cleared his throat.

"Well," he said, watching the stallion graze in the sunlit field. "I guess I should get back to my hut and gather my things." He watched her out of the corner of his eyes as she flinched and looked quickly at him.

"You are leaving?" she said.

"Yes."

"But why so soon?" she asked, trying to hide her over-interest in the subject. "Are you not comfortable here?"

"Yes, very much so." He was gazing at her, peering into the depths of her violet eyes. "But, I have much to discover about who I am. I do not think I will find out here, and I have an undeniable drive to move on. Plus, I think that my presence here has disturbed the fair ffolk of this village and I do not wish to upset the peace any more than I have."

"But, *Qaela*, you are an honored guest. Your presence has not disturbed our village."

"Yes, it has, Maelyrin. I can feel a difference just between today and yesterday. Your elders are tense, there is something wrong." She was shaking her head slightly.

"I explained about that. The Prime elder—" she stopped as he softly grasped her arm.

"Please, Maelyrin." He looked away for a few moments. "I don't know when, or where, or even how, but I have spent time with your people before and know that they are not easily flustered, especially the elders. Is this not true?" He looked back and into eyes that were becoming shiny with moisture. She turned away, closed them and nodded. "So I think it would be best that I go as soon as I can."

"You have suffered much. You should rest a few more days."

"No. I feel fine."

"Why not?" she said, a tiny flicker of frustration spicing the tone.

"Why are you so interested in keeping me here?" A look of shock crossed her features that quickly transformed into a look of ire and embarrassment. She stood rapidly and took a few steps away from the branch. With her back still toward Marc, she said, "Why do you say that?"

Marc smiled while looking at her lithe figure framed by the sunlight from the glade. His eyes flowed over the soft curves of her young body, accentuated by the dress she wore.

Her beauty was also heightened by the mixture of innocence and knowing that she displayed. "You tell me."

Slowly she turned, gazing at the ground. Her chest was heaving slightly, but when she spoke, her voice was level and placid. "I do not know why. You are the first human I have ever met and am not even sure others would have the same effect on me. But I feel an affinity to you that I have not experienced in a long time. I find it easy to talk to you. That is rare."

"Can you not talk to your own people?" She looked up at him, a maelstrom of sorrow, anger, pride, and frustration storming behind her eyes.

"My station is revered among my people, but also feared."

"I do not understand. Is it unusual for a woman to become a healer?"

"No." The hint of a smile began tugging at her lips. "A healer can be either a man or woman. I speak of a 'gift' bestowed upon me by my mothers before me."

"And that is?"

"I . . . *See* things."

"You are a seer?"

"No. Not exactly. It is difficult to explain, but I *See* into people and I know what they feel, who they are, and in some sense, what they are thinking. I perceive change, know things. It is a talent that is yet not matured, but it is said among my people that it will be our redemption for it is the one true way of understanding the nature of the Tears of the World."

"What are these Tears?"

"No one knows what they are. They are something we lost at the beginning of time, and it is our responsibility to recover them. All throughout the world, we ffolk are driven to find them, and it is for those of us with this ability to understand them. Only, the talent is becoming more and more rare. It is feared that one day, the ability will be lost to us and then so will we be lost."

"Is this why you are feared?" His look of confusion caused her to smile, even as the single crystal tear slid down her alabaster cheek.

"My people are extremely private, even amongst themselves. It is neither appreciated nor understood how I can know every intimate detail about everyone I meet."

"I see."

"Except you," Maelyrin said quickly. "I cannot *See* you and know nothing about you at all."

"Do not worry," Marc said. "I do not fear that. In fact, it would probably be helpful, since I don't even know anything about myself." He chuckled, then, Maelyrin smiled.

"I find myself wondering if you are the only one my 'gift' does not work on," she said, looked out into the glade. "It is refreshing."

"Refreshing?" Marc prompted.

The skin around her eyes tightened a bit and her jaw clenched. Several heartbeats passed before her face loosened. "I am a needed thing, but not wanted. None of my people can possible understand my Sight, and there are no others with this 'gift' that can help me . . . cope. I am a pariah among my kind. I did not realize how much until I met you and your . . . resistance."

"I'm sorry," Marc started, but stopped his next words when she began to shake her head.

"No. It has always lingered there. Your presence has only prompted me to look at it with more . . . more realistically."

"What are you saying?" Marc asked.

She suddenly looked at him, a flash of surprise crossing her fine features, as if he had just caught her slipping sleep herbs into someone's drink. "Nothing," she said.

He stood, casting another glance at Whitesteel, not knowing what else to say, not wanting to cause her anymore discomfort. Instead, he smiled and nodded. "I should be getting back. I am happy that you have found someone you feel comfortable talking with, but, as your people are driven to find these Tears, I am driven to find my identity. Would you escort me back to my hut, I probably will not be able to find it on my own."

She visibly struggled with herself, then smiled neutrally. "Of course, *Qaela*."

Chapter 13

Exploring the Wasteland

The line coiled out of sight, lost in the clouds of dust kicked up by the horses' hooves. Commander Marklin du Anlin, turned back forward in his saddle to look at the wasteland ahead of them. Behind him, trailing by twos were a thousand horse of the entire 3rd Regiment of the Imperial Cavalry spread over a mile back. Each man dressed in charcoal grey, lightly armored with muted steel breastplates, high black boots, wide brimmed hats to keep the sun off, all dusted with the brown of the dirt. Half the regiment carried lances and the other, short bows, and all were armed with long swords. Each were slumped in their saddles, relaxing as best as they could as their mounts plodded along. A symphony of snorts and whickers, coughs and sneezes, due to the drifting powder, sang counterpoint to the jangle of fastenings and creak of leather and thudding of hooves.

Anlin gazed ahead, blocking the ever-present noise of the regiment from his mind, having to squint even though the sun was balancing atop the sharp broken crags of newly formed mountains that walled them to the west. The land here was blasted, and dry, mostly a russet flat expanse of dust broken by tough scraggly bushes from which a high pitched constant buzzing often emanated, the work of large flat-gray winged bugs being called Bloodeyes by the men. Occasionally, towering outcroppings of rock thrust up out of the ground like terrible mockeries of stripped, limbless trees, casting stark shadows twice their lengths to point desperately toward the east. The air was still and heavy, but it was not overly hot, though the way ahead did shimmer. Still, everyone hunched uncomfortably in their saddles, patches of wetness staining their armpits and back, dabbing at faces with kerchiefs and sipping regularly at their water skins, not at all eased by the heat rising from their mounts. His preliminary reports of the area, at least, had been accurate, and they were the more prepared for it.

His orders had been to head up the east side of the mountain range from the new fortress of Nur that was being constructed within the bay just south of the Rift and probe the fortress of Tergaard, once guarding the southernmost border of the lands of the former ruler, Hedric. Scouts had reported that it now stood on the lip of the great rip in the ground, partially separating the continent, joining New Sea, which completed the break. Tergaard was reported as being deserted though only one of the five scouts dispatched to the mighty fortress had returned. If abandoned, it would be reclaimed and refortified if possible, a strong holding for the Empire in the lands south. If not, he would have to return to Nur with his reports of strength and defenses being maintained within.

Anlin looked around the blasted terrain, thinking that the fortress was more than likely abandoned. This area was once verdant grassland, but since the Dark Night, when the world tried to shake itself apart, the lands changed. The Rift appeared, a tremendous gash slashing northeast to southwest across the continent, impossibly deep, impossibly wide, cutting off all former trade routes and water sources from the northwest. Within weeks, the area this side of the cut dried up, becoming the wasteland they now rode in. More than likely, Tergaard, perched on the lip of the cleft, no longer had an available water source to support two people, much less a full regiment or more of the Imperial Army. Hopefully, for their sakes, there would be a stockpile of some sort. A contained reservoir for just such an emergency. Of course, five years was too long a time to hope for much. Even if the standing garrison left, the place would most probably have been plundered several times.

He cast a glance backward at the cloud of dust drifting along with them lazily in the over-warm air, shook his head. If anyone or anything remained at Tergaard, he hoped they were friendly, for they were sending them a nice big herald of their coming.

The parched top soil, still soft and loose, would make it extremely difficult for even just one rider to remain inconspicuous, much less a thousand. Begrudgingly, that was the only reason he could think of for the general's directions to send an entire regiment into what was considered hostile territory. The sheer number of armed and armored men should dissuade any opposition. Any unplanned opposition, that is.

Two distinct fans of dust appeared in front and to the left of the column. *Scouts*, he thought just as Captain Turcot beside him muttered, "Scouts!" and someone behind them, Makson he thought, yelled, "Scouts coming in!" Anlin snorted, raised his hand, signaling a halt and pulled his mount reluctantly to a stop. Behind him, the tumultuous jangling and snorting rose in response to the sudden change in the routine. The men, excited by the difference of pace, began yammering quietly, sounding like a dull roar in the stillness. Turcot drew in a breath, ready to dress them down, but Anlin looked at him and shook his head. The assignment and surroundings were bad enough. No need to kick their morale in the teeth with nit picking.

Standing still, not moving against the dry air, the heat coming up from the horse sweltering, caused sweat to bead quickly and drip down his face and form a runnel on the lower part of the brim of his hat. He thumbed away a large drop dangling from his brow, jiggling in front of his eye. Rushwind, his horse, tugged at his reins, snuffling at the dust for something to chew. Striker, the Captain's mount, stretched out, stiff legged, and began relieving himself in the dust, Turcot leaning forward to take some of the pressure from the animal's kidneys. The clouds continued to grow, looking like two flames made of dust, their cores, two dark figures on horseback.

Anlin scrunched his nose, never quite used to the acrid odor of horse urine though he had been around them since birth. The heat and dust only made it worse. "Hurry up!" Turcot mumbled while dabbing at sweat with the cuff of his uniform. *Yes do.* Anlin added mentally.

The two were at a gallop, closing quickly, now easily identified. Silek, on the left, gray travel cloak whipping out behind him had been with Anlin for a good ten years, one of the better scouts he had ever known; the best human scout, he had a special gift when it came to finding things. Anlin often wondered why he did not follow a more lucrative venture, like bounty hunting, instead of hanging around with him and whatever troop he currently commanded. He often considered that about himself. Why he still insisted on the hard, dull life of a soldier.

Next to Silek was someone who caused him much more concern. Maliss. Even in this heat, he wore his customary dark, nearly black, leather long coat that seemed to defy the wind his mount was generating, it was so heavy. A close hood wrapped his head and a kerchief covered the lower half of his face so that one could only see the dark, partially slitted eyes framed by thick green cast skin common to his Skoran heritage. No other part of his skin was visible, his entire body covered by some dark material of one type or another, mostly leather. He was the most recent assignment to the regiment, placed just before they left Vistan, by the Corps Commander himself, saying only that Maliss possessed special 'talents' that would benefit the mission. He did not go into any detail, staying professionally aloof to inquiries, as was Maliss. Rarely speaking at all in general, the Skor merely stared with a disconcerting blankness when asked questions regarding his background. Silek seemed to like him, what the connection was, Anlin didn't know, but they appeared to work well together. Under those circumstances, Anlin was willing to overlook the uncomfortable feel Maliss tended to leave with him; something akin to the slimy scum that forms on long standing water. Still, he would keep an eye out. It was always bothersome when his superiors intervened in something he was in command of, especially when he was not informed as to the specifics. It was more than irksome when they meddled in affairs that were strictly his bailiwick, like choosing and hiring scouts.

The two of them slowed to a walk only a few yards from the main body of the regiment as he continued his thoughts along those lines as far as he could. The dust cloud they had created rolled over them. Anlin bent his head forward, letting the wide brim of his hat catch most of the settling dust. Sweat dripped off the end onto the horn of his saddle. Out of the corner of his eye, he saw that Turcot was doing the same. After a few moments of silence, he asked, "Well?"

"We found water." Silek was smiling. He stood in his stirrups for a couple of seconds to stretch his legs and back. "Couple miles distant. Natural spring. Fresh."

"Where?" Anlin asked, suppressing his excitement. The previous scouting reports had mentioned both a flowing creek and a spring. When found, the creek was but a sandy memory and the spring had been fetid and undrinkable. It was not without a heavy feeling that he ordered them further into the wastes just on the off chance that another source could be found. Luck, so far, was with them.

Silek plow-reined his horse, turning him in a tight circle, then pointed northwest, towards the jagged mountains. "That peak with the three notches; at its base within the foothills is a spring bubbling down into a pool eight, maybe nine, feet across. The surrounding area is wide and flat with tall escarpments on three sides and a large outcropping of fallen boulders on a large portion of the forth. It might be a little tight, but I think it will shelter the whole regiment, though it will take some time to rotate them around the pool."

"Any grazing?"

"Some." He sighed. "But not enough for even one fifth of the regiment." Anlin repeated the sigh inwardly, realizing he had been getting his hopes too high. At least they still had some spare rations in addition to the packs the mules carried.

"Excellent," he said while grimly noting that Maliss had hardly blinked during the whole interchange. "You two go ahead and fall back to the rear and req some extra rations and take a break. Be ready to help guide, you probably will not being going out again today. Any sign of Melik and Danisek?"

"No," Silek shook his head, his face tightening slightly. "But we crossed their path earlier, heading further north than us."

Anlin nodded, a bitter taste in his mouth. Two of his ten scouts were long overdue, gone since the early hours before sunrise, with no explanation. It was tough to think they may have deserted, especially since he had a record of keeping scouts that out did most of the other officers he dealt with, and even tougher to think that something may have happened. Which was his first inclination; that being the most common problem he had had to deal with in his long career. If so, he hoped it was something simple, like a mount going lame. He hated to think of the worst, however much he had to. It was his theory that his concern for his troops was what kept him successful as a commander, but his fretting tended to have adverse effects on his digestive system; knots of frustration that upset his stomach being the norm. "Dismissed," he said.

"Sir!" Silek said with a half salute that elicited a half smile on Anlin's mouth. He peeled his mount away and he and Maliss nudged their horses into dust churning trots. Several of the men sitting behind moaned out some complaints about the cloud, but they were unheard or simply ignored by the scouts. Anlin turned in his saddle to peer back along the line, a common practice, almost a compulsion. Directly behind him and Turcot, were the bannermen, holding aloft the long staves that bore the Imperial and Regimental Colors, each standard a limp tract of cloth hiding the coat of arms they each bore. Without so much as a word, he gave the signal to move forward, angling Rushwind toward the notched peak Silek had indicated. By his estimation, they should reach the shelter by dusk.

Chapter 14

A Focal Point

"*W*hat happened?" Sandoren mumbled. Cotton clogged his mouth, throat, and brain. An answering *tsk*! brought his eyes around to Alexandra, who wore a half-impish, half-serious look on her face.

"After all these years, Sandy." she teased.

"Huh?" he answered groggily.

"You would think you would be a bit more careful, check for things like silver adders and such."

"Silver—" He groaned as he remembered the hiss and quick numbness. A fuzzy image of a serpent's head danced in his mind's eye. "Is it still here?"

"No. She has gone back to her nest to take care of her young. I swear," she continued unabashedly. "What would you do without me to pull your butt out of trouble?"

"Probably be married with six or seven children. Maybe even working a farm or something," he groused, struggling to sit up. His body trembled with weakness from the poison, even with the aid of Alex.

"I'm glad I am such a positive influence on your life," she retorted. "Thanks for the compliment."

"Any time," Sandoren said. With her help, he pulled himself back against the huge oak that dominated the hollow. "What about the boy?" he finally asked, gesticulating weakly with his hand. The large, meaty child now lay on his back within the nest of lush flora. His thick chest rose and fell in long rhythms; his welts were gone, cuts and scrapes, the pink of new flesh and the once dark bruises now soft yellow.

"He sleeps," she answered. "Whoever beat him did some mean work to him. Several broken ribs, cracked skull, internal bleeding. By all rights, he should have been dead." Her brow furrowed, unsaid thoughts crossing behind her eyes. "Were it not . . ." the furrow deepened, emerald eyes distant. He did not know what she was worrying over, but suspected. She had mentioned much the same about the man she Healed in the ffolk village. The one that carried the terrible poison. She was puzzling out a meaning he did not even begin to want to understand.

He was about to prompt her when she suddenly shook her head and said, "Were it not for what he is, he would be dead."

"Seems to be going around," Sandoren said, unable to completely hide his sarcasm. She merely nodded. "What is he?"

"I'm not sure, exactly," she answered while visibly pondering the sleeping form. "It's almost as if he is some sort of focal point, or something. He is incredibly strong with the Power. Many more times stronger than myself."

"Could he be an Earth—father?" he prompted, fumbling around the unusual word. She considered for many moments. "Fa 'Andel?"

"No," she finally said. "He is incredibly strong, but it is unfocused, amorphous. There is no direction or purpose," she cocked her head to the side, a motion he well knew. "It simply exists." She kept staring at the boy. "Besides, Dartaign has to draw the Power as well as I to use it. The boy isn't drawing it. . . He is it." To his knowledge, Alex had never met Dartaign, the only male that could touch the Power of the World, but she spoke as if they were old friends. Of course, he knew, though not through experience, that they were all somehow connected to each other. Bound in some way he did not understand.

"Where is Dartaign?" he asked suddenly for no other reason than to confirm that line of thinking. She looked at him, her eyes seeming to focus.

"What?" she said.

"Where is he?" he repeated. "Dartaign?" She pointed in a northeasterly direction.

"Somewhere far that way," She cocked her head again. "He's hurt, but not badly." She came to, quickly looking at him, saying, "Why?"

"Just curious," he said, unable to stifle the grin that tickled the corners of his mouth. Her own sudden grin sprang fully to her face, and she picked up a bit of nearby bark and tossed it at him. He blocked it with up flung hands.

"You're just trying to change the subject," she accused. He shrugged, still smiling.

"Maybe."

"Has your strength returned yet?"

He held up an arm and flexed it, feeling the tension in it. "It's getting there."

"Good," she said. "It shouldn't be too much longer before the after-effects of the adder's poison has gone. Then we can go." Sandoren was looking around him concernedly, causing her to smile again. "Don't worry, she is gone."

"What do you mean, 'worry'?" He drew back a little defensively. "I'm just checking around and making sure nothing is, uh, sneaking around while we sit here chatting."

"Sure, Sandy." Her comment caused him to squint at her in mock anger.

"What about him?" he gestured to the supine form again.

"He is going with us," she answered, her matter-of-fact tone reflected sharply in hard-as-steel eyes.

"What about his family?" he asked, masking his incredulity with studied effort. Alex quirked an eye at him and huffed.

"He has no family, Sandy," she stated. "We've been here for hours, and no one has come looking for him. He was badly beaten and near death. And he has to come with us."

"And if he doesn't want to come with us?"

She sniffed loudly and muttered something under her breath, so quiet even he, with his sensitive hearing, could not pick it up. He was about to argue further, but the stubbornness etched into her face was stronger than the rock that held up a fortress. Instead, he shrugged and cleared his throat and gazed out into the woods. "Yea, well," he intoned. "I suppose we will wrestle that bear when it rears."

Chapter 15

A Cause for Escape

"*We* gotta go 'ome." Bren whined. He was standing in the middle of a small clearing gazing up into the late afternoon sky. In one hand dangled the limp body of a squirrel that Colin had killed with a well thrown rock, in the other, a gnarled stick that had been his 'sword'. Several bruises dotted his arms and a blood encrusted scrape slashed down one of his cheeks.

"We can't go until we find Stupid!" Colin remarked. He, too, had some bruises, but not quite as many as Bren. "He's gotta be around here somewhere."

"He's probly l'ready 'ome." Bren mumbled. Colin spun on his heel, hand grasping tightly to his whipping stick. Even though Bren was far out of reach, he still took a startled step backward.

"And if he isn't?" Colin hissed. "We go back an' he's not, we get it good! We're already in for it now! I say we stay until we find him!"

"Then what?" asked Bren with caution.

"Then we beat 'im up some more, drag 'im home an' tell Burjon that he tried to run away an' we chased 'im and got 'im back."

"We're gonna get a beat'n anyhow." Bren offered.

"Yea," Colin turned away from him, swinging the stick in a slashing motion. The top of a thick weed fell to the ground. "but it won't be as bad." He began walking across the clearing.

"'Sides, I been thinkin' that I'm tired of getting beat by that ol' man."

"So?"

"So, I been thinkin' that the next time he raises that strap to me, I'm gonna kill 'im,'". Bren, who had begun dragging after him, stopped suddenly, his mouth dropping open and eyes going wide.

"Kill 'im?" he said. Colin walked to the clearing's edge and plopped down on a rotting, fallen log.

"Yea." He said, noncommittally.

"If you kill 'im, where'r we gonna get food." Colin stared at him for several seconds before scooping up a short, thick stick from the forest floor and hurling it at him. Bren threw himself down, a yelp of surprise escaping from him. The stick sailed harmlessly past where his head had been.

"Sometimes I wonder if you're stupider than Dummy!" Colin said when Bren's head bobbed up over the grass line. "Wha'?" he said.

"Bren, wha' did you have in your hand jus' a second ago?" Bren's eyes widened and he looked around frantically. After a few seconds, he crawled to the side and lifted the tiny corpse up over his head, a look of triumph on his simple features.

"Food!" he cried, grinning. Colin shook his head and stood.

"Come on," he said. "Let's get outa here and find Mudswine."

"Yea," he mumbled, scrambling to his feet. "Okay."

Colin was already walking beneath the thick canopy surrounding the glade, and Bren had to run to catch up. The two tromped through the woods for over an hour, speaking raucously, slashing plants with their sticks, throwing rocks and stones at squirrels and rabbits and other fauna. Once the light began to dim as the sun dropped lower to the horizon, even Colin had fallen silent, both dragging their feet, their sticks hanging limply at their sides. They were following a thin game trail, heading for an easy sloping knoll, when Colin suddenly went rigid, then knelt quickly, throwing an arm back to grab Bren.

"Wha—" he began, but was cut off by a low hiss and fierce look from Colin. Abruptly, he knelt just behind his companion, leaned over and whispered, "Wha' s'matter?" He received a sharp punch to the thigh, tried to stifle the grunt that wanted to answer the pain of the shot.

"Listen!" Colin spit, using his other hand to gesture toward the small rise ahead. Bren cocked his head, bringing a filthy hand to cup his ear. His brows crinkled together as he concentrated. Drifting to them just beneath the sounds of the evening creatures coming to life, was the distinct music of laughter, followed by the low murmur of softly speaking voices.

In a low crouch, Colin crept toward the crest of the knoll. Taking cover behind some brush and dead fall, he slowly raised up and looked over the rise, down the other side. He quickly bobbed back behind the screen and whispered something to himself before turning his gaze to Bren and waving him to come up, placing a finger to his lips and giving him a look to curdle milk. Bren cast a glance up into the boughs of the darkening trees, cringing slightly when he saw several bats flit by. As fast and as silently as he could, he scrambled up beside Colin, received another tag on the shoulder.

Slowly, both lifted to look over the deadfall. The knoll crested smoothly, but plunged steeply down the other side, eventually rounding into a deep, bowl-like depression. Near the center was a huge, spreading tree under which came the origins of the voices. Three people were standing beneath the bough near the gigantic bole, speaking and brushing their clothes of dirt, seedlings, and dried grass. Dummy was there, nodding his head, a smile on his stupid face.

He was only given a cursory once over, however, as the other two demanded more than just a glance. Bren, slack-jawed, could only stare. Next to Stupid stood a slender man in loose clothing, a slim sword buckled at his waist. Next to him was. . . he blinked several times, sighed loudly. The most beautiful woman he had ever laid eyes on stood right against the tree speaking with the hulking idiot in musical tones. Long, full raven hair framed a face right out of the stories. Bren was sure the man was ffolk, another one right out of the tales, and a warrior to boot, but he could not have been more interested. He figured he could sit there and stare at the woman forever.

As they watched, she turned away from the idiot and placed her hands on the trunk of the huge tree. A second later, small popping noises, like fat raindrops on dry leaves, filled the hollow. The tree, straight up through the center, seemed to peel away from itself as if it were splitting into two separate trees. The flaps then folded in on themselves, widening until a large hole waited in the center of the trunk, wide enough for two men abreast and maybe half again as tall as the idiot. Colin sat, mesmerized, and Bren had to jam his dirt encrusted fist in his mouth to keep from gasping.

The woman said something softly and motioned with her hands. Dummy lumbered forward, disappearing within the tree, followed closely by the ffolk with the sword. The woman waited only a moment before she, too, disappeared within the embrace of the tree. Bren slowly lowered himself and turned so he could lean against the deadfall. His eyes were wide and unblinking and just as he was about to garner enough strength to speak, Colin grabbed his shoulder and began pulling him over the brush. "Wha?" he gasped

"Come on!" Colin spit, letting go of Bren's dead weight. When Bren gained enough composure to turn and look, still crouching for fear that the strangers would suddenly pop out of the trunk and point at him, Colin was sliding down the slope on his heels, over half way down the bowl.

"What are y' doin'?" he hissed down at him. Colin hit the more level slope, stumbled, and ran toward the tree. Without turning, he called back, "Goin' after them! Come on!"

"What?" he cried. He instinctively ducked back behind the brush. "Uh. . ." Bren, realizing suddenly he was about to be left alone in the thick woods, night falling, evil things walking, jumped up and started after Colin, who was at the tree, inspecting the slowly closing hole, tripped and tumbled down the slope amidst fallen leaves, grass, weeds, dirt, grunts and squawks of surprise. Miraculously, he landed at the bottom of the deep slope on his feet and stumbled his way toward the tree. Colin was just within the threshold of the 'doorway' in the trunk.

"Shouldn't we jus' go 'ome?" he asked, breathlessly.

"Go if you wan'!" remarked Colin. "You can tell Burjon he escaped death while he beats ya' haf to it." The portal beyond was as dark as night, but like a tunnel, there was a small point of light seemingly far distant. Colin entered, began walking toward it. Bren, hands on knees, huffing, cast one look backwards into the hollow, in what he thought was the direction of the farm. If he went back, he would be beaten three times over, probably get locked in the barn and have to eat moldy bread and drink souring milk. He looked into the tree, barely making out Colin's shadowed form within, the sides coming closer together. He began to fidget, lick his lips rapidly. Death could be waiting beyond that portal. He looked at the farm far away, beatings, locked up, he realized too, he would have to do the work of three now that Colin and the Dummy were gone. A frustrated grunt boiled up into his throat, the hole was smaller still; he could no longer see Colin. He held his breath and plunged into the darkness of the tree as if jumping into the water hole.

Chapter 16

Departures

*T*he supple leather made a soft pop as Marc tightened the cinch around the massive barrel chest of Whitesteel. The horse whickered in response. Marc's eyes rested upon the hilt of the sword, tracing its length from the pommel to the cross guard, down the plain leather scabbard, which he had fastened to the saddle. He was not sure why he did that. He still did not remember anything about the weapon, save for a distant vague familiarity, but it had somehow seemed right to fasten it as he had. "Do you know who I am?" Marc whispered in Whitesteel's ear as he gently scratched the beast's cheek. The horse stamped his foot and snorted.

The amulet hung heavily around his neck, its weight slightly irritating. It still bore no familiarity whatsoever, unlike the indistinct impressions the sword did. Or the saddle. Or his other meager belongings. The Prime Elder had again probed him about the bauble after he had returned to his hut for a small repast of fruit. Although he denied it, the Elder expressed a peculiar intense interest in it and how it related to him, almost trying to force him to admit a history with it. Marc did not know why he did not leave it on the small table. Probably, it was that it was found in belongings that were his only by association, that it hung around his neck now. He touched it beneath his shirt, fighting down the frustration that tried to work its way into the sereneness he had been feeling. So many questions. . . .

He looked over the saddle at Maelyrin, who was quietly running her hand over the stallion's neck, following the motion closely with her eyes. Her face was relaxed, allowing joy to seep into the unguarded features. He smiled, slightly, glad that her troubles were ignored, even if it was temporary. When she found him looking at her, she flushed and hid an embarrassed smile behind a fall of silvery hair as she bowed her head.

Quickly, though, she built her neutral expression before handing Marc a wrapped and tied cloth sack over the saddle. "It's not much," she said softly. "Mostly just some dried fruit and some bread, but it should last a couple of days."

"Thank you, Maelyrin," Marc answered, grabbing the sack with one hand while taking hers with his other. She flinched, but did not try to pull away. "You have made my stay here more than tolerable. You have made me feel at home."

She stared at him deeply, checks flushing anew, but a determined effort not to look away strained them. Her large violet eyes, normally unreadable, became pools of emotion. "I am happy to have contributed to your stay," she spoke almost fiercely, as if she wanted to keep her words, her feelings, to herself but unable to. "I, too, am glad of your visit Qua—Marc. May you find what you seek, and may it be as well as you hope."

Her words, her face, her scent, barely perceptible over the odor of leather and horse but powerful nonetheless, stirred him on many levels, caused him a nearly uncontrollable urge to take her in his arms and kiss her, deep and long; to comfort and hold her. Not only as just a man. With much clarity, he knew he could care deeply for her; did care for her. In just the scant few days of meeting her, and despite their racial differences, they had found a bond, self-nurturing and growing strong.

Yet, he stayed his hand, the horse standing between them more than just a physical barrier. A voice deep within him whispered powerful warnings that to follow that path would not work, not for any racial or cultural differences, but for something deeper, darker. Something dangerous. Unexplainable, not understandable, but nearly palpable. Whatever its origins, whatever its meaning, it was sobering. Slowly, he released her slim hand as he would a pleasant dream; reluctantly, regrettably, and surreptitiously. He began tying the bag of food to the saddle, discomfort evident in his deliberate motions, but not before he saw the quick flicker of pain that flashed through those eyes. A rejection mutually agreed to but not wanted. Without a doubt, she would have returned whatever he might have given. It was a compelling truth, and it swayed him.

That voice, deep and penetrating, spoke again, pushed him away. He smiled lamely, received a pain-filled one in return.

Finally, Maelyrin stepped back a couple of paces, giving him the unconscious go ahead to struggle into the saddle, his muscles and tendons still echoed some weakness even though his wounds were healed. No other words passed between them, although her eyes told volumes, just as he knew his must. With one last, tight smile, he pressed his heels against the horse's flanks.

Snorting and nodding, Whitesteel pranced, excited to no longer remain idle. Marc gave the massive white steed his head, letting him trot his way from the ffolk village. Though he did not look back, he could feel Maelyrin's gaze resting on his back.

Chapter 17

Decisions

She watched Marc, this human who caused such fierce, confusing emotions within her, disappear into the thick forest surrounding the village. Even after he had gone, she stood transfixed, gazing at the point where she was last able to see him. Her lip trembled slightly and her eyes suddenly misted. It felt as if he were tugging at her, that, at any moment, something would tear painfully, separating them forever.

Without thought, she turned and ran the few hundred yards to her hut, pushing aside *valeurith* that was responding too slowly. Under the small bed of naturally shaped wood was a sturdy travel pack, grabbed hastily and tossed unceremoniously on the top of the soft linens.

She pulled her dress off quickly, almost tearing the thin fabric, and was halfway finished pulling on some durable breeches for traveling when she stopped suddenly. "What am I doing?" she said into the dimness of the hut.

"I can't do this!" she then whispered emphatically while pulling the pants up around her hips and tying them. Her breath was rapid and her chest hurt where her heart was thrumming solidly against it. Tears blurred her vision, hastily wiped away with one hand as she grabbed for a shirt with the other.

She could not believe the compellation was so strong, nor why. "I have duties! Responsibilities!" she hissed fiercely. *My people need me!* She paused in her lacing of the light blue garment, shook her head, finished tying it off just above her breasts. Reaching for the belt was almost as if something else were controlling her every move. Tears flowed freely down her face, even though she was willing herself not to. After many seconds, she buckled the slim belt around her waist, adjusting the long, thin, scabbarded hunting knife that went with it so that it was comfortable against her thigh.

The thought of leaving the village appalled her, caused her guts to twist. But going after Marc stirred such feelings that they overwhelmed and muted the dread. "This is foolish!" she repeated over and over, but somehow she could not convince herself.

Going after him seemed not only right, but inevitable. As if he had chained her somehow and was pulling her to him. "But I must stay!" she pleaded, hands balling tightly. Her entire body was shaking, tears flowing down cheeks red with emotion. Angrily, she began randomly stuffing the pack with items she would need. Flint and steel, herbs, dried fruit, extra clothes, all jammed into the heavy leather pack.

She had never journeyed far from the village. It frightened her ---*I must stay, they need me!*--- though she was well trained in surviving on her own.

"I cannot!" she huffed while tugging on a soft leather boot that reached her knees. Her head hurt, filled as it was with arguing thoughts about why she should stay; why she should go. Her people did need her, that was true. But they did not want her. She was feared, maybe even hated. She knew the truth, saw it, felt it in everyone around her, save one. And that one offered a hope she had not felt in many long years. Marc would not shy away, because she could not See him. Would not even if she could.

Still, her responsibilities to her people were great even if they did not want it. To simply leave like this was crazy and foolish. She did not completely know why she was thinking such thoughts as going through with this plan. Was going to go through with it.

Once she admitted it to herself; once the reality of what she was doing was finally plain to her, the conflict lessened. Her eyes dried and breath smoothed. The argument in her head and heart diminished enough that thoughts began to crystallize; plans began taking shape. It occurred to her that she had been waiting for something like this to happen. Some chance for freedom to present itself. Unconsciously, Maelyrin had been looking for this moment. Guiltily, she had long known that this day would come because she could not live the way she was. Loving her people was not the issue; not needing them like they needed her was. For so long she had wanted their acceptance, hoping for it, but it had burned itself out. Became a dried, empty husk held together by duties to them.

The last thing she grabbed was a small pouch from a table, its contents clacking together as she put it in the over-stuffed pack and drew it closed. Shouldered, she had to shift it several times until the weight felt comfortable against her back. Eyes teared again, her resolve threatening to crumble once more as one last look around was cast.

Before Maelyrin became caught up in another tumultuous dilemma, she strode out of her hut, stopping only to retrieve a bow and quiver of arrows that had been embraced by the *valeurith*.

Quickly, she made her way back to where Marc had departed and plunged onto the trail of pressed grass left behind by the great white stallion. Maelyrin did not look back, face a mask of determination though tears again streamed freely down her cheeks.

Chapter 18

Death Watchers

*F*ive sets of eyes stared as the greyffolk girl made her way cautiously across the glade below them, but only one of the dark robed creatures started reining his mount towards her, the horse's eyes white-rimmed round.

"No!" muttered Crowlin, adding *Teraard* on as an afterthought. Their names were useless, he knew, but he tried to keep them within his memory, lest he forget what they all once were. Teraard's free hand twitched spasmodically, counterpoint to a guttural mewl that escaped from hidden lips. He wanted to go after her, they all did, but now was a time for restraint. "We move and we break the dweomer that hides us!" he explained harshly.

"Why must we wait?" asked Reegan from his right.

"*He* says to!" Crowlin spat, swinging his suddenly blazing eyes from Teraard to Reegan. "No other reason! If you would like to ask Him. . . ." he did not finish, did not need to. Reegan was already shaking his cowled head and pulling back on his reins, forcing the frightened gray horse he sat astride to back up a few paces. *They were all frightened of Him!* Crowlin thought, placing himself in that category as well. A grim smile worked slowly onto thin lips. They may question him, Crowlin, but they would never challenge his leadership, else they would be linked directly to the Master.

Crowlin looked at the sunlit glade down the knoll on which they sat, invisible to all living eyes. The girl was no longer there, having moved on while he had engaged in the useless diatribe. A relief in more than one sense. He let his gaze drift back around to the North. A wishful fantasy, he knew. In reality, distance was nothing, though in his mind there was. The greater the physical distance from Him, the more comfort.

Finally, he wrenched his gaze away from his useless hopes and turned it toward where the village of greyffolk stood. His quarry was there, among the 600 some odd ffolk. Incapacitated. Another slow grin crawled onto his hood darkened face. After all these many years, he would get to finish it.

"Are you sure he is still there?" Reegan rasped, as if knowing his dark thoughts. Crowlin nodded shortly, angry at the unknown challenge, and replied, "The poison he took will keep him down for a long time," He snorted derisively, contemplating the ever-widening circle of withering grass that surrounded the group. "Even with his 'healing' powers. So *He* says."

Reegan grunted noncommittally and shifted in his saddle. Crowlin continued to stare at the blackness that seeped into the green. *Yes.* He thought. *Finally, I will be able to destroy Pendragon!*

Chapter 19

Crossing Old Paths

*7*wilight had nearly surrendered over to night when Alex, Sandoren, and the boy stepped from the embrace of the huge oak onto the soft soil of the forest floor not far from the ffolk village where she had taken the poison from the man she instinctively knew was part of her journey. The man she was told about by Gyssel so long ago. A faceless man with no home, without peace, tied by strings of Fate extending far back into time. An enigma she would know when she found him. A herald that the other would soon be discovered. That had been discovered.

Alex looked back at the boy, barely visible as anything but a shadow in the fading light, yet still able to see the slackness in his round face and dullness in his eyes. He had not spoken one word since he had awakened earlier, though he nodded responsively to her questions. He merely plodded along behind her and Sandoren as a lost, hungry animal might. She feared he was mute, possibly his mind damaged beyond repair from the beating that he had taken, and she could no longer feel the pull of power that had drawn her to him. The glimpse of what he was as he lay broken and battered within the hollow many miles distant now was gone, disappeared as the morning mist before the sun. She silently hoped she had not been wrong or misled. Alex shook her head suddenly to clear her thoughts and was about to begin walking when Sandoren's hand fell upon and gripped her arm, startling her.

Buried in her thoughts as she was, she had not heard his sword whisper from its scabbard, nor seen the intense look he now wore work onto his sharp features. Her skin began to prickle, her thoughts shoved aside by the instinct of survival Sandoren's face warned of. "What is it?" she whispered.

"Listen," he replied as quietly, grip tightening meaningfully on her arm. Staring into the gloom she focused her attention intently. Aside from the breathing of her companions, she heard nothing. Only deathly silence reached back from the darkness to touch her ears. No cricket chirruped, no night bird cried out. An icy shiver rode resolutely up her spine, raising short hairs.

Several tense minutes crawled by while they stood in a rigid half crouch, staring into the myriad shades and lines of starkness ahead that was the forest. A cool autumn breeze wafted from the direction they faced, bearing a faint acrid odor, sickly sweet, causing them to grimace.

Taking advantage of the moment, Sandoren crept forward slowly, releasing Alex's arm only when distance forced him to. She slipped backwards and took the boy's clammy hand, cutting a glance at him to make sure he was alright. The boy, though, was busily studying the contact between them. He looked up at her, a broad smile working slowly onto his shadowed face, apparently unaware of what was going on around them.

Sandoren had not taken ten steps and she was about to move after him when a low guttural mewl drifted to them from ahead, its unearthliness shocking them both rigid. With catlike grace and quickness, Sandoren was back at her side. "What now?" he said, leaning close enough that his lips were nearly touching her ear. While she thought, he returned to peering into the darkness ahead, holding his sword out before him comfortably, yet with deadly confidence. After a moment, she leaned over.

"We are all still weak and the boy is our main concern at this point. We must move away and find a place to rest and regain our strength. Tomorrow we can come back for the other one and hopefully avoid whatever thing is ahead of us." Something else was wrong, but she couldn't quite figure out what it was. She needn't worry Sandoren about it, though, until their current situation was taken care of, so she said nothing further.

Sandoren nodded, still gazing into the gloom. They waited a few more minutes, straining to hear more evidence of the producer of the nerve-jangling sound, but no more was forthcoming. Alex leading, pulling the hulking youth with one hand, set off in a southwesterly direction, away from the frightening noise maker, hurried but cautious, followed closely by a back-glance casting Sandoren.

In the brevity of the anxious moments, she did not check to make sure the Passage through the tree had closed itself, and they were well away from the area when the two boys stepped gingerly from the opening in the large trunk.

Chapter 20

Horrors of Old

*C*olin looked around, the silvery light of the ever-present moon defining the landscape in patches where the foliage allowed it to pass. A surreal definition, one both boys were used to due to their many excursions away from their beds when they were supposed to be asleep. Behind him, Bren whimpered something about being hungry and lost and no way to get back. The tunnel in the tree had immediately closed up upon their exit from it, leaving them with no notion about how to get back or, as the more he looked around, a clue as to where they were. Stretching away from them in all directions was not the brush and creeper-choked forest that surrounded the farmstead he and Bren had called home. Instead, huge reaching oaks spread before them, almost regularly spaced, sheltering a floor clear of the choking brush and deadfalls he was used to. A light stink hung in the air, pushed around by a faint breeze coming from, his best guess on their position, north. The smell vaguely reminded him of the blacksmith's shop back in Shady Glenn. Bren mumbled something, drawing back his searching attention.

"What?" he asked back harshly, unable to hide the irritation from his voice at his companion's constant complaining.

"I'm 'ungry." He whined.

"Would you jus' shutup!" Colin hissed. "I think there's a town up ahead of us. That's probly where they took the idiot. We'll git food there!" Too bad he had dropped the squirrel he had been carrying around when they came across the strangers in the hollow.

"'Ow do ya know?"

"I jus' do," Colin answered, gazing in the direction the smell came, wondering if his friend would ever be able to think for himself. Bren always relied on someone else to make his decisions for him, mostly it was Colin, though he was not adverse to complaining about them when they were made. It had been that way since they were small children, since the old man purchased them at auction, when Colin first met him. He was fairly used to it, but it still grated on him at times. "Come on!" he finally said and began walking nonchalantly toward the direction the smell traveled from.

It was not long before he wondered if he had been mistaken. The odor strengthened as they walked, quickly becoming a rancid stench. A sickly sweet smell that already had forced several gags from Bren and had Colin breathing through his mouth to avoid the full brunt of it. Still, he thought he could detect the odor of baking bread and cooking stew lacing the otherwise repugnant smell. That alone kept him moving forward. Had he not been hungry as well, he figured he would have turned back long before now.

Thinking it was merely a tangle of dark disguised roots, they were nearly stepping over the body before seeing what lay huddled at the base of one of the large sheltering trees. Bren vomited immediately upon the realization, emptying his stomach of his meager breakfast while leaning one armed against the oak, back to the grisly discovery. Colin, seemingly undaunted, dropped to a crouch to study it.

The body lay twisted and shattered at the trunk's base as if it were a rag doll casually tossed there by a bored child. The spirit that had been housed in it departed before it understood what had happened as an expression of grim surprise was still frozen on the ffolk's face and his hand clutched the hilt of his half drawn sword. Cold, still wet blood carpeted the earth beneath, turning the grass a darker shade of black, its metallic tang hanging closely about the body.

Colin let his eyes wander over the mangled corpse, intently examining it. He had seen death before, many times, but never this closely; never a man; never this violently. It sparked something deep within him that instantly frightened and fascinated him; repulsed and drew him. Almost of its own volition, his hand suddenly reached out to touch the dead man's hand. The cold, pallid, almost rubbery, flesh beneath his fingers caused his gorge to rise abruptly but he bit it back.

Behind him, huffing from lack of breath, Bren said, "Who?" voice hoarse from retching and bearing a liquid quality as he forced the question through another gag reflex.

"Ffolk," Colin answered absently, trying to work the rigid fingers that gripped the sword hilt with a steeliness only born of his death.

"Is it the one we're followin'," Bren asked, finally able to control himself enough to form a complete thought.

"No," replied Colin. "Different one."

"W-wha' are you doin'?" Bren exclaimed in a harsh whisper as he bravely drew closer to Colin to see over his shoulder at what he was working at.

"Tryin' to git his sword," he said without taking his eyes away from the dead hand.

"W-why?" Bren asked a little too quickly. "Why would ya do that? Isn't it bad luck t'take a dead man's sword?" Colin paused in his grisly task to look up at his companion. Bren's eyes were round and easily visible even under the shadows and, he thought, his skin a little pasty. Bren's obvious terror caused a little used compassion to steal into Colin's breast, and he slowly exhaled a half sigh.

"Because we need somethin' other than our slings for protection. This man hain't been dead long and his killer could still be 'round. What do ya say now?"

Bren nodded briskly, "Oky," he said quickly. "T-take it!" Colin gave him an affirming nod in reply and returned to his chore, working calmly while Bren fidgeted behind, an occasional, uncontrollable whimper escaping tightly clamped lips. The fingers refused to give away their steel-like grip on the hilt and Colin began to think that to retrieve it, he would have to break them. Finally though, as if in response to his unbidden thoughts, he was able to encourage them to loosen just enough that he could pry the hand away from the weapon and slowly withdraw it from its sheath. He stood, holding it as if it were a priceless treasure.

Ambient light gleamed along the surface of the metal. Colin took it in as he did the weight and feel of the slim weapon. As a man thirsty takes in water. The closest he had ever come to holding a sword was the imaginary ones born from sticks he and Bren used when mock fighting. It was heavier than he thought it would be, but at the same time, it felt more balanced, more easily controllable. It felt. . . powerful. Warmth and energy flooded him, a sense of invincibility working into every corner of his body. In his hands, he held the power to take life. A smile formed on hard lips, the smile he often had when telling Bren that the next time the old man hit him, he would kill him, or when he was taking his fury out on the idiot. It was a smile of triumph, of promises kept and goals achieved. In his hands, he held the solidification of those thoughts, its deadly simplicity, a confirmation of a destiny he often thought he wanted.

He took a couple of swings, listening as the keen edge sliced the night air, feeling the tension in his corded muscles. Smile brightening and eyes gleaming, he mentally decided that he would no longer be pushed around by anyone. Ever.

"Come on," He finally said, the steel of the sword now behind his words. Mangled corpse forgotten, Colin began walking north again, back erect, letting the odor guide him, knowing now what the stench was that was calling him. Bren, reluctant to press on, knowing his suspicions would soon be confirmed, but too afraid to go back alone, mutely fell in step a few feet behind him.

They soon found themselves on the forested edge of a large moon-bathed clearing, staring at trampled grass and silvery limned forms of pallid dead lying strewn in random piles, the fetor they had been following hanging thickly in the cool night air. The stink of death, charred flesh and spilt blood.

Colin wasted no time, strolling into the field as if the dead scattered about were only pieces of rotting wood instead of once living people. He bent once, stealing another sword from a pale, lifeless shell and held it aloft, by the blade tip, in Bren's direction.

Bren stepped among the dead, determined not to look, breathing shallowly through his mouth, but unable to keep his gaze from drifting over the tattered remains, touching briefly the gaping scorch holes or jagged slashes, dragging over faces frozen in waxen masks of fear and pain. His body quivered deeply from a coldness not born of the air, yet Bren could not wrench away his gaze from them. As much as he wanted to, needed to, look away, he could not, knowing that he had to see them. These men he did not know, but could have. Out of some perverse need, he could know them, and know Death, by burning their grisly images into his mind. Though Bren doubted his shocked mind could ever understand it.

Lost as he was in his horrified brooding, he did not see Colin or the sword hilt. Only when he came up against the cold metal, did his attention shatter into a thousand fragments, forcing a squeal from rigidly held lips and causing his body to react as if freezing water were suddenly dumped over him. Bren slapped blindly at the touch of the sword, thinking that while he looked upon death, it had crept upon him and laid its icy fingers on his soul.

A stinging slap across the jaw brought his world sharply back into focus. Tense, anger-filled eyes held his, Colin's hand poised for another strike. "I'm oky! Oky!" Bren stammered quickly, holding his own hands up to ward off the next blow. It did not come, though Colin failed to immediately drop his arm, instead continued to stare fiercely at Bren, searching, maybe even considering the actual worth of his frightened friend. Finally, though, the hand lowered and Colin's eyes began to lose the keen edge.

"What're ya tryin' to do, git us killed?" he hissed, his voice sounding profane against the silence. Bren replied with a shake of his head. "Here! Take this and follow me! Quietly!" he warned, grabbing one of Bren's hands with his free one and slapping the hilt of the sword painfully into it with his other.

Once Bren held the unwieldy object, Colin retrieved his, pulling it free of the soft earth into which he had thrust it. Without another word, he turned and strode the rest of the way through the death field, moonbeams dancing menacingly from his blade as it swung with his stride. Bren sighed heavily, hefted the sword he held and followed Colin as quickly and quietly as he could.

The village was apparently large and spread out though they never really saw anything that he could logically define as a building or house. Wherever Colin wandered, however, they found carnage equal to that in the clearing and worse. The bodies of men, women, and children were strewn carelessly about, some bearing scorch marks, some the effects of the reality that burdened his right hand. The first group of non-warriors they stumbled across had seen Bren hunched over again, trying to rid his body of the contents of his stomach, and even Colin had looked pale and a little sickly, but Bren's body and mind quickly became numbed to the terrible representations. That is, all except for a subtle terror slowly permeating his being. Throughout, the many casualties, whether armed men, or unprotected women and children, did Bren see any that were out of the ordinary. All had the look of the group as a whole; a part of the village. There were none that remotely seemed an aggressor. Whoever or whatever had done this horrible deed was either extremely conscious of leaving behind their wounded or dead, or, more frightening, were able to accomplish such an act without suffering a casualty themselves.

   The ramifications were not lost on Colin either, though his reaction was different. Instead of letting the fear running rampant through him control his actions, he worked to channel it into something else. Something more useful to him. Anger, rage, a snarling beast, cornered and ready to fight. So intent was he on guarding himself against his fear that he did not immediately realize that Bren had stopped dead. Only until he heard a choked gasp did he turn to find his sidekick.
   Bren was standing rigid, head turned and eyes wide, locked and staring. His face was drawn tightly and his mouth worked, hinging and unhinging as he silently mouthed something. The stark, utter terror on his face flew across the span between them and crawled tinglingly up Colin's own spine.
   Cautiously, he moved towards Bren, creeping slowly past a large bundle of strange vines that seemed prevalent to the area in which they searched. Bren stood between two such bundles separated by one of the huge oaks and a waist high shrub that ran the distance. Beyond, where Bren's gaze was fixed, was another of the large glades. He crept closer, clearing the shield of vines that blocked his full view of the meadow and, with nothing short of pure primal instinct, threw himself behind the cover of shrubs, heart clenching painfully in his chest. Without thinking, he scrambled the couple of feet to Bren, reached up and grabbed the front of his tunic and pulled. Thankfully, Bren reacted silently, though his movements were slightly less than violent, his head jerked downward, stretched eyes desperate in their seeking, hands flying to Colin's and grasping tightly, the once held sword thudding softly to the grass. After a very long second, Bren's eyes cleared enough to recognize Colin and allow him to drag the smaller boy down behind the screen of bushes. With finger to lips, Colin shot him

a fierce warning look, before lifting into a crouch and then a half stance so he could gaze out over the shrubbery at the nightmarish thing in the glade.

The moonlight was bright in the meadow, bathing it in a pure silvery wash, the several bodies appearing as pale fleshy mounds. It stood near the center of the field, stark against the moon glow; a tear in its near perfection, a mannish form, twisted and hunched perversely. Arms twice longer than what would be normal, legs bent as an animal's, supporting a thick trunk heavily muscled and corded. A physical manifestation of the stench and horror of the destroyed village.

It stepped lightly, powerfully, back turned toward the two boys, reached out with a knotted arm and casually flipped over a corpse, a low, hair raising mewl coming from an unseen throat. Pins and needles traveled the length and breadth of Colin's body, numbing it with rigid ice. Bren cowered beside him, quaking violently. Looking upon the thing caused Colin's insides to clench, stirred ageless instincts buried deep within him. He dared not take his gaze from it, however the pain of terror bled through him, for to do so would draw it near enough to feel its fetid breath against the back of his neck. He was hopelessly trapped between what he must see and what he did not want to.

The thing moved through the field like a terrible mockery of a farmer checking his harvest for rot or pests. Soundlessly, Colin knew despite his life's blood pounding in his ears, searching the corpses with a casual air of disdain. Every few seconds releasing a low, spine rattling mewl that was felt as much as it was heard. Comforted only by the blade he held, he still had to consciously tighten his grip several times against rebelling fingers threatening to let fall his only protection.

Time oozed from one minute to the next in the inexorable way it did in times of great stress while Colin stared at the creature and Bren stared at the ground, knees tightly hugged close to his chest. The monster seemed to glide from one corpse to another, peering down at them for a split second before tossing their already mangled bodies with its talon-tipped hands and knotted extra-long arms.

Suddenly, it straightened, extending itself smoothly with powerful grace, seeming to double in height, raising its head to the glittering curtain of stars above it. Sharp, short hisses worked past the pounding of blood and into Colin's numbed mind, clicking a response of recognition that started bubbling up through the morass his brain had become. The realization that the creature was sniffing the air came the moment it turned its head slowly in his direction and pierced him with eyes that suddenly illuminated in the moonlight like a cat's, a sickly metallic yellow that thrust jagged shards of ice through Colin's brain and into his soul, freezing every particle in his body completely and painfully. A dull thud drifted up from the ground as his sword slipped from nerveless fingers and fell to it. Through the shock and noise of utter terror, a voice whispered, telling him of the agelessness of the creature before him. It spoke of the power it wielded and the pure hatred that fueled it. Colin's hand jerked around futilely, trying to clutch the sword that was no longer within reach, even though, deep inside, he knew a mere construct of metal was nothing against this ancient evil.

The mockery of a grin split the jet blackness beneath the luminous eyes, revealing needle-like teeth glistening with spittle. Teeth that rent his sanity as readily as its eyes did, threatening to snap that tiny thread that held him just this side of the dark threshold of saneness. The whispers turned to screams of agony, repeating over and over something he could not understand.

Suddenly, his body reacted, stumbled backward away from it, tearing away the horrific, intimate gaze when he met the ground. Colin's trunk twisted, trying to turn his body over, hands clawed the loam, dragging him forward while his legs kicked violently, running on ground that was not beneath his feet. His eyes rolled back, attempting to regain the creature as his mouth gibbered and drooled and his ears tried to decipher meanings. His mind remained silent, cold as the corpses around then while Colin's body moved purely on instinct. Finally, his separately acting features pulled together enough to regain his feet and propel him into the darkness away from the creature.

Bren, knocked lucid by the words spilling from Colin's mouth, contracted the terror infecting him and found himself running hard after his older friend though unable to catch him. He could feel the creature's eyes upon his back like a physical thing, laying him open to his very soul, but the screams building in him could not break through his painfully clenched jaw.

The thing watched them flee, grin plastered on its face until they disappeared into the dark backdrop of night. When it could no longer see, hear, or smell them, it returned to its task.

They ran, Colin gibbering into the night, Bren grimly silent, the slight autumn chill freezing their clammy, sweat soaked faces, each separate yet drawn together as one in their terror. Blindly they moved, almost unwaveringly, hurtling bodies and low shrubs, crashing through or slashing at higher ones. Trees were dodged, but only just enough to streak past, often clipping and scraping against the heavy trunk, tearing away small showers of bark and bits of flesh. The landscape blurred on either side as they flew and fuzzy ahead from their self-inflicted breeze, air drawn tears streaking stripes along the sides of their faces. Distance and time became as nothing, pushed far back into their numbed minds, drowned out by the only conscious thought they had; that of escape from the terrible visage of death behind them. At some point, Colin went down, falling into a rolling heap as his feet unexpectedly found another body, coming to rest in an uncomfortable twisted pile cushioned only by stalks of wheat his own body pushed beneath him.

Lungs burning, breath short, Bren stumbled to his side to assist him, leaning over the sword as he used it as a brace.

But Colin's eyes were closed, his breathing ragged. Bren shook him, pushing weakly on one of his shoulders, but only receiving a low moan in response. His tired mind awake enough to tell him Colin had passed out and that he himself needed rest, his fear wrought strength now suddenly draining away, replaced by leaden exhaustion.

Bren stared down, trying to focus, the sight before him undulating as if he were looking through moving water. The earth seemed to clutch at him, was trying to drag his heavy limbs down to its embrace. Unable to resist, Bren succumbed to the demands of his overextended body, and as if leaning against an invisible pillow of air, slumped forward into the newly trampled wheat, the sword he had not consciously realized he still had, falling away from him in a dull gleaming arc, shoring up against the supporting wheat. *At least I will die in my sleep if it comes,* he thought, not knowing the thing in the meadow had not deemed them significant enough to follow; that it still picked through the dead in grisly concentration on some errand only it knew of. Within seconds, trailing that last thought, consciousness slipped from him and he, too, slept. Still a boy, but altered forever.

Chapter 21

Refuge in Thought

*7*he boy was asleep not five minutes after they nestled themselves within a small close copse of fir trees only a few hundred feet from a tiny creek wending its way south. He snored softly, curled up on the soft mat of old needles that carpeted the floor between the obscuring trees. He still had said not a word even though Alex had prompted him several times when she felt they were safe, but he simply smiled slackly at her.

Alex rested her chin on her knees. The temperature had become more chill as the evening wore on, but not enough to deaden the sap sweet odor that she breathed in deeply while waiting for Sandoren to return from his scouting patrol. Fortunately, the closeness of the firs insulated the interior of their warren from the cutting breezes without. She let herself relax, freeing her mind to drift into nothingness; far away from the stresses coming and gone. A lucid moment in her absence, it was a state in which she allowed only her senses to operate, grounding herself only in the present; past and future necessarily forgotten.

Deep beneath her, the thrumming rhythm of Earthblood as it flowed through deep channels became almost audible, its power prickling against the thin walls that held it from her during moments of inactivity; enticing her to extend her touch to it, to embrace it, to fill herself with it. Though the temptation was high, she refused herself the joy of doing so now. It was too easy to lose herself in its embrace, now that the power came so easily, no longer blocked by the diffusing wall that once allowed only a seepage of the power through to be gathered up over a period of time. Now, it was intoxicating in its abundant quickness, like a river no longer held back by the dam that once regulated it. No, it would not do to become lost in the ecstasy of its touch. With a will born of pure stubbornness, she pushed herself emotionally away from the prospect and concentrated on other things.

It was then that she realized what had been bothering her earlier. And just to make sure she had it, she let her awareness run in the direction of the man she had healed of the poison. The first herald. *Yes, that was it.* Alex could no longer sense his presence. The Air Bond she had established through the Healing was gone when it should not be. The man had amazing fortitude and healed quickly, according to the Faethe, but she didn't think that would affect the Bond, through which she could be able to sense how the Healing had taken. Distance yes, but she was now back within that range, so it should reestablish itself. But it hadn't. And why, she did not know. Perhaps her own ordeal with the poison had interfered with it. Perhaps her proximity to the boy, which was a peculiarity she did not yet understand, was interfering with it. Whatever the case, it was not worth concerning herself overly with it. Regardless of his healing talent, he was still human and it would be a while before he was up and around.

Sandoren returned, slipping into the enclosure like a shadow and sidling up to Alex. "So far, so good," he murmured. "I think we left it behind, whatever it was." He settled himself a bit more comfortably. "Do you know what it was?"

Alex shook her head slowly along the cup of her knees. She felt like a child again, full of innocence and wonder; maybe even a little frightened. "Don't know," she mused. "Something from the Age of Ellynthryll, maybe, or even further back. An

Eldritch, perhaps." The hairs on the back of her neck stood while prickles ran the length of her skin. "I really have no way of knowing unless I could see it and I certainly think that would not be a good idea."

Sandoren nodded.

"Hopefully by morning," she began after a long pause of contemplation. "the thing will have either moved on, or the ffolk will have driven it off."

"I don't know," he replied slowly. "It sounded too close to the village." Alex paused in her gentle rocking as she considered his implications, but, just as swiftly, she resumed.

"Creatures that survive that long do not do it because they are powerful," she reasoned. "But, because they are smart, too. Whatever drew it so close to a large community more than likely did not keep it there for long. It should be long gone by morning. Then we can collect the other and be on our way northward."

"I hope you're right, Alex," Sandoren said as he lay back in the bed of needles, pulling his pack underneath his head. "A change of scenery might be good for the both of us."

Alex smiled briefly at the sentiment. The road ahead was going to be arduous at the least, and the scenery they were heading for was not a thing to be happy about. Of course, she knew that Sandoren was well aware of problems that could arise. They had been traveling together long enough to know that easy or pleasant often were not terms associated with them.

Her longtime companion was asleep quickly, his soft breathing slow and rhythmic, leaving Alex with her thoughts and unspoken fears; decisions she knew she would be forced to make now that the boy was in her charge. Decisions she was already making. It was true, the things she had said to Sandoren about the creature. It was a thing from ages past. She could sense that; feel its existence as it blended with the ever-present life forces that were the backdrop of the world around her. It was something not unnatural though not wholly natural. Like a sudden knot in a muscle, it commanded attention, its life-force a super-heated pool of intense energy and seething hatred; sly wisdom beyond the rules of time. But she had sensed something else while standing beneath the shelter of the oak. Something wholly unnatural within the shadow of the greater being. A confusing sensation strong with the underpinnings of trepidation. Something intrinsically wrong that cried out to her, pleading for an investigation that she ultimately had to refuse for the sake of the boy. For the whole of the world, not just a part.

Long into the night she remained awake, tucked away in their tiny shelter, hoping against hope that her decisions were the correct ones.

Chapter 22

Routine Sleeplessness

*T*he murmur of many voices constantly undercut all the other noises he listened to, echoing as they did on the sheer walls around them seemed to turn one thousand murmurs into ten, all but drowning out the sounds of the crickets and miniature waterfall that fed the small pond. Randomly interspersed in the foreground of the voices were the contented nickers and snorts of the horses, the occasional bray of a mule. Cook fires crackled, then hissed when whatever concoction being cooked boiled over or dropped fat tears of grease. Utensils clinked as the last bite was scraped off the plate or the last gulp of *qaha* was taken. Somewhere in the distance, laughter. The soft melody of a hymn accompanied by a hand flute drifted from somewhere else. From behind him the constant scratch of quill to parchment as the mapmaker plied his trade. All working in concert to form a natural music. Music without meter or verse. Completely random.

Beyond the large tent was the soldier's song.

Anlin absently tapped his longpipe on the side of his thigh, vibrating loose the spent leaf to form a tiny pile of dark ash on the worn grass, then leaned back in the small fold away chair and propped his booted feet up on a nearby cask. He pulled a pouch from the pocket of his unbuttoned coat so he could refill the bowl.

The site had worked out fairly well save for it was a little crowded, turning out to be a canyon between two outreaching arms of the jagged, sheer mountain chain they paced. The water was clear and a little chill, spilling from somewhere deeper in the craggy rock face and flowing down into the pond. An hour gone since the last mule was watered saw all the mounts and pack mules picketed up against the cliff face in the center of the camp, the men now winding down from the weary day behind them. If Madlin was correct, they should reach the fortress by midday tomorrow. And hopefully bring an end to this part of their journey. Of course, it could be a different story if the place was being occupied.

He considered the mapmaker for a moment, listening intently to him as he scratched his notes onto the small bound book he kept. He wrote constantly, pausing only to eat or stare around himself. He never slept, at least, not that Anlin had ever seen in the two some odd months he had been with the regiment. Nor did he talk, could not talk. The story was that his tongue had been cut out during the rioting just after the Dark Night. It was said that his own guild master did it, driven insane by the changing landscape, and unable to cope with the skill Madlin had. However he was coping with his loss of speech, it certainly did not seem to affect his mapmaking abilities. If he had to make a judgment just based on the last couple of months, he would have to say that his skills were improving. After all, his suspicions were that he no longer had an excuse to talk. Now he could throw himself completely into his work without justifying his lack of social skills. Indeed, he often had a particular gleam of joy in his eyes that bordered on madness whenever he was busy, which , of course, was nearly all the time. A crooked smile worked onto his hardened face. *What a crew,* he thought, in no way dissatisfied, as he puffed his pipe flame into existence.

The lighting stick lay smoldering on the pressed floor, carelessly discarded as the tent flap rippled and drew back, the rustle of the heavy material pulling Anlin back to the present.

Captain Turcot stepped into the large tent, ducking under the low door while flapping his hat against his leg to disengage the clinging dust. Through the closing triangle of darkness, the flickering light from the several lamps inside touched briefly the dark mail of one of the guards standing just beneath the tent's large awning. His personal guard. Turcot maintained that it was his honor guard, though he could not quite convince himself of that. What honor was it to have to be protected by one's own charges?

"Evening," The Captain said. "Is there any more where that came from?" he added, gesturing towards the tin cup sitting on the corner of the low table to Anlin's right, half filled with now cold *qaha*. Several maps, unrolled, rocks holding their corners, dominated the small area, along with quills, ink, charcoal, markers and other mapmaking tools.

"Yes," Anlin replied, a brief smile touching his mouth, and pointed towards the entrance with his pipe. "Fresh pot boiling on the fire." Turcot turned to look at the flaps as if he could see through them, eyes weary and full of consideration on whether it was worth the added effort of stepping back outside to pour himself a cup of the dark bitter liquid. Instead, he moved to another of the chairs and sat down heavily, causing the wooden and metal supports to squeal in protest. "Maybe later, eh?" he said, tossing his hat onto the ground beside him.

"Not a worry," Anlin said around his pipe stem. "I have a Corporal *volunteering* his services. He would be more than happy to fetch you a cup." Turcot smiled broadly, both mischief and nostalgia brimming it. Anlin took a deep breath, winked at him and bellowed, "JARREN!"

A loud explosion of noise erupted outside the tent, exclamations of surprise mixing with the sound of wood falling against itself; a chair falling into the pike rack, the long shafts hastily grabbed before the flags they bore touched the ground. A second later, a blushing, nervous looking young man stood at attention within the tent, anxiously straightening and pulling at his uniform. "Yes, sir?" he stammered.

"Jarren!" Anlin said sternly. If possible, Jarren went even more rigid. "Go fetch the Captain a cup of *qaha*!"

"Yes, sir!" he said with a crisp salute and quickly exited. Anlin, no longer able to hide it, smiled broadly. Turcot, speaking from behind the hand that hid his, asked, "What did he do?"

"Left his weapon behind at morning's camp," he answered, a note of irritation clinging to his mirth. Turcot's eyes widened slightly.

"Left his. . . ." he started. "How do you leave your sword behind?"

"I don't know," Anlin answered. "Probably the same way a certain cadet at the old academy kept forgetting to wear his helmet until his instructor made him sleep in it for a month. He is just young."

The captain chuckled heartily. "A man never lives down those moments, does he?"

"Not at all," The tent flap splayed out suddenly and there was Jarren holding out a steaming tin cup and trying without much success to keep calm. Turcot reached out and took the cup with a pleasant, "Thank you.", then Jarren returned to his stance at attention. Captain Turcot stopped just shy of taking a sip and eyed the young corporal over the rim.

"Thank you, Corporal," he said pointedly after a moment.

"Yes, sir!" Jarren replied without moving.

"That will be all, Corporal," Turcot said, summoning up as much gruffness as he could muster on this weary evening, though the young man's grim face nearly made him choke on his own laughter. "You are dismissed!"

"Y—yes, sir!" he stammered while turning toward the flap. Anlin shot a wink at Turcot, then cleared his throat loudly. Jarren froze suddenly in half step, rapidly turned back and into rigid attention, a small wince just leaving his face.

"And, Corporal?" Anlin growled.

"Yes, sir?" came the meek reply.

"Don't let me catch you napping out there on that chair!" Jarren started to nod. "And move away from those banners!"

"Y—yes, sir!" he nodded vigorously and all but ran from the confines of the tent. The look on his retreating face said that that was not even fast enough. The two grizzled men broke out in hearty laughter while Madlin, the mapmaker, continued to scribble his notes, oblivious to his surroundings.

"Were we ever that bad?" Turcot said after bringing his laughter under control.

"I suppose we were, once," Anlin replied, taking a long pull from his pipe. He held it for a few seconds before exhaling, eyes looking into the distant past. "It's too bad we cannot hold onto that part where everything was fresh and exciting, even getting into trouble. It's also too bad that Jarren, there, will have to lose that, become hardened and jaded, like us. It causes me to wonder what these kids are joining up for. Is it for fame and fortune, like we did? Or is it for a different purpose? Jarren, there, has the making of a fine officer, despite his excitability."

"Do I detect a note of regret there, Du," Turcot asked soberly.

"No. Not regret. I'm just prone to wondering about how things turned out and where they are going. The purposes behind them."

"Ah," Turcot answered, leaning back and taking a sip from his still steaming cup. "Becoming a philosopher in your old age, are you?'

"Maybe." Another puff from his pipe. "Do not tell me you don't think about these things. I've known you too long to think you don't."

Turcot nodded, set his cup on one of the tables that ringed the tent. "Sure, I think about things. I wonder if I should have settled down, become a farmer, married a girl, maybe that one I knew in Merlankerr, had children, what not. But I try not to think on it too much, because it causes too much noise in my mind. Raises too many questions I cannot readily answer. I wonder if I'm too damn old to do this anymore. The Emperor's expansion policies are difficult to fit into the teachings I was given back in the day. I don't particularly like the changes, either, but I figure if I keep focusing on them, I will really be in trouble."

"You and me both," Anlin said after a moment of contemplation, nodding against his pipe. "And that is fact, I suppose. We have been soldiers far too long to consider anything else. You would last as long as me in a corn field, probably less than a day. No, farmers we are not, much to the disappointment of my father."

Turcot was nodding as well in fluid agreement, eyes looking up into the tent's ceiling. It was a common discussion between them, old and as comfortable as their boots, especially of late. A way of justifying the history they shared, a way of trying to explain their existence in these different times. For them, the battle was no longer on the field. That was routine, their battle was for survival in a new era of ideas and blood lust. A battle neither one knew if they were equipped well enough to fight.

"How is Marga?" Turcot asked suddenly, more to move away from the subject than sincere interest. Being Anlin's longtime friend, he knew nearly all there was to know about his family. Indeed, Anlin's family was more like his.

"Brutish as ever," He answered, equally aware and supportive of the intentions. "Her latest complaint is that she is about to run out of children to help her with the household now that Aron is about ready to leave."

"He still on about that foolishness about moving to Calif to study with those wizards!"

"He sure is," Anlin's brow creased. "He is convinced that he has a natural affinity for magic, and he is of age. . . ."

"But. . .?"

"But, I have a feeling that the same thing is going to happen to those Schools that happened to the Academies the Knights used to run."

"Even though Calif is still a Free City?"

"For now," came the stiff reply. "I told him my suspicions the last time I was home, but he insisted that was where he wanted to go, even demonstrated this talent of his. Made a plate float for a few seconds, nothing extreme. He should be just about ready to leave, should get there about the time of First Snow. That is if the weather is going to cooperate this year." He chuckled, took a pull from his pipe. "Funny thing is, Corin claims she is going to follow mine and Aiden's path and become a soldier."

"What?"

"Yes," He said, smirking. "She says next summer, she is going to apply to the Imperial Academy."

Turcot leaned back and stared for several seconds before a smile worked onto his face as well. "I guess if all this madness in the world was not going on, I would be surprised, but I suppose that that fits her. Even as a child, she had a certain 'disposition'."

"You mean that same 'disposition' that caused her to beat Aiden's friend, Willen, nearly half to death when he teased her for wearing a dress?" Anlin laughed at the memory.

"The very same," Turcot replied, adding his own chuckle.

Outside, a wave of sound approached, that of conversation pausing as soldiers and guards snapped to attention, the click of their heels and the clink of their mail. Anlin looked at Turcot, who was shaking his head. Baen was approaching, Anlin's 3rd in command, stiff and unbending and extremely formal. He had been one of the first to graduate from the Empire's new Military Academy in Vistan, only a year old, and a prime example of the type of soldier the School was churning out. He was part of the reason for their earlier discussion as Baen represented their future. Anlin's son Aiden, had also been one of the first through that new system and, luckily, came away with some of his humanity still intact. Of course, Anlin had been grooming him from the time he could stand with his teachings. Those teachings they both had learned from the Schools at Citadel City when they were Aiden's age.

Not that Anlin was not fiercely proud of Aiden, and for most things, the new Academy was an excellent institution in the ways of strategy in warfare, but, by Anlin's own admission, he felt that it lacked severely in certain areas. Areas he felt very important, such as governing principles like honor and compassion. There was more to war and fighting than just killing and subjugating.

The guards outside the tent snapped to attention, followed closely by Corporal Jarren's voice slipping through the canvas. "Sir!" he called. "Lieutenant Baen requests permission to enter!"

Turcot rolled his eyes. "Enter!" Anlin snapped loudly. Immediately the tent flap was drawn open and a man of medium height, but thin and with hard features, stepped into the room. Lantern light glinted icily in his blue eyes and heavily polished boots and buttons. His uniform was fastidiously crisp and neither men could detect a speck of dust on it. Anlin silently wondered if it was a trick of the light, but a voice deep in his mind told him otherwise. Baen stood at attention and snapped a salute. "Sir, reporting for officer's call, sir."

"Be at ease, Baen," Anlin said shortly. Baen relaxed rigidly, an expectant look plastered on his face. Anlin cleared his throat. "Report," he said after a moment.

"All mounts and pack animals picketed, fed, and groomed. All men present and accounted for, save for the two missing scouts, Melik and Danisek. We have enough rations for six days at full portion. No reported loss of equipment and all wagons are in good condition." Anlin winked meaningfully at Turcot, who, behind Baen's line of sight, looked at the tent flaps as if he could see Jarren standing outside.

Anlin stood slowly, easing his aging joints from their positions. Turcot followed suit and all three men crowded around the map table. Spread out in front of them laid an old map of the area around Tergaard before the massive land changes caused not so long ago. Crude charcoal marks and lettering in places denoted where those new changes were, drawn from the reports from the first scouting parties that made the trip to the fortress and returned.

Index finger resting on the area denoted as Tergaard, Anlin intoned, "According to our original reports, Tergaard now sits on the edge of the huge cut, called The Rift, apparently abandoned shortly after the Dark Night. The far eastern wall, including some of the outbuildings, have been destroyed and replaced by an upheaval of rock. The rest of the fortress is reported to be intact. I have dispatched two scouts to investigate the fortress." He slid his finger down the map along the edge of the smudged charcoal drawing of the mountain range that now paced them to the west. "According to our mapmaker's best guess," he said, indicating Madlin with his thumb. The man never looked up from his work. "We are approximately . . . here. About a half days march from the fortress." He paused to take a few puffs from his pipe. "Now, gentlemen, the original reports are almost a year old, so we do not know if a lot of this information is still accurate, though we should have a clearer idea on the morrow, when the scouts return." He pointed again, this time toward another drawing near the fortress. "We call this the 'Tooth', it's a large blade-like rock outcropping that angles southwest away from near the western wall of Tergaard and juts nearly a half mile into the open desert plain, separating it from the rest of the mountain range which apparently begins to tire out into low hills and buttes nearer the Rift. The rest of the area is open wasteland as far as the eye can see.

We'll break camp at dawn and hug the mountain range all the way to this point," he indicated the outcropping labeled, 'The Tooth'. "Here, the regiment will split. Lieutenant Baen, commanding this second group, will hold here, while I and the remainder of the regiment will move in to examine the fortress. Our goal is to confirm the original reports of the fortress's structural integrity, whether or not she still has stores and an available water source. If so, a small garrison will be left until the Imperial 1st Infantry arrives to take possession in about a month. The remaining bulk of the regiment will then continue on its prescribed route eastward along the lip of the Rift and eventually meet up with the 5th Imperial Cavalry, which is coming south from New Sea at a point southwest of Calif."

"The 5th?" asked Turcot suddenly. "Isn't that Aiden's regiment?" Anlin nodded, eyes bright with pride, and said, "2nd under Fembrin."

"Why, you old goat!" Turcot exclaimed, drawing a smile from Anlin and a half sneering twitch from Baen at his lack of decorum. "You never told me the 5th had the eastern probe."

"Can't tell you everything," he joked. Baen sniffed loudly. Turcot rolled his eyes. "Any questions?"

"Is there any resistance suspected?" Baen interjected before Turcot could answer the negative. The man's face was alight with anticipation.

"None is expected." stated Anlin. The man was maybe half his age, and he could remember being a young officer just out of the Academy and bristling for a fight, but Baen's interest was a little too intense for his comfort. "But, as always, we will be prepared for it." Baen's expression fell back to the rigid disinterest he normally presented, but his eyes continued to tell his disappointment. "Any more questions?"

Baen shook his head, while Turcot continued to remain quiet and unmoving. "Well, then," Anlin said shortly. "Let's be on about ourselves. We leave at dawn."

"Yes, sir," Baen said, flicking a quick salute and clicking his heels together. Turcot replied with a simple, "Sir."

Baen retreated quickly, moving back out into the cool evening air without another word. Turcot returned to his seat and took up his cup, casually watching after Baen, a contemplative expression on his face.

"Something wrong?" Anlin finally said softly, picking his cup up from the edge of the table and taking a sip. He grimaced.

"I just wonder about that one," he said, leaving his gaze attached to the tent flaps. After several minutes, his stare snapped and he brought his attention back to Anlin. "So! Who is going out ahead?"

Marklin sat down in his small camp chair, saying with a grunt, "Silek and Maliss."

"Hmm!" Turcot tipped back his cup, drained it, set it down and picked up his hat. He stood, and through a yawn, said, "Well, I'm off." Anlin grunted his reply. "See you in the morning." Pulled open one of the flaps and looked back at his friend and commander. "You should get some rest."

Anlin nodded absently, watching Turcot exit the tent without really seeing him. His thoughts mused on the two missing scouts and the day ahead. It rankled him to not know where they were. Bothered him on a level he did not always like to admit existed. Though not exactly common, scouts did tend to keep their own schedules and situations had happened before where they were past due, but eventually showed up no worse for the wear. Yet, he would never become used to it. His concern for his men dictated a lot of sleepless nights, and tonight would be one of them.

Chapter 23

Transitioning Thoughts

*7*he sun gazed through a latticework of long, thin streamers of clouds far to the southeast where Marc Pendragon and Whitesteel trudged along. Camp was broken more than a couple hours before the dawn and his intentions were heavily on the side of not stopping. Though his memories still refused to yield up any significant clues to his identity, he found that he seemed used to such activities as long days spent on horseback. And Whitesteel, it appeared, had plenty of reserve energy, especially given the leisurely gait at which they traveled during the large part of the day. Indeed, when they had halted for the evening previous, Whitesteel was overflowing with prance.

They headed, generally, in a southwesterly direction. Logically, he could not reason why, only that a vague sense of recollection told him it was the proper direction. And when allowed his head, Whitesteel unerringly chose to go that way. He could only assume that there was a destination familiar to the both of them or that that was the direction he had been heading prior to his stay at the village and his subsequent loss of memory. In an odd way, it was as if he had been born at the village and was now venturing forth from home for the first time in his life.

It was not long past noon, resuming after a short repast of dried fruit, that they broke out of the thick forest onto a lush plain of rolling hills. Whitesteel began frisking almost immediately, freed now from the confines of the trees and shrubs. Marc, too, suddenly felt unfettered by the wide vista before him and had but only to cluck his tongue to send Whitesteel launching forward into a full gallop through the waving sea of grass.

Marc's body instantly adjusted to the new, smooth gait. The sudden wind against his face and the loud pounding of the steed's hooves churned an abrupt thrill throughout him. Consciously, he could tell that he was quite accustomed to riding, but his current situation did hold some benefits. And at that moment, he did not think on what was lost, but reveled in what he had gained. It probably was not a common occurrence to experience something again as if it were the first time. Unstained by repetition; unbiased by experience.

Whitesteel's ferociously powerful strides churned up large tufts of grass and it was only seconds before he was at a full out run, his mane and tail whipping out behind him like pennants in a gale. Small tears formed and fell from the corner of Marc's eyes as the wind slid past. Concentrated heat began rising up from Whitesteel as he pounded up and down one hillock after another, grunting with the strain, but not slowing. Seconds turned into minutes as he ran, blending the surroundings into a blur of lush green and yellow, until, finally, Marc thought it prudent to have him rest. Whitesteel resisted stubbornly, biting loudly and shaking his great head at the gentle tugs on his bit, refusing to relinquish the exultant freedom of motion he was engaged in. Marc thought at first that he was going to continue to run until he dropped, but soon, he began slowing, albeit in a very gradual manner. After several more minutes, he slowed to a brisk walk, his barrel chest expanding and contracting in great huffs and snorts. A thin sheen of sweat had formed which lent an almost silvery quality to his coat.

After some soft words from Marc, Whitesteel stopped long enough for him to drop to the ground and pull the reins over the head and free the bit from his mouth. Marc's legs were hot and a bit shaky, probably still weak from his ordeal, and it took a moment for them to adjust to the solid ground. Whitesteel, in the meantime, began munching contentedly on the fresh grass, until Marc began walking, holding the reins loosely and patting the huge animal's cheek and neck.

Since dawn, the thin clouds overhead inexorably thickened and now, as Marc scanned the horizon, very little blue was available to the eye. He figured that by nightfall, the slate clouds would completely dominate the sky, and while he did not think it would prove much of a serious problem, he was not looking forward to the uncomfortable condition that the clouds were promising, especially now that the temperature was dropping during the hours of darkness. And now that he was not whipping along astride the running steed, he could feel a slight breeze that was threatening to become more stiff as the daylight passed. Marc resigned himself to the possibility that he would be wet and miserable this night.

Whitesteel stopped suddenly, momentarily cocking his ears vertical then quickly laying them back against his head. Marc, his attention drawn from the weather, paused as well and listened intently for the few seconds that the horse waited. Over the whisper caused by the breeze brushing past his ears, he heard a faint noise from somewhere ahead that he could not identify except that it was somewhat alien to the current milieu of sounds. Marc unconsciously reached back and unfastened the leather cord that kept the broadsword from bouncing in its scabbard, a physical reaction to the sudden uneasiness caused by the unknown sound. He began walking alongside Whitesteel, who had, only a moment earlier, decided to continue.

They were heading toward another of the long, low rises that rippled across the plain, its crest a smooth line against the graying horizon. As they started up the long incline, a few more sounds drifted over the top, still muffled by the growing wind and the hill, but more distinct than the former. The noises sounded like someone yelling or calling out, though he could not be sure because of the muted quality. Still, it cautioned him further, slowing his walk. His mind began to focus, pushing all extraneous thoughts aside.

The wind could not push away the noise the closer he came to the crest of the hill, where he was suddenly assailed with the clear sound of people fighting. The whisper of steel as the broadsword slid free of its scabbard comforted him on a level deep within, and brought a sharpness to his mind that tickled at his frozen memories. *Well, I guess I'm not a farmer*, he mused. Whitesteel nickered softly and nudged him with his nose, setting him in step again. He looked at the horse with a touch of surprise and found within the deep brown eyes a glimmer of intelligence that he did not expect to see and a touch of something more. Marc realized that Whitesteel wanted a fight. A true war horse. Marc nodded and strode to the top of the hill.

The knoll sloped down as gently as the rise, dropping down into a wide, semi-flat valley perhaps a quarter of a mile wide before climbing toward the crest of another hill. Forest land was encroaching from the south, moving up diagonally over the further rise. Below, in the trough, several wagons stood, others overturned, their pack animals either laying in arrow riddled heaps or wandering several yards away, dragging the remains of their yolks and ties. Several men on foot were swarming over and around the wagons, some ransacking their contents, others driving their swords into the last resistance of the train's owners. As he watched, the last defender, an aging man in ragged clothes, slid to the earth in the face of two darkly dressed men with cloths tied around their faces wielding long swords. A sucking gasp reached Marc after he lay still for a couple of seconds.

A burning anger deep within Marc's core flared into existence, and he unconsciously gripped the sword more tightly. But, before he could move, several whistling arrows *thunked* into the lee slope of the hill, digging in only a scant couple of yards down from him. His eyes flicked to the tree line along the crest of the opposite knoll and picked out five shadowed figures standing just within the break. They were moving quickly, nocking their bows with more arrows. As he took another breath, the small flight was arcing out over the brigands below, dark lines against the gray, bristling the downslope seconds later. A grim smile worked onto Marc's face. He was out of range.

A yell from the wagons drew Marc's gaze downward to rest on a man standing away from the wreckage, mask pulled down and pointing up at him with a blood dulled sword. His face was a white spot framed completely by dark hair and lined where his brows and mustache crossed the plane. Six pairs of eyes suddenly focused on him, followed by disembodied angry mutterings. Marc's smile widened as he stepped away from Whitesteel, bringing the sword up in front of him so that those eyes would not miss the gleam of steel. He did not know for sure if he was really capable of what he contemplated then, but the anger that burned within gave him a confidence that was unshakable. He waited, silently, watching the men as they visibly struggled with this new encounter.

Whether because of unsated blood-lust or just pack mentality, the decision on what to do was made quickly, and the six men charged past the dark haired man and up the slope toward him, yelling almost in unison. Marc stepped further away from the horse, wanting to keep the steed out of the brigands' line of sight, and gripped his sword loosely. Of its own accord, it seemed, his body relaxed into a stance ready to accept the charge of the six men.

The long slope, though gentle, worked quickly to separate and slow the rushing men, drawing them out in a ragged line. Marc waited patiently, his mind completely silent, his body in complete balance, as the first man closed in on him. Like the others, he was dressed in dark clothing and leathers that allowed them to hide easily within the shade of the close knit trees. In contrast, the cloth that was tied around his face was a bright red. The brigand reached the crest where Marc stood, long sword raised high overhead, another call exploding from his throat. Marc stepped into him, the bastard sword leveled out. The man's cry turned to an agonized wail as the sword bit fiercely, driven deep by the force of his run. Using the sword as a guide, Marc wheeled around the bandit, turning gracefully before ripping the blade free, letting the momentum carry it around in a powerful arc that cut a deep gash through the chest of the second bandit before even the first fell, lifeless, to the ground. Marc sidestepped to allow the second bandit to stumble past, gurgling out his final words. The third one came in a little more cautiously, his blade out in front of him guardedly, but not enough that Marc could not take advantage of him, bringing his blade up quickly to connect with it. The sharp clang of steel rang out as the swords met.

The man's eyes, all but hidden by a ragged brown mask, went wide in surprise as his sword suddenly jumped up from the blow, then in agony when Marc's blade slipped in under his guard and plunged into his belly. A wrenching shriek broke from the bandit, spraying spittle and blood out in a fine mist from underneath the cloth. A quick kick to his chest freed him from the grasp of the sword and sent him tumbling backward, his sword falling against Marc's with a dull ring. The weapon was flung out in a glittering arc as Marc had to move to block the swing of the forth. A weak blow and ill-aimed besides, the bandit's blade ricocheted away, exposing his side. Marc twisted his around and down, dispatching the man with a momentary flash of pity at these clumsy attackers. The fifth fell just as easily, screaming out his last breath while he fell to the ground.

The sixth was the only that showed any amount of intelligence since Marc appeared on the hilltop. He spit out a few expletives in a language Marc didn't understand, then turned and ran back down the hill. The leader, or, at least, the one that had alerted the others to his presence was also high-tailing it up the slope of the opposite hill. There was no sign of the archers.

Marc waited as the two men disappeared into the trees before he bent and wiped the blood from his sword on the clothing of the last of the bandits, noting grimly that he was not moved by the carnage he just wrought. Five dead in quick succession, all obviously unaccustomed to handling the weapons they had carried. He cast a glance back at Whitesteel, who was clipping off mouthfuls of grass, then surveyed the area again. Seconds later, he started walking slowly down the slope toward the wagons, keeping his eyes on the modified horizon for any suspicious movement. There was none, and, judging from the ineptitude of the bandits, he really did not expect any more trouble, but something second nature to him remained alert.

When he reached the valley floor and was closer to the wagons, he stopped and inspected the damage and death left by the brigands. There were seven wagons in all, scattered over an area of about a hundred yards, three of them overturned and collapsed, the torn grass and deep ruts evidence to their demise as their pack animals panicked and attempted to flee. Strewn in and among them were the vehicle's cargo: crates and baskets, clothing, casks and sacks, some that had burst open to reveal flour, sugar, liquid, nothing of outstanding value or conspicuousness.

The dead were even less so, aged men and women wearing heavy wool clothing of browns and russets that were very well worn lay where they were butchered. He saw not a weapon among them, not even a hunting bow, and the pack animals, both alive and dead, were not in the best shape. Everything about the wretches cried out poverty which made the attack all the more tragic and senseless. Marc's anger burned anew, not only because of the scene before him, but also because his lack of memory. If his mental faculties were in order, he might have an idea why inept bandits were killing indigent travelers.

A clatter of boards falling near one of the overturned wagons, brought his sword up. He began a slow circuit of the area, intent on putting some obstruction between himself and whatever made the noise and allow him to get a better view of the battleground. Mentally, he shook his head in disgust each body he passed or stepped over. When he came to the wreckage from which the sound emanated, and was assured that there was no one else lurking within or around the other wagons, he called out, "Come on out! I will not harm you!"

Stretched moments passed as he waited, scanning the wreck for any movement. When nothing occurred, he decided to level one more warning before investigating. If there was nothing there, well, only Whitesteel was around to hear him talking to himself, and he was busy catching up on some grazing. As he was taking another breath to expel his words, several boards on the opposite side of the wagon began shifting and falling away from something. Marc's sword came up again.

Long, dark hair and dirty white fabric emerged from behind the shelter of the upset cart, throwing off bits of debris. He blinked when the figure straightened, and he found himself looking at a young, disheveled woman. Lines of fright drew the pale skin of her face tightly around her eyes and mouth, but her stance and the solid way she wielded a long dagger before her spoke volumes as to her decision between fleeing or fighting. "Don't come any closer!" she stated, her voice tremulous.

Marc lowered his sword and straightened, held up his free hand. "I mean you no harm," he said . "I am not with those bandits." The woman cast glances sidelong and, unconsciously, chewed her bottom lip, obviously making sure she had an escape route. Ever so slowly, she relaxed, dropping her weapon hand to her side.

"They were not bandits," she said, stepping among the detritus of the wreckage. "They were deserters."

"Deserters?" Something twinged within the depths of his blocked memories.

"From Scandin." She came out from behind the collapsed wagon, watching him warily. Her dress, though dirty, was made of a finery that did not fit in with what the dead travelers were wearing, made of a satiny material of different hues of white. Though displaying an unusual amount of bravado, she appeared soft, her body used to a more sedate lifestyle, not at all akin to the calloused hands and corded muscles of the dead. "We found them hiding out at an inn in a small village back that way." She gestured south with her dagger.

"Why would they follow you, this group was no threat to them?"

"Old Hav—" A sudden hitch in her throat cut her off. She was looking at the body of one of the old men laying nearby. "Old Havlek recognized a couple of them. Apparently they were from the same town. He was angry at their cowardice. I guess they thought he would report them."

"Where were you going?"

"Hestaff." She sighed, suddenly looking frail, exhausted. "We were trying to get away from the Troubles." She shrugged. "Who would have thought they would have followed us all the way up here. . ." Her voice trailed off as her gaze wandered aimlessly over the southern horizon. After a few minutes of silent staring, she held out the hem of her dress and studied it, muttering quietly about how dirty it was.

Marc cleared his throat uncomfortably, startling her into looking at him as if for the first time. Her brown eyes were wide with fright, her mouth a thin determined line. The moment of their gaze passed as she began looking around her again. "Well. . ." she said. "I guess I'll be on my way. Th-thank you for your assistance."

"What?" Marc exclaimed, his incredulity tightly reigned. "What did you say?"

A glazed expression began to seep onto her face as any remaining color drained from it. "I-I guess I-I'll be going. . . now." She looked around at the ground blindly. "Just as soon as I find. . . ."

"Are you okay?" he said. "Perhaps you should sit down and rest."

"Y-yes. . . ." Her hand reached out and began grabbing for a hand hold as she started to sway. "I. . .I think that . . . might be a good idea." Marc started to move toward her, but the motion brought her eyes back to his face and the hand holding the dagger up. "No! Stay back. . . please." Marc's free hand went up in a placating gesture as he took a step back.

"Alright," he said. "Alright." More softly. She nodded, her head bobbing like a cork in water, and again resumed fumbling around with a hand. Within seconds, she found a place along the broken wagon and sat gracelessly, staring languidly at the bloody grass underneath her feet. Marc looked into the grayness, trying to judge how much more daylight was left, then tracked around along the hilltops, over the wreckage and death, and finally back to the girl. She had feinted, slumped over against the broken sidewall beams like a rag doll.

He huffed, stabbed the ground with his sword, and left it standing like a grave marker as he began the grim business of collecting the dead.

Chapter 24

A Long Day in the Sun

*M*orning came all too quickly, the sun brushing the sky several shades of rose before lifting itself above the fuzzy horizon. The chill began to recede, but only slightly, the men, bleary eyed and moving about sluggishly, seeking warmth within their uniforms and by standing close to their mounts, hands wedged under saddle blankets as they waited for the command to mount.

Anlin gazed over what he could see of the camp, sipping at his final cup of *qaha*. Stretching away from him was a veritable sea of men and horses, crowding together, their breath misting out before them like steam from hundreds of small fissures, all of them fuzzy, half shadows broken only by those frosty puffs. The air was moist against his skin and gave his view a glassy quality only available during these times just before the sun appeared. The chill reached him as it did all his men, but he had long since found a way to ignore the effects of the bite. Still, he marveled at the temperature, given the barrenness of the region.

Eventually, through the crowd of slowly organizing troops came Captain Turcot, leading both his horse, Striker, and Rushwind, both fully saddled. "Morning," he said as he drew near.

"Yes, it is," replied Anlin.

"Get any sleep?" he returned. Anlin glared at him over the rim of his tin cup as he took a swallow of the bitter liquid. Once done, he tossed the rest into the small fire, then hung the cup on a peg jutting from the nearest tent pole.

"Enough," Anlin groused, nodding to the men standing nearby. They broke quickly into action, gathering tools and equipment needed to take down the commander's tent. "Ready to go?" he asked, stepping from the shelter just as the sun broke the horizon. Sharp yellow fans of light washed down upon them, banishing the uniform greyness and the chill attached to it.

"The only thing I'm ready for is my next life," Turcot answered, attaching a salute to it.

"Yea," Anlin retorted, returning the salute, then taking the reins of Rushwind. He and Turcot pulled themselves up into their saddles, drawing expectant looks from those soldiers closest.

"Sound the prep!" Turcot barked. A scarecrow of a soldier, named Banek, standing his horse a few feet away snapped to attention then brought a gleaming brass horn bundled in colorful cords to his lips. A crisp tone split the morning placidity as it called out. Soldiers scrambled, muted conversations forgotten, loose equipment quickly bundled into their gear, to stand their horses, right hand gripping loosely their mounts' bridles, waiting rigidly for the coming order to mount up.

Anlin viewed it as he had thousands of times before, waiting silently as the preparation command swept through the regiment as a ripple moves through a mill pond. He waited the customary 100 heartbeats before nodding to Turcot.

"Prepare to mount!" he yelled, followed quickly by another call from the horn. The command was repeated, yelled over and over by the soldiers, fading away into the distance as they called and responded, stepping back and placing their left foot into stirrup, left hand holding the reins and grabbing a hold of the high pommel. "Mount!" Another wave as the men pulled themselves into the saddle.

Anlin watched with routine interest as commands were called; the horn sounded and the men moved, first into full rank line, followed by counting off, then into the long snaking line four abreast. The process took less than an hour. By the time they had finished and were waiting for the command forward, the sun was already beginning to make the temperature uncomfortable.

It did not let up as the regiment wound its way toward their destination. Indeed, the heat increased beyond what it was yesterday, steadily rising with the blazing ball. Anlin cast a quick look back, long enough to see the string of slumping men and dragging horses before turning back and gazing into the shimmering distance. Hand held at an angle to the brim of his hat to add some shielding to the blinding light, he vainly tried to pick out the two figures emerging from the liquid horizon that he had expected to see for a couple of hours now. Deep lines etched his brow, funneling sweat down onto the bridge of his nose and brim to drop onto the black leather of the pommel. "Where are they?" he muttered harshly.

"Don't know," Turcot answered, the heat weariness touching the edges of his voice. "But those two are the best." He cast a squinting glance up toward the sun. "They are probably just being smart and waiting out this flamin' heat in the shade of one of the bigger rocks. Like we should be doing."

As if in answer, a dusty trooper rode up alongside of Turcot, his mount snorting and coughing from the dust kicked up by its weary trot, handed him a piece of paper, saluted, then reined back once Turcot acknowledged him. Anlin's second grunted after scanning the script on the parchment.

"How many?" he growled.

Without looking up, Turcot answered. "Twenty-two more, bringing the total up to . . . seventy-eight."

"Damn heat," Anlin said. "Dispatch two additional men to stay back with the stragglers, help round them up and wait until nightfall to catch up with us. That will keep us shy of 100 down. At least for the moment. And get those physicians spread equally among the men to try to head off any forthcoming cases. Hopefully, we can hold out until that blasted fireball falls west far enough to afford us some shade!"

"Right," Turcot answered. A brief smile touched his heat chapped lips. "Think Jarren is up for some shepherd duty?"

Anlin snorted in spite of himself, a smile of his own breaking the cragginess of his face. "He is a fine lad," he said. "Sounds just like the thing to help him out. Make sure he has gotten himself another sword."

Chapter 25

Troubles From the South

*B*lue fire limned the body of the dead ffolk, radiating outward from the single touch quickly, consuming it and reducing it to fine ash within a matter of minutes without the detriment of oily black smoke and the overwhelming stench of burnt flesh. Alex straightened slowly and began shuffling toward the next body, Sandoren moving quickly beside her, placing an arm around her waist and supporting her tired frame.

"Alex," he said softly, but sternly, "You must rest. It's not going to do you any good to kill yourself like this."

"This has to be done," she returned quickly, irritation trying to pinch her exhausted face. Angrily, she kicked out at the next body, frightening away the most brave of the carrion birds that remained. They scattered, flapping sluggishly a few feet to settle on the next, dropping fat, greasy feathers in their wakes and calling out hoarsely in protest. "This has to be done!" she repeated vehemently.

"You are so stubborn!" he replied, his own anger showing, as she stooped and called on her powers to consume the corpse. It was coming more slowly, her exhaustion blocking her efforts, but it, too, was soon encompassed with the blue flame. She stood and began moving toward the next.

"Yea! Yea!" was her only reply before she began the ritual that had been required since she touched the first body earlier that morning. Scare the crows away, call on her power, move onto the next, in a seemingly endless cycle.

The ghastly, horror-filled masks of death blurred into insubstantiality, largely unseen as the exhaustive work was taking its toll. The razor edge of pain, too, long since dulled; her tears, washed away hours ago out of necessity. She acted mostly instinctively, driving her weakened, aching body mechanically to satisfy an unconscious need for absolution. Thankfully, the task was nearly finished.

The boy, all but forgotten, snuffled behind her. His eyes were wide, liquid, swollen and a deep frown covered the lower half of his moon face. Suddenly, Alex's legs gave out, and she began to stumble. "Sandy, help me," she gasped.

"I am," he replied, her croaking request deepening his concern. He squeezed her gently so she would know he was there, before helping her bend to touch the next body. Her body heat flared momentarily as she called forth her power. As the flame took hold and she released her Touch, she whimpered softly. Sandoren shook his head, clamping down on the admonition about to shoot past his lips.

Although accustomed to the sight of death, it still sickened him on some level, even more so when it was the slaughter of the innocent, and he could not help but nurse the burning anger at the atrocity. However, the majority of his thoughts, and a conflagration of conflicting emotions, lay on Alex.

He knew her drive, understood it less, and it grated to no end that he could do absolutely nothing to relieve her of it. And it twisted him deep down in his core that it was her drive that would probably kill her, as it was trying to do now. Despite all her talk about Balance, and health, and such, nothing could stand in her way once her instincts kicked in. It was all the more infuriating when she began to lecture him on not being so hardheaded about things.

She groaned softly, pulling his gaze to her tight and sunken face. *She hasn't had enough rest since her last ordeal.*

He thought morosely. Immediately, that part of him that called him coward, leapt upon his thoughts and fed off them, insinuating itself deeper into his soul, convincing him more and more that, had the opportunity truly existed to help, he would run instead of face the responsibility. It was more of a struggle to quell those feelings "Is that all?" Alex mumbled.

"Just a few more," he whispered back soothingly. "Then you will rest." Sandoren wondered briefly if all he was capable of was moral support, but quickly brushed it aside, instead focusing on helping her to the next, and hopefully final, group of bodies. He cast a glance back the way they came, seeing but not seeing all the body-shaped, ashed areas glaring whitely in the afternoon sunlight. Over 650 spots lay back that way, the only reminder that this area once supported people, and with the coming rain, not even those for very much longer. Whatever had slaughtered these ffolk had showed absolutely no mercy.

A sluggish black cloud lifted from the group as they neared, a few of the crows remaining behind and squabbling with each other. Sandoren yelled sharply, scaring them off, then swallowed hard against his rising bile.

Many long minutes passed before Alex completed her work with the three bodies. Once done, she sagged heavily in Sandoren's arms. He considered briefly, moved her to a small bit of shade nearby and was about to lay her gently down in the lush grass when he spotted a clawlike hand emerging from some dense shrubbery several yards distant. A sigh fell from his lips. He shook Alex gently, prodding her slipping consciousness with his voice until she woke enough to understand. As he feared, she decided to take on the task, waiting only long enough to gather the strength to stumble over with Sandoren's help. She, of course, curtly refused to be carried, saying that any pause now would mean an avalanche into unconsciousness.

When they closed within a dozen feet of the corpse, Alex suddenly pushed away from him, her features becoming darkly intense. "What?" Sandoren hissed.

"Someth—" A high pitched shriek burst from the brush, followed by an ebony blur that sent leaves and twigs spiraling through the air in an explosive cloud. Something hard and powerful slammed him in the chest and sent him sprawling backward, grunting in surprise. Hastily, he jumped back to his feet, sword sliding from its scabbard. The black thing moved again and hot agony speared up through his arm; his sword flew from his grip and disappeared from view, and again, he was thrown to the ground.

Cradling his arm, he rolled away several feet, before getting his legs under him and rising, slipping his dagger from his belt. His sword arm dangled uselessly at his side.

"No!" Alex yelled. She was barely standing, hands on knees, swaying, face haggard. "Wait!" she then gasped out when his eyes found hers. Immediately, they leapt to the creature which crouched between them. It was a dark, disproportioned thing, thickly corded muscles under skin the color of fetid, murky water; blacks and greens in a random patchwork mottled by irregular tufts of bristly hair erupting from it. Extra-long arms and a squat body, rows of needlelike teeth within a maw that split its feral face. An ancient odor of musky death surrounded it, but it was its eyes that drove thin lances of terror into his soul. Deep as the darkest night, they were filled with silvery red nothingness as old as the beginning of time. Within, the killing and devouring of hundreds of creatures. Thousands. Reflecting from that emptiness, vast pools of hate beyond any conceivable notion.

A shudder broke out around his heart and quickly spread throughout his body in numbing waves. How it remained hidden beneath the placid waters of his skin Sandoren did not know, but the shivers stayed deeply entrenched with his bones. Panic riddled and vulnerable, his fears gained credence, challenging strongly his confidence, subverting it. The most shameful thing about it was the creature was not even looking at him. His dagger slid from nerveless fingers.

Alex saw the utter terror grip Sandoren, the falling dagger, from the corner of her eye. She, herself, was suffering from an incomprehensible fear trying to permeate her very being, but she resisted, relying on her connection to the Elemental Powers of the Earth to help strengthen her resolve. The creature's eyes were fixed in the direction of the boy, who simply stared back at it with a slack look on his face though his eyes were lucid. The thing swayed back and forth, searching, facing her at least twice before swinging its gaze around at the ghost white figure of Sandoren and back. A peculiar whine deep within its throat broke the tense silence as it glanced around it, rocking in a slow manner from its malformed hips. Minutes dragged by, the creature intently looking around, blinking its silvery red eyes slowly. The boy, statue still, watched it with non-blinking eyes, until, without warning, the fiend sprang past him and loped away toward the forsaken village, leaving a noxious odor in its wake.

Alex exhaled slowly, casting a look at Sandoren who allowed a low quick moan to exit his mouth. He knelt in the grass and held his head with his good hand. The boy was smiling when she looked back at him, the dull glaze encompassing his eyes once more. She smiled back weakly, her adrenaline powered strength slipping quickly away. A haze was creeping along the edges of her vision, and her body was shaking. Before she knew it, she, too, was kneeling on the ground, pitching forward into the blackness of unconsciousness.

Chapter 26

Hell's Heat

"*H*ey," someone whispered, disturbing the uncomfortable darkness he floated in. The nudge that followed knocked him into blazing awakeness, spinning the entire sweaty, sticky, dusty world into his awareness. For a moment he did not realize that he was staring down at the pommel of his saddle, his head bobbing at the end of a limp neck along with the steady gait of his mount.

"What?" Corporal Jarren mumbled once his brain began working again. He continued to let his head bob, though, nearly hypnotically relaxed despite the oven surrounding him.

"Looks like you're still the Commander's campstool," Mandol Jorn said from his right, kneeing his horse, Rumble, closer so that he could lean near enough to whisper. Jarren cut his eyes suspiciously at the stocky, dark skinned man. A wide grin split his face and his eyes gleamed playfully. "Guess you didn't do enough penance last night."

"What are you yapping about?" he asked after a moment. Jorn answered by gesturing quickly with his head, never taking the grin and eyes away from his target. Jarren sighed inwardly, slowly lifted his head enough so that the brim of his hat unblocked the view in the direction of Mandol's gesture. Coming down the line in a slow, dust raising trot was

Sergeant Ganz, searching passing faces from the grim, pinched expression that normally adorned his weathered face. Though the odds were in his favor, Jarren knew Mandol was right. Ganz was searching for him; he could feel it deep in his guts. The accidental loss of his weapon had heralded a rise in his popularity that was more than he ever wanted and would undoubtedly be slow to recede. "Damn," he said, even though he knew his newfound conspicuousness was warranted. Mandol chuckled, reseating himself on his horse as the perfect cavalryman, as if the heat was not getting to him as it was everyone else.

Jarren, with deliberate effort, straightened himself in his saddle, absently pulled at the bottom of his uniform top to pull out the wear, as he watched the sergeant come closer. Several feet away, recognition dawned on Ganz's face; a deeper scowl that sent crevices crawling across the leathery surface. Jarren sighed again, the result of a pit forming in his stomach. He waited for him in the closest semblance to heat induced attention he could manage.

"Corporal Jarren," Ganz said sharply as he drew next to Jarren's mount. A couple of troopers looked over at him, but most remained in their individual trances, more than likely just glad the sergeant wasn't speaking to them.

"Yes, Sergeant," he answered, silently hoping the man would not catch his disdain, yet too hot and tired to try and mask it.

"Message for you from Captain Turcot," Ganz growled, holding out a folded piece of parchment, staring at him as if he were the child he never wanted. "Lose that sword again and I'll give you mine," he added.

"Yes, sir," Jarren said, snapping a crisp salute. Sergeant Ganz flicked a return, stared at him for a second more before turning back toward the front. Jarren scowled at his back while giving him another type of salute with his descending hand. The gesture was quickly forgotten, though, as he brought the message up, unfolded the heavy paper with his thumb and read the distinctive scribble of the Captain. "Damn," he said to the note once his eyes flowed over it two or three times.

"You got to go up there and polish his boots?" Jorn said, non-decorum now that the sergeant had gone.

"No," he answered simply, for once not reacting to the man's taunt. "I have to fall out and collect all the stragglers and catch up with the regiment after nightfall."

Mandol burst with laughter, pounding a hand against the pommel that caused Rumble to flatten his ears and issue the deep throated whicker he was named for. Through his laughter, Mandol managed to say, "Babysitting! Now that is a job for you!"

Jarren watched him, a quiet smile forming on his drying lips until the man calmed enough to hear the words he would speak. "Yea," Jarren chuckled along with him. "A real stable-clean type job." Mandol nodded with his giggles. "It's a good thing Captain Turcot thought the apple-pickup needed *two* people to do it."

Within a split second, stone-faced confusion swept over Mandol, stopping cold his laughter. "What?" he asked.

"Fall out, soldier," Jarren retorted. "You're going with me." Realization took hold of Mandol Jorn slowly, like mud drying on a day like today. When the glint of understanding finally reached his eyes, it was Jarren's turn to laugh while Jorn frowned and groaned.

"Aw, that's not fair, Jarren," he said.

"And who said life was?" replied the Corporal on the tail end of his chuckles. "Besides," he smiled evilly. "Think of it as earning the right to marry my sister."

"Right," Mandol leered. "Let's just do it and leave your sister out of it, yes?"

"Watch out. One day soon you're going to need my friendship," Jarren grinned. "Believe me. I grew up with her."

"Shut up, Kydel," He grumped, kicking his horse into a light gallop. Laughing, Corporal Kydel Jarren moved after him, angling his mount around the dust cloud rising from Rumble's hooves.

Chapter 27

Death is a Terrible Business

*T*he fire raged, sending noxious clouds of black smoke curling up into the slate sky and waves of acrid heat in all directions, while Marc looked on, a kerchief tied around his mouth that kept out only a minute amount of the sickly sweet odor that washed through the tiny valley. The girl, Anine, was further out, away from the stench and heat, sitting upon one of the refugee's nags that had remained nearby and unharmed. She had awakened not long after he had begun piling the bodies near the wreckage of the wagons and, without word, helped by moving less heavy items, wood, broken or smashed crates and supplies, onto the now blazing pyre.

At some point, she decided to tell him her name, assuming, he figured, that he meant her no harm. After the pyre had been constructed, while Marc worked at lighting the blaze, she gathered the nag on which she sat and some supplies from one of the other wagons and told him in passing she would wait. She only moved enough to get away from the billowing smoke and charnel stench. Whitesteel, too, stayed well away from the fire, grazing.

Marc waited patiently, ignoring the cloying odor as best as he was able, a shovel found among the wreckage in his hands, ready to stamp out any of the flames that happened to cross his hastily created fire break that surrounded the pyre.

Luckily, the grass was much too moist to catch easily, but he stood sentinel just on the off chance of it happening, noting grimly that the closest ring of flora was becoming dried and singed as the flaming pile reached its peak intensity. Thankfully, too, the nearby hillocks provided enough protection against the breeze that sparks were not scattered until their life-giving embers were too high and cooled by the same before drifting earthward.

Marc stood, watching the area beyond the shimmering curtain of heat and smoke with a peculiar sense of detachment that at once felt odd and normal, as if the grisly work were something seen hundreds, thousands of times before, though he consciously did not look at the blackened bodies piled on top of each other upon which the fire greedily fed. In that manner alone was a sense of recognition of his former life still locked away in darkness. The frustration of not knowing his identity overshadowed only in his wondering if, at these moments, he really wanted to know about his former life. Truly, he did not know if his memories would better serve him if he was able to unlock them. His guess up till now was that he might enjoy life a little better if he did not.

Wiping sweat and soot from his face, he pushed his thoughts aside and judged that the fire was on its downward spiral into death, and with the coming weather, it would do little harm should the surrounding grass catch. After casting a considering look at the wooden spade he held, he tossed it onto the fire and walked from the funeral pyre, grabbing up his sword as he passed by it. He gave a sharp whistle, it coming to his lips unbidden.

As he was wondering why he did it, Whitesteel came trotting up to him and nudged him in the back with his giant head, nearly throwing him from his feet. A smile came to him as the horse nickered softly in his ear, and he ducked down and back under his neck, patting it sharply. "Ready to go, old boy?" The horse nodded and snorted. As he slid the sword into its scabbard, after cleaning the blade of grime, his stomach growled loudly. Ignoring it, he swung himself up into the saddle, deciding to eat once away from this grim place.

He clucked his tongue, directing Whitesteel with his knee toward Anine, who watched him with a sullen expression on her alabaster face. "What now?" she asked when he sidled up next to her. He searched her eyes, her face for several seconds.

"I'm heading southwest," he said absently, scanning the heavens quickly before looking back at her. "It will be dark soon and the weather is probably going to be disagreeable. You are welcome to come with me until we reach a village or settlement."

"I was headed to Hestaff. . . ." she said haltingly. "But that was only because they. . . were. I don't see that I have much choice now. I will go with you if you don't mind the company." She tried a smile. It only touched the corners of her mouth and lasted but a moment. Marc nodded.

"Alright," he said. "Let us get away from here and find a place that may offer some shelter for the night. When was the last time you ate?"

"Early this past morning."

"We'll eat then as well," he replied, touching his heels to Whitesteel's flanks, causing him to start walking briskly. A moment later, Anine's nag snorted and trailed after them.

They traveled the remainder of the day, only a few hours, through thinning forests and widening plains, wordless, Marc and Whitesteel several yards ahead of Anine and her mount. Her horse was old and slow and anything but sure-footed. It was a relief when the hillocks became less and less until they had all but disappeared, if only so her mount did not have to struggle up each incline, breathe rattling from its exertions. It was a wonder that the beast still lived. It must have been dragged along with the small caravan unhindered by any supplies, as much trouble it was having now with the equipment it carried, head drooping low as it swayed. Marc did not think it would see out this part of its journey.

Twilight was upon them when Marc stopped within a small stand of trees wherein many saplings stood. With a few deft ties of his rope and the use of a couple of wool blankets salvaged from the wreckage, he created a small shelter that, while it would not stand up to a downpour, it would, coupled with the surrounding trees help keep the coming drizzle off them while they slept and ate. At least he hoped it so, as he hoped he was not wrong in his thinking that it would be just a drizzle. Several minutes later, a small fire crackled nearby, the horses' saddles were loosened and bedrolls were laid out. It was not cold, but Anine huddled close to the flame.

As Marc rummaged through his saddlebags for some food to warm, he turned and said, "You don't talk much, do you?"

It took a minute for her to look up at him, her countenance transfixed by the fire. She smiled thinly. "Actually, I have often been accused of being rather winded."

"Really?" The illumination from the fire bled shadows into the recesses of her face, drawing out the haggardness already there in sharp contrast to the underlying smoothness that must be characteristic. Hair dangling in front of her eye was brushed slowly back by a grime coated dainty hand. He found several pieces of jerky, sat down opposite her and laid them on a large rock to warm them

"Yes," she replied. "I was once someone who spent much of her time talking about new fashions, political intrigues, and other assorted gossip."

"Courtier?"

"Of sorts," she huffed a partial laugh, flicked her eyes to the flames and back again. "A wealthy merchant's daughter. It seemed so important, then." Her eyes drifted back to the fire, becoming far away. Minutes passed.

"And?" he prompted softly.

Without taking her gaze from the mesmerizing flames, she said, "And then the ruling Clans decided their partnership was no longer worth the effort."

"Why?"

"Don't know for sure," Her eyes, deep, clear, and filled with remembered pain, met with his again. "It all started with the Argath Clan claiming that the founder of their family line had risen from the dead to come back to them. Someone calling himself Hammunan, or some such. . . ."

"You don't sound convinced."

"The Clans' ancestors are supposedly always coming back from the dead at one time or another to assist them with problems and to give them insight. It's part of their religious beliefs. When this Hammunan took over, suddenly the *kuso* began challenging everybody and their retainers to duels, calling it *Du-othaa Morin,* The Spirit Warrior's Right, or something like that. They took on all four of the other ruling Clans, the twenty or so minor ones choosing up sides in order to gain more prestigious positions. It wasn't long before it turned into an all-out war."

"You speak as if you were not part of their society."

"I'm not. . . I mean. . . we were not." Her eyes misted a little. "My father sold items that were very popular in Scandin, such as silks and satins. We only lived there because of the business. When things became too hostile, and. . ." she smirked, "business dropped, we tried to leave. My father was killed in a skirmish between *kuso* of the Akla Clan and the Argath in an outlying town. I was lucky to find the refugee train."

"Indeed," Marc said, flipping the pieces of dried meat. "And these refugees?"

"They were *Henuai.* Common property of the ruling Clans. Farmers, servants. They are leaving in droves, headed north, ever since the fighting became so rampant that the Clans had to supplement their armies with the more able bodied. It's cruel and insane. The *Henuai* have been forbidden to fight and carry weapons for hundreds of years. The *kuso* give them spears and send them into battle," She grimaced. "It's truly barbaric."

"Yes," he mused. "It sounds terrible and explains much about those bandits' ineptness with their weapons."

"What about you?" she asked suddenly. "What is your story?"

Marc considered her across the undulating flames. "I don't know what my story is," he said slowly. "I seem to have lost my memory." Her eyebrow arched in disbelief, a corner of her mouth quirking. "I woke up days ago in a Ffolk village after being poisoned. All I can remember is the last few."

"Where are you going, then?" she said smartly.

"Don't know," he answered sheepishly. "For sure. Whitesteel and me seem to be drawn in that direction." Her face became more pinched as he stumbled around his explanation, her disbelief flapping at his own resolve in such a manner that he found it difficult to believe. "It's true, really," he finished with a marked clearing of his throat. Marc picked up some of the warmed meat and reached over towards her. "Jerky?" he asked, hope riding the question.

Anine took it with a half-smile. "Okay," she said. "I will take that. It really does not matter, I suppose, even if . . . . well, never mind." She took a bite of the meat, chewed, grimaced, swallowed. "It's good."

"It's venison," said Marc, smiling. "And it's not that good."

Anine chuckled, holding the strip of deer meat up as if in a toast. "I shouldn't complain," she said. "It's better than some of the things I've eaten since we left."

Marc echoed the salute and took a large bite of the tough, dry, gamey piece of venison, barely hiding his own grimace.

Chapter 28

Babysitting Duty

*A*lex blinked, found herself sitting against the large bole of an oak tree, her legs all but hidden by extremely lush, thick grass that curled up from the ground as if she had been shrunk and was now the size of a doll. Next to her, lying among equally healthy turf was Sandoren, sleeping peacefully, a soft look to his normally tense features. She was still tired and a little weak, but the ache in her muscles and the intense fatigue were gone. A yawn attacked her, bringing tears to her eyes. When they cleared, she saw the boy standing out in the glade beyond the tree.

He had his arm outstretched, palm up, and was staring intently at the doe that softly nuzzled it. After a moment, he stroked the deer's check, then dropped his hand. The doe began grazing. Watching him just then, she saw not the retarded boy that had followed her faithfully from the hollow yesterday, but got a glimpse of the greater person that she sensed in those first moments she saw him lying in grass similar to that which nestled she and Sandoren. He turned back and saw her looking at him and smiled broadly. The glimpse she had evaporated, his features returning to the slack look that normally covered them as he walked over toward her in a slow, lumbering gait. When the boy broke the shaded barrier, he squatted down, facing her and smiled again. "Better?" he said suddenly, clearly, though slightly slurred.

Alex drew in a silent gasp, nodded slowly, a smile working onto her face. "Yes," she said. "Yes, I am better, thank you." He nodded buoyantly, sat back on his heels, smiling loosely.

"That good," he said seconds later, then began looking at the reaching branches overhead, the glaze beginning to cloud his eyes again. Hoping to keep him from drifting back into that other world, she blurted, "What is your name?"

His eyes came back down and focused on her slowly, and for a minute she thought she lost him, but his brows knit in confusion. "Name?" he asked.

"What are you called?" she said then. He stared again for long minutes, then his eyes rolled up to the right and his mouth dropped open a bit.

"Dummy," he finally replied, then added, "Mudswine. Stupid. Lots names." He smiled, hurt springing into existence behind his cloudy eyes. He was too far for her to reach out and comfort him, so she smiled sympathetically.

"What would you like to be called?" she asked. Almost immediately, the pain left, replaced by a surprised look of joy. His eyes rolled back up to the left and he screwed up his brows in intense concentration. Again, after a long pause, he looked back at her, smiling broadly.

"Del," he stated. Her brow arched in consideration as she watched his bright expression, then she pushed the thoughts away and smiled as brightly, nodding.

"Yes. Del it shall be," she agreed, almost laughing at the expression of pure joy that passed over his features. He nodded to himself several times, then stood. Without looking back, he trundled back out into the glade, mumbling the name over and over. Alex watched after him in wonderment and some confusion at his actions, thinking on the name he had chosen for himself and how he came to think of it. And, more importantly, if he knew what it meant.

"Did I just hear him speak?" Sandoren asked sleepily, taking her away from her pondering.

"Yes," she answered, looking over at him. "Have a good nap?"

"I suppose so," he replied, gazing up into umbrella of limbs above. "Though I don't remember how I got here." His face turned toward her, an upside down expression of surprise behind the partially obscuring grass. "It wasn't that creature, was it?"

"No," she chuckled. He lifted himself onto his elbows. "I think it must have been him."

"That was kind of him," Sandoren said, then grunted, pulling himself backward so that he could lean against the tree trunk. Once situated, he let his head loll over to look at Alex. "Still a little weak," he stated. Alex answered with a nod.

"What was that thing?" he asked tentatively.

"An Eldritch," she answered softly, chewing her bottom lip. "A creature born of the world when it was created, but not exactly a part of it."

"Huh?"

"It's a natural unnatural thing," Alex replied with a matter of fact tone that caused Sandoren to draw his eyebrows together.

"You really know how to strike to the heart of an explanation, Alex."

"It was born of the world, but it doesn't follow the laws of Nature. It is a little complicated to explain without a full dissertation. Suffice it to say that it is very powerful, very hateful, and *very* old. We are lucky to be alive."

"Why are we alive?" he clucked his tongue. "I mean, that thing was so fast, I was on the ground before I knew I had been hit. I don't really remember a lot after that."

"I think it was after the boy," Alex remarked slowly, her eyes seeking out the youth. "But I think it somehow got confused when it came near. It seemed not to be able to see him when it was up close, like he suddenly became invisible, or disappeared into the background like a change lizard. It must have become frustrated, because all it did was run off." She looked off into the distance for several quiet moments. "It is out there still. Close. Watching."

"How do you know?"

"I can sense it. It was the same creature we heard last night."

"I found its tracks when I was making a circuit of the village this morning, but I could not identify them. I don't understand it, really," Sandoren mused over the problem for a bit. "That thing did not kill the villagers, I am sure. Swords killed a lot of them, and, I believe, magic killed the rest. Why, then, was it here? Was it waiting for us?"

"There is no telling," she said while pulling her knees up and leaning forward on them. "It could have been chance, it could have not been chance. Perhaps it somehow sensed we, or, he, would be in this area. The interesting thing is how it reacted when it confronted us, and, for that matter, how the boy reacted."

"I . . . um. ..I'm. . . ."

"It's alright, Sandy. I felt it too. The only reason I was able to withstand it was my ability. You were at no fault."

"Right," he said under a snort. "Sure. Okay. What now?"

"Well," She looked into what little she could see of the sky through the bough of the huge tree. "it is going to be dark soon, and the weather is turning sour. We have no more than several hours to find out where the man we are looking for went before the coming rains wipe out all traces. I suggest we see if we can find some sort of clue as to where he went before we are cast into the darkness of evening."

"That may not be as difficult as it sounds," Sandoren said with a smirk. When her brow cocked in a questioning, somewhat sarcastic, arch, he continued. "I found some interesting traffic traces at the southwestern end of the village. Someone on a single, iron shod horse left in that direction followed by someone on foot. One of the ffolk and obviously before the attack came. The marauders, too, were on horseback, but unshod. There were five of them. They came up from the south and apparently waited at the top of a hill that marks that end of the village for a time. There is a large area of blight up there. After the slaughter was over, they rode out toward the western horizon. The interesting thing is that the blighted area on the hilltop overlooks the path of the two travelers leaving the village."

"What are you suggesting?" she said shortly.

"I'm not suggesting anything. It's just another added coincidence to this strange occurrence. My guess is that your human left riding the iron shod horse and someone from this village followed him. Probably to make sure he did leave. I have a feeling that the ones that did this senseless act of violence fit in there somewhere."

"In what way?" she asked, watching him intently.

"The man was poisoned, wasn't he?"

"Yes. But by something that runs along the same lines as the Eldritch. It was an unnatural, evil poison."

"Could they not all be connected?" he asked, leaning forward. When she offered no more information, he went on. "It occurs to me that maybe the five riders may have been looking for this man as well, maybe to make sure the poison took. Perhaps so was that thing. Perhaps that thing poisoned him in the first place. But he slipped out before they caught up with him. Maybe they waited for him to leave before they descended upon the village. Whatever happened, there is only a few definitive points. The time the man on horseback, assuming it was the human, and the one on foot left was roughly about the same time the raiders arrived on the hill. Sometime yesterday morning. The murderers who did this. . ." his hand swept toward the village. "were powerful in their own rights. Five of them rode in, murdered the entire village before any organized resistance could be formed, and five of them rode out. No other unusual traffic has departed this village. Except for that thing."

"I'm afraid I still don't quite follow you, Sandy," she said curtly. "You're starting to ramble."

"Do you know anything about this man we are looking for?" he asked, staring at her intently. Her brows knit again in irritation. He held up his hands disarmingly as she was about to speak; an admonition coming to her lips, no doubt. "Look. We know nothing about this man, and this incident seems rather suspicious to me. The chances are pretty good that the killers watched him go. He was followed by another from this village who did not return. I'm merely suggesting that. . . ."

"I know what you are suggesting," she said with a hint of savagery. "and I think you are letting your prejudices run away with you!"

He stared at her for long moments, struggling to hide the pain that had sprung to existence behind the clearness of his large eyes. Pain that she inflicted, and now felt as solidly as if he had thrust a dagger into her chest. She could not even begin to know why she had said anything. In their long years together, it had been that same attitude that had kept them out of trouble on many occasions prior. "I'm sorry. I didn't mean that," came the afterthought.

"Forget it!" he answered, a line appearing between his brows in an attempt to cover the pain that still resided there in his eyes. His anger, however, was unable to wipe it away. "We should get out of here before that creature returns." He stood quickly, retrieved his gear that had been placed against the bole opposite them. As he was strapping his sword belt around his waist, he reiterated, "As always, I can't even pretend to know what we are doing, or even exactly why, but I do not have a good feeling about it. More than usual anyway."

"I know it," she said. "Me too." She diverted the sigh about to erupt from her throat into a loud exhalation from her nose. Slowly, Alex stood, watching the boy as he walked aimlessly through the field, touching some of the high grass every now and again. A lump of frustration sat heavily within her stomach. Something she figured would remain there for a while, a malignancy composed of things to come.

"By the way," he said once enough time had passed to assuage his fear, pain and anger. "What did he say?" he indicated their charge with a wave of his pack before swinging it onto his back.

"He said he wanted a name," Alex answered, a monotone quality creeping into her voice. He stopped with his adjusting to look at her. Though she was gazing at the boy, she had a faraway cast to her visage.

"A name?" he went back to adjusting his pack. "Didn't he already have one?"

"No."

"Well, what name did you give him?"

"I told him to choose one for himself."

"Did he?" she nodded, the mask of contemplation unwavering. "What did he choose?" Several quiet seconds passed, Alex giving no indication of hearing him. As he was about to repeat himself, she turned her head towards him, a deeply lucid thoughtfulness settling into her features.

"That's the odd thing," Alex said. "The name he chose is Del."

"Del?" he repeated, saying it twice more as if he were tasting it. "Del? Where have I heard that before."

"It's ancient Arquil," she said, a mysterious smile coming to her lips.

"Ancient Arqu--" His eyes searched the heavens of the inside of his mind until a lightness born of recognition began dawning behind them. "Doesn't that mean . . .?"

Alex was nodding. "Yes, it does," she said softly.

". . . Balance?" he finished, looking back at Alex. "That is odd."

Chapter 29

Chaos at Tergaard

The fortress shimmered in the distance, surrounded by clumps of the towering treelike rocks thrusting up from the barren earth, advancing out into the field before it, all but obliterating the once great paved road that met up with it at its gate. A single, triangular blade of rock speared at them from the edge of the shifting image of the keep; a tangible pointer toward their destination. Hemming in and supporting the thin rock face of the Tooth were low mounds and hills that emerged from the ground like uneven, cancerous gums, pockmarked with caves and clefts that resembled abscesses and open blisters. Connecting to it and moving from the western edge back near the fortress was the beginning, or ending, of the towering, sheer, mountain chain they had been following for three days now, the other terminus the backdrop for the construction of the fortress of Nur, their port of entry into this part of the world.

Beside him, Turcot exhaled heavily. The sun lay to the west, readying itself to plunge behind the huge wall of the mountains, to the east, nothing but barren, arid wastelands. But Anlin could only stare northward, at the fortress rising from the liquid metal-like ribbon that undulated on that horizon and the great nothingness of the Rift that could be sensed beyond it. It had taken them longer to get here, the heat slowing and confounding them at every second. Since dispatching Corporal Jarren to assist the stragglers, fourteen more men had fallen out with the heat sickness and six mules in the pack train far behind them had died of it, leaving necessary equipment and provisions to be claimed by this wasteland. And still, Silek and Maliss had not returned from their trek here. Some of the other outriding scouts had reported throughout the day of finding their tracks, but they were few, the trail wiped mostly away by the sharp quick winds that randomly blasted through, leaving only the earth near and around the rock pilings undisturbed.

It was at these times in his life that he wondered at and berated himself for ever becoming a soldier. It was at times like these that he questioned the orders he received from his superiors. It was at times like these that a knot of rebelliousness began rising within his gullet.

Marklin snorted, pinched and messaged his dust choked nose. This end of the Tooth lay maybe another few miles distant, the fortress maybe another after that. The sun would probably be dropping behind the mountains by then, still far from sunset, but, nevertheless, casting them into shadow. Hopefully a cooling one.

"Sergeant," Anlin called back. Sergeant Ganz immediately broke from his position behind the banner men and urged his horse forward.

"Sir?" he answered. Once near, the Commander looked over the aging soldier, his grim face worked over in deep tough lines, especially around his eyes and mouth, and graying hair showing from under the band of his hat, but still a solid man who refused to slump in his saddle despite the heat and the years seated in it. Ganz, another of the loyal troopers that had served him since the beginnings of his career as an officer, waited patiently, though his eyes told him he had better hurry or he was going to get off his horse and start looking for a tree stripling with which to beat him. Anlin smiled inwardly. The man took guff from no one, not even his commanders, though a more loyal and caring man did not exist. To everyone in the regiment, he was the embodiment of everyone's fussing mother and stern father.

"Fall back and fetch Lieutenant Baen for me, will you?" he said evenly. Ganz' face pinched more deeply. *Perhaps,* Anlin thought. *Not everyone's mother and father.* Saying nothing, Sergeant Ganz gave a quick, precise salute and began trudging down the long line of cavalrymen.

"You pissed him off," Turcot said quietly once the sergeant was out of earshot. He nudged Striker with his heels, starting the horse into a slow plod. Almost instantly, Anlin followed suit with Rushwind, the behavior so deeply ingrained he did not even notice anymore that he did it. The others, behind them, did not move nor look at them for that matter, quietly using the break to smoke or sip from their canteens while their mounts shifted, nickered, relieved themselves while swatting at biting flies and nipping at their neighbors. They were as used to their commanders' behaviors as they were the sun rising and setting.

"Yea, well, he'll get over it," Anlin replied. They stopped several yards from the bannermen, a comfortable distance proximity wise, but far enough to be able to converse openly. "He's been around long enough to see ten Baen's come and go."

"Yea, but I think he's getting meaner the older he gets," Turcot smiled warmly. "You best be careful, or you might find yourself on the wrong side of a hickory whip if you keep having him deal with him."

"Maybe," he answered, adding, "But, regardless of his personal feelings, he knows that Baen is a pretty decent soldier." Turcot snorted, and not to clear his nasal passages of dust. "You know it, too."

"He is a great parade officer," Turcot retorted. "But I think you overestimate his abilities in a field position. He has too much of a hard on for control and power. His ambition is not geared for your job, not even General Krane's. I think he's looking at the spire on the mountaintop."

Anlin visibly paled, the image of the black armored being that controlled the entire Imperial forces coming to mind. He gritted his teeth and shook away the unbidden scene. "That's insane. And if it's true, he's insane. Nobody in their right mind would even think of challenging Von Draden and, I think my friend, the sun is broiling your mind to be even thinking that yourself. They don't call him the Devastator for nothing, you know."

"Okay, okay," Turcot said, holding his hands up. "You're right, you're right. But Baen reeks of politician, Marklin. His abilities, I think, are more suited to battle within that arena than out here in the real world. You know it as well as I. He's only here to make a name for himself, and that's truth. Even I did not want combat like he does. I don't think he has ever taken a man's life before or I would think he would have less fire in those dark eyes of his when talking about it. He cares only for glory, and, mark me, he will do anything to get it, and that includes throwing away all his available resources."

"Just slow down, Larson," Anlin barked. "You're giving too much credit to his motivations. It wasn't that long ago that we were as full of ourselves as he is. He is anxious, and so what if he wants to make a name for himself. All officers do."

"Yea, but there is something else there, and you know it," Turcot said, holding his gaze for many tense moments. "Don't tell me he doesn't give you a creeping sensation when he talks about battle and such. You can't hide that from me, Marklin. I can see it in your eyes, hear it in your voice. The man bothers you more deeply than just his rigidness. The man craves for it just a little too much. You've said so yourself."

"Maybe you're right, maybe you're not," Anlin said. "But even so, there is nothing we can do for it now. We have no other choice but to trust in his training."

"Maybe you should consider letting him take his group into the fortress."

"Why?"

"Because I think, and you do too, that if anything happens up there and we see some action, Baen is going to conveniently forget about his orders and charge in like a maniac to save the day."

"No," Anlin retorted. "I think you're wrong. My wager is that Baen will follow his orders to the best of his abilities, because that is what he is all about, that is his training, even though he gets ticked off at it. *You* of all people should know that he is a stickler for the manual. And *you* have said so *yourself.* I think that sometimes you want him to mess up because you don't like him personally."

"What?" he answered, a line appearing between his brows, his voice raising. "That's not right, Marklin. If I didn't know you as well as I do, I'd knock your ass off that horse right now, Colonel or not. Don't you ever question my professional . . . ."

"Look, Larson, I apologize," Anlin said more softly, raising a placating hand. "I think this heat is getting to both of us. I know you do not compromise your ethics, I had no right to suggest so. I simply think that maybe you are not giving him enough credit. Yes, he is a little overzealous about making a name for himself. Yes, I, too, believe he is better suited to the political arena than out here. And, yes, I even think that he is a little too rigid and expects more from everyone else than he has a right to and that bothers the hell out of me. But, I think he will do what he was trained to do; obey the orders of his superior officers whether he likes them or not. First and foremost, he *is* a soldier."

"Maybe," Turcot said, his voice finding its normal tone and volume, though a swift undercurrent of non-belief backed his words. "I for one, though, do not like trusting my back to him, and many of the other officers and near-officers share my opinions. Don't trust him too much, Marklin, or you may find a Burnbeetle in your bedroll."

"Don't worry, Larson," Anlin replied, a smile playing on his lips. "Baen thinks your bedroll is mine anyway." Turcot looked at him for a few seconds, the anger in his face draining away before returning Anlin's smile and shaking his head in mock defeat.

"You're messed up in the head, Anlin," he laughed.

"Never denied it," came the reply. The two men moved the conversation to more shallow territory, leaning comfortably against the pommels of their saddles, waiting for Sergeant Ganz to return with Lieutenant Baen. Soon, Captain Turcot, leaning back with his right leg draped over Striker's withers, knee cocked around the saddle horn, turned to see the two men riding slowly back up the line toward them. With a sigh and slack expression working over his face, he pulled his leg back over, seated himself properly and said, "They're coming." Anlin grunted in answer, capped the waterskin he had been sipping from and replaced it back in its place against the saddle's fender just behind his leg. Rushwind snorted and swatted at it with his tail, prompting a firm pat on the neck from the Commander.

"Yes, sir," Baen said in greeting as the two moved in front of them and turned to face them. Turcot clucked his tongue quietly as Anlin looked over the younger officer. However he did it, Anlin could not guess, but Baen's uniform was mostly dust free, the soft substance only settling into deep folds and along seem-lines where it could not readily be brushed away, outlining the man in subtle lines of reddish-brown against the grey, something like a charcoal drawing. Sergeant Ganz, next to him, as well as Turcot and himself, were powdered with the stuff from head to foot, the brown grit bunching darkly only in places where sweat had soaked through. Baen's neck was even clean and Anlin would not be surprised if his back were just as dust free.

"Lieutenant," he began, a deeper, more formal tone in his voice. "As we discussed last night, we will split there," he pointed to the area ahead where the Tooth arose from the earth. "and you will keep your group behind the screen of rocks standing both in reserve, if needed, and to guard and round up the pack train. I'll take my group closer to the fortress, and, if everything seems alright, will move inside the gates. Once I have decided the area is secure, I will send a messenger back to get you. Any questions?"

"Sir, I would like to request that you send my group forward."

"No, Lieutenant. You will stay back in reserve and watch for the pack train, this is where you are needed, and I expect you to carry out your orders with the finesse and honor that I believe you to have. Is that understood?" Baen puffed up slightly at the compliment, but was still obviously unhappy with the decision. He looked at Anlin squarely for a moment before the barest twitch moved his eyes, a barely controlled glance at Sergeant Ganz, before giving a sharp salute.

"Yes, sir," he said. "Understood, sir."

"Sergeant," Anlin suddenly said, directing his hard gaze on the older man. He stiffened. "Fall back to your position and prepare Banek for the maneuver orders."

"Yes, sir!" he said crisply, with just the same amount of sharpness in his salute as Baen's. Anlin had a sudden picture of the future, as if the Sergeant sitting next to him were Baen in many years. If only Baen learned some compassion, that is.

He waited until Ganz was back at his position before returning his gaze back on the young Lieutenant, who, upon seeing him turn, straightened again and placed a carefully composed neutral expression on his face. Anlin did not miss the look of scorn there only moments before.

"Now, Lieutenant," Anlin said flatly. Baen straightened further, if that was possible. "I don't pretend to not understand why you made the request you did, because I was once a young lieutenant eager to test my mettle. You seem like a bright young man with a promising career, but right now, you lack the necessary experience. Agreed?" A thoughtful frown touched the corners of Baen's mouth and, reluctantly, he nodded. "Good," Anlin began anew. "Follow now. Lead later. Yes?"

"Yes, sir!" Baen said, saluting again, the sudden pride in his stance almost a nostalgic prod into Anlin's own past when his commander had expressed his compliments in much the same manner.

"You're dismissed," he said, then added, "Send up a runner when you have taken your position."

"Yes, sir," Baen replied, and with a final search of Anlin's eyes, peeled off and moved back down the line, prodding his mount into a canter once he passed the bannermen.

"Nice work," Turcot offered, turning back around in his saddle and gazing at the distant fortress. "You think he knows something we don't?" he asked suddenly, causing a pin prickle on the back of Anlin's sweaty neck.

"Nah," he replied, not completely sure he meant it. "Just anxious."

"Whatever you say," Turcot answered. Anlin shot him a withering look then held up his hand and waved the regiment into movement. Immediately the chorus of creaking leather and jangling harness overtook the silence as the lines moved forward. The Commander and the Captain waited the few moments for them to catch up to them before nudging their mounts into the slow walk forward. Minutes moved by slowly, the descending sun to the left measuring the time in grades of lightlessness as it slid behind the obscuring mountains. More quickly than he thought, they were moving past the edges of hills supporting the ascending blade of rock called the Tooth. Anlin turned and signaled with his hand. A series of short clarion bursts from the horn drowned out the sound of hoof on sand, the creak of leather. Within several minutes, he could see, far back down the line, the clouds of dust widening and the vague figures of Baen and the second half of the regiment split from the body and moved toward the awaiting arms of the angle made by the Tooth and the rest of the range. He looked at Turcot before turning completely forward.

His second was staring straight ahead; eyes fixed on the fortress, and, dropping his gaze, found that he had already unfettered the hilt of his long sword from its leather holding strap. "Worried?"

"You know I always like to be prepared," Turcot said in a low voice, the tone he dropped into before going into dangerous situation. He looked at Anlin, pinning him with a gaze filled with many years of seeing death. "You ever wonder if this is worth it?"

"All the time, Captain," he answered. "All the time." Anlin reached over and undid the binding on his own sword, gave Turcot a grim smile, then moved his gaze onto their target.

The fortress materialized from the shimmer, a behemoth of thick, hard stone with little ornamentation; the perfect decoration against the surrounding theme of barrenness and waste. It was cupped between the Tooth and another upheaval of rock on the far right almost as if it were a link in the chain and not something separate from it. From the distance, he was able to see the remains of the walls that had once housed the fortress' outbuildings, now torn and blasted by the strange rock formations thrusting up from the ground, large chunks of smoothed rock laying scattered around it, testimony to the force which destroyed it several years earlier.

He let his gaze wander over the remainder of the structure. Aside from a few scars, the rest was as intact and solid as when it was first built, but looking at it, he was disturbed by the stillness ahead. Even from this distance, he could feel the deadness of the halls before him though he was too far to actually see any movements on the battlements. Had there been any. It was instinctual, given over from approaching structures that housed the living thousands upon thousands of times; one could sense it as if the buildings themselves were living, breathing things. The feeling that crawled through him now was the same feeling he got when passing a graveyard, only more so; emptiness, stillness, death. Nothing.

And it settled deep in him, worsening when he looked to the left at the shadow darkened side of the tooth, the yawning holes of void boring into the stone gum line, staring into him, pushing a chillness into his bones. Absently, his left hand fingered the steel of his sword. Turcot, too, he saw, was struggling with his own sense of desolation and those behind him, like an extension of his body, were tensing with expectation.

He grunted, cleared his throat, and tried to shake the clutch of coldness from reaching his brain, telling himself his fears were unfounded. The fortress was obviously abandoned, and it would do no good to let the graveyard likeness bother him even though he was close to it age wise.

It was then that he noticed the silence beyond the jangle and creak, the thud of five hundred hooves behind him. The men were preternaturally quiet, and it bothered him anew that the Bloodeyes' buzzing calls no longer sang counterpoint to the noise of the regiment, and more so that he could not remember when the bugs had quieted. It somehow seemed very important that he remember that detail because his burdened mind was trying to convince him that it happened just before he thought of it.

They drew closer to the fortress, the gate gaping wide, giving view of the inner courtyard, barren and empty, affirming the feeling of abandonment. High up on the central tower, a lone ragged standard, dark blue fading in the sun, hung feebly on its shaft, limply resisting attempts of random light breezes to fill it and pull it away into the air. He silently begged for someone to walk past his view of the courtyard or between the low blocky crenellations that ringed the tops of the huge walls, just to allay the trepidation that refused to let loose from his bones.

He slowed, unconsciously pulling back on Rushwind's reins. For once, the spirited animal did not fight. Those behind and beside slowed with him, captured themselves by the oppressive weight of the looming dead edifice before them.

Without noticing, to the man, the column came to a slow halt; all eyes nervously pinned on the fortress. It just was not right for something so huge and once filled with life to now be void of it.

Anlin suddenly realized they had stopped and was about to give the command forward when something nearly tangible tugged at him to look to the east, pulling his gaze away from the fortress of Tergaard. From a little south of the outcropping rose the distinctive fans of two riders bearing down on them, one of the figures waving frantically and apparently calling out though the beat of his mount's hooves and the distance proved too overbearing to it. Anlin smiled, recognizing both as his scouts, Silek the one waving and yelling. His hand was half raised in greeting when ice trickled up his spine. Silek's posturing was not one of greeting. He was trying to warn him.

He was still looking in their direction, trying to decipher the barely audible calls coming from him, when a tumult of tense alarm arose behind. He jerked his head around to see the column bowing eastward, the mounts prancing, resisting their riders' attempts to control them. They, as well as the men, were calling out in surprise, whinnying and snorting with panic, some straining against their bits, bowing their heads back while their bodies tried to move away, others reared. Within seconds, the ordered column was succumbing to chaos and he did not even know why. He turned bodily in his saddle, looking at the indomitable rock wall to their left.

From the many caves and crevices lining the Tooth, it seemed the very shadows themselves were detaching and flowing from them in a flood of pure blackness, spilling out onto the floor of the plain, pooling, before coursing rapidly toward the column, causing the line to bow. Without thinking, he was screaming orders, simultaneously drawing his sword, calling for his men to stand firm, to bring back order and discipline to the expanding chaos, even though ice had formed just below the flesh of his body. The bugler, Banek, was blowing rapidly on his horn, adding the piercing calls to the cacophony.

Staring wide-eyed, mouth hanging open, a painful grip on the hilt of his sword, Anlin watched the terrible flow of black crash into the column like a giant liquid spear, splitting the line in a vicious explosion of screams and terrible, erratic movements as men and mounts flailed and fell against the onslaught, the flow itself breaking apart into its smaller components, splashing and splattering among the dying men.

Within the shade of the Tooth, creatures as black as midnight, vaguely resembling men, were suddenly distinguishable from the black tide as they tore into the column in a wild frenzy of hate filled viciousness, leaping effortlessly onto them and tearing into them with raking claws. From his side, Anlin heard Turcot praying loudly in a hoarse, fear filled voice.

The men, recovering from their frozen surprise by the instinctive discipline drilled deeply into to them, reacted to Banek's trumpet calls, turning their mounts toward the onrushing things, drawing weapons, some nocking arrows, and attacking with a fervor born of the most basic instincts of survival. Arrows zipped from their bows, swords gleamed in the dying light as they rose and fell, the creatures falling, the tide slowing, like water against a dam.

Suddenly, Anlin had no time to watch his men fight and die, as a stream of the inky creatures flowed toward them, bounding and leaping. Rushwind began backing up, lips pulled back and eyes rimmed white, a squeal-like snort expelling from him, but Anlin tensed his knees and rapped the animal's flanks with his heels, willing his horse forward into the fray. The creatures came on, the first leaping across a wide swath of ground to meet him. His sword whistled above Rushwind's head, meeting the thing.

In that instant, time slowed enough for him to look full at the creatures as his glinting blade sliced through it with as little resistance that it would take to cut a melon down the middle. It had no face. No eyes, no mouth, no ears, as if it were wearing a shiny black cloth that completely covered it, and it made no sound as the sword passed through its otherwise humanlike body. In fact, none of the creatures made a noise; only the agonized screams and angry yells of his men and horses filled the dying day.

It obviously felt pain, though, as it squirmed and spasmed in a frenzied seizure once his blade separated the top portion of its body from its lower and it fell in halves to the dirt beside Rushwind to be trampled by the animal's hooves. Time snapped back, yanking him from his observations to face the next aggressor, his sword whipping back, separating the thing's head from its shoulders, amazing him that there was barely any resistance at all to the inflicted wound. The body, flailing in its midflight death, rammed into his chest, managing to drag long, thin claws down one of his arms. He cried out hoarsely at the stinging wound, more from surprise than pain, and pushed the dying creature away from him. It felt solid when it had hit and could have thrown him from the saddle had he not been prepared, but it was not heavy, though more so than he would have guessed from the wounds he inflicted. He noted grimly that the things did not bleed either; that their separated body parts were whole unto themselves as if the creatures were composed entirely of the blackness that covered them.

He watched the headless body drop to the ground, turned his attention back to the oncoming attackers. The bannermen, unable to maneuver well with their weapons while still holding the standards, were steadily being pushed backwards, each encounter leaving long thin rakes on their bodies. Anlin yelled at them to drop the standards, but only one complied, the other yelling back that he would not. The Imperial standard fell to the dust, trampled by the various horses' hooves that clamored over the ground.

Anlin dispatched another of the creatures, noting with some confusion that this one wore the ragged, stringy remnants of dark blue cloth.

Appearing suddenly by his side, Silek yelled over the chaos, "Sir! You have to get out of here!" Anlin glanced at him, three long razor cuts bled freely along his cheek but he otherwise seemed okay, even relatively calm. Anlin cut another of the creatures down, then reached out his free hand and grabbed Silek's shoulder.

"Get out of here!" he cried, yanking Silek's arm to stop the protest coming to his lips. "You must warn Baen! The rest of the regiment is. . . ." he was cut off as another silent creature bounded onto Rushwind behind him and began clawing at his back. A couple of quick stabs from Silek's short sword sent it tumbling from the panicking Rushwind in a frenzied spasm. "The rest of the regiment. . . " Anlin yelled from behind a grimace once he fought Rushwind back under control. ". . . is waiting beyond the edge of the bladed rock! Tell Baen to assist. . . We need help!"

Silek was staring at him, locked in a moment of still time, uncomprehending the order, visibly torn between some inner struggle of loyalty, fear. He began shaking his head, eyes never wavering, entranced, until Anlin grabbed him again and pulled him across the span between their huffing mounts, and screamed at him, "Go!" It shook him awake, nodding briskly before turning his horse away and kicking him into a gallop, the large animal throwing and trampling the inky creatures that got in their way until he was free of the battle and speeding across the plain followed closely by Maliss, fans of dust rising to obscure them.

Commander Anlin allowed himself a deep breath, fanning a new flame to his hope as the agonized sounds of his men dying and mounts screaming worked to crush it. He was turning back to the fray when light exploded in front of his eyes, followed by a hollow pain, then . . . darkness.

Baen watched Commander Anlin's column file toward the fortress of Tergaard with mixed feelings, telling himself time and again that he should be going instead, that he should be the one with the honor of taking the fortress for the Empire; that he should be the one to face any foe that may be waiting inside. But, at the same time, deep down, knowing the Commander's words were correct. And made him feel a pride in himself he did not feel back at the Academy; that he was not allowed to feel. He struggled with it, even as his appointed second in command of his group, Bron Basek, told him something was happening near the gate of the fortress.

Anxiously, he stared at the column, though in confusion. The group was too far to see in detail what was going on, but the sudden cloud of dust that rose chaotically around them could only mean one thing.

Battle!

The impulse to set his spurs into his mount and charge came quickly, but he clamped down on that. He had orders. And even though it rankled him to no end, he was determined to follow those orders. If nothing else, the Academy had taught him that; drilled it into him so deeply that he burned inside at his inability to consciously countermand them. He was vaguely aware of Basek talking to him, asking him what to do, and he was equally vague in his awareness of his biting, anger-filled reply for him to shut up and be ready.

Frantically, his eyes flicked over the huge brown cloud, searching, every now and again seeing the distant figure of a trooper as a dark shadow materialize momentarily as the dust swirled a certain way. The failing light, too, was frustrating him, angering him more, challenging him, taunting him into going to meet his destiny. But he would not move, standing rigid, almost painfully, in his refusal to disobey.

A rider burst from the dust cloud at a full run, a second close behind. His salvation. A tremendous rush of adrenalin coursed through him so violently that his body began to quake. That was when he was knocked away from his euphoria by the screams and yells of his own men and horses. Turning quickly, the only thing that came to his mind was that giant ants were boiling from the nearby crevices and overtaking the tail end of his waiting column.

For a second, understanding was not there and the cries of pain and death reaching his ears were not absorbed into his mind, but it was only a quick lapse. The full impact of what was happening struck him and the excited rush washed back over him. He was being attacked. This was his chance for glory. Forgetting the two runners heading toward him, he drew his weapon and sent his horse charging toward the fight.

From his vantage in the false twilight, it seemed that the rear was being attacked by men in black armor. Men that would rue their decision to attack him. Behind him, Basek was yelling at him again, but he couldn't slow down to listen just then. He needed to get to the battle.

Men charging past him, going the other direction, caused him to slow, his head snapping quickly from side to side, watching soldiers rushing away from the direction of the fighting. Confusion attacked him again, striking his mind with numbing force and for a moment he could not fathom what was happening around him. He stopped and watched the route, face slack, until his anger burned through again. His men were running from battle!

Cowards!

His face knotting in fury, he began yelling at them, haranguing them to return to the fight. At his side, Basek appeared yelling that they must retreat. Baen called him yellow and struck him with his free hand, ordering him to get the men organized. Basek looked at him, a glaze working over his face and in his eyes. He had hit him too hard and stunned him.

With a frustrated cry, he turned back toward the melee, seeking an answer to the confusion that tried to unbalance him. The fighting ahead of him was furious, encompassing half the group, all knotted with the men in black in a maelstrom of terrible sound and motion, quickly being obscured by the coming night and rising dust. He railed at the gods for this treatment. This was not supposed to happen to him. His entire training in the Academy promised him glory, and this was not glory. His troops were cowards, the light was failing, the enemy was swift. He turned his rage back towards his men, screaming at their weakness, ordering them to their deaths. A young man near him turned and looked in his direction, drawn by his yelling, and spurred his horse over to his side. Baen ordered him back into the fray, but before he could respond a black shadow appeared out of nowhere, springing onto his horse. Clawed hands grabbed the man's head and twisted violently. The young man's eyes bulged as his neck snapped, the sound breaking through the tumult, flinging across the space between them to slam into him, forcing Baen's mind into a cold numbness. Spikes of ice slid down through his body. The shadow was battered away by another trooper while the young man fell forward onto Baen's lap. Instinctively, he caught him then looked down even though the battle was surrounding him; men fighting and yelling furiously against the strange shadow men.

Though he fell forward, the young man was looking up at him through red bulging eyes, a terrified grimace on his mouth, the ruin of his neck, darkly bruised and twisted, the odor of fouled blood wafting up from somewhere. The moment the boy groaned, splinters of fear shot painfully through Baen, stabbing into the heart which beat into his chest. The battle was forgotten, an envelope of terrible peace and otherworldly silence formed around them as he realized the boy, just a bit younger than he, was still alive. He could hear a slow long squeak as he breathed and watched as tears flowed freely from his wide, non-blinking eyes. His face was bloodless, pale against the twilight, and he could hear his struggling heart, thumping wildly within a chest cut off from its guide, cast into the dark as well, feeling the thud against his thigh.

Baen started to shake, then, a quaking that began in his marrow and vibrated outward through his organs, muscles, and skin, knotting it up around every hair, pulling it away from his teeth and from around his eyes; working until it reached into his brain. The young man's horse moved suddenly away, dropping the trooper from his saddle to hang limply over the side of his own. The man's body jerked spasmodically, and a gut-wrenching mewl fell from bluing lips. Baen's vision fuzzed, and he closed them to block out the gurgling sight hanging from his lap, but only making the situation worse as he could feel the quivering of the young man as his life trickled from him. He died with a final violent shudder that transferred into Baen's body, twisting at his soul, forcing his eyes open to stare at the ghastly mask of stark terror etched into the boy's pallid face. The last moments of his life, the sight, sound, smell and feel of the boy's death sinking indelibly into his very being, lodging there with the promise of haunting him for the rest of his life.

The cold chill of death brushed through him painfully, causing the restraining arms to shiver away and allow the limp body to ooze from his lap and fall to the earth below, adding itself to the sea of corpses, both human and not. Baen stared around him, still within the envelope, moving his eyes sluggishly from one dead body to the next, seeing blurry movements around the edges as the battle continued to rage, hearing the distant sounds of death. He was dimly aware that he dropped his sword and ignored the voice whispering to him from far away to defend himself.

Suddenly, the body of another horse intercepted his slogging vision, pulling it up from the morass. He was looking at a man he knew, Bron Basek, the span between them impossibly long making it difficult for him to recognize his second. Basek seemed to be moving in slow motion, his face carved from anger, blood falling from several long thin cuts. He moved closer while Baen stared dumbly, the sense of his body lost in a fog of hot ice. The last conscious sight he witnessed was the man's hand raising, gripping a piece of shattered wood. Baen's sluggish brain could not warn him in time that he had been hit. The envelope he existed in was complete.

Chapter 30

The Night Reveals Its Secrets

*J*arren considered himself lucky that the men in the regiment were, for the most part, above average in their intelligence. He and Jorn, once procuring a mule and extra supplies from the pack train, found them easily, clumped in small groups of twos, threes, or more, and huddling within the scant shade afforded by the tall rock-trees and squat outcroppings. Most had already been seen by a physician that had volunteered himself the duty of taking care of the heat sick and were rested and well enough for some travel. There were several that had not been touched by the heat, falling out with their comrades to render aid. By the time the sun had fallen far enough for the stars to find light of their own, Corporal Jarren had a small command consisting of seventy six men recovering plus twelve not, himself, Jorn, and a physician, a small man named Garman who claimed to be from the southern city of Sanquist, eighty one horses, three of which were coming lame, and two mules, the second found wandering a few miles behind the regiment.

Of the missing mounts, three were confirmed dead from the heat, the others considered to have wandered off in search of water, probably dead now as well. They had also found the bodies of five dead mules strung out along the regiment's path, still with all their supplies. His largest concern was the two missing men; though, none of the others had any knowledge of them. Jarren had to consider the possibility that the message he received had been wrong, but also the more dark reality that the message was correct and two men were lost, or worse.

Jarren was perched now atop a large rock outcropping, smoking his pipe absently while gazing southward, looking for the return of the two men he sent to the last campsite in the hopes that the missing troopers may have made it back to the spring. A weakly flickering watch fire burned near him, filling the air around it with a pungent stench that helped clear out clogged nasal passages, courtesy of the small, tough scraggly bushes that somehow clung to life in this blistering hell. A little further down the outcropping leaned Jorn, his only companion, the rest of the men encircling the base with the mounts, resting until he decided otherwise.

He wiped a trickle of sweat away from his temple with the back of a hand. The loss of the sun had not given them the loss of heat. Though not as uncomfortable as earlier, the land itself bled away the heat it absorbed all day slowly, giving little respite. A land of harsh extremes, he knew, and he hated it.

"How long are we going to wait?" Mandol asked quietly, picking aimlessly at the tough vegetation stalk he had, his normal propensity for goofing off subdued for the moment.

"Little while longer," Jarren answered, staring up at the crystalline night sky. "The longer we wait the cooler it will be when we begin. And we have to give them enough time."

"You think we will find some more on the way back?"

"Probably," Jarren said, a thoughtful tone in his voice. "The message I have said that any more that fell out would be directed to find shelter, build a signal fire, and wait for us."

"You realize that the rest of the regiment is probably living it up in that fortress by now."

Jarren glanced down at his friend, a dark shadow against the dark rock, the flickering light lining only a portion of his body. He waved his hand upward in a grand gesture. "And miss all this?" A twig suddenly hit him in the forehead and bounced back down onto the rock. "I see even you are not above criticism."

"Yea," Jorn said after a moment. "I do suppose it is sort of peaceful out here." Jarren let the quiet chirping of crickets and soft breeze whispering over the rock to sink down into his body, took a deep, filling breath. Somewhere far, some night animal was yapping. He could only agree. Overhead, the stars glistened against the velvet, the moons, forever at their zenith, glowed like a gigantic pearl in soft light. "That is, while the sun is down, anyway."

"You're starting to get a little too sentimental," Jarren said, sitting up slowly. He pulled his sword closer to him, the metal dragging against the stone surface a harsh reminder of the peaceful illusion. "We should get down and get mounted up. It shouldn't be too much longer."

"You said that already," Jorn answered, brushing bits of plant from him before starting the climb down. His loud scraping and grunting in the night pushed away the rest of the peacefulness. Jarren blew out a long sigh and rubbed at his stubbled chin and began gracelessly following his friend down the stone slope.

Not long after finding the soft sand at the base of the perch, the two scouts returned, bearing the news that the other missing men were not at the former campsite. Hoping that they just missed them on the way back, Jarren reluctantly had the men mount up. Soon, the ninety soldiers were trudging deeper into the wasteland surrounded by the stark shadows of finger-like rock outcroppings and stark blackness of the huge wall of mountains to the west that cut the glittering curtain of the sky off in a jagged line that ran toward the horizon.

Mandol, next to him, was busying his sense of humor by tickling his mount's ear with a stalk of the plant he had been stripping earlier, causing Rumble to shake his head and snort menacingly. Garmon, the physician, was somewhere back behind them, nattering on in his thick southern accent. The snatches of conversation he heard were about the dangers of the heat. Tack jangled and creaked, men murmured their concerns, thoughts, desires, into the night; horses snorted and nickered, the plodding of their hooves a soft crunch against the variably hard and yielding ground. The dryness of the raising dust drifting into his nostrils tickled the passages with the sharp odor of it, mixing with the scent of sweat matted horse hair. It was hypnotic; a comforting array of sounds and smells that coaxed Jarren's mind away from his troubles.

It didn't last long when a sigh erupted from him, the several hours ride ahead promising to be made longer by the knots of men he expected to find along the way. Knots of men he did not know the condition of. And the odd way that the temperature dropped suddenly early in the morning, settling into bones and chewing at the extremities made it even more concerning. Jarren's earlier sense of peace was going away, quickly being replaced by nagging suspicions and irritating thoughts that bubbled up randomly, settling in like the coming cold.

Less than an hour later, they sighted the faint flicker of a signal fire in the distance, its light casting a ghostlike yellow halo against the outcropping of rock that brooded near it. Jarren angled the small troop toward it, a building excitement encroaching on the trancelike state so easily fallen into while traveling. As they drew nearer, several calls rang out and shadows danced suddenly against the flicker. He thought he saw the glint of unsheathed steel, and called out to identify the group. An answering call returned a minute later.

Two men waited for them, keeping the small fire between them and the troop, both nervously holding onto their swords. Grim lines, made harsher by the wan light, etched into their faces. Jarren gave the order to halt then he and Jorn dismounted and moved slowly into the ring of light. The men relaxed visibly, their arms lowering and faces sagging at the recognition of soldier to soldier. Their weariness quickly overtook the grim expressions.

"How are you men?" Jarren asked cautiously, still aware that, though relieved, neither had put away their swords. The whinny of a horse sounded from around the sheltering rock.

"Well, sir," one of them answered, the older of the two by the set of his face. "Just tired, now." His companion, a lanky man who had replaced his hat with a moist scarf tied around his head, turned and gave a small whistle. Sudden scraping on the rocks above them nearly had Jarren reaching for his own sword until a third man materialized on its sloping surface, short bow in hand and an arrow sliding back into his quiver. "Sorry, sir. Gets a little jumpy out here after dark."

"It's alright," Jarren managed, reigning in his reaction. "I can understand perfectly. I'm Corporal Jarren. This is Jorn. We came back to get you. You all still have your mounts?"

"Yes, sir," said the man. "We have four mounts." He shifted nervously, the other man kneeling next to the fire, face taking on a strain that caused a knot to form in Jarren's gut.

"Who?" was all he asked. The older one swiped his hat from his head, watching it while his hands kneaded the brim.

He finally looked up. "Fedek," he said sternly, an obvious attempt to control himself. "Aston Fedek." He motioned with the hand that held the crumpled hat. Jarren, following with his eyes, saw just outside the fire light, jutting out from the base of the escarpment, a mound of dirt, a sword sticking from the head with a hat dangling from the hilt. "'Fraid the ground is really hard beneath the surface, so the grave's pretty shallow, sir. We did what we could, the three of us."

"That's fine, soldier," Jarren said sharply, successfully covering the hitch in his throat. "That's fine. Your names?" *Change the subject.* He thought. *Change the subject.*

"I'm Jander. That's Bevek," He pointed back with his thumb. "And that one back there is Lain. Fedek died of the heat sickness soon after we fell out, sir. We did what we could, but the ground is just too hard."

Jarren held up a hand. "You did fine, Jander. You did fine. Why don't you and your men get your horses and fall into the troop, yes?" The older man stood a little more straight, the weariness momentarily washing from his face, replaced by the pride of a soldier that has done his duty. He nodded. "Give the fourth mount to one of the troopers that are doubling."

"Yes, sir!" he said sharply, turning to the two others standing close now. "You two heard the Corporal, get moving." Bevek and Lain scrambled around the outcropping.

The troop was on the move again soon, the three quickly arranging their gear and falling into the line. Jorn went back to pestering Rumble with a twig while those behind fell into the natural rhythms of travel. Jarren, though, brooded. While one man out of about a hundred lost was not bad on the cold plane of parchment that became a loss report, it was still one man. A being whole unto himself and one that he took personal responsibility for even though, logically, he knew he shouldn't. It happened. That was the nature of being a soldier. Death was always on the horse next to you, and everyone, from the Commander down to the cooks, had to ride with Him.

But he could not excuse himself though the man died after he was sent back to get those already waiting. The image of the shadowed grave rested in his forethoughts as if it were a huge marble mausoleum, immovable and lasting, instead of a thing to be swallowed by the land, probably the next day when the wind kicked up. Try as he might, he could not banish it.

So, Jarren continued brooding, even as they began to steadily run into signal fires, finding more men waiting out the heat in anticipation of his small, but growing, detachment. Men reporting no other deaths. It gave him a sense of relief, but not enough to allay that one death.

"What was that?" Mandol suddenly whispered, his voice harsh against the backdrop of the noises of the troop. Jarren, slow to respond to the question, finally shook off his thoughts.

"What was what?" he answered, looking at his friend. Mandol wore a quizzical look, head cocked to the side. His look began to slacken.

"I guess it was nothing," Mandol said finally. "I thought I heard –" A faint sound reached them, sliding over the background noise like a wisp of air. An untraceable, indistinct pitch that prickled the back of Jarren's neck. Jorn straightened suddenly, grabbing his hat off his head as if that would help him hear better. "That," he said.

Jarren called a halt and waited the few minutes for the trambling noise of the troop to slow, then stop, the only sound above the sigh of the breeze the random snort or nicker of the mounts. He was thinking that they must be mistaken, that they were just hearing things over the wind; ghosts formed of the ambient sounds of the troop. But the hairs on the back of his neck were still rigid. He was raising his hand to give the signal to move forward again, when a short whine slid through the darkness from off to their left somewhere.

"Sounds like a wounded animal," Jorn said, though it sounded more of a question than statement of fact. Something familiar about it, though, prompted Jarren to lower his hand, reconsidering his intended actions.

"We'd better check it out," he said after the moment of deliberation.

"But if it is a wounded animal, we could run into some predators," Jorn warned. "Some of the reports I saw said there were some dangerous creatures that took up residence here after it turned desert."

"There's something about that sound," Jarren pressed, another whine reaffirming his decision. "Have Blevins round us up some torches." Jorn, reluctantly, complied after expressing his misgivings once more. Soon he, Jarren, and the stocky framed Blevins were riding out under the pale moonlight, using the sound and their undisturbed night vision to draw closer to their objective before pulling out the lengths of pitch coated clubs.

Getting nearer, Jarren heard the distinct sound of a horse snorting and nickering, now and then sending out a pain filled whine that needle pricked the heart each time its mournful tone drifted through the night. *Must be one of the mounts that wandered off.* He thought. *Dying.*

They continued to move slowly toward the horse, reluctant now to fire the torches for fear of frightening the animal into a panic, maybe losing it completely; maybe destroying whatever reserve it had that was keeping it alive. Besides, the eternal moonlight lit the plains with a ghostlike sheen that afforded them enough vision to see large shapes if not detail, and they only had three torches. If this turned into a longer span of time than the torches permitted, they would just be cast back into the darkness, probably at the time when they needed the light from them the most.

Ahead, suddenly, between two of the tall escarpments of rock, materialized the object of their search as a vaguely horse-shaped shadow. Jarren stopped them and waited. Very quickly, another whine reached them, coming from the shadow.

"Quietly," Jarren whispered to the others. "Dismount. Blevins. Stay back with our mounts while me and Jorn try to get closer." They nodded their understanding, as a unit, pulling themselves off their mounts to a symphony of creaking leather Jarren hoped would not startle the beast. Jorn and he quickly slid their swords into the wide belts at their waist as well as two of the three torches, made sure that they had a flint and steel, before handing over the reins of their mounts to Blevins.

Slowly and as quietly as they could manage on the loose sand, the two spread out and began moving toward the horse. When he looked directly at it, the shadow fuzzed against the pallid, silvery background, and even when he concentrated his gaze slightly to the side to allow the dark shapes to sharpen within his peripheral vision, it appeared that a large bundle lay across the back of the horse, which confused him. If it were a pack horse, then it didn't belong to the regiment. For the moment, that was all Jarren could think of. Nothing else came to mind.

The creature must have sensed them, because it suddenly gave a nervous snort and began stumbling away from them as if something were tangled in its legs, heading nearer the escarpments. Jorn began calling out to it with a soothing voice, as he and many cavalry soldiers did with their own mounts, the creatures often being the only companions to justify their need to speak. It worked, apparently, as the beast stopped and gave out an answering whicker.

"Turn around and light one of the torches," Jarren whispered across the span separating them. In the pale glow, he saw him nod in reply and turn and kneel. The clicking of steel against flint sounded alien to their surroundings, the large sparks generated by them, glowing faintly against Mandol's huddled form. A second later, yellow light flared as the torch hissed to life. The pitch covered wood popped a few times before reveling in its newfound life. Squinting against it, Jorn smiled at him then coughed as he brought the flame too close to his body and breathed in the black smoke, darker even than the night, that curled away up into the sky. Jarren moved nearer, beckoning him to stand and turn slowly to give them time to adjust to the flaring light.

Jarren's heart dropped into his stomach once the torchlight washed over the horse. It looked back at the two men with cloudy, fear rimmed eyes, the terror showing within them only overshadowed by the sick weariness that heralded a close coming death. Clumps and lines of dust laden blood crusted all along its body and flanks and down its legs. One of its front hooves was twisted unnaturally at the fetlock. Slumped over its back was a trooper, his clothes a ragged mess of ripped cloth, dirt, drying blood. His leg was cocked back, still in its stirrup, levered that way by the lance he gripped, angling out over the animal's withers and saddle horn, butt shoved down into the leather sheath connected to the stirrup covering. The soldier was motionless and, from the meager light of the torch, Jarren could not tell if he still breathed.

The Corporal stood rigid, not able to will his body to move, though Jorn inched closer around the side of the wretched mount to see the man's face.

"Oh, no!" he said suddenly around a choked gurgle. Jarren looked at him, somehow sensing the answer about to fall from the man's mouth. "It's Jarl, the Bannerman." He was stuttering, the difficulty he felt storming across his dark face in waves of confusion and pain. "He still holds the Regimental Colors."

Regimental Colors. . . . The words hit Jarren square in the chest, taking the breath from him and sending him spiraling away from the scene in stunned silence. An impossibly long corridor connecting him to Jorn and the Bannerman formed, made of circular walls of swirling gray fog that kept constricting. He heard himself say, "What?. . . .Colors. . . ." his voice far from him and strained, echoing and muted at the same time.

Something pulled him back, a deep thumping from somewhere behind him. Suddenly, he was staring down at the ground, the torch burning on the sand nearby, his chest aching and head pounding. Jorn was thumping his back, his voice at his ear a loud boom as it asked over and over if he was alright even though he was sure he was whispering. The earth wavered before his eyes, at odds with the swaying of his body being held by weak, shivering legs. He groaned, his stomach clenching but not expelling its contents.

"What happened?" Jarren finally stammered, voice liquid.

"You almost feinted," came the still disembodied reply. Shaking his head loosely, he pushed Jorn away and forced his body to comply with his stuffy mind's request to overcome his dizziness.

"No!" he barked, filling himself with an anger that burned away at his weakness. "No! Not me! Jarl!"

"I don't know Kydel," Jorn said, his voice beginning to take on a slight tremor. "I don't know. But he's dead." His last words threatened to unbalance Jarren again as the ramifications began to sink in. Where was the rest of the regiment? If the banner man was dead, what of the others? *What happened? What happened?* It was a question he could neither answer nor fathom, though it repeated itself over and over again in an ethereal voice that was both his and not. *What happened?*

"Blevins!" he called into the night. "Come here. Bring the horses." An answering cry came back to them and, within minutes, the man and mounts materialized into their torch-fire world. Using the presence of the other trooper for support, he marshaled his resolve against the dead banner man, locking it and all the questions surrounding it behind gates of discipline. "Go back to the detachment and wait for us, we won't be long."

Eyes searching his, the stocky young man finally said, "Yes, sir," before climbing on his mount and nudging him into a trot back the way they had come.

"You should've had him stay," Mandol said once he had gone. "We could've used his help."

"Maybe," he answered, his voice softening. "But until I have time to think on this, there is no need to upset the men." He cleared his throat, a futile attempt to dislodge something that was not physically there.

"Yea, well," Jorn answered. "We still could've used his help."

"Stand down, soldier," Jarren spat, more fiercely than he intended. Mandol snapped rigid, a conditioned response he was unable to forestall. "Let's get done what we have to do," he added after a minute, a touch guiltily. Jorn, face clouded with a mixture of emotion, nodded.

Neither man was ready for the grim duty ahead of them, each holding onto a false sense of themselves that was shattered once they brought the sputtering flame close enough to the dying horse to cast a light on the still form of Trooper Jarl, setting them trembling deep down in their beings, causing their insides to writhe in response. The pallid mask of pain Jarl wore glared at them sidewise, accusing them of the life they held onto. Jorn turned away quickly and retched, the sound of his gorge rising launching Jarren's stomach into his throat. As his body spasmed painfully, Jarren could not help wondering that people were afraid of the dark. It hid things that light should never touch. Like Jarl's dusty, blood encrusted glare that begged the question of why.

The Trooper's body was limp and rubbery and, once untangled from the standard and forced to release the sword his hand seemed a part of, slid off the saddle into their arms like an overlarge bladder of water. The sudden movement broke the mantle of blood covering his wounds, causing more to ooze from his ragged body. A rancid sigh slipped from the lifeless shell, startling Jorn to stumbling backward into the dirt, a cry bubbling from his lips and left Jarren under the flaccid weight of Jarl's body. He fell, too, landing awkwardly in the soft sand, rolling Jarl's corpse away from him.

Jander's words about the earth came back to him once he began stabbing into the dirt with his dagger and found underneath the soft top layer, a hard clay-like under layer that resisted attempts at digging. Together, the two men pried and chipped at the stuff relentlessly, letting their bitterness and horror at what happened to Jarl drive the blades. Sweat dripped freely from their noses and chin and down their backs. Their muscles ached, coming on quickly at the stubbornness of the earth to give up its hold on itself, and time slid by unnoticed, until each was grunting with each movement. At some point, they realized the torch had guttered out, casting them in the silvery glow of the moon. Neither bothered to light the other one.

Even still, the grave was shallow, only a depression that cupped Jarl slightly as they rolled him into it, the chunks of hard dirt a weak semblance to a cairn. They were able to find a few stones to add to it, found at the base of the outcroppings, but they, too, were reluctant to give of themselves, this land a selfish host. The rest of Jarl's covering, sand pushed over him in a thick layer, a wide circular baring of the hard earth beneath the result. Like Fedek's, now far to the south, Jarl's sword was hammered into the earth at the head and his hat placed upon the hilt, the only testimony to his demise.

Jarl's mount, coaxed down to the dirt with gentle urgings and tugs with reigns and soft vocalizations, was freed of its pain by a single, deft thrust of Jorn's dagger, glistening trails sweeping away dust from the man's cheeks. Jarren moved to the outcropping and sat down on a close lying boulder, impelled by the heaviness of the moment to put some distance between them, each needing a moment of solitude to deal with Jarl's death and its implications now that the burden of his burial was done. He watched as Jorn slid down against the now silent body of the horse and pretended not to hear the choked sobs he could see wrack him in the pale light of the uncaring moon above.

After some time had passed and each rebuilt the defenses that defined a ramshackle house of normalcy, Jarren had Mandol wrap the Regimental Colors in Jarl's cloak and bind it with his mount's reigns, then handed it to him once he mounted Rumble. In the wan glow, he could see the strained look on his face, knew that his own was a mirror of it, tried to ignore it. Failed. Pulled himself sluggishly into his saddle.

The ride back was slow and silent, neither men wanting to speak, both letting the quiet rhythm of the horses work out the aches in their bodies. A chill was in the air, a testament to how much time had passed, and wrapped them as completely as the silence, a soothing stillness wrapped in an arcing, glittering curtain of velvet ripped off to the west. A different face to the harsh, blasting, unforgiving land he was cursing from the time the regiment entered its unwelcoming border. A loving, comforting mother's hold that allowed him some peace before facing the men of his detachment, for all he knew, the last of the Imperial 3rd Cavalry.

They were waiting, bunched up where they were left, dismounted and in unorganized groups, their low talk as much of a guide-on in the distinct silence of the enveloping night as the small signal fire burning near its head. A deep hush fell about them as Jarren and Mandol neared, sensing them before seeing them, and the heaviness that had been lifted briefly by the cool silence settled back into Jarren's chest as he felt the eyes of his men find him in the dark. He would have to tell them what they found, tell them of Jarl's grotesque corpse, found accidentally, astride his dying steed still clutching the Colors. He would have to tell them what he thought it meant, what he was trained to think it meant, the truth of it lay in his guts like a rock. But not now. Not until he could come to grips with that truth.

Movement began, men standing and brushing futilely at their uniforms, more out of habit than anything, getting themselves ready to move, but waiting expectantly for answers as to why their current commander had been gone so long, the whisperings of Blevins not enough for the intense curiosity caused by his solitary return. Horses began to whicker and snort, waking from the lull in their rest period, some of them kicking at the dry ground looking for something to graze upon.

Stares riveted against them, at the staff Mandol carried, as if the very weight of them could peel back the covering and reveal what lay beneath. Grim eyes that sparkled in the glow of the moon though they did not understand what they looked at, but felt its importance as a harbinger of ill omen. They watched as the wrapped staff was secured awkwardly to one of the two pack animals.

Wordlessly, Jarren and Jorn returned to the head of the group and waited as it lengthened into its snakelike formation, the men not needing nor waiting for an order to do so. They simply did so, all of them feeling the heaviness that Jarren and Mandol bore and because they did not understand it, anxious to get moving, the sheer act of putting physical distance between this place and that an unspoken desire. After giving them what he thought was enough time, Jarren simply nudged his mount forward. As one, the column followed.

The knot of dread lying in the pit of his stomach grew the closer they plodded toward the fortress of Tergaard where the rest of the regiment was supposed to be. It was a cancer, feeding off his mind as it created scene after scene of what he expected, excuse after excuse for why Jarl was found the way he was. *His message could not mean what seemed so obvious,* his mind reasoned. *It had to be a fluke. Jarl simply got separated from the regiment and was attacked by one of the predators Mandol had talked about.* But in his heart, he knew the truth, he knew what to expect even though his mind tried to deny it, tried to wrest the truth away and create something less terrible to deal with.

At times, he thought he was going to sick up again, the way his guts clenched, but he did not. He did nothing, just stared straight ahead into the darkness, his aching body moving with the rhythm of the horse beneath him. For the most part, anyhow. A few times, he dragged his eyes away and placed them on Mandol, but didn't leave them there long when he made out the drawn, haggard look his friend wore. He knew Mandol's mind was doing the same thing as his, but though they both experienced it, they were separated by it, unable to use each other for support.

A faint lightening to the east and a deep chill in the air told them that dawn was coming. And about the time the thought bubbled up from the morass of stagnant dread which filled him, someone spotted the telltale flickering of a signal fire some distance away, held aloft by the dark shadows of a particularly large outcropping of rock.

Without thinking, he angled toward it, a small hope squeaking in the darkness of his mind that it may be the regiment. The thought trailing that his detachment should be fairly close to the fortress by now.

What they found, though, strangled that small voice in a gurgling, gut-wrenching minute, silencing it.

Chapter 31

Traveling Days

As he had expected, Anine's horse died in the night while they slept, huddled up under the shelter against the moisture that drizzled down through the canopy. They had taken what little supplies that they could, and he helped her up behind him on Whitesteel's flanks, giving the great beast its head as they road through the sprinkling day. Unerringly, Whitesteel continued to head in the same direction as the previous days.

Anine was a soft presence at his back that was difficult to keep from thinking about. And, for her part, she seemed in much better spirits than when they met, her face less haggard when she awoke, the rest of the previous evening obviously deep and healing. She was talkative too. Very much so, chattering on about anything she could.

Mostly, prodded by Marc, she spoke of Scandin and the surrounding lands and the customs of the people there. The rigid caste system, the ruling warrior clans, and the interaction between them. Anine's father had been a trader from Hestaff whose wares had sparked such an intense interest in the rulers that they had invited them to stay with them in the palace, a rare honor that was offered to few. The top five clans had established a stability that was also rare in an area with such a chaotic, violent history. Most of her talk was of inconsequentials, such as fashion and assorted gossip, but he did not mind, enjoyed it, as everything she said tickled the back of his brain. Each thought expressed seemed to bring him closer toward the portal that would lead to his former self.

That evening, just a few hours before darkness, they came across the wide, stone paved road that cut through the plains from the south and headed in a northeastern direction toward the city of Hestaff, a piece of the extensive web of such paved highways that once linked all the major cities on the continent. For many long minutes, Anine stood, fists kneading her back after dismounting for a rest, staring up the empty road, a thoughtful, sorrowful expression on her face. Marc left her to her rumination as he studied their surroundings until, with a loud sigh, she dropped her arms and turned back, asking if she could continue on with him.

"Is not that the direction of your home?" he asked.

"I really don't have a home," she answered. "At least not now. My father was the only family I knew."

He looked up and down the old highway, noting that it was pitted and weeds and grasses were growing between the large sunken cobbles. A disjointed memory told him that the road had been cut off to the south, by what he was not certain, but its appearance certainly told of its abandonment. With some trepidation, he agreed after Anine reasserted that she had no place to go; reasserted that she wanted to go with him even though he did not know where he was going or why. Casting one more, forlorn look up the road, she remounted, wrapped her arms tightly around his middle and nestled her head against his back and said nothing the rest of the evening.

They camped only an hour from the road, Whitesteel again headed the same direction. He built a small fire and warmed some more jerky before unsaddling and brushing down the great horse, not pressuring Anine to speak, sensing that she needed the silence to deal with demons of her past that the sight of the highway stirred up. They ate in silence, and when the fire had burned down to a dull glow, they laid out the bedrolls and went to sleep. Marc was later awakened by soft sobbing, and not knowing exactly what to do, asked her, lamely, if she was alright. In answer, she slid next to him and huddled close and cried herself back to sleep, leaving Marc bewildered and fighting back his maleness.

Morning dawned blue and dry, and they set out soon after the sun lifted itself from the eastern horizon, Marc again giving Whitesteel his head while enjoying the soft company of Anine as she settled back down into her chatter, speaking again of the comings and goings of the people of Scandin. The day passed, uneventful, as they traveled through wide, grassy plains interspersed with stands of oak, ash, elm and pine, Marc speaking only when she asked him a direct question or when she paused long enough that he thought she was waiting for him to.

They camped that night under the reaching canopies of one of the many islands of trees that dotted the plain, ate Marc's dwindling ration of dried venison and sipped water from his waterskin, spoke a little about the general nature of things, but mostly enjoyed the quiet chorus of night creatures and crackling fire. When they settled down for sleep, Anine, wordlessly, curled up next to Marc, her body heat and scent, still pleasant though traveled, keeping him awake for a large part of the night.

Chapter 32

Power Revealed

"The rain's wiped out all signs of his passing," Sandoren said, kneeling on the sodden ground, now aimlessly brushing at the grass with his hand. Alex patted Del on the arm then sat slowly on the grass in the small clearing, taking in the wet scent of it and the cold chill as it seeped into her clothes while the boy stared slackly into the gray distance. "Both of them."

The heavens opened up soon after they found a sheltered area to camp, not far from the village, just as twilight gave way to full darkness, and cried softly until well after the gaze of the sun lightened the gray curtain that enveloped them. Though not a harsh rain, it was steady and the land drank deeply of it, pulling it down into its loam, nourishing itself with the life giving liquid until saturated. Once the iron gray clouds exhausted themselves, the land was spongy and swollen, all former wounds healed and the grass newly lush.

"What do we do now?" he asked after a minute, looking up at the uniform haziness. Alex ignored him, instead letting her body relax. When he turned his gaze on her and saw what she was doing, he stood and stretched, and moved off toward the nearby sheltering trees.

She watched him go with little thought, closing her eyes after a few moments. Releasing her mind was quick now that her body was emptied of tensions, and she sank down inside herself; felt as if she were sinking down into the ground itself until the press of it on her body became nonexistent. She waited only the span of a couple of heartbeats, then let her senses reach outward. To any but her, the sudden rush of sensation would drive splinters of pain into the brain, tearing the mind in a sudden shock of lightening. But she was ready for them, allowing them in stages, embracing them, filling herself with them.

The pungent, sweet odor of wet loam wafted through her like a breath, clinging to her body as readily as the droplets of moisture adhering to the tough, spun fiber of her clothing. Above her, the moist air currents swirled sluggishly, the cool temperature and low pressure held in by the encompassing cloudbanks, promising more rain throughout the coming days. She felt each and every blade of grass beneath and around her, the fibrous material permeated with water, and could sense the changes taking place within them as they drew nourishment from the soil. Nearby, the ageless forest stood, individual trees, hard bark softened by dampness, timeless rings growing, weaving, sap moving up and down throughout each trunk into the limbs, bringing food to limp leaves, combining with each other to form the body of the woods, a wide, flowing presence not unlike the grass. Far beneath, the Earth thrummed in slow, powerful beats.

Slowly, deliberately, she let her awareness grow in a widening globe, seeking. She passed by Sandoren and Del, feeling and hearing their breathing, heartbeats, and churn of internal organs as they intersected the growing boundary. Passed over hundreds of smaller creatures, ants, flies, worms, spiders in their webs, rodents in their warrens. Let them fade into the background, not lost, but largely ignored, as she sought out what would help her. She found her less than a few hundred yards away, watching them through the trees, hidden from even Sandoren's keen senses. She smiled.

-*Come*- she whispered to her, waiting a short span before an answering –*Yes*- came back to her. Alex let the sphere of awareness recede quickly, allowing it to disappear only after savoring the feelings and sensations for as long as she could, nearly forcing it from her. Her eyes opened, trailers of her awareness bringing the world about her in almost glaring reality. Everything was fresh and new, the colors of the grass, trees and even the clouds. Each a scintillating myriad of shades, made darker by the wetness, but no less brilliant; textures standing out sharply and individually. She had to blink a few times, a small feeling of sorrow settling deep within her as the colors and textures muted into the normal. Her mind became clamorous as thoughts began breaking the silence.

Movement from her right drew her attention. She smiled again as Sandoren crouched next to the tree he had been leaning against, staring off into the waterlogged forest. Within seconds, ghostlike, a large shaggy wolf appeared, padding through the soggy underbrush with a faint whisper, giving Sandoren a wide berth before breaking the boundary of trees and drawing near. She sat on her haunches directly in front of Alex and gazed at her with deep, murky yellow eyes. Her nostrils flared a couple of times.

Alex, smiling warmly, held out her hand for the wolf to sniff, waiting patiently while she took in her scent before scratching the animal along the jawline. She used the touch to facilitate the contact between them, a less tiring way of communicating. –*Thank you*—Alex whispered into the wolf's mind. –*Help me?*—

-*Yes*- came the reply, more a sense of affirmation than actual word. Alex touched her mind more closely, sending her an image of the man she sought followed by his scent as she remembered it from the dark hut in which he lay as she leeched the poison from his body only days earlier. The interchange lasted but a second. –*Will return*-- the wolf sent as she padded back into the woodline.

"Now!" she called to Sandoren. "We eat and wait. You have breakfast ready?" He grinned and shook his head.

They ate some fruit and berries taken from the orchards in the village, sitting quietly under the drooping forest canopy.

Several times, she tried to engage Del, but he seemed more withdrawn than normal, his slack expression and distant eyes not wavering as he chewed slowly, a line of juice from the corner of his mouth down around his wide chin. She gave up and contented herself with gazing at their soggy surroundings.

"When's she going to be back?" Sandoren asked after they finished and repacked the supplies.

"Don't know," Alex replied.

"We're losing time," he remarked. "This man we're chasing is sure not going to wait out the weather." Alex turned to face him, sitting cross-legged and leaning forward slightly. He watched her, letting his eyes wander over her moist, unkempt hair, twisted and pulled over her left shoulder, an ebony stain against the green of her cloak, before meeting her emerald gaze.

"What makes you think that, Sandy?" she said, the corner of her mouth trying to smirk.

"I don't know," Sandoren answered, looking down and clearing his throat. She reached out and took his hand, drawing his gaze back. "Just antsy, I guess."

"Look, Sandy," she said, studying his sharp features and large eyes. "I know you too well. You're antsy only when you're nervous, confused, angry, or scared. I know you don't trust this. I'm not sure I do either. But he's necessary."

"Why?" There was anger, sudden and hidden quickly, in his eyes. It drew her up short, but only for a second.

"I don't know why," she said. "But it was told to me that he is important to what we are trying to accomplish."

"How do you know?" he replied. "You only said that we would find them close together. No description. No name. How can you be sure that this nameless man is the one we need. Or the boy for that matter. Have you noticed that he isn't normal."

"Have you noticed you're not quite normal?" she retorted, brows arching and a flicker of flame sparking to life in her eyes. "Del is not normal, no. But he is one of two that we need. This man is the second."

"But, how do you know?" Sandoren said flatly.

"I just know," Alex answered with an end-of-discussion tone. "On both counts." She dared not reveal to him how she knew. What happened within her when she first saw him, gaunt and glistening in the lamplight, his body full of a poison that should have killed him outright, even she was not sure of, but it grabbed her and held her tightly.

"Okay," he said, holding his hands up. "Okay." He leaned back against the tree, looked up into the branches. "Whatever we do, we better do it. Your man is on horseback, we aren't. And Del, there, isn't known for his speed. Regardless of whether he is moving now or not, he will steadily get ahead of us. He has about two days on us now."

"Don't worry, Sandy. The wolves will help us."

"They're a little small to be carrying us, don't you think?" he said. Alex smiled.

"Just wait," she said, placing herself back up against the tree on which they leaned. Del stood almost statue-like, undisturbed by their spoken words, now staring off into the gray sky above. He was swaying ever so slightly from side to side. She was about to take her eyes away from him when her skin prickled sharply, drawing a gasp of surprise from her.

Energy coalesced almost visibly around him, coming in from every direction like a whirlwind drawing the air into it, swirling and growing in a furious rush. His eyes, blocked partly by the tilt of his head, were large and liquid, filled with wonder and curiosity. And power, pure, terrible in its strength, so much so that she was frightened by it, her breath held tightly. It grew, charging the air around them with such intensity she expected him to suddenly burst into flame and light, the pressure becoming so great as he held onto it. Yet, a small smile curled on his lips, simple, filled with innocent pleasure.

Alex stared in horrified wonder, feeling the Earthpower surge and swirl around and through him, knowing that he held far more than she or the rest of her sisters combined could ever hope to. The grass around him swelled and twined around his ankles, growing larger and more lush as the seconds slid by. Then, just as quickly as it coalesced, it dispersed, a fast stream of tingling bursts against her senses.

Del continued to stand, staring upward, the smile gracing his lips, lush grass enveloping his legs up to his calves. She released the breath she had been holding. Watching. Waiting. Sensing something.

Above them, the clouds began moving, sluggishly, swirling away from themselves. Minutes later, blue opened above them, allowing the sun to beam down upon them, warming and dry, chasing away the cool moistness for a brief time. Del was smiling broadly, eyes closed, as he rotated his face to bathe it in the sunlight.

"Rain passing?" Sandoren said idly, looking out into the sun laden glade with sleepy eyes, drawing a half smile and cut off chuckle from Alex. He did not know, could not know, what had just taken place.

"No," she said softly. "Just a fluke."

"Too bad," he replied slowly, voice reflecting the grogginess of his eyes, and shifted against the wet trunk. "It'd be nice to be dry again." His eyes closed.

Del held his face to the sky even after the clouds reasserted themselves and closed the window to the blue he had opened. She studied him, pushing back at the fright that still drifted like a haze within her, confused by him, by his actions, by his demeanor. Sandoren's words came back to her, haunted her. *Am I truly convinced that the boy, and the man, are the ones we seek? Was Gyssel right when she told me to seek them out, that I would know? Why am I having so many second thoughts? Is he the one? He holds Power I never knew was possible, but does his crippled mind understand what just happened? Could he understand the power he just wielded, the Imbalance he created just to feel sunlight on his face?*

An innocent display, to be sure, but as dangerous as cornering a wounded animal. With more, devastating, consequences. Alex wondered if she could truly believe this boy was the one she sought?

Doubt continued to work into her mind, growing within the cracks like the roots of a weed, forcing her stone-like convictions about him apart, slowly, inexorably. Sandoren's concerns adding the fodder needed to keep them growing, his prejudiced tendencies seeming more wise now after Del's unconcerned, unbridled display.

With some effort, she blocked those thoughts, plucked out those weeds of skepticism, telling herself that she was right, that she was sure. But the roots remained.

Del was looking at her, his eyes still large and luminous, full of clarity and as depthless as time itself, just as she saw yesterday just before he spoke to her for the first time. A motherly smile of concern worked onto her face, chasing away some of the tenseness she felt around the corners of her mouth and eyes and hairline. *Is he?* The thought came in the guise of Sandy's voice, causing her to reflect briefly on his undisciplined display and its terrifying possible consequences.

"No," Del said quietly, his tone almost musical. It shook her from her thoughts, surprised her as much as he had yesterday, and sent tendrils of confusion creeping into her again. She was about to ask what he meant when she saw the clouds flow back into his eyes and his face begin to relax into its normal rubbery expression and, instead, shook her head in defeat. *How can I be sure*, she thought, *when he only slides out of the darkness of his disability randomly?*

Chapter 33

Powerful Attention

*F*ar to the northwest, in the great besieged city of Vistan, the seat of power for the Northern Empire, the Emperor stopped suddenly, rigidly. Turning slowly within the dark, mirror polished hallway of the cyclopean construct perched above the city proper, eyes gazed south east, looking through the nearby castle wall. They stayed there, fixed, for a long time, before the mouth behind the mask muttered.

"Tempest," it said, drifting in the silence.

Not as far away as Vistan, a single traveler, a woman wrapped in a voluminous cloak carrying nothing, stopped and looked east, long obsidian locks floating on the stiff breeze. Her eyes glittered with a dark light and her full lips quirked into a slow smile that never went higher, a chilling smile that may have saved the ten or so bandits lying dead several miles south had they but seen it beforehand. She began walking again soon, less concerned about the disturbance than the Emperor, far to the north, but just as curious.

Chapter 34

The Shock of Reality

*M*aelyrin gagged reflexively, a cloth held tightly against her mouth and nose that did little to block out the charnel smell that filled the bowl of the tiny valley. A chill drizzle that seeped deep into clothing and skin and down into the bones caused her to shiver, though it was the sight before her as much as the cold that contributed to it.

The black mound, reaching nearly waist high, thought at first sight when she topped the hill to be the remnants of a bonfire, turned out to be a tangle of wood, cloth, and bodies, all charred with a ring of white ash surrounding it. A sickening sheen of moisture glimmered across the whole of its irregular surface, the obvious end to the all-consuming flame that once engulfed the hastily erected pyre. Several small trailers of smoke and steam still rose from deep fissures, a testament that, within, the heart still burned. Small hisses sounded periodically. Nearby, four other wagons rested, wood dark from the weather, some with their soggy contents for the most part still intact.

Maelyrin looked around at the uniform grayness and misted ring of hillocks. Marc's trail had led here, but the hours of light rainfall had all but obliterated any distinguishable trail away. At least, that is what she hoped was the reason she had not found anything beyond the churned turf around the wagons that would lead her to think otherwise. As she perused the pile before her, her only hopes were that he was not among the twisted, carbonized bones that made up the majority of the heap. She looked around the trough again, eyes lingering over the bloated bodies of pack animals. Among them, she did not see the corpse of the magnificent white stallion Marc had named Whitesteel. It was a good sign for her fluctuating emotions. Silently, she wished she had found a mount herself. Then she might have been able to catch up with him instead of steadily falling further and further behind.

When she had seen the building clouds on the horizon yesterday, a pit had formed in her stomach. A pit that stayed with her through the cold night and miserable, wet morning. It grew heavier now as she wondered desperately what next to do. Maelyrin's only consolation was that Marc had headed unwaveringly toward the southwest. If she could not pick up his trail within the relative shelter of the nearby trees, she, at her figuring, had a direction in which she could head. Before she relied on that train of thought, though, she decided to make one more circuit of the area, convincing herself that she had missed some clue the former two times she circled the trough. Taking one final look at the grisly remains of the pyre, she turned toward the likely direction Marc would have left had he kept to his pattern and began scanning the ground for the telltale markings of Whitesteel's prints.

Where she stood, the ground was too torn by the previous battle, the skin of grass ripped in too many places revealing the dark muscle of earth beneath, so she began moving slowly outward in a wide spiral, studying closely the area just before her feet. It was not long that she was angling up the slope of the nearest hill. She stopped momentarily and kneeled, eyeballing the grass along the rise for any irregularities. An uncharacteristic curse rose from her throat. The light was too vague to pick up any shine of pressed grass and the fresh moisture helped whatever flattened greenery to relax and reform.

The unmistakable *pop*! of breaking wood resounded throughout the tiny valley, shooting ice up her spine. Her head whipped around to stare back down at the wagons, the sight below causing her body to go rigid. Several human men stared up at her, standing around one of the wagons. Two of them were helping a third stand from among the broken side rail of the wagon where he either stumbled or simply leaned against the old sodden wood. The rest of them wore grim, hungry smiles that advertised their intent more sharply than words ever could.

She cursed again, glanced quickly at the wagon where her bow, quiver, and pack leaned, then back at the grass. With a surge of energy, she launched herself upward, clawing fistfuls of grass and soil for leverage as she bolted for the tree line that lay not far over the crest. Several barks and roars broke out below, suspiciously full of glee. She did not need to look back to know her flight was not the only one.

Biting back her urge to shriek, she instead channeled her fear into the muscles of her legs and arms as she scrambled up the slope. Though relatively gentle, the ascent was long and soon her breath was ragged and burning as she neared the top, finding a slight rush of energy as the ground beneath her feet began to level. Keeping herself just this side of panic, Maelyrin's eyes searched out the haven in which she was sure to lose her pursuers. Her breath caught momentarily when she found that the tree line doubled back on itself on the opposite side, cutting back several hundred yards before winding back over the next hillock, leaving another quarter mile or so of open plain for her to race.

The lapse in concentration cost her as her foot found a depression in the loam, jolting her sense of balance in a rapid blink that she could not readjust to. She stumbled, the downward slope pulling her stride farther and farther more erratically, until her momentum and irregular gait was too much to compensate for. An unconscious yelp burst from her lips as her body pitched forward. Pain lanced from the shoulder she, at first, landed on, bringing more grunts and cries from her throat as she began tumbling down the slope, the pain exploding and flashing through her body, matching closely the way her vision became jumbled and blurred. Grass and dirt flew into her mouth and eyes, and she lost all sense of time and direction even though there was a vague impression where the ground was located.

She had come to a stop long before she realized it, her mind unable to stop spinning and the aches in her body still throbbing so that it felt as if the pain was still being inflicted. When her vision and mind cleared, she found that she lay on her back somewhere near the bottom of the knoll. Drifting down to her were the voices of the men chasing her, calling out to each other in a language she did not understand. She lifted her head slowly, aware of the precursors to the pain she would feel in the moment she committed herself to moving, and gazed up the slope. They were on the crest, dark shadows against the lead of the sky, pausing in their objective most likely to make sure she had not killed herself. Her movement pushed them mobile again, bounding down the hill like wolves on the hunt.

Instinctively, she tried to crawl backward, a burning agony flaring in her shoulder bringing her up short with a cry ripping from her mouth and a reddish haze that swirled through her vision. Forcing away the after effects, she took several deep breaths, prepared herself, then rolled over the uninjured side to find her feet, crying out again as the pain shot through her. Using the remaining slope for help this time, she got herself into a crouch and launched herself down the hill again, her left arm dangling at her side, each step sending pulses of hot agony radiating from the shoulder.

Tears ran unchecked from her eyes as she tried to put more distance between her and the hooting predators behind her. Maelyrin's only thoughts focused on moving her hurting body into the safety of the woods where her naturally raised abilities would end the chase, though she increasingly began to think that she was not going to make it. That her flight was in vain. Anger shot through her, and, this time, she yelled out in rage. It forced another surge of energy into her failing body.

She was struggling up the side of the opposite hill, it seemingly becoming steeper each step taken, when, suddenly, whatever reserve of willpower she had expended itself. Maelyrin slipped to one knee on the wet grass, angled her body away from the injured shoulder as the ground came up to meet her. The pain and exhaustion became too much even for her fear, pushing everything back behind a dark mist that encroached on her consciousness. She slid to the ground, a cloudy hope that she would be out completely by the time they caught up.

Something heavy and large flashed overhead, felt through the squeezing darkness, moving down the hill, colliding with the men chasing her, their boisterous yells turning quickly to screams of pain. With some effort, she forced her eyes open to see what was happening, deciding that she was hallucinating once she did. A giant stood on the down-slope between her and the men. They were screaming and falling to the sides amid arcs of blood and flying body parts. In the grayness of the light and drizzle it seemed there was a silver flickering shield around the huge figure, laying open each man that came too close in a cloud of red mist. Once she decided she was just seeing things, she let the exhaustion take her.

Chapter 35

The Days Revelation

The glare of the morning sun held no warmth. It was a ball of freezing fire that cast its yellow rays across the blasted sand and rock in sparkling sheets, revealing glittering patches of frost that clung to the ground like white moss. Fragile things that died quickly in the cold light, dissipating into sickly trailers of mist that crawled across the sand, drifted among the grotesque mounds as if drawn to them, to caress their twisted forms, maybe to share in their mortality, maybe to draw forth whatever life might be clinging to them. Jarren wondered briefly if it wasn't mist at all, but the silent release of souls, unable to cling to the vessels that once housed them. He wondered briefly if the deep shivering of his body was his own soul trying to find its own release so it could join its brethren, instead of it being caused by the intense morning chill.

It was only a thought. It was born, it lived, and it died in the infinitesimal eternity that was a thought. Only a thought. But it seemed his body shivered more violently, quaking harder against the cold, yet unable to drive his eyes away from the ghastly sight, nor to cause him to unhinge his rigidly held body.

He really couldn't know, though. It was a numb, unfeeling thing, his body. A cloudy mass of nothing which stray thoughts drifted through. Like those mists before him. Or those souls.

Behind Jarren, he knew, were many more sets of eyes, red rimmed and scaled, listlessly devouring the sight over which they looked. He could feel nothing for them, either, though there were thoughts of them. Somewhere.

He told himself that he needed to do something, but the mind that belonged to Corporal Kydel Jarren was silent. That thought drifted away, too, nothing anchoring it to any action. Jarren simply could do nothing but stare while his body quaked.

Spread out before him and the remainder of the regiment, humped and twisted, was half of the 3rd Imperial Cavalry, their bodies and those of their mounts sprawled in a flaccid 'V' shape in front of the huge quiescent walls of the fortress. They looked like clumps of black coal amid leaning spikes and spines in the morning light, dark blots without identity. He had been told that the other half had suffered the same fate, but he could not see past the blocking view of the sheer blade of rock where they were supposed to be tucked behind. Even though it had been delivered to him upon his arrival at the huge outcropping a few hours ago by a pale rendition of the scout, Silek, Jarren had placed himself at his chosen post and stared into the night anyway, not able to completely acknowledge all the evidence present to substantiate the claim. Even now, with all the dark bodies scattered there, he couldn't quite believe it. Jarl's bloated, torn face seemed to be looking at him from somewhere far away, accusing him.

It was just a thought.

"Sir?" the voice was low and full of stun. It also had a tone that had only begun showing up in the last few hours. It parted the mists of his mind enough to let consciousness slip in, bringing with it the harsh reality of his aching body and iced extremities, the ragged edges of his sanity. He preferred the place he had been. He preferred the nothingness.

"What is it, Mandol?" he said, his voice raw. A second or an hour could have passed before he answered, he didn't know.

"What are we going to do now, sir?" Mandol asked. If he hadn't seen the man's shadow out of the corner of his eye, a swaying brush stroke on the rock beside him, Jarren would have thought that it was his own mind still, as many times as it whispered that question over the past few hours.

"Stop calling me 'sir'," he said, blankly. Mandol shifted on his feet several times, kneading his hat in his hands, an intense war of emotions raging across the planes of his dark face. Finally, he sat roughly by his friend and grabbed hold of his arm. The wool of his uniform was sheened with cold moisture.

"Kydel!" he hissed. "Need I remind you that you are the highest ranking officer now? Do I have to forget your rank long enough to kick some sense into you, along with some teeth?"

Jarren's head swiveled slowly in his direction, the dullness in his eyes parting before a bright, flickering spark of anger, bringing a tiny smile to Mandol's face and a quick satisfied nod. "Good," he said. "It's good to see that there is life still in there." Jorn let go of his sleeve. The rumpled material slowly reasserted itself over Jarren's arm. "Now, sir," he said. "What are your orders? Sir?"

The anger smoothed over a little. "Let's prepare the men to move," Jarren answered. Mandol instinctively went rigid. "And send Silek over here."

"Yes, sir!" Mandol said, a questioning look crossing his eyes that said he was reconsidering his previous remarks. He scrambled up, groaning something about his age and rocks and such, and clambered across the low, wide boulders. Jarren returned his gaze toward the fortress, toward the mass of death that sprawled there, among the thinning mists. His anger blazed suddenly, burning whatever fog that remained in him away in a white hot stroke.

"Why have you done this to me?" Jarren spat. An instant of guilt spiked up, but he crushed it, allowing his fury free reign. "Why? How could this have happened? I didn't want this! I'm not ready for this!" He cursed his situation soundly, blaming everything there was to blame, looking for a solid surface to stand on, letting his anger exhaust itself.

"You sent for me, sir?" Silek said. Jarren hadn't heard him come up, didn't know how long he had been talking, wondered how much the scout had heard. By the tremble in the man's voice, he could have been there awhile. But then, most of the men spoke with that tremble now. A disbelieving, shallow tremor that could barely rise above a whisper. *Shock*, Jarren's brain suggested. *Pure shock*. Still, he was suddenly uncomfortable and had to clear his throat a couple of times while he stood. It helped that his body cried out in prickling agony against the motion. *Shock*.

"Yes," Jarren said, once he forced himself erect, fists levering into his lower back. A small voice noted that Silek was older than he by several years, and it wondered why he had called him 'sir'. Shock was the only answer he could come up with. "I need to know what your eyes have found."

"Sir?" Silek answered.

"We have to get these men somewhere safe, tend our wounded. You are the only one that can guide us. That is, after we tend to the dead." He said the last absently, but it looked as if Silek had suddenly had a bucket of freezing water thrown in his face. It tightened and paled so rapidly that Jarren thought the man was passing out. "What's the matter, Silek?"

"We. . . uh. . . we can't tend to the dead. . . sir," he said. Silek was visibly shaking, not violently, but it was there. "I'm sorry I didn't tell you before. . . ." he went on. "But . . . before you arrived, we. . . uh . . . we formed a detail to get out there and look for the wounded . . . ."

"And?"

"Well, sir. . . they wouldn't let us." Cold fear and anger mixed in Jarren's guts at the scout's words.

"What do you mean?" he ground icily.

"Those. . . those . . . things. . . ." Silek's eyes were clouded with fear. "Those things came back out when we got close. . . . hundreds of 'em . . . . They stood there like statues. . . . like statues made of night, sir. Two of the men went in. . . in too. . . near. They. . . they . . . fell on them before they could get ten feet. . . . They ripped 'em apart." Silek gulped loudly. "And then they came after us. But they only chased us to the edge of the old road. Then they stopped. . . . They just stopped and went back."

"Well," Jarren said slowly. His guts were churning and his spine was an icicle. "It looks like they left before the sun rose." He had heard tale after horrid tale of the inky creatures that had wiped out the regiment since he arrived. Enough that he actually could believe them, all but that tiny fire of doubt that refused to be doused no matter how much proof surfaced. But the look on Silek's face didn't change, may have even become paler.

"That's just it, sir," he paused to take another rattling breath, as if he had been holding it since he had spoken last. "We thought that too. . . that they were gone. . . . But, sir. . . they were there. Those things were laying with the bod. . . . regiment. . . . waiting. . . ." It felt like small, tiny spiders were scuttling up the back of Jarren's neck, disturbed from whatever sleep by Silek's words. *Laying among them, waiting. The Creator save us all.* "Maliss says they are still there. . . sir."

Jarren needed something, a hand hold, a foot hold, something before he slid off the cliff of his sanity. "Maliss? How does he know? Where is he?" It came out in a rush and Jarren had to mentally backpeddle to try and get control of himself.

"He's gone again, sir," Silek answered, then hastened to add, "He went out again, sir." when the Corporal's face pinched angrily. "He's been coming and going all night, sir. He's been covering our backs." Silek visibly relaxed when he saw Jarren do so.

Jarren turned away, allowing his shoulders to slump a little, watching the puff of cold vapor that rode the huffing sigh he exhaled. "Then there has been no word on whether the Captain or the Commander are alive? Maybe hiding somewhere else?" he said as his eyes passed quickly over the dark figures scattered carelessly near the fortress. *They're out there, now, watching us.* He thought, throat tightening. *They're out there and I can't pick them out. But I can feel the truth of his words.*

"No, sir," Silek said, quieter still. "Ganlin said he saw. . . the Commander fall. Before he died, he said he saw them both fall." Jarren stared at him, hope rising at Silek's start, but it crashed onto the stone as he finished. *Ganlin, the banner man for the Imperial Colors.* The thought was grim, but the one that followed almost choked him up. *Both Colors recovered, but only a breath of the regiment left.*

"What about the men under Baen's command?" he asked hopefully.

"Don't know, sir, we were cut off while trying to deliver the message for him to move forward." He gulped again. "They must have been taken from behind, but we weren't able to reach them. That's how we ended up here." Silek straightened a little. "We did all we could to get survivors here."

"Well, it appears that we can move neither forward, nor backward. . . ." Jarren's musing, though, sparked some life back into the scout's eyes. He arched a questioning brow.

"To the east, not far, we found a river," Silek licked his lips excitedly. "And forage."

A shadow of a smile appeared on Jarren's face. *Water and forage. East. Thank the Creator*, he thought. "Then, I guess, east is it," he said softly, bringing a slow nod from Silek. "Perhaps we can meet up with the 5th after all."

"The 5th, sir?" he asked, sudden confusion rampant on his slowly coloring face.

"The 5th, Silek," he said. "They are coming south down the coast of New Sea on this side of the world."

"H-how. . . .?"

"I heard it," he answered quickly. "There are benefits to having to be so close to the Commander's tent." Silek nodded, finally, his confusion swept aside by a glimmer of hope. "You'd better go and get prepared. We leave soon."

He straightened, saluted. "Yes, sir." *Yes, sir.* It echoed in Jarren's mind, a foreign thing that just did not feel comfortable, would not feel comfortable. Jarren watched the scout as he moved up the sloping sides of the rock outcropping toward the clusters of men huddling up there against the cold and the deeply imbedded fear. Ragged forms in the pale, cold yellow light of the morning sun. Below and around the side of their position, within a group of enclosing rocks, he could hear the horses whickering and snorting, coming alive after the longest night of his life. The sunlight, though still chilly, warmed him inside, gave him some hope that they could get to the rendezvous point, despite their diminished number and diminished supplies.

Jarren couldn't help but look back at the scattered bodies of the regiment, guilt and shame pooling inside him, rising slowly. He couldn't leave those men out there, but he was. He had to. But it wasn't right. And he could not let his thoughts dwell on the fact that the Commander's body and the Captain's body were out there, baking and drying among the others. Perhaps Silek was wrong. Perhaps they were not out there.

The thought was cut off sharply, and his breath caught painfully in his throat. *Had something moved out there? In answer to his thoughts? Could he have been mistaken? Maybe just a bug zipping through his peripheral vision?* Jarren stared hard, willing the thing to move again, willing his eyes to try and view it closer, as if he could make them the eyes of an eagle. But nothing stirred. Nothing moved except the hair on the back of his neck. He tried to convince himself that it was his imagination, but the argument was weak. Something had moved, a sluggish settling of something bloated after a feast. A predator not interested in prey, but warning that it wasn't unaware.

The thought caused his guts to churn again, but he had to force himself to turn away and to the task of getting the survivors of the regiment moving.

Chapter 36

The Emperor's Curiosity

*A*lex was napping against the tree trunk when she
suddenly became aware of the she-wolf returning and woke
herself. Sandoren stood within the glade, back to her, looking
up into the uniform gray. Del was sitting near him, observing
intently a meaty hand crawling with all manner of insects. She
smiled, taking in the scene as a mother observing her family in
moments of solitude does, a gentle warmth filling her, her heart
swelling. She let it flow through her, time standing still, as a
cool breeze wafted by.

Sandoren tensed suddenly, a subtle winding of a spring
that was not visible to the untrained eye. To her, as predictable
as the sunrise. He turned, looked at her while his hand dropped
to the hilt of his sword, but relaxed once he saw she was awake
and unconcerned. A second later, the wolf materialized near
her, sitting next to her as she did previously, waiting
expectantly until Alex rubbed her beneath her slim chin. She
peered deep into the animal's murky eyes, experiencing deeply
and all at once the she-wolf's life in this world, her hunts and
kills, her litters of pups, her place in the Balance of life. *–Can
you help?–* she sent.

-Yes.- the wolf replied, sending back a combination of
scents and visuals that told her more in that single instance than

simple spoken language. Immediately, she knew that the man she sought was nearly a day ahead of them, moving southwest with a companion. And, in the next moment, the wolf provided her with information that would help them catch them. She smiled warmly and scratched the animal beneath the chin again.

"Thank you," she whispered. The she-wolf gazed at her for many moments, nostrils flaring slightly as she stored Alex's scent within her memory. Then, she disappeared into the trees without looking back.

"Well?" asked Sandoren, coming closer now that the wolf had gone.

"He's not as far as we thought, only about a day, traveling that direction," Alex pointed while standing up and absently brushing bits of grass and weed from her clothing. It wouldn't take them long to close the distance enough that she could use the Air Bond to track him. "But we have to go that way," she said, pointing north, over her shoulder with a thumb. Sandoren cocked an eyebrow sharply. "You certainly don't think we can catch them while on foot, do you?"

"Going almost the opposite direction isn't my idea of closing the gap," he griped. "Why don't we just *treewalk* like we did a few days ago?"

"Because I don't have the strength," she answered simply. "And I cannot sense him. He's too far yet." Sandoren grunted while picking up his pack and slinging it on his back, both an answer to her statement and a reaction to his still aching body.

"Let's get going, then," he muttered. "The Maker only knows how much time we've wasted."

"What's eating you, Sandy?" she retorted. "You've been moody for days now."

"I don't know," he answered a little too quickly. His irritation flared sharply across his features and was subdued just as fast. Their eyes locked for many moments, a tenseness between them that was a rarity. Each struggled to determine the cause, yet each sidestepped their own concerns and answers;

silent fencing that deepened the discomfort and placed a wedge between them that left them in unstable territory. Shaking his head, he broke contact and began walking north, his stride stiff with angry pride.

Alex watched him, a deeply intense musing that revealed nothing to her but the outer formation of the thunderheads hiding the storm within. A silent sigh escaped her as she threw the thoughts from her. "Del," she called softly, turning moments later when there was no forthcoming answer. He was intently studying the insects around him. "Del," she said a bit louder.

No response. With an eternal patience that seemed an unusual reaction to her, she called several more times, finally walking to him and placing her hand on his shoulder. He flinched at the touch, stirring up concern within her, the memory of how they found him flashing up before her mind's eye, but he smiled brightly, slackly, once he turned to look up at her. Del stood slowly and allowed himself to be led after the receding Sandoren. The insects that had been crawling all over his hand began dropping off of their own volition.

They went back to their tiny lives, the insects, disturbed by the one that disturbed them in such a way that was completely unnatural and against all the behaviors of their primitive brains. Yet, it was something more than natural, a higher state of being. Over a span of only inches, a multicolored grasshopper regarded the large hunting spider that had been stalking it prior to the distraction. In return, ten beady ocules were held riveted on the prey while the warmth overhead moved for several minutes. The spider turned and wandered into the forest of grass, while the locust leapt and grabbed onto a higher reaching weed stalk. All throughout the small glade, the miniscule life forms paused in their hunting, fleeing, eating, hiding, and resting, experiencing a peaceful solitude for many minutes, unknown to them, before reverting to their natural inclinations.

The spider went back to its hunt, sighting a large green and orange caterpillar munching obliviously on a leafy weed. The grasshopper was being targeted by a small bird sitting on a limb not far from the overhanging weed on which it clung. Life went on as usual, the visitation of the wash of calmness forgotten, the one who generated it long gone. The source of warmth and light above them diminished steadily, becoming only a thin red stain against the far horizon, alerting those creatures of daylight to give way to the orchestra of nocturnal creatures. Creatures that knew nothing of the passing peacefulness.

The spider, sated temporarily of its hunger, crawled sluggishly toward its burrow, while the grasshopper, alive but missing one of its rear legs huddled beneath a rotting stick. The bird that had attempted to take more than its leg nestled back on its branch.

Suddenly, everything stopped for the second time. The crickets' song cut off midway, the spider quivered in its burrow, the grasshopper froze completely by the antithesis of the warming breath of peace experienced.

The creature stepped from the gloom beneath the trees, materializing from the pooling shadows directly beneath the branch on which the bird sat, its tiny heart suddenly thumping so wildly that it over strained itself and seized violently within its chest. The bird's lifeless body, eyes still wide, dropped from its perch and hit the ground, the only sound save for the whispering breezes. However, it did not cause a reaction from the thing that stepped from the shadows.

Dressed in a long coat blacker than the night, its pallid face seemed disembodied and floating as it moved out to the center of the glade. Above, the unmoving full moon cast down its silvery light, but in vain, as it slid away from the dark man.

He knelt at an unusually lush patch of ground, eyeing it with stygian darkness where his eyes should be. Turning his pale face north, in the direction the trio left only hours ago, his hand idly touched the luxuriant growth. The grass drew away, withering and blackening from the rancid touch.

The man stood suddenly, tense, a wickedly thin sword appearing from the depths of the light swallowing coat, glittering in the silvery moon beams as if it alone could bear the glow that the rest of him defied. In a wary stance, he surveyed the intensely quiet surrounding trees, peering into the wells of darkness bleeding through them. The wan light at the very edge of the western horizon thinned, slowly, then disappeared altogether.

Shrubbery near the edge of the glade exploded outward violently as the demon-like creature sprang from its concealment, its luminous eyes leaving faint glare trails in the night. A piercing scream split the terrible silence as it barreled toward the dark man near the clearing's center.

The shadow man spun away from the creature, blade licking out, spraying hot ichor in a fan as the Eldritch flew past, claws ripping. Carried by the momentum of its rush, it was several feet away when it whirled back to face its opponent. The combatants stalked each other, wary now that they each knew they could be wounded by the other.

The Eldritch flashed a saliva shiny grin then launched itself again, trying to rake with its claws once more, but the dark man dodged and stepped through, drawing the thin sword along the creatures ribcage. It mewled in rage, touching the new wound and looking at its glistening fingertips. Its eyes suddenly took on a darker shine as it swiveled its head around to look at the man.

They circled, taut springs ready to release, the creature's eyes blazing, the dark man's empty beneath the eye lids; twin motes of utter blackness within the pale face. The creature sprang first, leaping high and over the man, a dark blur in the moonlight, momentarily catching him off guard. Knifelike nails dug deep past light swallowing cloth into pallid flesh and bone, the blow throwing him backward into the grass.

He was up quickly after a twisting tumble to get feet under him, his sword arcing around to meet his opponent. The creature was close to his back but sprang away from the gleaming metal. Only a moment's pause slipped by before it came in again, hunched down, ripping furrows in the field with all four clawed limbs, screeching out its fury. It barreled into him, lifting the dark man from the ground and flipping him over its back.

The shadow man landed like a cat as the Eldritch twisted back around. Before completing its turn, the man lunged forward and drove the blade deep into its body. It roared, arching away from the bite of the blade, ripping it from the hands of the dark man, slashing out wildly while backpedaling. Long streaks appeared on the pale man's face, widening then spilling dark fluid down his cheek.

The creature, huffing violently, pierced the man with its horrid glare, ignoring completely the thin blade angling oddly from its knotted body. A deep mewling growl began in its throat, growing quickly in intensity and finally erupting in a violent scream that silenced the nocturnal orchestra for miles around. Eyes blazing in the dark, it launched itself at the man again, shifting rapidly as he tried to sidestep and slammed into him, driving him backward, claws ripping savagely along his back and teeth gnashing into his chest.

The dark man struggled furiously, silently, lashing out with kicks and punches, refusing to give in even as he was smashed resoundingly against a tree trunk then savagely hurled backward into the clearing to land in a skidding heap that churned up the earth. He was up again, quickly, but staggering, one shoulder hanging low, the arm connecting dangling lifelessly. He was turning when the Eldritch crashed into him again, wrapping its overlong arms around his chest and arms, bearing him down and raking its back claws viciously along his belly like a cat and biting into the flesh at his throat, ravaging it.

The dark man, the Shadowman, servant of the Emperor, took a long time to kill, struggling fiercely as the Eldritch shredded and gnawed, clasped about his body like a python, leeching its life force away. The thing finally, suddenly, stopped fighting, its body rent.

The Eldritch stood slowly and snuffled at the air, then looked down at its side as if noticing for the first time the sword sticking out from it. It pulled the blade free, studied the dark ichor that covered it for a moment before tossing it on top of the flayed body of its opponent. It sniffed again, looking north, then loped after its quarry.

Chapter 37

A Refuge in No Memory

*7*he plain slowly lost ground to the forests again the further they traveled, the stands of trees becoming larger and larger until, to the north, there was nearly a solid line of them. The routine did not change. They rode the never tiring Whitesteel, Anine talking about her life in general while Marc listened and commented where appropriate, enjoying the soft presence at his back. They rested often, stopping and dismounting to stretch worn muscles, before moving on, while the sun, bright in the clear blue sky, drifted above them, showering them with a comfortable amount of warmth. As the great ball began dropping toward the western skyline, they found themselves heading into a wide glade that swept down a soft incline at the end of converging tree lines in the middle of which stood a single dwelling, small but sturdily built from the heavy timbers of the surrounding oak, hickory, and walnut. Next to it stood a stable about the size of the house, surrounded by a heavy fence that gave whatever animal kept there a large area in which to run. A crystalline stream flowed from the embrace of the trees to the north and curved down behind the dwelling, following the fence line several yards back before re-entering the trees to the south east.

"Where are we?" Anine asked, again kneading her back with her fists.

"I am not . . . quite . . . sure," he said softly, an inkling trying to flicker in the wet wood of his mind. He helped Anine down before dismounting himself. Whitesteel whickered and nudged him with his nose. Absently, Marc reached up and scratched the horse behind his ear, staring at the house as if the mere act would answer Anine's question. Though he could not remember any significance of this place, his logic began drawing its own conclusions.

Whitesteel nudged him a little more roughly, using his entire forehead, knocking him off balance and drawing an irritated look back. "What?" he asked. Whitesteel threw his head back in an exaggerated nod and whickered again, snorted and stamped a foot. Marc smiled then chuckled. "Alright, alright."

"I guess he wants to keep going," Anine said off to the side, patting the animal's chest.

"Yea, I guess," Marc stepped back and quickly released the bindings that held the scabbard to his saddle. Anine, walking around the other side, gave him a quizzical look. He shrugged. "Just being cautious," he said a moment later.

"Seems safe enough," she replied.

"Yea," Marc said, looking back down the small slope at the house. "I guess that is what bothers me."

"Do you know this place?"

He continued to stare at the house and its stable. "I'm not sure," he answered, again after a thoughtful pause. "I have an idea that I do. . . but. . ." It trailed away as he began slowly walking toward the house, hefting the scabbard in his hand as if uncertain of its weight. Absently, he reached out without looking back, a gesture meant to maneuver her behind him. Anine's warm hand, as it slipped into his waiting one, surprised him slightly, causing him to stop and look at her. She smiled. He returned it, continued on toward the house. Behind them, Whitesteel snorted and followed, his heavy footsteps muted by the lush grass of the glade.

Trepidation began mounting within him the nearer the house he came, confusing him, beginning to battle the thoughts his logical mind had implanted. His breath quickened just a touch, accommodating the increase of his heartbeat. If this place was what he thought it was, how would he know? Eyes roved over the wood of the building taking in the grain and knots, studying the way the timber was joined, feeling a subtle stirring of severed memory, as if he recognized that knothole, or the uneven mud plaster that filled the seams between that corner piece. But it was fleeting, a flash of light in the darkness that blinded and left afterimages that could not be focused on.

Marc almost balked, suddenly thinking that maybe he did not want to find out if what he was thinking was correct. His presence here was at once comforting, a strong sensation of a place known, developed, but vague and haunting as if it were a dream half remembered in the full light of day.

He must have slowed because Anine was suddenly slightly ahead of him and pulling him gently without realizing it. Consciously, he made an effort to speed up. Several feet from the house, Marc stopped and pulled her slowly behind him. With a deft flick of his hand, he grabbed the hilt of his sword and let the scabbard slide from the blade to thump softly on the grass.

The place appeared deserted, the surrounding turf overgrown and encroaching upon the natural areas of travel in front of the door. But it was the door that caused him concern, standing slightly ajar as it was. He stepped closer and used the tip of his blade to push it open the rest of the way, the silence of the glade suddenly disturbed by the creaking of its hinges.

Light fell onto the planking of the interior and illuminated the dust motes that drifted about from the movement of the door. He moved across the portal, allowing his eyes to adjust to the still shadowed inside. The room was large and layered with dust and sparsely populated with several pieces of furniture. Two archways led deeper into the house, yawning blackly. He knelt, studied the floor, then chuckled.

Crisscrossing the dust in the worn wood were the distinctive tracks of small animals.

"What is it?" Anine asked.

"Masked Bandits, I'd wager," he replied, standing. "Would you mind handing me my scabbard?" She moved back with a nod and a quick, nervous smile. He watched her for a moment, letting his eyes wander along the curves of her body, then turned into the house, working slowly across the floor, some of the boards creaking beneath his boots. The sounds tickled the back of his mind.

His eyes played over the room, taking in the austere appearance. The furniture was functional, made from the same timber that the house was constructed of, layered with thick heavy blankets for cushions. A small table stood near the door, empty across its dusty plane. The hearth was blackened with soot, but the rack within without wood and the floor of it barren of ashes.

Marc stepped through the first arch, mid-wall to his left, and he looked in on a modest kitchen area. Dominating the far wall, a large cast iron stove squatted under a shuttered window and to the side of it, a narrow door. Dust laden cut-wood was piled next to it, and on the other side, shored up by a long heavy cutting table that pulled back along the right hand wall. Pegs pounded in the plane above it held large pots and skillets, also cast iron and well used. To his left, flanked by two ladder back chairs was a small sitting table that allowed its occupant to view the glade from a long low window, it, too, shuttered against the light, keeping all but a thin beam from shining through. With little thought, he moved to the second arch and peered into the darkened room. And froze.

Anine's shadow fell across the doorway. "Do you know what this place is?" she called quietly in the gloomy room.

"Yes," he said, his voice muted. "I think we are in my house."

"W-what?" she said, surprised, walking the span of the large entry room to peer around his frame.

Within the dimness beyond, a large, heavy framed bed emerged off to the left, but it was what stood directly across from the doorway that Marc stared at. Had he not been standing where he was, it would be able to be seen, at least partially, as anyone stepped across the threshold of the front door.

It was a huge lacquered cabinet, a massive oaken thing with ornate designs carved into the open doors and legs, the joints reinforced by gilded braces. A piece of finery that didn't belong in the house, making the surrounding building seem more a shanty than a well-built cabin. Within, as if the gloom nor the dust touched it, was a full suit of plate and chain armor glinting in the meager light. A large shield stood at its feet, a heraldic device etched into its face, a curling dragon in gold clasping a disk on which several raised lines radiated outward from the center. The whole was surrounded by nestling dark cloth that lined the interior of the closet. It was something he expected to see within a noble's house or the court of a ruler. Out here, in the middle of nowhere, it was a complete surprise.

"What makes you think this is yours?" Anine asked. It was a soft whisper directed at his ear, her hand waving out in front of him to gesture at the wardrobe.

Marc said nothing in reply for a few seconds, instead pulling something tied on a chord from under his shirt and pulling it over his head. He placed it in her outstretched hand, saying softly, "This is why."

Even in the dim light, she could see the amulet at the end of the chord was an exact replica of the disc held by the dragon herald on the shield. Strange as the situation was, the odds suddenly shifted into his favor. "What is it?" she asked.

Marc stepped forward, taking his eyes away long enough to give the entire room a cursory glance, then moved across the floor until he stood in front of the cabinet. Tentatively, he reached out and touched the design emblazoned on the shield, studying it closely. "I'm not. . . sure," he said over his shoulder. "But I have no doubt this is mine." The final answer was etched into the shield along the top edge. Several runes played across it. Though he couldn't read them, they were exactly the same as the ones that graced the base of the blade that he held loosely in his hand. In fact, close now to the closet, he could see some inconspicuous brackets near the shield that looked like it could accommodate the sword.

Wordlessly, he placed the blade within their embrace, a perfect fit and a feel of completion that wasn't there before.

A solid lump of lead formed in his stomach, and, not understanding why, he lifted the sword from the brackets and shut the doors to the cabinet with his empty hand. They closed silently on well-oiled hinges, and he noted that not a trace of dust filmed the polished wood, probably a minor piece of magic. Once the doors had blocked the view of the armor, the disconcerting feeling in his gut lifted. *Odd*, he thought.

He waited, looking at the gilded, ornamented doors as if he could see through them into the dark interior at the armor, willing his memories back. Still, though, nothing but the past few days were available to him. Anine became a soft presence at his back as she stepped behind him. Forcing the strange feelings and thoughts, he turned, smiled at Anine, and asked, "Shall we find something to eat?"

She was looking at him strangely, her eyes smoky, a quirk at the corners of her mouth. A tingle worked down the back of his neck, starting at both sides of his head where his jaw connected to it, causing his mouth to water. Almost before he could swallow, she leaned in and placed her lips softly against his. Heat moved down his body, her lips lingering. Their touch against his, ephemeral with gauzelike softness. His heart rolled.

"Thank you," she whispered as she pulled away.

"For what?" he asked, finding his voice a bit ragged.

"For coming along when you did," she said. "For helping when you didn't need to."

"It was chance that I. . ."

"Shh!" she said, placing a finger to his lips. "Don't mess up the image I have." The finger was removed only when he nodded his acquiescence. "Yes. Let's get something to eat."

"I'll see if there are stores," Marc said quietly, his body still reacting to the kiss, a knot of anxiousness growing in his chest. Anine stepped away, grinning, pulled her dull hair around in front of her face and looked at it quickly before flipping it back over her shoulder.

"While you do that," she said, a playful glint in her eyes. "I think I will take advantage of the stream behind your house." She left him then, heart pounding, Marc's mind a windfall of bafflement as his emotions warred. A carefully timed smile thrown back over her shoulder as she stepped through the front door caused a more intense heated rush within his blood.

Marc lingered for several moments once she had disappeared, watching her lithe form in his mind's eye, smelling the soft floral scent that existed under the smell of dirt and sweat, feeling her touches upon his skin, the press of her body while they rode. With a deep, forced sigh, he propped the re-scabbarded sword against the threshold she passed through and moved himself into the kitchen area and to the slim door.

It opened easily, squeaking only slightly, revealing a tight rock path that led to an outhouse straight out from the door and moved back along the side of the house to another one several feet down the wall. It was locked, a simple key and bolt embedded in the wood below the handle. Without thinking, he reached to the top of the frame and found the old key that rested there.

He was placing it within the key hole when he smiled broadly, realizing the infinitesimal triumph his subconscious mind just had. The tumblers rolled and the bar slid back, allowing him to push the door open, another smile coming to his mouth.

The oddly protected room was a pantry, lined with shelves full of preserves, stores, and casks. A very narrow, steep stairwell plunged into darkness near the back of the pantry from where cool brisk air wafted. A cold storage. *Tonight*, he thought. *We feast.*

The cold room was several yards beneath the ground, lit only by a small oil lamp he brought down with him from its place on a shelf up in the pantry where it sat next to a piece of flint and steel. The light was wan, but it glittered back at him from the millions of tiny ice crystals that frosted the walls and ceiling. On the floor in the center of the room was a large smoothed over lump of ice about the size of his head. It was colder near it.

He toed the lump, studied it both standing and kneeling, touched it, wondered about it, knowing that his locked mind held the answer. But he decided the mystery would have to wait when his stomach growled out in frustration. He looked around the tiny room, found what he thought might be some smoked and cured ham, grabbed it, looked under the stair and saw a rack filled with bottles, slid one from it, and retreated up the stair.

In the pantry, he added some things that caught his attention, and, arms full, backed out, closing the door awkwardly with his foot. The oven was quickly filled with wood, lit and stoked, his choosings spread out over the preparation table as he trundled about looking for utensils. As a second thought, he started a fire in the hearth, more for light against the coming darkness than for heat, as the air outside was comfortably warm.

Anine returned just as dusk was giving way to nightfall, his feast nearly finished, not noticing the growing dimness, lost within the menial task. His heart leapt when he turned and saw her, her fresh appearance newly startling. She wore clean, un-ripped clothing. It was a pale plain dress that was obviously too big for her frame but ingeniously tucked and tied with a belt such that it still accentuated the curves of her body. Her skin was pristine, unmarred now by the dirt of the road, and her hair, wet still, gleamed in the flickering light. Anine seemed even to stand with a more stately posture, and her eyes seemed more lively, the surrounding skin smoothed and relaxed.

"What took you?" Marc asked idly. "You have been gone quite a while."

"I brushed and fed Whitesteel," she answered with a silky voice. He arched his brow, another elusive memory floating through his brain.

"He let you?" he replied.

"Of course." Smiling around the answer as if she knew beforehand what his question was. "He is quite magnificent."

"I suppose he is." He gave in, turning back to the oven to stir the contents of one of his pots. Marc turned back to see her moving around the large sitting room, checking and lighting the small oil lamps with a burning ember from the fire in the hearth, bringing into being a soft cozy glow that reached into the corners and formerly dark places in the rafters. The flickering embraced her slim figure, highlighting her dark hair and soft skin, evaporating her clothing just enough that it revealed the silhouette of her body beneath. He could do nothing but allow his eyes to travel the slopes and curves, his chest tightening pleasantly around his suddenly thudding heartbeat. When she turned, a knowing smile came to her rose-petal lips that turned his blood molten and sent a flush of heat up his face. But she said nothing, walking slowly through the sitting room toward him.

Stepping under the arch, she, likewise, began lighting the lamps in the kitchen area, moving slowly and silently, eyeing and smiling at him every so often, brushing up against him as she passed, her flowery clean scent causing him pause as it embraced him, tantalized him, leaving a faint touch in the air that stood separate from the smells of the cooking meat and vegetables. It became incredibly difficult for him to concentrate on the meal, his hunger suddenly not for food.

Once finished, she retired to the sitting room after gracefully accepting a cup of chilled wine from Marc, courtesy of the mysteriously cold storage room, to sit and gaze into the flickering hearth fire. Watching the dance of the low flames, her legs crossed and tucked back, cup held loosely in her lap, she looked at peace. The light from the glowing lamps softly lining her face was markedly enhanced by her smooth features instead of the other way around, as if it were originating from her skin. Marc stared for many long moments, unable to break the line of sight.

Hesitantly, he finally turned and tended the finishing meal, the raging fires of his emotions working against his thoughts, drawing them away from the food he was preparing and leading them into the room where Anine sat, wondering about her sudden affection, wondering at his own feelings, a maelstrom of pleasurable straining spinning around a tight reluctance he had felt before, with Maelyrin, just before he left the ffolk village. What it was, he did not know, much less why. But, he knew he should. Somehow, he knew it was vitally important, yet, still, his clogged mind returned a staunch refusal.

They ate, silently, at the small table in the kitchen area, the shutters thrown open, a cool breeze wafting through, carrying the buzz and chirping of crickets and other night insects. The meal, a thick vegetable stew with slices of smoked ham was a delectable king's feast compared to the dried, cured jerky they had been subsisting on for the last few days. Each bite was savored by both, more so by Anine it seemed. Between small mouthfuls, she watched Marc, caressing his eyes with an intent, deliberate look that he reflected back to her, body reacting, heart clenching, mind rebelling.

With an uncomfortable clearing of his throat, he began picking up the dishes once they had finished their meal. The touch of her hand was a sudden shock, so heavy in its lightness, that it stopped him cold, drew the gaze of his eyes into hers. She rose slowly, never breaking the physical connection as her hand slid up toward his elbow.

Their intense gaze raged furiously, their needs and wants communicating themselves across the tiny span. His arm wrapped her quickly, but he needn't pull her. She stepped into him voluntarily, their lips meeting in a trembling, needful kiss; a soft exploration of their souls.

Time stopped.

Marc forgot about the dishes.

They separated after a long tremulous span that sent the world spinning away and back again. The light seemed softer, the warmth greater. Emotions raging, he stepped away to catch his breath and get a handle on himself, the knot of discomfort growing with the maelstrom. Before thought could reassert itself, they stepped into each other's embrace again, the kiss becoming more stormy, their arms beginning to clutch.

Longer moments passed before an unwilling break occurred, both of them pulling away from each other, breath heaving from their chests, color rising in their cheeks. Her gaze was a smoldering mix of embers behind the brown of her irises; his, a fiery look that strode the line between man and animal, the slate intense. The space between them, a void of coolness wrapping the flames.

"I need a moment," she said suddenly, her voice husky. His brows drew together, confusion working onto his face. She nodded toward the kitchen door, beyond it, holding his gaze with hers until the light of insight burst, and he smiled and nodded in return.

Pulling away was almost painful; a slow, subtle detaching of an envelope that blocked out the rest of the world, letting in, first, the crackle of the fire and chirp of crickets, then the scent of the food and pungent smell of burning oil, then the individual beacons of light and the materialization of the surrounding house and its furnishings. Lastly, he felt his place in the room as the earth pulled him down against the floor. All the sights, smells, sounds flowed into each other, coalescing into the singular reality normal to him as Anine disappeared through the thin side door, pulling the wooden plane closed behind her, snapping the final connection they had just been sharing. He sighed, roughly, pushing his feelings back down into the pit of his stomach, and quickly slammed back the remaining wine in his cup. The sweet alcohol tingled against his tongue and down his throat. He huffed again.

The night air was cooling against her skin and the door, rough through the thin fabric at her back. Her hand on her chest did nothing to quell the thudding of her heart. Anine just needed a minute, a strengthening of resolve and a last questioning of herself before she became swept up in the rush of emotion she was experiencing. Just a pause before she returned to the man that had become a major stabilizing part of her otherwise shattered life, Marc, a hero sought after and found, a light in the darkness.

While scanning the moon swept glade, she wondered about the rushing emotions she felt, just as Marc did, unbeknownst to her. She thought it had been growing since she saw him standing within the gray light, pinched between the obscuring boards of the overturned wagon at the site where Havlek and his family were murdered, growing slowly, overtaking the cold emotionless void she had been in. Like a flame intent on engulfing wet wood. Each time he had chosen not to take advantage of her situation, each time he lent himself as a shelter for her crumbling spirit, only strengthened the fire until it was a white blaze that beat back that cold dark and warmed her in ways she had not felt in many years.

She stepped from the house and walked along the path toward the privy, lifting her face to the swollen moon, staring at its stationary position in the sky, a large round pearl amid a glittering field of diamonds scattered on a dark velvet curtain. Calming even if it no longer rose, set, or waxed and waned, a singular full presence that illuminated the darkness with its silvery light, sheening the ground and sparkling along the flowing water of the stream in molten slivers. It was something she had rarely noticed in her short life.

Anine questioned herself not on what she was about to do, not about what she was going to give the man that kept her from careening into an oblivion that she must surely have descended into, but whether her motives were right. Whether she was doing it out of some necessity or compensation rather than because she wanted to; whether her feelings for him were true and not born of a desperation caused by her recent losses. She questioned the swelling in her chest as she thought of him, of his rugged handsomeness, his patient kindness. It was not an easy thing for her. Anine had always been able to know, understand, and, mostly, control her motivations before when her life had been the daughter of a wealthy merchant, when the most important things in her life was what fashions were popular, and what new gossip was making the rounds. In retrospect, she chided herself at her stupidity, her incessant clinging to the mundane, lost in a veil of idiocy, sheltered as she was.

Anine hadn't known what life was really like. She hadn't known the horror that must be a part of it. She hadn't known the face of death so intimately. Until a few weeks ago, it was an illusion that others talked about, that happened to someone else to add flavor to the rumors. Her education, though, had been fast, furious, and a terrible realization that she was not immune; that money, no matter in what amounts, could not buy the veil back. Since then, that horrible day when the clans declared sacred war with each other, when her father had been dragged from his carriage, his cries hoarse in the din of a raging battle, the scream of the horses as they died. Since then, she had hidden in sewers, eaten things that crawled in the muck, stolen, and even killed, all in the name of life. Survival. Anine remembered the many times she wondered if life was worth that much fight. She remembered the many times she placed the tip of the dagger at her breast or the blade against the veins in her wrists, unable to summon the strength to push or pull; to end it. For a while hope was a lie, life was a forgotten dream.

Anine changed in those few, long weeks, in ways she didn't understand, but somehow treasured. Now, it was almost a fulfilling; no longer an inscrutable void within that oppressed her outwardly and kept her focused on the unimportant. So, for perhaps the first time, powered by her newfound joy and sense of being, she questioned her motives in ways previously ignored. From the standpoint of giving, instead of taking. Of her chance of redeeming an otherwise worthless existence. She wasn't sure if what she was doing was right, but it felt that way, and the fact that she was scrutinizing her feelings and motives affirmed her decisions. Now, she was stalling, reining in the fear that accompanied unexplored territory.

The snorting of the horse did not shake her from her thoughts. Her mind, distracted as it was, flicked out the idea that it was only Whitesteel, settling in for the night. The realization never came that the steed was safely behind the bolted door of his stall within the barn at the other side of the house. It was only until movement at the far corner, near the storage room, disturbed her deliberations, and, at first, she dismissed it as her imagination. But, she froze where she stood when the horse stepped from under the eave, a thing made of formless shadow sitting astride it, hunched over as if sleeping.

Twin points of sickly light flashed in the vicinity of its head.

Her throat constricted painfully, cutting off any alert she had been about to call out when a second amorphous rider prodded its mount from the tree line to the left, near the tiny outbuilding. It came out beneath the silvery glow of the moon, its form limned with the pale light. It, too, was hunched and twisted beneath a dark cloak. Under the hood, a twin flashing of the first.

Ice slid into her belly, chilling her deeply. They were, both, staring at her, their gazes heavy on her soul, matched pairs of formless figure and immutable glare, unmoving now that their presence was known. A breeze quickened, flowing through the glade in a rush. The flapping of their dark clothing was like thunderclaps in her ears, and a faraway part of her brain could see the mounts they sat upon trembling, eyes wide and rolling while mouths worked silently on bits that were not there. The knots in her stomach worked through the ethereal cold crystallizing her soul and she croaked out something undecipherable, the clench in her barren throat unyielding. . . .

Inside, Marc sipped slowly at a newly filled cup while staring through the warm yellow flames that feasted lazily on the wood within the hearth, staring at the wall of his mind that separated himself from the past few days. Absently, he set the cup down on the small square table near the door, the clocking sound it made setting his thinking into motion. *Anine should be returning soon*, he thought, his chest swelling and blood rushing at the picture of her that came to the forefront. Her lithe figure, glistening hair, the flowery scent and the soft press of her body. The feel of her lips still lay upon his and her taste still in his mouth. Marc wished that he could tap into the wellspring of his past before the inevitableness of the night occurred, wanted to tell her more of himself before their lovemaking, needed to give more of himself before she gave herself. . . .

And the nagging discomfort that seemed to swell when his emotions did, increased as his arousal did. The elusiveness bothered him as much as its appearance. Not knowing what it was frightened and angered him, a knot in the pit of his stomach that was at the core of the other feeling, swallowed by it as if to mask that, too, from his prying curiosity. "What *is* that?" he whispered at the fire. A moment later he shook his head and pushed the discomfort away and its surrounding thoughts.

Through the thick walls, he heard Whitesteel neigh loudly and wondered if Anine were spending her thoughtful minutes with the giant steed, knowing that she must be having similar self-conversations that he was. Knowing that she was as frightened as she was excited about their evening. No memories, he figured his insight must only be a result of his age. A sideline thought surfaced, telling him it had been some time since Anine stepped outside, and he wondered if he should go to her.

The decision came quickly, but as he reached out for the handle, something heavy thudded against the door and the swing bar lock began to shake and shimmy rapidly. His brows came together suddenly, confusion and concern rolling onto his face. "What the. . ." he began.

Something slammed into the door with a resounding *thock*! the wood splaying outward from the smooth plane where the steel head impacted. Splinters shot out from the upper corner, flashes of white that flittered through the air and onto the floor. A spine-splitting scream shattered time.

"*Anine!*"

Marc heard himself cry out above the echo of the cracking wood. His hand shot out, angling toward the sword that leaned against the frame. It halted, inches away from the leather handle.

The dam in his mind fissured.

He stared down at his hovering hand, shock spreading quickly over his features. Outside, several fleet knocks followed by a straining, "Marc. . . .please!" He forced his hand to move. It did not.

The cracks in the dam spidered across the face rapidly, chunks of it beginning to fall away. . .

"Marc!" Anine sobbed, rapping heatedly, panic seeping through the wood. *Marc*. His name echoed in his mind. *Why?* He screamed silently at his impotent hand. A strong hiss and another steel shaft thudded into the wood higher up, drawing a frenzied shriek from behind the thin, infinite, barrier between them. ". . . please!"

Holes appeared in that mind barrier, the structure unable to hold as the cracks continued to race. Things began slipping through.

"Marc!" she pleaded again, her pounding desperate, the sound blanketing the room. *Marc . . . Marc. . .* Thunder boomed from the barn as Whitesteel's hooves met the heavy timber of his stall, his scream, fury that ran the length of the glade. Tears, angry, frustrated trails, leaked from his eyes. "Marc!" her terror filled voice reached into him and gripped his heart. "Marc! Please!" *Marc. . . Marc. . .*

Aeric. . . .

The dam holding back his memories fell inward on itself, his former self surging forward, sweeping away the remnants of the false life only several days old. He cried out, tried to thrust his hand at the hilt with pure, terror-wrought will, eyes clenching and heart leaping when nothing happened. Whitesteel kicked the stall harder, the sharp cracking of wood riding his furious screams. Beyond the door, Anine pleaded, begged him to open the door, her voice splintered horror that ripped into his being and shredded him. "Please! Please. . ." *I can't!* he shouted into the silence of his mind, fighting the pain in his soul.

His eyes widened. The hiss heard from far off, stealing forward in the night in terrible slowness. Whitesteel screamed, Anine implored, his mind and soul tore asunder as his hand refused to move, his entire body rebelling against him. The shaft buried itself, thrusting out a horrid grunt that shot through the barrier and slammed him hard, stopping his heart. "Nooo!" his voice ripped out, a long shriek that didn't block out the heavy thud against the wood. Whitesteel squealed again, thrashing against the door of his stall as Marc fell into the plane before him, his body finally reacting as if a coiled spring, his hand coming against it roughly, another shriek flying from him. He slid down, dimly aware of the many stinging splinters tearing into his face; his hand, somehow free to move now that the sword was not its target, tried to grip through the wood, scrabbling painfully against it like a wounded thing. Harsh breathing filled his ears, counterpoint to the blood rushing through it and a bright red light shone up at him from his chest. In the barn, timber cracked like thunder, shattering and falling with wooden clarity.

Something dark pooled on the hard packed floor, flowing beneath the space under the door, liquid, hot, seeping into his clothing and scalding his skin. He watched it dumbly, eyes vacuous, dipping his fingertips in it and bringing them up into the light. A second later, a ragged whisper reached him through the door, "Marc. . . please," it said, followed by a strangled, single cough. "No!" he sobbed back, his hand clawing the door, dragging bloody furrows in the surface. "No. . ." Water streamed from his eyes steadily, clouding his vision, and a ringing buzz droned in his ears, adding to the agonizing deafness that was somehow unable to block the frayed breaths vibrating through the door, carrying torn whimpers and gurgling pleads that shredded his being.

Anine's final agony-filled sigh drove a spike deep into him, laying him open as readily as the ragged claws of a beast ripping his flesh. The frenzied crash and squeals of Whitesteel disappeared, his mind blocking out everything but that last exhalation, clasping it, trying to hold it forever, even though it cut deeply, its edges razored and ragged. He could only stare at the puddling dark ink, wondering what it was. . .

. . . *blood*. . .

wondering why. . . .

He heard the voice through the haze of shock, replaying it after the fact, it sounding like sand grinding under stone, coming slow like the oozing of molasses, or blood. "Too bad, Pendragon," it cried. "you would be dead by now if you hadn't escaped."

. . . *Crowlin*. . . his splintered mind whispered.

"Unfortunately, your death has been postponed," it said after what seemed forever. "But we'll be sure to visit you soon."

"Anine," he whispered, his voice croaking past a raw throat, eyes and hands clenching.

"Enjoy your woman," it came back through the sudden thudding of several sets of hooves. "We did!"

"Anine. . . No!" Planting his knuckles against his forehead, he squeezed tightly, eyes, fists, teeth, body. "No." *Please. . . please, Marc. . . .*

He sprang to his feet, screaming out his rage and pain, a long, wrenching wail that shattered the silence once more. Arm shooting out, no longer constrained by the need, his hand grasped the hilt of his sword in a fierce grip, ripping it from the floor, the scabbard launching away from the gleaming blade and clattering somewhere in the next room. He stared at it, eyes wide and red with madness, huffing hoarsely, his breath steaming along the flat of the blade held close. He could see the tight pallid features and the ragged crimson cheek, the steel of his eyes broken. Anine's body was a heavy presence beyond the door, Crowlin's voice a grating in his brain, his rage expanding like a conflagration in dry grass. Whitesteel, fitful in the barn. . . .

The sword bit fiercely into the table, wood shattering loudly and wine becoming a crimson spray. Another shriek erupted, releasing his fury in a glittering arc that crashed again and again into the broken table, then the nearby chair. Wood and cloth splintered, ripped and flew, a raging hurricane that destroyed unheeding. The fire spat and hissed, a splattering shower of oil awakening it, its container, a torn brass receptacle blackening quickly, sending sparks and embers bouncing out onto the carpeted floor. Chips peeled away from the walls, mud concrete exploded, clouding together with the thick smoke from the lamps and coiling up from the smoldering carpet each time the ringing metal bit into something.

Marc raged, screaming out his agony, demolishing everything around him, bent on shattering the mocking blade, himself even, driving around the room in a loping stumble, throwing things that got in the way that was too close for the sword; chest heaving in terrible gasps, vision fuzzing around the edges, breath harsh and throat burning. He lurched through the archway into the bedroom, his exhaustion pulling the sword from his hands and flinging it across the darkened room. The staccato crash of exploding porcelain flew back at him, washing against him without effect as he tumbled forward into the cabinet, his swiping hands flinging the doors open, as his failing body drove him to his knees before it.

Looking on the old armor, hands outstretched as if pleading, he stopped and stared, eyes taking on a clarity that would have startled him had he been looking in a mirror. He gazed at the set for many seconds before a ragged, soul-broken sob wracked him. "Why?" he begged to it. "Why?"

He cried far into the night, fighting back his exhaustion with pure anger for as long as he could until he simply fell over in sleep, huddled by the cabinet containing his armor. Armor belonging to Aeric Pendragon. . . .

Chapter 38

States of Mind

*A*lexandria's chest clenched, sucking in a loud breath as she drove up out of her dreamless sleep, clutching at the clothing covering her heart. The breath was locked away, refusing to break from the prison of her burning lungs. Her heart pounded like thunder. Then, after many seconds, her breath exploded outward, "Aeric. . ." her mouth blurted. *Where did that come from?* The burning pain in her chest began to smooth out as her body picked up its natural rhythm.

Next to her, Del slept soundly, a slight snore punctuating the slow pattern of his breathing. A moonbeam slanted through the overhanging branches to caress his face. She scanned around with misty eyes. Sandoren was nowhere to be seen within the pale moon-spotted shelter, nor in the glade beyond. Behind her, one of the horses they had procured earlier in the day whickered softly. Alex glanced in its direction, saw three large shadows, and turned back, still clasping the shirt over her heart, it still thumping wildly within her heaving chest. South of them, not far, only a few miles, the Eldritch stirred the backdrop of the Natural, remaining the ever-present loom of death that shadowed their every move.

Alex cocked her head a little. It seemed a little more cautious today than normal, and she wondered if it were due to the pack of wolves that paced them to the north. The family of the grizzled she wolf that lent their help to her, an Earthmother.

In fact, it was a wonder the female wasn't near. She must have moved off to hunt after they had turned in.

She waited for many minutes until the pain left her breast and it settled down, wondering what had awakened her, knowing the answer as soon as the question floated up. The man she sought. Aeric. And he was in pain. She felt it although she didn't know the reason, and now, conscious, the feeling faded, dispersing like mist.

They were close now. The wolves keeping track of him relayed that to them earlier, several hours ago, that he and his companion had stopped at a structure. A house. They should catch up to them by tomorrow unless the stopover was just that, a warm shelter before traveling on. At any rate, she was close enough that the Air Bond that connected them was faintly felt. Then she could chase him into Perdition itself, as long as she kept within that distance.

Alex looked up through the shadowed maze of tree limbs, barely able to see a sliver of the moons through them, and she huffed a little. Since the Dark Night, the celestial lamps had refused to move from the vantage directly overhead, a ghost that stayed throughout the day, quietly blotting out the noon day sun during High Summer, two months gone, though, by the incessant heat. . . . Its lack of movement worked against her attempts to gauge the passing of time. The trees, the shelter they gave broke up the heavens enough that she could not identify any of the stars that she could see winking through the canopy. She finally closed her eyes and let the Earth itself tell her how far morning was.

Several hours still, though her intentions were to leave in only a few, using the remainder of the night to close the gap. That is, if Sandoren returned before then. His activity was normal; there was no doubt in her mind that he was scouting around, forever restless, but it was his erratic behavior that troubled her though she understood the driving motivation behind it. His discomfort around others was being severely tested, first with Del, now with the other. *Aeric*, she corrected mentally. In all their years together, contact with others was generally kept to a minimum, more out of necessity than anything else, at least from her standpoint. His was voluntary. Even now, she was not quite sure if it was his discomfort around others, or his uncommonly large preference for solitude. The combination, though, proved unshakable. And here she was telling him they were going to travel extensively with others.

A nightbird suddenly broke from its perch and flitted through the branches near her, the sound interrupting her thoughts. Alex looked to find what had disturbed it, thinking it Sandy, but it was the wraithlike form of the she wolf padding through the trees that she found, nearing to a respectfully close distance and laying down for the night. Her luminous yellow eyes flashed twice from the moonlight before closing for the few hours of rest she would get.

A sudden yawn assailed Alex, and she decided to follow the lead of their silent companion. Still concerned over the pain that woke her, Aeric's pain, she lay back down on the soft ground, letting the night work on her eyelids. She was asleep in moments.

To her mind, it was only minutes later when she felt a hand on her shoulder, shaking her softly, Sandy's voice drifting through the haze of sleep, saying, "Alex, it's time to go. Alex . . ."

She sent him an irritated moan, wanting very much to nestle back into the obliviousness of sleep, but the shaking and speaking persisted until it snapped the umbilical keeping her in that realm. Frustrated, she swam upward into full consciousness. One eye winked open, seeing the dark blotch that was Sandoren's face above her. Even though blacked out, she could tell he wore a grim expression. It irritated her further. "Okay, okay," she hissed. "I'm awake." The shaking stopped and he moved away, toward the horses.

Alex lay a minute longer, her body leaden with sleep, yawns systematically attacking her, bringing tears to still tired eyes, before struggling her muscles into motion. She saw that Del was already awake, his stupefied expression compounded by his own tiredness. He gazed dully up at the moonlight, and she couldn't help recalling the intense vortex of Power he generated yesterday morning. And she couldn't help the shiver that rose in response to the thought. Alex hoped that, for whatever reason she was sent to find him, she would be able to teach him to control the vast amounts of energy he could draw before he Extinguished himself. Or them for that matter.

Sluggishly, joints popping, Alex stood, stretching out the last vestiges of her shortened rest, noting glumly that the air was still warm. It would prove to be a stifling day, even though the sun was moving south and the light it cast onto the world placed it in perpetual morning; normally a peaceful non glare that carried a comforting coolness on its back. Maybe, if they were lucky, an afternoon shower would chase away the heat for a while. Of course, she couldn't feel the flows of the Elements that would grant such a reprieve. It was still too early to really be sure, but her bet would be that there would be no rain today. At least, however, they might get one step closer to the goal she was chasing, whatever that was.

The Living Trees could be somewhat nebulous in their desires, to put it lightly. Alex snorted quietly and smiled. That was a very mild explanation. They were extremely vague. Her smile reversed quickly when she remembered that nearly all of them were destroyed not too long ago. Another disabling loss to that so precious Balance. Sandy's mordant complaints of fighting a losing battle were not as far off the mark as he thought, his sarcasm being more a prod at her stubbornness than a known fact. Perhaps if he knew the truth, he might be a little more accepting of the others.

But, what to do? Where did the pieces fit? She knew that Del and Aeric were integral in connection with the Wound, but how? She knew the Wound had to be closed, but how? *How?* How, how, how was she supposed to close it? It was far too powerful for her to even get within miles of it. And it was getting stronger each day. It was as if it were a cancer that grew within her, that she was constantly cognizant of, even while asleep. A gnawing itch that couldn't be healed and was feeding itself with her own life force, consuming it. Inevitably, the Wound would throw the Balance so far off kilter, that the world would not be able to restore itself. Of course, that was exactly what the various races were doing, only, nowhere as quickly.

There was still hope for them, at least.

The arguments she had with herself were old. Combined with the disparity of her sleep wasted attitude, it was not something she should be entreating with herself about just now. Trying to force calmness into her frustration and anger, Alex pushed back at those thoughts and set about getting ready to move on.

Unfortunately, Alex found she had nothing to contribute to or occupy her mind with. Sandoren was tightening the girth-straps of their mounts, their supplies already tied in neat bundles behind the cantles of their saddles. It did nothing for her irritation. Instead, she stepped close to the first horse and touched its cheek, sending calming energy into the animal just before she released her Healing into the beast, drawing from all the Elements around her. The horse jerked, but only slightly, a quickly cut off neigh disrupting the silent morning. Alex let the rush move through her for several minutes, feeling the animal's systems and organs strengthening, before moving to the next.

They had found their mounts only about an hour's travel north of where Del had unleashed the vortex, trapped behind a rotted fence surrounding a wasted pasture connected to a dilapidated farm house. They were malnourished and abused. Skittish animals that at first refused to even come at her call, instead crowding the fence directly opposite them, finding safety only between themselves.

The farmer, a middle aged man just as dilapidated as the farm had run out at them with a pitchfork, shakily threatening them to be on their way. It took little to convince him to alter his course, Sandy sliding his blade half way from the scabbard, with his left hand no less, to show the enraged scarecrow the gleam of the blade was enough. He agreed to Sandoren's alternative more quickly than she would have thought, throwing the pitchfork down within moments and backing away a few steps, gnarled, work-callused hands held up in placation.

When he was informed, rather sternly, of their plans for the horses, he bitterly protested and threatened them with all manner of bodily harm, all the while backing up toward his leaning domicile. He hurled one last threat, punctuated by rapid fist shaking before slamming the door at them, the force yanking the top hinge from its mooring and causing the door to sag awkwardly, revealing the dark interior of the place. He didn't show his face again until they had nearly disappeared into the forest line.

There had been four of the pathetic creatures, stubbornly, fearfully resisting any attempts to bring them closer, their skin, thin coverings over skeletal racks, making them look like blankets draping overturned chairs and stools. So badly were they neglected that she, at first, thought that it would be better to simply put them down, and, in the end, she had had to hasten the death of one of them, painlessly stopping the creature's heart, the normal sweetness of using the Power leaving a bitter taste in her mouth. The horses were still young and the death was a terrible waste and an affront to all that she stood for. She cremated the body as she had those in the ffolk village, more to keep the farmer from using it for food, or any other purpose he might profit by.

The others were, thankfully, just shy of the brink, and she was able to conduct her Power into them in a more gratifying manner, its Energy pulsing through them, energizing them, healing them and nourishing them. Causing their salient fear to disperse and their trust of her become complete. Though not the best alternative, it was the most advantageous, for them as well as the horses, since they had neither the time to properly nurture the animals back to health, nor would it have been an easy task had they had the time. The creatures' health was so bad, their bodies were just as likely to reject any nourishment as they were to accept it. Out of necessity, she gave them more than they should have had, herself threatening to tip the Balance so that they might catch up to their quarry before too much more time had passed, but they drank in the Power as they would have food, allowing it to work with them instead of against them.

The tack and saddles had been found among the clutter of unused tools and stores within the dry rotted barn, all worn, but not in terribly bad shape. The drying leather needing only some of the same care, nourishing oil and some new rivets. The saddle blankets, of course, would have to be replaced when they could, but the moth eaten wool still had some fluff left in them.

The Power she now directed into them was far less than before, their short ride yesterday interspersed with several resting and grazing periods helpful. The lush forage they had received would do them far more good than what she could give them.

She finished up, scratching the third horse, a roan that Del had named 'Day', behind the ear a few dozen times. Alex felt better, her frustration receding into the background of her mind to fret from the shadows. Unfortunately, it didn't vanish altogether, and Alex thought she might warn Sandoren. She suspected he knew already, however.

And with his attitude shifts, the coming day should prove an interesting one.

Chapter 39

Languishing in the Aftermath

*I*t was funny how the mind worked. In the dim light, he could plainly see the scuffs up the insides of his boots where the stirrup straps constantly wore, but he could not bring forth the face of his wife or his children. His bones ached and the thin long stinging wounds on his body burned, but he was more concerned with the ragged holes in his wool uniform. His longest friend, confidant, and companion lay dying next to him in the squalid, rank cell, and he was fussing over a missing button.

How they got there, he did not know. How long they had been there, he could not tell. Light filtered in from somewhere beyond the small barred window in the heavy iron door, but he could not fathom from what. The corridor outside extended both ways beyond his angle of view. The only thing he was certain of was that they were deep underground with tons of oppressive rock above and around them. They were in the fortress of Tergaard.

Next to him, Turcot moaned and listed on his side, drawing a look from Anlin. The pale fuzz of light glimmered across a sheen of sweat on his face and, in the coolness, he could feel the heat radiating from his body in thick, oily waves. Somewhere, water dripped hollowly and loudly in the terrible, otherwise silence. There was no one else in the large, moist cell. And if there were anyone in any cell near them, they were more silent than the dripping *plock!* of water.

Anlin's body shivered, a quick reminder of the sunken chill of the place. But it was not completely the chill that brought on the spasm. Underneath the fog of his brain, in vivid flashes that caused his wounds to twinge, bounded the utterly black creatures that had attacked the column. Deathly silent creatures of ink. Long claws, empty faces, terrible death boiling from the ground itself, the very darkness of shadow coming to life to destroy them. Even with it behind them, the very thought made his guts freeze.

Suddenly, once acknowledged, Anlin was wrenched from the moist cell and dying friend and thrown back into the battle, the sun now a blazing orb of fire above shining down on the flat bodies of them, surrounding him and his men like a plague. He reached for a sword that was not there, unable to close away the screams of his dying troops. The sand was red from bloody rain and time after time one of the things charged him, an insanely fast leaping gait that furrowed and tore the crimson sand. He watched, his inability to close his eyes painful, as they came closer, each time to inevitably be intercepted by one of his soldiers or a horse.

Anlin found he was able to walk freely among the carnage, untouched, as though his was a vortex of calmness in the violent storm, watching in horror as those he knew, he commanded, fell under the sea of terrible blackness. Brak, Ferlnan, Pilek, a flood of names slid by him as horrid death masks passed before his eyes. But though it seemed he was safe, he felt that it was a ruse, that the things were massing behind him, poised to rip him apart as well. However, when he turned, he saw only more of the same massacre.

Something was there, though, he felt it, tickling the hairs on his neck like a foul breeze. Or breath. Staying just out of view, around the darkened corners of his vision. His throat was tight and a coppery taste lay within its depths.

The something shifted, a shuffling grating against stone that brought him around quickly. Anlin's eyes stared at a heavy door that, for a moment, he didn't recognize. A deep bone shiver awakened his senses and he realized that he, too, was gripped by a fever. His wounds cried out icely.

The shuffling noise filtered through the door again, pimpling his flesh and placing barriers between his sudden lucidity and the fever wrought visions. Still, it took a moment for him to realize that something was moving in the corridor beyond their cell, something furtive and languid. Something bulky that had to drag itself through the wet darkness.

He held a painful breath, straining to hear against the buzzing deep in his ears. Nothing. Nothing but the steady plocking of water and the wheeze of Turcot's breath. *I'm still hallucinating.* He was thinking when the bulk moved in the hallway again.

Anlin's body reacted, pulled itself up against the moist cold stone of the wall, one hand flailed about looking for something; a loose stone, length of wood, anything that could be used as a weapon, while his eyes gazed heavily upon the rust flecked slab of thick iron. It moved, paused, then moved again, each cessation an interminable span of painfully held breath; each shuffle, a terrible grating sigh that exhaled through the tiny square window, focused by the rigid lines of its frame in such a way that he could almost feel a rancid wind against his face. The wan light peering through it wavered, a dark bar of shadow sliding against it, making it wink.

The sound slumped closer, its shuffling louder with underpinnings of bone dragging against stone, the dark bar growing until it blotted out all the dim light. Anlin's body continued to scrabble backwards, trying to press himself into the wall, even though he could not tear his eyes from the window. Beside him, Turcot's breath had become hollow and rapid.

The quivering returned, the deep infestation of his fever sparked by the terrible fear gnawing at his numbing mind. His hand, unable to find a weapon tried to dig itself into the floor. Flashes of molten pain shot through him as his nails peeled away from his fingertips.

He cried out when he saw a beady yellow eye materialize between the bars in the small window. It seemed to glow and cocked up and down as if taking in the entirety of the cell. With terrible finality, it settled on him, and its gaze was leaden. Anlin clamped down on his tongue painfully to keep from yelling out again.

The eye rested on him for an indeterminate time, digging into him with slow deliberation, peeling away the layers of his humanity. He could do nothing but stare back while forcing himself to suck air into his clamping chest and squeezing it out in rough sighs. Suddenly, the eye flicked downward and the tumblers in the lock thundered throughout the cell as they rolled. A loud thud against the iron sent the slab squealing open, the sound a forerunner to the cloud of utter stench that surged forward into the portal and flooded the room. Anlin gagged and choked as eons of rotted cloth, decayed flesh, and ancient dirt flowed thickly into his nose and mouth.

Beyond the door it stood, a humped figure draped in mottled layers of rotted clothing, edged by the dim light in the corridor. An elongated head jutted from the bundle, a beaked buzzard-like head that jerked and cocked continuously from side to side, first bringing one of its beady eyes to bear, then both, then back to the opposite single gaze. A whining squawk issued from its beak, standing the hairs on his neck, before it shuffled into the cell, its eyes playing first across the prone body of Turcot, then him.

Anlin growled in fear and tried to press into the wall again. He was sure the temperature dropped several degrees. The thing let another questioning whine issue from its beak followed by a series of short squawks that rattled his spine, then stared at him, its head cocked. Its eyes blinked rapidly. Anlin could only stare back, unable to distinguish details, only blocks and shades, as if its very presence swallowed his ability to see straight.

After moments of tense silence, another series of squawks issued from the creature and it shuffled forward a couple of steps, its eyes narrowing in the dimness. The sound of its scraping feet in the room echoed in his teeth and he, once again, strained against the cold stone, trying to move away from it as unrelenting fear prickled through him.

It waved one of its hands, a quick flicking of shade that caused him to flinch and then it huffed, blowing a rancid wind that enveloped his head in numbing stench. The air tingled around him.

"Death will come mercifully if you tell what I desire," it screeched, the words falling from its mouth, perfectly understandable Arquil dragged across gravel. The sound of it pinned Anlin to the cold stone and gripped at his throat. Something squeaked from it, an answering whine he couldn't hold back. In the wan light, he thought he saw the corner of the thing's beak curl up into a smirk. The long drawn whimper came again, eliciting a low grown from Turcot. "Your friend, yes, as well. Merciful death." It nodded, then shuffled forward a step. Anlin saw that the hunched thing leaned on a cane and it clicked on the floor. "Yes. . . You will tell me of those you call master." The cane tip was a brutal flare of pain on his thigh. "Who is the one who commands your army?"

His throat was ragged and his voice came haltingly, but Anlin was finally able to force the fear back long enough to spit, "I am!" The pain of another cane thrust drew a gritted moan.

"The commander of the army whose emblem you bear!" The cane tip struck a third time, landing harshly against the Imperial Coat of Arms embroidered onto the left breast of his uniform coat. There was a dull pop and liquid fire spread through his torso.

Many ragged breaths came and went before he could answer, each one a stab of fluid agony. "One. . . called Von Draden."

Another thrust, another groan. His fever flared with the pain and storm clouds began to form around the peripheries of his vision. Thankfully, his body started to numb itself. "Describe him!" It squawked, another tingle flittered through him, pulling at his vocal chords. Haltingly, far away, he heard himself describe the looming black-clad man. The thing stepped back and gave a pleased whine and nodded to itself again. After many moments, the thing turned and shuffled out of the cell. "Sent them here, yes, yes. He knows I am here." It said it as if talking to itself, but stayed with the Arquil as if solely for his benefit.

The door squealed and shut with a piercing clang and the thundering of the tumblers followed, ratcheting around the cell for what seemed eons and slowly replaced by the steady plop of the dripping water. Anlin groaned, looked at the door, at the single beady eye that stared back at him through the old rusting bars. "Now, yes," its voice was muffled by the door, but it speared him awake just enough to send splinters of ice into his heart. "You will die mercifully."

Anlin's scream followed the creature as it humped down the hallway. And it continued after it was gone, echoed up and down the corridor until his voice gave out. Finally, spent, he lay back against the stone, his body quaking again even though a cloud of heat seemed to surround him. His chest burned fiercely and his breath was short; his mind screamed for rest but his frayed nerves would not allow him to.

Time passed in steady *plocks* of invisible water and ragged moans and breaths of Turcot, each one an anticipation of the next, each one possibly the last. His own body, free now of the monster that had looked upon him with its baleful gaze spasmed regularly in icy hot quivers and a clammy sweat covered his body, soaking into his cloths and keeping whatever warmth they might have lent away from his skin. His eyes wandered over the rough, slime encrusted stone of the cell, a tapestry of dark shiny shades of black running together like watered inks.

Many times, while staring at the wall, the sun would come back, burn deep into his eyes, take him away and leave him places, at times to let him visit with his family, sometimes with the regiment and happier times. Other times he would visit various battlegrounds, watch as death walked among fighting men. The last battle before the Dark Night at the Steps of Ellynthryll against the dark armies of Gelron the Deadlord. Further back, the Border Wars against the united lands of Rendor and Parlin when he was but a young man, and, inevitably, the slaughter of his regiment at the front gates of the fortress. Randomly, he would be drawn back to stare at the blank walls for unknown amounts of time, and it became too difficult to distinguish between hallucination and reality. Whatever part of his sanity remained chose his various trips abroad as the reality he sought, since they were not filled with choking, bone quivering chills and ragged, pain filled breathing.

The noise of clinking metal was as a fly walking on his eyelid, an irritant that returned as soon as the feeble wave of a hand passed by. A spirit wailed in the night, a raucous, hair whitening squeal that drew frightened curses from his mouth and shattered the place where he had been, his wife shimmering like water and vanishing before his outstretched hands, only to be replaced by the dark form of a shadow that meant nothing to Anlin. Even as it slid through the dark place of pain and cold and picked up Turcot.

The dark shape carried the moaning man from the cell while Anlin watched dazedly. It was furtive and quick and a small sane voice whispered through his fever and told him what the creature was. Briefly, he watched more of the things as they ripped his men apart, their screams of death silent in his ears.

It seemed a blink of an eye when he looked up and saw the ink-creature standing over him. He let out a terrified cry and tried to back up, only something cold and hard prevented him from moving away from it. He cried out again. Rough hands fell upon him and jerked him upwards and he thought he could feel the steel-like claws pierce his skin. He struggled, a feeble attempt thwarted by his own weak body. All he could manage was a few epithets directed at the creature as he was lifted and draped over its shoulder.

The rough handling and bouncing was too much for him. A knot of pain pooled at the point where his eyebrows met, pressed against the inside of his skull for an intolerably long time before it exploded in a white flash of light that sent him spiraling back down into blackness.

Chapter 40

Introductions

*M*aelyrin's head was pounding; the reason why she was waking up, she guessed. Something heavy lay across her body, keeping it warm, causing her to want to nestle back into sleep. Her duties could wait. The Faethe could do without her for one day. She needed rest. Her body, a dull aching following the thud of her head, needed rest. She decided to go back to sleep, pulling the blanket up around her chin.

Something nagged at her, kept her from drifting back into the quiet oblivion where her head and body aches disappeared. It started her brain working, rolling things over and over. Whatever the problem was, it was elusive, staying just out of the wan light she was casting around in the dark cavern of her head.

Maelyrin's eyes flashed open, then clenched shut as needles of light stabbed her vision and made her head squeal. She groaned.

She was not at home, she realized suddenly, the images of the past few hours rushing at her out of the dark like a cornered animal. Marc, the bandits, her flight and tumble. . . .

Slowly, she reopened her eyes, allowing the still gray light in slowly, biting back the pain it caused. Covering her was a heavy cloak of some sort, soft, but thick, russet in color, unrecognizable, with a musky scent. Certainly not hers.

"Where did this come from?" she mumbled. The haze in her mind refused to part, her last memory that of the ragged men that were chasing her. Fear swirled and churned anew. *Did they catch me?* She doubted it the second she thought of it. Somehow, Maelyrin figured, if they had caught her she wouldn't be alive now to be wondering about it.

It was then that she remembered the giant, the whooshing air and deadly silver sheen, the cries and screams of dying men. . . . She sat up slowly, gritting against the tightness and ache that flared at the movement, especially in her shoulder. She lay on a soft patch of moss under the spreading limbs of an old weathered elm, its leaves still full and green, even though autumn was supposed to be upon them. A small fire crackled nearby, drawing her sleepy attention. A pot dangled over the low flames from a metal tripod, wisps of steam escaping from it, liquid within gurgling riotously, sometimes spitting some of itself out over the lip to hiss on the fire below. Arranged neatly upon a straw mat placed near it were several utensils, cups, and bowls. Further away was a large leather backpack that she did not recognize either.

Above, through the limbs, the sky was still slate, making it difficult to tell what time of the day it was, though she suspected it was late in the afternoon. She rubbed her eyes with the heels of her hands then slowly wound her hair back and tied it with a leather thong she kept loosely about her wrist.

She took the cloak off of her, studying it as she folded it. It was finely made, tightly stitched. She shrugged and set it aside, looked at her own clothes, dry now but still soiled. She clucked her tongue, then, carefully, brought herself into a kneeling position and looked at her surroundings. The elm was on a gentle rise that sloped away several yards before rising once more, a mild, undulating sea of green flowing away from her between large, reaching trees. Elm, oak, hickory, and several different types of fir.

Movement from the left, a flicker amongst the closeness of the trees not far from where she sat grabbed her attention, led her hand to find the knife at her belt. It wasn't there. Her heart leapt at the realization that she was unarmed. Ignoring the burning pain in her shoulder and body, she twisted, looking frantically for a stout length of wood, her eyes falling on the side of the tree she had been sleeping under and causing her pause. Leaning against the trunk were her pack, her bow, and quiver, still full. Her knife was tucked under the flap, its hilt peeking out from under the worn leather. She relaxed, a little, then reached forward and slid the knife from its sheath as she crept around the trunk, using it as a screen. She waited, listened, then moved slowly forward toward the next, and the next.

Moving silently, using the trees and vegetation to her advantage, she slid forward, farther than she had first thought, catching flashes of movement through the screen, more steadily the closer she got. Finally, she stood at the edge of a break in the trees, shielded from view by a clump of dwarf firs. She tucked the knife into her belt.

It was the giant.

He moved through the small glade, fluidly, powerfully, in a dancelike manner, his companion a slim, long, slightly curved sword that glittered in the muted light of the slate day. From her vantage, she could hear it slice the air, whistling sharply, and it seemed to disappear and reappear as he moved, at times turning into a silver blur that surrounded him and brought forth the fading memory of what she saw just before she passed out.

Maelyrin watched in awe as he moved, standing on one leg one moment, arms held wide, sword moving in a slow arc in front of him as if of its own accord then, with sudden, liquid grace, crouching in a deep stance, the sword circling back and down to slice back to his side in the next moment. So mystified by the strong yet soft movements that, for many long minutes, she failed to notice the giant's height, his pale blue skin and jet eyes.

Had she not been held in thrall by the fluid motion, she might have reacted differently, seeing something frightening or ugly in the visage of the giant. But, in the alien beauty of the deadly dance he performed, the rippling blue of his muscles, glittering black of his eyes, long thick whiteness of his hair and height greater than her reach while standing on the tips of her toes, only blended with its graceful splendor as if one could not be separated from the other without losing the whole. And his face, rugged and not quite human, had such a serene quality to it that she became relaxed and could see nothing ugly or frightening in the creature that had saved her life.

Then she *Looked* at him, in him, through him with her Sight, and was at once calm and at peace with him. What she Saw was a deliberate emptiness. The serene quality of his face was merely a quiet reflection of the utter sereneness within him, a soft, flowing tranquility that was, at once, stronger than the strongest steel, unbreakable, yet fluid and passive. Nothingness that was as much a part of what he was doing as the physical motions. Maelyrin guessed she would be in awe of him if he were merely walking if that serenity were a part of it.

She settled back, got comfortable and watched him as he moved from one stance to the next flawlessly, gracefully, his sword arcing and sliding through the air in impossibly complex patterns. A fine sheen of sweat glistened along his cerulean skin, moistened the loose fitting white shirt in patches under the arms and down the back. He was tireless, whether moving quickly or slowly, and equally powerful. She lost her sense of time, in a way becoming a part of the dance he wove, becoming submerged in the water of serenity that flowed from him.

It was twilight, the gray growing slowly darker when he spoke, his voice soft, yet a rumble that rivaled that of thunder. "You are well?" he asked, his Arquil thick with the lands south. He was standing statue still on one leg, sword vertical in front of his face. It surprised her, first that he appeared to be moving into another stance and suddenly stopped, and secondly, she thought she was well hidden behind the firs, her view of the glade nearly one way.

Maelyrin stood slowly, her muscles screaming in protest, and brushed herself off. He turned toward her in the interim, the slim sword sliding into its scabbard without him having to use his eyes. The movement in and of itself a testament to the danger he posed. She nodded, hiding the wince that had crept onto her face.

"Come," he said, striding toward her, placing a smaller scabbarded weapon in his belt alongside the larger one. The movement startled her, causing a flinch to run through her body. Her knife was up before she thought about it. The giant never stopped, never flinched, nor even looked down at the blade. His eyes, black as midnight with pinpoints of white for pupils, rested almost lazily on her face as he drew close then continued past, forcing her to crane her neck as he stepped by.

Maelyrin let out the breath she had been holding. His lack of reaction spoke volumes. He was either a fool, or so comfortable in his abilities that her feeble show of aggressiveness meant little to him. She knew it was not the former, could sense it, even without the benefit of the past display. Without doubt, the giant was no fool.

Uncomfortably, she fumbled the knife into her belt, amazed that she did not cut herself, and hurried to keep up with the long strides of her blue-skinned rescuer. Once back at the fire, he took the swords from his side and with simple reverence, leaned them against his large pack, then knelt in front of the small mat. She sat down opposite him after he beckoned with a wave of his hand. Without word, he took the kettle from the fire and poured the contents into one of the larger bowls. Steam from the water curled up in the fading light. From several small pouches, he took something and began pinching it into the bowl.

A pungent aroma drifted up with the steam, curling in her nostrils. He stirred it briskly with a small whisk then filled one of the small wooden cups.

"Drink," he said as he held the steaming liquid across the fire toward her. "Your shoulder was badly loosed from its socket. I moved it back. This will ease the pain and help to heal it more quickly." He gestured with the cup again.

She took it from him gingerly, feeling the warmth through the wood spread into her hands. Reluctantly, she sniffed it, pulling back and wrinkling her nose. Across the flames, the giant smiled. Maelyrin smiled back, a slightly distrustful one, and sniffed at it again. And again. Finally, she took a breath and took a sip.

The hot liquid was bitter and, at first, she had to struggle just to keep from spitting it out, much less swallow it, having to force the muscles responsible into working. Wincing, she looked back at the giant. The amused smile still touched his lips and his eyes, glittering ink, seemed to look through her, causing her to feel naked. She concentrated on the liquid, taking another sip. It warmed all the way down into her stomach. She took a third sip. Like magic, the bitterness became less and the aftertaste became a pleasant sweet taste, and she found herself gulping the stuff down, the warmth beginning to spread through her body.

With an embarrassed smile, she held the cup out toward her rescuer. "More, please?" she asked meekly. His smile grew, revealing teeth like an animal's, sharp and gleaming. He must have sensed her sudden discomfort because his smile lessened, becoming the thin lipped amused one he formerly wore and resorted to simply nodding before taking the cup, refilling it, and handing it back.

"Careful. Sip it," He said. "Works better the slower you drink."

She nodded, stopping the gulp she had been about to take and turning it into a modest sip. "It's good," she stated over the lip of the cup, taking another sip. "What is it?"

He made a rumbling growl in his throat that she realized was a chuckle. "Just tea," he said. "with some added herbs."

"Thank you," she said, adding after a moment, "For this and for saving my life." She shuddered. "Those men. . . . "

"Were desperate and base," he finished for her. "It was a terrible shame that they chose to die."

She shuddered again, both at what might have happened to her and at the hazy remembrance of their cries of pain and his whirling blade. Pushing the thoughts aside, she concentrated on the warmth and taste of her tea. Now, it was delicious and already the aches and pains in her body began to smooth out. Then a thought struck her, one that almost made her chuckle. "Who are you?" she said, smiling, thinking it odd that it hadn't occurred to her sooner to ask, thinking it almost the way it should be to think of him as 'the giant'.

"Is it important?" he asked. It caught her off guard, and she thought for a moment that he was mocking her, but the serene look on his face shifted her thoughts away from that. She nodded that it was. "I am called Kiyomori Sen. You may call me Ki if you find that too difficult."

"Ki," she murmured, then more loudly, "Quite a mouthful." She cocked her head to the side. "Does it have a meaning?" she asked, an inkling of recognition in the roll of the name. For the first time since seeing him did a ripple of disturbance wash across the placidity of his demeanor. Suddenly, he looked a bit sheepish.

"Yes," he nodded. "It means 'Seeker of All Wisdom'."

"What is wrong with that?" she asked, a smile curling on her lips, a small maneuver at making herself feel a little less intimidating by taking advantage of his sudden discomfort.

"It was given to me many years ago," Ki said, a touch of reluctance in his deep voice. "It was a reflection of my ambition. Not something to be proud of."

"I am not sure I understand," she said, slowly, unable to press her advantage.

"It is called '*argaat en saiga*'," he explained softly, his honesty sounding something of a confession. "It means 'an anchor for the ego'. A crude, but accurate translation. It was given to me to teach me humility." He chuckled then, the deep throated growl she heard earlier, and while she really could not tell by his eyes, themselves, the face surrounding them said that he was looking back into his past at a more pleasant time. His nostalgic journey was quick, the placidity of his normal expression smoothing over his features once more. "That was long ago."

"Did it teach you humility?" she asked pointedly, her mouth moving faster than her mind. Another rush of heat traveled up her face, and she was silently glad the fading light hid her embarrassment.

"That is not for me to judge," he answered without pause, smiling again. "Now, you should rest more. Your ordeal has left your body much too . . . *annit*. . .out of balance. Rest will restore. Yes?"

"Where are you from?" she asked, not hearing him above the murmur of her curiosity. "The *Traelynn*, my people, are not familiar with your kind."

"Tippon-ya, a chain of islands south, off the coast of Scandin Republic, is the home of . . . my kind, the *Turgatha-mal.*"

Ice slid down the back of her throat and crystals of it formed beneath her skin, numbing it and bringing water to her eyes. Her spine went rigid, painfully, the warmth of the tea gone. *Turgatha-mal.* . . .she thought frantically. *No!* The *Traelynn* knew of the *Turgatha-mal,* but by another name. *Andelyn da Molithe*, the Blue Demons. Killers of her people.

Her knife was at her hip, but might as well have been three leagues away. The paralytic ice freezing the entirety of her body kept her hands tightly folded on her lap, unable to move the tiny distance to the leather hilt. It would be a futile gesture anyway against the killing efficiency of the *Turgatha-*

mal, even without the deadly blades that now leaned against his pack. Blue Demons were killers as children.

Out of the shadows of her mind, voices cried out, screaming at her every story and fable told her about the Blue Demons as a child, shrieking the horrible truth that now sat across from her, the placidity she had seen earlier now the calm patience of a coiled snake, waiting to strike at its unwary prey. How had this happened? How had she not recognized the monster, the slaughterer of her kind, when she had first seen him? Or even when he had spoken?

Maelyrin needed to find a way to escape, to get away from the killer before he decided to tire of whatever game he was playing with her. Before the evil that was the *Turgathamal* asserted itself and put him into action. For a moment, she knew the pain of the cruel, slim sword passing through her body, felt it as if it already had. Yet still, she could not move, could barely breathe. Each stroke of her heart was a peal of thunder in her ears that repeated every few minutes.

Across from her, the flickering of the fire against the darkness causing his visage to waver before her, the creature watched, silent, unmoving, black eyes glittering from the yellow light; a pillar of death that urged the shrieks of terror within her. How could her Sight have lied to her? How could he have hidden his true self from her?

"No. . ." she mumbled, her voice sounding a slow scream to her. The pounding became worse, a sudden pressure at her temples that formed rings of fog around the peripherals of her vision. Her body was quaking, her breathing shallow and painful. The sound of her own voice an echo in her suddenly silent mind.

She moved, her body lashing out of its own accord, not waiting any longer for the messenger from her mind to bring its commands. The embers of the fire exploded along the ground sending coals scattering out. The pot and tripod flew up and over onto the woven mat, spilling steaming water amid the wooden utensils. At least one of the bowls shattered. She was backpedaling, arms and legs working furiously to carry her away. Something hard and rough stopped her. A cry of pain and fright escaped from bloodless lips as the injury to her shoulder flared anew, the joint re-dislocating with a loud pop.

Above her, the tree began to sway back and forth like liquid, each breath a pain filled treasure clutched close as if her last. In her swimming vision, she saw her killer stand, the burns on his legs standing angrily out against his skin even in the near darkness caused by her flight. All around her there was silence, only the low hum of her pain known to her. Her heart must have stopped because her chest was knotted agony, but it was somehow far away. Maelyrin watched him step toward her, a single stride that seemed slow in motion, his visage fuzzed and rippling as the tree, her downfall.

The Blue Demon must have tired of the game, or maybe, the burns she caused enraged him. It was time for her to die. Maelyrin knew it even before he bent over her, blocking her view of the reaching limbs of the elm above her. She fought against the tide of fear and pain in her, determined that she would watch her death bravely, to make sure he knew it. But, as before, her determination was not enough. Her vision darkened just as she felt the killer's hands upon her.

Chapter 41

Rest and Tension

𝓘t was a modest home that they looked down the slope at, constructed from the very trees encapsulating it and the wide soft-green glade in which it sat. At first, it had appeared to them that the place was abandoned, the only thing convincing them that it wasn't a picture, the sparking ribbon of water that ran along the back side of glade. But then, moments later, from behind the large barn near the house, a snow coated stallion stepped into view, grazing contentedly on the lush grass.

Alex glanced over at Sandoren. A tight expression dominated his face and, even though it was cooler here among the trees, sweat drizzled down the side of his cheek. He didn't return her glance, nor did she try to draw it. Their long ride here was accomplished with not more than a few words exchanged, neither of them in the mood to assist each other out of their sour attitudes. Attitudes that worsened as the heat grew, an oppressive stillness made much worse by the body heat rising from the horses. All in all, a miserable combination.

Del was slumped over the pommel of his saddle, patting Day's drooping neck as he nipped listlessly at the grass. His dullard's eyes were alight with that peculiar combination of joy and vast intelligence that was, at best, fleeting. He had been another source that fanned her irritation, since departing their campsite, lagging behind and straying off, sometimes so much so that either she or Sandoren had had to head back to retrieve him, often finding him staring at the dapple on the forest floor, or dumbly studying an insect, bird, or other creature. At one point, she had looked back and found Day plodding along, head hanging low, ears bouncing, without Del astride him. When they had backtracked, they had found the boy standing under the shade of a tree, brushing the bark up and down slowly with his fingertips. It took them several seconds of calling his name before they got his attention, a wide, slack smile answering them. Sandoren had exploded then, yelling and cursing at the trees and sky in his native language until finally falling into the torpor that now held him.

From then on Alex held onto Day's lead line, the rest of the morning passing miserably without incident. Now, the sun nearly at its apex, a full body width between it and the ghostly moon and glaring down at them from a cloudless sky, they stood their horses on top of the slope leading down into the glade where the man she sought was supposed to be; where Aeric was supposed to be. Her heart felt a bit hollow. He was here, though, somewhere. She could sense him, but wasn't quite sure where, the grueling last few days fuzzing the edges of her senses and her connection to the Earth. She needed rest. Plain and simple, but didn't know if that would be possible.

Below them, threading through the wood line, away from the house, were several of the gray and white figures that had been their silent scouts, fanning out and working around and through the trees . The Link she shared with them told her that the wolves were wary, scenting something in the clearing that agitated them; something they were unable to clearly relate back to her. Not the Eldritch. They were just as aware of it as she was, somewhere behind them, too far to be overly concerned about. No, it was something else that they sensed, a lingering taint that clung vicariously throughout the area, a phantom that moved about almost randomly. Each sensation spiked their hackles before they became conscious of it.

They also scented recently spilled blood, near the dwelling, though none felt comfortable breaking from the pack to investigate it further. A slow clench in her guts reminded her of her disturbed sleep last night.

Without warning, the wolves dissolved deeper into the trees, a final message drifting back into her mind through the Link. *He comes.*

Alex's chest tightened, then her knees, setting her mount, Clover, into motion, directing the mare toward the house. Her focus laid on the door, she, nonetheless, noticed the white stallion, off to the right of her gaze, watching her intently, ears laying back in loose warning. Sandoren grunted from behind and, following that, she heard his mount's hooves begin to shuffle in the high grass.

Clover walked more briskly only after patient urging from her, and they covered the last few hundred yards quickly, and tensely. The white stallion snorted harshly, then whinnied from his corral. Clover answered with a shake of her considerably smaller head, followed closely by an expulsion from Veraddin, Sandoren's mount. Why he chose that name, she wasn't sure, but it pricked her still. He should have chosen the *Faellyn* word for 'spite' instead of the one for 'stubborn'. Of course, that fit him just as well as it did she.

Alex was so intent on the door, that she didn't readily notice the large stain darkening the packed earth near the threshold, nor the black shaft piercing the wood frame near its top. When she did, her heart leapt and her throat clenched. Clover stopped, her senses telling her that she yanked the reins. From the stain, her eyes traveled up the door, saw the ragged hole in the planking, let it linger there for a second, before moving to the bolt at the top, her mind asking what had happened.

She might have studied the scene longer, but something moving through the trees opposite them caused her to pull her gaze from it. Alex's heart, still beating anxiously at the tense realization of a purpose mixed with the anxiety of the possibility of that aim being ripped away prematurely, flipped and rolled with greater vigor. Her eyes were locked onto the sound as if she could see through the screen of trees and brush, and she held her breath. *If he is mortally wounded, what then?* She didn't think she had enough strength to Heal him. . . *It couldn't end this close. It couldn't.*

He appeared like a spectre from the undergrowth, moving slowly, weakly along a small path that entered the clearing, his clothing tattered and filthy with grime and the russet color of dried blood. He dragged behind him a spade, its blade scratching the dirt in a soft, thumping rumble. Had she not been sure that this was the man she Healed of poison only days ago from the Air Bond, she would never had been able to recognize him otherwise, the dust covering his face a backdrop for dark lines where sweat cut through it only to be dusted again looking like long, vertical cracks in a clay facade. His eyes were hollowed out pits surrounded by taut, drawn skin, a mask of pain and exhaustion that wrenched the viewers and forced them to give thanks that they had been spared of whatever horror he wore.

He was beyond the tree-line when he finally noticed them, sitting atop their horses near the house, and tensed with the quickness of freezing water, stopping sluggishly. His eyes, though, rapidly became steel, newly forged, bright, clear, and hard. The spade swung slowly in front of him with deliberate purpose. "What do you want?" he said in a husky, tight voice that sounded as if he had rocks lodged in his throat.

Beside her, Sandoren went rigid. "We are looking for someone," she said softly. "A guide. Someone called Aeric." he flinched visibly, but stolidly refused to speak. Beside her, Sandoren turned a surprised look on her. "We were told he lived here about."

"You were told wrong," he retorted, his voice gaining some strength in his sudden anger. "No one by that name lives around here. Now leave."

"Show some respect when speaking to an Earthmother, you. . . " Sandoren suddenly burst out, stopping only when her hand came to rest on his arm. The man flinched again, and recognition flashed across his face, but it was quickly swallowed up by the hardness that spread from his eyes.

"Do you know where we might find some lodgings this night, then?" she said quickly, drawing his hard gaze from Sandoren, watching his face soften, but only slightly.

"Go back the way you came," he answered, stammering slightly, though still gruff. "Turn north where the forest breaks and follow it until you come to a small road. There's an inn there, and a village further up the road." He began walking again, a stumbling gait toward the house, pointedly ignoring them.

Sandoren began fingering the hilt of his sword, his eyes ablaze with indignation. *Would this never stop?* She asked herself. "Thank you," she said. He said nothing more, staring deliberately at the door, mentally staving off their presence as if they were not there. Clover turned at the press of her knee, but not before she watched the man disappear into the building and slam the door behind him. Not before she saw the darkened interior, the floor beyond filled with shattered pieces of wood and shredded cloth. She gave Sandoren a grim look before nudging Clover into a slow trot back up the slope. Halfway, she cast a glance back, noticing he wasn't with her. Tugging gently on the reins, she turned the horse around to wait. Clover protested with a snort and a jerk at the bit, but complied.

Sandoren was on the ground, kneeling near the tree-line opposite the door and studying the ground intently. Veraddin grazed on the lush grass near him. After several minutes, he stood and pulled himself back into his saddle, shot an intensely dark look at the cabin before tapping Veraddin into a trot. He passed her, moving up the hill quickly, a haunting glance at her overshadowing the fiercely held anger steeped into his face. She shook her head and followed him.

They rode in stone silence for many miles, looking only forward, listening only to their inner voices. Alex spent the time pushing back the feelings that raged in her. The sudden change in circumstance stunned her, deflecting her with such quickness that all she could do was retreat and try to regroup. That she was angry was a foregone conclusion. That she was confused was as well. Disbelief and even a bit of embarrassment bubbled in there among the cracks, and she chided herself for becoming used to how others treated her. The bowing, the scraping, the sometimes obsequious respect that commonly followed her around. She had become used to getting her own way by merely asking, or even looking like she was going to ask, her only challenge of spirit coming from Sandoren. She was used to it and apparently expected it. Aeric's sudden resistance found none of her own. Luckily, her tongue hadn't been as frozen as her brain and allowed her a graceful retreat.

Sandoren was another matter. His anger an odd behavior for him, not because of anything but the length at which he held it. He was hot-headed, yes, but he was also quick to rid himself of it. The look he gave her coming up the slope made her insides clench.

As if on cue, Sandoren finally spoke, saying, "What now?" A brooding grunt that was a vain attempt at calmness.

"We find this inn and rest," she answered shortly.

"Good," he said, voice smoothing out a little. "Good riddance."

"Sandy?" she began, but he rounded on her, chained fury working his features.

"No, Alex!" he nearly yelled. "No! We do not need this man! This . . . this disrespectful . . . He cannot be the one!" His tirade caused her to glance back at Del, who stared at them with wet saucer eyes filling with fear. She clenched her jaw, tried to remain calm.

"You're frightening the boy," she said slowly.

"I don't care!" he burst back. Veraddin pranced and shook his head, ears back. "To the Flames with them both! To the Flames with this blasted charge! And this day. I don't care! It's futile, Alex. Don't you see that? The Balance has tipped too far toward Chaos. We can't tip it back."

"It's only because I know you are as drawn out as me that I don't strike you across the face," Alex hissed, her green eyes piercing him with reflected fury. He blinked, stunned, then his face began to knot, his mouth opened and closed and he gulped air, then frowned. Finally, a frustrated growl erupted from his throat and he spurred Veraddin into a fast trot, placing enough distance between them for their anger to find a comfortable cushion.

From behind her, a snuffle came that stabbed her heart. She suddenly felt like crying herself, something she rarely did, but she clamped down on it, anger still blazing enough that she could. She pulled back on Clover's reins and slowed enough to let Day come aside.

Del was rocking back and forth over the pommel, tears streaming down his slack face freely, eyes far away and whispering to himself. "No pain, no pain," he called to himself over and over, the chant cutting cleanly through her anger into that part of her that accepted the hurt and turned it into the soft need to help. Alex moved Clover close and leaned over and held the boy to her in a one armed hug. She did not cry, but a single tear did escape her efforts to close the gate and glide down one of her cheeks.

She held him for only the time it took for him to dry up and give her a slack, loving smile that drew from her a returning one and a scrub of her hand through his shaggy hair. From then on, her heart was a little lighter.

It was nearing dusk when they intersected the hard packed road that emerged from the trees to their left and curved in a north-easterly direction only to disappear again within the enfolding tree lines heavy with pines and hardwoods. It was not a wide road but it was well traveled and only slightly rutted. And there, sitting near it, cupped by the woods that curved back around behind it and overtook the road not very much farther on, was a well-kept, two story building made of heavy timber. Oil lanterns already flickered against the coming darkness on each side of the door and each visible corner. A sign swaying slightly with a breath of wind alternately obscured one of them, but they were still too far to read the words carved into it.

Behind and to the side stood a large outbuilding with large doors and a wide fenced area. The barn doors still stood open, and they could see someone moving about the dimness among the bobbing heads of other horses. Oil lamps flickered on the corners of it as well. The wafting breeze carried the sweet scent of hay and honeyed oats, stirring their mounts into constant nickering and barely restrained prancing. A quick paced tune drifted from the interior, the fluty sounds of an ocarina, maybe, the staccato slap of a few hands clapping accompanying it. To her it was soothing and familiar and she saw a joyful awe spread onto Del's face. Sandoren remained a tense statue ahead of them, a souring effect that warred with everything else.

The whickering horses must have alerted the stable attendant, for a moment later, they were being approached along the sunlit side of the inn by a reed-thin middle-aged man in worn russet clothes dusted with clover and hay. He smiled and nervously dry washed his hands, then began bobbing his head like a rooster. "Evenin' mams and sirs," he said, his Leeran accent a bit of a surprise. A Leeran this far north was definitely a sign of changing times. "Must to take your steeds?"

"We would be most gracious," Alex said, swinging her leg over the pommel and sliding to the ground. A wave of dizziness assaulted her when her feet touched, and she had to lean heavily against Clover holding tightly to the pommel while her vision began to clear and her stomach began to settle. When her body was hers again, she looked up and saw the stableman craning his neck sidewise, looking at her anxiously, and behind him, Sandoren, still astride Veraddin, his face momentarily washed with concern. He looked away uncomfortably as the stableman said, "Does mams well?"

Alex swallowed hard, nodded. "Yes. I am well," she said as she pushed herself away from Clover. Apparently, her exhaustion was catching up to her. The stableman took the reins from her with a look that said he did not believe her one bit. His look changed, though, when she produced several silvers and handed them to him. "Make sure these three horses receive double the amount of feed," she said quietly. His head began bobbing on his stalk-like neck.

"Yas, mams, yas," the Leeran answered, excitement flashing in his eyes. He turned quickly and sought the next pair of reins, obsequiously thanking Sandoren, then Del, though he stopped and stared at the vacuous boy for a second as he almost snatched the reins from his hands. Sandoren's upper lip curled, his disgust worming slowly onto his face, and he huffed. Del simply watched the stable hand as he led the horses toward the barn, a weed trying to pull them faster than they wanted to go.

Casting a disappointed look at Sandoren, Alex straightened her shirt and pulled her forest cloak from her shoulders and folded it over her arms. She reached out and took Del's hand, who flinched at the touch and had to peer down to see what was against his flesh. Momentarily, that happy smile adorned his face as his gaze traveled back up to her own. She led him toward the door, silently grateful that he helped to mask her suddenly swaying gait. Sandoren walked slightly ahead of her, a brooding guard. Alex felt like she was falling asleep even before walking through the door.

Everything after had a dreamlike quality. Their entrance only disturbed the patrons between their clapping. There was a smiling hefty man in an apron and serving wenches in long skirts and wide bodices. Sandoren made the arrangements, deftly keeping her within his envelope of protection. The stairs were ahead, she felt as if she were floating. . . The last thing she remembered was the soft bed as she lay down, Sandoren and Del shuffled off to another room by the aproned fellow. . . .

Sunlight peering through the crack between the shutters caused her eyelids to flutter open. Then, a long yawn. Alex sat up slowly, her mind fogged with sleep, and she ran her fingers through her dirty, tangled hair. Fuzz lined her mouth and moisture rimmed her eyes, drawn up by the several yawns that followed the first.

At the foot of the bed, taking up much of the leftover room, was a porcelain tub, steam curling up from the rim. Alex smiled, not remembering if that had been here when she had come in or if it had been brought in afterward. She felt rested, but she sat on the bed, legs curled, one under the other, hair dangling raggedly around her face for many minutes, savoring the silence in her mind. Then, slightly drugged, she stood and stepped over to the window, enjoying the light-caused pain as she pulled them open, then pushed up the sash. Brisk air followed the light into the room, prickling her skin, raising chill-bumps along its surface, and causing her to suck in a breath and hold it for a second.

She looked out over the clearing and into the nearby woods, watching the predawn mists drift through and along the ground like lazy spirits. The sun had not yet peered above the tall timber. Once she became used to the coolness wafting in, she breathed in the soft pine smell and pungent loam of the woods deeply. This was her favorite time of day, the peaceful pause just after the nocturnal creatures returned to their daylight resting places, and the diurnal creatures were just beginning to wake from their nightly sleeps. It was a time that stood still, only for a few moments, but for an eternity in its own right.

Alex let the cool air caress her face for several more minutes, enjoying the sight of the drifting mists, the smell of the forest, and the sound of the preternatural silence, before turning away from the portal. She disrobed slowly, even though the touch of the chill air against her bare skin caused her to shiver every once in a while, clucking her tongue as she inspected the worn and travel dirty material. Her shirt, once white, would need several washings before it started to even resemble its original brightness, and her breeches were beginning to wear too thin around the knees. She smiled again, shivering at the same time, when she saw a spare shirt, trousers, and under-clothes laying over the arm of the bedside chair. She made a point of thanking Sandy when she saw him next, even if he was still sulking.

Alex pushed those thoughts aside, and the other ones that were beginning to percolate within her brain, and stepped slowly into the steaming water. She allowed herself to hiss, half from the hot water against her skin, and half from the idea that she was actually taking a bath after so many days of travel. Even though she spent most of her life outdoors, it did not mean that she disdained the creature comforts of society. Indeed, silently, she reveled in them, feeling something she supposed royalty felt when pampered. As she slid down into the invigorating water, she allowed a second "ahh." of pleasure to escape her lips. It *had* been too long. As she took the floral scented soap and sponge in hand, she tried to remember when the last time she had a hot bath was.

Of course, she could simply use her powers to clean herself up; use them to knock the dirt from her skin and hair. But then, it would defeat the purpose of the bath. And she was not about to deprive herself of the soothing time by herself.

The smell of boiling oats, frying bacon and eggs, mingled and drew her down the stairs, her stomach rumbling so noisily she almost blushed, thinking that the cooks and kitchen maids would hear her coming. Almost running into her near the bottom of the stair was the hefty man she remembered from the previous evening. He was muttering over some pieces of parchment and didn't see her until her shadow fell across his balding pate and down onto his papers. He looked up quickly, not quite able to hide the sudden fear that leapt up into them. A broad beaming smile, though, quickly washed it away, replacing it with warmth and kindness that deepened the brown of his eyes. "Ah, Mistress Alexandra," he said while holding out his free hand. "I trust that you are well rested?"

"Yes, thank you, Master. . . . ?" she said, tentatively, embarrassed that she could not remember whether or not he had introduced himself last evening. She gave him her hand, which he grasped warmly.

"Abyl, Mistress Alexandra, just Abyl." he said, gently shaking her hand. "You were quite exhausted upon your arrival, so do not be concerned if your memory is slightly blurred. It is well that you are rested." She arched an eyebrow. He spoke too well to be a simple innkeep, and she could hear a subtle twang in his accent that said he may have once been from the north, possibly as far north as Vistan, or even Calif.

"Thank you, Master Abyl," she answered with a smile, tacking on the honorific despite his protest. He smiled, flushed slightly, and nodded, then began backing down the stair.

"I must give my thanks, Mistress," Abyl said. "It is a rare gift to have an Earthmother grace us. *Tus'stair no areylan.*" He bowed at the neck and brought his hand to his heart. She paused, her brows arching again, while her heart flipped in her chest at the ancient acknowledgement: *Your presence graces.* It took her a moment to remember the appropriate response.

"*Areyla'ana no layne'ar tol.*" She answered. *Your graciousness blesses me tenfold.* She then placed her hand over her own heart. He nodded.

"You have a visitor awaiting you in the common room." Abyl said after a pause, then backed the rest of the way down the stairs and moved off down a small hallway that obviously led toward the kitchen since the smells and clanging of pots came from that direction.

A visitor? she thought. *What an odd way to refer to Sandoren? For his knowledge of ancient Arquil and custom, he couldn't have missed the fact that he was her Guardian.* Alex stopped dead.

Standing near the window, looking out onto the green in front of the Inn, dressed in functional finery, a loose fitting pale blue shirt and black breeches that disappeared into high travel boots, was Aeric. The morning light sheened softly the side of his freshly shaven face and the gray patch of hair at his temple.

A large sword swept down the back of his thigh, held there loosely by a hand resting on his hip between the hilt. He turned, as if musing over something, then straightened rigidly when he saw her.

His face had softened considerably since yesterday, but beneath the planes of his weathered skin, and especially in the steel hardness of his eyes, she could still see the pain, disgust, and anger smoldering there. She stepped off the last stair into the room.

"Grand morning," Alex said, only partly feigning indignance. "What brings you out so early, Master. . . .?" She sure was asking that question a lot this morning.

"Marc," he answered, either ignoring or simply missing the ice that drove her words. "Just Marc." And she was hearing that answer a lot, too.

"Well, Marc," Alex said. She took a seat at the nearest table, sitting as primly as she could, thinking it was a good thing she started off the morning feeling like royalty. "You're here, why?" She was aware that he had rode nearly half the night to be here now, but his rough treatment of them yesterday did not brook a reprieve quite yet. She thought she saw him flinch at her words.

"I came to apologize," he said quickly. "I know what you did . . . for me, and I am thankful. And I apologize for my behavior yesterday. I was out of line." He cleared his throat in discomfort. It softened her, but not completely. His stinging attitude was not quite smoothed over yet.

"If you are aware of who I am, are you also aware of what happens during a Healing?" she asked. He shuffled his feet and swallowed roughly.

"Yes," he said finally. "I am aware of the Air Bond."

"What do you know about the Air Bond, Marc?" Alex let the iciness creep back into her voice as her anger began rising again.

"I know that it allows an Earthmother to sense those they Healed for a short time," he said. "It allows them to make sure that the Healing takes or if there is another wound. . ."

It seems that this was a day when she would run into all the people in the world that knew something about history. "Do you also know what can happen during times of great stress suffered on the Bonded?"

He nodded after a moment's pause. "I am."

"Then can you give me a reason why you lied to me," she said coldly. "Aeric." It was a soft utterance, but it hit him like a brick. He flinched, a definite flinch, then his face contorted as all the pent up emotions he hid flash-flooded over it. It was fast, and he quickly took on a neutral expression. All but his eyes. They hardened even further. And his voice became the backdrop for his anger.

"Aeric Pendragon died a long time ago. My name is Marc," he stated. "I thank you again for helping me, but I must be on my way."

"You certainly rode a great deal just to say that," she said quietly. He was already turning away, his hand on the door handle, when her voice reached him. Marc froze for a moment before pulling open the door. He froze again on the wide step just outside when she spoke again. "I heard about a man named Aeric Pendragon, once." she drove on, striking out in places that were partially blind to her. "Many generations ago, there was a High Knight of Ellynthryll who bore that name." He did not turn, but he did not move either. If she was right, he was listening with his entire being. "It was said that this man was one of the greatest of the Order and his name, in some places, still lives on in legend. Even his fall was once sung throughout the lands. They say he died defending his wife on his wedding day. And there is even a monument on the hill on which that occurred, so I hear." He flinched again, and it pricked her heart. She took a deep breath, ignored the pounding in her chest, then bore on. "A great tale. . . if you like tales." She paused again, took another breath. Hurting others was something she hated deep down in her core, and now she was going to do it purposely. She was going to sacrifice what she held dear, for a boy she wasn't sure of, for a cause that may never be. "But there was another story. One only spoken of by few, because it was such a terrible thing to think of, such a tarnish on an otherwise brilliant legend*." Forgive me!* she cried silently. "That story said that this man, this High Knight called Aeric Pendragon, stood by and watched his new wife die upon another's sword without lifting a hand in aid, that he was cursed from that day forward to wander the earth to suffer his cowardice. While not believed by the masses, disdained almost as blasphemy by them, those tales eventually reached a certain historian, Kandis Karvalion, I think his name was, who wondered why these brushfire stories existed. It is an even more unbelievable story than his greatest deeds, but the details of this man were more crisp than any other documentation of his earlier life. Apparently, there were many witnesses to his terrible disgrace and Karvalion recorded testimonies from some of them, the rest already passed on by the time he was intrigued enough to investigate the tales. All of them, though the actual act was confused, could recall the knight with such detail, that just reading the records, one could see the man in the mind as clearly as if he stood in front of them. And all of them spoke of his sword, tied as closely to his deeds that it was as much a part of the legends as he was." One more breath. "It was a sword remarkably similar to the one on your hip. Though, history also speaks of the many copies that were forged at the time."

She stopped, and had to bite her lip to keep it from quivering. Several slow minutes crawled by, silent save for the clinking of pots in the kitchen that rang hollowly into the room. She even thought her heart had stopped, but she realized soon that the burning in her chest was stale breath that she was unconsciously holding on to as if she were submerged in a chilling, deep water. Where she should be, if she was correct in her deduction. The silence between them became more oppressive at each passing second.

With a sudden finality, his shoulders slumped. "What do you want from me?" he said, still without turning, but the agonized defeat that sounded in his hoarse voice reflected all the ice that she had used in her delivery and drove it straight down into her soul.

"I need your help," she said simply. She could not force any more words from her mouth than that, before her throat tightened. Another lengthy pause passed before he slowly turned and looked at her, his gaze reaching through all her defenses and gripping her heart strings. His eyes, so steely hard before, were lucid and deep, and the horrible agony that lay within their depths was so unbearable that she had to tear her own gaze from his and look down at the tabletop.

"You have a funny way of asking," he said gruffly.

"It's complicated," she said, an embarrassed flush beginning to crawl up above her neckline.

"Is it?" he shot back, the hardness coming back into his gray eyes. That was worse than the clearness of pain that was just there. Without warning, Sandoren appeared from the hallway leading to the kitchen. He had been saying something, whether to her or someone behind him she wasn't sure, but he had been relaxed and wearing a comfortable look. Whatever he was saying stopped suddenly and his posture tightened when he stepped into the room and first looked at her, then to the person standing in the front doorway. Anger moved across his face like storm clouds across the sun and, after staring at her for a couple of seconds, he wordlessly stomped up the stair. "I will think on it," Marc said from the doorway. "I will return this afternoon to give you an answer, whatever I decide. You have my word on it."

She looked up. He turned to leave and then stopped again. His shoulders were lifted back in the way she had seen him at the window, a comfortable confidence that was no longer consciously felt. Marc turned back to her, his eyes grabbing hers in a clenching grip, accusing in its hardness. "There are many myths and legends connected to the

Pendragon name. More beyond count. But you got that story wrong," he said in a harsh monotone, then watched her for an indeterminate time, his silence terrible in its reproach. Before turning back out onto the green, he said, "The sword that killed the man's young wife was his own," he paused, this time to watch her flinch. "The hand that killed her was his, too."

The door shut with barely a whisper, dousing the room in dimness, leaving her staring at the planking, alone, everyone else staying away out of respect or just practicality. She was alone. And she wept.

Chapter 42

Thoughts Over Tea

*M*aelyrin came awake slowly, swimming up through thick syrup from the depths of oblivion. Something cool and moist lay across her forehead. The pain in her shoulder throbbed slowly. A newly built fire crackled nearby, the smell of cooking meat heavy in the still air, the sizzling of dripping fat loud. It was still warm even though dark, and, above, through the tree limbs, stars winked and glittered. She yawned, deeply, then tried to sit up, finding that her left arm was bound tightly to her side with long, wide strips of cloth.

A thought struck her, sending her head in a jerking motion to look around. He sat across the fire from her as before, on his knees, back straight and stock still, his black eyes glittering. Her guts churned, her panic rising quickly into her throat.

"You must rest," Ki said evenly. "You injured your shoulder worse. You will not be harmed by me." His voice had the effect of an overdose of mint leaves; an instant, complete relaxation washed over her. Maelyrin's mind whispered to her, echoing his voice, reminding her that she was not dead now or harmed, except by her own doing. It was confusion that assailed her then, willing the muscles in her throat to move.

"Why is it that I. . . " she stuttered. ". . . you. . . Why am I alive?" she finished lamely.

"Should you not be?" he asked.

"You are *Turgatha-mal*," she answered as if that were enough.

"And you are *Traelynn*," he replied. "Am I to judge you by your heritage as readily as you have mine?"

"No," she said softly in reaction to the sting from his words, dropping her head back to the moss. "I'm sorry."

"I understand your fright," he explained. "My people are known for their brutality, especially against those we have shared the world with since the beginning of time. But we are often swayed in our thinking by what we have seen or have been told. Our cousins, the Eldythians, are thought universally to be noble warriors, but does that make them any less violent in nature."

"No. I suppose not," she answered quietly. She struggled with her right arm to drag herself to the weathered trunk of the elm so that she could lean on it and be more comfortable instead of trying to look at him by lifting her head off the ground. Ki stayed motionless across the fire, no doubt unwilling to cause another panic reaction. "I have often . . ." she said, once settled, breathing heavily, her hand folding the moist towel that had fallen from her head absently. ". . .thought that my people were . . . too stringent in their reclusiveness."

"Perhaps, then," he gestured with his hand, "that is a good lesson."

Maelyrin looked down at the tight wrappings around her arm and body, smiled wanly and shrugged her uninjured one. "Thank you," she said. "And I apologize for my reaction."

"No need," he said, a smile touching his lips. "Again, I think there must be a lesson there." Despite the pain it caused, she laughed, albeit a short one. "Are you hungry?"

The question was quick and simple but aroused a fast, furious reaction, stomach rumbling. Her mouth watered so badly, she could only nod in answer, her eyes dropping, pinning themselves to the spitted fowl above the flames. He lifted the food from the fire, juices running down the seared meat and dripping loudly into the flames, and sliced from it several pieces with a knife.

She took the strips from him, shuffled them from hand to hand, blowing on them before tearing into them greedily. A little embarrassed, seconds later, she slowed, smiling sheepishly across at Ki who was chewing slowly on his.

The meal was finished quickly and silently, Maelyrin asking for more twice. The bird was a little tough, but she was too busy eating to complain. Afterward, Ki set his pot on the tripod to boil some water for more tea, which she waited for in anticipation.

Over a steaming hot cup of the bittersweet liquid, she asked, "Why are you so far north of your homeland?"

"I don't have a homeland," he answered, giving her a start.

"But you said . . ."

"I said that Tippon-ya was the homeland of the *Turgatha-mal*. I have no home, nor a clan."

"You are a wanderer, then."

"Yes, mostly." He poured himself another cup of tea and sipped at it.

"Mostly?" she prompted. He nodded and sipped. After several minutes of waiting, she asked, "Then, where are you going?"

"North," he said.

"Why?" she pressed, a touch of discomfort rising within her at her impertinence. He studied her for several moments, took a long sip from his cup, held it before swallowing.

"I am searching for someone," he said softly. His voice still rumbled like thunder. "One like me. One like what you thought I was. A killer of the helpless."

"*Turgatha-mal*." she whispered, throwing her eyes at the flames and suppressing a shudder. When the panicky feeling left her, she returned her gaze on the one before her. "Why do you seek him?" Asking was a struggle and she suddenly could not understand the uncontrollable fear that knotted her guts at the thought of another Blue Demon. Perhaps just the sudden appearance of one after all the events of the past few years. . . .

"Why do you seek your Marc Pendragon?" he asked. She stared, eyes wide, all former thoughts spent like embers in rain.

"W-what?" she sputtered. "H-how did you. . . ?"

"You spoke about him while you slept," he said. "It seemed very important that you find him."

Embarrassment awash with anger flooded her. "I-I s-spoke . . ." she tried to get a handle on herself. "How. . . How long was I . . . asleep?"

"A day."

"A day?" she almost spilled the rest of her tea. "Oh, no," she then whispered harshly. "I have to. . . ."

"Calm yourself," Ki said, tone even, as before, it seeming to echo in her mind, cooling her exploding emotions as if a fresh mountain spring opened up from above spilling snowmelt down on her. She sat back, her tense muscles loosening, the tight pain spreading out and dissipating.

"What did you do to me?" Maelyrin asked after a long calm pause.

"I did nothing to you," Ki replied, drained his cup and began to pile the utensils in a neat stack. He stood and stretched, a column of taut muscle that rivaled the huge trees surrounding them. She watched him quietly, her Sight peering into his soul, wondering about the discomfort that rippled the otherwise vast sea of calm within him. A tiny wavelet, to be sure, but powerful in its wake. He was finished speaking, at least of himself.

Falling back into a semblance of calm, a yawn crept up on her, unstifled. Even though asleep for a day, her watery eyes became heavy and her limbs leaden. The throb in her shoulder retreated. She drained her own cup, savoring the bitter sweet liquid, mildly thinking there must be more in the tea than just tea, and handed it back to Ki wordlessly.

"You should sleep," he said, taking the cup and placing it with the others. "Your body needs more rest. I will wake you when the sun rises, if you should wish it, so that we may begin looking for your Marc Pendragon."

She nodded, the fog of sleep growing in her mind blocking the last of his words and the questions they tried to dredge up. Slowly, she eased herself down the trunk, watching the blue giant fade into the darkness, the swords back in the belt around his waist.

Chapter 43

Waiting

The fire burned lazily in the hearth, sending a comforting heat out into the large room while Master Abyl moved about wiping the small tables off with soapy warm water. Alexandra watched him silently. She was sitting in the same seat that she had been in when Marc had left that morning, and had been sitting there almost the entire day. Abyl had cleaned them twice already today, even though there had not been a soul that had stopped by.

Travel had been slow, Master Abyl had explained, since the trade routes to Hestaff had been cut off from Mithron and Symond to the south by the breaking lands. He said he preferred to keep the tables clean to keep himself busy than for any other reason. Kiers, the Leeran, and a young woman by the name of Mira were the only two others about, and both went about their business just as Abyl did. Though it had an undercurrent of anxiousness, it was normal, and it comforted her. If only a little.

Sandoren disappeared shortly after Marc left and hadn't returned, while Del had taken to following Kiers around as he worked in the stable. She was thankful that the man was kind to him. Del's mental state made him an easy target for others, his scars were evidence enough of that, and he had a tendency to fray nerves. Kiers, so far, seemed to have infinite patience with the boy. As for herself, she could only sit. And wait to see if

Marc returned. And Sandoren. And wait for her guilt to subside.

I must do what I must do. She thought, but it was ashes in her mouth. There was no forgiving what she was doing, just as there was no certainty that she would accomplish what had been set forth for her to do. Whatever that may be. Exactly.

Just then, the door opened, allowed a gust of cold air to rush in, caused her heart to leap. But it was only Master Abyl preparing to light the lamps flanking the portal. The view beyond was dim, banks of ominous clouds had been settling above them all day and it made the coming twilight early and lent a stiff chill to the air. There was a good chance that the weather would turn. . . return to a semblance of normalcy. Of course, she knew she was wrong. It would be a long time before the weather was normal again.

Master Abyl came back in, huffing slightly and blowing into cupped hands. "It looks like we are in for some angry weather," he said as he closed the door behind him. "Mistress? Is there anything I can get for you?"

"Some mulled wine, please," she answered softly.

"Right away, Mistress," he answered, nodding. "And will you be taking some dinner, as well?"

She shook her head. "No, not right now, thank you."

"As you wish, *Mal 'andel*," Abyl answered, a bit like a protective parent that wasn't happy at hearing his request denied. He bustled from the room and returned in moments with a goblet and set it down in front of her before going back into the kitchen. She took a tentative sip, not really tasting the spiced, honeyed wine, lost as she was in bitter thoughts, gazing into the languid fire.

"What kind of help do you require?" said Marc. She cried out in surprise, the fire coming back into conscious view just before her head twisted toward the door. The thoughts she had been entertaining evaporated.

Marc stood in the doorway, a heavy dark blue cloak draping his wide shoulders. Beyond him, the light cast from the lamps fuzzed a backdrop of mist laden darkness. The ghostlike form of the great white horse stood further out. And, as if in answer to her gaze, a low whicker drifted inward. He looked at her with those hard, hurtful gray eyes for only a moment longer before shutting the door.

She was about to stammer out an apology for her words earlier, but his gaze kept her from it. Instinctively, she knew it would do no good, nor would he accept it. An apology now could only hurt matters worse. "I need you to come to with us to Calif," she said instead.

"What for?"

"A-ah-I need a guide," she answered. He smirked.

"Your Guardian should suffice," Marc said shortly. "Besides, since when does an Earthmother need a guide at all?" he strode the short distance and sat down heavily across from her. "You don't need a guide."

"No," she looked down into her goblet. "I don't need a . . . ."

"Ah, Master Marc," said the innkeeper from the kitchen door. "I thought I heard the door open, but wasn't expecting to see you twice in one day."

"Hello again, Abyl," Marc answered, turning his granite eyes from her. There was warmth in his voice and his eyes softened a little. "Just taking care of some business." Abyl glanced at Alex, a slightly startled look crossing his face.

"Mira almost has eveningfeast ready," Abyl said in a questioning tone, recovering quickly from his apparent surprise.

"Sure," Marc answered with a nod.

"Yes, good. I will leave you to your conversation, then," Abyl said, inclining his gaze toward Alex. "Mistress." He backed out of the room into the kitchen and closed the intervening door.

"I cannot give you a reason why because I do not yet know myself. I just know that I need you to come with us,"

Alex said simply once the innkeeper vanished into the kitchen. Marc pushed back in his chair, started to rise.

"That's not a good enough reason," he said shortly. With surprising speed, Alex leaned over the table a grabbed his hand before he was half way out of the chair. That tingling shock that he had felt when she laid her hand on him during the Healing ran up his arm, giving him pause.

"Please," she said, not keeping the urgency from her voice. Slowly, he sat back down, eyeing her stonily.

"You do not know what you are asking," Marc said in a harsh whisper. "Associating with me can only cause you problems."

"It must be so. That is why your arrangement will be as a guide." She paused, the deep green of her eyes piercing. "I know who you are and what it is that burdens you. At the very least, you may discover the path to the absolution that you desire."

He stared long into her eyes, the process of his mind reflected back in the slate orbs. After moments, they softened ever so slightly but it was as much a testimony of his tired defeat as the slumping of his shoulders was earlier that morning. But there was hope there, too, a sudden fierce burning that arose and found life. Still, he continued to stare into her eyes, the flames reaching deeply, daring her. Time slipped tensely by.

Finally, he nodded, breaking the bond their eyes, her emerald, his steel, made. "I will go with you," he said quietly, a warning deep undercurrent to his words, as if he were condemning her request by agreeing with it. "When do you wish to leave this place?"

"Tomorrow," Alex answered.

Chapter 44

Soft Commune

*N*ot far from the little house Marc called home was a wide low hill that offered a spectacular view of the surrounding woodland and the sparkling stream that wound around the knoll and back through the trees to eventually kiss the edge of the land on which the cabin stood. At its apex, sunken and grown over with grass, was a weather-beaten stone of obsidian. It had once been chiseled with words and crisp corners, but time had eroded them away and rounded the edges, making it just a nondescript stone sinking into the top of a hill. But to Marc's eyes, it had not lost any of itself. To him, the chisels still caught the light and shadows and threw back words as cleanly as the day he had chipped the letters out. So long ago.

Marc sat next to it companionably, looking up into the sky at the slate clouds gathered there while his hands braided blades of long grass in slow, measured ways. A small pile of them lay at his hip. Whitesteel grazed down the slope, near where he had been unhindered of his saddle and tack.

He came here during those periods when he knew his identity and when he was not drifting aimlessly about the lands of Arquilon searching for answers to long dead questions. It was a place of peace for him, which was an odd contradiction. But being at the resting place of his wife seemed to bring his deep seated agony into a focus that was small in comparison to how it raged when he was abroad. And surrounding that small, tight knot, was a calm emptiness. It helped him sort through thoughts and feelings that he needed to give serious consideration.

Of course, at the same time, he could not remain for long. The intensity of that pain, condensed as it was, brought about vivid memories that bordered on reality. Reliving the last few moments of her death like that tended to drive him forth into the world again to balance out the effects. Eventually, the cycle returned him here to this hill, next to this stone that all but he had forgotten the significance of. It was one of the reasons that he did not necessarily need to look at the stone to see it or the words that were once carved on it.

"I'm going again," he said softly, briefly gazing down at the green braid. "I don't know why." He crumpled the braid quickly and threw it to the side. "I can't do any good for these people!" he hissed. He stared at the rumpled grass clinging to the tops of the unpicked blades. "I think it must be part of the curse that people seek me out." Down the hill, Whitesteel snorted.

Minutes crawled by in ruthless slowness, each one an echo of the crawling lead above him. Occasionally, he squinted up at them, chewed his lip, sucked his teeth, some idiosyncrasy to man the walls of his defenses. "It doesn't get any better," he finally said. "After all these many years, it never gets better." He shook his head. "I'm sorry. I know how selfish that sounds. . . This last time, I was away for at least a week. I was completely different. . . No. . . I was the man you knew. . . once. I was that one, except untainted by all the blood I've spilt, all the things I've done, all the things I've become." He harrumphed. "How I miss that person." Tears suddenly stung his eyes. "How I miss you, even now." He gulped, let a few of them roll down his cheeks as he worked to keep the straining focal pain from exploding. The struggle went on for many moments, the only sound, a breeze hissing among the grass. "Well, enough of that. . . ." he finally said, his voice horse in the breeze. He stood slowly and turned toward the stone, looking down on it with a strained expression. "I won't be back for some time, I imagine," he said as he shifted the sword on his hip, his eyes flickered back and forth along the weathered stone. He smiled wanly, "When I return, I'll . . . uh. . .I'll tell you all about it." He looked at the sword's pommel, cleared his throat and pinched his eyes for a second. "I'm sorry I couldn't stay. . . longer. . . I'm sorry I. . . ." He sucked in a deep breath and let it out. "Goodbye for now, Kayla. . . ."

He walked back down the hill and began to saddle Whitesteel despite the horse's protests.

Chapter 45

Side Treks on the Road

"*C*ould he have gone north?" Maelyrin stood by the ancient paved highway, leaning on her unstrung bow, looking up its body as it snaked northward, the worn cobbles of its scales shining dully in the afternoon light, a maze of stone bordered and lined by a net of unkempt grass. "To Hestaff?"

"It is possible," answered Kiyomori softly, his figure a looming presence behind the smaller woman. His great russet cloak lay about Maelyrin's shoulders, a warm barrier against the sudden chill that nipped at her, but he seemed unaffected. "But does not seem likely since his trail has been southwest the entire time you have been following him. It would have been just as easy to head north from the beginning."

Her head fell forward and she snorted. A furrow appeared between her brows. "Do you have to be right all the time?" she said. He smiled just a bit.

"On the contrary, I am right only part of the time," he answered, drawing a chuckle from her that expelled some relief into the coming bitterness of weather. Her shoulder twinged at the effort, but that was all. The tea must have held more than just warmth.

"What do you think we should do, then?" she asked, gazing back up the road, then turning to look south, a questioning look on her face. "Maybe he went that way."

"Perhaps," Ki said. He was studying the leaden sky that had been creeping up on them all day, casting a drab blanket over them. Surrounding them, several miles distant, was the uneven green of the tree lines blending down into the grass of the plains, their high stalks shimmering dully as the late afternoon breezes slid by them. The only life they saw were several flocks of birds wending their way towards their evening roosts. A couple of crows in a nearby tree called out with mocking self-assurance. "There is a village not far from here," He said after several minutes of contemplating.

"What? Where?" she said, looking around quickly. "How do you know that?" She looked at him, then said, "I thought you said you haven't been this far north?"

"I did not, but I have not," His cryptic answer caused her to take a moment to decipher it. When understanding passed over her face, he continued. "Those carrion birds are too fat to have lived on wild seeds and insects and there is the faintest touch of wood smoke on the air. "

"Where?"

"That way," Ki said, pointing north a little away from the road. "Probably beyond those trees."

Maelyrin pondered that for a few minutes. The thought of going into a village of any other race than her own made her nervous. In fact, a sudden fear welled up in her, her mind going back to her first encounter with humans outside the safety of her own village. She drew the cloak around her unconsciously and shivered. However, she remembered the stories the Faethe used to tell her when she was little about his travels abroad when he went in search of the Tears. Tales of huge soft feather beds, bustling people, carriages, fine clothes. His old words sparked her curiosity higher than her fear, and a sudden gust of wind that threw back the cloak's hood and caressed her face with an icy touch, tipped the scale. She suddenly wanted to experience a blazing indoor fire and a soft bed with heavy blankets. "Okay then. Let's get going so we can get there before dark." She received a grunt from the giant in answer.

They continued on up the barren road, the once great highway now a headstone to an ancient time. Kiyomori walked slowly, but Maelyrin still had to keep a quick pace to stay up with him. They remained silent while they moved, a common pattern established earlier. It was second nature to Ki. She figured that he probably spent the majority of his life alone and the addition of someone to speak with was not enough to begin to change that. It was just as well, his pace kept her concentrating just on moving her own legs, much less conversing. It was a tiring pace and the muscles in her thighs seemed to be grinding together. The dull throb, though, was not on the top of her list of worries.

For at least an hour, they kept to the highway before coming across a rutted dirt road that joined it, running back to the west into the woodland that now paralleled them. They turned onto it. This road, too, bore the markings of disuse, tufts of lush grass and weeds encroached its borders and rode the hump of dirt in the middle, and fresh, windblown dirt was slowly filling the ruts. Further along, the trees converged until they were riding the banks of the path and the reaching branches of the elm and oak formed a tall arch that at once cut the chill breeze and blocked much of the fading daylight, casting them in a twilight gloom full of hoots, chirps, calls and buzzing of woodland creatures.

The road wound about like a river through the great trees and enveloped them in a feeling of peacefulness, but it wasn't long before they fell back away, the end of a natural covered bridge, revealing ahead spans of field bearing crops that should have been harvested by now. Row upon row of drooping, wilting wheat stood untended on either side of the path that arrowed through for maybe a mile before plunging into another thick stand of trees. A small house was hiding far from the road near the wood line in the northern field. Even from their distance, Maelyrin could see the gaping hole where the door should be and the beam of its tall roof was lined with black shapes. More crows. They called harshly, warning off the two interlopers that the place now belonged to them. Several more of the birds moved slowly along the weed choked ground, sluggishly pecking at overripe and rotting kernels that had already fallen from their dying stalks. Occasionally, one looked up and cocked a beady eye in their direction.

It made her shiver.

Kiyo paused only long enough to look at the house once they drew closer to it, said nothing. Neither did he seem to mind when Maelyrin stepped closer. Once they moved under cover of the trees, she relaxed. Until she looked up and saw more of the fat, oily black birds perched on the limbs nearby and glaring down at them. A tightness grabbed her spine at the back of her neck and a sickness dropped into her stomach. She thought about stringing her bow and shafting a few of them.

They passed a few more small farms in the same condition. Islands of dying wheat between enclosing trees being slowly consumed by an army of crows. She also saw flashes of movement deep within the trees. The first time she tensed unconsciously and half drew her knife when Ki's large hand came to rest softly on her shoulder. "Wolves," he said. She shivered again, but put the knife back and moved on.

"What has happened here?" she whispered. It sounded harsh and still too loud.

"I do not know," he said moments later. The next farmhouse they came upon, he walked over to, leaving her standing in the center of the road bundled in the heavy cloak. Clouds of angry crows flew up from the field, crying out their terrible calls at the disruption at his passing. There were far more than she realized. He circled the dwelling, studying it, before stepping up onto the porch and reaching out to push open the door. He paused, then, after a moment, he backed away, turning only when his feet touched the ground.

She watched him, *Looked* at him, a curious random activity that she allowed herself. Only a ripple rolled across the placid calmness that defined him. She still couldn't decide whether it helped to comfort her or disturb her, but it was the same nearly every time she *Looked*. Calm emptiness was the closest she could come to understanding it.

His long strides brought him back through the cackling wheat field quickly, her trepidation lessening the closer he got, but not before she nervously called out, "What is it?" Her voice sounded somehow alien and many crows answered her in loud, mocking *caws*.

"Plague," he replied simply. "The door has been marked."

"Plague," Maelyrin said, a hitch trying to jump into her throat. Before it could grip, she prodded her Healer's instincts into action. "How long?"

"It's been some time," he answered, his black eyes playing across the fields and tree lines. "The mark is several weeks old." He looked back down at her. "That explains the poor state of these fields."

"It is passed, then," she said, he nodded.

"Do you wish to continue?" she nodded.

"We may be able to find someone who has seen him." Maelyrin huffed, then eyed him critically. "It would seem logical for him to seek out a settlement after spending so long in open territory, would it not?"

Ki chuckled his growling chuckle and grinned, showing a goodly portion of his sharp teeth. "Perhaps," he answered. She smiled back. There was only a twinge caused by the sight of his smile now.

"Let's go before I lose my nerve," she finally said.

The Lonely Traveler Inn sat within bowshot of the outskirts of a village. It was boarded shut and, by the looks of its dry timbers, missing shingles, and faded sign, had been so for some time. There were no markings on the door in either red or black. The plague was not responsible for this one closing. Maelyrin looked at it for several minutes, allowing its overall blockiness to become a little less alien to her. Then, wordlessly, they moved on, heavy of heart. At least she was.

When they sighted the first of the villages' buildings squatting ahead of them within the trees, another raucous cry went up by several sentry crows that flapped into the air and flew from them lazily. Maelyrin paused again, her legs locking of their own volition. The smell of old death hung in the air, faint, ghostlike, and the only sound she heard was the clamor of the alerted crows. Her mind said it wanted to hear the murmur of voices, the whisk of cloth, the whicker of a horse. Her eyes sought movement, anything other than the small fluttering of black things, but she could see no one moving there, like there should be.

There was, though, the smell of wood smoke hanging on the air, but without the accompanying noises and sights the Faethe described to her seemed only to prompt the ominous feeling in her chest to become heavier. She had to mentally force her legs to continue.

Ki slowed while gently moving her behind him with a wave of a hand. The skin of her neck crawled. "What is it?" she asked quietly at his back. He seemed to be moving differently, more fluidly and completely silent. The air around him felt as if it hardened and veritably crackled with energy.

"I sense danger ahead," he rumbled softly in reply.

"Great," she whispered as she slid her knife free.

They moved cautiously, drifting toward the left side of the road, Ki, a coiled, but somehow relaxed, spring. The road widened as it entered the village, but was no more kept up than the rutted one. It was chewed and turned as if hundreds of horses had ridden through it after a stout rain, except that it was dry; a hard mass of tiny cliffs, mountains, slopes and valleys.

Lining it, like old sentinels, were dilapidated wooden houses and shops spaced randomly, crowding trees, the road, and each other. Many of them stood shut away from the outside, large black or red circles or 'X's painted on the rickety doors, but others gaped, their doors thrown wide, as if in disbelief that they had been abandoned. "Stay behind me," he said.

"Sure," she answered quickly. "No problem."

Ki moved along the front of the first of the houses, glancing inside as he passed the yawning door. Ahead of them, perhaps a quarter of a mile, was a large palisade of sharpened stakes that cut the road in twain and appeared to surround two opposite facing buildings. Two of the more prominent buildings of the village, three story structures that lorded over the rest of them. Smoke poured from the chimney of the most visible one.

As they hove near to it, about half the distance from the palisade, a voice rang out in the silence. "Stop there!" it cried. A cacophony of noise arose from suddenly disturbed crows and a bunch of them took flight. Maelyrin's eyes were jerked up and she saw a shadowed figure in the topmost window. "Don't move!"

A sudden flurry of action behind the tree-trunk wall brought her gaze back down. Figures moved rapidly and noisily behind it, people with picks, pitchforks, bows, and some swords. They arrayed themselves in some semblance of battle readiness, dirty faces appeared between the stakes. Desperate faces, belonging to both men and women. Clouds of black birds took to the air, calling in harsh protest.

"Send your speaker out!" Kiyomori bellowed, causing her to jump. Several of those behind the barrier did as well and many faces disappeared behind the protective trunks. A loud yammering that rivaled the flapping crows arose. She heard, "Eldythian" several times.

"They are frightened, starving, desperate," Maelyrin murmured. "Don't hurt them."

"Yes, they are," he replied softly. "No, I will not." His tone sounded hurt and it brought up a guilty hitch in her throat.

"Go away!" someone yelled. Several echoes, male and female, followed.

"Step to my right, not farther than an arm's width and let them see you. Then, repeat my call," Ki said.

"What? Me?" she stuttered. More cries for them to leave called out, more cries from the crows pealed from the rooftops where they settled and watched with unsettling interest. "What if they panic and shoot at me?"

"You will be protected," he answered. "Do not be frightened."

She mumbled an expletive into his back, nodded to herself, then stepped quickly out to his right, sucking in a loud breath as she did so. Immediately, another low rumbling rolled out from behind the barricade. "Please," she called, pausing to swallow against the aridness of her throat. "Send out your speaker." She heard several hushed words, several times, unmistakably, "Greyffolk." floated back to her. Heads appeared and disappeared; the tops of pitchforks and hoes bobbed and moved about brusquely. After many tense minutes, a couple of the stakes were pulled away, and a woman stepped out onto the road.

She was pallid and her features were sunken and dirt smudged her cheek just under her left eye. A wide fright filled eye that matched the right. She sported a heavy, thick leather coat under a ragged gray cloak and held a longsword that was dull and nicked. Puffs of dust rose from the road where she stumbled. Maelyrin gave her a comforting smile, cognizant of the dozen eyes at the end of drawn bows trained on them. It did not seem to affect her much.

"A-are you alone?" she said, gazing past them, down the road.

"Yes, just the two of us," Maelyrin answered quickly. "You have nothing to fear from us."

The woman's eyes flickered over her and came to rest on Ki, where they fluttered briefly between him and the road. "A-are you Eldythian?" she stammered.

"No, I'm not," he said softly. "Why have you blocked the road?"

The question startled her, making her eyes go wide. "Bandits," she choked past her fear.

"Bandits?" Maelyrin asked. "How long have you. . . ."

"Thirteen days!" she hissed, her eyes working up and down rapidly. They stopped, stared at her. "Do you have any food?"

"Just some dried meat," Maelyrin said, then, after a moment, rummaged through her pockets and came up with an oiled leather wrap. The woman's lips pulled back in a rictus smile, and her eyes stabbed at the package. Maelyrin tossed it. The package was snatched from the air and greedily tore open, while her sword fell to the street with a dull clang. The woman thrust the revealed strips into her mouth and devoured them before they could be chewed more than twice, while a whining ruckus started behind the barricade. Hands shot out between the stakes, grasping the air for the food. Kiyomori and she were forgotten, by all of them.

"Why haven't you sent out foragers?" he said suddenly. The rumble of his voice startled the woman so that she nearly dropped the last of the meat. The leather wrap hit the ground, and she smoothed out her clothes and dark hair as she swallowed the last bit in her mouth.

"T-too dangerous," she said shortly.

"So you choose to starve," he stated, a touch of anger tainting his voice. "Why haven't you fled?" She gazed at him, dumbstruck, while seconds slid by. Then, a look of utter fury stormed onto her sunken face.

"Because this is our home and no flaming looter is going to take it away from us!" she hissed. "This is our home!"

Maelyrin looked at him, at the planes of his bluish face as he gazed back at the woman with that unsettling cool gaze. He nodded. "You cannot fight off both them and hunger," he rumbled. "Which do you wish to succumb to?"

"Neither!" she said hatefully. He nodded again.

"Then you need to get food and get organized," he answered. "Or that waiting host will be the only thing well fed around here."

She studied him, his face, his black eyes, her fury turning into a slow burgeoning hope. Her fright at them evaporated. Without much more deliberation, she nodded while kneeling to pick up her fallen sword. "Wait here," she said. Ki nodded.

"What happens now?" Maelyrin asked as the woman backed out of earshot and moved into the enclave.

"Now, they discuss it." His eyes never left the palisade. "She convinces them, then, they live."

"And if she doesn't?"

"They die." It hung in the air like black smoke.

There was a loud, frantic, and ultimately short, argument within the compound, a few male voices singing a husky counterpoint to the woman's. Only minutes later, she stepped back through the palisade followed by two men, their sunken eyes studious of the ground before them. She no longer held the sword in hand, the dull, chipped blade slid down into the leather strap that wrapped twice around her waist. She stopped about the same distance she had been before, wariness in her step and set of her shoulders, though, obviously, a trait not strong enough to withstand her hunger. "I am Jana," she said forcefully. "The mayor of this village. If you offer help, then we accept it." One of the two men grumbled something into the dirt.

"I am called Kiyomori Sen." he said, bowing slightly at the waist. "This is Maelyrin Traelynn. We are glad to be of service." Even though Jana seemed expectant of his words, the very act of hearing them caused her shoulder to fall forward in relief.

"Thank you," she said as she strode forward. "What must we do?"

"First, we must get your people some food, then we can turn our attention to defense."

It took Jana all of a couple of minutes to relate the last thirteen days. Maelyrin thought it senseless, like much of what she had been doing for the last week, following a human man

she knew nothing about. Could know nothing about. The
bandits had come demanding they turn over the town to them.
Jana refused. They were given a day to reconsider. Then, they
left. It was as if they thought they were knights following the
codes of conduct when preparing to lay siege to a fortress.
Their arrival the following day was brutal and quickly over and
several villagers lay dead in the street. The bandit leader called
it an incentive and left again. The palisade was built and the
remaining villagers barricaded themselves within the small
compound with any weapon they could find and what food they
could carry. From then until now, it had been a constant wait of
anticipation, a wondering when they were going to return. The
fear alone was enough to keep them holed up. The food had
gone four days later. They had been too frightened to even send
out hunting parties. Luckily for them the barricade enclosed the
village's well, behind the town center, the three story public
building from which they were spotted. Otherwise they would
all have been dead a week ago.

"Why did you not eat the carrion birds?" Ki asked
pointedly as twilight began to fall on them. Jana looked as if he
had just turned into a spirit and floated away; the color bleeding
from her face so fast that Maelyrin was suddenly afraid that it
was not Ki turning into a ghost. Her own stomach turned at that
notion as she looked upon the patiently waiting host, and swore
that they looked back. Jana regained her composure slowly,
righteous disgust bringing her color back three fold. Her arm
flinched as if about to do something on its own, but she stopped
it.

"To eat the flesh of the Destroyer's Children is to lose
the soul that the Creator gave us," she said flatly. Ki nodded
again, a twitch of his brow the only show of his bothered
calmness.

"Send out hunters, now, in pairs," he said. "There is
plenty of game in the forest. Have them come back
immediately when they get a kill. Send out others to get
preserves and such."

"What if the bandits come?" she asked breathlessly.

"What if they do?" The question slapped Jana squarely in the face. She sucked in a breath loudly, but couldn't seem to let it out while the fog behind her eyes began to clear in a violent whirlwind. A fat tear fell from each of those brown orbs as understanding reached down into her and gripped her heart. A look of shock froze her face. "There is no time for that, now," he continued. "How many of you are there?"

It still took her some moments to gather herself, but she did, admirably. However, she seemed unable to stop the flow of water from her eyes. "There's only forty-nine of us now, including the children. Most of the villagers were taken by the plague this past spring. . . . twelve have been taken by the. . . . bandits."

"Where do you keep the dead?" he asked, his pointedness startled Maelyrin and Jana alike, but it was Jana that flinched several times. Her frayed sanity was about to unravel, and Ki's questions were only going to hasten it, and it angered her. Jana was a strong woman, and she did not need her *Sight* to know that. How she had become the chosen leader of this ragged band was not evident, but not a surprise. What her *Sight* did tell her was that she was lost in a world she knew nothing about and was operating only on the strength of her will and that will was cracked and battered and would soon give.

"We've wrapped them in linens and keep them in the tradesman's shop until we can care for their souls properly," Jana said, shaking visibly while lifting a loose hand and gesturing toward the second of the barricaded buildings. Maelyrin's stomach lurched. Jana suddenly turned from them and barked, "Karn! Santef! Go get the others together! Get as many of them as able to go out and hunt! In pairs! Send some others to get stores and millet and barley for bread."

The two men jumped at suddenly being addressed and the grumbler replied, somewhat belligerently, "What about the bandits? They'll come back."

"Not tonight!" Jana yelled, her voice splitting the silence like the chipped blade she carried in her belt. The two men, each one and a half times larger than the smaller woman, jumped and cringed back. "Tonight, we flamin' eat! Now get them to their tasks! Understand?"

Slack jawed, the grumbler finally nodded and turned, slapping the other man on the arm and drawing his attention away from Jana, but not before she received some haunted looks. When they both disappeared behind the fence, her shoulders slumped again, just before she started to stagger.

Maelyrin rushed over to support her as her legs began giving way. "Thank you," Jana whispered hoarsely. "I'm okay now." It was obvious that she was lying, and it was obvious that she knew Maelyrin knew she was. She continued to lean on her all the same.

"Where do you rest?" Maelyrin asked softly.

"Take me to that Inn," she said, gesturing to a building near them, two up from them and three down from the palisade. The sign claimed it to be the Everful. Maelyrin smirked at the irony. At least this one wasn't boarded up like the one on the outskirts of the village. She mentioned as much, that and the oddity of their names in comparison. Despite her recent ordeal, Jana chuckled. "A rivalry between brothers back when there was more travel on the road. Merchants and such." She sobered quickly. "It seems so long ago."

The Inn bore a layer of dust that seemed a lot thicker than a two week blanket, but everything was well ordered. The benches and long tables in the common room still stood in neat rows, and there were kegs stacked on rack behind a counter, waiting for a tap that would be long in coming. The mallet hung on the wall near them.

Maelyrin took it in quickly and stored it away to be looked at when time permitted, though her first impressions were not what the Faethe had been able to give to her when she was younger. In all his stories, she did not remember him speaking of how rigid these buildings were, their sharp edges, planes, and corners. Nor how dim inside, blocked away as they were from the sunlight. Like small sharp caves they seemed.

She had to remind herself that she was not in a major city; that the things that the Faethe had told her would not likely be represented here in this small place. That kept the smallness of the tiny bedroom and bed from bothering her sensitivity to the new experience, but not by much. The wooden frame creaked out in protest as she helped Jana lay on the thin mattress, causing her teeth to grit. She looked over the woodwork and sniffed. It was like a puzzle, all hooked together with joints and pegs of wood. It served its purpose, she supposed, but it was no work of living art. A sudden pang of homesickness arose in her.

"Thank you," Jana said, adjusting herself. Her voice took her away from the pangs and brought her back to the moment.

"You're welcome," she answered as she unfolded a blanket that sat at the foot of the bed and draped it over the scrawny woman. "How is it that you came to lead these people?" she asked to while the time.

"My father was mayor before me. When he died, they all figured I was the natural choice." she laughed. "Little did they know."

"Don't be so hard on yourself," Maelyrin said. "You did as well as you could under the circumstances. How many are sick?"

Jana's face widened in surprise for only a second. "What do you mean? The plague came through. . . ."

"No," Maelyrin interrupted, placed her hand on Jana's. "How many are sick because of hunger."

"Oh. . . Only a few," her eyes watered again and her face flushed. "I can't believe that I. . . ."

"Shh. You did what had to be done. There is no point in worrying about it now." Still, the flood came, Jana sobbing in great huffs. Maelyrin pulled her close, lending her strength that she wasn't certain that she possessed and held her for at least half an hour while she cried. Jana gave out finally, the exhaustion, hunger, and stress taking its toll on her body, and fell asleep. Maelyrin left, pulled the door to as quietly as the hinges would allow while marveling at the construct; even though she saw the inherent inefficiency compared to *valeurith*.

She cared for the six that were hunger sick while Ki looked over the defenses. Sunken-eyed villagers, those that had not left to forage, watched them both with a heady blend of distrust, fear, and hope. The village center was large enough, just, to accommodate all the defenders as long as comfort was not a condition of measure. The children, those too young to use a bow anyway, were kept inside much of the time, cared for by the elders remaining, which were not many. The rest took up pick, or ax, or whatever was handy, and waited. They took whatever position was available, took shifts whenever exhaustion demanded, their fear driving them beyond the boundaries of their bodies. They were uniformly pallid and hollow eyed. Their clothes were ragged and filthy. The smell of stale sweat, excrement and vomit clung to the area in wafting clouds that never completely went away. Near the other building hung the unmistakable reek of death.

After she had seen to the sick, she went looking for Ki, who had disappeared outside the palisade. Night had fallen by then, and the clouds thinned enough to let in some moonlight. Crickets began to buzz, the first of nocturnal sounds to arise. She shivered. Though silent, the waiting crows still lined the rooftops, and their eyes caught the moonlight. Tiny pearls gleamed in the darkness, blinking occasionally as heads swiveled or eyes closed. Unconsciously, she moved faster, nervously.

She found him outside the barrier on the western side of the palisade. He was squatting, searching the surrounding buildings and trees while brushing the churned up dirt slowly with a hand. "Interesting predicament these people are having," he said when she had come within earshot.

"What do you mean?" she asked as he stood, his large form blotting out the shadowed edges of the nearest building. He didn't answer, simply walked further down the road, kneeled, brushed the ground again while looking at his surroundings. Confused, Maelyrin followed. "Ki?"

He looked up, and his eyes shone like the crows' did in the moonlight. Her throat dried.

"Have you noticed anything unusual about this situation?" he asked quietly, his voice seeming to blend with the night sounds.

"No," she replied. "They are very frightened and very determined."

"Yes. Yes, they are." He turned his gaze back to the road. "But what are they hiding?"

"What do you mean?" she said, gazing at him intently as he pondered the surrounding woods. "Are you always this distrusting?"

He chuckled, the growling noise eerie in the night. "Only when death is involved," he said. Ki stood and looked at her, eyes bright in the moonlight. "That is something you will learn in time." When she did not reply, he reached out and pointed back toward the barricaded buildings. Several cheers echoed hollowly back to them; the hunters beginning to return with food. "Why do you suppose they were able to take time to build that wall but not enough to get food?"

"They were frightened."

"Yes. . . Now, tell me, have you seen any fresh tree stumps nearby?" he asked. She blinked, then looked around. Trees lined the road on both sides and even though dark, her eyesight could penetrate further back behind the nearest ones. Nowhere could she see the telltale signs of a woodsman's ax. Confused, she looked back at him.

"I. . . .I don't understand," she finally asked.

"If they were too frightened to gather enough food, why did they take the time to carry the timber in from somewhere else?" She was about to speak, when his voice rumbled again.

"And these tracks, only three sets, do not lead toward the village, but away."

"What are you saying?" she asked quickly. Her voice was angry, an irrational reaction to the challenging remarks he was offering up.

"I'm saying that the story we were given is not what is really going on here."

"But they are truly frightened and desperate. . . ."

"I do not dispute that," Ki said. "But their behavior does not reflect the facts. Those people in there are guarding something."

"Yes, the town," she snapped. Ki shook his head with patient slowness.

"They are guarding something inside that barricade," he said. "And they are waiting for retribution."

Maelyrin stared at him, her confusion twisting her anger up into a white hot barb. "So! So what if they are? Does that change anything? Are we going to leave them to that retribution?"

"No, it doesn't," he said, his voice, still waters. "But if we are to help them, if we are to expose ourselves to danger, then it is important that we are not deluded by false impressions."

His answer pricked the bubble of her anger and let the air out of it. As so many times since she had met him, she was ashamed of her outbursts that seemed such an alien part of her. "Well then. . . . What do we do, then?"

"We let them eat and sleep," he said. "It will better prepare them for the battle they are waiting for. In the morning, I will give them some idea of how to fight."

"And me?"

"You will stay close to me and be wary. Whatever they are trying to protect can easily sway them to turn their suspicions on us once this threat has lessened."

Chapter 46

A Thicket for Comfort

A thick blanket of snow covered the ground when the sun hefted itself above the horizon. The clouds responsible for the whiteness were long dispersed, allowing the light to reflect brightly off the pristine surface. It kept Alex squinting against it as they rode, following the trail Sandoren's horse left for them when he rode ahead before sunrise. Beside her, whispering quietly to himself, rode Del, humped down within the voluminous clothes Kiers rounded up for him, replacing the tight, ill-fitting ones they scavenged from the ffolk village. Marc rode a couple of lengths behind them, bundled in the heavy blue cloak he had worn last evening. He remained silent, not even speaking when asked a question, only giving long, stony looks in answer. Earlier, his slate eyes had made her shift uneasily.

Now, she was angry, both by his silence and by her reaction to it. She huffed, blowing out a breath that misted thickly about her face. Clover snorted. There was no use in worrying it. The fact that she had to cajole him into coming still lay in her stomach, a lump of guilt that wouldn't let her breakfast settle. Adding anger on top of that only made it worse. In an effort to pull her mind away from it, she focused her attention on the double line of holes in the crust of the snow ahead of them.

All that did, however, was shift her thoughts to Sandoren's brooding behavior, which kept becoming more odd.

Instead of waiting for her to rise this morning, he left before dawn, leaving a note with Master Abyl that he would be scouting ahead and would meet up with them later. She shook her head and gritted her teeth, asking herself why things seemed to be falling apart now.

Of course, that didn't matter either. She had something to do regardless of casualty or consequence. Something that warranted that neglect even by doing so. She was working against every fiber and value that she was, that she stood for. Her head hurt.

Behind them, somewhere, the ever presence of the Eldritch itched the back of her mind. It was closer today and she somehow thought it less reticent. She would have to tell Marc about it soon, once he got over his steadfast silence. Alex found herself reconsidering her earlier decision not to ask the wolves for any more help.

Sometime around mid-morning, it began to snow again, a rain of small pellets made all the more unusual since the sky above them was still a clear, clean blue. It startled Alex out of her reverie, but did nothing to alleviate it. It added to her heavy thoughts. She had not sensed it. Even now, she could not sense the Patterns even as the freezing balls fell softly against her face and melted.

She smiled and chuckled, realizing suddenly that she was just as guilty of brooding as Marc and Sandoren were. Her eyes closed, and she allowed herself to sink into the motions of her body as Clover plodded along. She breathed in deeply, the cold air seeping into and energizing her. She let go, disappeared into the place where she could feel the throbbing of Earth's Blood beneath her and Earth's Breath as it streamed by, then let her awareness reach out in an ever widening globe. The refreshing smell of snow filled her nostrils, the pungent under layer of loam following it. Her body relaxed and the tensions left her mind. Only seconds later, content reflecting on her features, she opened her eyes and accepted the pinch of the heightened blare of the world around her.

The immediacy of her calmness would only be temporary, but it brought her the balance that she needed. She would have to take some time later on and do it again to strengthen the stability the new pile of stress was working hard to undermine. For now, however, her brief respite was enough to bring clarity of mind.

Sandoren met them not long before the sun reached its zenith, appearing from a nearby grove of snow laden trees only when the obscuring fall allowed him to identify them. Veraddin was nosing around in the white at the grove's edge, clipping grass he unearthed. Sandoren's face was grim and drawn by tension, and he gave the trailing Marc such a fierce look that she at once thought that he might free his sword from its scabbard.

"There's a large group of men up ahead, camped out along the cross road we want," he said quickly, tonelessly. "About thirty of them. Humans. Bandits, I think. It might be a good idea if we camp out until they move on."

"How far ahead are they?" Alex asked.

"Couple of hours," he said. "More, if this. . ." he looked up through the falling snow at the still blue sky. ". . . continues to fall."

"What's going on?" Marc said, stopping his large white horse near her right stirrup. Disgust washed across Sandoren's face and his sword hand flinched toward its hilt. If Marc noticed the gesture or the look, he didn't acknowledge it with either words or expression.

"Sandoren said there is a group of bandits camped up the road," Alex said, heading off the biting comment that she saw rising in her companion's throat. "He suggests that we begin looking for a place to camp until they move on."

Marc looked at her, a flurry of movement behind his eyes as if he were in the middle of a harsh memory, then he nodded. "Very wise," he said. His voice too, was toneless. "There are many groups of such men raiding up and down the roads these days."

"And that. . ." Sandoren began, but was cut off as Marc continued.

"Is it possible to go around them?" he asked, turning his flat gaze on the tall ffolk.

Sandoren's face reddened quickly, but he replied evenly, "Yes, but we'll lose more time than if we wait." Marc nodded as if disinterested, then backed Whitesteel away and moved down the road. Sandoren watched him with serpent's eyes, hand gripping his belt tightly. Alex rolled her eyes.

"Well," she said, breaking the tension. "Let's get as much distance as we can get today. Do they look settled in for more than just a night."

Several moments passed while Sandoren struggled against himself, his face carved of rough granite. "No. They won't be there long," he said. "They're probably waiting out this strange weather. If it stops they'll probably move out tomorrow." He gazed back up into the falling balls of snow. "If it doesn't, I don't know when they'll leave."

"Hopefully, it'll stop soon then," she said offhandedly, herself looking up. The snow looked like little bits of gray radiating out from the blue above. She didn't notice his sudden questioning gaze.

"Can't you tell when it will stop?" he asked. His tone changed, losing its anger for a brief second to be replaced by concern. She looked at him, his face seemed shadowed, and she shook her head.

"No," she said softly. "I can't sense this. Even now."

"What? Why?"

She looked at him, a pinch of pain followed by that touch of fright in her breast. "It's not natural," she said simply. Without another word, she nudged Clover into action, following the quickly receding Marc. Sandoren watched her for only a moment before going back and retrieving Veraddin.

The strange snow kept falling the next few hours, growing steadily heavier until it was too thick to see very far ahead, much less the sky. Above, though, Alex could sense clouds rolling in, natural clouds that promised to drop natural snow. As much as that was not a comforting thought, it eased her mind a bit.

Finally, Sandoren led them into the encroaching woods and found a place relatively sheltered from the fall and far enough from the road that, should it stop snowing, the fire they were going to build to keep warm would not attract any undue attention. Her longtime companion, for his part, dismounted away from the rest of them and went about gathering the wood they needed.

Marc moved to the opposite side of their chosen camp site as far as proximity would allow. It was as if both men were being kept at bay by an invisible bar connecting them to her. A bar stronger than any steel that would neither keep them from drawing too far nor bring them closer. *Perhaps, in time*, she thought, watching him as he began caring for his horse, first taking the bridle then the saddle off. He rummaged through one of his saddlebags and brought out a brush with which to clean the day's ride from the magnificent beast.

She turned and helped Del down from Day. He gave her a slack smile, but that was the extent of his interaction. Del had remained deeply withdrawn all day, rocking in his saddle and mumbling softly to himself. The coat that they had procured for him was thrown open, exposing the thin shirt beneath, but he seemed comfortable. Still, she buttoned the coat up while he stared off in some space only known to him and led him to a spot near the center of their site. "Del?" she said, holding his shoulders while peering into his far away eyes. She continued to say his name until, slowly, he was looking at her. "Del?" he nodded, slightly. "Are you hungry?" He nodded again, smiled. "Okay. You stay right here and I will get you some cheese, alright?" He nodded a third time while she brushed at his ratty hair with her fingers then left him standing while moving over to Clover's saddle bags.

While digging through the leather satchel, her attention was drawn back to Marc when the sound of long brush strokes reached her. She stared. It was as if she were looking at another person. All of the stiffness and gruffness was gone from Marc completely and replaced by a tenderness that startled her. As he brushed the magnificent beast, he patted and stroked him and, she cocked her head to make sure, was whispering to the animal. Whitesteel returned the kindness, whickering softly and nuzzling the big man. He moved to the other side, brushing every inch of the animal, his face, normally etched from stone, was soft and relaxed, and he was even smiling, eyes lucid.

Suddenly he looked up, over the horse's broad back, catching her gaze in his and stiffened. The relaxed, caring expression he was wearing vanished like an extinguished candle, and his eyes went steely hard. A deep frown creased his face. The guilt she had been hiding welled up again and the anger with it. She cleared her throat and turned away quickly, though she could still feel the heaviness of his gaze on the back of her head. A minute passed. Alex realized she was holding her breath and had to force an exhale that sounded too much like a sigh.

Anger flared again, indignation and embarrassment that she had to force down. The sound of the brush strokes starting again relieved some of the pressure even though they were short and clipped. Silently, clenching her jaw, Alex took the wrapped piece of cheese and a waterskin back to Del, who was sitting at the base of a tree and staring at the ground, his coat unbuttoned again and his hair messy. It took several tries to get his attention long enough to take the small hunk of cheese and water, which he took with a slack smile before returning to his study of the several insects crawling around in front of his legs. She gave them a cursory once over before returning to Clover to brush her down.

When she finished, a small fire crackled in the center of their clearing, Sandoren squatting near it feeding small, dry twigs to its licking flames. The light from it, even though it was still daylight, albeit dim, accentuated the course lines scrawling over his face, giving him a surreal expression of angry frustration. Marc, on the other hand, was already lying down, his saddle bags his pillow, face relaxed in pre sleep. Whitesteel stood over him and suddenly seemed menacing. She sighed, this time a genuine one, and sat down near the fire, leaning back against her saddle and began chewing absently on some cheese and bread. It appeared that the rest of the day and coming evening would be spent in silence.

The night brought another bout of snow, natural snow, that fell so thickly that some of it filtered down through the tight canopy above them. The sunrise was a miserably slow lightening of gray, the clouds packed thickly over their heads though unseen through the branches. When she awoke, shivering beneath her blankets, she found Sandoren sitting up beneath a nearby tree and watching her. At first, he didn't notice her looking back, his eyes distant. *He is thinking about his situation*, she thought, mildly. *About his anger and all the things causing it.* She smiled sympathetically into her blanket. Sandoren was a good man and friend. He would try to accept the changes that had been thrown on him, but it would be hard. He was stubborn in his convictions. "Did you sleep at all?" she asked quietly, startling him.

He smiled thinly, only for a moment, before the tensions settled into his features again. "Some," he said hoarsely and scooted over to the fire to stoke up the coals and put more wood on it. "It's tough going."

Alex nodded, sat up slowly, drawing her blankets more tightly around her frame. "For all of us."

A shadow crossed his face. "Yes," he mumbled. "Do you want some warm jerky?"

Her stomach rumbled. "Yes, thank you, I'm starving," she said, bringing another small smile across Sandoren's face.

"You're always starving," he said and handed her some strips of dried meat. He sat back on his haunches and began chewing on his own breakfast.

"Do you think they have moved on?" she asked.

Sandoren shrugged. "I wouldn't bet on it since it snowed again last night," he said around a mouthful of food. "But, then again, they may not care about the snow at all. It might have been the strange weather that stopped them. Remember that story we heard about the fire raining from the sky south of Render?" he waited for her nod. "Maybe they heard it, too, and decided to stop for fear of being burned to death."

"Yes, perhaps," she said thoughtfully, then seriously, "Sandy, are you alright?"

The clouds passed over his face again. "I mean it, really alright?" she reiterated. His face turned sullen, then angry, then neutral, and he nodded.

"Yes, I am fine."

"Don't lie to me, Sandy," she said, the sternness in her voice only partially true. "I have known you far too long for you to be able to hide things from me."

"You have already heard my thoughts," he answered levelly, hollowly. "There is nothing else."

Liar, she thought harshly. *You bald-faced liar.* "Fine." With some effort, she fought to keep the harshness out of her voice. It didn't work. Sandoren felt it and flinched, then clenched his jaw and stood.

"I will ride ahead to see if the bandits have moved on," he said flatly. "Stay here until I return."

Alex nodded, and when he left, walking Veraddin out of their shelter, she wiped at the tear that had fallen down her cheek. Next to her, Del moaned and tossed, chasing off some unpleasant dream thought. He was uncovered and bare chested, his shirt and coat wadded next to him as if he squirmed out of them in the night and used them like a stuffed animal or similar snuggle toy. She reached over and placed a hand on his bulky side, then pulled it back in surprise. He was hot. She checked again, placing her hand on his skin. Warmth not unlike that of the fire chased the cold from her fingers.

Frantically, she slid over enough that she could place her hands on his face, calling on her healing powers. His face was hotter still, but dry, and he was breathing deeply and rhythmically. The growing fear of a fever began to wane, replaced by curiosity. But, still, her instincts told her something was wrong, that the heat rising from him indicated something was amiss, that it was anything but normal . . . .

"It's normal," Del said softly, his voice deep and sonorous rather than that of a boy. It surprised her again, and she quickly pulled her hands away while simultaneously leaning forward to look at his face. His eyes were still closed, and his breath came in the same measured strokes. She thought he was still sleeping.

"Yes, I am still asleep," She backed up quickly, a primitive reaction that leapt before she could think. He spoke in the same deep voice. The voice of someone else; a man.

"Del?" she asked softly. Tentatively, she reached over and shook him. "Del?"

He answered her with a groan and a smacking of sleep coated lips, pulled the blanket over his face as he rolled away from the direction of her voice. Hastily, she glanced around, stopping suddenly when she saw Marc gazing at her with those steel eyes. "Did you hear that?" she asked quickly.

"Hear what?" he asked. His face was clear and unfettered by sleep. "The boy speak?"

Alex nodded. He nodded back. "Some people talk in their sleep," he remarked, then pulled something rolled in cloth from his saddle bag, unwrapped it, then began putting small bits of it into his mouth. She relaxed a bit, pulled the blanket around her more tightly and watched him as he stuffed a few more bites of his breakfast in his mouth. "Yes, of course," she said.

"Is your Guardian always so pleasant?" he asked absently, looking in the direction the ffolk had gone. It spiked her.

"Are you?" she remarked.

He looked at her then, calmly. "Not always," he began. "Only when I'm forced."

"Point taken," she said hastily, an angry tone working into her voice.

"The boy," he said, gesturing with a hunk of bread toward the supine form. "He's daft?"

His comment inflamed her more. "He happens. . . ." she began harshly, cutting herself off when the thought struck her that he was merely curious, not necessarily being crude. Quickly, she backed down and took a few deep breaths. "He may be?" she said cautiously. "Sometimes, he seems very aware, but most of the time he is as you've seen him."

"Is he why you are traveling north?"

"Yes, partly," she answered, drawing her blanketed knees up to her chest. "He is a key in a large, complex puzzle." After a thoughtful minute, she added, "You are, too."

"I am what?" Marc was grinning, a sardonic crease. "A puzzle?"

"A key to a puzzle," she said. He gazed at her for a few minutes, a unwavering stare that became heavy and uncomfortable. Just as she was about to make a comment about it, the man pushed himself up from the ground.

"Well, you will find out your mistake soon enough," he said bleakly. "In the meantime, we should be getting ready to ride. Your crusty sidekick should be back soon. We are not. . . ."

"Be careful of what you say about Sandoren, Aeric!" she spat. Marc winced, but didn't look at her. "His worth will not be compared to his disposition. You, of all people should understand that!" He flinched again.

"Yes, well," he answered. "If he doesn't learn to control his temper, he is going to get sloppy. And getting sloppy can get you killed."

"So can. . . ." What she almost said, she clamped down on, quickly finishing with, "anything else." But the pause was terrible in its honesty and Marc did look at her then, pain awash on an otherwise stolid face. He knew what she almost said. And, he knew she had meant it, hiding it only because it was in her nature to.

"At least," he said, his voice icy. "The odds need to be decreased. Maybe you should restrain him a bit through your Bond."

"We aren't Bonded," Alex retorted. Marc's brow lifted sharply. "Besides, what you profess cannot be done."

"Sure it can," He answered "But, since you're not Bonded, then it is not important. You should still give him counsel. A Guardian who is controlled by his feelings is not a Guardian."

"You let me worry about Sandoren," Alex stated. "You worry about whatever else you want to worry about." His comments, though, burrowed into her mind and lodged there, refusing to budge. They reinforced her own thoughts and feelings about her companion. His answer was a shrug that preceded a turn back to his task of saddling Whitesteel. Silently, she chewed on her own breakfast, watching him as he moved, his breath forming slow clouds in the morning air. The horse, for his part, waited patiently until the girth straps were threaded and pulled tightly enough to keep the saddle in place before going back to quiescent grazing.

They were all awake and ready to move on when Sandoren returned, each inside a bubble of silence not unlike what would be if they were individually alone. Del was as slack jawed and distant as ever, so much so that he didn't even bother to examine the multitude of bugs that seemed to conglomerate around him whenever he stayed in one spot for more than a few minutes. After an epic battle of trying to get him to eat some bread, which she lost, Alex was actually relieved to see Sandoren's taciturn face appear from the thickets that surrounded their camp

"They've gone," he said without preamble when he drew nearer the fire. "Headed east along the road just after sun rise."

"Good," Alex answered, brushing crumbs from her cloak. "How about the northern road?"

"It's clear," he answered quickly. "For several miles anyway."

"Good," she repeated while wrapping the rest of the hub of bread back into its cloth. She glanced past her Guardian and watched Marc pull himself up onto Whitesteel's back. It was not difficult to picture him in full armor, a shield strapped to his arm and that infamous sword at his side. After all, she had been raised on the stories of the High Knights of Ellynthryll. That time when such men were still a common site. Before the Knight Wars wiped the rest of them out. Of course, that was many, many years later than Marc's service to that Order.

She looked away before he settled himself in the high cantled saddle and had a chance to let his gaze wander over to hers. When she peered up, though, she found a stony gaze bearing down on her. She gave Sandoren a sheepish smile then said, "I guess we should get going then."
A line appeared, then disappeared between his brows before he nodded sharply. "I'll scout ahead," he threw back over his shoulder when he turned. She watched him disappear back into the woods, a curse whispered in answer to his gruff reproof. Alex shrugged it aside and returned to packing up the rest of the food.

Chapter 47

The Battle for the Village

*M*aelyrin looked up from her cup of tea to see if Kiyo's eyes were open yet. They weren't. She shivered, the small fire built earlier warmed only a portion of her, and the chill side won out in a brief battle. Her eyes flicked in the direction of the village, which lay just out of sight beyond the thick trees, then back to the small clearing that had been trampled bare of snow by Kiyo's flowing exercise earlier. They had been there since sunrise. Once he had finished, he sat down across from her and, apparently, went to sleep while sitting up. Why he had to do it out in the snow, she had no idea. At least, the hot bitter liquid helped keep the cold provided by the white blanket away. Mostly.

She shivered again.

Actually, the blue giant wasn't really sleeping. Her *Sight* told her that it was something more, something deeper. Almost as if he had died without letting his body know it. The utter serene-ness had been reestablished, too. The slight ripples of disturbance the villagers were causing with their constant, unusual lying were gone now.

She couldn't say much about herself, though. Her neck muscles tightened reflexively just by thinking of them, and her emotions ranged from pity to fright when she was among them and their furtive glances and covert gestures at keeping them from the abandoned trade building.

Luckily, Kiyo quickly organized them into more defensible positions, gave them an idea of what battle was like and showed them how to use their weapons more effectively. He sent out foragers and hunters, and had the elders set up a hospital within the three story public building. The tasks were met with confusion and constant yammering, but it kept them busy and restored to them some sense of self-worth, giving them a reprieve from their very real fear. All in all, it had proven to be a very frustrating day.

"They come," Kiyo said softly, the rumble of his voice startling her. His eyes opened slowly, the glassy black of their surfaces revealing nothing of the thoughts that must be behind them. Only the calmness could be *Seen*.

"What?" she replied. "Who?"

"Many horses from the west," he said. Lead dropped into her stomach.

"Is it. . . .?"

"Possibly," he rose slowly, calmly. "If so, I want you to stay close to me."

"No need to worry about that," she said as she hurriedly put the tea utensils in its small pack. Once finished, she stood, shouldered her own pack, and picked up her bow and quiver.

Kiyo's leisurely pace served only to agitate her more than she already was. Her heart fluttered wildly and her pace quickened and, for once, she found herself flitting about the longer strided giant like a swallow harassing a hawk instead of trying to catch up with him.

When they arrived back at the village, the first sounds of the thundering hooves was just being noticed. Shouts rang out. A barely controlled panicked race for the battlements ensued, the villagers calling out their fears in quick bursts as they took up their arms. Amazingly, the previous day's practice seemed to be less confused now that their lives depended on it. As they moved into the barricade, they found them staring wide-eyed down the road while fingering weapons as if they itched. From the second story of the town center, several pairs of frightened eyes peered out from just over the window sills, both young and old.

Jana rushed up to them before they were three steps within the little gate, her hand clenched around the hilt of her beat up sword. "They are coming!" she blurted, her breath pitched higher than normal.

"Yes," Kiyo answered simply, evenly.

"What do we do?"

"We wait." Maelyrin couldn't help but smile slightly when she saw shock and awe pass over the woman's features. "Also, remove a stake from this side of the barricade, close to the town center."

Jana and Maelyrin both stared in surprise. "W-what?" Jana finally managed.

"Remove a stake so that I may leave if it comes to fighting," he explained. She stared again, her mind working over his statement. When understanding rose behind her eyes, she turned away from them and began barking at the two burly men that seemed to be her seconds in command, Karn and Santef, who promptly began removing a large enough stake for him to slide through.

A preternatural silence settled over them suddenly, the only sounds, the pounding of distant hooves, the whisper of a breeze, and the occasional muted caw of crow. All of them gazed out at the blanket of white and vertical dark lines of moist tree trunks, jets of harsh breath rushing from frightened mouths. A noticeable pall of tension grew with the closing thunder. Maelyrin's own breath was shallow and her chest hurt with tightness while the coppery taste of fear crawled up into the back of her throat. A drool of sweat at her temple caused a shiver to run through her. With controlled nervousness, she withdrew an arrow from the quiver at her hip, and slid the nock into place. The dull gleam of the steel tip caught her eye and she realized that she may be taking a life today.

She swallowed. Hard. Tried to breathe deeply, but couldn't. "Taking a life," she whispered. "How can I take a life? I'm a healer."

A soft, but firm, hand came to rest on her shoulder and she looked up into the twin obsidian orbs. "You will do what you must." It felt like ice was cracking and falling away from her spine when she nodded her answer.

They came around the distant bend at a leisurely gallop, appearing suddenly in a cloud of mist and kicked up snow, men bundled in furs atop them. Across the span, eyes met eyes, and one of the horsemen flung up a hand. As a group, they reined in, the horses whinnying and snorting, some of the riders calling out in surprise. For several seconds they glared over the distance while their mounts pranced back and forth, then, the sunlight began glaring off steel as weapons were drawn from scabbards and holders. Swords, axes, and broad headed maces appeared.

A low murmur ran down the length of the barricade, the silent spell broken in the face of reality. The horde came forward at a trot, a snorting, growling thing churning up the snow, turning white to black as hooves gouged up the moist dirt beneath. The clouds of steam puffing from mouth and nose seemed fierce in the dull gray morning light. Just outside of effective bow range they stopped and one of them yelled through a misty breath, "Give us what belongs to us and no one will be hurt."

Nervous eyes looked back at Kiyomori and Maelyrin and at each other.

"Begone!" one of the villagers yelled. "You'll get nothing from us!" This time, many of the horsemen's eyes looked among themselves.

"Then you will all die!" the voice snarled back. Another ripple of anxious murmurs went through the villagers. But they did not come forward. They waited, allowing the last of the words to sink down through the grayness and settle into the spines of those behind the bristling wooden fence. Their horses

pranced back and forth, churning up the earth and squealing
into the chill air. Bursts of mist formed an occluding screen.

Kiyo glided to the opening, surprising Maelyrin.

"What are you doing?" she asked once her mind clicked
over and allowed her to speak.

"I want you to stay inside the palisade," he rumbled
softly. "And be aware of all that goes on around you."

"I thought you wanted me to stay close to you?" she
said with some ire stirring within the musical tones of her
voice. He quickly turned and looked down at her, his face in
complete relaxation though it was set stoically.

"I want you to be as safe as you can be," he said.
"Inside the walls is best."

"But. . . . ."

"You will stay," he said, the tone in his voice an
evenness that echoed through her mind. She blinked, held her
breath as she suddenly lost the drive to follow him outside.

Mechanically, she nodded.

As he moved to the hole in the fence, she shook her
head and wondered why she was still standing there. *What did
he do to me?* she thought.

When he slid through the small opening and walked
with graceful power to the center of the road, the horde, as a
whole, stilled and, even across the distance, Maelyrin could see
their faces change expression. Bewilderment replaced the
menace, and a new anger rode closely behind it. Several of the
aggressors began muttering chaotically. All save for the few in
the front, who leered forward at the figure of the giant. Shortly,
one of them turned and barked at the others, silencing them.

"So," one of them spat, the foremost of them, his head
wrapped in a fur cap like the others, but she could see a dark
red beard pushing its way out from the collar of his heavy coat.
"You fled this way after you killed my brother."

Confusion swept over Maelyrin, and she heard herself
mumble, "What?" Kiyo, though, said nothing, didn't even

move. He simply stood facing them like a large bluish-cast statue.

The bearded one turned to his nearest companions and said loudly, "I guess we get more for this than what we came for." It was the second time there was an allusion to another reason for their presence. Absently, she looked at the tradesman's shop, and when she swung her gaze back out to the street, she found Jana looking at her, face tight. Maelyrin looked at her for a few seconds, discomfort rising in her belly. When she was able to pull her eyes away, as if there had been nothing but that gaze, she heard one of the bandits saying, " . . . looks different."

"No!" exclaimed the bearded one. "I'd know those cowardly eyes anywhere." Under Kiyo's gaze, though, the men were becoming more silent, almost meek. A nervousness seemed to be overtaking them, even the speaker, as if his words were only to buttress his resolve. "Today, we get revenge as well as rich."

It was only after a moment of silence did Kiyo break his. "What you seek is not yours to take," he called, voice booming along the empty corridor of snow swept trees. "If you value your lives, then turn back now." All of them sat up and back, white faces going slack, and she thought she heard an echo of his voice. The simultaneous actions of the men would have been comical if the situation wasn't so tense.

They stared, horses breathing great plumes of mist, for many moments, and then, without warning, the man next to the bearded one screamed out in fury and kicked his mount's flanks. The beast leapt forward, its rider screaming shrilly, brandishing a long sword in circles above his head. Maelyrin froze, almost dropped her bow. The villagers, too, were caught off guard. As she watched the wild man harangue his horse into a full out run, bearing straight for Kiyo, several arrows sped by him, some of them lodging into tree trunks, others slamming into the dirt to be trampled by the mount's hooves.

Kiyo remained stock still, hand on the hilt of his unusual sword, watching the horse and rider flying across the span as if it did not exist. Apparently stunned by their companion's rash move, the other bandits remained where they were, riveted by the spectacle.

Hooves thundering, sword gleaming dully in the gray light, the bandit screamed out his fury again, his face becoming pinched with rage. She couldn't blink, couldn't breathe. He drew closer, but Kiyo still didn't move. She suddenly feared for her friend, who seemed oblivious to his impending death. The bandit drew closer still, began leaning in the saddle. Kiyo seemed determined to be trampled.

Just before death took him, Kiyo moved. Maelyrin wondered if she blinked, it happened so fast. Villagers cried out as the riderless horse crashed into the palisade while trying to turn away. It squealed as the sharpened wood bit into its flesh, and it staggered away, blood streaming down its side. The bandit, his scream of rage curdled into pain and suddenly silenced, lay several feet from the giant, twitching in the snow covered mud, his body contorted awkwardly, gashed and gushing. Kiyo was standing from a deep sideways stance, flicking his blade quickly. A line of crimson flew from the metal, streaking the whiteness to his side.

She had to watch the bandit die in retrospect, her mind putting the pieces of the flash of movement together so that she could now comprehend what she was looking at. The memory of a shining shield around Kiyo came to her again. Someone near her vomited.

Kiyo waited until the last possible moment, letting the man lean out to strike him with his long sword, when, suddenly, the blue giant moved like quicksilver to the opposite side of the horse. His blade slid from the scabbard, lightning swift, effortlessly slicing through air and bandit equally without touching the neck of the mount, sending the horribly wounded man flying from the saddle into the earth. His death was quick; probably never knew it happened. And now his shell lay mangled, twitching in red steaming snow while his horse stumbled toward the woods to die. Kiyo, faster than she could believe, snapped the blade back and sheathed it, then took his place in the center of the road, not even peering back to see if the man were dead. He already knew it.

For moments, the rest of the horde was shocked silent. Mouths hung open and arms dropped slowly. The bearded one's face suddenly contorted into a hideous mask of rage, and he stood in his saddle. "Kill them all!" he screamed.

As if they were straining against an invisible barrier that instantly disappeared, the horde surged forward in a mass of furious roars, their shock finding release as readily as the charge. Quickly, they fanned out along the road as well as they could and many of them intent on the tall solitary figure standing in the center just outside the palisade.

Around her, bow strings began twanging, the sound nearly lost in the impending rage of the howling mass. Villagers cried out in fright and fled their posts, some seeking shelter in the building, others simply threw themselves down into the mud and huddled in quivering heaps. Only a few remained in their positions, grim faced and pale.

For Maelyrin, who had never seen battle before, it felt as if every hair on her body was crying out and a heaviness landed on her rib cage. Within her head, a steady thudding fought with the thundering hooves and hollering men for dominance and the world around her suddenly seemed painfully bright. Dimly, she was aware that she was bringing the fletching of an arrow to her cheek and sighting past the shaft.

I'm going to kill a man, her mind whispered loudly. *I'm going to kill. A man.* A cold shiver ran through her body and runnels of sweat began itching through her hairline and down her temples. She loosened her grip, and dry swallowed. A woman near her cried out, drawing her gaze. Maelyrin stared dumbly at a feathered shaft that had sprouted from her chest. It wasn't until another one zipped past her head that her stupor was shaken off and she sighted her own shaft again. Gritting her teeth and clamping down on her mind, she loosed the arrow.

It sped away into the tumult, and a man fell backward off his horse, but she wasn't sure if it was her arrow or someone else's. Quickly, she was loosing another, then another, her mind quiet in spite of the horrible scene before them. Worried, she flicked a glance at Kiyo.

He stood as he did before, sentinel still, a single tree against the onrushing hurricane, waiting patiently for the death that seemed imminent. It was obvious that he would be trampled by the mass of horsemen, that he wasn't going to get away with a feinted sidestep this time. Instead, he sprang straight up, impossibly high, twisting around in the air as the overzealous bandits rushed by underneath, startling them. Horses stopped and tried to rear but were slammed into by others behind, pushing them into the sharpened spikes of the barricade. Men fell, screaming, to be trampled while their mounts cried in agony upon the impaling spikes. Maelyrin didn't see him come down, but more terrified cries from behind the crowd, told her that Ki was working his grim work out of sight.

More was not possible for her, as the sudden press of bodies against the fence forced her attention back to her immediate situation. A cloud of rank odor rolled past her, horse, sweat, and blood, that worked against her breathing. The yelling was deafening. Many of the nearest bandits were hacking at the fence with swords and axes, trying to get at the villagers. Wood chips flew in showers. Arrows ripped through the air, fired by bandits and villagers alike. Men and woman and horses fell.

A black cloud began to obscure the periphery of her vision, and her breath came in ragged wheezes as the reality of the situation sunk into her. Something blurred past and stung her cheek. Her fingertips came away crimson. She stumbled, moving like her limbs were coated in sap, searching for cover. She came up against a heavy door.

Shakily, her hand found the latch and pushed it open, revealing a yawning mouth that breathed out the stink of rot. Maelyrin's stomach lurched painfully, and the tunnel of her vision constricted, but she moved inside nonetheless. Instantly, the sounds of the battle became muted once the thick wood of the building stood between it and her. And it was cooler within its depths, more chill than the air outside. Despite the stench, the space enabled her overworked senses to settle, but, for a while, only the hardness of the wall she leaned on was real.

The wan light creeping in through the cracks and crevasses of the shutters and door helped her eyes adjust to the dusty dimness once the constriction of her mind let up enough. The room spread out before her, a wide space of empty and broken shelves pushed up against the walls and far merchant's counter. Motes drifted lazily through beams of cold light slanting down across several long, wrapped bundles stacked near it like cordwood.

Another chill swept through her, though not from the cold in the room. The breath she finally released coned out visibly, obscuring her death grip gaze on the bundles only a little. Despite the icy scuttling along her spine, her mind silently counted the white linen wrapped packages. There were eighteen. *Hadn't Jana said twelve villagers were killed?*

Pushing a wayward strand of hair from her face, she began creeping toward them, moving slowly and as silently as she could. Even though the roar of battle still raged outside, every creak of protest from the dry floorboards froze her in her steps. An overreaction, she knew, but she could not help herself. All the silent looks, all the obfuscation surrounding this building nesting deep down within her since arriving began hatching and worming around inside. Yet she was drawn to the bundles. Somehow, they were wrong. And she needed to know why.

The closer Maelyrin drew, the worse the smell became as she penetrated the invisible cloud held at bay by the cold. Already, she was breathing shallowly through her mouth, but the cloying decay coated the back of her throat and clawed up into her nose. She could feel it on her skin like oily dew. "Twelve," her mouth said. "She said, 'twelve'."

Maelyrin paused, remembering the conversation they had with Jana the first day. There should only be twelve bodies here, not eighteen. She counted them again, studying each and the pile as a whole. Eighteen separate bundles. Each body was wrapped tightly, thickly with heavy cloth and lay underneath a layer of dark dust. Those on top were still defined, body shaped ghosts neatly stacked. But those few beneath were more amorphous, bearing unusual lumps and edges that seemed unnatural.

She gulped.

With her bow, she reached out and gently prodded one of the bottom-most bundles, clenching her jaw and squinting in disgust, already anticipating the sudden release she was about to cause. Instead of the soft yielding she expected, the tip encountered something hard that shifted. Even over the outside noise, she heard a muffled 'clink' slip out from beneath the pile.

Her brow arched.

Another, more firm, prod produced a distinct 'thud'. "Interesting," she muttered and knelt to study the bottom bundles more closely. There were six of the unusual sacks in all, and each, after a hesitant poke, yielded the plain sound of metal moving against itself. Setting the bow down, she cast a glance backward at the door, then drew her long hunting knife. Another furtive look at the entrance, and she scooted to the sacks, knifeless arm thrown across her mouth and nose. Quickly, she slashed into the material hiding the contents of the original sack she tested.

An unmistakable gleam caught the stray light as something slid out of the slit, rang on the wooden floor and rolled in a tight staccato tone until it lay quietly at her foot. A single coin. Gold. She stared at it for only a moment before using the blade tip to open the cut enough to visually explore inside the wound. Other, larger shapes and forms were revealed. The stark lines of a gold embossed box, the delicate curves of a silver goblet. Other, smaller items. Gleams and sparkles of different colors caught ambient light.

Six of the eighteen 'bodies', it appeared, were a wealth of treasure. Maelyrin did not know much about the world outside her own little village, but it seemed odd to her nonetheless to find this type of riches hidden in a tiny farming community such as this. *Where did all this come from?* she wondered. As she was about to confirm her suspicions about the other five sacks, though, the battle roar suddenly became louder and gray light flooded the room.

A husky voice said, "What're you doin' girl?"

Maelyrin spun around to face the door, her heel striking the coin near her foot and sending it ringing across the floorboards. The light behind him made it difficult to see his features, but she could tell it was Santef by his build. She also knew his eyes were not on her just then, but the coin as it flashed away from her. Outside, the sound of battle paused as if an omen. "I knew you couldn't be trusted," he said darkly. "You'll have to pay for your treachery." To accentuate his statement, he motioned with the sword in his hand. The crimson-stained silver glittered evilly in the grayness.

Maelyrin froze, locked in mid-breath, hand clenching painfully around the handle of her woefully inadequate knife. Her mouth became arid and coppery while her eyes suddenly began watering and seemed to bulge in their sockets.

Santef strode purposefully in her direction, his shadowed face all too plainly showing his intentions. His movement shocked her backwards, sending her stumbling into the pile of bodies and loot she forgot was behind her. Her chest screamed, deprived of breath, and her knife wavered out in front of her as her other gripped at the linen wrappings. Her eyes were pinned against the darkness of Santef's face. Briefly, it passed through a slant of light, an illuminating heartbeat of utter hate.

His sword raised, impossibly long and sending off flames of silver red. Maelyrin's mouth peeled back from her teeth and her entire face felt terribly sunburned. A hissing squeal of breath reached through the loud thundering of her heart that would momentarily end. She wanted them to, but her eyes refused to close.

Santef's sword fell from a suddenly limp hand and clattered to the floor. Dumbly, she watched as his eyes rolled back in his head, and he slumped to the floor, a flaccid slough of skin that revealed a hulking dark demon beneath. She screamed, though her constricted throat made it a croak of surprise. Something echoed in her mind. A voice that threw her panicked mind into sudden silence.

"You are safe," Kiyo said, the rumble of his voice a release valve. She stumbled into him, clutching him tightly and sobbing greatly into his chest. Several minutes slogged by as she cried, struggled to get her panic under control while Kiyo's huge arms wrapped her in comfort. When she was able, she drew back and looked down at the supine form of Santef.

"Is he dead?" she asked quietly, forcing it out between the trailing spasms of her sobs. Absently, she stepped away from the gruff looking man.

"No," Kiyo said. "I put him to sleep for a while."

Maelyrin found herself wishing otherwise. And the thought of her knife, laying on the floor near the bundles, came, unbidden, to her. She admonished herself even as that part of her wished his death. "He was going to kill me!" she hissed, anger mixing with astonishment mixing with horror.

"Desperation, whatever the cause, can have an odd effect on people," Kiyo soothed. "Let us go now."

"W-what?" she asked.

"It is time for us to leave," he said simply.

"But. . . . What about the wounded?"

"What about them?" he asked. His gaze passed over the bundles.

"We have to help," she stated weakly, pushing back her raging emotions. Kiyo looked down at her, his relaxed face taking on a sympathetic look. Slowly, he shook his head.

"We've helped them as much as they will allow," he rumbled and motioned at Santef. "He has compromised our staying any longer. For your safety, we must leave." As if his words were prophecy, the door creaked open, pushed by a haggard looking Karn. The hard breathing quiet of battle's end followed. Behind him were more of the villagers. Eyes flicked at the bundles, then to Santef, then to them. Beneath the gore of battle, their expressions were uniformly grim. And something else, something more haunting to her. It was a malignant distrust. It was a primal greed. Karn's blood splattered sword came up, much the same as Santef's did minutes earlier. "Stop," Kiyo said, just over a whisper and tonelessly as she had heard many times before.

Karn's face went suddenly flat, and he stopped. "Drop it," Kiyo continued. The weapon clanged as it hit the door jamb. "Back up." Karn began backing out, pushing the others back with him. Kiyo looked at Maelyrin briefly. "Come," he told her.

Shaken, Maelyrin quickly retrieved her knife and bow and followed the giant. He moved slowly, ducking under the jamb once the villagers were away from it, blocking her view outside. When she stepped out onto the stoop, her stomach turned violently at the sight before them. The dead littered the area like a terrible storm tore through the enclave. Men and women lay in heaps and dangled from spikes, twisted and broken, their faces glaring the torment of their final moments. Weapons, broken, bloody, in lifeless hands and piercing lifeless bodies were scattered throughout. Part of the fence had been torn down, and men and horses clogged the blood soaked opening, some of them twitching in death spasms. Maelyrin could see that none lived. Not bandits, anyway, though she could hear moans of pain filtering out from the town center. The way they were eyeing them, she could not imagine that any of the aggressors were among the wounded within the building.

The villagers continued to give them wide berth; Kiyo's will pushing at them and keeping them at bay while they gingerly maneuvered toward the break. The squelching of mud beneath her feet caused her guts to lurch. Just looking at the carnage, she guessed that over half of the villagers lay in the wet earth. Outside the fence, once she stumbled out around the bodies, was just as bad. Bandits and horses lay in their own gore, some sprouting shafts, but most bearing terrible slashes and missing limbs. Some of the many crows and ravens were already squabbling over rights, the rest peering down through the gray as if shocked still by the display of violence. A few horses, still living, picked their ways slowly around the edges of the road, snuffling at and shifting snow aside to get at the grass beneath.

Kiyo, backing out of the ragged gap, made a clicking sound and held out a hand while continuing to stare down the villagers as they crowded around the opening like the carrion birds roosting nearby. One of the closer horses pricked its ears forward then came over to nuzzle at the giant's blue hand. "Can you ride?" he asked. In his other hand, he held their packs, somehow gathering them on the way out.

Maelyrin nodded, then said, "Yes," when she looked back to see that he was watching the villagers. Her throat was dry and her answer came out in a cracked tone. She tried to block the slaughter from her as she moved to the horse's side. Absently, she patted the animal's brown hide and let him sniff her hand. His hot breath relieved Maelyrin of some of her shock. It was alive, gloriously alive, and it reminded her that she still was. Nimbly, she swung up into the low cantled saddle and settled in as Kiyo led them further down the road.

Maelyrin watched over her shoulder as they moved away from the village, peering back at the many sets of heavy staring eyes. They just stared, the survivors, and she couldn't suppress a shiver that raced up her spine at their hollow gaze. Confusion swept through her, shaken loose by her chill. They had helped these people. Had risked their lives to save theirs. And were being repaid with hate and threats of death.

Suddenly, she wished she were home. Aside from Kiyo, her experiences with the outside world were proving to be terrible beyond anything the Faethe had ever told her. It was better to be in a place that she wasn't necessarily wanted, where she was feared even, but at least, where she was safe. Right then, the distant company of the Prime Elder was preferable to this. Only the village and hate filled people now stood between her and her own home. And, of course, there was Marc to consider.

Will I see him again? That human that caused her heart to stir even over her fear when she thought of him. His steel eyes and the piercing way he looked at her. The way she could not *Look* into him, discover all his secrets, and ultimately drive him away because of it. She had to believe it, hold on to the thought of seeing him again, otherwise, her fear may just drive her insane. Her grip on it was tenuous at the moment.

She shifted into a more comfortable position once the view of the village was swallowed by distance and the encapsulating pines. She relaxed a little, breathing out a thin sigh into the cold and let her body begin to sway to the rhythm of the horse. After a while, exhaustion bubbled up into her muscles, turning them to lead, making her feel drugged. Her shoulder even began to ache. "What is wrong with me?"

Kiyo looked back, regarded her with his black eyes only momentarily before returning his gaze forward. She thought she saw him smile. "It is a side effect of battle," he said. "Your body expends much energy during demanding situations. It will pass."

Maelyrin grunted a response. Kiyo, of course, was relaxed and full of energy. He walked easily, loosely. *Why aren't you exhausted, then?* She thought at him.

"I know how to conserve my energy," he replied, startling her into a confused pondering on whether he was reading her mind or if she spoke out loud. She was about to ask when the thud of hooves coming up the road behind them caused her body to go rigid. Kiyo stopped and turned to look down the road. Maelyrin twisted in the saddle to do the same.

Around the curve, coming at them at a full gallop, was Jana. She was waving to them and her mouth worked, yelling something that was lost in the sound of her mount clobbering the ground. The sizzle of lightning zipped up Maelyrin's spine, and she almost kicked her horse into a run before she caught herself. Jana was alone. There was no need for her fear. She sucked in a breath and instead, prodded the animal to face her.

Jana was breathing heavily when she pulled her mount to a fast stop in front of them, its hooves ripping up and throwing clods of wet, dark dirt toward them. "Wait. . ." she was saying. "Wait, please. . . ." Maelyrin's lip curled like an angry dog's and she stiffened, hand on knife hilt. Beside her, Kiyo remained as placid as ever. He waited patiently for Jana to catch her haggard breath.

"Please," she said finally. "Don't go." Maelyrin almost growled, but waited for Kiyo to speak. When no reply was forthcoming, Jana shifted uncomfortably, cleared her throat a couple of times. "I. . .I must apologize for the actions of the others. They. . . they have been through much the last few weeks."

"I can see how stealing and hiding treasure can be a difficult trial," Maelyrin snapped. Jana reacted as if suddenly slapped. She stared at Maelyrin, red seeping up into her face and the eclipse of shock in her eyes moved away to reveal controlled rage.

"You don't know. . . ." she began, teeth clenched.

"I know that Santef tried to kill me when I found out! I know that Karn and the rest of the villagers wanted to as well! I know that we helped you people and you turned on us. And I suspect the dead piled on top were not due to natural causes!"

Maelyrin was nearly yelling at the woman, her lethargy consumed in a conflagration of anger and fear revisited.

"How dare you!" Jana shot back. "You don't. . . ."

"No! How dare you!" Maelyrin yelled, standing in the stirrups and pointing sharply at the other woman. "If it were not for Kiyo, you'd all be wiped out right now and your precious treasure gone! If it were not for him *I* would be dead now! Killed silently by your goons!" Each word was punctuated by the stab of her finger, and each stab made Jana flinch, clench her blood flecked jaw, brought tears to her eyes.

The woman started to say something, caught her breath, then opened her mouth. Just as Maelyrin was about to lance into her again, Kiyo's hand came to rest softly on her shoulder. Instantly, she calmed, as if he suddenly stole her anger with his touch. "We had no choice," Jana said, her eyes wide with pain. "All of our crops were failing. The plague wiped out most of the able bodied. We couldn't tend them properly. We couldn't find help. Then, some strangers came through. Seven of them. Stopped at the Inn. They were mean tempered and dirty. Drank heavily and ate heartily even though we could not spare the extra food. The ale loosened their tongues. They bragged of their raiding to the east. Of their horde. Even where they left it, in the woods, while they were in town. As the night wore on, they became worse, began insulting everyone, throwing things, bellowing out threats against the whole town. Then, one of them grabbed. . . ." She paused to swallow past a hitch in her throat, her face tightening as she looked backward. "One of them grabbed Lina and began to maul her." She looked up suddenly, looking at them with wide, wet eyes. "When she struggled, he stabbed her. And stabbed her. And stabbed her. Over and over. Then the rest of them began attacking the others. We killed four of them, but only after they slaughtered eight of us. Three of them escaped, fled west.

We thought they were lying about the treasure, but we sent some villagers out. We were wrong. They were not lying. Before he died, one of the men told us the rest of them would be coming for it and would punish us. We saw an opportunity to use it to buy the needed food to get us through winter. We hid it and prepared for the rest of them to come. I told them you weren't part of them, but Santef didn't believe me. I'm sorry."

As she spoke, a fountain of guilt sprang up in Maelyrin that flash flooded through her, washing away the anger she had been harboring. "Why did you not just tell us?"

"I should have," she answered, letting her eyes fall. "But Santef and the others thought it would be better if you didn't know, in case you were with them. At the time, things were so bad, I thought it easier."

"What about killing us?" she asked, only a portion of her anger coming back. "Was that part of the plan, too?" Jana could only look at the horse's mane. "I see," Maelyrin said after a slow moment. Still, she couldn't find it inside her to hate either Jana or the other villagers.

"Please, forgive us," Jana whispered.

"Of course we will," Maelyrin's mouth flipped out before she could think. It surprised her, but, simultaneously, a warmth began in her chest. Jana's face brightened, and she looked up from her focal point on her horse's neck.

"You will help us?" she asked, though it sounded more a statement of fact.

Maelyrin was nodding when Kiyo said, "No. Our service to you has ended." Both women looked at him, shock registering on their faces.

"B-but," Jana stammered, "we have wounded."

"Yes," Kiyo said. "That is often the case where battle is concerned." Maelyrin could only stare while Jana's mouth gobbled around silence, her eyes wide.

"Some will die," Jana finally managed.

"Yes," he said simply.

Jana continued to pale. "I do not understand," she said, her voice shaking. "Why will you not help us?"

"We already have."

"But the wounded?"

"The threats against Maelyrin's life has ended the help we can give you," he said.

"But, I have explained," she stammered. "I have asked for forgiveness."

"And we have given our forgiveness, to you, whom I believe is sincere. However, you do not speak for your people."

"But I am their leader."

"No, you are not," he commented, as if it were the weather he was talking about. "Your people have become a pack, feeling as one. They are led by desperation and greed. Even I cannot protect her from a blade from the shadows."

"But. . . ." Kiyo held up a hand. A softly powerful gesture that stopped her completely, an end to their conversation. They stared at each other, while Maelyrin bounced her gaze between them. Jana paled even further, if that was possible. Her stringy brown hair, sunken eyes, her expression, she suddenly looked like an old woman though she couldn't be more than twenty five years. Tears formed and fell, each one a dull reflection of her exhaustion, frustration, and now, despair. Slowly, painfully, she nodded and pulled back on the reins. Her horse backed up like it was the one bearing the weight of disbelief. When more than a length, she pulled sharply, the tug of its bit forcing the equine's head to turn away followed by its body. With a terrible cry, she kicked the beast into a run, tearing up the turf as they headed back to the battle-ravaged village.

Once Jana had disappeared from sight and Maelyrin was able to find her voice, she rounded on Kiyo, anger thundering from her mouth, sparking from her eyes. "How can you be so cold hearted!" she hissed. "Those people need my help."

"Help them if you wish," he remarked. "Only consider that you know a secret that nearly all of them don't want known. That they were willing to kill to silence that knowledge. That still, they will."

"But Jana explained all that," she argued. "She asked for forgiveness."

"You hear only what you wish to hear," he said, then began walking away from her, down the road, his stride purposeful. Her mouth dropped open, then clenched shut, her face pinching in frustrated anger. She looked back the way Jana had gone, and, with a grunt, set her horse in motion at the same time she reined in. The horse started forward, snorted, jerked back and raised up. Snorted again in frustration.

Maelyrin looked back at Kiyo's diminishing figure, then turned back to look toward the village. Her teeth gritted together. *What should I do?* Her instincts to heal were strong, but she knew, deep down, *Kiyo is right*. The survivors of the fight were driven by greed. Not just survival. She *Saw* them.

Maelyrin kneed her horse after Kiyo, nursing more guilt. Her decision came after moments of self-engagement, emotions swirling like a storm through her. Anger, rage. Ultimately, her conclusion to follow Kiyo was simple. Fear. She was afraid of them, of what they were capable of. And it willed her to push aside what she thought she was.

Chapter 48

Questions and Musings

"*W*e should kill them," Reegan's raspy voice crept over his shoulder and into his hood where it was captured and devoured by an absently attendant ear.

"No," Crowlin replied after a moment. "He said to wait and see what they are doing."

"Why?" Meerdon coughed behind them. Crowlin considered the question, for the moment the quick flash of anger that normally came with a question to his orders, was ignored. He was wondering the same thing, entertaining the strong notion of disobeying his orders and allowing himself the ecstasy of taking their lives, watching Pendragon's hope fail before plunging a blade into him. Doing so even though every ounce of his being would be filled with the flames of his punishment. *Ah, sweet, terrible pain.*

"The woman is an earthwitch. He wants to know what she's about," he sneered.

"What about the boy?" Teraard hissed. "I can taste his life force from here. He would sustain us for a long time." One of them whined hungrily.

Crowlin nodded into his cowl. "Yes," he whispered. He could feel it, too, like a deep breath of icy air. Something so tantalizing that his hand strayed away from the leather pommel and grasped in the direction the ethereal-like scent came from. It quavered, then clenched, and he forced it back to its rest.

Already, the sustenance derived from the innkeeper and his workers was fading, being replaced by the constant gnaw deeper than his belly. "He said, 'No'!" Crowlin suddenly hissed.

The loud '*thock*' of a crossbow wrenched his mind away from the pull of the life force, and his head jerked around just as the sharp yelp flew back at them. Something white and heavy flashed among the trees, thrashed a couple of seconds, sending loam and brush scattering just out of sight. Then, it was quiet. Crowlin inhaled, took in the tang of blood on the air mixing with the smell of decaying leaves and dirt.

When he looked back, Gorn, the fifth of them, shrugged crookedly and croaked out, "Wolf."

Crowlin breathed in the scent of death again, let his gaze drift back toward the direction of the small party they followed. Had they been on a hill or near the road with them in sight, the woman's sudden flinch and sharp indrawn breath would have sparked a suspicious connection, but, since they were using their other senses to follow their quarry, he thought nothing of the animal's death. It was a pastime he found allowable as it kept the others in check, to some extent.

"What about the Old One?" Reegan's query was distant to his ears, but when it reached into his mind, he looked over the hunched figure slightly behind him.

Crowlin had to shrug helplessly. "We leave it alone, too. For now," he said. "He wants to know why it is following them."

One of them growled, an echo of the frustration they all felt. They were the cat's paw. Their lot was to play a game so old that he sometimes forgot the purpose. To obey or be destroyed. Or worse. That was why they were there, sitting astride dying horses, waiting, wanting. It was a lucid moment in which he could part the sludge of his memory enough to regret leading them all into the cave to find shelter from that storm. Such a trifling thing then, sheets of water. Discomfort, the only reason for it.

Of the five, he was the only one able to understand the true irony of their transition from that night long, long ago to their presence there amid the trees, killing animals instead of the ones they wanted to kill. Hungering for those they were not allowed to feed on. Wanting freedom that would only come with a death they were all denied. The price of their bargain. His bargain.

The rest of them, he mused, were safer in their evolved ignorance. They no longer realized their past existence, nor cared, he supposed. Theirs was a day to day drifting from one feeding to the next. By measures, at any rate. Reegan had windows to their long past that he stumbled onto every now and then, while Gorn was, by far, the most evolved into that state of unawareness. Teraard and Meerdon were somewhere between them. None of them, including himself, were the men they once were.

Crowlin didn't know if the Master knew his thoughts or not. Didn't know if his level of awareness was known to Him. Not that it mattered much. He still did the Master's bidding. Just as he had for these many years under His yolk. And if he obeyed, they would obey because they knew no better. They knew they didn't want that mantle, either.

With a grunt, he kicked the gaunt flanks of his dying mount. The creature was too frightened to make a sound, but it jerked into movement quickly enough. He considered taking a more hardy beast next time. Like a lizard mount.

Chapter 49

History and Curses

"*I*t will take us two, maybe three days to get through Dedlan's Pass," Marc said casually around a sip from his water skin as he stared at the mountain range ahead of them. Beads of sweat were trickling down the sides of his weathered face and the back of his neck, a response to the unusual heat that was beating down on them. "Another four, maybe five, until we reach Hestaff. . . ."

"I think we are pretty aware of that fact, human," Sandoren sneered. "We've traveled these lands for many years now and seldom get lost." Marc looked at the ffolk, his face calm, but his eyes steel hard. Alex shook her head. For two days now, when he wasn't scouting far ahead of them, Sandoren continually sniped at Marc over anything he could find to argue with him about.

"Yes, I am sure you do," Marc said, dangerously low. "But do you know of the Cloister high in the White Rocks where we can stay?" Sandoren shifted, still glaring. Alex raised an eyebrow. They were not aware of it. "Or do you know about the ruins of Khemosh, on the other side, where spirits and other things make their dens? Do you, perhaps, know of someone in Hestaff who will ferry us across the waters so we don't have to ride around the new inland sea? Do you maybe have a way to find out what news from the north may be filtering down?" Sandoren's stare continued to become heavier, his eyes darker, while he chewed the inside of his lip as Marc drove on in that quietly calm but harsh voice. Finally, with a loud grunt, he kicked Veraddin into a cantor, leading the spirited animal away from them. Del, behind them, muttered something to himself, over and over, while they watched him go.

Shaking her head, Alex said, "Now he'll be gone for another day or two."

"Maybe I should have warned him about the serpent vines," Marc quipped.

"He knows about the serpent vines!" she lashed, drawing those cold eyes from the retreating figure of Sandoren to her own, where they lingered for several uncomfortable moments.

"I apologize for my rudeness," he finally said, obviously not. "But he is becoming more and more dangerous to your safety."

"Just leave Sandoren to me," she stated.

"That's what you said a few days ago, but he worsens. You should use your Powers on him to control him."

"You know that is not our way," she retorted; she was angry, but tiring, and it sounded weak, even to her own ears.

"That is not *your* way," he said, returning his gaze toward the sparkling peaks not far ahead, Sandoren now completely out of sight. "That is evident. Though that was not the case with some of your sisters in years past."

Uncomfortable now, she shifted in her saddle. Clover took the movement to step up the pace, making her rein the horse back. "Yes, well," she said. "Even though I have been alive for a couple of generations, I certainly don't have the flawless recall from ages past that you have stockpiled in your mind. It is not a practice we now follow." She finished softly, her anger gone, a puff of smoke in the wind, but added, as an afterthought, "however convenient it may be." And thought she saw a wan smile crease the man's otherwise grim countenance. It was the first time she had seen such since that day in the clearing when she had been watching him brush down his huge steed. Although a small change, it made a vast difference in his visage, and, for a moment, she got a glance at the man he must have once been, so long ago.

"There are still holes," he remarked.

"What?"

"In my memories," he explained. "They aren't flawless. There are many holes and spaces. Probably keeps what sanity I have from leaving completely." Alex knew he was speaking lightly, but couldn't help but sense an undercurrent of despair. "At any rate," he continued without pause. "You may want to reevaluate that rule, before he does get himself caught in a serpent vine. And not the kind up in these mountains."

"Just leave him be," she answered shortly. "He will be fine."

"You know him best, I suppose," Marc stated. "He sure wouldn't be acting like this, though, if he weren't . . . ."

"Weren't what?" she asked.

"Didn't have so much hate and distrust for others as he does," Marc finished. *Liar.* She thought at him. Alex let it drop, however. Whatever was bothering Sandoren would eventually come out and be resolved. It always did. Arguing with Marc about it, though, would only serve to exhaust her more than she was already, even if he did have some insight into the odd behavior her longtime companion was displaying that she did not.

They rode on silently. The two of them anyway. Del chattered to himself incessantly, sometimes giggling softly, as several small birds and flying insects alighted on him and Day, adding their chirps and buzzes to his conversation while setting aside their natural urges of predator and prey. The boy remained withdrawn, though it seemed to come and go in cycles. Or like waves, rather, with crests of near lucidity and deep troughs of obliviousness. She saw none of the wakefulness he showed the day he chose his name, nor had he had, thankfully, another of the episodes like he did in camp the other morning. Neither the first time, nor the last, she wondered if he had always been this way, or if his dazedness had something to do with the manner in which she and Sandoren had found him.

A burst of anger went out to whomever had beaten the child nearly to death.

It pleased her, however, that he was joyful in his state. The way he reacted when Sandoren was overly upset hurt her deeply, allowing her to see a portion of his past and of the people he put up with, just as she had glimpsed the person that Marc had once been. The feeling was, of course, instinctual. That, logically, there was nothing that she could possibly do about it except to try and keep it from happening to him again. Nonetheless, that frightened her.

Whatever this boy's destiny was, she was sure it was going to be a difficult path, and she wasn't sure how long she could protect him. Or from what. The Eldritch, perhaps? Once it got its bearings? If, of course, Del was the reason the thing was following them. A creature like that was motivated by ways she could never understand.

And what of the other strange presence that seemed to be shadowing them? It was an inconsistent feeling, but it was there. The same sort the wolves impressed upon her back at Marc's cabin, when they first met him. Like the bitter taint of just spoiling meat. Somehow, the death of the wolf two days ago was connected to it, but, they, as well, were being unusually silent about what had taken one of their brothers. Not a deliberate silence, but more of a lack of expression, just as she was having.

And what else was in store for them? Not one to worry over the future much, she nevertheless was curious, and more than a little frightened, by what the Living Trees near Calif were going to reveal to her about the Wound that she could feel, even a continent away, right now bleeding off the Earth's Power. Throwing the Balance so far into Chaos that, eventually, there could be no moving it back. That if left unchecked, would eventually rip the world apart in a death so violent as to be unimaginable.

What of Marc? His figuring in the tableau was completely beyond her comprehension. If he was truly the man that he seemed to be, how could he help them. Aside from his evident, extraordinary circumstance, he did not possess skills that Sandoren and she did not already have between them. Even if he weren't cursed as he was. His presence with them was an anomaly. Even an added frustration. His shaky relationship with her suddenly vacillating companion seemed to be compounding Sandy's behavior.

So many questions. So few answers. *And time*, she thought, not for the first time. Alex sighed quietly and gazed up into the clear blue above them, letting the unusual warmth play across her face while, beneath her, Clover's rhythm helped her release her dark thoughts, draining them out of her mind as she would a water basin.

Too bad there are no inns between here and Hestaff, she thought. *I could really use another night in a soft bed.* Her mind began chiding her, telling her she was getting old and growing weary of the Earth beneath her when another thought bubbled up. She turned her face away from the heavens and asked, "What is this Cloister you spoke of earlier?"

Marc looked at her, his expression saying that she brought him away from some deep thinking as well. At least the placidness of his face told her they were not the dark and brooding kind that seemed to be surrounding her of late. It made her smile, especially when understanding of what she was asking entered the universe behind his eyes.

"A group of monastic wizard warriors live up in the high valleys of the White Rock Mountains," he said loosely. "Been up there for, well, for a very long time."

"Interesting," she said. "Sandoren and I have passed through Dedlon's pass many times over the years, but I have never heard of there being any community there, monastic or otherwise. The locals tend to avoid the mountains altogether, for the usual reasons. Ghosts, superstitions." She paused to gaze at the sharp, mostly forested, pinnacles ahead of them, squinting slightly as the sunlight glittered off the bare peaks like thousands of tiny stars. The crystalline makeup of the rocks catching it and throwing it out like so many diamond like gems. "Not that the stories are completely unfounded," she continued. "But I would have thought some of them would have mentioned a town or a village or something."

"The Cloister is very well hidden," Marc relayed. "Both physically and magically. Enough so that even those with overly sensitive perception miss it. Much like those fey places in which imps and such reside. Unless they want to be known, they are not."

"Ah, yes," she nodded. "And how is it that you know of this place?"

Marc shot her a grin that was suspiciously coy, and replied, quite bluntly, "I helped build it."

Alex almost choked. "How long did you say it's been there?"

"That's not important," he stated, a strangely wistful look crossing his face. "The important thing is that it is there and hospitable to travelers who know of it and respect its existence."

"What do you mean by that?"

"I mean," he said, grinning again. "that if your Guardian doesn't behave, he may find himself well removed from its confines."

Alex slitted her eyes suspiciously, "What kind of people did you say live there?"

"Harmonists," he said, pinching his brows together in thought. "I guess would be the best way to describe them. You will have to see them for yourself before you understand exactly what I mean. They are those that choose to separate themselves from the world so that they may delve deeply into themselves, and, well. . . you'll see. They are amazingly like the Earthmother in their ways, but not. . . ."

"You don't sound so sure of yourself," she said. "I suppose you don't go there much."

"Not exactly," he answered. "I go there often, though it can't be measured in spans of time. It is a sanctuary that I go to when I need to. . . ." His face was taking on the solemn sadness that he normally wore.

"Retreat from the banality of everyday life?" she said, trying to keep him from the precipice he was heading for. She didn't know quite why, but his silence now would bother her. Right now, he was open, lucid. He was allowing her to look inside the dark shell he was, thus far, very protective of. Not only might it give her some hints about her own questions about where he would fit into her task, it also served to keep her away from those black thoughts. And, somehow, it was relaxing and energizing at the same time, as if, by being so, he was able to take her fatigue from her, convert it, and give back strength that filled her with flowing warmth.

"Yes," he said, smiling again. "That is a good way of putting it. 'The banality of everyday life'. There is a certain peacefulness there."

How nice that will be, she thought soberly. If it were so, she might have them stay there a day or two more, putting off the urgency to get to Calif so that she could get the much needed rest her body was crying out for. And the intriguing possibility that these monks utilized Elemental Powers excited her. Men able to channel the Powers of the Elements were always rare. Historically, there were only a handful. Dartaign was even more of a rarity, now that her sisterhood in general was scarce. She often wondered if there were other men, somewhere, with the abilities that were, traditionally, the birthright of women. It was something that never fit well with the Balance. For her, anyway. Some of the others seemed never to give it a thought, and there were even a few that disdained the very idea of men being able to utilize them. *Used to be*, she mentally corrected herself, remembering that most of her sisters were dead now, since the Dark Night, or, as they that survived called it, the Night of Agony.

She shuddered, unconsciously, as her body remembered the terrible, wracking torment it suffered that day as the world tried to rip itself apart. Thankfully, it passed quickly, a pinprick in the greater scheme of Life.

Alex hoped it were so, these men, for countless reasons.

"And what of you?" Marc asked, sliding the subject away from her prodding mind. "From what Circle do you hail?" The question caught her off guard, even though he was who he was. Little was known about their society, outside of it. Mostly due to their own counsel on the subject, of course, but over the last few hundred years, those outside the calling of Earthmother simply were not interested about them. Over the last few generations, their presence as a significant balancing force in the world as teachers and healers had waned, just like the moons did after their fullness. Moon, she corrected. Since the Dark Night, there was only one moon where there had been two, and that one never moved nor waxed or waned, always hanging above their heads like a perturbed spirit. "Ah, I hail from no Circle," she finally said, wondering if he knew as much as he seemed or was just repeating something he may have heard.

His eyes widened in surprise. *Yes*, she realized. *He knows.* "Then, you are the First?" he asked. She could only nod in response. Of the few remaining, Alexandria was the oldest and the ablest, by the process of selection.

Marc suddenly looked troubled. "What of Gyssel?" he asked, sparking sorrow for one of her closest friends. Gyssel had been the First before her.

"She died in the hours after the Troubles," she said simply, keeping her pain of remembrance to herself. Marc settled back in his saddle, a thoughtful expression on his face, taking the news as if it were a simple government proclamation.

"I did not know that," he said softly.

"Did you know her well?" she prompted, wondering how he knew of her, since the woman had been very reclusive the years before her death. Marc smiled warmly and nodded slightly.

"Yes," he said, gazing into the distance. "I knew her very well. I watched her grow up."

His comment was solemn but somehow flippant, and it was her turn to be surprised. She was never sure of her exact age, but Gyssel was certainly on the far side of the mid millennium mark when she succumbed to the pain of the breaking world. "Even taught her a few things, like how to handle a sword."

"You're the one . . . ." she blurted, a realization that came before she had a chance to mull it over. "She spoke of you, on occasion, though never named you." Saying it, she could hear the woman's voice, full of fondness, eyes wistful while talking about the man and patting the hilt of the odd accouterment to her raiment. Alex remembered Gyssel carrying the blade with her wherever she went, an unusual behavior for someone so well versed in the Elemental Powers, and, to Alex's knowledge, that was all she ever did with it. Carried it; never wielded it for the reason it was forged. When asked about it, she smiled her fond smile and said it was a gift. Somehow, she never connected the weapon or the name to the wandering Pendragon, who was spoken over at meals and other such mundane times when the mind tends to wander. The parallel between the mysterious gift giver and the wandering hermit just never intersected until now.

Marc flinched a little at her comment, and his eyes became liquid and deep with memory. "Everone," he said, to himself. A reminder. "I've not heard that in a long time."

Alex's perspective shifted, allowing her that small insight that opened and shut quickly, but left behind a residual feeling of insignificance. Like standing on the shore of the ocean and realizing its infinite power, or gazing up into the heavens at night, into its endlessness, and seeing herself from that point of view. Gyssel found her as a small child, raised her in the Ways of their calling, showed her as much as she was able to understand and even more than that. To Alex, Gyssel was more than a good friend, she had been a parent, a teacher, a protector, helping her to flourish as an Earthmother. So much so, that she grasped more than most about the world around her and the Powers that gave it Life.

Yet, here was someone who had been alive at the time of Gyssel's birth, had watched her grow up. Had even been a teacher to her at one time. The feeling of insignificance and awe that suddenly washed up in her like a tidal wave of that ocean nearly caused her to slide from her saddle in shock. Up until that moment, he was just a man. A brooding man, at that. One that she could somehow compel to do her bidding. Had compelled, using information provided by the woman she called friend and mother. Someone so vast in experience and knowledge that the guilt she felt for using that information rose from its place and grew tenfold. "Marc," she asked, barely keeping the hesitation from her voice. He turned his eyes to her and she saw his age in them; a near infinite depth. Old eyes. "If you don't mind my asking. . . How old. . . .How long have. . . ."

"I don't really know, anymore," he answered her, looking far away, back into his past. "After a while, you stop measuring time with years and dates. Especially when calendars change from the ashes of one empire to the next. Start forgetting about names and places, as if your mind is like a cup and can only hold so much. I was around long before this road existed," he indicated the deeply worn, cobbled highway beneath the hooves of the horses. "This was built at the height of a peaceful Empire called the Tamulsek Regime that spread over the whole of a continent that is much smaller now. I remember the sacking of Khemosh, the ruins that lay on the other side of these mountains, by the warlord Fallenfrost and his armies before even that. I remember the vast city of Vistan as a small village without a name. The famous Inn, the Silver Unicorn, not even a whisper. Not many historians even know about Ellynthryll, but I do. I remember the Knight Wars, when the High Knights turned against each other. The downfall of that great kingdom came soon after, which led to the great Migrations that nearly depopulated these lands, but it's mostly a foggy distant dream now.

I know that the world beneath our feet is far, far older than the mistiness of my memory. That even before then, there were even greater Empires and Kingdoms that ranged farther than the imagination. The knights of today are but a shadow of what they once were, as those of my time were but a shadow of those before them.

Mostly, I remember people. Your lineage, for instance, is far older than I am. Gyssel. And before her, Naom. And before her, Bella. The line extends until time began, I imagine. I remember the founder of the Hedric line, a man named Ussander, a strong, intelligent man with a meanness straight out of Perdition. Quite the opposite of his more sedate, unifying progeny. He was a conqueror, like so many before him and since. Some of the Heroes of Legends, too, I knew. The stories told about them by bard or book today have nothing to do with who they really were, or in many cases, what they did. Mander Frostglider, for instance, who is said to have single handedly wiped out the Evil Cities of Gohthra and rescued countless peoples from fates worse than death was actually a drunken pig of a man who got lucky, once, by killing a man in a duel of The Great Game who happened to be an invading general who was, himself alone, spying out the city he was planning to sack. And the Evil Cities of Gohthra, to my knowledge, only existed in the flagrant mind of a wandering minstrel who met Mander after the duel.

That Karvalion fellow you spoke of was a pompous windbag that met death on the end of a dagger in a rundown tavern in a city that no longer exists. All the information he dug up on me, he actually stole from a real historian by the name of Nedron Bantholam II, who got his information from his teacher Gan Lemmock of Hegria, who learned his information from me when I stayed at his estate for a time. Nearly two generations before Karvalion supposedly 'interviewed' witnesses.

Other things, I remember not at all. Like the mysterious disappearance of other races. The great Beasts, the Reptizar, even the tiny Blossom Fairies. It seems to me that the Scandin Empire was just there, one day, as if Night birthed a whole nation in one cycle. This pendant," Marc absently tugged the piece free of his shirt, let it dangle in front of him, catching light and sending off sparkles of bronze and ruby. "I have no recollection of how it came to be in my possession, or when, or what it is, exactly, though I recognize it as part of my family crest. I believe that some of the symbols on it mean Balance. It has been with me, I think, for much of my unholy life.

My mind is like the sandy bottom of a river, flowing along with the current, burying and revealing rocks in random ways, sometimes during the light of day, sometimes with the fall of night. At times I remember much; at others, nothing. Mostly, though, my memories are like those stories you hear as a child. So real they seemed, when your parents were telling them to you then, but now, you know them for what they are. Stories."

"Sometimes it's difficult to tell where the past ends and the present. . . .hello, what's this?" he said it while holding up the pendant at eye level and studying it while it swayed and twisted to the comfortable gait of Whitesteel's steps.

"What's what?" Alex asked, looking over the jewelry herself.

"The stone. . . ." he said, glancing in her direction. "It's glowing. . . . I thought it was just the sunlight. . . .but it just flashed brighter. . . ." Alex leaned over a little and peered at the twisting medallion. The smooth ruby red gem in its center indeed seemed to be brighter, but she thought it had to be from the sun. She looked over the rest of it, noting silently the opposing sides of the straight and curving starburst.

"The entire thing means Balance," she remarked. "The straight lines represent Law. The curving ones mean Chaos. It's very old and embodies a simple yet complex . . . ." The red stone pulsed, slowly, growing bright and then dimming over a span of several seconds. There was no doubt in her mind, now. "That's peculiar. . . . You say you don't remember where you got it?"

Distractedly, he looked at her and shook his head slightly. "No, but there is some recognition in this . . . . like something is trying to come up to the surface, but can't. . . ." Marc shrugged and dropped the pendant back beneath his shirt once the jewel seemed lit only by light of the sun. "Oh, well, it will come sooner or later." He smiled, a bit shallowly. She said nothing in return, even when his hand went conspicuously to his sword hilt and deftly undid the thong that kept the blade in place when not needed, though she did wonder if he knew more than he was telling. He looked up at the sky.

"We may be able to reach the Cloister by nightfall," he said casually, though he seemed like a taut spring ready to explode. "You think the kid and these nags your riding can handle a little exercise?"

She arched a brow. "Nags?" she said. "Let's just hope your sour barn horse can keep up." Whitesteel snorted at the comment, laid his ears back and tossed his head a few times. Marc laughed, bellowed a full hearted bawl that surprised her. "Del?" she called, turning around to look at the boy. She had to call his name a couple of times, but he finally looked at her and gave her a wide smile. "Run?" she asked and a spark lit in the slackness of his face. Day neighed and before anyone could react bolted forward, passing Alex and Clover opposite Marc, while Del yelled with delight, leaving behind a cloud of confused bugs and birds.

Clover began prancing and snorting until Alex relaxed the reins a bit, then, she followed Del, quickly achieving a full out run. Alex smiled into the wind, taking a little pride in the effects the Power had on these animals, now full of health and vigor within just a week of being near death. Behind her she could hear the thundering of Whitesteel as he pounded the dirt just off the edge of the cobbled highway. She led Clover to the other side, the softer, smoother surface allowing her to surge forward.

They ran, full out, for several minutes, before prudence took a hold of her, and she slowed Clover to a light gallop, not knowing how her healing would hold during extended exertion. Marc drew up alongside, apparently having to struggle to slow the white beast he rode. Whitesteel was taller than Clover by several hands and definitely broader. His muscles were well defined and rippled with the movements of his gait. The horse certainly wanted to keep going. While Clover was settling well into the gallop, Alex could sense that the burst of energy she had was gone. The mare had her head lowered and her stride lengthened. But Whitesteel. His head was up, ears forward, and he was prancing beside them. It seemed there was no end to his energy level. She thought he might be able to run for hours.

Over the wind they were generating, she yelled, "How old is he?" Her thinking was five, maybe six years old. A stallion just coming into his prime.

Marc looked at her, and a small smile twitched at the corner of his mouth. "He's as old as I am," he yelled back. She could have fallen off then, would have if she wasn't more prepared for these types of surprises than the average person, the news glancing off the armor of her experience. *What did he mean by that,* her mind cried, the pounding of Clover's hooves vibrating up into her thoughts.

"What do you mean?" she yelled, her disbelief making the request for reinforcement.

"Whitesteel's been alive as long as I have!" he called back, a smug look crossing his bouncing face. She pulled back on the reins, slowing Clover enough so that the sound of her hooves didn't interfere as much with her cogitating brain. Marc slowed Whitesteel with her.

"How is that possible?" she asked. *Yes, how could it?*

Marc shrugged, the smugness changing to a perplexed gratification. "Don't know," he said, looking at the horse's head. Whitesteel's ears were cocked in frustration. He wanted to run. "He somehow got caught up in my curse. Whitesteel, the Everhorse." He laughed a bit, Whitesteel threw his head and pranced. "Uh," Marc said suddenly, gesturing forward with his head.

Alex looked, and gasped. Del and Day were growing smaller as the boy and horse were one in their running. Del's arms were stretched wide, and they could barely make out wisps of his calling glee. "Wups," she said, tapping Clover's flanks with her heels. The horse jumped forward, falling back into the comfortable gallop that, she thought, would gain on the happily racing duo. Whitesteel was right there with her, on the other side of the road.

Del and Day disappeared around a small bend obscured by one of the many clumps of trees that dotted the plains they traveled. Logically, she knew her loss of sight of him was merely temporary, but her insides, her heart, plummeted with concern, asking things like, *What if he falls off? Or runs into a tree?* Alex had never bore a child in her many years, but she instinctively understood what it was like by the way she reacted to Del's sudden disappearance from view. She urged Clover faster.

It was her that almost fell off, though, as they plunged into the wooded area and was nearly hit by a frightened, wild running Veraddin. Something manlike, dark, hairy, was astride the beast, dancing and jumping crazily with its upper body while it hooted and squealed. Beside her, closer in the encompassing tree line, Marc cursed loudly, but it was mostly drowned out by the roar of blood rushing from her face. Her thoughts suddenly, unilaterally jumping to Sandoren. She yelled, tried to pour more energy into Clover who was beginning to snort tiredly. It must have worked. She noticed grimly that she was starting to outpace Whitesteel. The thought gave her an odd sensation, momentary confusion, but she brushed it aside.

Around her, the land began to swell in places, and she realized they were now on a small incline. Soon they would be entering the pass proper through the White Rocks. The trees were becoming thicker, more packed together.

Dimly, her mind spit back the name of the creature on Veraddin, but it only confused her more, and she argued with the recall. "Epas are too shy to come close to people," she insisted, her voice shrill, nonetheless, carrying over the pounding of Clover's hooves like a whistle.

They broke from the trees just as suddenly as they had entered them, and she looked across a rolling landscape of grasses that inclined sharply near the line of forest that blanketed the lower reaches of the mountains. Del and Day were not far, stopped now and staring at the spectacle ahead. She glanced back, but did not see Marc.

Even from this distance, she could tell they were Epas. Gangly, hairy humanoids that generally lived deep in the forestland. There were many of them, jumping, howling, and swiping at a dangling Sandoren, who was awkwardly tangled in serpent vine, a few feet above the ground, trying not to struggle. In his only free hand, was his sword, which he was using futilely to keep the creatures away from him. At first, she thought they were playing with him, as was a common belief if they caught someone within their rangeland. Epas were not known to be aggressive. She almost smiled as they blew past Del.

But as she drew closer, their body stances and howls told otherwise, and she could see crimson on Sandoren's thigh. The Epas were enraged and out of control. The numbing realization was only kept at bay from being total disbelief when she looked up and saw the serpent vines wrapped around Sandoren's neck, his other hand thrust up between it and his throat, caught there, his struggles causing the vines to contract, cutting off his air. Already, his face was contorting, lips bluing, mouth wide but unable to draw life giving breath. Yet, he still fought. Though his bulging eyes could not see the angry mob below, he struck out with his blade each time one of them jumped at him, scoring, however lightly, nearly each time.

His time was growing short, though, his strikes becoming weaker. Alex screamed, trying to scare the normally fidgety creatures as she bore down on them. They merely turned toward her in surprise, then howled out a challenge. Half of them rushed her.

Clover spooked. She tried to stop, squealing in fright, and turned her body, throwing Alex from the saddle. She hit the ground rolling, air bursting from her lungs, followed closely by the panicked horse. Clover's fall, a sudden, heavy crash near her. Before she could recover, Alex was gripped in several places and hauled up into screaming chaos. Nails burned down her skin in several places and she cried out. Dark forms danced in front of her face as she tried to get her bearings and catch a breath to fill her searing lungs. Something hit her shoulder, pain exploded. Something else hit her in the back. Then, a hailstorm of pain broke out all over her body. Dimly, she realized the raucous host was pummeling her with their fists.

She tried to throw up her hands to defend her face, but they were held fast by unseen bonds. Frantically, she twisted and turned, trying to move, escape, look for help. She called out shrilly, painfully, as the blows rained, seeing only wild hairy faces with snarling mouths and mad eyes.

"Marc!" she yelled, finally, able to gather enough air for the purpose. She feared, though, that it was lost in the wails of her attackers. A fist belted her in the cheek. Light and pain exploded behind her eyes, and her head was thrown back. Luckily, the creatures were not terribly strong, but the blow caused her consciousness to slip one notch away.

The raining strikes seemed to become distant, and a dull ringing took up residence in her ears. It allowed her a moment of respite, however, and she was foggily able to cast around her eyesight in an effort to get her bearings. She was facing the road and Sandoren was off to the right. He was hanging limply while his tormenters took turns leaping up and dangling from his legs and body. His sword was gone. Off to her immediate left, was Clover. She was trying to stand, but having trouble as two of the Epas were jumping up and down on her side. Over the bell in her ears, she could hear the horse screaming in pain and fright. Slowly, she jerked her head enough to look over the raging creatures and back down the road.

Del was still sitting Day, obviously outside the Epas immediate awareness, tears streaming down a pale and slack face, his mouth hanging open. Next to him was Marc, on the ground standing next to Whitesteel, watching them die, a grimness etched into his face. Their eyes locked, briefly.

Alex was hit in the face again, this time knocking her stunned consciousness back into place. The roar of the world came back, full of fury and pain. Her body sagged, held up only by those punishing her. Closing her eyes, she tried to block out everything, though the worst came from her mind as it panicked and told her she was going to die and Marc and Del were simply going to watch. A sickness formed in her belly. *Why?* She yelled silently at him. *Why aren't you helping?*

You know why, another part of her mind wailed back. Yes, she knew why, but Marc's betrayal was a terrible agony deep inside her, much worse than the clobbering numbness the Epas were giving her. She was going to die, and no one was going to help.

Silently, she fought back, that part of her that was a rock, that stubbornness that could not be broken, pushing back the tide of her pain, panic, and fading body, enough that she could reach out and grab it. She closed her eyes, ignoring the pummeling, and drew deep of the Earth beneath her, pulling power up and quickly into that knot of indomitability, concentrating it, compressing it until it would be compressed no more, and then, with an angry yell of defiance, she released it.

The Power exploded outward, like a bubble that took all sound, movement, everything away in one moment of ecstatic pain. The Epas shrieked in agony as they were thrown back by the blast, forced to release their hold, they bounded away in a frenzy, slapping at sizzled fur and clawing at singed eyes. Alex lay on her back, the rush of power gone, her body numbly throbbing. Shakily, she looked up at Sandoren. A controlled but weak wheezing filtered down from him.

She drew again from the Earth and Air around her, this time more slowly, letting it fill her, permeate her being, energizing her and pushing away the pain. Her beaten body mended itself, cracked ribs knit and torn muscle mended. The bruises receded into yellowish underpinnings, and the only blood on her was that which was drying on her lips and chin. Within moments, Alex was as she was prior to the attack, and though her body was still weak, she climbed, trembling, to her feet.

The serpent vines released Sandoren as Alex reached out and relaxed them with her touch. He gasped, drew in a loud, ragged breath when the clamp around his neck loosened, and he fell forward onto the cobbled road, trying to pull precious air into wounded lungs. Alex moved to him and directed the Power into his body, Healing him just as she had used it to Heal herself. When he was breathing slowly and rhythmically, she turned her attention to Clover.

The horse was standing, eyes wide, nostrils flaring. She was in shock and favoring one of her legs, but was otherwise unharmed. Once she directed the Healing Flows into her, even that was only a memory. When she was finished, she, reluctantly, released her hold on the Power. Immediately, she was grabbed and held tight. At first, she stiffened in response, her body thinking it was being attacked again, but she relaxed and stroked Del's hair as he sobbed into her shoulder.

"You son of a whore!" Sandoren said raggedly behind her. She looked up to see Marc walking toward them, holding Day's reins, Whitesteel behind them, moving of his own accord. He was stone faced and his eyes diamond hard. "You just stood there! You were going to watch us die!" Sandoren stumbled toward him as the accusations fell from his lips. Marc stopped.

When Sandoren's intentions became evident, Alex yelled, "Sandy, no! He couldn't. . . ." she was cut off as Marc's head jerked back violently from Sandoren's strike, blood splattering out from his nose, across his lean face, running freely as he righted himself. His expression never changed, nor did he utter a sound, or even move to defend himself. Marc simply stared at Sandoren with dead pan eyes.

"No," she yelled again when she heard the snick of Sandoren's knife coming free of its sheath, but he was beyond hearing her just then. Still Marc did not move or blink.

"I'm going to cut you open, you bastard," Sandoren hissed, pulling his arm back to slice. Suddenly, he went rigid, and spit out a grunt of surprise. Alex gently pushed Del away, holding onto the Power as well as her exhausted body could. "Alex?" the ffolk stammered.

"Damn it, Sandy!" she said, her anger bubbling up into her tone. "I said, 'No!'." Slowly, she walked toward them. "He cannot help, you stubborn fool!" she spat once she came around to look at the rigidly held Guardian. Alex didn't look at Marc, even though consciously, she understood his inability, it was something that the rest of her was unwilling to deal with just yet. Fortunately, he didn't take his flat stare away from Sandoren.

"He is cursed!" she yelled into her companion's held face, watching it try to pinch under the blanket of hardened Air which enveloped him. Her resumption of her tirade blocked out the large man behind her completely. "He can do nothing to help anyone in times of need! Physically unable, just as you are right now! He's been that way for generations, living countless lives of an estranged observer. Do you understand, you horse's ass?"

Sandoren blinked several times, then hissed out a, "Yes," through his clenched jaw.

"You better because he is wrapped up in the journey that I must make! No 'maybe's' or 'if's' about it, regardless of your petty feelings, got it?" she waited until he blinked. "If you can't handle it, then you need to move on because your childishness is putting us in danger, you got that? I will not have you jeopardizing the life of this boy or the task with which I have been given, understand?"

"Yes," he hissed again, his face reddening with shame and anger. "I understand."

"Good," she said flatly, and released her hold on the solidified air. Sandoren relaxed reflexively, an unconscious move that did not release the humiliation that bound up in him. "Because this is the last I am going to speak of it."

Sandoren nodded curtly, stepped past her and began walking back in the direction Veraddin went without another look or word. Alex could feel the gap between them widen even more, becoming too wide to ever really repair, and, internally, she wailed in frustration. She knotted up her anger, steeled herself, then turned to Marc, about to unleash her fury on him. Something slapped her hand and she looked down to find Day's reins resting in it.

"I told you, you would regret it," Marc said in a low, hate filled voice. Before he stepped away to mount Whitesteel, she caught a glance of his otherwise elusive face and saw a sadness and self-loathing so deep beneath the surface of his eyes that she forgot her anger and whatever else she was going to say. Without looking at her, as well, he nudged the great horse to a trot and headed into the foothills, leaving her standing there with a slack jawed Del and her own terrible feelings of guilt.

Slowly, numbly, she dropped the horse's reins and moved to where Sandoren had dangled near death and retrieved his sword from the brush. The weapon was a heavy, awkward thing. To her, it had always been so. A thing of death, but necessary. In Sandoren's hand, it had been a thing of life, something that kept Death from her time and again, just as her powers had thwarted that Apparition from taking him, too. *A Balanced Set*, she thought suddenly, then added angrily, *No more.*

Alex used the unwieldy blade as a walking stick for her aching, tired body. Whatever she had done to the Epas took a lot out of her. When she turned back to the road, she found Del feeding Day grass pulled from the edge of the road.

"Del," she called softly. The boy turned his attention to her and smiled with drool slicked lips. "Are you okay, now?" He nodded after a pause in which his face took on that empty look.

"Yes," he said.

"Are you hungry?" she asked. She stepped forward, realized her legs gave out just before her knees hit the ground with a jarring halt. Pain shot up and through her body, causing a hiss to escape her clenched teeth. A clammy sweat broke out on her skin, and her body began trembling violently. A cloud encroached on her vision and the curse that fell from her mouth was distant and muted as if she were under water.

"You tried to take in too much," somebody said through the blackness surrounding her. She thought it was Del, but she remembered he was feeding the horse. Besides, the voice sounded different. "You are still a child in relation to the Powers now available to you and must be more careful," the voice continued. She whimpered, or thought she did.

The light hurt her eyes and glared off everything, but she looked up anyway. Something blacker than night moved among the trees on the other side of the road, nearest to Del. Neither he nor the horses sensed it. She tried to warn him, but nothing came out. The Something stepped onto the road, all teeth, it seemed, and grinning.

Without warning, a vortex of Power steeled through her, taking her breath. It was icy cold and burning hot at the same time, and she gasped as it moved about and through her. An echo of words spoke into her cloudy dizziness. *Careful. Too much. Careful.* It stormed, pulling her this way and that, stealing from her all that she was, then, became a breezing, cooling and peaceful flow that refilled her. "There," that voice finally said.

Her vision cleared, the dizziness gone. She heard herself say, "Del, are you hungry?" The boy smiled and shook his head and went back to feeding his horse blades of fresh grass. Alex looked around, shaking her head slightly. She was standing again, leaning on the sword, using it as a cane. *Didn't I fall down?* she thought hazily. *What happened? Something happened.* She looked around for a beast that was all teeth and black as night. There was nothing there. *Wasn't there?*

Alex shook her head again. *Must be seeing things*, she thought. *I must be really beyond the edge of exhaustion if I am.* Though her body was still weak she felt strangely refreshed. *Got to be more careful with the Powers next time.*

A few minutes later found them atop their mounts once more, walking them in the direction Sandoren had gone. Within a few more, they saw him riding towards them around the bend in the clump of trees where the horse had nearly bowled them over. There was no sign of the Epas and Veraddin seemed no worse for the wear. They stopped and waited for the Guardian, offering his sword to him when he was near.

Sandoren took it without looking at her, his face a carefully sculpted mask of neutrality. The pain inside her couldn't have been worse if he drew the razor-edged blade along the flesh of her arm as he took the sword back. Once it was placed in its scabbard, he moved up the road ahead of them, Del turning Day just as he passed. Alex stared down at the pommel of the old saddle she sat astride and struggled for a few seconds with her emotions before following them.

They rode silently, plunging deeper into the woodland that flanked the steepening road. Overhead, the sun made its way slowly to the horizon as they pressed further into the pass. Without knowing when, the land rose on either side, becoming high forested slopes and precipitous walls of rock, enclosing them within the cut. Birds of prey glided over them, and the normal sounds of the wild made it hard to believe that anything was wrong with the world.

As Night threw her veil of dusk over the land, readying them for the darkness to come, they found Marc waiting for them at a high point in the pass before it began to decline. The view ahead was staggering, even in the dim light. The high hills they had just traveled through became nothing compared to the sheer, craggy cliffs and peaks before them. The White Rock Mountains glittered like diamonds in the last of the sun's rays, the crystalline walls like giant teeth catching and rebounding them back, showing off the reason for its name. Alex, and even Sandoren, had to stop to take in the view, though each of them had seen it many times before.

"Come," Marc said hoarsely, turning Whitesteel down a small trail that she could not remember seeing before. Del moved in behind him, talking softly to some furry animal nestling in his arms. When Sandoren made no move to follow, Alex nudged Clover onto the path with a sigh. Sandoren and Veraddin came last, giving the group a wide lead.

The trail wound down around the hills, into untouched forest, almost parallel to the pass they left, but then, it turned east and began up again, steeply, into the mountain. For hours they walked, all silent except for the occasional whicker or snort from one of their mounts or the soft chatter of Del. The temperature dropped, becoming increasingly chill while the night sky glimmered cleanly above, through the canopy of surrounding trees. Alex thought she must have dozed off, because, at some point during the early morning hours, she found herself in front of a tall wide wooden gate. Two small lanterns glowed warmly on either side, casting yellow light out into the darkness of the thick, chirping wilderness.

Minutes later, the left side of the gate swung open silently, and Marc waved them forward, disappearing first through the portal. Once inside, they found him dismounting, Whitesteel's reins held by a robed man that said something to Marc in a language she did not understand. He replied in kind, using the same language as the robed man did, briefly gesturing in their direction. The robed man turned to them.

"Welcome," he said softly with a slightly musical tone in his voice. "We have been expecting you. I am Aldmerron. The chosen Speaker for your stay. We have prepared rooms and a hot meal for you. Please follow me. Your horses shall be tended to." Aldmerron finished and handed off Whitesteel's reins to another robed man who suddenly seemed to appear next to him. He and Marc began walking up a wide path, speaking to each other in the unknown language earlier used. Behind her, Sandoren grunted something sarcastic.

Alex dismounted, yawned while holding out Clover's reins to the man, and looked around. The horse whickered softly. They were in a huge sculpted garden. Shrubbery and bushes of many different types decorated the spaces between interweaving paths and small streams that trickled throughout the area. Above, spreading their branches aesthetically, intertwining with each other, were several varieties of trees, some of which she had never seen before. Small lanterns glowed throughout, giving an etherealness to the place. Immediately, she felt relaxed, safe, more at peace. She reached out, briefly, finding an abundance of life and Power here.

After a moment of breathing in the beauty and calmness around her, she started up after Marc and Aldmerron, following Del who, somehow, got down off Day and got ahead of her before she knew it. Behind her, Sandoren was dismounting, still grumbling to himself.

Chapter 50

Rest, Comfort, and Apologies

*W*hen she awoke, Alex was as refreshed as if she had slept for four days. Four deep, dreamless days. The soreness in her body, the weakness, was vanished and her mind was clear. She sat up and looked around the austere room constructed of daub, the pallet she had been sleeping on giving only a token squeak of protest. The aroma of fruit blossoms and other flora wafted through a window, brought by a comforting breeze. She smiled and set about dressing herself.

Outside, the air was softly cool and more aromatic, the gentle breathing of it swirling countless flavors to and fro among the sun dappled garden. Small paths radiated out from where she stood intertwining with trickling creeks and shallow pools further out. Flora of all types blended within the spaces between them, juniper, jasmine, rose bushes, lilacs, and lilies. Countless in numbers and varieties, they were well tended and sculpted with the practiced eyes of an artist. Even some of the rarer fireflowers and muskbush were evident, as were swanplants and sunflowers. Above them, the sheltering arms of oaks and ironwoods, willow and wideleaf, chestnut and elm, spread over and among many types of pine, and spruce, and aspen, whispering quietly with the sway of the moving air, lending their own earthy scents to the slight intoxicating perfumes of the many flowers. Birds filled the air with song and small animals moved about on the ground and in the branches, chittering happily. The garden seemed to extend forever in every direction, rolling and flowing with small hillocks and knolls, revealing partly concealed daubed buildings. Several of the robed men moved about within sight, some tending plants, some walking the paths, some sitting quietly, tucked within the bushes as if a part of them. Alex could not help but simply stand there and take several deep breaths, wondering how, in all her life had neither she nor the other sisters known of this place of beauty.

And power. Yes, much Earth Power resided here. Life giving and stable, infinite and healing. Alex had sensed it last night, but, now, after her deep rest, which, no doubt, was aided by the very Nature that surrounded her, it felt like an almost palpable presence. She half expected to turn at some point and see one of the great Living Trees overlooking the area. She stepped away and began strolling down the nearest path, not knowing where she was headed, nor caring. At the moment she did not think of anything else but the sculpted, natural beauty around her.

Some of the robed ones nodded at her, some simply looked her way, while some completely ignored her. Aside from their uniformly light green clothing, the only similarity they seemed to share was their silence. Though they were as diverse as the flora, human, skor, ffolk, one of the swamp dwelling reptilmen, not one spoke or otherwise made a sound. Even a gnomite, known for their inexhaustible speaking abilities, was preternaturally close mouthed. All went about whatever business they were about.

As did she, which was simply walking and enjoying the surroundings.

Alex was far from where she started, farther even than the robed ones, the path continued to curve around through the vivacious garden, leading her to nowhere in particular. At first, she thought the man was simply working the soil, the way he was kneeling, back to her, hood thrown back. It wasn't until she saw Del near him, sitting and studying the ground, that she recognized the broad, strong back and graying hair that belonged to Marc. She changed direction and made her way toward them, curious as to what he was doing, kneeling in the grass.

He seemed to be reaching for something, only to stop and withdraw his hand before trying again. She thought she heard a grunt, maybe a curse, come from his direction, a profane sound in this place. Her interest piqued; she slowed and crept toward him until she could look over his shoulder. Alex was amazed he had not heard her, his usual alertness must be completely caught up in the task he was performing.

On the ground, near his foot, squirmed the gray-pink body of a featherless hatchling, opening and closing its beak silently. Alex looked up to see a nest resting in the crook of a low hanging branch, about the height of her head. Marc was reaching for the hatchling, his hand getting maybe a quarter of the way out before stopping and vibrating as if electrified by lightening, then, with a grunt of frustration, withdrew back to his knee. He did it several times before his body went suddenly rigid. Moments later, a tired voice said, "Can you help me?"

Alex moved next to him and knelt, looking down at the dying creature. "There's nothing I can do," she said softly, studiously watching the baby bird, but able to see Marc's strained face out of the corner of her eye. "Once the hatchling has fallen from the nest, the mother will no longer accept it as her own."

He reached for it again, grunting with effort, and pulled back. "Then kill it," he said. "Put it out of its misery."

She thought momentarily, then summoned power from around her and held it in her hand until she formed the flow that would take the creature's life quickly and painlessly, and reached for the bird. A shadow falling on them gave her pause, and she looked up and saw Del looking down on them intently. The expression on his face caused her to pull her hand away. It was knowing, sad. His eyes were luminous, and he shook his head.

Del knelt suddenly, reached out and scooped up the flailing hatchling softly in two meaty hands. Alex quickly grabbed his wrist and said, "No, Del. The mother will not take it back." For the first time, soft anger flashed over his features, and he shook his head sharply.

"No," he said, shaking off her tenuous grip and standing.

"Del," Alex said, also standing. "It will be better if. . . ."

"No," he said with more forcefulness and turned, reached up and deposited the baby bird in the nest it had fallen from. The vortex of Power she felt the day he opened up the sky for sunlight suddenly surrounded him, making her gasp as if cold water were dumped over her head. An instant later, it was gone, snapping as if it were a bent twig. Alex reeled a little, still stunned though experiencing it before. It was fast, then gone, but it was powerful beyond anything she ever felt before. Alex was not surprised when she saw a couple of the robed ones come around a group of high shrubbery to stare in their direction.

Seconds later, as if on cue, the mother bird winged down through the branches and settled in the nest, oblivious to the onlookers, and began preening the younglings who were starting to squeak hungrily. Alex had to blink past held open eyes when she watched her feed the fallen hatchling as if nothing had ever happened. Once she realized what Del had done, shame began to fill her. She could have done the same thing he had, taken away the moment of eminent rejection by taking the foreign scents from the tiny, squirming body. Reflexively, she took Del in her arms and hugged him.

"See," he said finally, going back to his former task in the now lush and unruly grass. She nodded, thought of Marc.

He was walking away, the three robed ones bowing their heads at his passing when she sought him out. Marc's head, too, was down, cowled and his shoulders were slouched. She had to rush to catch up to his long strides, noting briefly that the three remained in that bowed position, hands tucked into sleeves, as she went by them.

"Marc," she said, once she closed the distance.

"Leave me be, *Mal 'andel,*" he answered, making the ancient honorific sound anything but.

"Please, allow me to walk with you," she pressed.

"As you wish," came his disgusted answer.

They walked quietly for at least a sun's width, weaving through the garden's many paths. Alex hoped Marc would say something, anything that she could remark to so she could open the conversation she wanted to explore. But he said nothing, did not even look in her direction. The only visible part of his face was the tip of his nose, peeping from the heavy green cloth. She sighed inwardly. Grudgingly, she decided to attempt to get him talking and said, softly, "Marc. . . ."

"Look, lady," he snapped, stopping long enough to turn a shrouded look of anger in her direction, using a finger to punctuate each word he spoke. "I don't know why I'm here, but I am. I don't know why you want me here, but I guess it really doesn't matter. What I do know is that you will be much better off if you leave off trying to get to know me."

She stepped back unconsciously, her jaw locking from the indignant way at being treated so. Marc's eyes were slits beneath the hood, and his finger hovered just below her chin. Several heartbeats passed while she struggled to swallow the lump of anger that knotted the back of her throat, her eyes steady against his. Finally, he grunted and whipped away from her down the path.

Alex blinked several times, his departure suddenly releasing the bonds on her throat, the lump sliding free like bitters into her roiling gut. "I'm sorry," she called suddenly, her voice rough. Marc stopped again, his head going back to look up into the trees while a sigh escaped him.

"What for?" he said.

"For dragging you into this the way I did," she answered. "For not knowing why. For whatever reason." She was still angry, but she was able to keep that aside while she spoke. Marc turned, looked at her.

"There's no need to apologize," he said after a long moment. "It is I who must apologize, once again, for speaking so harshly. However, I think you should reconsider my importance to your journey. Ultimately, I will prove to be its downfall. The incident at the mouth of the pass should give you some indication of my worthlessness."

"Is that the way of it, then?" she asked. "The curse, I mean."

He swallowed hard. "For the most part, yes," he said. "I cannot give you aid in any way. Especially when you need it most."

Alex smirked, but smoothed it away quickly when Marc frowned. "Then that shouldn't be a problem, since I do not need your aid."

"Then what do you need from me?"

"I don't know," she said, then, when he arched a brow, "Truly. I was told to seek out the boy, that you would herald my finding him, that I needed both of you to help me seal the Wound."

"The wound? What is that? And who told you this?"

"A terrible. . . hole. . . a mountain that is spewing forth the death of the world. . . northwest of us. . . in the Starlight Mountains," she said.

"The volcano?" he asked.

"Partly. . . It is drawing Power directly from the World and throwing it out, causing severe strain and Chaos in our world. If I don't find a way to stop it, it will destroy us and the world. . . .It's difficult to explain, but, on the Dark Night, it appeared . . . ."

"Threadbearer. . ." Marc whispered.

"What?"

"Nothing. A thought came to me. . ."

"Did you say 'Threadbearer'?" she asked. He nodded and a small smile creased her lips. "Where did that fable pop up from?"

"Don't know," he answered. Then, changing direction, "I hear there is a great, dark cloud covering much of the lands northwest."

"Yes," she said. "It emanates from the Wound and is poisoning everything it shrouds. A terrible side effect to the actual Power bleeding from it. Before she died, Gyssel told me to seek out the boy, and you, though she could not tell me why, only that you both have something to do with my . . . quest . . . to Heal the Wound."

"Gyssel, eh? Headstrong wench," he said. Alex nearly snapped something about respect, but the loving tone he used gave her pause. "Even in death, she finds ways to bother me." He smiled then, looking backward into a private past, then chuckled. "You old bat."

"Old bat?" Alex snapped. Marc coughed and looked at her again

"Sorry," he said. "Not you." His face tightened and his eyes took on their normal hardness. "I said I would go with you, and I will. For whatever reason. But, be warned. My curse manifests in ways that can cause your quest to be undone."

"I'll just have to take that risk."

"Yea, I've heard that before," Marc said, blowing out another sigh. "Often times, people rue that comment." He trundled down the path, leaving her to her thoughts.

Chapter 51

The Emperor's Ire

"*There* it is again!" the Emperor roared, though there was no one around to hear. Not even one of the *Sceaduwen*. "Is that you, Tempest? What are you doing? Are you trying to tempt me away from my goals? Are you testing my patience? Destroying one of my children. . . that was a terrible thing to do. But you will feel retribution soon enough." Turning from the direction from which the flood of Power came, a pulse, quick but terrible in its strength, the Emperor turned to a nearby table. Several maps lay unfurled on it, the topmost showing the whole of the small continent with several markings on it. The emperor perused it for a few moments before scratching another mark on it. "Getting closer, I see. . . Do you have business in the north? Yes, yes, keep coming. . . you might walk into your destruction. Yes, yes, one less of us to disturb my plans." A gloved finger smudged markings at the bottom corner of the map. "Cabal, you are there, are you not?" It slid toward the middle. "And Skek, is that you? Got to dig Hoblin out of his hole and get him working on the ships, yes, yes. Only two recovered, but you need to get us more."

A *Sceaduwen* materialized from the shadows and waited while the Emperor mumbled a few more comments to no one. "Go seek out this disturbance," the Emperor finally said. "Be cautious, the last one never returned." The Sceaduwen bowed and silently stepped back into the shadows and disappeared while the lone ruler considered the space where the thing was standing, looking far away. Finally, nodding, he went on, "Yes, yes, Tempest, you will be the first. Yes, the first. . . ."

Chapter 52

The Philosophy of Death

*D*eath. Destruction. Death and destruction seemed to be only what the outside world was. Where was the beauty and magnificence? Where were the glorious buildings, the strange carriages, the people that her teacher had told her of in those rare moments of nostalgia? Could it be that the Faethe was lying? Or could he just have been wrong, thinking the world was something it was not? Like when a dream seems so real that it is difficult to distinguish between it and reality when wakened. Maelyrin didn't know. Really did not want to see anymore death and destruction. In fact, she wanted to go back home, to the village of her birth and take up her duties as the Faethe's apprentice again. Even the cool, fear-wrought respect the villagers gave her seemed more than tolerable now. She knew now that she was just being foolish. Within just scant days, the world outside her village had taught her that her life there had been better than most. The guilt she felt for having left was a becoming a constant reminder of her youth and inexperience. The horrors she witnessed was teaching her quickly. Whether she wanted it to or not.

However much she thought about going back, to rejoining her haven, she could not justify leaving behind the reason she did it in the first place. For her, Marc Pendragon was the driving force behind why she was headed north instead of east. It was as if he, this man, this human, was an ideal or even something more obscure that she could not deny. Inside herself, she emphatically knew her decision to follow him was the correct choice. How she knew did not matter. It simply was.

But it did nothing to keep the horrors away.

Maelyrin studied the mane of the horse she sat astride, Kiyo's loping gait a presence out of the corner of her eyes. The tears were gone now, but not anything else. The Inn was the worst yet in a growing list of things, events, terrible visions, that would haunt her for years to come. A lynchpin to the dam of her tears, that, once pulled, had kept them running down her face for the better part of the morning.

Her head hurt, right above her brows, her eyes stung, her throat felt raw. Her cheeks felt as if tree sap had run down them and had hardened and would crack if she but smiled, or grimaced, or had any other expression other than the one she wore now. A deep, neutrally sad look that seemed to sag from the bones of her skull. She was sapped, all the strength she had rolled down her face and dripped from her chin, and all she could do was sit slumped in the saddle staring down at the black hairs of the mane while her body floated to the rhythm of the horse's gait. She was trying not to see the images of the dead. Not that it mattered much now, since the sobbing left her body numb.

But, they came, floating into her mind's eye like a fly, powerless now, but no less irritating. She wondered if it would have been less of a shock had not the survivor told her their names. If, somehow, the twisted creatures that had once housed living beings would have been easier to look upon, to bury, had not he given them lives and identities. Silently, she cursed the man with the strange accent who told her the names of the dead. Master Abyl, the innkeeper. Mira the cook and serving girl. Tam, their only customer since the others left. It would have been better for her if they were just three twisted, horrible dead things without a past.

No it wouldn't, she thought. It would only have made her wonder who they had been; given her a terrible sense of aloneness for them in a way. The masks of terror they wore in death would have been infinitely worse, coming to her in her dreams to torment her, asking, *Who are we? Who are we to have suffered this?*

At least now, she had a way to put them to rest, their horrible visages as well as their bodies.

And, at least, bearing witness to their frightful end had yielded much needed information. It gave her direction to an otherwise directionless quest. It reset her on the path of her goal. At least, the man with the odd tongue had been able to tell her the way Marc Pendragon had gone and to where he thought he was headed. How fortuitous it was to have found him. Amid the death and destruction, amid the confusion and aimlessness, amid her very own doubts of ever finding Marc, the only one to have seen him, a man that missed death by a matter of minutes and obscuring trees as he chased a customer's escaping horse.

She could not swallow the irony. And it did nothing for her tears.

"Is the entire world this terrible," she said, not really expecting an answer, speaking only to give her pent up thoughts another release, since her eyes dried up. But Kiyo answered evenly, not tired in the least by his exertion.

"There can be much cruelty in the world," he said. "And there can be much beauty. Do not judge the whole by the smallest of its parts."

"This is not the time to get cryptic!" she lashed, her flaring anger a brief burst that reverted back to somberness. Kiyo stopped walking, and she was suddenly afraid she had hurt him or angered him. The horse she sat upon struggled against her urgings, unused to her as master, but finally stopped as well. She had to turn in the saddle to await the admonishment she expected.

Instead, Kiyo waved his hand in a large level circle, saying as he did so, "Look around and tell me what you see."

"Trees," she answered quickly.

"Is the sun shining? Is the air warm against your skin?" he continued as if he had not heard, then stopped and looked at her expectantly. She nodded.

"Yes. The sun is out and it is warm on my face," she snapped. "But what does that have to do with anything?"

"Would this be something that you would normally find pleasant?"

"Of course, but . . . what about it?"

"Are you enjoying it now?" he asked

"Of course I'm not enjoying it now," she retorted, her voice starting to rise in pitch. Kiyo's, though, seemed to soften.

"Why are you not enjoying it now?"

"You bloody well know why!" she yelled. "We just spent half the day burying those poor people back there." Her breath was heaving, she noticed, and her hands were gripping the reins so tightly they were beginning to ache. She stared at the giant, silently wishing him pain for being so cold, so obtuse. "What does any of this have to do with anything?" she said finally, forcing her muscles to relax, which they did so only a little.

"Nothing," he said simply. She sputtered, tensing again, but unable to find words with which to vent the sudden terrible anger that seized her. *Calm yourself*, came a drifting thought that seemed to match the movements of the giant's mouth, though all she could hear was a pounding hiss thundering in her ears. Just as quickly, the storm fled, and she sagged, still unable to speak, but from exhaustion rather than fury. "You will learn that, ultimately, you are responsible for what you carry with you," Kiyo said once she was breathing again. "That it is your choice whether to enjoy the sun on your face or to worry over the dead."

"Are you saying I should rejoice in the fact that those people are dead, or that the people back in that village tried to kill us?"

"I don't presume to dictate how or what you should feel. I am merely saying that what you carry does not have to be the burden you are making it. What happened to those people was, yes, a horrible thing. However, you were neither responsible for it nor for the care afterwards, though you did honor to them by seeing to the burial of their vessels. It is good that you feel the way you do, that you do not deny your feelings, but be wary that it does not dominate you. That it does not become a shield from which you are unable to see around. After all, you are alive, and the sun is shining. Whether that is a good thing is for you to decide, but it still *is*. The past will remain unchanged and the future will remain undetermined. That leaves only the present in which you can actively take part in."

"I don't understand," she said after a moment.

"You will," he answered. "In time." Without another word, the blue giant began walking again.

Chapter 53

Crowlin's Impotent Rage

"*We* lost him," Reegan croaked.

"What!" Crowlin raged. He grabbed Reegan's cloak and pulled him forcefully within a hair's breadth of his face. "How?" he growled.

"Don't know," Reegan stammered. "The stone makes no tracks. He must have turned off the path." With another growl, Crowlin threw the other back. Reegan stumbled and fell to the rock without a sound, while he scanned the sharp crystalline peaks surrounding them. Out of frustration, Crowlin pounded his thigh several times until the pain seeped up into his brain. Dimly, he was aware of one of his fingers snapping with the effort. The burning sensation started his mind rolling. "Is there any other way out of this range?" he asked with controlled fury.

Reegan groaned his way to a standing position. "No," he rasped.

"Then—" Crowlin began but was cut off when a white fire burst inside his head. He could feel his teeth grip so hard they chipped, and he leaned far over, his body turning into a tight rigor. Words flowed into his blazing mind, leaving scorch trails on the inside of his skull. Several minutes passed before the agony that raged in him stopped. And several more went before he could recuperate enough to pull himself back into a standing position. The Master's sudden presence always left him shaking with weakness. The stares of his companions were heavy, but not one of them would accept what had just happened. When he could again speak, he said: "We go ahead to Khemosh. Whether he is ahead or behind us, we can get there before him and awaken some of the Chyldren. We'll set a trap and wait for him there."

"T-the Chyldren?" asked Reegan. He stumbled backward again as Crowlin backhanded him sharply.

"What are you afraid of, Reegan?" he hissed. "Death!"

While he was picking himself up again, Teraard asked, "Why don't we follow the Old One?" Crowlin turned and looked at him.

"It's disappeared, too," Reegan said around grunts.

"It matters not!" Crowlin yelled. "We go forward to Khemosh! If you are afraid, you can go back to Him. I am sure He will be more forgiving than the Chyldren." No remarks from them followed. "Well, then. . . let us go." Crowlin swung up into his saddle and kicked the flanks of his mount, starting the decrepit beast across the stone path deeper into the gleaming range. Seconds later, he heard the hooves of the others' mounts clattering unsteadily behind him.

Chapter 54

Frustrations of Tracking

$\mathcal{M}$arc was sitting in silent meditation when he heard the first rending scream. A piercing, inhuman sound that tore at the recently fallen night like claws tearing flesh. Before even his eyes were open, his hand was on the hilt of his sword which lay on the floor beside him.

Again it split the darkness, a high pitched squeal of fury and frustration that rattled his teeth and bounced his heart. A vague sense of recognition flitted around the edges of his mind, but it was shattered when the scream came again.

In the next moment, he was outside, his *kobokh* robe hanging loosely about his large frame, his sword preceding his movements. The lanterns randomly spaced throughout the garden and on the daub buildings cast their soft lights in a manner that seemed suddenly eerie this night. Several of the other men were already outside, looking all around, calmly but like predators readying themselves to pounce.

Another scream. From a different direction. Heads turned in that direction. Alex appeared near him, and he saw Sandoren moving about down the path, moving fluidly, pacing like a caged beast. His sword gleamed as it caught the glow. He was making his way towards them and even from the distance and the pale light, Marc could see the fear etched on his face. It was a knowing fear. He knew what was stalking the outer boundary.

It was Aldmerron that finally gave a name to the fury outside. *"Brehnduk,"* he said when he neared.

"Brehnduk?" Marc said, recognizing now, what the squeals did not permit his mind to reach on its own. "Are you sure?" He needed not ask. He knew, but his seeking mind wanted confirmation.

When Sandoren hove closer, he looked to Alex and asked, "Is it the Eldritch?"

She nodded while Aldmerron answered Marc. "Yes," he said. "It can't get in the Barrier. It's angry."

"No ribbing," Marc said. "What's it after?"

"I do not know, Menla," Aldmerron said, unruffled by Marc's sarcasm. "There is no reason. . . ."

"It's after Del." Alex said finally, drawing everyone's attention.

"What?" Marc said.

"We think it is after Del," she repeated.

"And you were going to tell me this. . . when?" he asked.

Alex looked at him pointedly. "Now," she said flatly. "It seems to get confused the closer it gets to him, so it has been staying pretty far behind us. The Barrier you spoke of. . ." she indicated Aldmerron with a nod, but did not unlock her eyes from Marc's. ". . .is probably confusing it more. It might be thinking that it's lost him."

"Why does it seek the boy?" Marc asked and received a shrug in response.

"Who knows why the Eldritch do anything," she said.

"Well, it looks as if there is nothing else to do then, but go back to bed," Marc said. Another scream protested. "Or, at least, back to our quarters." He turned to Aldmerron. "I don't suppose there is a possibility it can get in here?"

"I do not think so, Menla," he answered. "The Barrier is woven strongly. Nevertheless, the Wen will spend the night at guard. Good night, my brother."

Marc returned the reverent bow that Aldmerron gave him. "Good night, Brother," he answered.

"Do not fear, Mal 'andel. You and your companions will come to no harm while under the protective arms of the Wen. May you rest well despite the night's baleful music." He bowed to her as well.

"We thank you for your kindness. . . Fa 'andel." Her comment caused his eyes to go wide momentarily before backing away a decent distance before turning his back on them.

With a last look of disgust, Sandoren slid his sword back into its scabbard and faded down the path, no doubt going to spend the night patrolling the grounds, untrusting of the Wens' reassurances. Alex watched him go, an expression of studied neutrality on her face. When he was gone from view she looked around and saw Marc looking at her.

Quickly, to avoid any more argument or uncomfortable discussion, he gave her a slight bow, saying, "Good night, Mal 'andel."

She blinked, inclined her head, "Good night, Marc." When she moved down the path toward her dwelling, he went back inside to return to his meditation while the beast, the Brehnduk, the Eldritch, howled and screamed in frustrated hate.

All night, it prowled, wailing out its concern, but when the sun crept high enough for the crystalline peaks to catch its rays and spray them out in glittering colors across the land and garden, it fell silent.

Chapter 55

A Decision is Made

*C*orporal Jarren drew shapes in the sand with a stick, shapes that had no definition or form except to some primitive portion of his mind. Shapes that represented sluggish creatures made of blackness that ripped flesh from bones. It was something that he had been doing for the past few days. Some sort of purging that was almost obsession.

Only inches from his feet was the lip of the river, a wide, flat ribbon of glorious water flanked by wonderful greenery undulating eastward across the blasted plains he and the remainder of the 3rd cavalry had been inhabiting for the last few forevers. The water lapped at the gray beach with comforting regularity, and he found himself most calm when sitting next to it, even though moisture tended to soak into the seat of his pants and chilled his flesh. It was a discomfort he was prepared to surrender to. Anything was better than being outside the boundaries of the huge cottonwoods and high grasses where the sun beat down on a man with such mercilessness that death was a comforting thought. Better than dealing with the parched lips, burning eyes, and baking skin. He had on more than one occasion since the remnant of the 3rd arrived, thought to stay here where there was plenty of food, both for them and their mounts, and water. And cool shade. Firewood. Everything that there wasn't in the wasteland beyond.

At least they could move east along the bank until it reached a terminus. While they did that, he intended on moving very slowly. That is, if he decided to move them from this spot. Move them from where they literally collapsed upon arriving two days ago. And while no one bitched about being here, he was loathe to even think about moving. He just as soon build himself a shelter near enough the shore that he always had a look at the water, enough sand and enough sticks to draw in it with.

But that's just wishful thinking, isn't it? Sooner or later, we are going to have to move on. If they dawdled here too long, they would miss the 5th on its track south. But then, right now, service in the Imperial Cavalry was the furthest thing from his mind. And the minds of his men.

Surviving was the first priority. And once that notion had settled in on their numbed spirits, then resolve would have to be reached. After that, morale had to be raised. After that . . . . There was an infinite number of objectives he could think of before returning to Service in the Imperial Cavalry.

Halfheartedly, he threw his stick into the lapping water and scraped his hand across the doodles in the sand, turning the dark lines gouged into a whitish background into a single plain of darkened, wet dirt. Jarren breathed the fresh water and loamy smell in deeply, looked out over the glimmering surface as he let it out, then picked up another stick and began dragging it through the swath of sand between his outstretched legs.

The sun was still climbing the eastern side of the sky, an impotent ball of fire made so by the many overreaching, leaf-abundant limbs that split the harsh light and stippled it across the ground in harmless shards.

He decided they weren't leaving today. Maybe tomorrow, but not today.

Footsteps on the grass and twigs pulled him from his train of thought and placed it in a quiet place not unlike that when in the heat of battle. He waited. The tromping noise died out several feet behind him. "Sir?" Mandol's voice asked.

"What is it?" Jarren answered, his voice still rough and grainy.

"Sir, Maliss is returning," he said.

"So?" Jarren snapped.

"He's got someone with him, maybe two others, we can't be sure. Silek is riding out to greet him," he said.

He has someone with him, maybe two. The thought turned his head around to face his friend, the flare of hope burned in his chest. Mandol wore a mask of exhaustion, like they all did, but he saw within the withered depths hope as well. A clang of jealousy vibrated through him, leaving behind a trail of disappointment. In himself mostly.

Jarren stood, biting at the scream his muscles and tendons put out, wavered a moment, then approached Mandol. "Where?" was all he could muster.

"This way," the man said with a weak smile and turned away, but not before he lay a supporting hand at the back of Jarren's elbow. It felt warm and icy at the same time, sending a prickle through his skin. The touch was like a thirsty man needing water but spitting it out when he got it because his body was too parched to take it.

Jarren let the sensation seep down into the numbness that yet lay deep within him as they made their way slowly through the brush fall and along the small animal trails cutting into it. Mandol kept silent as he led them toward the boundary that marked this paradise from the arid hell beyond. Over the last few days, every one of the hundred and fifty so men had become tombs of silence. For a large part, he had too, and was accustomed to it from everyone else. However, a part of him howled at the unnaturalness of it. A part that longed to hear the sound of the cavalry he had come to love. The low murmur and quiet laughter of men that lived and died together. That part of him wanted noise, any noise, even if it were cries of anger.

When they broke from the tree line, he had to stop and look out at the desolation ahead of him for a moment so its reality could make the transition from the unreal sensation that struck him suddenly. His throat dried painfully, mimicking the arid landscape that seemed to go on forever from the place he stood. With a small force of will, he swung his gaze up and down the borderline of trees and brush, looking for other men, but he saw none. Then, he let his eyes slide over to the plumes of dust framing the dark shapes of riders. This too, he had to make a conscious effort to transcend back into reality. For a moment, he thought they might have been illusions.

"Who's on picket duty?" he asked.

Mandol looked at him for a moment, then said, "Blevins is in charge."

"When we find out who this is, have him move their line closer to the edge," he said.

"Yes sir," Jorn said.

Jarren saw the smile on Silek's face before he could make out its details and it filled him with hope and energy. *No more bad news.* He thought it as a wizard would cast a spell. And maybe it was a spell of some sort. One that might banish all he had seen and give them luck, at the very least.

Something coiled in his guts.

Of course, no spell could do that, could it? Either erase the past or give them exceptional luck. He didn't know for sure. He would have to ask a wizard the next time he saw one. Then, Jarren smiled. *When was the last time you talked to a wizard? Never! When do you think you will ever have the chance to? Never!*

He hadn't realized he was mumbling to himself until he noticed the concerned look Mandol was giving him. "What?" he challenged.

"Uh . . . Nothing," he said. "You feeling alright?"

"What do you think?" Jarren said.

"Yea," Mandol said. "Enough said."

He immediately felt a stab of guilt, but put it aside quickly, and just let the sound of the breeze in the trees take over. After several minutes, the staccato thump of the horses' hooves on the dirt reached him, and it wasn't long after that,

that the horses were slowing to a trot. Maliss' and Silek's mounts largely blocked the third, and it wasn't until they were stopping that he was able to see the roan that trailed behind. Two men in ragged uniforms slumped in the saddle and, his hope starting to whither, he saw the captain's insignia on the shoulder of one of them.

Captain Turcot, it seemed, was alive. But by the way he slouched, like a rag doll tied to a family pet, he wasn't in good shape. The second man's face was eclipsed by Turcot's body, and he could see no insignia on his shoulders, though he wore an Imperial Uniform. The numbness was reeling up, swallowing whatever feelings of excitement he might have had when Silek said, still wearing that big grin, "It's the Commander."

"The Commander?" Jarren said, confusion working up from the numbness into his consciousness. "You mean Captain Turcot."

"Both of them," Silek said. "They are both alive."

Jarren stared at him for half a beat then switched his gaze to the piercing eyes of Maliss, who looked out over the veil covering the lower part of his face. They were dispassionate, not even reflecting Jarren's curiosity. *He's as dead as those men on the horse behind him seem to be*, he thought with a shiver. And then, what Silek said sank in. *Commander Anlin and Captain Turcot lay slumped on that horse.* His voice spit out, "Both of them are alive?"

A shadow fell over Silek's face. "Yes, both of them, but they are injured and ill."

"What?" Jarren said. "Ill?" He looked at Turcot, at the skin visible on the back of his neck and his hands. Pallid white glowed back; sickly white, and, while he studied those terrible places, a shudder rolled through the whole of the Captain's body. Again, the ghost of Jarl the Standard Bearer rose up in his mind's eye and pointed an accusing finger at him. He felt himself start to swoon and mentally reached out and pushed the dead man from him. Though he knew the story backwards and forwards, he still didn't *know* what happened to the 3rd Imperial Cavalry. He didn't think he would ever know what happened. "Well, get them to the physician," he finally said.

"Yes sir," Silek said and nudged his horse into a walk. He tugged on the reins of the third horse, startling it into motion. One of the men on its back let out a moan, he didn't know which. Maliss turned his and kicked it into a trot angling away from them, back out into the desert.

"Where is he going?" Jarren asked.

Mandol shrugged. "Dunno," he said. "Maliss listens to no one but Maliss. It was so even when Commander Anlin was in charge."

When Commander Anlin was in charge. "Commander Anlin will be in charge again," Jarren said without feeling.

"I don't know, Kydel," Mandol said. "I've seen the dead look better than him."

"Does that include Jarl?" he was yelling, the pain he had been holding back suddenly breaking free like a hungry beast. "Does it? Or how about all those poor wretches we left in front that accursed place? Do they look better than he does? Or maybe—"

An explosion of light went off in front of his eyes, and the world reeled. When he hit the ground, the air whooshed from his lungs and tried to stay there, burning even while refusing to breathe in. When, after an eternity of horrible clenching, his chest finally began working again, he looked up from his encapsulating mattress of grass at Mandol. Tentatively, he touched the throbbing patch of skin that was swelling his left eye shut. "You hit me?" he said.

Mandol, who was standing over him with his fists still clenched, said, "Yes I did, you pitiful jack."

"I will have you lashed for insubordination!"

"You go ahead and do that, Kydel," he spit. "If you think Commander Anlin will allow it! Or is the mantle you wear just a convenience when you need it and something to whine about when you don't want to bear its weight? Get it through your head, dolt, that out of a thousand horse there are only a handful left. No officers. No under officers. Only you, Corporal Jarren. You are in command, not Anlin, not Turcot. At least until they look better than they do now, which I somehow think will not be by breakfast. Do you get me? So, if you need to pad your poor wounded pride, then you go ahead and have me lashed, or drawn and quartered, or whatever you want, but know this. . . I will beat you every hour of every day if you continue to whine and pity yourself because you are the only one suffering in this mess. We are soldiers. Death is our bedmate whether we like it or not!"

Jarren watched, too dumbfounded to say anything, as Mandol stalked off into the wood line and disappeared into the greenery. He rolled over and picked himself up while he gritted his teeth from the flares of pain that spread out from his left eye. He managed to get himself into a kneeling position when the dizziness struck him, an undulating wave that rolled over his vision like a gray cloud and tried to squeeze his stomach into giving up its breakfast. When the attack passed, the tears came, and he had to settle back on his knees while he cried out his frustration into dirty hands.

Once both the tears and dizziness left him, replaced by a dull tiredness, he brought his body up, then stood for a few minutes while the hot breeze dried the tracks under his eyes into a tight-feeling covering of salt. Absently, he reached for his sword, but his hand grasped air before he remembered that the blade was still by the river.

Jarren spit out a ragged laugh. He didn't carry his sword anymore on his hip. Just moved it back and forth wherever he happened to be going. Jarren laughed again. What an odd behavior for him to do when the hordes of blackness that decimated the regiment could be sweeping towards them right now.

Jarren laughed yet again, this time like he cried, a long ululating crowing that filled the air around him, sent birds a-wing. While he did so, something seemed to slide into place, something that thumped down into a socket fit for it. He laughed until he couldn't breathe, then kept doing so, his chest heaving without sound, aching and burning, until his body stopped of its own accord. Once that too had passed, and he leaned against himself, hands on knees, eyes staring at the ground, at his feet while he gasped agonized breaths, the fog in his mind that had plagued him since the attack cleared away.

And, though his body was physically tired, it no longer bore the heavy sodden feeling that had lain within his marrow, and he felt light and free moving.

Jarren gave himself a few more minutes before heading towards the hospital they fashioned out of the only officer's tent they had. Every now and again, he prodded the swollen eye and smiled. *Thank you Mandol. . . . But I owe you one.*

When he arrived at the tent, he was composed, face neutral and head held up, back straight, yet he still paused. Mainly to prepare his nose for the reeking odor the flaps held in, a rotten cheesy smell that set his throat to watering and gagging no matter how much he tried to breathe through his mouth. He stopped also to clamp down the resolve he felt. Not that he needed to especially, but just as a precaution. After a moment, he leaned in, grabbed the heavy fabric and pushed his body into the opening.

The fetid cloud of rot met him. Worse than it was yesterday, it oozed around him, clung to his skin. It was overly cloying and left an oily residue on the back of his tongue. It was the disease of death that floated around the tent. Or maybe it was Death itself. The men lying here were the men who got away from the battle though were severely wounded, all of them bearing long gashes in their ashen skin. Fifteen of them, most lying quietly on pallets of grass wrapped in saddle blankets, while shivers moved through their drugged bodies. Bandages, yellowed from discharge, wrapped them all in various places, heads and faces the most common.

Garman, the physician, was looking over the ghostly figure of Captain Turcot and didn't even look up when he entered, though Mandol, standing nearby, did. His eyes were hard but thoughtful, and he saluted with a formalness unlike him. Jarren saluted back and winked at him, giving him a start that turned into a slight grin. Silek was nowhere about, which surprised him. He expected to see the scout. In fact, expected to see him over Mandol's presence. But it was a mystery that he could worry about later, if, indeed, he decided it was worth pursuing.

For now, though, he wanted to find out about the Commander and the Captain, and moved through the tent towards the physician to that end. It took clearing his throat twice and a gentle tap on the man's shoulder before Garman's attention pulled away from the waxen, trembling Turcot.

"How is he?" Jarren said, looking down at the gaunt, drawn face of the Captain. The man's skin was so pale it seemed translucent; he fancied he could see the man's pupils beneath their lids. Waves of soggy heat radiated up from him carrying the rank odor of sickness.

"He's not good," the physician said. His voice was sluggish and deep inkwells lay beneath his eyes. "He's in worse shape than the others. Like the fever has gone all the way into his bones." He squinted. "What happened to your eye?"

"Will he live?"

Garman stared at him for a long time, though Jarren didn't think it was because he was measuring him up. More, he thought the physician slipped and fell into a well of unconsciousness and had to climb out again. "I don't think so," he finally said, his voice thick.

"What about the Commander?" Jarren said, a little too quickly. His composure was beginning to wear thin around the edges, and he wanted to get this over with as soon as he could. He looked at the other man, Commander Anlin, seeing him for the first time since the morning before the attack. His weather-beaten face was drawn like Turcot's but he wasn't fish belly pale. However, his cheeks were high with color. Too high. Every few seconds, his lips peeled from each other and moved briefly before closing again, whispering something none could hear. Absently, he picked up Anlin's uniform coat from the foot of his makeshift bed and looked it over. The insignia, his insignia, was gone from the shoulders, the only evidence that they ever existed, a few loose threads emerging from the heavy material. A ragged hole replaced the Imperial Coat of Arms that resided on the chest. *Why did he do that?*

"He seems in better shape. But he is in the longsleep," Garman said. "And I do not know when, or if, he will wake."

Jarren nodded, dropped the coat back on the Commander's bed, looked around at the other wounded men. "Keep me informed," he said. "And get some rest, Garman. You need it as much as you prescribe it."

"I'll see what I can do after I finish examining them," Garman answered, a wan smile trying to work on his mouth. "And you take care of that eye."

"Good," Jarren said before turning into the door flap. He pushed outside and immediately took a deep inhale of fresh air, then started when he looked up and saw dozens of eyes staring back at him. The men, probably all of them, ringed the little shelter. They stood like ragged statues, their faces masks of exhaustion and glumness, their eyes full of questions. Now, he understood what happened to Silek. He already heralded the return of the Commander and Captain.

"Commander Anlin and Captain Turcot are alive and under the care of the physician," Jarren said, noting the presence of Mandol right behind him. "But there is little else that I know. You men go back to your bedrolls, get your rest. When I know more, you will know more."

They wavered, and whispers flew back and forth between them, but they didn't leave. A knot tried to form in Jarren's throat, but he swallowed it quickly. "Go on. Get back to your rest," he said, his voice rising and deepening at the same time. "We are likely to be moving very soon. Go. Now."

Still they stared, gazing at him with sallow eyes, unmoving. Jarren met their challenge stare for stare, looking at them squarely one after another. Sweat sprung out from his pores, but he didn't acknowledge it, instead he became mindful of the fire in his belly, grasped it and stoked it. Minutes passed. The call of the birds became distant. The sun got a little higher in the sky, heading for the pale globe of the moon hanging over them.

Finally, someone looked away, and then, another one turned and shambled back through the brush. The lynchpin. After that, all of them began turning away from his heavy gaze and moving back to their temporary homes. When they were out of sight, Jarren slumped a bit, let himself breathe again, let his muscles unkink. The only eyes now, that he could feel, was Mandol's on the back of his neck.

He smiled, then walked away himself, heading for the riverside place he had become accustomed to.

Chapter 56

Traveling Blind Through the Pass

"*What* was that?" Maelyrin said, lifting up out of her
exhausted rest at the insistent keen. She looked around,
blinking the sleep from her eyes. It was quiet again, the sound
of a normal night, but the horses were restless, whickering and
snorting and stamping the ground with a nervous hoof. Kiyo
was sitting near her, cross-legged, looking around.

"Creature of some sort," he said. "It's to the east of us.
Fairly distant." As if summoned, another scream whistled
ghostlike from the direction he was looking. It rose hairs on her
neck and began her heart pattering. They were not yet into the
steep cliffs and crags of the mountain proper, but she could
hear the wail echoing off the sheer rocks followed by a far off
humming. Minutes later, the crack and tumble of broken rock
reached them.

"And that?" she stammered.

"No doubt the scream is vibrating the glass rocks ahead
and causing a rock slide," He craned his neck a little and tilted
his head. "That could be a problem, if it continues crying on the
morrow. At any rate, it is far, you need not worry. You should
try to get some rest. The pass looks like a tough trek, you'll
need your energy."

Another wail drifted to them, followed by the echo,
followed by the hum, though, this time, there were no sounds of
rocks falling. "Sure," she said. "Easy for you to say." He, at

least, smiled a little, as she snuggled back down into her bedroll and pulled Kiyo's cloak over her.

The thing kept screaming, sometimes causing rock slides, sometimes not, but the terrible sound always clawed icily up her spine. She tossed and turned, even tried to block the sound by covering her head with the cloak, but it crept into the folds and creases and found her ears. At some point, her exhaustion took over and she slept fitfully, the keening reverberating through her head as disembodied bolts of ragged lightening. They ran together and seemingly went on for an eternity, and even in her sleep, she became frustrated and angry and frightened.

When the sun rose, she didn't know it. Not until Kiyo gently shook her did she realize day had come, but not before she violently slapped at a terrible dark thing that sprang from her imagination and was accosting her. She was vaguely aware of a squeal from her own lips, but it all shattered into warm colorful light as her eyes flashed open and she saw Ki's face. Maelyrin forced breath to come more slowly and sat up.

Once she had gathered herself, she was amazed at the sight before her. The peaks ahead of them sparkled like tremendous drops of dew, throwing off rainbows of shimmering colors as the angled morning light struck them. She had to shade her eyes from the piercing glare but could not look away. Though painful, the shards of crystal light reached right through her sight and shattered into the back of her head, dazzling her with a dizzying array of colors and melting warmly into her soul.

So transfixed was she, that Kiyo's snapping fingers in front of her face did little to bring her attention away from the fiercely gleaming peaks. Maelyrin only wanted to sit and look, ignoring the burning in her eyes, but Kiyo finally shook her, breaking the link, and she came away with another frustrated, pain-filled, cry.

Tears were streaming from two flames that had replaced her eyes, and no amount of clenching and rubbing helped

alleviate the burning itch that resided there. For several
minutes, she worked as if sand were thrown in her face: rub, try
to open an eye, clench, more tears, wipe, until she felt cool
moisture on her face as Kiyo dabbed at her eyes with a wet
piece of cloth. After an indeterminable amount of time, she was
able to falter her eyes to a semblance of being open. They still
leaked steadily and the burn was nearly alleviated, but glare
ghosts danced in front of her vision. She felt Kiyo's large
thumb on her eyelid before it was pulled up and a shadow fell
across her face. He repeated the action with the other eye. "No
lasting damage," he rumbled. "But you might not be able to see
well for a while."

She grunted.

"I'm going to wrap a moist strip around your eyes," he
said. "I want you to leave it there until this night, understand?"

"How am I supposed to see where I'm going?"

"You are going to use your ears, your sense of touch
and balance," he said. "And you must trust your mount. Think
of it as a lesson in survival."

She said nothing, didn't think she could say anything
without letting her shame out, but when Kiyo wrapped the cloth
around her head and cast her into darkness again, a sudden
panic geysered through her, causing a gasp to escape her lips.
She heard Kiyo say, "Relax," in the strangely monotone voice,
but this time, it only helped to push the anxiety down and mute
it, not get rid of it completely. To help belay it or just to keep
her mind occupied, she touched it, adjusted the wet folds,
instinctively wanted to rip it down, to let the light in, but she
resisted the urge. Barely.

"Relax," Kiyo said again, this time without the peculiar
compelling inflection. "Resist the want to pull at it or take it
off."

"But I cannot see," she complained, still prodding at the
cloth experimentally. Maelyrin knew the words coming out of
her mouth were inane, even sniveling, but she could not help it.
Giving her anxiety a voice helped, in its way, to control it.

"Yes," Kiyo agreed. "It can be discomforting, but it is only temporary. More so if you leave them be."

She nodded, able to almost echo his words as he spoke them. How many times had she told the children of the village not to pick at the cuts and scrapes she treated. Indeed, how many times did she have to counsel the adults for the very same thing. She knew very well the body's capability to heal itself. But she also knew what it was that prompted her to repeat herself to those very same people. Regardless of how logical or correct that assumption was, or no matter what caused it in the first place, her body rejected the idea. Both the injury and the subsequent means to heal it. It was unnatural to that part of her that knew she had eyes, had just been using them, was unprepared to have them taken away. And it required a conscious effort to quell that side of her as it reacted to the misunderstanding.

And it was a battle. Thrust into darkness as she was, it suddenly felt to Maelyrin that the earth she was sitting on kept tilting to the side in an effort to send her sliding away, and she had to thrust a hand down to the side to hold up her imaginary fall. Several times, she heard alien noises that kicked her heart, took her breath, and forced her head around to locate the frightening sound, only to realize it was an animal moving in the underbrush or her horse pawing at the ground when her mind caught up to it. When she was taking her meager breakfast, several times she missed her mouth, pushing the dried meat into the skin of her chin or cheek. She tripped while standing up and would have fallen face first into the stony ground had not a huge hand caught her. And when, after many tries, she was mounted on her horse, she had to clutch painfully hard with her thighs while leaning far forward and clasping the beast around the neck with her arms because of a terrible vertigo.

At some point, Maelyrin grew comfortable with the gait of the horse enough, even the random stumbles it had, that she was able to sit up, though not all the way. She maintained a slightly hunched form over the pommel of the saddle, still unable to trust completely the unusual motion. How long it took before she was able to sit up she did not know. The passing of time was nonexistent. She could feel temperature variations as they rode beneath sheltering rock or back out into the sunlight, but where the sun was in the sky, she could not begin to guess. They were headed up on an incline. Of that she was quite sure as it helped her keep her distrusting hunch.

Kiyo remained silent for the most part, talking to her only when she began to panic, or, out of frustration at not being able to use her eyes, she attempted to take the cloth from her face, or when he moved ahead or dropped behind because the invisible path she followed narrowed between the great cliffs.

However, it wasn't completely discomforting. After a while, she noticed that her sense of smell and hearing sharpened. It seemed that Maelyrin could detect the dryness of the very rock around her and able to scent the fresh living odor given off by shrubs, trees, or even grass when the pass afforded the proper environment for the plants to cling to. Several times, she picked up the musky smell of some animal that made its life here.

The most intriguing thing she sensed was the hum. The rocks themselves sang a chorus of various pitches and tones. Whether from the sunlight beating upon their crystalline structure or the breezes sailing against them, she did not know, but the tones were continuous as they rode, sometimes becoming so loud that she could feel vibrations purr across her skin, coaxing the fine hairs to dance along the bare flesh. Several times, again, she was prompted to take the cloth down so she could see the wonderful melody being played out in the array of colors she remembered upon waking that morning. But on those occasions, she didn't require Kiyo's assistance. She only had to remember the burning pain and the reason why she now wore the cloth, and she was able to push the urge aside.

Kiyo stopped them many times so her horse could rest and she could stretch out her aching legs or eat a little food.

Each time, she hurt more, and each time she wondered when they would stop for the night. When that time came, finally, it surprised her, and she half expected that she would have to drag herself back up into the saddle.

Once she believed it to be true, she began working the kinks out of her ache-filled body, first trying to straighten her cramped back, messaging her neck, then her wobbly, crying legs. Once she reestablished the blood flow to her muscles and rid herself of some of the travel, she said, "Can I take this cloth off my face now?"

"Yes," Kiyo said. She thought she detected a hint of scorn. "But keep your eyes closed as you do and open them slowly."

She almost cursed at him, but decided she was too tired to argue that she already knew what to do, that she was only trying to make conversation, no matter how foolish the effort. Instead, she turned her flagging attention to removing the dry and stiff strip of cloth.

Maelyrin opened her eyes to a silvery glimmering of moonlight reflecting off and through the many crystalline stones. The entire area was awash in the pale light, sparkling deeply in the rock, flowing over the ground, and, seemingly, shimmering in the very air, taking the ever-present moonlight, storing it, compounding it, and releasing it. It reminded her of hoarfrost at night, only brighter and more alluring. She could only stare around her, taking it in as she had the morning light, though this time the sight was soft and did not leave her trying to peer through glare ghosts. Which, fortunately, were gone now. "I'm glad this day is finished," she remarked.

Kiyo grunted in answer as he went about setting out his bedroll, then, done with that, offered her some dried meat. "Are you not going to make a fire?" she asked. Now that she was off her horse and her muscles were more relaxed, she was more aware of the chill hanging in the still air.

"No," he answered in a low voice. "We are too high up and the rock will reflect the light far more than would be prudent."

"But you are a great warrior," she said, the sarcasm in the tone turning her own mouth down at the corners. She did not realize she was harboring resentment until the comment came flying out, but, it was there. She wanted some comfort after the grueling day's ride, some warmth. Not a night spent with cold cramping in her tired arms and legs.

Kiyo snorted. "Just because one may know how to fight," he said. "does not mean he invites it."

"I apologize," Maelyrin said quickly. "I meant nothing by it."

He grunted again after taking a bite of the scant piece of cured meat he held.

"I said I apologize!" she spat, the ache in her muscles, the long dry ride, the quiet fear of losing her eyesight, the exhaustion transforming itself into the sudden heat of anger. A sharp hum replied quickly to the rise in volume of her voice. The rock was warning her.

"You did," Kiyo said softly. Though tired, Maelyrin could *See* that he was unruffled by her outburst, which stoked her own furnace higher. Instead of letting her mouth go, she bit off a frustrated growl, threw out her bedroll, and lay down, her back to the giant. She covered herself with his large cloak and chewed hastily at the meager supper.

She realized her actions were childish, her behavior inexcusable, but just then, she did not care. All she was worried about was her screaming muscles, growling stomach, and chilled skin. She was still fussing at herself when Sleep crept up behind her and cracked her over the head.

When the sun rose, it was Guilt which sat down next to her as she broke fast on the same dried, tasteless meat. It held her ear and didn't let her look too closely at Kiyo's broad face, and it rode behind her all that day, breathing against the back of her neck as they made their way along the winding trail through the sharp crags and glistening crystal cliffs. At some point, Guilt left her, pushed aside by trail weariness, and she found they were headed mostly downward, not consciously aware of when they crossed over the peak in the long pass. By dusk, they were descending once again into lush forest land, a blanket of deep thick green darkening with the evening shadows.

After spending the day in the heat, sweating uncomfortably in glittering rainbow light, she was relieved to see the promise of cooler air in the woodland carpet, but once they penetrated the green, she found the temperature cloying, moist, and no less warm. Creepers choked the trees on either side of the path, dangling in wide leafed vines in places and hanging like curtains in others. Eventually, the path leveled out, and, within the gloom on either side, she could see old structures and ruins peeking out from the encapsulating ivy, the bones of a once city. Mist was beginning to coil among them. Clouds of tiny gnats hung sluggishly over the road, getting into her eyes and nose and sticking to the sheen of sweat that coated her skin, prompting her to swat and spit at them. It was preternaturally quiet, as if an invisible fog settled over them and muted away all sound. All except the distant hooting of some bird or something.

She sniffed loudly, of course, when she saw that Kiyo seemed undisturbed by either the temperature or the bugs, though he occasionally flicked a hand in front of his face. She thought it might be an unconscious gesture, but Kiyo seemed to do nothing 'unconsciously', or maybe did everything that way. She sniffed again in rebuke, too late to catch herself or the gnat that got caught in the wake and begin tickling the sensitive membranes. Maelyrin went into a sneezing fit that had nearly the same effect on Kiyo as the sniff. Not one.

They continued into the descending darkness. The ivy choked trees seemed to crowd the path the darker it became and the hoots became more numerous, louder, and more eerie, echoing lengthily despite the muting nature of the forest. The road became a thin strip of pale moonlit mist which she studiously kept to the center of, her horse's footsteps swirling and breaking up the light blanket, leaving a noticeable wake behind them for some few lengths. Finally, the thick woods peeled away from the road, creating a small place cleared of brush and trees. Kiyo stopped and looked it over, then said, "This should be a good place for us to rest out the night."

With an exhausted sigh, she slid from her mount.

Chapter 57

A Night In Khemosh

*M*arc swore under his breath and reined Whitesteel to a halt as the noise faded. The great horse snorted and shook his head. Marc shushed him as if he were a person, leaned forward in the saddle and cocked his ear toward the trees. Alex stopped Clover and had to reach over and grab Day's reins when Del didn't respond to their sudden pause.

"What is. . . ." Marc shushed her, too. A moment later, a faraway hoot drifted through the otherwise silent evening. It was answered quickly by two more. Marc cursed again and sat back.

"What is it?" Alex said again, quickly, so not to be hushed.

"We're in trouble," he said simply. She was about to ask him to explain himself when she heard the sound of Veraddin's hoof beats coming up the path and, instead, turned to watch Sandoren coming toward them, dispersing the thin layer of mist on the ground into scattered tendrils.

"We may want to consider stopping for the night," the ffolk remarked as he neared. He spoke only in Alex's direction, not completely looking at her and using the tone she only heard when he addressed other people, a neutral, cool voice that barely hid his contempt of them. "The two travelers ahead of us are making camp not more than a few leagues from here."

Alex peered first at Sandoren's shadowed face, then beyond him at the pale lighted figure of Marc. It was a slight, but definite shake of his head that answered her. When she looked back at Sandoren, she could tell his brows were pinched in anger. "We keep going," she said.

"Why?" he asked, his voice carrying a harsh edge. "It's too dark for the safety of the horses and I thought we were being cautious. One of the two ahead of us is an Eldythian, I think. And you know how quick they are to herald their way into other people's business." Several hoots echoed him.

"Marc seems to think it will be in our best interest if we continue," she said.

"I thought he wasn't able to act in anyone's best interest," he hissed. A hoot infested pause ensued as they stared at each other.

"You hear that?" Marc said softly. His voice was tired.

Sandoren refused to take his moon glittering eyes away from hers as he answered, "What of it? Night birds are commonplace."

"Those aren't 'night birds'," he replied.

"What are they, then?" Sandoren spit, finally taking his gaze from Alex and placing it on Marc.

"The Chyldren," Marc said. "They're awake."

"What?" Sandoren said at the same moment that Alex asked, "The Chyldren?"

"They're the Guardians of Khemosh," he said. "Or it's Curse, whichever story you believe."

"Khemosh!" Sandoren nearly yelled. "Everyone knows that Khemosh is a fabled city, like Lhahast, or. . .or Mythcharon. . . .or. . ."

"Where do you think you are?" he said.

"Sandoren," Alex said.

"Glasdon," Sandoren snapped.

"Glasdon," Marc echoed with a nod. Several more hoots measured his pause. "Glasdon, yes. You must be right, then." He nudged Whitesteel into movement.

"Marc, wait," said Alex, then held her breath until he reined back again, before saying, "Maybe we should go back."

Marc looked behind them and shrugged, "Might as well continue forward."

"If these things are dangerous," said Alex. "Then why tempt it?"

"Because they are behind us as well as in front," he answered. "It'll be just as dangerous whichever way, but if we go back, we will have to wait until they go back to sleep. Our best chance is to keep moving." As if to punctuate his statement, several hoots cried out from the direction they came. The answering cries came from all around them. Suddenly, Alex felt cold.

"What are these things?" Sandoren asked, for the first time in a long while sounding coherent and serious. Marc turned and regarded him silently across the span of night.

"You'll see," he said. "Before we get out of 'Glasdon', you will be well acquainted with them."

"Perhaps it would be best to go forward," Alex said. "We might be able to help the two travelers ahead of us."

Marc snorted then chuckled dryly. "I wouldn't worry too much about them," he said, his tone dry.

"We know why you're not going to worry," Sandoren snapped. *Marc's right,* Alex thought. A thought tired and tinged with diminishing denial. *He's becoming dangerous.* "But why shouldn't we?" he finished.

Marc stared at him, and she thought she could see the hardness of his eyes even though his face was cast in shadow. She thought she saw a terrible, grim smile crease his mouth. The expression of someone who knows all the darkness in the world and no longer tries to warn others about it. The knowing smile of the mother who tells her stubborn child not to reach out for the candle flame because it will burn but realizing that is exactly what has to happen because that is the only way the baby will learn. When he spoke again, the plainness with which he said it gave her a shiver. No remorse, no feeling. Marc simply said, "More than likely, those two are already dead."

Chapter 58

Tḥe Cḥyldreɲ

*7*he fire was small, but it illuminated a wide area, flickering and chasing shadows against the backdrop of trees and vines that gave Maelyrin the impression she was inside a large dome. The mist layering the ground seemed thicker now and, though it kept away from their camp, cast aside by the warm flames, it gave the wood around them an ethereal feeling, as if it were only an illusion.

While Kiyo laid strips of dried meat on a rock near the flames to warm them, she finished rolling out her blanket and sat down on it. The loam beneath her was soft and inviting, lulling her exhausted body towards the rest it desired. She pulled her knees up and laid her head on them. Maelyrin's eyes were drooping and moist, her body aching from the long hours in the saddle, and her mind was numb. Yet something nagged at it. Moments later, she realized what it was.

"The birds got quiet," she said, her voice sleepy. Kiyo's hand froze over the rock and he dropped the strip. Not only had the strange hooting sounds quieted, but the entire surroundings were silent. Not a buzz, or howl, or the scuttle of a small creature sounded. Not a breeze touched a wide vine leaf. It was as if the world were holding its breath. Anticipating something.

She was lazily looking off across the path when she saw it. A flash of pallid white. Gone quickly. So fast she wasn't certain she saw it, but her head was off her knees and her eyes wide. "What was that?" she asked, her voice quavering. When Kiyo didn't answer, she glanced over and found him gazing intently across the road. Further down the path, she saw another pale something flit between the trees, leaving curling tendrils of disturbed mist to mark its passing.

Kiyo was on his feet, Maelyrin not far behind. "Quickly," he said softly. "Gather your bedroll and pack."

Maelyrin did not realize what he said until her horse whinnied and began pulling at the lead rope she tied around a nearby tree limb. And then, she could only nod stupidly before turning to gather her things. Beyond the firelight, a vague, man shaped shadow flashed between two trees. A knot formed in her throat and icy water drizzled down her back. In a flurry, she grabbed up her blanket and pack, her exhaustion and achy muscles completely forgotten, and quickly tied them to the back of her saddle.

Something moved off to her left, yanking her head, but nothing was there except a memory of waxen white moving within the trees and settling fog. She noted from far away that her hands were shaking, frustrating her efforts at threading the cinch through its rings once she threw the saddle over the fidgeting horse.

"Don't move," Kiyo ordered softly. His voice seemed to thunder about in her skull and she reflexively sucked in a loud, painful breath and clamped down on it. She found him focusing his gaze behind her. Her shoulders tightened and the whole of her body began to wrack itself with deep shivers. Slowly, rigidly, she turned, unable to follow Kiyo's directive. Whatever he was looking at was far worse in the night of her mind than seeing it with her own eyes. Or so she told herself, anyway.

Maelyrin wasn't aware of the horse flinching away from her, whining, exuding a stench of fear sweat through its coat. Nor was she conscious of Kiyo's presence across the flickering flames. She was only aware of the thing standing only a few feet away from her.

Maelyrin might have thought it was a man if it was further away, except it was completely unclothed and corpse white. Inquisitive, bright eyes looked out from a vaguely human shaped head atop a thin neck supported by a spindly frame. But there, the resemblance stopped. It had no nose and its mouth was tiny and puckered, surrounded by bloodless lips that made soft smacking sounds. Two frail hands hovered out in front of its hairless, sexless body in a supplicating manner. Surrounding it like a cloud was the odor of freshly baked bread and that of cut grass, sweet and cloying. Its delicate appearance assuaged her numbing fear enough to unlock the muscles of her throat and lungs. She took a breath and was able to say, "What is it?"

Kiyo's answer was, "Very slowly, move back." It perplexed her, but she slid back a step. The creature cocked its head and issued a subdued hoot then stepped forward in a way that seemed both subservient and curious. Dimly, she was aware of her horse whinnying with anxiousness but she dared not take her eyes from the pallid thing. She thought its little mouth smiled.

"It seems harmless," she said, beginning to loosen from her rigid fear. It made another soft hooting sound, smacked its miniscule lips and cocked its head in the other direction. She started to repeat herself when, in an eyeblink, the thing flashed forward. Liquid molten fire leapt up her arm. She was hurt, but had to look down and see that the creature had her wrist in an impossibly harsh grip before her mind could comprehend it in its entirety. The smacking it was making became intense and eager the closer its tiny mouth came to her.

A hiss and a flash of silver and the tension popped and she found herself suddenly stumbling backward amidst a high pitched squeal. Her wrist burned fiercely, the thing's severed hand still clutched around it. Her mouth cried out in frustrated pain as she struggled to rip it free, throwing it into the fire once it released its foul grip.

Several more of the corpse white creatures exploded from the trees, moving impossibly fast, each meeting Kiyo's deadly blade in frightful squeals as the sword danced from one to another, slashed them and sliced them while he stood like a stanchion by the small fire. Maelyrin was unable to follow much of it as she struggled to maintain her footing, fighting a swaying body filled with dizzying pain. A dark blotch encircled a wrist that hung limply on the end of her arm, each step or shuffle of her feet sending jarring bolts of liquid agony flinging up the appendage and into her head.

She swooned.

And found that she was looking down at the mane of her horse, lifted quickly by Kiyo and placed in the saddle before she could comprehend the action. His free hand gripped tightly her mount's bridle, keeping the beast from rearing and struggling too much, while he sliced and cut with the other.

They moved quickly, heading down the road, Kiyo jogging beside the trotting horse while Maelyrin held the pommel of her saddle with her good hand, trying to keep conscious as each step of the mount caused flaring pain that burst brightly behind her eyes. Between each flash, she caught glances of pallid flesh as the creatures, wary of Kiyo, zipped along beside them, shadowing them through the trees. Every so often, one had a surge of bravery and leapt out from the protection of the foliage, only to meet the silver blade. Kiyo seemed to anticipate the attacks seconds before they happened, and no matter how they chose to throw themselves at them, he invariably sent them squealing back into cover. Eventually, she noticed the things were lessening in their attacks and simply following along beside and behind, hooting loudly to each other as they loped along with them.

Then suddenly, they were gone, cutting off and disappearing so quickly that she wondered if she had slipped into unconsciousness. The hooting fell behind them, carving a receding path back the way they had come. Bodily, she relaxed slightly, not realizing that much of her pain was due to tenseness for fear of her life. But it didn't go away quickly.

Indeed, an overwhelming cloud began forming around her and pressing down heavily. Dread. Slick fear. She wasn't sure which. Or why. It seemed they were safe, the pale creatures gone, but she sensed something near. Something dark.

"Kiyo," she whispered, her voice raspy. Her warning came too late, however, as the moment her mouth uttered his name, a flurry of shadow broke from the brush beside them. Kiyo grunted, the horse cried out and tried to skitter away, jerking at the giant's hand. It struggled and tried to rear, forcing her to grip at its mane just to hold on. She heard the clang of metal against metal and felt the released spring effect as the horse was freed, and she had to clamber to keep from being thrown off.

Quickly, the wind was in her face and thunder in her ears as she was suddenly flinging down the road, desperately hanging onto the bolting horse with only one arm. Furiously, she tried to get the terrified animal under control, fearing that, in the gloom it would trip, killing itself and her. But the horse fought her, refusing the pain of the bit, snorting and crying for many long, frightful minutes, until, more out of fatigue than any of her efforts, he slowed to a gallop, then a trot, then stopped altogether, huffing loudly in the night. His breath was a mist in the moonlight even though the air was not that chill.

Maelyrin was exhausted as well; the energy it took to hold onto the beast escaping into darkness like her mount's ragged breath. Her thighs trembled, her uninjured arm hung loose like jelly, the throbbing in her other, a salient echo of her still racing heartbeat. With some act of will, she was able to knee the horse around and prod him forward, back toward her companion. The fact that the horse could only lumber slowly was not a concern to her. To her, and her wounded, tired body, it seemed the beast was trotting.

She need not have bothered, for, very soon, Kiyo loped out of the shadows at, for him, a slow jog. His night darkened face was set and he silently took the bridle again, turning the horse even as it was mustering itself for another spook, and dragged it into a trot.

For a while, they ran, the jolting cadence of the horse forcing a tingling numbness in her body. Only after the beast had stumbled for perhaps the fifth time, did Kiyo let the creature walk. She didn't know how long they traveled, and really had not a care on the subject, this night's trials having long since worked its terrible ways on her, but they finally broke from the encapsulating woodlands onto a silver limned plain of tall grasses and wide views.

Kiyo immediately left the trail, striking into the waist high stalks, heading northeast as the moon stared down on them in studied disinterest, and continued on for an indeterminate time that way, until, on some unheard cue, he stopped them.

"We shall rest here," he said, his voice queerly low. "We should be safe here."

"Good," was all she could muster, slowly, painfully oozing from the saddle onto firm ground, where her legs rebelled and tried to buckle. Maelyrin had to lean against the beast's side, letting its bulk hold her up. The heat from its body was stifling, a steamy, smelly emanation that she had not noticed until she was off of it and able to catch a whiff of cool breeze. When she thought enough hours had past, she slowly moved around the front, clutching her hurt wrist gingerly to her chest, ducking under the drooping neck of her mount.

Kiyo was kneeling, moonlight splashing across his wide back because he was leaning forward, supporting himself with one hand. His head was down, his white, tied hair, shifted forward and dangled down over his shoulder.

He looked like he was praying, supplicating himself to some deity she knew nothing about, when she noticed the dark blotches in the moonlit grass and his other arm pressed into his side in a stiff angle. For a moment she stared, not understanding the picture she saw before whatever numbness possessed her mind popped like a soap bubble and she was able to will her body forward. "Oh my. Kiyo," she breathed. "You're hurt."

Chapter 59

The Flight Through the Ancient City

*T*he first of the creatures to present itself stepped out on the path in front of them, startlingly quick and fluid in movement. It simply stopped and peered at them, its head cocking from side to side like a bird's while it softly cooed questioningly from its tiny mouth. The meager light from the moon seemed to catch its already pale skin on silvery fire and the way it held its hands in front of it gave Alex the thought that it resembled a servant of some kind.

During the time between Marc's mentioning of it and now, a span of only a handful of minutes, she was able to dig through the chests in the attic of her memory and unearth an old legend about a city called Gommsh that suffered under a dire curse by the name of J'harycha. When the thing stepped out from the brush, it jolted her mind into remembering that J'harycha was a term the Mannic Peoples used to describe 'an unholy child'.

And indeed, she could understand why. The creature looked innocent enough, but she could sense its depravity and hunger behind the masking gestures and comforting hoots. This was a creature unnatural, even compared to the Eldritch. It was a thing of senseless death. It was. . . .

Her thoughts were cut off as it suddenly lunged forward with incredible speed straight at Sandoren and Veraddin, who, by contrast, seemed to be swinging his sword through jellied air. Instinctively, she held up a hand, simultaneously drawing on her reserves and releasing the Power outward. Thin spidery bolts of lightning arced from her fingertips and lanced into it just before it latched onto Veraddin and threw it backward in a crackling howl of blue white light. It landed in a smoking heap, thrashing wildly as it keened through its tiny orifice. Just as quickly as it was downed, however, it sprang back to its feet, large black, smoldering patches on its otherwise unblemished whiteness.

Sandoren, needing no cue, swept forward and slashed the creature across the chest as it bunched itself for another lunge. It squealed again as it stumbled backward from the blow, then turned and bounded into the waiting trees.

"So that was one of the Chyldren, huh?" he said, looking back at Marc. "Doesn't seem so dangerous to me."

"For such a long lived race, you sure are a stupid representative," Marc said, his voice neutral. "If we live through this, I hope you bring something more akin to the wisdom the ffolk are known for from it."

"Don't speak to me of wisdom, old man," Sandoren sneered. "You're not exactly packing a full skin of it yourself." With some audacity, he sheathed his sword. Marc looked him over and shook his head before kicking Whitesteel into a trot, his own blade catching the beams of moonlight from above as he cradled it on his shoulder.

Alex, glaring at Sandoren, trotted after him, holding Day's reins, but not before she said in disgust, "You can be a real dumb ass, Sandy." And not before she saw the flash of pain that washed over the man's face. She had little time to regret her words, though.

At first, their small group was only met by a few of the Chyldren in much the same manner as the first. Stepping onto the road and watching them, though they were not given the time to make the terribly fast lunge at them. Marc, ahead of Alex and Del by only half a horse's length, sped up each time, swinging his sword in large arcs that hewed the things deeply, sometimes severing completely an arm or head, but usually sending the creatures sprawling backward.

However, it wasn't long before more of their brethren threatened them. And with more aggressiveness. Leaping out at them from the entangled growths along the sides of the path, the pale Chyldren began attacking in greater numbers. Soon, all of them but Del, were defending themselves furiously.

Marc moved completely ahead of them, his sword tirelessly hacking along each side of Whitesteel's flanks, while the great horse reared or bucked as necessary, pounding the decrepit looking things with his fore or rear hooves. More than once, one of the Chyldren flew toward them, courtesy of one of Whitesteel's powerful kicks, only to be trampled by Clover or Day.

Though she could not safely glance back, she could hear Sandoren's exertions behind them, his grunts and Veraddin's snorts forming the rear guard.

She defended their immediate flanks, catching the creatures more often than not in mid leap with the lightning from her fingertips, casting the smoking, writhing, keening forms back into the woods from which they attacked. It was a methodical well working defense, allowing them to press forward, however slowly, without wasting too much effort, waiting for them to come to them.

Alex realized their folly once the things began falling from above. Hidden by the ivy choked trees, they were able to maneuver out over the road and remain hidden until the small group was nearly under them. All at once, their forward motion was halted, the first few to drop being too near a miss to risk continuing.

A numbing shock began working up her limbs, as if she were suddenly submerged in icy water. A combination of the constant surging of power and a fear that Marc was correct in his appraisal of the situation: that they were not going to make it through this night, that her mission was going to grind to a halt, right here, in a deep, ivy-choked forest among the ruins of the ancient city of Khemosh. She blocked it off, buttressing against it by emptying her mind of all thoughts or feelings, losing herself in the ebb and flow of the Earthpower as it manifested at her request in scintillating bluish arcs of electricity that burned and tossed the tenacious creatures.

But, still, they came, in a seemingly endless flood, all around them, leaping, crawling, hooting and smacking, trying to reach them, trying to place those puckering lips against them, to rend them. She cast about, quickly, methodically, taking in the scene through the heightened senses imbued by the rush of Power running through her body.

Marc and Whitesteel were pushed backward until the great steed's body was angling across the path Clover and Day faced, while, similarly, Sandoren and Veraddin were pressed into their hind quarters. Both men were breathing hard, grunting and straining as the sea of white continued to boil from the undergrowth. Though battle raged around them, she was able to see that Del was sitting silently by her side, staring straight ahead at nothing, his lips moving silently in the din. And, for once, she was glad of his 'awareness'. She couldn't help hoping that, if it came, his death would be quick and painless, as much as she realized the creatures surrounding them were capable of making it otherwise.

Amazedly, however, in her movements and blasts, she noticed that the side of the path and woods on Del's side of their tightly packed box was relatively free of the hooting, corpse white things, and those that were, were merely staring up at the boy in the supplicating manner with which they first revealed themselves. The dazed expressions they wore reminded her of the Eldritch, the time it attacked while they were in the razed ffolk village, standing only a breath away from Del, swaying back and forth as if it were unable to see him.

In answer to her silent summons, the irrefutable wail of the Eldritch drifted over the bedlam, behind them still, its call one of rage and frustration, not unlike that of the night it was trapped outside whatever barriers the brethren at the cloister had woven. It, too, was certainly being beset by the throng that was the Chyldren of Khemosh.

When the sputtering sensation swept through her, interrupting the flow of Power such that the ends of her fingers merely sparked, she realized with dawning horror, how tired she was, how used up. The constant flow of energy through her was beginning to take its toll on her fragile human shell. If she was not more careful she could easily kill herself before the Chyldren did, consumed by the very life giving Power flowing through her.

She concentrated, pushed aside her concerns and drew forth the Power again, sending a weak but effective lance of bolts into the next springing creature. The effort drained her further, more quickly than she thought possible. Suddenly lights and blots of darkness began dancing in front of her vision and it felt as if Clover had disappeared beneath her and she was about to fall to the ground. She began panicking, feebly reaching for something solid, struggling to keep her stomach from emptying its meager contents. A sudden flash of paleness in the background of her dancing vision warned her of her impending doom and she threw up a hand out of futile, primordial defiance.

She cried out as the icy rush pounded through her, arching her body rigidly, and when her vision cleared, she saw the creature who had heralded her death fly up and away from her to crash brokenly into a tree trunk. Surprised at the instant clarity, she looked around wildly and found Del's hand on her arm. He was looking at her with bright lucid eyes, and, when Alex's eyes traveled up the meaty arm to see his face, he nodded once.

Her skin tingled as if all her pores had opened at once and she could feel each individual fiber of clothing that lay against it, each bead of sweat that formed and ran down it, every breath of breeze that touched it. Within her, the rush of Power built tremendously fast, more quickly than she could release it, and she began to fear that whatever Del was doing was dangerously close to what she had nearly done seconds before.

Alex relaxed, consciously, and pulled back mentally, gathering her will. In a span of less than a second, she thrust her hands out toward the flank she was defending and completely released the dam that was holding back the Power.

Hot, blinding lances of lightning fanned out from her hands, crackling loudly, exploding into the throng of Chyldren to their right. The closest were incinerated instantly, before even their great speed could help them, while those behind were flung away like sticks in a tornado, dancing wildly in glowing clouds of electricity and fire, squealing in a horrendous cacophony. The ivy clogging the tress withered and peeled away and the darkness brightened to artificial day.

The burst lasted for only a couple of seconds, ending as quickly as it began, leaving behind trace glows of crawling lightening and luminescent balls hanging among the distinct roll of minute thunder. The stench of burnt flesh, wood, flora, and ozone permeated the area along with the grassy-bready scent given off by the keening Chyldren. As with the surge of energy she was able to summon at the beginning of the pass, when they were attacked by the Epas, she began to crumple under the sudden absence of the filling Earthpower.

Around her, everything unexpectedly stopped. Thankfully. Since the blasting light had the unforeseen side effect of blinding her companions, both Marc and Sandoren covering flash burnt eyes with hand or arm. The Chyldren stood away from them, hooting softly and dry washing supplicating hands while cocking their heads avian like.

Whitesteel turned enough so that she caught a glimpse of Marc's chest and the muted red glow that emanated from it. She struggled for a few moments, warding off the terrible weakness and threatening unconsciousness with only the last shreds of will still available to her.

"Marc," she whispered, her voice full of sand. He was blinking away flash ghosts, holding his sword defensively out in front of him, though he obviously sensed the attack had paused.

"What?" he replied, his voice as ragged as hers, his chest heaving with effort. She knew the sudden pause in the battle could only be detrimental as the body sensed it no longer needed the extra energy reserves they had been operating on. Even now, Marc's shoulders were trying to sag, though he kept moving them up and back when he noticed.

Weakly, herself slumping over Clover's withers, she thumped her chest, and said around a heavy breath, "Amulet,"

He looked down, saw the red light shining through his shirt. A momentary perplexity coursed over his slacking face.

The newly agitated hooting of the remaining Chyldren caused him to dispose of whatever thoughts surrounded it, and with an effort he raised the tip of his sword, which had been drooping too. He fixed her with his eyes, though surrounded by a tired face, his eyes were still iron hard. "I'm finished," Alex said suddenly. "My Powers are fled." He nodded, the skin around those steel gray orbs tightening. She turned her head enough to see Sandoren out of the corner of her eyes. Though vague, she could see him slumping in the saddle slightly as Veraddin fidgeted. He was pale and dark lines ran down his face. Though unable to look directly, she knew it was blood. Beside her, Del appeared to be sleeping. His eyes were closed and he was relaxed, his breathing measured.

In that moment, there was nothing. Though the Chyldren were beginning to recover from their surprise, she saw none of them. "Sandy," she forced through tired lips, her tone deeply serious. Alex saw him nod, knowingly, and heard the unmistakable snick of his knife being pulled from its sheath. There was no anger in him now, no hatred as he urged Veraddin up next to Day. Only a lucid acceptance of the promise the encircling horde was about to fulfill. Only a grim sense of duty to spare the innocence of the boy dozing next to her. A detached tear rolled down her cheek, the emotions that formed and followed it, blocked away behind layers of exhaustion and imminence. *What a terrible waste,* she thought.

Alex closed her eyes, tightly, and turned her head away, unable to watch, to even face the direction. Any second now, the Chyldren were going to leap en masse and destroy them, but it didn't concern her. The only thoughts she had lay on Del and whether or not he would be spared of the coming doom, though she cowered from the task, or the proof. Her heart clenched and her mind nevertheless threw up images of Sandoren's blade doing its work. *How did this happen?* She wondered.

"They're backing off," Marc said, his voice so low she almost did not hear it, so rough with exhaustion that that was what alerted her to its presence. Her eyes flashed open, the scene before her swirling madly, painfully in the backs of tired eyes. Shakily, her mouth coughed out a quick, "Stop,"

When the wave of nausea passed, she saw there was no need. Sandoren was staring up the path, his body rigid. The killing dagger was back in its sheath. Dragging her heavy gaze away from him, she looked up at what he was fixed on. The Chyldren were backing off, literally, reinforcing her first impression of them being servants. They continued dry washing their hands and cocking their heads from side to side and seemed to be bowing reflexively as if just having been dismissed.

All of them were quiet, neither hooting or smacking their tiny lips, as they moved away, forming an aisle along the path, letting something else through to them. Something shrouded in misty clothing that seemed to float around it as if a breeze wafted on the dead air.

The preternatural silence that preceded it deepened, creating a void around them that did not seem menacing in any way. As it drew closer, its glide like walk carrying it more swiftly than she at first thought, Alex was able to make out more of its features under the pale light of the never changing moon above.

Whatever it was, it was humanlike, or ffolk-like, very tall and wiry, almost frail, underneath the billowing clothing, though its features were sunken and tight. Old leather stretched over a bony frame in which shadows pooled like ink, drawing stark lines that brought out the stiff angles of its face. From this hollowed plane shone two orbs of silver that cast a pale glow, like the moonlight. Wispy white hair framed it, flowing down into the robes it wore.

It hove within a few feet and stopped, studying them coolly for many minutes while all of them but Del struggled to control their breathing and keep from falling from the saddle from fatigue. At last, it inclined its head in a graceful bow and said, "Trav lynen oth' maris' tal, feorna?" The dialect was thick but unmistakable; ancient Arquil. *Weary travelers, do you not know this cursed place?* Before a reply could be given, it continued, "Fantain 'ul, tharis Mal 'urna photh la sin'fee, ul Mal 'andel." *But then, you carry a piece of the Life Giver and with it comes its maiden, the Earthmother.* Its silver eyes looked at her. "Tus'stair no areylan." *Your presence graces.*

Though fighting to stay conscious, Alex managed the proper reply, the ancient words difficult to her tired mind but nonetheless still able, "Your graciousness blesses me tenfold."

Marc also gave a traditional reply, his own use of the Old Tongue startling her until she remembered what he was. He said, "Much gratitude for your concern. How may we be of service?"

The creature seemed to smile at the proper responses. At least, it seemed to her that the corners of its thin lips curled up at the ends like old parchment. It responded in kind, its heavy accent making it hard on her to translate, "Your kind offer is not required. I was awakened by the disturbance of the Foul Ones and paid heed to its reasons. Interlopers were near, whom I chased from the presence of the Living Magic and bade the Cursed to return to their unwholesome Slumber. You may pass here without further peril."

"We are indebted to you more than I first surmised," Marc said. "Is there not some service for which we may repay your courtesy."

"There is not," it replied. "It is for this that I exist and require nothing in kind."

"Please excuse my impertinence," Alex interjected, her tongue becoming tired at making the fluid, rambling sounds. "But may I inquire from which House you are in Lineage to?"

The creature chuckled, a dry crackling of autumn leaves. "I belong to no race anymore, but once hailed from the House of Fraelyne' se, but now I am only a Bael, the Guardian over its Memory."

At the mention of the name, Alex flicked a glance over at Sandoren. Though his eyes were weary and carried a haunting of their recent dealings with the Chyldren, he still managed a scowl, however slight. She shook her head. *Hopeless*, she thought. She heard Marc mutter, awe in his rough voice "A Crypt Keeper."

His statement raised a question in her mind that she pushed backward so she could peruse it at a later time, and said, "I am grateful for your presence and will trouble you no further with ill-mannered questions."

The Bael waved one of its sticklike hands in dismissal. "No need. Often it is not that I entreat with the Living. . . discourtesy is not a consideration."

"We are again thankful of your aid, then," Marc continued. "But also regretful that you were Wakened from your Long Sleep for such as us." The Bael flicked its hand again.

"It is pleasing to me to remember and mourn. Be not regretful for that which you had no control over." The Bael pointed at Marc's chest. "The Light has faded, so then, the Interlopers that roused me and my Fouled brothers have passed beyond its Rays and the road ahead is now secure. Be safe and keep well, friends of the Living, for my influence lasts only until the tree line." As it finished, it bowed its head again then stepped to the side of the path.

"Rest well Guardian over the House of Fraelyne' se," Marc said and urged Whitesteel ahead. The horse rumbled a protest but started walking.

Alex nodded at the creature as she passed with Del in tow. The Bael murmured a respectful departing phrase but did not look up from its bowed posture even as she gave the required response. Sandoren followed closely, struggling to maintain control on a tired but still frightened Veraddin.

Out of curiosity, she glanced back only to find that there was nothing there but trees, ivy, and the blanketing mist. The Bael vanished back to whence it came.

Chapter 60

A Small Rebellion

*T*he horses were being pushed far too hard. Crowlin could hear it wheezing terribly even over the thunder their hooves were making on the ground and the rush of the wind past his ears. He could feel it, too, the jerking of its sides and the erratic motion of its gait. While the negative life energies they imbued the beasts with made them stronger, faster, it ultimately sped the creatures' deaths. It did not help that they were slowly being drained of their lives just by the close proximity of him and his cronies.

However, that was only a thought. One that had little, if any, concern attached to it. The horses meant only a mode of transportation to him. What concerned him most, at that point, was why the beasts were carrying them away from their quarry. He shook his head and jerked back on the reins violently, causing the creature to scream out in pain as it dug into the loam.

Everything was going accordingly. Or had been. Except for Teraard's unforeseen attack on the two other travelers in the wood. Except that it appeared that they had wakened too many of the Chyldren. Except that they spent more of their time keeping the creatures away from their own position rather than monitoring what was going on. Everything else seemed to be going well. The forest resounded with the calls of the Chyldren and they could sense Pendragon and his party approaching, their life forces a beacon in the darkness of their hunger. Especially the unidentified one. The boy. They were able to sense that one farther away than the Earthwitch. But something happened, something he could not remember. Instead of the secluded place they waited, they were suddenly running away, in a direction he didn't know, their prey fading from their senses. . . .

Crowlin shook his head again, waited for the others to drag their mounts to a standstill. All of them but Teraard reacted quickly, stopping nearby. Teraard's mount slowed its headlong gait further away, stopping, it seemed, of its own accord because its kin so did. Teraard was humped over the saddle like a sack of dirt.

Impatiently, Crowlin turned to Reegan and asked, "What happened?"

The other stared blankly at him from under his cowl for several breaths then shook his head. "Don't know. . ." he said. "We must have been Compelled. . . ."

"By what?" he asked, anger rising quickly inside him, starting to spill out into his words. Reegan nudged his mount further away so as not to be the recipient of its inevitable surge.

"Don't know," he said again. "But I feel the remnants of a dweomer . . . . We must have woken something else besides the Chyldren."

"You think?" Crowlin yelled while he pounded his leg. A string of curses followed as he raved out his frustration into the night air. When he was finished, he looked around and said, "Where are we?"

Reegan shrugged. Crowlin cursed some more. Teraard slid off his horse onto the ground.

They turned their heads and stared at him, waited for him to move. When he did not, Crowlin let his shoulders slump forward. "Pick him up," he said tightly. Reegan dismounted and stumped over to the inert form, dragging his bad foot carefully through the tall grass.

"His Essence has fled," Reegan said after turning the empty body over and checking it. ". . . Must've had a magic blade."

"What?"

"The giant," Reegan replied, more to himself. "Must've had a magic blade."

"The giant," Crowlin repeated, remembering the tall one when the other two travelers came out of the misty darkness followed by a small group of Chyldren. He silently cursed Teraard's lack of self-control. Whatever the giant was, it was fast with a blade. Not fast enough, but still . . . He pushed it aside. "Now his recklessness has cost us," he said. "Pick him up, tie him to his saddle. We have to feed, get fresh mounts, and restore him." He pointed in their direction.

"What about Pendragon?" Reegan asked after hefting Teraard's shell onto the back of his decrepit mount. "What if he is still alive?"

"He probably is. . . ." Crowlin said. "Pendragon is harder to kill than you are. Whatever the case, the Master will tell me. . . .Right now, He is quiet, and we need to regroup. Pendragon can wait."

"Is that wise?" he asked. "If Pendragon survived the Chyldren, maybe we should go back and finish him."

Crowlin stared, fury boiling up inside him. Granted, Reegan was preoccupied with trussing Teraard's shell to his horse and maybe did not sense his more than overt misstep, but it was still there. A direct challenge to his authority. It didn't matter if he was right. It didn't matter that he wanted to kill Pendragon. Indeed, killing him might mean a brief reprieve, a small freedom. The thought even occurred to him that feeding on Pendragon would serve several purposes. Not to mention the woman and the child. Together, their combined essences might give them the power to break away from His grasp.

But they had been forbidden from that course of action. He couldn't understand why. This game had been going on for so long, he hardly understood any part of it. The Chyldren had not been his idea, nor the thing that left him near death on the outskirts of the ffolk village. In fact, now that Crowlin thought of it, they were rarely, if ever, directly involved with his destruction.

But then, Pendragon was still alive, wasn't he? Despite all the machinations the Master involved them in, the man was still foiling His attempts. At times, it seemed He wanted Pendragon dead. At others, captured. And, at still others, just to suffer. Now, with his mind clear of His presence, he was more confused than normal, and his burning hatred of the man was quickly pushed aside by curiosity.

For as long as he could remember, they, the five of them, roamed the land, following this man, causing him pain. Injuring him and those he cared for, executing schemes created by the Master. But why? The Master had so many other worthy goals, like Cutting the Thread, but Pendragon seemed always to the fore, pushing aside all other objectives. For the first time since his transformation, he wanted to know what this man's importance to the Master was and why they spent an inordinate amount of time chasing him around the whole of Arquilon.

Flashes of intelligent thought were not something that happened regularly with Crowlin, and it would require much more contemplation. For now, he would leave Pendragon to his fate. He was still his Master's servant and would continue to be so until he found a way to break away from His grasp. However, he was not above small rebellions every now and then. Taking his four brothers away from here was such a time.

Crowlin looked around, over the moon limned trees, into the cool breeze. The path his mind took him down was new, and rugged, but proved exhilarating. His sudden heightened state even allowed him to overlook Reegan's impertinence. At least this time. "Come," he said imperiously. "Let us go."

Reegan nodded into his cowl and slung himself into his saddle as Crowlin nudged his failing horse into a trot.

Chapter 61

Visitors on the Plain

"Kiyo, wake up," Maelyrin said. "There're riders on the plain coming this way." She reached out and touched his shoulder. A reluctant move. Afraid that by doing so, she was going to confirm the terrible thoughts that had been plaguing her since he lay down and closed his eyes. All night and all this day he hadn't moved. Even when she cleaned and dressed his wound with some goldenseal and bandages made from a spare shirt. Maelyrin knew that when she touched him, she would find his skin the cold, waxen rigidness of the dead. And out here, alone, it was a thought that knotted up her insides and caused a clammy sweat to break out on her skin.

His eyes opened like the rise of the sun in the morning. "How many?" he said, his voice edged with roughness but otherwise as strong as normal.

She was able to release the breath she had been clutching. "Four."

"Assist me to stand," he said. She shook her head.

"No, you must stay down," she said. "Your injury-"

"Will be well," he said. "I am indebted for your help, but I must stand. Where are they now?"

She rose up enough to look over the high grass. "Headed right for us. Not far. They must've seen the horse."

His hand drifted down to his side and inspected the bandage wrapped around his waist before working over to the other side. "Where are my swords?"

"Oh," she said and crawled closer to the horse. "I had to move them. They were tangling in your legs. Here." She laid the larger weapon at his side. The smaller one she left propped up against Ki's pack.

Kiyo nodded, paused, sat up. Though he remained silent, his face bore the strain of the sudden movement, paling most around his obsidian eyes. She silently hoped his wound didn't reopen though it was inevitable at this stage. "Be careful," she said. "We have no more water. I can't make another poultice to keep your wound from festering." He nodded again and slowly rolled to a kneeling position.

Biting back the flash of heat that rose with her frustration, she moved to his support. Together, they stood and she handed him his scabbard, the sword nearly as tall as she. He slid it into a belt tied hastily around his middle.

The four horsemen closed with, it seemed, confident cautiousness, and Maelyrin breathed more easily when she saw they wore the armor that identified them as knights. The Faethe had stories of men of such honor. They stopped several yards away, and the one leading dismounted, handed over the reins to his brother knight, and began striding toward them. "Greetings," he called, holding up a gauntleted hand in supplication. His other arm was blocked off with a large shield coated blue with black stipples in an ordered pattern across it. In the center was a representation of a black lion. "Are you in need?"

Maelyrin started to answer when Kiyo's hand settled on her shoulder. She held her tongue and waited.

The knight wore a smile that the setting sun didn't hit right. His face was heavily pocked on one cheek, unable to be hidden by the four day growth of beard. Like his face, a large dent pocked his breastplate just above his heart. The right side bore an embossed symbol of some type of bird. "I say, are you in need?" He readjusted the shield, pushing his arm through the thick hand strap so that it rested on his back like a pack

"No," Kiyo said. "We are not in need."

The knight blinked and looked at Kiyo as if seeing him for the first time. "You an Eldythian?" he said quickly, then: "We have a camp nearby you're welcome to rest at. You look like you've seen enough action to last awhile." His eyes slid to Maelyrin and crawled over her. "Are these the only possessions you have? My men can help-."

"We have no need of any help," Kiyo said. "Sir?"

"Tolliver," he said, his eyes flicking back to the giant, taking in the stained and ripped cloth of his open shirt. "You may want to think about my offer. There are many dangers on the plain."

"No, thank you," Kiyo said.

Maelyrin suddenly realized the other three knights were closer than before, sidling up their side while being engaged by Tolliver.

"You and your men should go," Kiyo was saying, his voice taking on the odd undertone. She watched the man blink several times. A languid smile began creeping back onto his face.

"I really think you should come with us," he said.

"I think not," Kiyo said, again using the voice. This time, the man's face cinched up into an elongated scowl. He took a step back, his hand jerking across his stomach toward the sword cradled in his other. Kiyo moved, a flicking motion that sang in the evening air with a clear tone. That silver blur fanned out and Tolliver was suddenly stumbling back, both hands trying desperately to hold back the tide of crimson that erupted from his throat. He gurgled and fell backward into the grass, the look of utter surprise etching itself into the already disfigured face.

The other men, fanned out on their flank, stopped. One of them yelled, kicked his horse and fled. The remaining, after a moment, followed him, calling back threats.

Maelyrin stared at the unmoving form of Tolliver. Blood sheeted the breastplate, pooled in the dent, and drooled down its sides. She could hear it *plocking* on the back of the shield beneath him. Her guts roiled and her throat clenched and salivated heavily. She had to struggle for some time to keep her body from going through with what it was trying to do. When she tried to speak, her mouth gobbled without sound. Finally, she was able to force out, "How did you know?"

"Come," Kiyo said. "We must go, quickly, before they bring others."

"I don't understand. . . ."

"Maelyrin," he said softly. "We must go."

She heard him, but his words slid past her mind into some nether region, unable to gain roots in a place so occupied by yet another shock. Eyes locked on the body, part of her brain kept saying it was a knight. A man of honor. A protector of innocents. The stories the Faethe told her said that was what they were supposed to be. Had she been alone. Had Kiyo truly been as she thought before his eyes opened, she would have trusted this man. At least until she used her *Sight*. By then, though, it would have been too late.

Again, her name drifted through the clamor. Again, it disappeared into a dark place.

Maelyrin was able to take her gaze away from the dead man only after Kiyo gently pulled her body around. Once disconnected from the vision, reality crashed in on her. She was shaking and her knees buckled and she sagged against Kiyo. A flood of tears rushed from her eyes and sobs wracked her body. The giant held her, let her spill her pent up emotions onto the cloth of his shirt clutched in her hand and held tightly against her face.

When the tears dried and the sobs became sniffles and she was able to begin replacing the dam that held them, Kiyo said again, "We must go."

"How did you know?" she said through a breath spasm.

"His armor didn't fit properly and his shield device was different than that on his breastplate."

"So?"

"Come," he said. "Let us go. I will explain once we are away from here."

Maelyrin nodded into his chest, took a deep breath and stepped away from him. He flashed that toothy smile that once seemed so threatening. She found herself smiling back and felt lighter. But when she started to move past him to the horse, her eyes moved over the bandage and lead dropped back into her stomach. "Your wound has reopened."

He nodded. "Yes," he said and gently pushed her probing hand away. "We must go."

Despite the resistance she threw up, she found herself mounting, his odd voice tone an echo in her mind. In retaliation, she threw the rest of the bandage shirt at him. "Fold that up and place it on top of the soiled one beneath the binding." He smiled again and nodded. When they trundled off, the sun stood a hand span from the thin line of the horizon, burning the sky with bright orange and red streaks.

It was diving below the line when they made out the tents in the distance. Their goal, the road, lay not far beyond the grouping. "Is that the bandit's camp?" Maelyrin said, her voice rising too quickly.

Kiyo grunted and said, "Look closely and tell me."

Despite the flash of heat at being denied relief and comfort, she studied the shapes they were creeping up on. The tents were square and looked like little houses with sharply peaked roofs. They were striped and limp pennons dangled from the center posts, though, in the disappearing light, she could make out only shades of dark instead of colors. There seemed nothing out of the ordinary, but there was something wrong with the scene besides the crawling fear that it was the bandit's camp. It was like an itch at the base of her skull, deep in the bone. She then realized the camp was lifeless. No one moved between the tents, and no horses grazed nearby. The flicker of newly built fires was absent. "It's deserted," she said. Hearing the rise in her voice, she was suddenly not sure of herself.

"Is it the bandit camp?"

"I don't. . . How?"

"Look at it again."

She stared at it. Now that she was silent, she was again sure that it was derelict. There was absolutely no movement. No one was out there, but that itch still pestered her. *Is it the bandit camp? How could I know? They're tents. Abandoned tents. Tents standing out in the middle of the plain like a well-kept orchard. How am I—*

"No, it's not the bandit camp," she said.

"How do you know?" Kiyo said.

"The tents are whole, identical, and they are arranged in neat rows," she said. "I don't think a bandit would bother with the order, if they had tents like those at all." The itch was gone.

"Good, good," he said, nodding. "You are learning."

"Not fast enough!" she said, nearly yelling. She had to consciously release her death grip on the saddle even though her strained wrist pained her. "If you weren't here, I'd have died long before now."

"You haven't," he said. "have you?"

That brought her up short, her brows pinched. "What?" she hissed.

"Died," he said.

"No. But what does that have to do with anything?"

"It means, beware of 'ifs'," he said. "They mean nothing and fixing on them can only cause you problems. Take heart that you are learning and that you still live." She sucked in a breath, ready to speak, to tell him they had no supplies, or water, and death was not far off, but he continued before the thought could move onto her tongue. "And beware of trying to foretell the future. You will find yourself against walls stronger than anything constructed."

She clamped her mouth shut, wondering how he knew

what she was about to say. *Maybe he could read minds.* A shiver flew up her spine, the heat of her anger changed into gut wrenching discomfort. Her mind spun downward into an oblivion, spawned by the thought, whether it was real or imagined. If he could look into her mind. . . What could be kept from him? All her dreads, desires, even the thoughts she was thinking would be laid to bare like the insides of a wound, to be scrutinized, judged, used. She wanted to vomit, though it was her brain that churned instead of her stomach. Maelyrin wanted to hide. She wanted to find a way to shut off her mind from prying eyes, even though it was Kiyo and she believed he would never do something so despicable as use her thoughts against her.

Isn't that what the villagers think about you? Another cold streak shot through her body, freezing her mind. Maelyrin looked around to make sure it was a thought and not someone speaking to her, so clear was the voice. Her voice.

She clenched her eyes and jaw. *Yes. Yes. That is how they feel.* The admission, however, did not rid her of the sensation. It made it deeper, thicker, and it seeped down into a body already leaden with exhaustion, beyond her ability to prod it for more understanding, but not enough to keep it from scraping the insides of her guts. "What are we going to do?" she said.

"We are going to find Marc Pendragon," Kiyo answered.

She smiled in spite of the muck in her stomach. "I mean about that," she said, waving a hand in the direction of the tent group. He looked at her and blinked. "Are we going to investigate it or pass it by."

"What reason would we have to investigate it?"

"We need supplies?" she said.

"Are you prepared for more death?"

"What," she asked, swiveling her head to look at him.

He pointed into the distance and said, "Look there."

Maelyrin followed his finger and gazed out at the flatland and saw. . . nothing. "I don't see anything."

"Look closer,"

She shrugged, looked again, this time squinting into the dusky light. Still nothing. She scanned. Nothing. Her body began shaking, the fizzle sparking once more. Brows pinched, she looked back at his hand and with an exaggerated movement, leaned out to look in the direction he was pointing.

Luminous pinprick eyes peered back. She jerked upward and bit her tongue, lost the image and had to look for it again. It was a big plains cat, hunkered down near the camp, nearly invisible in the tall grasses, staring at her and Kiyo. Obvious intruders into its immediate situation.

"What is it doing?" she asked. "Is it hunting?"

"Sometimes hunters scavenge and scavengers hunt," he said. "It's been attracted here by something. Given the nature of our altercation with Tolliver, I think you might well be prepared to see more death."

"I don't see any scavenger birds," she said.

"Nor I, but that means little."

She slumped more and drew back on the reins. While the horse was still unused to her, it was beginning to respond to her prods and pulls more readily. It stopped. The struggle went on for minutes while Kiyo surveyed the plain. Finally, she clenched her jaw, said, "Let's go."

She viewed the camp through a protective tunnel, scanning it only forward, ignoring everything in her peripheral vision. Mostly because things moved around there. Shadows, flitting things. Though her resolve was there, it was shaky, and paying attention to anything other than what she was directly looking at only made it crumble. The plains cat's gaze was heavy and did its own chipping away at it. Every few moments, she was forced to search out the creature and meet its stare, one that she found more satisfied than hungry.

Confirmation did not take long when Kiyo moved the flap aside on the first tent they came to. A cloud of black buzzed out at him, daring him to enter, but the flies did not obscure the naked, still foot revealed by his action. She thought she might, at least, be somewhat desensitized to the sight, but her stomach lurched anyway and a metallic taste glazed the back of her throat. The cone of her vision swung away from it quickly.

The rest of the camp was the same. Most of the tents contained bodies and a resident cloud of feasting flies and other insects. Pieces of armor sometimes glimmered in the fading light, left there casually or purposefully, there was no telling. The stink of death did not yet infect the area, but the air did waft out the coppery reek of spilt, putrid blood each time Kiyo moved a screen aside. Of supplies, there was none. All the former knights' weapons, packs, waterskins, were missing, picked clean of the corpse of the camp by the murdering thugs that raided it.

"I don't understand this," she said, voice quavering. "These are knights. Fighting men."

"Your northern knights are over-dependent on armor," he said. "And even knights have to take it off to sleep."

"But didn't they post guards or something," she asked.

"More than likely," he answered. "We'll circle out around the perimeter and check. It's a standard strategy, but, out here, an armored knight can be outmatched by foes that don't follow standard rules of engagement."

She nodded in agreement though she understood little of what came marching out of his mouth. Silently, they finished investigating the camp then, on Kiyo's lead, began working out in an ever growing circle around the camp. She had a brief flashback of the brigands that accosted her so many days ago and shivered.

They quickly found the first perimeter guard, laying on his back, staring up into the darkness through milky orbs. A grimace was chiseled into his waxen face. One hand clasped the side of his neck. From between two fingers protruded a long thin barb. Unlike the others, he still wore his armor, though his sword was gone. His helmet, which could have protected him from the dart, lay at his feet. Kiyo knelt and examined the barb in the silvery moonlight. Then, he moved toward where he said the next should be.

Maelyrin followed him, keeping silent while he looked at everything, even though her mind chattered with questions. She thought she heard something move in the grass, followed by a contemptuous growl. Of course, it could have been the breeze licking at the blades. That is what she told herself. They were headed towards where the plains cat had lain.

When they found the next corpse, she understood why the cat had been lazily watching them and had to turn away to keep from retching. The large beast, hunter that it was, had settled for a meal less motivated, and the savaging the corpse took seemed reflected on its grimacing face. Thankfully, Kiyo moved on quickly, and it was easy for her to turn her self-induced tunnel vision such that it was quickly lost.

There were four guards in all, one at each compass point. All of them, apparently, died in the same manner, a dart in the neck. Kiyo indicated it was probably poison, fast acting and painful. After standing up from the last one, Kiyo looked out over the moonlit plain and said, "We must be going."

"What? Aren't we going to bury these men?"

He looked at her. "What do we have in the way of supplies?" he said.

"Uh. . . none," she said. "No water, no food. My bow string is broken and I don't have any more."

"Burying them will be too taxing on our bodies," he said. "Our priority now is to find food and water."

"And we're going to leave them to be picked clean by scavengers?"

He turned and gave her a long look, his eyes sparkling in the pale light. "What do you think happens when their bodies are committed to the ground?" he said. "It is time for us to go."

It hit her like a slap and she reacted instantly, the heat rising quickly into her face. A thought struck and she pushed it aside long enough to *Look* at Kiyo. As usual, he was a study in calmness, but some ripples were making its way across the placid surface. Ripples of discomfort. He didn't like this situation either.

"Alright," she said finally. Stifling a groan, she climbed up into the saddle.

When they intersected the road, she could no longer see the death camp behind them. It disappeared in the moonlight like ghosts, but not from her mind. There, it joined the other specters of this violent world.

Chapter 62

A Brief Respite

South Watch lay a little over a day's journey south of Hestaff. It was the southernmost bastion of the now defunct Hedrican Order of Knights, guarding over empty plains and restless winds. It was more a trading post and stopover for merchant trains and the nomadic peoples of the expanse than a strategic military outpost. The last time Marc saw it, it was simply a large keep and its surrounding curtain walls. Now, several other buildings flanked it, and the road and they could see several figures, both on horseback and not, moving in and around the new construction. It also looked like an outer wall was being built on the near side of the grouping, as some excavation and scaffolding scarred the otherwise green ground northwest of the keep.

Marc took in the view with the same manner he always did. A studied disinterest of the inevitable. In his mind's eye, he could see the scene ahead as it had been when nothing stood on the low hill overlooking a nonexistent road. Of course, his companions responded with the same lack of concern, only their reaction was based on a picture that always was there, except for the newest construction. Perhaps Alexandra was old enough to remember when the castle, alone, stood on the motte. A very different structure before it was reconstructed with the curtain walls and battlements. Or, perhaps not. He briefly considered asking her but thought better of it when he glanced at her sagging form.

Since the events with the Chyldren, all of them had been keeping to themselves, more or less, for the last couple of days. Alexandra's Guardian remained completely silent; his jealous anger swallowed by the terrifying experience that still haunted his face in dull waves. The boy seemed not affected at all, while Alexandra rode slumped over in her saddle, her features drawn, large blots under her eyes. She rarely spoke, and her Guardian cast many glances in her direction that were wide and filled with worry, that is, when he wasn't reliving the ordeal himself. Marc knew full well the man's concern was valid. She expended much in the fight with the Chyldren. Too much. Just like Gyssel used to do. Now, she was clinging to the small amount of life force she had left with a tremulous grip. She needed rest and healing. And a place out of the unforgiving sun above them. At least, she should be able to get two of those requirements today.

Rest and a place out of the sun was something they all needed.

As they neared, a group of mounted men, riding in disciplined formation, spilled from the gate keep and headed toward them. Sunlight gleamed off polished armor and shield. Those in the rear carried lances, the pennons at their tips fluttering in the breeze. They were not close enough for them to make out the heraldry, but Marc guessed they still bore the markings of Hedric's Order.

Sandoren, ahead of them by a couple of horse lengths, slid and arm over and tested the pull of his sword within its scabbard. Marc intoned, "Knights," and waited for a snide remark from the Guardian, but the man's arm dropped back to his side.

It was unusual for them to send out such a large party to greet them, but not unheard of, especially with all the refugees moving through the area. Still, subtly, he reached down and released the thong holding his own sword in place. As if rehearsed, they reined in their mounts and waited as the patrol of knights drew closer.

The company stopped abruptly at a tautly raised arm from the lead knight, a man stiffer than the others and with a terse bearing. The purple plume in his helmet matched his personal coat of arms, a purple griffin against a silver sky emblazoned on his shield and again on the shoulder clasp of his deep blue cape. It was smaller, but more ornate than the simple device of the Order of Hedric, that of black starbursts on an azure background.

He was young, but the lines in his face and the shock of white in his close cropped beard spoke of a hard life. The imperious look he wore gave Marc the impression that he was likely to be responsible for much of those creases. "Identify yourselves," he demanded. Like his bearing, his voice toned haughty.

"This is the Lady Alexandra Moonglow; her Guardian, Sandoren; Master Del, and I am Marc Pendragon." The knight's eyes fluttered as he said it. "We seek the Sheltering arms of South Watch, sir. . . ."

"You will address me as Lord Edric," he said sharply. "What reassurance do I have that you are not bandits?"

Marc's eyebrow lifted. "It seems to me that you have all the reassurances you need right behind you, Edric," he said. Next to him, Sandoren stiffened and cocked an eye at him.

Lord Edric's face soured more than it already was, and his sword hand came up and over his saddle. "Do you realize who you are addressing, sir," he spat. "I am. . . ."

"I really don't give a good damn who you are right now," Marc retorted. "If you recall, I have entreated to you for shelter under the Codes which back that Device you're wearing. Now are you going to oblige me by giving me the correct answer, boy, or are we going to sit here under the hot sun and bake inside these clothes? There are some of us who need rest more than the need to know who is keeping us from it." One of the knight's behind him smirked. Edric sneered, his hand flinched closer to his hilt while Marc glared at him with piercing steel flints. "Go ahead," Marc continued, his voice low. "You know the penalty for acting against my petition." He tapped the pommel of his sword meaningfully.

Tense moments stretched out as Lord Edric glared at him, hand on his sword hilt. The corner of his mouth above the white patch twitched. An uncontrolled spasm that cracked the plane of his rigid lips and revealed the sharp whiteness of his teeth behind them. Marc readied himself for the man to lose his battle with himself, but, surprisingly, the twitch slowed and his hand pulled away from the weapon's handle. "Of course, my pardon, sir," he said tightly. "Peace find you within the Arms of South Watch." He turned his head inside the visored helmet and leaned back slightly. "Sir Hallivor," he barked. "Escort this party back to South Watch and arrange for them lodgings and meals."

"Yes, Lord Edric," the knight that smirked said immediately. "Right away."

Lord Edric waited until the other knight stepped his mount from the column before waving the rest of them onward. He waited for them to pass, continued to glare at Marc as they did. Once they had moved beyond Marc's small party, he sneered, and said, "May your stay be enjoyable, sir."

"You can count on it," Marc returned. Edric kicked his mount into a quick trot, leaving them with an amused looking Sir Hallivor.

"Greetings, my Lord Pendragon," Hallivor said once Edric was beyond hearing range. "Lord Baland speaks of you often. It is an honor to finally meet you."

"Please," Marc said, biting back his discomfort. "Just Marc will do finely."

"Marc, then," he answered, smiling broadly.

"Baland's still fighting back Old Mors, eh?" Marc said.

"He is," Hallivor agreed. "Keeps that Old Reaper on his toes, he does."

"Yes," Marc agreed. "he's always been tougher than a four year rooster."

"Six year," Hallivor laughed. "Come, let us get you into some shade and get some food into you."

"Best idea I've heard all day," Marc said and turned in his saddle to speak when he saw Alex regarding him from under her brows. While her hair was straggly and face sallow and drawn, her eyes were bright and clear and full of emerald tinged curiosity. "Ready?" he said, a flush of foolishness washing through him when nothing more appropriate came out.

"Yes, Marc Pendragon," she said softly. It was obvious to him that speaking was difficult for her but her eyes never wavered. He returned a feeble grin then nudged Whitesteel forward, ignoring Sandoren's sudden, veiled look. It seemed that Clover moved on her own, and Alexandra nearly slid off the animal's back, but was able to access some hidden reservoir of strength and managed to cling to the beast's neck. Marc swallowed hard and silently cursed himself of his ineptitude, then urged Whitesteel ahead next to the waiting Hallivor. If he couldn't break the curse, he could run from it. And while he told himself that, he could almost believe it.

To get his mind away from his guilt, he asked Hallivor, "Where is your wayward Lord Edric heading off to?"

The man blew a harsh breath through his thick mustache, and said, "One of our patrols hasn't returned. The Lord Captain Edric felt it necessary to go find them."

"How long overdue?" Marc said.

"Two days," he answered.

"Two days? Isn't that a little presumptuous?" Marc asked.

A thoughtful expression crossed the man's face. "Realistically," he said slowly. "No, not with so much activity on the plains these days. Though the trade routes from Mithron and Symond have been cut off, we have been seeing much more traffic. Refugees and such. And where a lot of desperate people are found. . . ."

"So, too, you find those who prey upon them. . . ." Marc finished the saying.

"Bandits," he agreed. "Some of them are very daring. Have even attacked a couple of our columns. It's the Lord Captain that's the problem. He has us prancing up and down the road, showing off our armor and swords, hassling anyone we find. I suppose from where he hails from, the bandits hang out along the side of road waiting for him to arrest them."

"Where's he from?"

"Telas," he said.

"Ah, Telas," Marc replied, smiling. "That explains it. Bandits do wait around by the road to be arrested in Telas." Hallivor laughed loudly.

"I've heard stories about how stiff necked Telasians are," he said when he was able to breathe. "But I never knew it was true. At least not until I met Lord Edric."

"Edric," Marc said, more to himself, musing over a thought that trickled down at his words. "I believe I've heard that name before."

"You have, but not his," Hallivor said, his voice filled with pride. "His brother, Sir Balistan Edric. He was among the knights that led the first charge against Gelron on the outskirts of Galin. He and Sir Jason Sulinaard cut all the way to the Deadlord itself and even wounded the vile creature before it unleashed its terrible powers and destroyed them both."

"Yes," Marc said, nodding. But it wasn't his deed that caused the flash in his brain. He remembered meeting the man several years ago, north of Render, during a minor skirmish with some marauding Skor. He was in the company of the one now called the Owl. The man vaguely resembled the other Edric, but only around the eyes. There, the similarities stopped. Where Lord Captain Edric was hawkishly rigid, Sir Edric goosely soft. Where Lord Edric wore a permanent frown, Sir Edric was quick to smile, like Hallivor. Where Lord Edric overdid his knightly image, Sir Edric seemed 'unknightly' in some of his doings. "Is this a case of personal jealousy then?" he suddenly asked.

"Hmm? Oh. Yes. That is the opinion of many of his peers," Hallivor said. "He is often heard berating the younger Edric's deeds."

"He's quite the charmer," Marc observed. "How long has he been stationed out here?"

"Only a few months," Hallivor said. "He has been up in Peldar in the new Motherhouse there, since we became outlaws of the *Empire* and were forced out. I think he thinks he is still there."

Marc grunted in response, understanding the sudden spike in Hallivor's demeanor as he spoke about the knighthood's ousting from the former lands of Hedric. He doubted a hundred years would heal that wound.

"Were it not for all the lands and titles he lost to him, I sometimes think he would be happier serving the Emperor," Hallivor was saying.

"Such blasphemy you speak," Marc said, causing another burst of laughter from the knight.

"Being this far out does that to a man," he said, choking down his chuckle enough to speak. "Cynicism is one of the unwritten Codes out here."

"Sounds like you've been out here awhile."

"Couple years now," he said. "It's quiet. . . well. . . was quiet."

"Yea," Marc said. "Change comes to all things. This place'll be a metropolis someday." He ignored Hallivor's sidelong look, and gazed at the emerging 'metropolis' before them, now that they were closer. Of the four buildings, not including the keep, three still wore the veil of newness, pale boards gleaming whitely in the sunlight. Squatting directly across from the gate keep was the old trading post, its wood gray and starting to curl. Beyond it, crowding the road, was probably an inn, given its relative size and two stories. The other two, obstructed by the post and inn were probably a gambling house and, maybe, a farrier, trying to horn in on the castle blacksmith. His uncertainty was on the near side of that hill. He had seen too many towns spring up in places to know that the first buildings were generally anything but what he thought they were.

Standing in front of the trading post were a handful of men haggling over the prices of pelts, strapped in bundles on the backs of two mules. Two of the six tending the mules, Mannics, were gesticulating, causing the bobs on their hide, bone, and metal armor to glint and sparkle in the light while the other four were leaning on their long handled axes or holding the reins. One of the two traders was holding up something on a string and gesturing back while the second was examining a pelt. Beyond them, a man, stripped to the waist, his skin bronze and sheened with sweat, maneuvered a hand cart toward the mass crawling about the scaffolding while knights pulling guard duty stood by the gate keep and along the battlements with anything but interest. The ambient heat caused them to shimmer as if they were badly made illusions.

"Why the new wall?" Marc asked. Hallivor let his eyes rove over the new construction and shrugged.

"The council wants a new wall," he said. "I don't ask questions. I don't see a use for it since the bailey can hold all the people about, but it keeps us from getting too bored. The Tantee peoples have brought rumors with their goods, but no one knows which one, if any, are true."

"Rumors?"

"Yea, regular stuff," Hallivor said, shrugging again. "Skoran hoards . . . dragons . . . any other conceivable beast about to descend upon us for being in their lands. The funny thing about it, they still come to trade their goods and drink."

"What kind of things are they trading for?"

"Foodstuffs, leather goods, whatever," he said.

"Weapons?" Marc asked.

"Sometimes," he said. "Those scavengers take what their pelts and stones will buy."

"Stones?"

"Yea," he said, "semi-precious stones, agate, amethyst, quanrime swirl, that sort of thing. Hamper pads the prices anytime they're around but they don't complain. I think they know he's gouging them, too, but they give him all he asks for, then they go over to Tonk's and drink, then they disappear again."

"Anything else unusual?"

Hallivor's face screwed up a moment, then relaxed and he shook his head. "No, can't think of anything — wait. . .No."

"What?"

"Well, we haven't seen the Bors around lately." His eyes cinched up again. "Almost three months now. They have been coming around here twice, three times a month on a regular basis for years."

Marc nodded. *Interesting.*

The guards at the gate keep straightened up when the small party arrived and waited for Hallivor. With some pomp, he stiffened in his saddle and called, "These fair travelers seek the Sheltering Arms of South Watch."

"Then they shall seek no further," came the reply from within the gate keep. "South Watch accepts them into the protection of her arms. Enter, and be at Peace."

Within the stone of the gate keep, the winches turned. Clanking like metal thunder, the great chains lifted the portcullis with agonizing slowness. Once it stopped, Hallivor lead them into the yawning mouth of the gate keep, past empty arrow slits and heavy doors, beneath closed and silent murder holes, and back out into the sunlit bailey.

The sound of hammer on anvil, muted outside the walls, echoed around the inner curtain, its origin from one of several small buildings hugging the inside wall to their right. It overbore the other noise within the wide courtyard. Hoof and wheel on stone, the buzz of conversation, the clang of weapons in practice, and the various whinnies, clucks, and lows of livestock. Men in azure livery swarmed from the stables at the left side of the keep proper and headed in their direction.

Marc unlashed his scabbard before handing Whitesteel's reins over to the young, pale complected man. "Behave yourself," he said into the beast's ear, causing it to flick and receiving a snort that he interpreted as, "Not on your life." Smiling, he patted the horse's neck sharply. Sandoren was already helping Alexandra down from Clover's back. Del was staring at something no one else could see.

The keep was a bulky square affair with rounded towers at its two corners that dominated the back end of the bailey. Hallivor led them up the steps to the large iron bound doors across the flat expanse that made up its front. The smaller, inset door was opened by a guard at their approach, and he ushered them into the entry hall, a spacious cavern that seemed more oppressive than airy with its dark stone, heavy tapestries, and large crossbeams. A huge iron chandelier hanging from the center rafters flickered candlelight into the corners, giving it a semblance of non-life. Blobs of tallow pasted the floor below it in tiny waxen stalagmites. A handful of servants in finer versions of livery than that of the stable-hands waited for them, blocking much of the room at their level, but not the dim view of the balcony at the rear or the steps leading up to it.

"They will see to your comfort while I arrange for you some rooms," Hallivor said, turning to Marc. "Is there anything you specifically require?"

"A healer for the lady would be welcomed," he said. Hallivor looked beyond him at the sagging form of Alexandra, and his face softened.

"Sir Dalek knows a bit about herbs," he said. "That is the best we can do out here. I'll send him around when we get you settled."

"Well done," Marc said. "Thank you, Sir Hallivor."

"My pleasure, Lord—er, Marc." His ruddy cheeks flushed a little more before he turned and exited through a nearby archway.

Immediately, the lead servant, an older man graying of hair but erect as a stanchion, moved to their left and opened a door. "This way, please," he said, waving a hand in that direction.

It was a sitting room he led them into, occupied by large, soft, but worn looking furniture. Candles sat on many small tables between them, sputtering in protest at the opening door. Still, it was a stark place, no adornments on the walls or ceiling, except sconces sporting pitch covered torches waiting to be lit. If comfort was the goal, it was way off some standards that Marc had seen. Of course, it was far better than some of the accommodations he'd suffered in the past.

Sandoren helped Alexandra onto a long couch. The back of Marc's throat went dry when she sank down into it. Her body seemed small and frail against the dark red satin of the lounge, her skin pale and drawn tight, smudges of ash collected in the sinkholes under her eyes and cheekbones. Her luxurious dark hair, too, seemed ashen and thin.

Before the servant had time to ask them for anything, Marc said, "Bring water and mulled wine. Chilled if you have it."

"Right away, my lord," the elder said and snapped his fingers. The loud pop sent feet scurrying, and he stepped back from the door.

Marc propped his sword against the arm of a nearby chair and sunk into the waiting cushions. He wiped his brow and ran his hand through his hair, noting the stiffness and sweat that coated it by turns. His eyes traveled around the small room, taking in the stark details of the stone, the over plush furniture, the worn side tables, the silent, still form of Alexandra. From a separate, objective part of himself, he realized no matter where his eyes roved, they eventually bounced back to the woman, moved along her frame, peered into the pits of her closed eyes.

His chest tightened.

Do not be concerned for her. Do not think you can care. You know what will happen.

He swallowed. Attempted to crush the thoughts. His heel ground the stone of the floor of its own will.

Marc counted his heartbeats, listened to his breath. He was able to insert himself into the oblivion formed over the years for the purpose of maintaining his sanity. However, he was unable to be sure it was working. His stability reestablished, he moved his eyes from Alexandra to the servant.

The man was too stiff, his features too used to an expression other than that of a servant. "How long have you been here?" Marc said, watching the man closely. When he responded, opened his mouth to speak, Marc interjected with: "Sir. . . ."

"Bevins," he answered immediately. A quick shadow passed over his stony features. "I've been here for sixteen years."

"And before that?"

"Telas," he said. "And before that, Vistan. . . My lord."

"Hedric's personal guard?" Marc said. Bevin's brows knit, just for a moment, then he nodded, once. A flood of relief filled the crevices of his face when the other, younger servants, actual servants, squires, stepped into the room carrying silver trays, goblets and pitchers occupying the flat surfaces.

"Wine, my lord?" one of them asked, a lanky youth with a mop of unruly brown hair. His smock bore a wet stain at chest height. He would take a tongue lashing for that.

"Water for me," Marc said. "Wine for the lady."

"She'll have water," Sandoren's sudden entrance into the present startled the young squire. One of the goblets fell against the cloth of his livery, and liquid sloshed from the silver pitcher, splattering on the tray. Bevins hissed. "Jared," he said.

"My apologies," the boy answered, too quickly. With such an intense look of concentration, Marc thought the tip of his tongue was going to stick out of the corner of his mouth, Jared puffed out his chest, slowly, until the goblet righted itself after a ringing dance on the platter.

Sandoren, himself pale and drawn, could only manage a partially fierce look, strained by exhaustion and chaotic fear. "Water for her," he said.

"Suit yourself," Marc said. "Though wine will help get her blood flowing better."

The Guardian gave him a long, slow stare, his mind working groggily behind it. Like warmed ice, he began to sink down on his perch on the end of the couch. He looked like he was about to change his mind when his face went rigid and he reasserted, "Water."

Marc shrugged, took the goblet being held out in front of his face. The quaff spilled cold liquid into his mouth, causing a tingle to run down the back of his throat and spread over into his extremities. *Thank the Creator for Coldstones.* He drained three full goblets quickly and was nursing a forth when another liveried servant entered and whispered to Bevins.

"Your accommodations are prepared," the servant not servant said. "If you will follow me, my lord." Marc handed off his goblet to the mop headed servant, picked up his scabbard, and watched Sandoren struggle to get a limply mumbling Alexandra standing. The ffolk tried to glare at him, but it was a weak attempt. Still, it cut Marc deeply. Without word, he passed from the room and followed Bevins as he led them deeper into the keep.

Once settled in the spartan room, Marc changed out of his road worn clothes, cleaned himself off with a rag and water provided by the servants, and put on a fresh change of clothes, also provided by the staff. A loose shirt and trousers. He sat down on the bed, a stout oaken frame surrounding a large feather packed mattress. When the knock came, softly, against the door, Marc found himself refocusing on the textured stone of the wall, the rest of him drifting back from the nothingness much more slowly.

"Yes," he was finally able to coax from his mouth.

"My lord," a voice said, filtering through the wood just as softly as the rap. "Lord Baland will see you now."

"Okay," Marc answered and quickly pulled on his boots, putting aside the distant vision he had been watching. A fast paced remembrance of the times shared with Gyssel, from youth to matron, no doubt dredged up by her very similar pupil, Alexandra. A long time ago, like most of his thoughts.

He opened the door and found Sir Hallivor waiting for him. "Personal escort duty?" he asked when he saw the still armored knight. The man shuffled from foot to foot until Marc smiled.

"Lord Baland speaks highly of you," he said, straightening.

"He does, does he?" Marc said, clipping off the words carefully that Hallivor did not detect the sudden flash of heat in his voice, a combination of embarrassment and anger. The man seemed not to notice. "Well, lead on," Marc added when it dawned on him that Hallivor was going to stand there like a fencepost until directed to do otherwise. The knight clicked his heels together before turning and heading through the dark, wide corridor.

"Your companions are settled and I summoned Sir Dalek to look after the Lady," he said. "That Sandoren fellow gave him such a stare when he showed up that I thought I might have to stay and stand watch. He's probably still there, glaring, unless his exhaustion has won out."

Marc chuckled, "He takes his Guardian duties a bit too far sometimes."

The offhand remark brought Hallivor up short. "Guardian?" he said. "You mean the Lady is an Earthmother?"

Marc nodded, eliciting a wide grin on the other man's face. "Well, well," he said and began moving again. "It has been long since an Earthmother has graced a place such as this. In fact, the last time I was lucky enough to be near one was during the siege at Galin. . . . Can't remember her name, but she was with that darkman, the false ffolk that calls himself the Owl."

Marc grunted, not wanting to comment on Hallivor's prejudice. When he had met the man called the Owl, he did not travel with an Earthmother, but he recalled hearing about her in the years since. Absently, he wondered if the ffolk's obvious differences to the norm were as much a hindrance as his own, unseen, curse. No matter, though. If he was who he was whispered to be, his obsidian skin and whatever else made him different, was not likely to be able to combat the strings of Fate.

Hallivor continued to chatter on about Earthmothers in general in the same rhythm and pitch as when he was escorting them in. An easy tone to tune out, and one easily encouraged by a random grunt, nod, or agreement.

The deeper they went into the keep, the more he anticipated seeing the old knight, Baland. It was at least seven years now since they had spoken. One of the men he allowed himself a fondness for. It was easier to allow himself to relax around those that chose to face death on a regular basis. It relieved him of a certain amount of responsibility. Unlike those that needed the protection that he was unable to give.

Hallivor's knock on the heavy door was answered immediately with a loud, "Come." The knight opened the door and held it.

"Enjoy your conversation," Hallivor said. "I shall stop by to see you later, if that is alright with you."

"That will be fine," Marc said and stepped into the room. "Though you know how long-winded Baland can be."

Hallivor's laughter echoed down the hallway as he left.

"Pendragon," a gruff voice said. "You old scoundrel, how be you?" He was standing in the center of the room, arms wide, his aged but still thick body wrapped in plain, heavy robes. Since he last saw him, Lord Baland's hair had thinned and turned from course gray to fine silver and his nose seemed wider, more bulbous. The fine spiders' webs that scrawled his sun worn face were deeper, more defined, but his mahogany eyes still retained that lively sparkle. He embraced Marc in a grip that told him his strength had not diminished at all, either.

"I am well, you old goat," Marc said once the man released him and held him out at arm's length. "And you?"

"Finer than some, worse than others," Baland answered. "I have some prime Leeran wine, just sweet enough for you to commit to the jump. . . Want some?"

"Graduated from the rough stuff?" Marc said. "Showing your age are you?"

He chuckled. "You haven't had Leeran wine, I see."

"Sure, I'll have a glass," Marc said.

"Good. Sit. Get comfortable," he said, indicating one of two chairs facing each other in front of a large fireplace. A lazy haze of fire covered the embers laying in the bed of the hearth, breathing out a comfortable warmth into the spacious room. As soon as he was sitting, Baland handed him a goblet.

"Not chilled?" Marc said, smiling. Baland sat, a little slowly, winked.

"You'll find it better without the cold added."

Marc lifted the goblet in salute, confident that he had, at some point in his everlife, sampled the substance. He told himself it couldn't be any worse than the sand bitter taste of Lysteyran Ale and tipped the goblet against his lip.

An explosion of apple and maple went off in his mouth and swept down his throat, causing his spit glands to go into spasms and his windpipe to tighten. The taste quickly transmuted, fading from the intense sweetness into the more tolerable taste of fermented fruit. That was when the burn started, and within mere moments, it felt like he plucked a coal from the fireplace and swallowed it. Marc's eyes watered and the constriction in his throat grew so strong he couldn't let out the breath he had taken in before sipping the beverage. Sweat popped out on his skin as the heat washed through his body, emanating from the white hot coals of his gullet. And then it passed, dissipating as quickly as it came, allowing him to breathe out in a great whoosh. Baland, who had stared at him from the moment he took the goblet, began laughing. His booming voice filled the room.

Marc began to set the goblet aside and was stopped by Baland's hand. He was still snickering, his eyes watering, too, and said around the laughter, "Take another sip." Marc started to shake his head, but put the glass back up to his mouth when Baland urged him a second time. After a brief pause in which he prepared against the sweet burn, he tasted the liquid again.

Nothing but a slightly sweet wine trickled into his mouth. Creasing his brow, he took another gulp, swishing the wine around in his mouth before swallowing. Still nothing.

"That's it," Baland said. "Only the first sip is the cliff fall. After that, it tastes like wine. You have to let it get through your body before the effect happens again."

"Interesting," Marc said, noticing that his brain had already started buzzing. He started to set down the goblet, looked at Baland and waited him to acquiesce, then placed it on the small table between them. "Lot of activity on the plains these days," he prompted.

Baland leaned back, took a sip of his wine and sucked his teeth through the explosion. It was over in an eye twitch. "Hallivor is a good man, but can't keep his trap shut to save his life," he said.

"Don't need Hallivor to know that," Marc answered after his own chuckle.

"Aye," Baland said. "that is true. Bandits and refugees thick as dirt."

"Hallivor alluded to something more," Marc said. "though I don't think it has occurred to him."

"The plains dwellers are moving, a big movement," Baland said. "Some of the rumors say the Flesheaters from the west are pushing them. Still only rumor, but even some of the more warlike of them have been acting strangely. Trading for preserves and other walking equipment. A lot of them still say we are bringing death upon our heads for being here, but they've been saying that for generations. Even some of the tribes that appeared after we got here," he chuckled. "Anymore, I think they respect our presence and are giving us warning about things without compromising their traditional hatred of us."

"That what the wall is all about?"

Baland nodded. "Aye," he said. "The Order believes we may have to shelter more than the usual amount should the rumors prove to be true. And I am inclined to agree. I've been around long enough to witness the unusual patterns that come about from sentient people. What do you think?"

"I think your instincts are sound," Marc said. "There hasn't been any major migrations in hundreds of years. The plains have supported the Nomadics for so long, it has become ancestral to them. If there are already some that have left their traditional haunts, then I'd say there is a problem. However, the masses of refugees and bandits moving through could just be the factor. It's difficult to tell. Better to be prepared, yes?"

Baland nodded. "True. And it does keep the men from getting too bored."

Marc laughed. "Hallivor said something similar."

"Hallivor would." Baland took a long pull from his cup and placed in on the table. "So, to where are you going on this trip through?"

"Calif," Marc said.

"Ah, the gateway to the east," Baland mused. "If I were trying to take over the world, that would be my next target."

"Granted," Marc said. "It's not the first place I'd choose for a sojourn."

"Then why go?"

"I am traveling there with the Earthmother," he said. "That is her destination. Have you heard any reliable news from there?"

Baland's brow was arched, but it went away once the question was asked. He shook his head. "Nothing significant lately. Like most of the lands north, they are suffering from the influx of refugees. The crazed weather is wreaking havoc with their crops. Much more I don't know. I hear that witch friend of yours is up the road in Hestaff, though. Perhaps you can get some more information from her."

"Sharla?" he asked. Just saying the woman's name made his blood stir. Baland nodded, sipped.

"Edric had an unpleasant run in with her several days ago while on a supply run," he said, face set in mock seriousness. "He just recently has been able to sit his saddle without grimacing."

"So that explains his sour demeanor," Marc said.

"No, that is his normal attitude," Baland remarked. "So then, I guess you met him."

"He met us leading a patrol, out on the road," he said. "He sent Hallivor back with us."

"Ah," Baland said, smiling. "Then you are probably now on the better part of his bad side. He and Hallivor don't get along well."

"Hallivor seemed to think that not many get along with him."

"That's true," Baland said. "He's from Telas."

Marc laughed. "Heard that too."

"Edric is a fine soldier and one you would want by your side in a fight," Baland said. "But that's about the only time you'll want him by your side. His family has a long lineage in Telas," he snorted. "Even the commoners in Telas think the nobles are too stiff."

"How did he get way out here?" Marc asked.

"Need a refill?" Baland said as he stood. Marc looked at the goblet, waved his hand.

"No, thank you."

"The Council wants him to cool his heels, so they sent him to us. When we were declared outlaws by the *Emperor,* all his lands and titles were seized and his surviving family arrested for aiding a known criminal. A few months ago, he received word that they were executed. His mother, sisters, uncles and cousins." Baland blew out a harsh breath. "Wiped out the whole line, but him. When he heard, he set out to destroy the Emperor that very day and, I hear, he was threatened with arrest and review before he came back. Two days later, he was sent here."

"Tough," Marc said.

"Yes," Baland said, placing the glass cork back in the wine snifter. The clink it made somehow relieved the tension in the man's shoulders. "Only I don't think they sent him to the right place."

"You think he should be in a more active place," Marc asked. Baland shook his head so that his jowls waggled.

"No," he said. "Blazes no. I think he should be sent to Leera to establish our first base there. They put him somewhere near anyone resembling an Imperial, there might be an incident that, at this point, would not be a good idea."

"You think he is that far over?"

"No, I think he is that rigid," he said. "Steel breaks, iron bends. And Lord Edric is far harder than steel." Baland sat and took a sip, looking over the cup's rim at him.

"So, that explains his demeanor," Marc tried again.

"No, I already told you, that is how his attitude always is." He chuckled.

"Hallivor mentioned his brother," Marc said. Baland rolled his eyes.

"Guess I'm going to have a talk with Hallivor," he said. "That's another hornet's nest. Balistan should have chosen another career. Being a knight was never his calling. In fact, he was up on review for several Code violations, before he went and surprised all of us by pacing Sulinaard the way he did. In one fell swoop, he not only paid his penance, he carved his name higher in the Annals than most any of us can jump, including his brother."

"I suppose he doesn't take that well," Marc prompted.

"Right on the lance rest," Baland said. "For someone who has so dedicated himself to being a knight, it has to be a crack across the chin. It was widely thought that Balistan entered the knighthood just to impress Landol, which was the wrong thing to do. Landol couldn't stand Balistan, for obvious reasons, and his entering the knighthood really irked him. You want to get on the bad side of his bad side, ask him about Balistan."

"I might just do that," Marc said, grinning, causing another roll of the eyes from Baland.

"Is it going to be my lot in this life to clean up after you every twelve years or so?" he said.

"Twelve? It hasn't been that long?"

Baland laughed. "We mortals measure time a little differently."

The conversation moved on to other, more mundane topics. Friends, family, battles, politics, following the ebb and flow conversations take between friends long separated by time and distance. There was a deep undercurrent of many such conversations that allowed for the quick continuance of anything left unsaid previously. Time slipped into an oblivion measured only by the largely ignored candles placed throughout the room and the slowly devoured wood occasionally tossed into the hearth by Baland. Like a spell, it worked on Marc, loosening muscles that rarely relaxed and allowing him to slide into a forgetfulness that gave him a respite from his curse. A tiny pause in his existence, but yet another sanity saving device.

It wasn't until the conversation began flagging that he realized all but one of the candles were nothing but cold blobs of wax in their bowls, and both were looking at each other through red-rimmed, watery eyes. Standing was like wakening from a nap, a dull hollowness of form that moved only sluggishly and under the most direct commands from the mind. "I guess it's not just us immortals that lose track of time," Marc said after a series of yawns set off by the realization.

"Go rest, my old friend," Baland said. "Perhaps we can have another opportunity before you breeze out of this place. How long are you staying?"

"Alexandra is hurried," Marc said. "But we won't be moving until she is able to travel."

"Soon, then," he said. "We'll be able to talk again, though, I fear it will probably be our last and worth savoring."

A pang thrummed through Marc's chest. Yes, it probably would be the last. "Then I will be sure to attend," he said, holding out his arm. The two men gripped forearms tightly, then embraced again, before Marc stumbled from the room and wound through the old halls until he found his. Hallivor was sitting outside his door, chair propped up against the wall. His eyes were closed and a soft snore filled the air around his face. Though the walls muffled, almost eliminated, all sounds from outside, he swore he heard the crow of the roosters signaling the coming dawn.

As silently as his cotton filled body would allow, he opened the door and closed it softly, leaving the young knight to his slumber. He would be sore when he awoke, but Marc was not about to deny him that. Could not.

With a grunt, he lay down on the bed, not bothering to remove either his clothes or pull back the blankets covering the mattress. He was asleep before he could close his eyes.

It seemed only minutes later that a soft rapping on the door stirred the waters of his dreamless sleep. With a groan, Marc rolled up into a slouch and washed his face with his dry, callused hands. "Come," he finally said.

Hallivor leaned inside, his eyes bleary. "Sir Dalek says the Lady Alexandra has fallen into the Longsleep."

"What?" Marc said. His mind clutched and his heart skipped. Hallivor's comment sliced cleanly through his after-sleep state, but revealed thick fog beneath.

"Lady Alexandra," Hallivor said. "She's fallen into the Longsleep."

The fog thickened, as did his blood. "She's dead?"

"No, no," Hallivor said, shaking his head vigorously. "No. She lives, but will not wake up. Sir Dalek says it's serious, though."

Marc breathed, the giant hand squeezing his chest loosened. And then a rush of fire gushed through him. "Why are you telling me this?" he said, not bothering to moderate the anger in his voice. Hallivor backed up, his face crimping in confusion.

"I . . . I thought you might want to know," Hallivor said.

"There is nothing I can do about it," he spit, raking his hand through his bedraggled hair. Hallivor stiffened further, his eyes narrowed.

"Sir Dalek was under the impression you might know what caused her condition, Lord Pendragon," Hallivor said. "He says it's not just exhaustion she's battling, but something more. I will explain that you cannot help."

He immediately turned and was several steps from the door when Marc launched off the bed, grabbed the frame and leaned out. "Wait!" he said, his voice sounding harsh in the enclosed hallway. Hallivor stopped and looked over his shoulder. "She drew too much on her powers and drained herself."

"I'll tell him," Hallivor said.

"Where do you draw your water here?" Marc asked.

His brows knit. "From a well," he said. "There is an underground stream."

"Is it accessible to people?"

"I fail to see how this is doing anything useful, my lord," Hallivor said.

"Humor me," Marc said, voice dropping in pitch. Hallivor's hand twitched toward his sword.

"There is a tunnel. . ."

"Show Sandoren where it is," Marc ordered. "Tell him to immerse her in the stream. He'll know what to do."

"How is a bath going to be helpful?" Hallivor said.

"Do it!" Marc said, steel eyes flashing in the darkness. Hallivor began puffing, readying himself to defend his honor. They stared at each other, the hall, walls, keep, disappearing into a blur of flickering darkness. Marc's muscles became fluid, strong, and he settled downward, rooting himself to the thick stone of the keep as every battle he ever fought washed over his mind, leaving it clear of thought, with only purpose. Hallivor sensed his impending death and backed up a step and blew out a heavy breath.

"I will do as you direct, Lord Pendragon," Hallivor said, turning and walking quickly down the hall, his boots clacking against the stone floor, leaving Marc coming slowly out of his battle mind. He was suddenly wishing for some ale. A lot of ale. Or any other drink that would erase the last few moments of his life.

Chapter 63

The Spawn of Darkness

*J*arren spent the rest of the day looking out over the river and planning the troops eventual movement down its bank. Occasionally, he scooped up some of the cool water and gently patted his eye with it, wincing when the liquid touched his skin even though he barely felt it. When the sun peaked, one of the men brought him a plate with some stew on it. He accepted it, no words passing between them. The man disappeared back into the woods. He didn't know his name. Couldn't remember it. Suddenly, it seemed important that he should. That it needed to be done. As he shoveled rabbit stew into his mouth, he wracked his brain, but it still wouldn't come. Once he set the empty plate on the sand next to him, he decided to ask Mandol. Instead of getting up and doing so, he leaned against the tree he sat under and dozed off.

It seemed almost instantaneous that his eyes flashed open. Darkness met him and panic rose up and shivered into his body. His hands scrabbled and clawed the tufts of grass he sat on. It took only a moment for him to realize that night had fallen, but it took a little longer before his body followed his mental directions. The memory of a scream drifted past his wakening mind, but only the chirping night met him now. *What was that?*

Another scream ripped through the evening air as if in answer to his thought. It was followed quickly by numerous shouts and calls that echoed the length and width of the camp. They were panic stricken cries.

Jarren was up and racing before he remembered both his sword and his boots. He stopped only long enough to scoop up the sword. The scabbard slid off the blade into a bush. The flat surface gleamed in the wan moonlight.

Most of the calls were coming from the center of the encampment. *The hospital!* Torchlight was throwing yellow flickers into the trees. Jarren compensated and crashed through some bushes, howled as something tore into the pad of his foot, but kept going nonetheless. Men were running to and fro, some half clothed, some unarmed, all with wide eyes and rabbit movements. There was a circle of them ahead, creating a human boundary that lined the clearing that held the hospital tent and the picket line for the pack mules.

"What's happening?" he yelled as he grabbed the first person he came in contact with. The man jumped and nearly ran him through. Luckily, recognition crossed his features before that awful swing followed. "What's happening?"

"One o' them things, Cap," he stammered, using the blade which had nearly sliced open the corporal's gut to point into the clearing.

"What things," Jarren said, turned away before the man could answer and pushed his way through the yammering crowd.

It was a hunched, skulking thing made of the inkiest black. Arms ending in long clawed fingers scratched at the ground, tearing chunks and gouges out of the loam, filling the air with its smell, comingling it with the cloying rot cloud hanging around the tent. There was no face. Only a head with divots and bumps where eyes and a nose and a mouth should be.

Jarren was struck by its movements, jerky and shaking, like a newborn calf trying to stand. It looked around, or rather, pointed its empty face at the encircling men and stumbled a bit. Some of the men yelled in surprise and backed up. When he took his eyes away from it, Jarren found several of the men looking at him, questions forming up there like swamp bubbles.

They were waiting on him. Waiting for him to do something or say something. There was no doubt in his mind that this was the type of creature that destroyed the regiment, but why was it here, and why was. . . . *It may not be alone!*

The thought spurred his legs, and he stepped into the clearing, almost like a man about to get into a barroom fisticuffs over a bet. The thing swiveled its head around toward him, to the collective gasp of the innermost ring of the men, and its body followed it sluggishly. Drunk was the only word that kept coming to mind. Gritting his teeth, he stepped toward it, holding his sword in a guarded position.

It stumbled backward, then forward, stopped, and seemed to shrug. It made not a sound. The weight of everyone's stares sunk into Jarren's muscles. In a lurching step, it came forward and stopped again in that sluggish sway.

Jarren's sword swipe was quick, defensive, and hit the inky creature mid-chest. The blade passed through the body as if it was hardly there. The resistance he expected was not there and threw him off balance. It felt like he was cutting through a melon, a momentary catch on the blade as it sliced into the rind, loosening up as it passed through the fleshy center, and catching again as it exited. But no noise. No crunching or squelching. And the thing made no sound, no crying or yelling, even as the top half slid from the bottom portion and hit the ground in twitching spasms. The pieces were complete, solid, inky all the way through. No internal organs. His stomach began to churn; his blade was clean. No blood, either.

The two halves of the body continued to jerk and twist. Disgust shot through him, and he hacked and stabbed at them until they stopped. Sweat broke out over his skin, turned clammy as the breeze touched him.

He looked up finally and found all the eyes of the men still staring at him in various shades of shock and fear. It suddenly made him angry. "Form up squads!" he barked and started pointing. "You, you, you, you, and you! Everyone else on them!" He addressed the ones he pointed out. "Sweep the area. Make sure there aren't any more of them."

The men he singled out gaped at him. "Go!" he roared. The waiting throng broke into chaos, but structured chaos. Now that the men had a definite objective given to them in a manner they were used to, a breath of life flowed into them. The breath of purpose. And the chance to rectify something that had cast a pall over them the last several days. Once he was certain the men were doing what he wanted them to, he shoved into the hospital tent, covering his mouth with his hand.

Everything was undisturbed, Garman was sleeping on an empty pallet. He moved over quickly and prodded him with his free hand, bringing him into a verbal half wake state, just to make certain of his health, then went around the tent and checked briefly each of the men laying within by placing his sweat coated palm near their noses. All of them breathed, to some extent. He finished his round at the cots of the commander and Captain Turcot. The commander seemed well, but in the dimness, The Captain's face looked almost gray and seemed somehow softened, or rounded, as if someone had taken a piece of grit paper and worked it against a wood carving of the man.

Jarren rubbed his eyes, felt a slight headache coming on behind them. When he looked again, the captain remained unchanged. A growing concern in his belly prompted him to awaken the doctor fully, but as he turned towards Garman's cot, the captain jerked. More precisely, it seemed that something jerked the captain's supine form. Jarren turned back, a hitch forming in his belly.

Turcot jerked again, and it seemed as he did so that his face became . . . fuzzy and doubled. Jarren stepped back, stopping only when his calf found the edge of the commander's cot. The captain began shaking violently, caught up in some sort of fit, a gurgling sound ripping out from deep within his body while Jarren stared, eyes unblinking. Seconds went by before the shaking form stopped.

The corporal stared, his mind incapable of thought or action. When the captain's graying skin suddenly darkened, a moan issued from Jarren's mouth. An inky shape climbed out of Turcot and sat up.

Jarren tried to turn away but fell over the commander's cot pitching him and Anlin's comatose form to the sandy floor. Another sound escaped him, a squeal, before sand entered his mouth. He struggled to disentangle himself from the commander and scramble forward at the same time desperate to look behind him, to find the thing that Captain Turcot was spawning. Huffing breath, thudding heart, a panicked thrashing found Jarren standing unsteadily in the center of the tent, staring wildly back at Turcot. The thing was still there, turning its faceless head to and fro. A muffled exclamation off to Jarren's right told him that someone was awake but not in tune to the situation yet. The distant, detached part of the corporal told him it was probably Garman, but that voice was quickly overthrown by the present situation.

A wave of nausea assaulted him, causing him to bend and stagger. Jarren saw he still had hold of his sword, but couldn't remember what to do with it. The dark thing coming out of Turcot seemed to be struggling itself, trying to pull free from the chain of the captain's body.

Garmon shouted something. A second later it translated into Jarren's brain. "Watch out!" But by then something slammed against the back of his head and bright flashes of light were dancing in front of his eyes and his ears were singing. The ground came up to meet Corporal Jarren just as the inky creature put its first tentative step onto the floor of the hospital.

Chapter 64

An Uneventful Trip

7onk's, though comparatively new, was in bad shape. The tables and chairs were mismatched, and many of them were patched with odd bits of wood and scavenged parts, some held together with strips of leather. The floor bore long gouges, worn, stained, and re-gouged, as did the tabletops and portions of the walls. A large wood-stove, that provided warmth during the winter months, stood in the far corner, its hatch open and the end of a brown bottle sticking out from it.

Tonk, himself, was a wasted man bordering on scrawny. Someone who could easily be starving though he didn't bear the bloated stomach of such an unfortunate. One of his eyes was clouded and wore a permanent squint, just like his voice. It took the threat of bodily harm for Marc to get a drink that wasn't watered down.

That was hours ago, and the tankard still sat in front of him, mostly filled. The sweat that had coated the outside of the large mug had long since dribbled down the sides and soaked into the table. It was just as well. The stuff was ash-bitter in Marc's mouth.

He took a sip, forced it down his throat, sucked air through his teeth, set the tankard back on its stain ring and gazed across the empty room. That was the extent of his movement, repeated once every hour or so it seemed. The activity became so ingrained that he did not, at first, notice the shadow that briefly darkened the doorway. When she spoke, his eyes and heart leapt.

"Someone said you were in here," Alexandra said. She was walking slowly, and her face was still drawn, but there was color in her flesh and the dark circles underneath her eyes receded significantly. With some effort, she sat down across from him.

"Glad to see you up and around."

"Thank you," she said, "I might still be sleeping had it not been for your advice."

Marc sat back and looked through the slightly skewed window. "I did nothing," he said.

"You told Sir Hallivor about the water."

"Yea, well, your Guardian would've thought about that sooner or later."

"But he didn't." She reached over and clasped his hand, sending the tingling up through his arm like lightening. It lasted for several moments after she withdrew it.

"When do you think you will be able to ride?" he said, took a hasty sip of his ale.

She gave him a wan smile. "We can leave tomorrow, Marc Pendragon." He nodded.

"It will be another day until we get to Hestaff," he said. "If we can find a ship, we can be in Calif within the next few weeks. Since you are well, I will go get some provisions."

Alex's brows twitched together, she frowned then gave a sharp nod. "Very well then." When he pushed back his chair and stood, she looked at him. "Help me stand, please."

Marc's mouth went dry and lead dropped into his stomach. His shoulders slumped. "I cannot help you," he said. "You know that."

"Sorry, I have forgotten," Alex remarked, held out her hand. "Please allow me to shake your hand then. For remembering the water before Sandoren."

Marc bit his tongue, trying to stave off the shame that billowed around the lump in his gut. Reluctantly, he held out his arm, preparing for the lightning strike her touch would bring. She looked at it before placing her hand in his. Quickly, she wrapped her fingers around his thumb and slid from the chair, allowing her weight to pull him off balance. "What—" he said, tensing and bringing his arm in close to his chest while leaning backward to compensate, in the process lifting Alexandra to her feet. "What are you doing?"

Alexandra withdrew her tingling touch then gently patted his stubbled cheek. She smiled, her bright green eyes full of mirth. "Thank you for helping me stand," she said softly. "Marc Pendragon." The woman left him standing by the table, stun worked all across his face in tight lines.

Seconds later, he rushed out onto the porch in front of Tonk's, the stunned expression replaced by a stormy one. "Why are you playing with me like this, lady?" he yelled at her back. "Who do you think you are?"

"Just think about it, thick-head," she called back, a laugh trailing the partially muffled comment. When she said nothing else, he sent a fist careening into a nearby post, relishing the burst of pain traveling from his hand up his arm then stomped back into the tavern and slammed back the warm liquid in his tankard, draining it without taking a breath. After wiping his mouth with the back of his sleeve, he flung a silver coin onto the bar, tromped into the dusty street, and proceeded to the trading post.

The rest of the day was spent in fuming silence and clipped remarks while he arranged for provisions, making the mundane task drag out into long minutes that lasted for days. When he and Baland got together for their last conversation after a quiet supper alone, he was soaked through with indignation that bubbled and festered at irregular moments. But he and the old knight talked through the long night, Baland ignoring his sullen behavior as a man nearing his death would when speaking to a good friend. The old man's intoxicating presence eventually swept the feelings into a dark corner of his mind, a place that could be disregarded. But only for a while.

The conversation eventually became stunted, like the candles, each of them looking across the bleary eyed space in the dimness of the room. Outside the door, movement. Footsteps on stone. Muffled voices speaking to each other, low and filled with sleepiness, then moving on. The whisk of straw on the floor. Drifting scents of cooking meats.

They both seemed to realize the keep awakening at the same time and stood, slowly, and embraced, the old knight patting his back like a father to a son, though, by far, Marc was the older of the two. In this instance, however, Marc was still the child. He did not know the inevitableness of impending death. Aging past the point of fearing it, watching it, to that point of peaceful acceptance that showed in the old warrior's eyes.

"Good journey to you, old friend," Baland said, taking his hand and clasping it. It was still rough and strong, and brought a weary smile to Marc's face.

"To you, as well," he answered.

"Aye, it shall be," Baland said, walking him to the door, his hand resting at Marc's elbow. "Send word when you arrive in Calif, yes?"

"Of course." Baland's eyes were teary and Marc didn't think it was all due to sleepiness.

Marc strolled through the keep, buzzing with the false awareness that came with long stints of wakefulness followed by sudden activity. When he retrieved his belongings from his room, his sword and travel cloak, he made his way down to the kitchens and packed himself a meager breakfast to eat on the road.

Sunlight lanced into his eyes when he stepped outside, a surprise to his fogged mind. He didn't think his time spent with Baland lasted so long. And the events of yesterday seemed very far away, a journey in and of itself. After the burn left his still watery eyes, he drew in a long breath through his nose, filling his lungs with the fresh smell of morning.

Whitesteel was clean and already saddled when he

entered the stable, the telltale *wisk!, wisk!* of a brush on his flank reaching his ears. A head bobbed on the other side of the horse, moving to the rhythm of the brush against his skin. Whitesteel looked bored, one of his ears flopping forward like a lop-eared rabbit. When he saw Marc, his bottom lip began trembling in greeting. A second later, he nickered and turned his head backward. The stable hand cried out in surprise at the nip. It was the mop headed young servant, Jared.

"My-my lord," he said after he recovered. "You are early."

Marc glanced back out the door. "Yes, I suppose I am," he said. "What are you doing?"

"Sir Bevins gave me some extra duties," Jared said, a sheepish look on his face. "For spilling the wine."

Marc chuckled. "Good thing you didn't break the glass," he said. Jared nodded.

"I-I was about to saddle the others' horses," Jared said. "I was not expecting anyone so early."

"I could go back inside and get something to eat."

Jared flushed, "Uh. . . No, my lord, that will not be necessary."

"Would you like a hand with that?"

"N-no, my lord," he said, paling. "That would not be proper."

"Proper?" Marc chuckled. "I suppose you want to be a knight?"

"Why. . . Yes, I do, my lord," Jared said, stiffening. "Very much so."

"How long have you been squired?"

"T-two years now," Jared said.

"You're a little old, aren't you?" Marc said.

"Yes, a little, my lord," he said, shuffling from one foot to the other. "I come from a poor family, we could not participate in the trials like most."

"You're a personal recruit, then," Marc said. "Who is your sire?"

"Sir Bevins."

"Bevins?" Marc said, his eyes widening. "Well, that explains some things. How did he happen upon you?"

Jared shrugged. "I fought off some bandits raiding my family's farm. . . well, I was holding them off when Sir Bevins came along. He paid my father and brought me here."

"Excellent," Marc said. "I'm sure you will make a fine knight someday."

"Thank you, my lord."

"I'll let you get back to your work, then, young Jared," Marc said.

"Thank you, my lord."

When Marc walked back into the still morning air, Whitesteel followed him and nudged his shoulder a couple of times. "Yea, yea," he said, called back to Jared, "You have any sweet lumps with you?"

"Uh," he said, bustling from the barn, checking the pockets of his smock. That look of tongue-sticking-out concentration worked onto his face, but was soon replaced by dawning triumph as he held out some rounded pressed honeyed oats.

"Yes, thank you," Marc said. "Always keep sweet lumps in your pockets and even your steed will thank you." He held up a lump between them. Whitesteel snorted and jolted his shoulder again. Marc laughed while Jared held a hand over his mouth. "Here, you nag!" he said, handing the lump to the seeking horse. Whitesteel took it, gobbled it, nodded his head in exaggerated waves while pulling his lips away from his teeth. Marc gave him another one and wrestled with his head. When he looked up, he saw Jared back in the barn, pulling Clover from her stall and getting ready to pick her hooves. He smiled, a nostalgic flashback of his days in the stables drifting up from his long past.

Marc strapped his sword to his saddle and led Whitesteel down into the bailey proper. Several knights were assembling near the gate keep, a patrol about to leave. Their armor sparkled in the morning light and the rattle and scrape of the pieces sliding and knocking with their movements echoed around the area. They spoke amongst themselves in the comfortable manner that only comes from battling alongside each other; the tightness of brotherhood that gave any mundane subject a deepness that non-warriors would never experience.

Others moved about in the early air, servants in nondescript livery going about duties just as nondescript. The blacksmith was heating his forge for the day's work, while stable hands carted used hay and manure out and fresh hay in. A portly woman in an already dirty apron was dumping scraps into a pig trough, and younger women were tossing seed to the chickens from cupped aprons.

All the terrible things going on in the world and still the daily grind went on. And would probably go on until the end of time. How remarkable it was that people could sink into their normal tasks. Or ignorant. He didn't know which, maybe both. But then, he could hear the voice of Mistress Vance yelling at him from across the ages, from a time when he was young and serving his squiredom doing chores in the chapterhouse. "Chickens don't eat, chickens don't lay," or "Pigs don't eat, we don't eat," and other such wisdoms. The memories tickled his heart.

Whitesteel let out a snort, sending a cone of vapor into the crisp air. He could taste winter in the early morning though it was still a couple of months away. Of course, with the weather acting like it was, winter could come next year, or the year after. Or even come full force tomorrow morning. He considered the travel cloak draped over his shoulder, then rolled it up and tied it to the back of the saddle. Winter wasn't today, and the chill would be going away when the sun was higher in the sky.

Marc saw Sandoren striding through the courtyard, heading toward the stable, while he was finishing the adjustments to his tack. His walk was loose and unhindered by stress, and his face was relaxed. When he looked in Marc's direction, he nodded instead of scowled. Marc returned the nod and tightened the girth strap around Whitesteel's middle.

When the others were ready, Marc was waiting by the gate keep after taking Whitesteel outside and allowing him to warm his muscles with trots and canters. The exercise wound him up, and he was prancing and stomping in response to Marc's attempts at keeping him still.

"Good morning, Marc Pendragon," Alexandra said. Her face was fuller yet and her eyes shining in the sunlight. She also wore a subtle smug expression that jabbed at his pride.

"Good morning," he answered. "You are looking well."

"I feel well, thank you," Alexandra said. "And you?"

"Fine, fine." Sandoren seemed not to be paying attention to the interchange, and Del was completely oblivious to his surroundings, his eyes foggy and a line of drool spilling down his chin. The familiar retinue of animals and insects was not in attendance this morning. "Is he?"

"He is more withdrawn than usual," she said in a low voice.

"Why?"

Alexandra shrugged. "Don't know. I'm not so sure anybody would."

"Well," he said, nodding. "I suppose it's time to be off." He looked up into the sky, scanning toward the direction they were going to travel. "We should be in Hestaff by nightfall."

"Excellent."

They rode out of the burgeoning village around the keep at a leisurely pace, letting the horses walk unfettered. Not more than a half a mile out, something tickled the back of Marc's neck, the tiny spider of watchful eyes. He turned to look, but against the backdrop of the keep and the plains beyond, all he saw were a couple of travelers. One of them appeared to be an Eldythian, as tall as he was, reaching evenly to a fair haired person on horseback. They were slouched, even the horse, and shuffled slowly toward the Inn. It comforted him that the Chyldren had lost out on that count.

"What's wrong," Alexandra said from his right. He looked at her, at her emerald eyes, and had to force himself to breathe.

"Nothing," he finally managed.

The rest of the morning was spent in quiet musing, the horses alternately walking and galloping. Not long after the sun was lining up by the stationary moon, they began seeing small houses ahead of them, separated by plots of land big enough to support individual farms. Though the ground had yet to be turned, some were marked off with stakes tied with cloth. The buildings were new, simple wood dwellings sealed with mud and straw. Faces, white moons from the darkness within, peered out at them from roughhewn windows. All of them wore guarded expressions and did not turn away until the little company was past them.

"Interesting," Marc said.

"What's that?" Alexandra answered.

He waved a hand at the dwellings. "Looks like Hestaff has grown some," he said. Her answer was a long roving gaze over the plains ahead followed by a nod.

They smelled wood smoke and brine long before they saw the port city's walls, and the clumps of houses and people increased steadily the longer they moved. The closer they got to Hestaff, the less worried the looks, the less longer the stares. Most of them were not inclined to head into shelter when they saw Marc and his companions, and some even lifted a hand in greeting after a slight pause from working a churn or pounding a rug.

It was not a surprise to Marc, then, when they saw Hestaff ahead of them, framed off by a thick line of blue that seemed to float higher than the stone walls. It seemed to him that the city's populace had swollen and washed over the walls to flood the low plains surrounding Hestaff with a huge tent village. When the cooling, salt scented breeze shifted just right, it carried up the smell of thousands of people, their cooking food, their animals, and their garbage. A dull murmur of many voices rolled up toward them like distant thunder. Unconsciously, the little group drew closer together.

Marc was mentally prepared to be mauled by a mob of beggars, looking for any handout, stealing anything loose, but was surprised when they were met with indifference. Barely anyone looked at them, even the people sharing the road, all of them going about their daily chores. Fires crackled underneath bubbling pots held by wooden tripods. Wood was being chopped in central areas, carted in from nearby woodlands. Children played. Dogs barked. Multitudes of different languages chattered throughout, forming a cloud of comfort around the temporary town.

As they moved through it towards the huge gates of the city, Marc was able to see a definite striation between the groups, turning one huge tent city into several smaller ones abutted up against each other. The bulk of the people, by the sound of rambling language from small framed, bronzed humans with uniformly black hair, were Scandanese. But he also saw some tall, pale, blond headed Leerans; stocky, barrel chested Symonites; and even some lanky, yellow cast Mithronites. Patrolling through and around the wood frame, cloth covered dwellings, were the sable and azure adorned soldiers of Hestaff. No doubt peacekeepers between the various cultures, though their uniformly bored expressions said their efforts were more than paying off.

His heart panged in his chest when his mind suddenly dredged up a memory of Anine and her destination when he had found her. He swallowed it, trying to drive it back down into the muck of his recent past. It went, but left the dry flavor of talc in his mouth. Luckily, the growing crowd swallowed his attention.

A large, milling throng waited, bottlenecked at the gate while the guards regulated the entrance and exit into the city, and it caused them to slow nearly to a standstill. It would have been nearly impossible to advance had they not been on horses. As it was, the press was so much that the normal berth walkers generally gave horsemen was shortened to little more than a hand span from their stirrups.

Marc had little difficulty dealing with the proximity of the yammering crowd, but Sandoren's face was tight, his jaw clenched, and several times he snapped at anyone that got too close to him. A line appeared between Alexandra's brows, as well.

"Nervous?" he said, leaning over so he would be heard.

"A little," Alexandra said with a smile. "Crowds make me jumpy."

"At least they're just people, this time," Marc said.

She laughed.

It wasn't much longer after that they finally reached the gate and the somber guards monitoring it. The man that looked at them stared for a few moments before saying, "Identify yourselves." He could still be considered young were it not for the tightness around his eyes and mouth.

"Marc Pendragon," Marc said. "The Lady Alexandra Moonglow and her Guardian, and Master Del."

The soldier didn't even blink. "What is your purpose here in Hestaff?"

"Passing through, going north," Marc answered. The man studied him for a moment.

"Coming from where?" he said.

Marc arched a brow. "From my home, a week's travel south," he said. The guard stared again as if not comprehending him. Finally, he stood aside and waved a hand.

"Proceed," he said. Whitesteel did not have to be nudged. Hearing the tired voice of the guard, he began walking on his own. The other mounts fell in step, and they entered the cool shaded breezeway created by the gate keep.

Though the day was moving towards its end, the city was still bustling. The streets just inside the gates were packed with peddlers and hawkers, yelling about every sort of ware available: chickens, fruits, nuts, clothing, jewelry, etc. Wagons moved up and down in a clatter, and even some more elaborate carriages and hand born limousines passed by in a rush. Among them passed people dressed in many varieties of clothing ranging from rough, functional woolens to finery made of silk and brocade.

The wide avenue they tromped down sliced the city in half, running straight from the gate keep all the way to the wharf in a long slope, throwing off smaller arteries, side streets and alleys in random patterns. Unlike Vistan, Calif, or many other, larger cities, Hestaff was unremarkable in its architecture. Simple stone buildings lined the roadways, each maintaining a squarish theme, though they ranged in size and stature, some structures reaching four stories in height. But nothing like the twisting, graceful towers of Calif that pierced the very sky, nor the massive, elegant works that gave Vistan its distinctiveness. However, many of the buildings were wrapped in new scaffolding, and several lots where once Marc remembered ramshackle dwellings were cleared of rubble and new foundations were being laid. From their vantage, they could see the harbor was bristling with many masts. A forest of them. That too, a change since he had been here last. Hestaff had, for many generations, been a major port of call, but its harbor was never able to support such a flotilla.

It looked to Marc that the Dark Night, as everyone tended to call it, was more of a boon to Hestaff than a detriment.

Marc turned them down an intersecting street, immediately relieving them of much of the murmuring crowd and led them only a few buildings down before turning into a large yard fronting a three story inn called the Gaping Grouper. A polished wooden porch wrapped around the building and spiraled up each story, forming a triple-tiered balcony connected by long, steep stairwells on the side of the edifice. Lounging on the porch, on heavy outdoor furniture, were several hard eyed men that gave them quick once-overs before glaring back onto the road.

Before they came to a complete stop, a young man in a clean woolen smock walked out the front double doors. "I'm sorry, my lord," the man said. "But we have no rooms to let."

Sandoren hissed.

"That's too bad," Marc said. "My companion, Baland, will certainly be disappointed."

"Is your companion tired, my lord?" the man asked without pause.

"No," Marc said, "But he heard you serve a fine venison fillet."

"We don't serve venison here, my lord," he said.

"That's okay," Marc said. "Baland doesn't like venison."

The man smiled and straightened his smock. "Please, my lord, come in," he said and clapped loudly. Several grooms appeared suddenly from the left side of the building, came over and took their horses' reins. When he dismounted, he saw Sandoren and Alexandra looking at each other, eyes wide, and stifled a chuckle. He patted Whitesteel's neck before stepping onto the porch.

"You coming?" he said when he turned around and saw them still sitting their mounts.

"Uh. . .yes, of course," Alexandra finally said and swung off Clover. Sandoren followed her lead then lent a hand to Del.

The man held out a hand to Marc and shook it warmly. "I am Justan Smyethe," he said. "at your service. Your rooms have been prepared and supper awaits you in a private dining room."

"You knew we were coming?" Marc said.

"Of course," he said, his smile stretching. "Lord Baland sent Lord Havel word by pigeon early this morning. He suggested we put you through the paces once you arrived. May I present Telan, Lanwick, Carol, and Nesmet." He turned to the porch sitters, who now wore smiles themselves and gave them nods.

Marc nodded in return and said, "This is Mal' andel Alexandra Moonglow, her Guardian, Sandoren, and Master Del."

"*Tus'stair no areylan,*" Smyethe said, placing his arm across his chest and bowing his head. The gesture was followed by the other men.

"*Areylan' an no layne' ar tol,*" Alexandra answered, returning the salute, only with the opposite arm. Her eyes were still wide and held a curious surprise.

"Please, allow me to show you to your rooms," Smyethe said. "Baths have been drawn for you as well."

"Excellent," Marc said and followed the man into the Inn. The door opened into a large foyer of dark teak and mahogany. Right above them, from the beams of the very roof, hanging down a full two stories and wider than the double doors, was an enormous crystal chandelier, the glittering, jewel-like ornaments a very effective veil covering the thick, sharp downward pointing spikes that were part of the fixture's structure.

Across from the door was a wide split 'T' stair case made of the same dark, heavy wood as the floor and wall boards that connected the first floor to the balcony of the second. Stairs, sturdy and wide enough to allow several men to descend side by side. Tapestries adorned the walls in many places, depicting pastoral scenes, though Marc suspected that behind those coverings were arrow slits and reinforced walls.

Marc already knew the keystones were rigged to come out at a single stroke of a hammer, bringing down the entire structure on the heads of anyone unfortunate enough to be inside, and there was an escape tunnel leading somewhere to safety. He looked at the nearby window and smiled. The curtain rod was a spear.

Smyethe led them up the right fork of the stair then left on the second floor, into a corridor that led deeper into the Inn. The building was larger than it appeared from the street. He stopped quickly and drew a door open. "My lady," he said.

"Your room." The door next to hers was indicated as Sandoren's, the door across from his, Marc's, and the one directly across from Alexandra's, Del's. "When you are ready, the dining room is around the corner, servants awaiting you. Please take your time and make yourselves comfortable. You shall have no worries while you are here." With a slight bow, Smyethe left them.

Sandoren's brows were still lifted and Alexandra wore the pinched expression of concentrated curiosity. When they no longer heard their host's footfalls, she looked at Marc, a mirthless smile on her face. "What just happened?" she said.

Marc laughed. "It's a safe house run by the Hedrican Order." The two relaxed a little. "They run them in most cities. You just have to know where to look."

"Interesting," she said. "And that little ritual out front is supposed to confuse people?"

Marc grinned. "Probably not," he said. "I'm sure around here, many people know about this place, but in 'knight unfriendly' places, you would find it terribly difficult to see it."

"And all these persons are knights?" she asked.

"Most of them, yes," Marc said. "The men on the porch. Smyethe, maybe, but I think he is a Warmage. The stable hands were squires, and the servants we meet at dinner will be squires or the Trusted."

"Interesting," she said again. "It seems a bit un-knightly, doesn't it?"

"On the surface it does, I suppose," Marc said. "But it is necessary. It helps them keep an eye on things and serves as a well-established way of moving people around while keeping them safe and obscure." She arched a brow. "Important refugees and such. How do you think most of them got out before the Emperor could crush them?"

"Point taken," she said. "Now, are we going to eat first, or clean up?" Her stomach made a rumbling noise. "I think we should eat first." She smiled.

"Agreed," Sandoren piped in.

They followed Smyethe's directions and found themselves in a modest sized room taken up by a long table with several place settings already laid out. The room was lit by six-prong candelabras placed strategically along the table, their flickering wicks sending light out into the corners and casting a warm yellow glow throughout the room. Two servants in sable livery trimmed in silver flanked a closed dumbwaiter door. When they entered, one of them reached up and tugged a tasseled cord hanging near it, then moved to direct them to seats. From somewhere below them, a crank turned, and the clank of a chain reached them.

Broiled chicken, basted and on a bed of steamed greens, appeared from underneath silver domes amid puffs of steam filled with aroma. A porcelain plate was placed in front of each of them, and the glasses nearby filled with a wine that exhaled the subtle fragrance of strawberry.

Sandoren immediately began slicing into the meat, while Alexandra leaned over and, with closed eyes, breathed in the scent of the prepared food. Marc watched her intently until she opened her eyes again, and then began cutting into his chicken. He smiled under her gaze and sudden, slight grin. Del, of course, was staring off into space, though, thankfully, he wasn't drooling all over himself anymore.

The chicken was soft, succulent, and made his mouth water even before he took the bite. An explosion of taste went off, causing the sides of his jaw to cramp slightly, followed by a tangy aftertaste. He looked across the table. Alexandra was chewing slowly, eyes closed again, her hair, released from its binding earlier, flowing down over her shoulder.

Marc's throat hitched and he nearly coughed. He swallowed his bite and relocated his attention away from the Earthmother. Glancing past Sandoren, who was studying his plate and half eaten food, Marc let it wander over the polished walls and finely shaped, silver sconces dotting it.

Time stretched out with the silence and became complicated as Marc tried to keep his eyes from wandering back to the woman who sat across from him. However, each second that crawled by seemed to make her stand out more and make the rest of the room blend into the nondescript. Her hair seemed to glisten, her chewing became seductive, her eyes, when open, sparkled more brightly. It became difficult for him to chew his own food, and he found his chair grew uncomfortable by measures and no amount of shifting helped. Several times he had to clear his throat or quaff a hefty gulp of wine to rid himself of the lump in his throat that wasn't caused by his chicken.

He was thankfully relieved by a soft knock on the door and the entrance of a man wearing a white, loose fitting shirt tucked into brown pants tucked into soft brown leather boots. He was tall and had to duck his head as he moved through the doorway. Still, his black shot with iron hair, brushed the jamb. The two servants stiffened noticeably, but he didn't look at them.

"Greetings, I am Lord Havel," he said, resting his mahogany gaze on each of them for a heartbeat before moving it. When they reached Marc, recognition flared and a thin smile pushed up the heavy mustaches that graced his upper lip. "I hope that I am not disturbing you."

"Not at all," Marc answered. He saw Sandoren frown into a hand. "Please. Sit."

Lord Havel nodded then looked to Alexandra. "May I, Mal' andel?"

"Please, my lord," she answered. "We would be honored."

"Thank you," he said, taking a seat at the head of the table. "I trust your travel from South Watch was uneventful?"

"Very much so," Marc said.

"And you had no trouble with the Gate Watch?"

"Less than I anticipated," Marc said. "I have to admit, I was surprised by the reception."

"The guards?" Havel said. "Or not getting mauled in Tent Town?"

"Both," Marc chuckled.

"Quaint name," Alexandra remarked.

"Yes, it is so," Havel said, turning his attention to the Earthmother. "Especially since every city from here to Calif boasts one." He laughed, a hearty tone. "But I'll wager a month's rations that this one is different from the others. I have it on good authority that Silver Nook and Galin, at least, are suffering under the yoke of the refugees."

"And Hestaff isn't?" Marc said.

"No, actually," Havel said. "Hestaff is flourishing under the influx."

"How?"

"All refugees are required to indenture themselves to the city if they decide to stay. In exchange for food, shelter, and even a modest income, they provide a work force for whatever project is required. Some work in the mines, others in the fields, and so forth. Some of them are very specialized. We have many shipwrights that have proven ideal for Hestaff's new needs for sea trade."

"For how long?" Sandoren asked suddenly, surprising Marc. His tone was neutral, but the ffolk was unable to disguise all the contempt that he tried to hide. For his part, Lord Havel seemed not to notice, turned to Sandoren as readily as he had for Alexandra.

"Six months," he said. "By that time they can become citizens of Hestaff, or move on, as they choose. Obviously, most of them choose to stay."

"That is a very interesting approach," Alexandra said, drawing Havel's attention back to her.

"I thought so," he said. "And a surprising one, considering the normal daftness of Lady Halloran and the House of Lords."

"Daftness?" Alexandra said. "Problem with women in power?" She was smiling and her eyes held a gleam. Marc didn't think it was entirely in amusement.

"Women?" he mused. "No, not at all. I have a problem with daftness. A couple of months ago, she tried to convince the House to tear down the walls around the city to provide a better view for the residents."

Sandoren choked, and Marc stared. "Surely it wasn't that bad," Alexandra said, her brows peaking.

"No," Havel said. "What was worse was the House passing the motion."

"What?" each of them said in unison.

Havel was laughing and holding up his hand. "Don't worry. Leland, the Watch Commander, and Fra' Neln, Commander of Hestaff's standing army, set aside their differences for a time and convinced them the error of that choice. This latest idea seems to have worked out much better than it sounded at first."

"Apparently," Marc said.

"Except for the extra duty the Watch has to put up with."

Marc smiled and Sandoren grunted. Alexandra did not have an expression to speak of. The stress of so few trying to control the movements of so many seemed not to occur to the Earthmother. But then, why should it? He was thinking like a warrior, about tactics and morale of deployed troops. Sandoren, also, understood. Though he appeared unstable, he moved and thought like a warrior. At least much of the time.

"Where are you headed," Havel said. "That has you passing through our fair city?"

"Calif," Alexandra said.

"Ah, the City of Towers," he said, leaning back. "Have you arranged for a ship to take you?"

"Not yet," Marc said. "That's on tomorrow's agenda."

"Please, let me take care of that detail for you," Havel said. "Blason Sor of Blason Shipping is sympathetic to our cause and will assist you in your travels."

"Thank you," Marc said. Alexandra saying almost simultaneously, "We are indebted."

Havel held up his hand and smiled. "No need," he said. "It's not often that we are blessed with the presence of an Earthmother and a dear friend. Do you require anything else?"

"No, Lord Havel," Alexandra said. "We have been well looked after. By you and your friends."

"Excellent," he said rising. The others did so as well. "I shall leave you to the rest of your meal. Should you find you do want something, the squires have been relegated to serving your needs. Be wary, though, their enthusiasm of getting away from their normal chores can cause you some discomfort. Growling at them will generally do the trick. Good night, then," he said, giving them a slight bow before turning out the door, leaving them with two meek looking squires.

"You certainly have a lot of friends," Alexandra remarked as she sat.

"One tends to get around when you're as old as I am," Marc replied. She smiled, and took a bite of her dinner.

"Can we trust them?" she said, almost absently. He stopped chewing.

"Can we. . ." he said around the mouthful. "I'm rather surprised that you asked that and not him." He pointed his fork at Sandoren who shot back a frown that was not completely serious.

"He's thinking it," she said, smiling at Sandoren. He grimaced again and went back to his food.

"When do you want to move on?" Marc asked.

"You didn't answer my question."

"Do I need to?"

"I suppose not," she said. "I still need some rest, and I need to spend some time at the coast. . . How long will it take to procure a ship?"

"Don't know," Marc replied. "With all the ships in the harbor, I'm hoping it won't be difficult to find one leaving within the next couple of days."

"Could it be longer than that?" Sandoren asked, his voice flat.

"Yes, it could, but I think the odds are in our favor," Marc said. "There are more ships in harbor than I've ever seen. And if this Blason person is part of the network, then, more than likely, he will have a ship waiting just for such a situation."

"I hope so," said Alexandra. "I sense our time is getting shorter, though I'm not sure why."

"Lady Fate has been smiling upon us lately," Marc said. "Perhaps she will continue to do so."

"Lady Fate, eh?"

"Any help is good, real or imagined," he said, shoving a piece of chicken into his smiling mouth.

"How long until we get to Calif?" she asked.

"Not sure. Since the lands have changed, I haven't been up that direction. I don't know what obstacles are in our path. Normally, by ship. . . a month. Month and a half. By land, a little less. "

Alexandra nodded, answering something inside herself. Sandoren grunted and pushed his plate away as he wiped his mouth with his hand, his linen napkin still sitting, folded, by his plate. Immediately, one of the two squires whisked the plate away. He stood slowly and knuckled his back. "I'm going out to tend the horses," he said.

Marc nodded and Alexandra said, "Alright." As the Guardian exited, Marc dabbed his mouth with the napkin and handed his own plate to the other squire.

"Will you take me to the coast, tomorrow?" Alexandra suddenly asked.

"Why?" Her brow twitched.

"My strength has not returned," she said. "I need the sea to facilitate my recovery."

"Why not take Sandoren?" he asked.

"Sandoren doesn't know how weak I am," she said. "I don't think he needs to know."

"He'll be more suspicious. . . ."

"Perhaps," she mused. "I will send him to get some more provisions."

"Why me? Why not go alone."

"Because you know more about me than Sandoren ever will," she said. Her eyes were luminous in the lamplight and took on a pleading look that had not yet crept into her voice. "About us. Earthmothers. You, at least, have an idea of the dangerous ground I'm on. Since the fight with the Chyldren, I have been near death, sustaining myself only through the faint touch with Earth's Blood."

"If something goes wrong," he said. "you know I can do nothing to help you. Why would you ask that of me?"

"I'm not asking for help," she said, her voice taking on a shaky tone. "I want. . . . It will give me comfort to know someone with your knowledge of our Ways is present."

Marc forced his air out in a sigh. "Okay," he finally said. "I shall go with you. Midmorning?"

"Closer to noon. I need as much sleep as I can get tonight."

Marc nodded, a thoughtful expression on his face. "Alright then." He stood up. "I shall see you at noon. Will you be retiring now?"

"After I see if Del will eat and get him to his room," she said. Marc regarded the youth for a few moments. Del's blank eyes revolved into his gaze and solidified briefly. The boy gave him a slack smile before the clarity went away. He was staring at nothing again when Marc nodded.

"Right," he said, pulling the door to when he moved out into the hall. He stood there for a moment, hand on the lever, wrestling with the urge to return. Both to refuse her request and just to talk to her. After several flickers from the nearby lamp flame, he sucked his teeth loudly and went to his room.

Chapter 65

News and Hope

*M*aelyrin leaned on the railing, breathing in the cool morning air. Her eyes drifted down the road toward the north between long blinks, then moved over the handful of buildings this side of the castle squatting at the other end. While she never saw such a structure, she could not help but look away from its rough, sturdy construction into the emptiness of the plains beyond, trying to bring forth the image of the travelers she saw leaving when they arrived earlier. Particularly the white horse and the person riding it.

Her heart skipped each time she thought about it. *Could that have been him?*

She asked the innkeeper when they arrived, but the ugly little man behind the bar said no one by the name of Marc Pendragon in any shape or form stayed at his establishment, and if she didn't produce some coin she and her Eldythian friend would not be staying there either.

A tired smile crossed her lips at the thought of the wracked human trying to threaten her, and she wondered if he was still skulking around the kitchen where her tongue lashing had sent him. Kiyo, quiet and withdrawn, had chuckled at her brazen candor.

Kiyo was upstairs in a room now, sleeping. What she should be doing, but couldn't. Her brain whirled and heart thumped inside of her. She was certain that the man she saw was Marc, and her reaction fought back the slogged, sodden feelings in her muscles and drove her eyes wide and searching the northern horizon as if the man she sought would suddenly appear there, riding to her, knowing of her search.

She was about to go back inside, if even just for the act of trying to sleep, when her eyes swept south and saw him. Her breath caught in her throat, and stayed there a moment, burning, while her mind tried to work. It finally came out when she realized it was not the person she wanted it to be.

Still, something was wrong. At first she thought the man was standing in the road, but he seemed to be moving very slowly in a lurching manner. His body hunched and dipped at each dragging step. The sun glinted off armor but in many places it was muted by something. Her foot was off the porch, when several shouts emanated from the castle's gate and several guards began rushing in the direction of the man.

They reached him before she was halfway there. He fell into their arms, a disembodied grunt followed by sharp calls from the guards. He was covered in crimson, the visible flesh between the dried and drying runnels ranging from pasty to black. His face was distorted by swelling, and his right arm was hanging limp amid a wash of blood showering down on the cobbles of the street. The armor that once covered that side of his body bore great rents, almost as if the metal was torn rather than pierced. Amazingly, the hand at its boneless end still gripped his sword, the flat edge of the broken tip ringing hollowly on the stone.

When she closed in on them, the guards were supporting him, moving slowly towards the gate house. Though his head bobbled on his neck, his eyes were still open, dark slits beneath puffed, bruised brows and a gurgling mumble issued from his mouth. They pushed past her, one of them saying, "Stand aside."

"I'm a healer," she said, but all but one ignored her. The man that heard her just looked at her blankly, then, they disappeared down the tunnel that led into the castle walls.

Maelyrin could only blame her exhaustion for her lack of ability to hold onto any concern and, after casting another look to the north, she shuffled back across the road and into the Inn.

Kiyo was sitting on the nearest of the two beds, legs crossed and eyes closed. His large frame made the bed seem like a child's. She *Looked* at him and found him in the deep trancelike state he had been in before, out on the plain. The dressings on his side were still clean, and she was thankful once more that the wound had not festered after it got reopened in his quick battle with the bandit.

She lay down on the second bed and stared at the plain, unvarnished ceiling made of wooden planks. She was considering the oddity of the hewn wood when she slipped into dreamless sleep.

Later, body thick and brain filled with cotton, she awoke and stumbled downstairs to arrange for a meal after lighting the small oil lamp on the bedside table. Kiyo was in exactly the same position as when she fell asleep, a giant granite carving sitting on a semi soft bed. She got him a bowl of thick stew anyway. If he didn't eat it, the way her stomach was rumbling made her believe there would be no waste.

The ugly man had been replaced by a stout woman with a slightly more pleasant attitude than him and went about getting her the meals without argument. Maelyrin sat down at one of the scarred tables and placed her floating head in her hands.

Something shocked her awake. She was looking at the stained wood of the table when she remembered it was the sound of the door opening and looked up. A cool fresh breeze caressed her face. Someone was standing in the doorway, but she looked beyond him, out into the darkness. It took a moment for her to realize night had come, and she groaned inwardly. Sleeping the day away was something she had not wanted to do. But then, it was too late to worry about it, and once the realization sank through her clogged mind, she focused on the man standing there.

"Are you the Healer?" he said. "The one traveling with the Eldythian?" His voice was full of the timbre of youth and reflected on his smooth skin and lively brown eyes.

She blinked several times then made her head nod in reply. Letting them think Kiyo was an Eldythian was a choice she felt was safer than the alternative, but it was secondary to the reason she refused to correct him now. She was just too tired to form too many words.

"My name is Sir Levett," he said, taking a step forward. "I was asked to summon you to the keep, if you would be inclined. Our physician would like some assistance with the man that came in wounded this morning."

"Of course," Maelyrin said, pinching her brows together and placing her hand on her forehead as if those actions would help hold in the thoughts that bounced off her brain. "Of course. I'll come as soon as I get some food to my companion."

"The Eldythian?" he said, his voice peaking. "Can I meet him? I've never met one before."

Maelyrin stared at him for a moment, her sleepy mind freezing on his request. "Uh. . . . I don't think that would be a good idea. . . . he's wounded as well and needs to be left undisturbed."

"Of course," Levett said, straightening. "I apologize for my forwardness."

"It's alright," she went on. "I will be ready as soon as I get him some food."

"Yes. . . excellent," he said, seeming not to notice her repetition. "I shall wait for you out on the porch."

"Alright," she answered as he gave a slight bow and turned on his heel. She watched him march the few feet out the door thinking that he seemed too stiff, too straight. Not like the fluidity that permeated Kiyo's being. Powerful, but graceful at the same time. And not the comfortable way the giant seemed to be in his own skin. But then, in retrospect, most of the fighting men she had seen in her limited travels seemed stiff and unbending somehow.

Except for Marc Pendragon, that is. He, too, seemed to possess the gracefulness of a plains cat, though, again, it was in retrospect and part of her mind told her it might be just something she thought he should have. That thought was quickly pushed aside, however.

Thankfully, she didn't have to wait long for the woman to bring out two bowls of steaming stew and set them down in front of her. Her head was trying to ache from the thoughts and, in turn, her gut tightened. Still, her mouth began watering uncontrollably when the scent of the stew wafted up and curled into her nose. The charred odor of boiled meat and vegetables that had been in the pot too long rode the smell and the stuff lay in the bottom of the heavy wooden bowls in a lumpy brown mass, but that didn't keep her stomach from rumbling.

She shoveled a spoonful into her mouth and chewed rapidly. The concoction was mostly bland, the only tang from being scorched. And hot, burning the roof of her mouth. But it was certainly better than the dried strips of meat she and Kiyo had been eating. She quickly gulped down several overfull bites before she picked the bowls up and headed upstairs, then took a few more once she was there. The little table between the two beds held them both when she left, not disturbing Kiyo from his strange sleep. He would smell the stew and would eat if he was hungry.

Her pack in hand, she left the Inn, met the waiting Sir Levett, and headed for the castle, now a gloomy, stiff blackness looming in the darkness ahead. Her body prickled from the coolness of the night air. The closer she got, the more her stomach clenched. Logically, she saw no reason for the foreboding feeling that radiated out from her guts, but it was there. The clink and scrape presence beside her made it more tangible, and a shiver not born of the cool air crawled through her once the heavy stone of the gate keep surrounded her, blocking out the stars, moon, and sky. The heavy musty smell of the entrance invaded her nose, causing her nostrils to flare and eyes to narrow.

There was a brief respite when she broke out into the wan moonlight bathing the large courtyard between the walls and the castle proper, but it was quickly washed away when she looked upon the oppressive structure crouching on a low rise at the back of the open space. It lorded over several smaller buildings scattered around the inner walls like some giant spider watching over the prey snarled in its web.

And she was being led right to it. This time, the shiver stayed at the nape of her neck, a sort of hovering tickle. This was a marvel of the outside world that she decided she could do without. How unfortunate that she couldn't have come up with that conclusion upon exiting the structure, instead of entering it.

After a brief nod to the guards flanking the doors, Sir Levett opened it on a sudden constriction in her chest and a difficulty in breathing as he led her inside. The thick stone walls seemed to form very narrow alleyways even though she couldn't touch both with outstretched arms. Dust scent was strong here, and it mixed heavily with the odor of oil and pitch burning in lamps. It made the air seem dense and only aggravated her strained breathing.

At some point, Sir Levett asked her if she was alright and was answered with a terse nod. Her focus was pushed ahead of her, leaving her peripheral vision washed out and gray. All except for the figure of Levett, which became an anchor for her senses so they wouldn't be swallowed in the oppressive stone around her. Everything else was ignored or proved a distraction that made her throat coil.

Eventually, Maelyrin's guide brought her to a room in which an older man with a careworn face and tired eyes greeted her. Sir Levett introduced him as Sir Dalek, the outpost's physician, before he bowed out of the room, leaving her without her mental support. She found herself sitting in a hard, high backed chair, looking over a plain of wood at him. He was a big man, even if slowed by tiredness.

"I apologize for rousing you at this hour, but one of the men said you are a healer," Sir Dalek said after Levett pulled the door closed. "Is this true?"

She nodded, her throat as yet too dry for her to form words without a croak. His eyes fluttered.

"Excellent," he said. "Are you a true healer?"

"I am not sure I understand," she answered.

"Are you a healer by virtue of faith or magic?"

"No," she said, watching the light of hope in his eyes begin to fade. "I am a natural healer. An herbalist."

Dalek had been sitting forward like he was straining against bonds holding him in his chair, but her news sent him sinking back into the dark wood, deflated.

"Is this not the news you were hoping for?" she said.

"Not exactly," he said. "It was a long shot, but I had hoped you were a healer of the magical sort."

"Why is that?"

"The man you saw this morning. . . ." he said. "Has not responded well to my ministrations. . . . Perhaps the Ffolk have a remedy?"

"What happened?"

"He was attacked by something. . . we don't know what . . . I've worked on him all day and the wounds don't want to close. He's feverish. . . I'm at my wits end."

"I don't know if I can help," she said. "But I am willing to help wherever I can."

"Thank you," he said, standing. "I shall take you to him."

"Ah," she said. "My supply of herbs is low. I may need to borrow some."

"What kind?"

"Um. . . I won't know until I see him," she said.

"Of course." Dalek moved to the door, he was stooped and walked a little slowly. His tired body popped and crackled at the sudden movement. "This way please," he said holding the door open.

Maelyrin swallowed hard when she followed his movement with her eyes and looked out into the gaping corridor. It took a force of will for her to get up and follow him. She didn't realize the room offered a break from the stifle and, immediately, the oppressiveness of the keep settled again around her when she stepped after Dalek.

He moved along ahead of her, a great shambling bear of a man that blocked a lot of the view from her. The plain woolen robes he wore whisked soothingly along the floor. It helped, tremendously. The walk through the halls from Dalek's office to the room they had sequestered the injured man did not seem quite as burdensome as the one that brought her to the big man's office.

The man she saw earlier that morning lay on a large bed. He was clean now and pristine bandages wrapped his chest and arms and part of his face and neck. Though thick down blankets covered most of him and sweat beaded and trickled down his forehead and face, he shivered in occasional wracking bursts. His skin was still pasty in places and bruised and puffy in others. He looked about as well as the bandit did after meeting with Kiyo, only he was still breathing. Or trying to. The man was drawing in long wheezing breaths and releasing shuddering guffs of air. A stench hovered in the air, something like over-fermented yeast. Reflexively, she gagged and had to stifle it with the back of her wrist.

"He's hovering on the brink of death," Dalek said. "And has been that way since we brought him in."

"What have you done for him so far?" she said, sliding up next to the bed and sitting down on a stool placed there.

"Cleaned his wounds with melaleaf salve and gave him some willowbark tea," he said. "It helped, but only a little."

"Do you have any ashroot?" she said, looking up at Dalek. "And meadowsweet?"

"Yes," he answered, his brows raising. "But. . . won't ashroot kill him?"

"Not if you mix it with the meadowsweet," she said. "One part for every two of the meadowsweet. It fights fever better than just willowbark. Though, he might have contracted a poison. . . You may want to try out some leechseed oil, if you have some."

"We can get it in Hestaff," he said.

"It would be better if you knew what attacked him," she said. "Though the leechseed oil works well as a general nullifier. What's his name?"

"Lord Edric," he said.

Maelyrin turned her eyes back onto the man lying in the bed, Lord Edric, and touched him softly on the head, neck, then wrist, letting her fingers linger as she did so, concentration etched on her face. She shook her head. "Whatever you do, I don't think it will be enough," she said softly. "His lifebeat is weak and irregular. Is he strong willed?"

Sir Dalek snorted. "Lord Edric? Yes, extremely."

"That may be what keeps him alive over the next few hours, maybe days. Are there healers?. . . In Hestaff?"

"Yes," he said. "In fact, an Earthmother and her companions just left for Hestaff this morning. Too bad they were gone by the time Lord Edric returned."

"An Earthmother. . . this morning?" she said, Lord Edric forgotten as her interest spiked.

"Yes," he answered, a blank look on his face. "She and her companions."

Her heart began thrumming rapidly. "Was one of them a man named Marc Pendragon?"

Dalek blinked. "Why. . . yes, as a matter of fact Lord Pendragon was with her," he said. "You know him?"

"Yes," she said. She couldn't contain the smile that swept across her face, cramping her cheek muscles. "We are trying to find him."

"We?" he said. "Oh. . . the Eldythian . . . Well, they are in Hestaff by now."

"How far is it there?" she asked, her breath coming quickly, her pulse racing. It was, again, one of the moments she had longed to hear. Confirmation. It was him she saw this morning. She was very close.

"Just under a day's travel," he said. "You can be there by tomorrow evening if you leave in the morn---Where are you going?"

"I'm sorry, I must go," she said, gathering her pack from the floor and standing. "Prepare the ashroot and meadowsweet as I've said and it may help Sir Edric. The leechseed oil, too." She went through the door and stopped suddenly, then looked back with a sheepish smile. "Ah," she said. "Would you kindly show me out."

He nodded absently. "Yes, of course," he said.

Relief flooded into her when she was on the road again and running toward the inn. She still had difficulty breathing, but it wasn't from the oppressiveness of the stone keep now, but the excitement that was running through her, making her heart pound, her spine tingle.

Maelyrin could barely contain it when she slammed through the door, trotted across the common room floor and up the stairs. She stopped only when she was outside the door to the room she shared with Kiyo took a few moments to compose herself, then gently pushed the door open. The giant was still sitting in the same position he was in when she left and the stew remained, untouched, on the table, no longer steaming.

Her heart fell, splashing down in a guilt ridden puddle. Aching, she sat down on the bed and put her face in her hands and dry washed her skin in a long stroke that ended with her chin rested on closed fists. She stared blankly at Kiyo while she tried to rid her mouth of the bitter taste that just crept into it.

What she had been contemplating, she could not do. There was no way without jeopardizing Kiyo's safety.

She blew out the breath she had been holding, uncorking the disappointment she had tried to keep bottled.

They would have to wait. They could not go after him tonight, maybe not even tomorrow. Her only hope was that Marc Pendragon and his companions were planning to stay in Hestaff for a while, at least until Kiyo and she could catch up to them. She gritted her teeth momentarily, clenched her hands and lay back heavily on the bed, a sigh breaking from her. Ignoring her frustration was difficult, but she was able to push it out of the forefront of her brain long enough to admonish herself for her selfishness.

The yawn that came next surprised her, but also seemed to settle into her body like leaden rain. The journey, it seemed, was taking its toll on her body, one not accustomed to the rigors of travel. Whether from defeat or just need, she squirmed around lengthwise on the bed, trying to simultaneously kick off her boots. When it didn't work, she sat up, frustrated, pulled them off by hand and tossed them to the floor. Then, she drew back the blankets, turned down the lamp, and curled up in the instant gloom.

Her mind wanted to dwell on the previous excitement of her nearness to her goal, and she allowed it to for many long minutes, then moved her thoughts to more mundane things when it began to become an ache of anticipation. She even thought about eating the rest of the stew then decided against it. The gray mass of glop it became upon cooling was far from appetizing, and though she needed it, the anxiety she was ignoring cinched her stomach up enough that it was silent.

Instead, she concentrated on going to sleep.

Chapter 66

Distractions

*7*he pink eastern sky found Marc strolling the near empty streets of Hestaff after a deep dreamless sleep of only a few hours. Above him, stars still glittered in the deep blue welkin not yet touched by the coming dawn. Whispering silence wrapped him in an envelope of peacefulness, and he all but ignored the slinking figures and peering eyes that followed him from the black curtains draping the alleyways. Footpads and cutpurses that took only moments to make sure he was not a guard. Or a victim. The lingering chill invigorated him while the breeze kept the sour smell of the city and dead fish odor of the wharf from settling.

Marc walked down wide avenues and narrow streets, down to the docks and back again, on roads traveled hundreds of times in the past and some never trodden by his boots. Thoughts meandered through his mind, some flittering by without pause, some gliding by drawing some interest. Most thoughts that hung full in front of him were of Alexandra. And him. And his curse.

When he finally got back to the Inn, he veered toward the stable instead of the main building and stepped into the dimness. He looked around while taking in the heavy scent of hay, sweetened oats, and alfalfa. Several of the stalls were occupied by steeds that were anything but nags; stallions and mares that bore the strength and bearing necessary for mounted knights, even ones that didn't seem like it. Whickers and snorts reached out from the tiny pens along with contented munching and the occasional hoof against wood. The stable hand was not inside, but the other door, at the end of the wide aisle he stood in, was open.

Marc took a brush from a nearby peg and headed for the stall in which Whitesteel was residing. The horse greeted him with a soft nicker through quivering lips once he spied him coming down the aisle.

"Hey, boy," Marc said, patting the great head when it hovered over the stall door and nudged at him. Whitesteel whickered again. "How are you this morning? Being treated well?"

Whitesteel snorted and pulled his lips back from his teeth. "You've seen better, huh?" Marc said, smiling. "You haven't bitten anyone have you?"

The horse nodded his huge head, eliciting a soft chuckle from Marc. Patting one strong cheek with his empty hand, Marc started brushing the other with the brush he held. Whitesteel nudged him once before stilling for the attention.

Marc quickly lost himself in the activity, brushing the stallion's gleaming coat with long, slow strokes, working the whisk along his cheeks and neck while minutes slid by. When he finished the areas he could reach beyond the wooden barrier separating them, he caught the latch in his hand and was about to throw it when a rose petal scent flowed around him and tickled his nose. He smiled even before the dusky voice whispered through the dimness.

"I thought you might be in here with that old mule," she said. Whitesteel snorted, his ears laid back in warning. Marc moved his vision from around the blocking head of his great steed to look at the visitor.

"Hello, witch," he said to the woman leaning against a nearby post. She calmly reached up and brushed fiery red, full wavelets of hair from the flawless plains of alabaster skin and deep icy green of her eyes. Her hip moved, ever so slightly, allowing her long silken skirts to split and slide away from her leading leg, revealing the toned, tan limb from ankle to soft, buttery upper thigh. Though Marc knew it was intentional, the maneuver didn't keep his blood from rushing, stoking his body to react.

"Witch?" she said. "Is that any way to greet me after all this time?" She stepped up into him, parting her full lips slightly and tilting her head up. Immediately, Marc's arm wrapped around the small of her back and drew her into his tense body tightly as he met her mouth with his.

The kiss lingered for several intense seconds before he pulled away and said, his voice low and hoarse, "Hello, Sharla. It's been awhile."

"That's better," she said, lips drawing back from ivory teeth for only a moment before she returned heatedly to his mouth. Minutes passed as they explored each other's awakening passion.

"What are you doing this—"

"Shhh," She placed a finger across his lips and said, breathless, "It can wait until after we make up for lost time."

He grinned and asked, "What about the stable boy?"

The smoke within her eyes parted enough for mirth to show through. "He's busy chasing a loose horse," she said, moving languorously against him.

"A horse?" Marc said.

"Does it matter?" she replied.

"No." Their mouths found each other again as gripping hands moved and explored plains of muscle and skin beneath material. Marc maneuvered her until her back was against the ladder leading to the loft. With a heavy sigh that did not break their intensifying kiss, she stepped onto the first rung, lifting her body without the use of her eyes. He followed, stepping on a protesting rung each time she moved higher. When he lost contact with her mouth, he went immediately to the soft flesh of her neck, caressing the hollows and contours while she curled slim fingers into the hair at the back of his neck to keep his hungering lips against her.

They inched their way up the ladder, sinuously entwining and disentangling as they moved, but never enough to part from each other's anxious grasp. Heavy breaths and impassioned sighs filled the stable, and the musk of their eagerly clasping bodies filled his nostrils.

Finally, Sharla topped the ladder and slid backward onto the hey strewn mat that covered the floor of the loft, dragging Marc with her with burning, frustrated lips. They twined their bodies again, fiercely, Marc searching out her mouth with his as his hands moved over her body. Gasping, Sharla frantically pulled at the bindings of his clothing. With ardent knotted confusion, they both worked to free themselves of the material obstacles while unwilling to relent their desire for even the briefest moment.

Outside, Alexandra turned away from the open stable doors, her face an unreadable mask of neutrality. Quickly, she walked from the Inn grounds and onto the street where she could hail a carriage to take her to the coast, all the while ignoring the muffled sounds coming from the stable loft.

Chapter 67

Unexpected Gifts

*G*olden light spilled in through the thrown sash and immersed Maelyrin in cozy warmth which coaxed her into a semi-consciousness that allowed her to enjoy the nestled snugness provided by the thick blankets wrapping her body. Several times, she turned over and stretched slowly, exposing cool skin to warm softness and warm skin to cool breezes. She thought she could hear the sonorous tones of the Prime Elder as he spoke to someone else, probably the Faethe, and smiled against her pillow.

But in her fuzzed state, the smile flipped, and her brows came together. Instead of the fresh loamy scent of her hut, her nose picked up a spice laced odor. Instead of the quiet murmurs of her village, her ears vibrated to sharp noises. The clop of hoof against worn cobbles. The creaking of wood and metal. The quick, harsh cries of loud voices. Her first thought was visitors in the village. Maybe a trader caravan, or lost travelers.

Maybe it was an attack.

That thought brought her from the comfort zone into stark awakening quickly, and she bolted upright. So fast that a wave of dizziness undulated across the front of her skull. Her eyes went from wide back to heavy lidded and felt like they were going to fall out of her head. The Prime Elder's voice dispersed like mist.

The realization that she wasn't in her village sliced her insides as it passed through her. She was still in South Watch, a place not far from her home in physical steps, but far, far away with the passage of time. The frustration she felt the night before rolled up through her spine and lodged into the corners of her eyes where they burned like salt.

It took several heartbeats of messaging her temples and wiping her eyes for the tears to clear and the pressure to release enough for her mind to begin clicking over. The half dream of being home faded into the background noises just as Solarin's voice had.

At length, her head drooped and she began looking around the room in a sluggish sweep while trying to rid her mouth of fuzz. The window was open, looking out on the never ending plain of waving grass, letting in the gentle breeze and autumn-slanted sunlight to wash the room with clean air and comforting light. Stray dust motes gleamed momentarily as they drifted through direct beams.

Maelyrin stared out the portal for a time before sweeping her gaze across the surface of the neatly made bed next to hers, over the clean table between them, up the wall, and to a point on the ceiling directly above her where she affixed it on a squashed bug carcass as she breathed in the refreshing air in deep, full rhythms.

Again she began thinking of home, this time with the cool assertion of nostalgia wrapped in the cotton of her will. It seemed to her the longer she was gone, the less she remembered the looks of fear and hiss of whispers. She remembered more the quiet laughter, and soothing, musical tones. Mothers singing to the young, fathers teaching them about the woodlands. The Faethe's instructions and sentimental ramblings. The Prime Elder's careworn eyes and stolid face.

A wan smile worked onto her mouth. *Funny how quickly things can change*, she thought. *Not so long ago, I was only concerned with how everyone was treating me. Now, all I can think about is how much I miss them. I must be suffering from some sort of brain fever.*

She suddenly blinked as another thought slid into her mind. *The bed is empty.* Her head jerked down, and she stared at the emptiness next to her. Her heart leapt and, for just a second, she wondered if she were still stuck in the half dream she had been entertaining only minutes ago. "Kiyo. . . ." she said, as if invoking his name would cause him to materialize in front of her. *Where is he?*

She rubbed her temples again in an attempt to banish the lingering fog clogging her brain. Another thought occurred to her, and a metallic tang ran down the back of her throat. *They found out what he really was and came and got him. . . .* the thought whispered. Maelyrin was suddenly alert as the room took on a sinister presence, like a slime trail left by a slug on a branch she was about to pick up.

A cold, wet trail. She shivered at the possibility the room was violated while she slept, unknowing.

"Stop it," she said, gritting her teeth. "You're being childish." The fluttering beneath her breastbone did not stop, though, and it caused her to move rapidly to the door and down the stairs in her bare feet, leaving the door half open on cringing hinges. The floor was rough and protested loudly even at her slight weight, but she ignored it, not caring if it became a harbinger to anyone waiting for her downstairs.

She pounded into the common room, squinting against the bright sunlight beaming through the open windows and doors facing the ancient road.

Kiyo looked up from a steaming cup and flashed one of his fierce grins. "Good morning, Maelyrin," he said.

The only other person in the room was the squirrelly, slinking creature she barked at the day before. She ignored him and crossed the room and sat down across from the giant, the table absurdly tiny against his frame. No words formed for her to speak although she tried to say something several times.

"What is wrong?" Kiyo said.

"Ah . . . You're well. . . ." she finally was able to blurt. He grinned again.

"Yes, the wound is better," he said. "My thanks for watching over me. The food you acquired was revitalizing."

"The stew?" she said. Her stomach burbled and her throat clenched. "Ah. . . you're welcome. Are you able to travel?"

"Yes," he said. "We can leave as soon as you are ready."

She struggled, but the wide smile broke out on her face. It took her a couple of minutes to wrangle it back down into something more manageable to speak around. "Are you sure?" She waited for his nod, then said, "Excellent."

"I sense we are close to your Marc Pendragon," he said.

It was her turn to nod. "Yes, he was here yesterday morning. His party is in Hestaff. A day's travel from here."

"How did you find this out?" he asked.

"The local healer told me," she said. Suddenly, she felt guilty, remembering how she ran out of the keep last night, leaving him with the wounded man who deserved more than she had given. *How selfish I am*, she thought. *To have let my personal feelings get in front of someone's pain and suffering. I must apologize. I must see if there is more that I can do.*

A part of her yelled out a refusal, claiming time lost. It clenched her guts and dredged up more guilt. She wrestled it, kept it at bay with promises that it wouldn't last long. That there was little she could do for the man. That his life was up to his own stubbornness. But she had to check on him, as much to allay her guilt as genuinely make sure there was nothing she could do. Maybe she overlooked something in her rush to leave. *How childish I was.* "I have to speak to him once more before we leave," she said.

"Very well," he said. "I shall finish my broth and prepare for our departure."

"Yes. I will return." Maelyrin was standing before she finished and leaving the tavern before she thought to say anything else. A moment later, standing on the porch, she noticed her feet and, sheepishly, returned to the room to put on her boots.

The point below where her thin eyebrows met itched dully and the back of her neck was tight. The discomfort she felt, the uncertainty, cast her back when she was a child under her father's scrutiny. Awkward, gangly, unthinking. Only it was ten times worse now because she was a grown woman. Or was supposed to be. Maelyrin couldn't shake the feeling that, somehow, she would always feel inadequate; feel like she was making one rushed mistake after another. Especially around someone like Kiyo, who seemed to have an answer for every situation.

So thoughtful was she that she stumbled on the small stairway in front of Tonk's. Her face went red, and she was suddenly hot. Though she wanted to look around, on some level, to see if anyone was staring at her, Maelyrin instead fixed her gaze on the worn stone of the road in front of her and picked her way toward the keep with careful abandon.

She went through the gate keep unhindered but was met with resistance when she mounted the steps in front of the large doors. Her request to see Sir Dalek sent one of the bored looking guards through the inset door while the other three eyed her intimately. Maelyrin shifted from one foot to the other in an attempt to ignore the looks, but they left her with an oily feeling on her skin. She held back a sigh of relief when the smaller door reopened and the bearish face of Sir Dalek squinted out at her.

"Hello, child," he said with a tired smile. "What can I do for you?"

"I came back to check on . . . Lord. . . Edric," she said.

Dalek stared a moment. "Yes, alright," he said, pushing the door open further. "Come in. We shall go see him together."

He led her into the yawning darkness, the bang of the door making it worse despite the flickering lamps that lit the way.

"From the way you left out of here last night, I would have thought you would be half way to Hestaff by now," he said.

"I want to apologize for that," she said. Her voice echoed in the corridor like some unrested spirit. "I got a little over anxious."

"No need," he said. "I was young once."

Her step stuttered. *What is that supposed to mean? That I'm foolish?* "Has. . . uh. . . Lord Edric responded to the ashroot and meadowsweet?" she said. *I am foolish. A foolish little girl.*

"Yes, yes," the shambling man replied. "Quite well actually. You have our gratitude. He hasn't awakened, yet, but his wounds are beginning to close."

"The shivers and pallid skin?" she asked.

"Not as bad," he said. "We've sent a runner for some leechseed oil." He turned a corner and surprised the knight sitting outside Edric's door. The man stood hurriedly, wiping the blear from his eyes. Dalek waved him back into the chair he had been dozing on, then opened the door.

Lord Edric still lay as he had the night before, but his color had returned. The bruises he bore were just starting to yellow around the edges, and the swelling that disfigured his face was significantly less. *Good.* She sat on a stool that stood next to him and checked his heart beat under the skin of his wrist. A stronger, more insistent thud greeted her probing fingertips. *Good.*

Like a fog before bright sunlight, her feelings of insecurity vanished as the years of her training took over. She was focused, mindful only of the man lying before her. And now that she had a clear direction in which to proceed, now that she knew where Marc Pendragon was, she was calmer, unable to be distracted, like a river widening and deepening after confining rapids, allowing the water to run still.

She moved her fingers up to the lifebeat at his throat. A shiver rolled through him and he moaned, but it wasn't as strong as the tremors that shook through him last night. His eyelids fluttered. Maelyrin nodded. "He's doing much better," she said.

"Excellent," Dalek said.

Maelyrin looked at his forearms, pressed in the flesh and ran her fingers along the veins and arteries that lay beneath the muscled flesh. Replaced his arms and lifted the bandages on his face to look at the gashes beneath. "I don't think the leechseed oil is necessary, now," she said finally, then looked up at Sir Dalek. His bushy brows lifted.

"He's not poisoned?" he asked.

"I don't think so," she said. There was a questioning tone in her voice that belied her true meaning. He was not poisoned. She was sure of it.

"You're certain," he said.

"Yes."

"How can you be sure?"

I don't know! "I just am," she said. "Though you can still use the leechseed once you get it, if you're not sure. It will do no harm."

"No, no," he said with a huff. "I trust your judgment. If it weren't for you being here in the first place, he probably would not have lasted this long."

"I think it's fair to say that we just got lucky," Maelyrin said. "Or, he did." She glanced at the still sleeping form of Lord Edric. A sense of relief washed through her and she smiled. "Is there anything else that you might require?"

The big man returned her smile warmly and shook his head. "No, no, you've done more than enough," he said. "Now, what can we do for you and your companion?"

"Uh. . . ." Her words caught in her throat. *Nothing. We require nothing*, she was about to say. It was a reflex and stop gap saying that she used many, many times for those in her village for false gratitude that never really covered up their fear and distrust. Now, she caught it and *Looked* at Sir Dalek. Consciously, she bypassed the exhaustion that permeated him and found a genuine gratefulness there within him. And also a wish to assist her. Tentatively, she rolled her mind over things they needed, things lost or used up during their harrowing flight from the forest and those. . . creatures. Those hideous puckering demons that, even now in the safety of the keep, made her shiver. "We need some herbs and such, and I lost my bow. If you can spare one, I would be grateful."

"Done and done," he said. "Come, let me take you to my stores, and you can take what you need while I arrange for a bow."

"Thank you," she said.

It took her only a few minutes to pick out the herbs she needed, mostly ones that helped close wounds and kept out the poisons that could get into an unclean one. Some meadowsweet, ashroot, goldenseal and dragon's blood among others. She also picked out ones that would help pain: willow, some choice peppers and mints. When she was done, she had a wrapped bundle that fit comfortably in the crook of her arm. Comfortable on more than one level.

Sir Dalek returned carrying a fine ash bow and had a full quiver of arrows which he handed over with a grateful smile. "I also took the liberty of talking to Lord Baland," he said, pulling a sealed scroll tube from his robe and handing it to her.

"What's this?" she asked, her brows knitted and pinched.

"Present this to the door man at the Gaping Grouper Inn in Hestaff," he said. "It is where Marc Pendragon and his party went."

"It is?" she asked, looking at the scroll tube as if doing so would call him forth. "W-where is this . . . Inn?"

He withdrew a folded piece of parchment and handed that to her as well. She was beginning to get overloaded, and he took the bow and quiver from her so she didn't end up dropping everything she had in a bumbling shower. "I took the liberty of drawing you a map."

"Thank you, Sir Dalek," she said. Her eyes started to moisten "You don't know how much this means to me."

"Just be well," he said. "The further north you get, the more chaos you will find."

"Thank you, again," she said.

"Please," he said, holding an arm out to the corridor. "Allow me to escort you out."

The walk out was a slow lifting of clouds that pressed in on her. Even with the elation she felt from the news and assistance Sir Dalek gave her, the heaviness of the stone around her was still a presence felt. The daylight beyond freed the binding from around her chest. Maelyrin was grateful of the escort, and thanked him again just before they parted company at the gate house. "Know that you are welcome here anytime," Sir Dalek said as she began the walk through the airy tunnel, and she thanked him again.

Sir Dalek lingered at the inner gatehouse, watching the young woman glide through the wide arched passage. When she was out on the old road and heading back toward Tonk's, he strolled underneath the shaded area until he was standing by the outer gatehouse. The nearby guards were standing at sudden, surprised attention, but he largely ignored them, instead, pulled a pipe from a leather pouch he carried and thumbed some tobacco into the bowl, packed it in, then looked around for a splint to fire on a nearby lantern.

Once he was puffing contentedly, he lay his gaze on the small building across the worn highway, hoping to catch a glimpse of the Eldythian and leaned against the heavy cool stone. It had been a long time since he saw one of the blue giants but it was not something he would forget. Nor the way the huge, armored creature cut his way through a hoard of Skor regulars during the siege at Barrist Castle all those many years ago when he was young and full of spit.

He missed the chance to speak with him then, and, now, with another in his midst, he half considered talking to the young Traelynn's companion. Just to find out what he was like. What made him the thing that everyone populating the aging stone edifice behind him was trying to emulate whether they knew it or not. Dalek wanted to know why they were the epitome of knighthood and why it seemed so easy for them. He half wanted to, anyway.

Like Baland, he was getting too old to wonder too much about anything but getting through the day, and the next and the next. But still, it was something to think about. Dalek doubted very much he would approach him. It was only a passing interest. Some kind of throwback to what might have been; some kind of grasp at a youth far gone. It was not enough to interrupt the smooth taste and pungent comforting scent from his pipe. There were very few things important enough to disturb that, and nostalgia just wasn't one of them.

Several minutes later, that little rat of a man, Tonk, brought about the woman's horse from the stables and tied the newly saddled beast to the hitching post near the entrance stairs. Dalek took a few slow puffs of the pipe, eyes fixed on the doorway, even as it faded from view behind a wave of white smoke. He didn't have to wait long before the woman was standing on the porch, a travel cloak clasped around her neck, a pack strapped over her shoulder, and proudly holding the bow he had given her.

When the giant ducked under the door and moved down into the light, he took the pipe from his mouth, blew out his puff, and crossed his arm. He had to squint, the morning sun still glaring at him from a still low angle in the sky, but more because the scene before him wasn't right and was working through the attic of his mind. Once he came upon the trunk he was looking for, his sword hand moved towards a weapon that rarely hung at his belt, that was now leaning against a chair in his chambers.

The girl's companion was not an Eldythian. He knew
that the moment the creature stepped into the light and wasn't
decked from head to toe in strange, glimmering armor. Though
that long ago time was only a memory, it was a vivid memory.
And what other knowledge he gathered over the years about the
unusual race all worked against what he watched. Indeed, the
giant looked very much like an Eldythian, and he could see
how easily one could come to that conclusion. Except for the
white hair, he might have made the same assumption had the
creature been wearing the armor.

No, the young Traelynn's companion was not an
Eldythian. He was, or was closely related to, a Turgatha.

His gaze flicked over to the silvered haired woman, now
sitting astride the horse and speaking to the Turgatha with such
candor and air of trust that he resisted his impulse to sound the
alert and have the despicable beast put under the sword. Had he
wandered into the area on his own, he might have done so,
despite his thoughtfulness about the world around him. There
were few things that warranted that type of behavior. One was
when facing a full unit of armed Skor after they send the
Parlayer back in several pieces. Another was the Turgatha
anytime they set their filthy murdering feet outside their
islands.

Nonetheless, he stayed his voice and forced himself to
lean back on the building as if the cool stone could somehow
help him study the situation with a clearer point of view.

The last he remembered, even the Traelynn attacked the
Turgatha on sight. Sometimes to their own detriment, but here
was a fair, young, and even innocent Traelynn woman openly
consorting with the racial enemy of her people. Not only that,
the Turgatha was speaking and interacting with her in a manner
that was anything but the violent, terrible nature that he was so
accustomed to. In fact, didn't he see a report several months
ago about a Turgatha up north. One that massacred an entire
village just to sate his own bloodlust. And standing before him
was another one.

Yet, this one wasn't massacring anyone or anything. At least not now. Could there be a peaceful one among them? Like the rare but real, Skoran guides, or a Reptal priest? He wasn't convinced, but he decided he would not air his concerns. At least not at the moment. More time would give him the answer, and the men at the safe house in Hestaff, whom he decided to contact in a day or two.

When the odd companions began moving down the road, he placed the end of his pipe between his teeth and drew in a long breath that brought nothing but the ash taste of tobacco that no longer held an ember.

Chapter 68

An Unexpected Answer

"So what brings you to Hestaff?" Sharla said, kissed Marc playfully.

"Hmm?" Marc was idly caressing her belly, watching the tracks he made in the sheen of sweat with his fingertips. Although their breathing was returning to normal, the heat they generated still wrapped them in a comforting blanket. His body was loose, his mind lucid, but not groggy or tired. However, his thoughts were silent, and his ears far away.

Sharla nibbled at one then whispered her question again once she had his attention.

"What brings you to Hestaff?" Marc said, still watching his gliding fingers against her tight skin. "Ouch!"

"I asked you first," she said after withdrawing from his earlobe. Marc laughed.

"Heading to Calif," he said, looking into her eyes. He suddenly realized how similar they were to Alexandra's. Deep, icy, knowing. "What about you?"

"Setting up a safety net for the resistance," she said.

"The resistance?" he said, pulling his head away so he could see her better. "What are you doing working for the resistance?"

"With the resistance," she retorted. "There's a difference."

"Oh, yea, big difference."

She smirked and tugged him in for another kiss. "Haven't you ever done anything just because?"

"What do you think?"

"That's not what I mean," she said, then nipped his lip.

"Sure," he said through a wide smile. "I wander up and down the whole of Arquilon."

"Well," she said. "I help out a resistance once in a while."

"Really?"

"This one is different," she said, her face setting. "This one is important."

"So I've heard," he said. "How long have you been involved."

"Since its inception," she said, looking past him at the bird limed rafters. "I helped found it."

"You helped. . . . Why?"

"Because it's important," she said.

"But I thought this Owl person was supposed to found the resistance," Marc said.

"He disappeared shortly after the Dark Night," she said. "And no one has seen him since. The resistance cannot wait until his cowardliness drifts away with the dandelion seeds."

"That's a little harsh, isn't it?" Marc said.

"Maybe, but the result is still the same. He isn't supporting the cause that he was supposedly born to. If there is any chance at all of opposing the Emperor, it is now, when he is still garnering his power. If this person calling himself the Owl is who everyone is waiting on, then he needs to help us rather than hinder us."

"How is he hindering you?"

"Pardon me for saying this, but his remaining in hiding is causing a lot of resistance from others in committing," she said. "There are a lot of small groups of rebels, but they are separated by distance, views, whatever. If he is who he is supposed to be, the Owl can unify these smaller groups and draw the reluctant to join the fight."

"You're really involved in this . . . ." Marc said.

"How could you tell?" she quipped.

"It's been a while since I saw you so interested in something," he said.

"Really?" she said, her fingers playing down his chest. "And you call this a chore?"

"That's not what I mean," he said and finished his echoing remark by grabbing her lower lip with his teeth and letting go. She pulled him in for another round of kisses.

"Now," she said once they stopped. "Why are you heading to Calif with an Earthmother, her Guardian, and a young boy?"

He blinked, looked at her for a few beats of his heart. "How did you know about them?" he said.

"I saw you come in with them," she said. "I was waiting to see you."

"Oh?" he said. "And how did you know to wait?"

She studied his eyes for a moment then looked down between their bodies and tapped the pendant he was wearing. "I always know where you are. . . with this."

"With this?" He pulled the amulet up by its thong and let it dangle between them. The jewel in the center caught the dim light within the stable and glittered. Sharla nodded. "What is this?"

"You've forgotten. . ." she said. "But then. . . I guess you are supposed to."

"What?"

"To protect you, it."

"I don't understand," Marc said, looking from the pendant, to her, and back again. She coiled some of his hair around her finger, studied it for a second, smiled.

"Marc," she said. "It's a piece of the Heartstone."

"Heart. . . you don't believe in that myth do you?"

"You have forgotten," she said, brushing the hair back and drawing her hand softly down his cheek. Her face suddenly took on a deeply serious expression. "Listen, be careful. The

Emperor has a standing bounty on Earthmothers and those she travels with."

"We're going to Calif," he said. "Not into Imperial lands."

"The Tricouncil is flirting with the Emperor for assistance," she said. "To get them through their problems and the upcoming attack."

"What attack?"

Sharla's chuckle was partly dry. "Sorry," she said. "I sometimes forget I get information more quickly than some, though I thought your knight friends already knew that Balinoch has declared war on Calif and Flandric's armies are marching on it as we speak."

"No. I knew nothing of the sort," he said. "I suppose that explains what you meant by 'safety net'."

She curled into him, possibly a response to the dissipating heat, though he suspected there was also a need for comfort there. "Yes," she said. "If the Tricouncil comes to some alliance with the Emperor, our base of operations will be compromised. I've been setting up a new one down here. I'm going back to get the rest of the Ten ready to evacuate."

"When?"

"Today," she said.

"When today?" he asked.

"Soon," she said. "Soon." Sharla reached up and pulled his head against her insistent lips again, this time letting it linger until his blood was stoked to boiling. "Just long enough," she whispered in his ear, her pause not giving him time to answer before she was exploring his mouth once more with soft probing kisses. He met them with anxious fierceness, pulling her close, devouring her taste as his hands moved along silky skin, grasping, clutching, as if he could draw her body into his.

Long, slow minutes flowed by as they moved together, the energy of their heat and desire exchanging, combining, coiling them in a single envelope of rushing intensity that swelled with each passing, timeless moment in sweet aching, until, in one forever flash, it burst in furious utterance and melancholy release.

Though spent, they nevertheless held each other tightly, reluctant to completely break the pause in time they shared, even as the envelope slowly dissipated, even as their breathing slowed and lengthened, even as their bodies reached equilibrium. They caressed each other, loved each other with an intimacy born of many years of friendship and a somber grasping of the inevitable that finally came when Sharla moved away with a final kiss and smile, restarting the suspension of time and passing the moment into memory.

They dressed slowly, silently and withdrew from the loft onto the floor of the stable where the whickers and snorts of the horses reached a realness that didn't exist only minutes prior. Again they held each other, filled with enlivened exhaustion and quiet contentment, and kissed for several seconds, this time with salient completeness rather than reckless abandon. "I must go," she said once their lips parted.

"Must you," Marc said. The intrusion of normalcy was coming too fast and he wasn't willing to acknowledge it yet. Sharla nodded into his chest, looked up with lucid, moist eyes.

"Yes, I must," she said. "I don't have much time."

"Nor I," he said. "It seems. But I don't want to let you go yet."

She tightened her grip around his large frame. "We can wait until the stable boy returns," she said, just as the sound of huffing and snorting and stomping hooves reached them from outside the back door. Marc sighed heavily and hugged her closely before letting go.

"Is Marrillon still knocking about up there in Calif?" he said.

Her face, relaxed into soft neutrality, took on the look of seriousness once more, her brows knitting over a frown. "Yes, why?"

"Something wrong?"

"Perhaps," she said. "Why are you asking?"

"Can you deliver a message to him?" Marc pressed.

"Why?" The crease between her brows deepened into a crevice.

"I need him to do something for me," he said.

"Do what?" she said.

"I get the feeling that you're not too happy with Marrillon these days," he said.

"He's. . . well . . . he's changed over the years," she said.

"How so?"

"What message do you want me to give him?" she said.

"You're changing the subject," he pointed out.

"Yes, I am," she said. "What do you want me tell him?"

"I need him to supply my cabin for me," he said.

"Is that all?" she said.

"Yes," Marc said. "That's all. . . That and tell him not to let anyone know we're coming."

"Yes, alright. . . yes, I can do that," she said. "But Marc, he's not the same anymore, I don't think you can trust him."

"Don't worry about me," he said.

She touched his cheek. "I can't help it," she said. "The closer you get to Calif, the more dangerous your journey gets for you and your friends."

"I'll be careful," he said.

"You care for her." It was not a question. Marc stared. "Don't even try to lie to me, you big dolt, I've known you for too long to allow a falsehood between us."

Marc expelled his breath and finally nodded. "Yes, yes I do."

She arched a brow. "She worth it?"

Marc smiled.

"Well, then," she said. "I suppose I can share you again."

"Really," he said. "How generous of you." His comment elicited another wide smile and a quick kiss on the cheek.

"Be careful, Marc," she said. "I mean it. Though I know who you are, what you are, I still don't want to see you hurt."

"I will," he said, looking back at the door where the noise of the stable boy and his charge was growing. "And you do the same. Especially now that you are playing with fire."

The door began creaking open. Sharla hugged and kissed him once more before stepping away from him, breaking completely the physical bond between them. "I will see you again," she said, backing toward the front of the stable.

"Promise?"

"Of course," Sharla said, and then was gone, not entirely outside before she faded from view courtesy of the powers she commanded. Marc stared at the place he last saw her until the surprised gasp of the stable boy flitted across the room from behind him.

"M-my lord?" the boy said.

Marc turned and studied the stable hand for several seconds, noting that he couldn't rightly call him a boy, but not yet a man, his young face just stained with a darkening fuzz around his mouth and up the sides of his face. "Yes?" he said, arching his brows with a sternness he didn't feel.

"N-n-nothing. . . .I mean. . . . How may I serve you, my lord?" He was kneading the leather lead line he held so tightly, Marc thought he might break the tough material.

"Prepare my steed," he ordered, inwardly smiling at the young man's flinch. "I shall return shortly to take him."

"Y-yes, my lord," the boy said. "Right away, my lord."

Marc had to turn quickly to hide the smile that suddenly broke onto his face, but he was able to bark out a passable, "Very good," before striding from the stable. His hope that he had the young man off kilter enough that he would not notice anything untoward in his disheveled appearance. Or anything else for that matter.

He angled quickly toward the Inn after his glance up into the sky revealed his interlude with Sharla lasted longer than he thought it had. The sun was nearing its apex. He had just enough time to slip into his room and straighten up before meeting with Alexandra.

Once done, he crossed the hall and gently knocked on her door. A second later, he knocked again, leaned in towards the stained wooden plane and listened, then knocked a third time. No answer came back to him and just for one brief moment a spider crawled through his guts. He checked the knob and found it unlocked, so turned it and looked through the slim window formed by the opening portal. The room was empty.

Confusion replaced the crawling spider. He drew the door closed and made his way downstairs. Marc found Smyethe reading in a sitting room right off the entry hall. His face was pinched in concentration, and he didn't immediately notice Marc even though he blocked a large portion of the light coming from the front windows. After a minute, he rapped softly on the door jam, startling the young man from his study.

"Lord Pendragon," he said. "I'm sorry, I didn't see you arrive."

"Marc," he said. "And that is alright. Have you seen Lady Alexandra this morning?"

"Yes," Smyethe said. "I saw her a little over an hour and a half ago. She said something about going to the coast."

"Did she," Marc mused.

"Yes," he said. "If you like, I can locate her for you."

That caught him off guard though he had a fairly good idea about the man's occupation in relation to the Hedrican Order. "Ah. . . . Will it take long?" He swallowed hard while silently berating himself for his lame question.

Smyethe smiled wanly and closed the book around his fingers. "No, not at all."

"Alright, then, yes. That would be well appreciated." Marc said around the dry lump in his throat.

"Very well, then," Smyethe said. He reached into a pocket of the livery he wore, then withdrew a hand closed about something. Without pause, he then closed his eyes and tilted his head back slightly. His lips moved briefly. His eyes began rapidly moving beneath the lids, as if he were deep in the throes of sleep and viewing some particularly horrendous dream. A small clock ticked off seconds from its perch on a mantel above a small fireplace on the opposite wall. Its breathing the only sound in the room and, seemingly, within the whole Inn. Finally, Smyethe opened his eyes and looked over at him, his eyes bleary and his neck taking on a rubbery aspect. "She's near Mordland's Cove. About three leagues up from the westernmost dock," he said, his voice a bit slurred.

Marc nodded. "Thank you," he said.

"No problem," Smyethe said and pulled his book back into his lap with noticeable lethargy. Marc realized that though the young man may be a Warmage, he was still largely inexperienced. And if a simple use of magic drained him as much as it seemed to, he would be quickly taken out of action should any situation occur that forced him to draw on his limited skills. Not a good sign.

Marc thanked him again, left the young man to his semblance of reading, and quickly made his way back to the stable. Whitesteel was waiting outside the stable door, tied loosely to a hitching post with his lead. The stable boy was moving through the small, fenced in exercise yard on the other side of the stables, running a rake through the ankle deep sand. The horse nipped Marc on the shoulder as he undid the lead.

"What'd you do that for, you old goat?" Marc said, looking into the horse's huge brown eyes. His answer was to nudge him roughly. "Hey!"

Quickly, he tightened the cinch strap the wily animal kept loose when the saddle was put on him by inhaling a deep breath and holding it while the stable boy worked the straps previously. The beast tried to bite his thigh and received a soft swat on the nose for his efforts. "Why are you so ornery today?"

Whitesteel snorted and laid his ears back.

"Yea, yea," he said, pulling himself up into the saddle to the creak of straining leather. He wasn't so busy with Whitesteel's behavior to notice the buffed shine in the tanned hide and to take in the heady scent of saddle soap mixed in with the leather. He would have to thank the stable boy once he returned.

He felt Whitesteel tense beneath him and drop almost imperceptibly toward the ground. "Don't even think about trying to buck me off, you mule," he said, taking up the reins. "Remember the last time you tried that stunt. Remember the big knot on your hard head from my armor. Just because you don't like Sharla much, doesn't mean you have to take it out on me."

Whitesteel threw his head up and down and nickered loudly.

"Keep it up," Marc said. "And I'll retire you to a meadow full of other swayback nags." He nudged him around with his knee, briefly considered kicking his flanks just to get his point across, but decided against it. He was still too contented to allow Whitesteel's surly behavior to affect his mood. In answer, Whitesteel feigned a buck, but quickly fell into a relaxed walking. As Marc had bluffed, so had his steed.

The two quickly merged into the congested traffic along the thoroughfare leading back toward the main avenue. Hand wheeled carts vied with horse drawn wagons that competed with any number of travelers on foot. Street merchants hollered out their wares. Buyers yammered to each other and the merchants. Money changed hands, though some of it unknown to the person getting pick pocketed. A plethora of smells mixed and drifted among them. Sweet apple curling around stiff tobacco dancing with crumbly cinnamon clinging to dead fish smell and horse sweat moving by the breath of a salt gritty breeze coming up from the harbor.

Unbidden, Marc suddenly missed the tranquility of the small Traelynn village. Maelyrin's village. Already a lifetime away, his thoughts still bubbled around the idea of going back.

The sounds here were harsh to his ears, had always been, he surmised. So were the smells. Though he served many roles in his long lifetime, seen many things, lived many lives, he still yet remained a solitary person. For the most part anyway. And however calm and desensitized his life span made him, a tiny kernel of discomfort remained around the bustling crowds of city life, like the dust mote that irritates the eye when it lands just so. He would be glad to be moving on from here. While Hestaff was small compared to some of the sprawling great cities of Arquilon, like Vistan, it was far too large for his sensibilities.

Yes, leaving soon will be welcomed.

He turned Whitesteel away from the dock wards at the road closest to them and headed west. The thoroughfare was much more crowded than the avenue of the city, not only bearing the people and their modes of transport, but also huge bundles of wrapped cargo clogged the artery. Casks and boxes and bundles and sacks, stacked neatly but strewn along the street and docks, cramming movement for the most part, even stopping it to a drip in others. Bare-footed sailors crawled over everything like ants, cursing and spitting epithets. Dockmasters replaced the hawkers in their yelling, while gulls shrieked from dropping coated masts and berths. The air above was full of undulating waves of them, while cheaply dressed strumpets leaned against posts or sat on the steps to many of the harbor side businesses, mostly taverns and sordid flop houses. Overall, the populace took on a seedier, nearly sinister, look. Eyes followed him, from heavy lidded to jittery, but, by and large, a wide berth was granted Whitesteel and him as they moved along the dock street.

It wasn't long before a transformation took place in this part of the city of Hestaff. The buildings were suddenly new, mostly large warehouses leering over other, more respectable places of business. Shipwrights. Moneylenders. Mapmakers. So fresh that the area was not yet infected with the decrepitude only a few yards back. It would be a couple more years and a few harsh storms before the new ward was openly overrun with strumpets, drunks, and ruffians. Now, the City Watch made a good show throughout the area. Across the road more docks and piers were still under construction.

At length, they even passed the new construction, came out of the heavy traffic and crowding buildings onto a stretch where only the road marred an empty field off to his left and a rocky drop off to licking water on the right. The road ribboned over the field for at least half a league before meeting the outer wall of Hestaff. Though he had seen the city many times in the past, it still left him a small amount of admiration for the founders of Hestaff, who had the forethought to build for expansion, unlike most other cities that surrounded themselves with battlements but continued to overflow them until they had to build another wall. The result being several concentric walls surrounding distinct cities within the city. He saw the huge, sprawling city of Vistan in his mind's eye. Saw its own series of concentric walls, including the huge, fortified roadways that connected Vistan to its smaller, sister cities, Saroton and Merlankerr. All roads lead to Vistan, it seemed.

He shook off his thoughts as the two hove close to the gates. There were only a few guards present, leaning sleepily at their posts. Quite a change from the main gates leading into Hestaff, where the huge tent city lay. And only a few leagues from where he was. He snorted at the irony. The eastern gate was probably just as unpopulated, and he thought it possible that pulling gate duty here, or there, was something more akin to a reward than a punishment.

"Odd times," he said. *But, then, I've seen many such oddities throughout my forever life, haven't I?*

The first guard that noticed him, straightened quickly then slapped his partner on the arm. Two sets of eyes looked at him. Then four. Then all sixteen. The one that noticed him first began walking out from under the protection of the gatehouse, holding his halberd loosely beside him. "Something I can help you with, stranger?" he said.

Marc reined Whitesteel in and leaned forward onto the pommel of his saddle. "Is this the way to Mordland's Cove?" he asked.

"Yes," he said. "About a league from here. Follow the road until it begins to bend south. You'll find a small trail that will take you there."

"Thank you," Marc said and nudged Whitesteel into a walk again. The guard hurried to catch up.

"Will you be gone long?" he asked.

"Don't know," Marc said. "Why?"

"We. . . uh. . . close the gates at dusk," he said. "And don't reopen them until sun up."

"I don't expect to be gone that long,"

"Very well," the guard said. He stopped near his former post and watched as Marc led Whitesteel beneath the gates. He was grumbling to himself, but Marc ignored him, setting Whitesteel to a trot once they were out of the gate's shadow, and kept him going until the road made a noticeable bend to the south. A distinct trail led off into a thick copse of oak and poplar that began pacing the road. It meandered through the strip of woodland, rising gently and then sloping, until it broke onto a wide beach that curled around calmly lapping water. Further out, the cove opened onto the sea proper around a mouth flanked by large craggy rocks upon which the water crashed. Sprays of white shot up around them, followed by the distant thunder.

He stopped.

Alexandra was sitting on a small rock near the water's edge, dangling her legs in the rippling surface while running a brush through her long hair. She wore only her shirt, draped loosely around her shoulders. The rest of her clothes lay folded nearby. Even from his vantage point, she seemed . . . fresh, more energetic, though she was only brushing her hair.

He clicked his teeth, and Whitesteel started down the beach. She looked over at him coolly when he stopped near her clothes. "I thought you wanted me to come along," he said as he swung down off the large white beast.

"I didn't want to interrupt your rendezvous with the strumpet," she said.

"Strumpet?" he said. "Sharla?"

"I don't need to know her name," she said, pulling the brush with a quick stroke that belied the calmness of her voice.

Marc looked away long enough to loosen Whitesteel's saddle and tie the reins and lead up so they didn't drag on the ground. "Something wrong?"

"Not really," she said, sniffed loudly. "I never pegged you for one to fraternize with whores. It surprised me."

"Really," Marc said. "I would have thought that someone that ages as slow as you do would understand."

"No," she said. "No, I don't."

He moved over and sat on the bank near enough to keep from raising his voice and far enough away to see her plainly. "You don't get urges every now and again? Don't take a lover that has no real meaning so you don't lose your sanity while you watch your cherished grow old and die before your eyes? Don't you ever need the touch of another human, no matter how fleeting?"

"N-no. . . I do not," Alexandra said, this time peering out over the cove while brushing.

"Well, then," Marc said, picking some strands of grass from a tuft near him. "You are certainly stronger than I. A veritable pillar."

"And that is supposed to mean?" she snapped. Her eyes flashed in the sunlight.

"That means I don't believe you," he said. "That means you can certainly dish out harshness, but can't take it. That means you certainly can jump to conclusions quickly." He stood, tossing the grass aside.

"What?" she said, her voice cracking.

"You figure it out Mal'andel," He said, spun on his heel and strode toward Whitesteel.

"Wait," she said as he worked the cinch strap free so he could tighten the saddle. He paused. "I'm sorry," she said. When he turned around, he found her looking at him from under her brow. She wore a frown. "You're right."

"About what?" he said. Marc didn't think she would take the bait and answer. Thought the ever-present pride she seemed not to notice would keep her mouth locked.

"I know I can't take harshness," she said. "And I did jump to conclusions."

A swirling funnel cloud of guilt rose in him and tickled the back of his throat, causing him to clear it loudly. After a moment he huffed and returned to his seat, immediately picking more blades of grass. "Sharla is Magus," he said. "One of the most powerful in the world. I've known her a long time and care for her deeply. On the surface, we have a strange relationship, but not to those of us who live so long."

"I'm sorry," she said. "I didn't know. It's not a situation I am familiar with."

He studied her for several seconds. While unusual, it wasn't unheard of. Alexandra seemed like one that would be too involved in her profession to be bothered with such things. He still didn't believe she never had urges or feelings, however deeply she was enthralled by being an Earthmother. "I suppose it would surprise you to know I had the same type of relationship with Gyssel," he suddenly blurted.

Alexandra's eyes bulged. "What?" she said.

Marc nodded, calling to mind the woman's face. So long ago.

"You're fooling me," she said a second later, her eyes still locked on him and wide.

"No, I'm not," he said.

"She never told me," she said, her body relaxing from a stiffness caused by her shock.

"Why would she?" Marc said. "It only concerned her and me."

"I suppose so," she said. "But it doesn't seem like her."

"Why doesn't it?"

She shrugged. "I don't know," she said. "She always seemed so. . . strong. She never seemed to need anyone."

"Strength and need are two different things," he said.

"How do you . . . have . . . ." Her face was washed with a coat of innocence that he found refreshing.

"A relationship like that?" he said. When she nodded, he continued, "We needed it. It was simple. . . clean. . . if that makes any sense. All of us knew the pain of loss, experienced it many times throughout our long lives. It seemed the natural thing to do. Each of us had . . . well . . . eternity, almost, to live. Sharing our experiences kept our sanity, drew us together. . . When you spend more than a lifetime with someone, you grow close in ways that is impossible to describe. . . in ways deeper than anyone else is capable of understanding. Social norms tend not to come into play."

"Were you Bonded?" Alexandra said.

"Ah. . . No," he said, looking away briefly. When their eyes met again, the set of Alex's face told him she knew she was out of line. Long moments of discomfort ensued. Marc finally broke the silence by dropping the grass braid he had been unconsciously coiling and slapping his knees. "Well, I didn't come down here to bore you with the details of my life."

Alex smiled, a slight movement that bespoke cut off curiosity. "What did you come down here for?"

"For one, I agreed to come down here," he said. "For two, Sharla gave me some information that might affect our travel plans."

"And what would that be?"

"King Flandric of Balinoch is marching his army on Calif," he said.

"How long?"

"Soon," Marc said. "I'm not sure. But I know this . . . our time grows short."

Alexandra leaned back a little and gazed into the sky, a fine line appearing between her brows and her jaw muscles clenching. The action, small as it was, showed him in no uncertain terms how relaxed and at peace she had been. Regret pricked him, and he wished he could take back the news and save it for later, once she was more prepared it. "We have to leave," she suddenly said.

"Are you well enough?" Marc asked.

"Yes," she said. "For the time being. I've cleansed myself and am recovering my strength rapidly."

"Good," he said, looked around as if seeing the place for the first time. "How did you get out here?"

"I took a carriage to the gates then walked the rest of the way."

"Well, if we start now, we can be back before dusk." Marc stood up and brushed absently at his clothing. "I shall take Whitesteel up to the wood-line while you get dressed."

She looked down at her bare legs and shirt as if noticing her appearance for the first time. "Ah . . . Yes, that would be appreciated," she said.

He didn't have to wait long before she met him at his chosen place within the shade cast by the reaching trees, tying her hair back with a length of leather. His heart fluttered, and he was suddenly glad she was alright. "Wouldn't it be faster if we rode?"

"I thought you walked?" he said. She arched her brow and gestured at Whitesteel with a nod.

"Do you think that beast can support the both of us?" she said.

Marc looked at the horse in wonderment, still not fully aware of the connection she was trying to get him to make. Whitesteel looked up from the tuft of grass he was munching and nickered at him. "Him? He can probably support us plus Sandoren and Del. Why?"

"For someone who's been around so long," she said, smiling. "You sure can be dense."

"Huh?"

"Nothing, just get on the horse," she said.

"I'm not going to ride while you walk," he argued.

"Humor me."

Marc looked at her for several seconds, his face knotted with confusion and frustration. Finally, he shrugged and turned to tighten his steed's saddle. He looked at her once more when he was finished, shrugged again when she said nothing, then lifted himself up into the saddle. Instantly, she was next to him.

"Now help me up," she commanded.

His shoulders tightened so quickly they pinched and his breath caught. "Why do you insist on tormenting me like this," he said after he was able to breathe again. "You know I can't assist you."

"That's fine," she said and held up her hand. "Take my hand."

He twitched, his hand moving toward the outstretched hand, his arm froze, became numb. He strained, tried to push it forward while he clenched his teeth. Moments later, he pulled it back and huffed. "I cannot!"

"Stubborn ape," she said. "You're thinking too much. Can you do this?" Alexandra held her arm out to the side, palm up. "Forget about me wanting help!"

He stared again, this time his face crawling with anger and self-loathing.

"Just do it!" she said, her voice raised and shot through with an iron bar.

"Damn you," he hissed between locked teeth, his anger flashing through his eyes so quickly he couldn't see as a curtain of white fell down in front of them. When his vision cleared, he was holding his arm out. Automatically, he began drawing it in, not wanting to suffer the impotence his curse formed, but Alexandra caught his arm above his elbow and jumped.

Marc was suddenly back at Tonk's when she did the same thing to him before they left South Watch. His body immediately compensated. His hand clasped her arm and he leaned toward the other side so her weight did not topple him from his saddle and, perhaps, hurt them both. A grunt found his ear, but it was Alexandra as she threw her leg over Whitesteel's rump and tugged herself up behind him, all the while her touch sending waves of shocks through him.

Once righted, she said, "See, you can do it."

Marc said nothing, instead turning his stunned, buzzing attention forward, barely noticing her slight press against his back and the ring of pressure around his chest where her arms encircled him. Whitesteel began moving on his own, picking his way up the small trail. His mind was empty, but his body was filled with the itching and burning of a storm of conflicting emotions. Anger, guilt, frustration, sadness, elation, agony. All of them trapped behind a wracking, tingling, crumbling wall of numbness.

When they crossed under the shade-throwing gate, the guards snickered, nudged each other, and muttered obscenities that were lost on him, though he was aware of Alexandra tightening up behind him. Only because she was directly connected to him, though it wasn't the physical touch that weighed the most. It was the icy splinter of knowledge of what she had done that made him more attentive to her than anything else.

A question beat relentlessly against the chaos within him, however. One that shouted its position so clearly only because there was no other logic competing against it. Alexandra had found a way around his curse. Not once, but twice. The question was: could he?

Marc could do nothing but try to sort out the raging feelings in relation to the pounding question. Alexandra said nothing, made no moves, maybe sensing his need to think, to be lost within himself as he was. The hour long ride back to the Inn was over quickly in his mind, like the morning after an exhaustive day followed by a slow dive into comfortable bed. A second after the eye closes, there is the sun, peering through the window as if it raced quickly around the other side of the world. Alexandra disappeared into the Inn after she slid from

Whitesteel's back, giving him only a thoughtful glance and reassuring smile before she turned away.

With all the thought process of the walking dead, he went about seeing to Whitesteel with mechanical slowness. He handed him off to the stable boy only after the young man touched him on the arm and spoke his name a couple of times. Then, he shuffled into the Inn, up the stairs, into his room. The tumblers of the lock turning over thundered in the small space and drew tight eyes to its casing. Marc's fingers played over the brass to check its reality. Then backed away slowly when he couldn't place it. He sat on the bed, unable to stand anymore. He remembered catching the Traelynn girl as she lost her balance on the limb he had sat on, not too long ago. A simple gesture. One that would mean nothing to anyone else. The wall containing his emotions was cracked and holed. It collapsed.

Trembling all the way down into his marrow, Marc put his face in his hands, and wept.

Chapter 69

Changing Plans, Changing Tides

*A*lexandra listened to the muffled sounds with more than a mixture of guilt and sorrow. Every once in a while she had to pinch the ridge between her eyes to keep tears from falling from them. She knew it would take a long time before Marc rid himself of the realization she caused in him. When it happened, she sensed his dawning horror as years, centuries, of living with his curse came back to him in a single instant. She saw the 'what ifs' passing through the cool slate of his eyes like jags of lightning in storm clouds. Saw him count the numerous times he could have acted but was held up by what he thought was his curse. It was an instantaneous explosion that must have ripped him into a million pieces. At least, the sobs coming from his room told her so, filled as they were with generations of agony.

It was something of a surprise when they fell off, but when she looked outside and found that the sun had been swallowed by night, she simply understood that she had lost track of time, enthralled as she was by the big man's tears.

And now that they no longer bled through the wall separating them, she was able to turn her attention away from her silent empathizing and place it on the news he had brought her. If Calif was under siege when they arrived, she might not be able to get to the Grove. Not to mention that it would put the Living Trees in serious danger. It was going to be at least three weeks if they made across the sea then went overland from there and that was the shortest option Marc had given her. Balinoch lay a little over half of their journey there and though an army tended to move slowly, it was sure to beat them by more than a week.

That is if they hadn't actually started marching. That is if the information passed on to her was the customary warning and the army of Balinoch was still being raised. In either case, normal travel would bring them too close to the army threatening Calif. Of course, 'normal' didn't necessarily have to apply to her.

She reached out to the Earth, floors beneath her and spread her senses outward from it, toward the coastline, doing what she could to ignore the poisons irritating it where the city sat. Several minutes of sensing passed before she found what she was looking for, something that was adequate for her needs, only she did not know if what she was thinking about would work. Alex never tried over water before, especially one so expansive. After probing a few more seconds, fixing the position in her mind, she pulled back and reluctantly let go of her Touch.

A soft knock on her door cut off the slight mourning she went through each time she closed off the conduit from the Earth's Blood. "Yes," she said.

Sandoren looked in and said, "Dinner."

"Great," she said with a smile. "I'm starving."

"You're always starving," he replied. An old routine, but there was no life in it.

"Where have you been?" she asked.

His eyes slitted and the corners of his mouth went down, only momentarily, as the suspicion rolled by. "Just seeing the sights," he said.

"Really," she said. "See any good ones?"

"Yea," he answered. "There is a very nice glade not very far from the walls."

Though delivered in a stark monotone, it still made her chuckle. "You're never going to change, are you?"

"No," he said. "You coming?"

Trying to elicit a smile from him these days was a little too trying, and after what Marc had been going through and the residual effects of Earth's Touch, his stubborn numbness echoed back and clouded her attempt at lightness. Heavily, she got up from the bed and followed the man out. Sandoren. Someone she barely knew anymore. "Will you be ready to leave in the morning?" she asked as they turned the corner that led them to the dining room.

Sandoren grunted his assent, and it ignited a flame of anger in her belly.

"What about tonight?" she said. "Will you be ready to leave tonight?"

Sandoren stopped and turned his gaze on her, ire and confusion glittering in his eyes. Just as quickly, they went dull again. "Yea, sure." No questions. No arguments. Just that infuriating answer delivered with all the energy of peat moss.

Alex, fuming, locked her jaw to keep from saying something that would only make the situation uncomfortable, and turned into the room. Del was already sitting at the long table, looking off into space. Several moths fluttered in lazy patterns around his head, completely ignoring the many flickering candles that lit the room. She took the seat she occupied the night before and was immediately set upon by one of the two squires given the chore of serving them tonight. He held out a frail looking glass filled with an amber liquid. "Wine?" he asked, his voice carefully softened.

"Thank you," Alex said as she accepted the glass. Sandoren, who was still yet standing, looked at her with a thoughtful expression. She took a sip of the bittersweet fluid, and the thoughtfulness was gone when the glass touched the table cloth, replaced with that indifferent flat look. He sat down and poked at the place settings as if seeing them for the first time ever.

Just as the squires began placing the covered plates on the table, Marc walked through the door. He, too, wore a

carefully neutral expression, but his eyes still bore the redness
of his revelations. His voice, however, was strong and deep,
bearing no indication of raggedness caused by his torment.
"Good evening," he said, taking his seat.

"We have to leave," Alex blurted.

"Yes, so we discussed," Marc answered.

"We have to leave tonight," she said.

Marc's brows reached for the top of his head while the
hand about to drape the linen napkin on his lap stopped and
hovered above his thighs. "What?"

"After we eat," Alex said.

The napkin dropped onto his thigh, was absently
smoothed, as he said, "I don't think the ship has been arranged
for yet."

"We're not going by ship," she said. "We are riding."

"Riding?" he said. "That will take longer than just by
ship. If Flandric's army is already on the march, they will
surely get there long before we do."

Sandoren was eyeing them both with little interest,
spooning up mouthfuls of beans, even though Marc hadn't
received his meal yet and Alex's was still covered. "Who do
you think you are speaking to?"

"A lunatic?" Marc said, smiling. It was wan, but
genuine, and tugged at her lips.

"Yes, maybe, but besides that, I think I have a way to
get us there more quickly." She lifted the lid over her dinner
and waited for the steam cloud to disperse so she could get a
look at the repast. "How long will it take to be ready once we
eat?" Her mouth was watering, and she had to catch herself
before she drooled.

"The horses are rested, and we are fully supplied," Marc
mused. "An hour? Before half-night at any rate. Are you sure
you don't want to wait until the morning?"

"No, we must leave as soon as we can," she said. "Our
time is very short, and we have to get to Calif before that army
does."

"Why, exactly?" Marc asked.

"A Grove lies there, on this side of the city. The battling may put the Living Trees there in jeopardy. I must not allow that to happen. We must leave tonight!"

"Okay, alright," Marc said. "We'll leave as soon as we can." He looked to the nearest squire. "Boy. Rouse the stableman and have him prepare our horses immediately."

"Yes, my lord," the young man said with a click of his heels and a slight bow at the neck, and was gone from the room.

"What about the gates?" Sandoren asked around a mouthful. "Aren't the gates locked at night?"

Both Marc and Alex looked at him, Marc's face beginning to sag, while a smile was working onto hers. "Yes," Marc said. "That's right. I'd forgotten for a moment. I guess we'll have to wait—"

"We won't be leaving through the gates," Alex said.

Marc's brows reached back again, but Sandoren's face dimmed into disinterest. "Yea, alright," he said, and stuffed another spoonful of beans into his mouth.

Chapter 70

The Price of Hubris

7he tree was old, huge, a gnarled timber roped in thick, tight vines that reached up into the darkened sky with limbs draped in leaves that shined silver in the moonlight. Beyond it, the wide vista of the sea sparkled with silent magnificence. A salt tanged breeze made its way up the beach and tickled the leaves, making them shimmer.

Alexandra caressed the ancient bark, letting her fingertips move along the rough crevasses and scaled husk while her palms picked up the long slow beat of its life force. Warmth and life flowed from it in strong waves despite its age.

The more she probed, the more confident she became in what she was going to attempt. An easy thing to do over land, but never done over water. For not the first time since leading them here, she thought, *I hope I know what I'm doing.* The consequences of failure was an icy hand gripping the base of her spine. But she had no choice that was better than the press time was putting on her. What she contemplated, she had to do. She felt it, deep down. Otherwise, the direction she needed would never come once the armies of man destroyed the source. *Of course, if this doesn't work, then it won't matter.*

Failure equated to being buried alive in porous sand. A slow, suffocating death. Her bones shivered.

"Are you thinking what I think you're thinking?" Marc said. Since filing out of the Inn's grounds, he had been thoughtfully quiet. All of them had been. And now, his voice seemed alien in the drifting night air.

She turned and looked at him and nodded. Sandoren, a few steps behind Marc, was staring at the glimmering water, his face and eyes flat with disinterest. "I think I can do it," she said, just before realizing she was talking to herself more than Marc. *Can I risk him, or Sandoren? Both know the dangers. But what about Del? How can I risk his life?*

How can I not?

Her heart tried to rend when she looked at the boy. Marc and Sandoren were both warriors, risking their lives almost on a daily basis, so there was only a glint of guilt that bubbled up in her when considering them. But with Del, there was a geyser.

The boy was sitting on Day, staring up into the night sky, his slack expression pinned to the gibbous ball above them. Drool shined wetly on his wide chin, and his eyes were hollow. Whatever presence spoke through him from time to time had yet to reappear since their encounter with the Chyldren. She still didn't know what that other was. Perhaps his true self, perhaps someone or something else. Just as he, himself, was an anomaly, so was the Speaker.

Alexandra smiled. The ever-present swarm of bugs dipped and hovered around him in a loose cloud. Lightning flies this time, twinkling enough that a greenish yellow glow limned his wide face. The innocence she found there hurt her. More because she knew she would risk his life. Had to. It was a quick stabbing pain that made her turn back to the tree.

Alex laid her hands against the tree again and fell in on herself, creating a conduit between the thrumming Earth's Blood beneath, up through her, and into the ancient tree. The Power that flowed within her both chilled and exhilarated her, seemed to shift her out of phase with herself to blend with both the tree and the ground. It took a moment before she could refocus on the task at hand.

As she began forming the thoughts, the will that directed the Flow, the great oak began to respond. Its slow beat increased, its fluid channels quickened. There was a slow sigh in the being as its trunk began shifting, separating. Slowly, the doorway opened, as it had the last time she Treewalked. It seemed so long ago.

However, the ease with which the doorways usually opened was not present. Extending the ephemeral tunnel that connected this tree to one so far away pulled at her life force, felt like her stomach was getting tugged through her throat. Her head began to throb and sweat broke cold over her entire body, intensified a hundred fold by her connection to the Earth Power.

She struggled, pushed the concentrated sense outward toward that distant point. Time dragged as the tunnel extended, ever so slowly. Her breathing became ragged and her chest burned, but she continued nonetheless, until, finally, the tunnel touched that other, connected the two and formed the doorway on the other end. A sudden snapping back of the strain pushed her back from the tree in relief, where she sagged against her knees and attempted to catch her breath while maintaining the doorway. Though there was a pressure, a sense of walls enclosing her and moving in an inexorable pace, it was far easier to control than the energy she had expended just trying to form the door. It was only a temporary respite, more like she was just slowing to a jog to be maintained over the next few hours after running full out until unconsciousness nearly took her. The fight was merely beginning. "Quickly," she gasped. "We must ride."

But moving quickly was something she could not do. Not now. Sluggishly, she turned and looked at Marc. He held Clover's reins and looked at her with a face carved of neutrality. She didn't know if he heard. Sandoren was staring at her, eyes smoldering. "Give me your hand," she said, croaking through a dry throat. Marc pinched his brows together and clenched his jaw, seemed to tense against himself for a moment. *He's resisting himself, enacting the curse.* "Just do it," she nearly yelled.

Marc jumped at the sound of her voice, and Whitesteel moved forward of his own accord. With a stuttering movement, he coaxed his arm out as he had twice before on her request, confusion swept his face, and that deep unutterable sorrow welled in the gray of his orbs.

Alexandra grasped his hand, her expanded senses noting every ridge and muscle of it, and a charge of lightening zinged through her. She tried to yank, then fall, forcing him to react to keep from falling from the saddle, but he was already lifting her when her nerves began reacting to the commands. Exhaustion assailed her, made her body sodden and she found it difficult to throw her leg over Whitesteel's rump. Marc stifled a groan and hefted while she finally snaked the foot across. Once settled, she fell against his wide back and breathed.

Marc tapped Whitesteel into a walk, tugged on Clover's reins. The beast stepped up into the doorway, which was at least three horses wide and maybe half again as tall, which gave them just enough room to ride single file but little else. Cool air scented with the fresh smell of leaves and water wrapped them in a soothing envelope and the floor had a slight spongy feel to it. Sandoren urged Day in and then followed. Once within, Marc released Clover's reins to allow her enough maneuvering room, then kicked Whitesteel into a gallop.

The beast reacted instantly, joyfully, his powerful legs heaving them forward into the loamy tunnel, kicking up a refreshing reverse wind. Hooves thudded on the soft flooring, sounding like the rapid heartbeats of many giants instead of the normally high pitched clopping she was used to. The sides of the tunnel, the whitish, woody substance invariably covered by the tree's bark, only elongated and disproportionate by the power of the earth she had used, began to blur into moving white walls. The only light, a pale, disembodied phosphorescence also imbued by the act.

Alexandra lay loosely against Marc's back watching the waving play of the wall as it seemed to whoosh by them and deliberately pulled in the fresh, earthy tree scent in slow deep breaths. The rhythm of Whitesteel's running was easy and level, which kept her from having to physically struggle to stay on. It was well that the powerful horse was so smooth, otherwise she would be having a greater difficulty maintaining the corridor. As it was, the constant pull on her was growing stronger, a tugging on her very soul that was beginning to give, to rip. The ancient trees, too, were feeling the tension. Groans reverberated through the tunnel walls, a terrible wooden grinding that underlay the pound of the horses' hooves and the rushing air. Only she could hear it. Only she suffered their misery.

Time began to drag even though the horses were running at a good clip, and her eyes began to droop. Not from sleepiness, but from exhaustion. Yet again, she was putting herself on the brink after only another brief respite, and it seemed to her that even those small rests were not keeping fatigue away for very long, like, deep down within her, icy crystals of weariness had formed and none of her breaks were able to melt them. And, quickly, they spread once she was drawing on the Earth Power within and around her.

Her eyes flashed open and she went rigid.

How long, her mind screamed. *How long?* Alexandra looked frantically at the walls. The trees' groaning had become louder, more insistent, and a fast look behind told her that the corridor was collapsing. Slowly, but drawing closer nonetheless. She closed her eyes again, this time in concentration, as she forced the tunnel to stop its inward motion. Her Touch was sluggish, and when she was finally able to draw from the Power, something inside tore in a liquid rush of fire. It was ephemeral, a rending of something not physical, but it caused her to gasp in pain and a knot of lead settled into the place between her eyebrows. Grey mists began to seep around the edges of her vision.

Marc said something, but it was only a rumble of thunder in her ear as his voice traveled through his chest. It was also something she ignored as she fought to reassert control over the failing tunnel. The Flow of Power she held began to sear and itch against her insides as it licked and each passing moment made her body heavier with sodden wool, but thankfully, the collapse slowed bit by bit, then finally stopped, and she was able to relax, if only a touch.

She took a deep breath that rattled in her chest and tasted like wet fungus. Returning her head to Marc's back was like plummeting through thick cotton. Her head still pounded, sending shards of glass from that point in between her brows radiating outward into the whole of her head and down her spine. She heard herself say something, but not what, her mouth working on its own. It could have been a curse or a retch, she didn't know. Nor care. The different parts of her body seemed to be disconnecting from her mind and moving away like leaves falling on the turgid motion of pond water.

The drone of Whitesteel's hooves and the rhythm of his body moved through her in metronomic waves, tempting her with the caress of sleep again, turning her eyelids into ballast. She could feel the tenuous grip she had on the corridor start to slip. Silently, she screamed into the darkness surrounding her.

It caused her eyes to widen with temporary wakefulness, but it only lasted moments, a heartbeat at the most. Although, she couldn't tell how long the beats of her own heart lasted. The passage of time, to her, became the ooze of sap. She could only guess that it was the briefest of moments before the thin coverings over her consciousness began their downward plunge once more.

Ironically, it was the hurtful moaning of the trees that kept her completely from that oblivion. Jags of ice splintered into her with each mournful plaint. Though she had stopped the tunnel from its premature closure, the trees' pain did not abate. The connecting abutments of the corridor, the Life Points so necessary to this form of traveling, were straining under the pressure of so ambitious a stunt. What was she thinking? She should never had tried this, knowing full well that the proximity to the nurturing Earth was too far removed between the trees. *It was a mistake to do this.* A mistake, she realized, that would kill all of them, taking away the only chance to stop the Wound that was already killing the Earth.

She suddenly needed to tell Marc, though she couldn't figure out why. It was just there, a thought that bubbled up through the swamp of her mind. However, it wouldn't form anything on her thick tongue. No words would come. Nothing could force her mouth back into its proper place, so she let the words disperse.

It was her vision that drifted away from her mind next, refusing to translate the scenery into the correct pictures in her brain. Dimly, she was aware that the flash of whitish walls nearby were no longer. Darkness replaced it. The mists, it seemed, had turned into a thick fog while she wasn't paying attention. A fog limned in a pale silverish light.

It was then that her grip on the Flow slipped free. There was a clacking sensation, like her fingers banging together, and a jolt went through her. With a sluggish twist, she looked behind her. Sandoren, Del, and Clover, she could not see, but with a clarity that shocked her, the tunnel filled her vision. The white walls were slumping in on themselves. Tortured wails filled her ears. For some reason, she could see the second Life Point, a tree as ancient as the other, but more stout, without the arm thick vines coiling around it. Its bark was getting lighter, withering, as its reaching branches began twisting and warping in a cacophony of popping and crying wood. Leaves were falling in a blizzard, drying to deep browns even before coming to rest on the ground.

Alexandra screamed.

In pain. In horror. In fury.

Reality slapped her. They were out of the corridor, on the other side of the sea from Hestaff. They stepped out into the cool star filled night just before she let go of the Flow. Out of the corners of her eyes, she saw the shadowy forms of Sandoren on Veraddin, holding the reins of Day as Del stared off into nothing. However, that was only a passing thought. One that was thrown from the storm of her emotions, flashed across her mind's eye, and flew into some nether place.

Alexandra tried to scramble from Whitesteel's back. She had to stop the collapse before it killed the Life Points, but something was holding her, clamping her to the beast's back. With the last of her reserves, she squirmed and spit and fought and managed to slip the grasping bonds and fell from the horse. She hit the ground, cried out as pain lanced through her shoulder and lightning scattered across her eyesight. Yet, she quickly yanked herself to her feet then opened herself to the Earth Power while walking toward the withering tree.

Something wrapped around her and lifted her off the ground.

"NO!" she screamed. "Let me go!" Her head whipped around trying to find what was restraining her, but she only succeeded in thumping her face against rough cloth and catching glimpses of a shadowed figure.

"It's too late," someone said. Someone close. His voice nearly a yell but filled with concern.

"No," she said, struggling against the arms that wrapped her. She was rapidly losing whatever strength she had been able to summon. "No, I have to stop it." The tree's grinding cries of pain ratcheted across her heart. The tunnel was nearly gone, only a gnarled rip in the trunk that seemed to go on forever. "I have to—"

"It's too late," the voice said again, its timbre familiar but still unidentifiable. The grip around her middle tight, unrelenting, yet, in a way, gentle.

"No," she screamed again. "I can stop this!" *I must stop this!*

With the terrible rending sound of creaking wood, the tunnel finished collapsing, closing off its ephemeral existence to her with finality but leaving a deep ragged scar in the whitening trunk of the great oak that had been the anchor for their travels. Across the span of water that lay far from where they stood, she could sense the agony of the other tree as it gave up its life.

Alexandra screamed again, an inarticulate howl, and clawed at the arms that held her.

"No," that voice said, this time at her ear. She thrashed her head, felt a satisfying but painful thud as she struck something there and continued to claw at the arms.

With a last tortured sigh, the tree before her went rigid in the pale moon light, its branches grasping at the night air as if it could hold on to precious life. The bark went ashy and the last of its leaves, only a couple, broke free from their moorings and drifted down from the heights in languid fluttering arcs until rasping against their dead kin. A pungent, deadwood smell wafted from the hulk in vapor tendrils, curling in her nostrils.

Still, she struggled and screamed and clawed. A part of her could hear the protesting yells that ripped from her throat and that calm, contemptible voice speaking to her. *It's dead. There's nothing you can do. It's dead.*

It's dead.

It whispered through her mind like a phantom.

It's dead.

"No," she said through a raw gullet, but let her body slump into the restraining arms. "No." Hot tears were spilling from her eyes, thankfully blocking out the sight of the dead tree before her. "It's dead," she whispered. *I killed it.*

I killed it.

It was too much for her. The lead lump in her head pulled at the front of her skull. Breathing was a chore forced through scourged passages. The tears kept coming, rolling down cheeks from stinging eyes. She could only feel the rest of her body as a thick numb weight dangling from the back of her neck. She begged silently for a release, but it wouldn't come. Perhaps as punishment, she stayed conscious, bearing witness to the terrible murders she committed.

Next to her, someone coughed. Sandoren.

The arms around her middle lifted her slightly and turned her in its grasp, so that she faced the wide plain of Marc's chest. Reflexively, she wrapped her tingling, quaking arms around him and began sobbing into the cloth of his shirt.

It lasted a long time.

Chapter 71

Rage

*C*rowlin let go of the desiccated corpse, watched it slide to the ground in a papery heap before he lifted a wide, satiated grin up to the shining moon. The muffled agonized sounds drifted from the remaining gate guards as the others finished feeding and made his grin crack wider. Fresh, clean energy seeped through him, invigorating his every pore, tightening his skin around his bones. It would be a brief sensation, lasting only moments before the corruption within his body soiled the newly acquired life-force.

Once the wave of ecstasy passed, he looked down at the armored husk and nudged it with a foot. It rustled like dry leaves and fell in on itself, the face, a drawn mask of horror, disappeared in a flaking shower. Left behind was a pile of clothes and armor surrounding sticks and falling dust. Another grin wormed onto his face.

Lazily, he moved to the gear works and threw the lever. The giant, chain-wrapped spindle squealed into its spin, crying out into the night like a wounded thing. The counterweights dropped in rattling thunder and the huge, well-tended portcullis rose ponderously into its sheath of stone with a final clanging boom, letting the eastern gate of Hestaff yawn into the darkness beyond the flickering torchlight that surrounded it.

Not long afterwards, the mounts were led into the enclosing walls by a weakly slumped Teraard. Himself unable to partake of the treat that lay near Crowlin's feet, too feeble since his restoration to do anything but sit his horse, he had been left the task of bringing them through. Even from his vantage within the winch house, Crowlin could feel the waves of jealous hatred sloughing from Teraard.

"Guess you'll think twice before acting rashly," he said into the room, not intended for Teraard's ears, but the other reacted just the same, shifting within his cowl in jerky movements to face Crowlin. The other was waved on by an absent flick of his wrist though Crowlin could feel his defiance as a tangible thing. Silently, he willed Teraard to bring forth his hatred and anger into physical action. He wouldn't mind restoring him again, but the moment passed as Teraard moved into the small courtyard surrounding the gate and turned his gaze away.

It was something of a letdown. His body relaxing felt more like a sigh of disappointment, than an uncoiling of stored energy. Crowlin let his hand play over the cold metal of the winch lock, using its feel to move him from the immediate concern to the ultimate goal.

Pendragon was not far.

And the woman and the boy were with him. Both bright suns of lancing life force, one much stronger than the other. Though he had just fed, the hunger for those sparks rose in him like a tidal wave, washing over him in such a furious rush that he swooned back against the winch for a moment.

It was Pendragon, however, that damped the craving enough to let his hatred and passion reassert itself, placing his control back in his hands. After the debacle at Khemosh and the subsequent side paths they took to both restore Teraard and find new mounts, Reegan picked up Pendragon's cooling trail just outside the fortress of South Watch. Now, he was going to find him, risk everything, and destroy him. The Master would not be pleased, but, he hoped, the two guiding compasses of life force traveling with Pendragon would serve to keep him from the suffering he, no doubt, had waiting for him. Would finally free him and his company from generations of slavery.

As long as the Master continued His silence, he could keep his thinking clear of the fuzz that his head filled with after that sickening yet invigorating touch of the Master's mind. Everything hinged on that one happenstance. The silence of his Master was most important to his plans.

The rest of them were mounted and looking in his direction as he strode from the gatehouse. Several other piles of arid corpses lay scattered around the open courtyard. Parts of them rattled against the cobbled street, caught by the passing breeze and dragged across the smooth stone before disintegrating. He glanced at the armor and weapons with contempt. Behind him, a throbbing, pulsing sprawl of disdain lay at his back. Given the time, he and his companions could easily wipe these mortals from their festering city. Perhaps, once they were free, they could come back here and destroy Hestaff and feed until they could feed no longer.

But, for now, they had to take care of Pendragon.

He swung up onto the ragged beast currently serving as his mount. The others were jittery tense, sitting their saddles like coiled snakes. Though he didn't tell him his plans, he sensed they knew what he was about. He sensed they suspected his impending rebellion against the Master. Whether they sensed his ultimate plans for their freedom or just wanted to see him rent he didn't know. And it really didn't matter. One or the other was his destiny, and he was willing to take that path wherever it led instead of staying in the boundary separating them.

He kicked. The horse squealed and started to buck, but a quick shot to its ears changed its mind, instead sending it bolting down the cobbled road. Crowlin yanked at the reins once they moved beyond the East Gate and forced the animal northward, toward the sea line and the running jumble of thick woodlands that marked this deserted part of Hestaff, the two traveling with his quarry, beacons in the moon splashed landscape. Drawing him like a Heart Arrow.

Anticipation lay in his mouth like a Sugarburst, and he found himself grinning so wide that his jaw creaked. The thundering of the hooves on the open turf filled his ears, bringing back long memories of times past in similar situations. Times when they were dealing death and destruction, satiating their bloodlust on any that stood in their way. It was one of the only real sensations he had anymore.

Crowlin was enjoying the cold rush so much that, at first, he didn't notice the beacons moving quickly away from them, and when he did, he thought he was mistaken. The thought that they could move away from them even though they were moving faster than their mounts could normally carry them was not a large stretch, but his prey seemed to be moving north, over the water, faster than he could fathom.

When he began to think there was something amiss he could see the grove where he sensed them, or had sensed them. A tracery of their life forces still resided there within the enclosing trees, but the pulsing brightness they bore seemed farther away, leaving behind a thin line as if giving up minute parts of themselves as they went. Like a spider spinning a web. He didn't know of any that could do so over water.

Though not unaccustomed to magical forces, he had not yet made the conscious connection that these bright beacons, these so very tempting essences of nourishment, had such power. Despite the fact that the woman was an earthwitch. It simply wasn't something that he could accept just as he was on the cusp of success. Not until they drew near the huge old tree that that concept began working into his occupied, obsessed, mind.

There was a large, vertical slash in the tree's trunk. Witchlight spilled onto the ground from it in a pale greenish splotch. Standing in front of the tree was no one. Not Pendragon, not the woman, or the boy. Not their horses. Nothing but that glowing tunnel.

Crowlin screamed, drew his sword and kicked the beast underneath him into a faster pace. He flew straight for the entrance, his cry driving forward as he left his companions behind. At first he intended to steer the creature into the tunnel, but a primal claw gripped the back of his skull and made his arms draw back on the reins enough that when he flung himself from the saddle he didn't shatter his legs. He hit the ground running, raising the sword.

The tree groaned so loudly, it stopped him and his continuing wail stitched off.

He stared down the corridor, vaguely aware of the others drawing up a bit away from him, but could see nothing of his prey within its oval walls. However, he could feel them, ahead. Somewhere. He stepped toward the tunnel. A nauseating pain flickered through him. And at the same instant, another groan creaked from the tree. Another step brought another flicker and another groan.

He stopped and pushed his mindset for vengeance aside, looked at the tree wholly for the first time. A slide forward brought another flicker, only stronger, through him, echoed by a cricking moan. *Could it be so?*

Crowlin took a breath and crept the rest of the way to the tree, despite the increasing flare of pain that rolled before the groan of the oak. When he stood next to the trunk and opening, largely ignoring the constant throb, he reached out a tentative hand and laid it against the bark.

And snatched it back before even the hiss reached his ears.

He examined the hand for a second. Only long enough for the tiny trailers of smoke that curled up from the tips of his fingers to disperse. Then, he turned his attention back to the tunnel opening.

Crowlin stepped into the corridor.

Screaming agony bolted through him like lightning, and for a moment, he felt the tree's pain as he felt his. And felt the outcome of his remaining inside the corridor in a flash of clairvoyance that immediately drove him backward without the thought to urge his legs. Were he to stay within the confines of the tunnel, both he and the tree would die, killing each other as surely as if with swords or dark power. Momentarily, he was stupefied. There were very few things on the earth that could destroy him. That it would be a common oak tree never occurred to him before.

Of course, this might be a special case. Somehow the earthwitch created an umbilical in which she and Pendragon traveled. His very corrupted nature—

They've slipped from your grasp.

The thought dribbled ice water onto the back of his disfigured neck. *They've slipped from your grasp. Pendragon is gone. Your hope for freedom is gone. And to a place you cannot follow.*

"No!" he croaked. The dull throb of pain from being close to the tree itched at him, only infuriating his frustration. "No!" he repeated.

Crowlin cried out as his sword flashed out and bit into the tree. A grating moan came back to him that did nothing to relieve his fury. He slashed out again. And again. And again, until he was oblivious to the wail of the tree and the flashing pain that lit through him at each contact of blade on wood. He screamed, an incoherent ululating screech that blocked the tortured pain of the oak from anything else that could possibly hear it. Chips flew. White, moist chunks fell to the ground and rolled away from the humped, root supported base. Sap oozed down the bark, sparkling like tears in the moonlight and witchlight from the opening. He slashed and slashed. The pain jolting him through the contact burning him more and more. Leaves began falling around him like rain. Dry raspy things that scraped and clung to his cloak like skeletal claws of the unresting dead.

At length, he saw the pale glow of the doorway begin to fade and doubled his efforts, hacking into the wood with furious abandon. The opening began to twist and slide together as the umbilical within began falling in on itself. The fiery lances of pain receded along with the closure.

He stopped only when the doorway closed and the pale witchlight died. Left behind was a silent, twisted mass of gray wood, grasping at the moon with warped, claw-like limbs, denuded of leaves and tracing contorted black lines against the glittering heavens. Long, cloven wounds and deep gashes crisscrossed the dead trunk, its cut away mass, shavings, chunks, and splinters, laying in a rough semi-circle around the roots and clinging to his dark clothing like blood spatter.

Dimly, he was aware of the tendrils of smoke drifting from his cloak, and his skin itched and burned in stinging waves. Behind him, he felt the others staring while their mounts snorted and whined. Crowlin stepped back and slid the undamaged blade into its scabbard. His tendons and muscles creaked and popped, as if by killing the oak, he had taken on its wooden essence. Temporarily, his frustration lay under a thin layer of peace brought on by his destructive fit.

"Crowlin," Reegan rasped from behind him. He ignored him, still staring at the dead hulk as if the doorway would suddenly open and spit out his prey. "Crowlin."

His head twisted around and he speared his companion with his eyes. The thin covering of peace split and tore. "What?" he hissed.

"What about the Old One?" the tracker replied.

"What about it?"

"It's near," Reegan said. Crowlin stiffened and let go of his anger long enough to sense the things around him. The trees, grass, water. And the Old One. The creature was standing only a few spans away, at his back, watching them, gauging them. He didn't know how long it had been there, but he thought it might have been long enough to see him tear the oak up.

He silently withdrew his blade again as he turned to face it, even though the dark wrought metal probably would do little against the ancient creature.

It crouched near the up-thrust of a split trunked oak, all but a part of its shadow, its shining eyes and glittering rows of teeth betraying its hiding place. If that was what it was doing. Crowlin didn't think so, knowing it was so when he met the thing's gaze and felt the weight of eons drifting from the two orbs.

A cold sliver of fear slid into the base of his spine. Something much more tangible and lead tasting than when he realized the tree could destroy him. It was something he was sure he hadn't felt when he faced the Stone Guardian deep in the Starlight Mountains on the eve of the Dark Night.

But then, it was foretold you would survive that encounter, wasn't it. That you would destroy the Life giving Threadbearer. There is no such guarantee here.

He gripped and curled the sword in his hand with unconscious nervousness. Near him was a thing outside the ages, something born of the world when it was formed. It had roamed the wastelands of darkness long before light cast its cold glare across the landscape. His Master was but a heartbeat compared to its existence. Looking at it caused a withering inside him.

Behind him, the others were shifting from their saddles. The snick of steel leaving scabbards reached him. He briefly saw in his mind the dead guard and the armor that couldn't protect him and wondered what it was they thought they were doing. There was a shadow of contempt that rose up into the back of his throat. He considered sheathing the sword, but his hand didn't move. Oily darkness pooled in his empty hand. Underneath his feet, the grass blackened and crackled in a growing circle as he drew the life from it and perverted it into deadly power.

The creature flashed a grin at him, making him flinch. When he cocked his arm back to release the darkness, it flashed another grin then turned away from the tree and sped off toward the water. He was paralyzed by surprise for a moment, the dark power in his hand dispersed like mud in water. His legs were moving before he realized it, carrying him after the Old One.

It ran ahead of him in long, relaxed lopes, using its lengthy arms to propel its thick, ropy body as well as its legs. Turf churned at its passing. It was terribly fast and flitted from shadow to shadow as if it traveled only within them. Crowlin was able to keep track of it because of his closeness to its black essence, but it still proved difficult, and he knew he couldn't gain on it. Suddenly, it sprang into the air and sailed out over the moon sparkling water lapping at the shoreline. It seemed to hover for a split moment then plunged into the inky, silvery liquid.

Crowlin stared at the undulating water, sure that the creature would surface somewhere in the mercuric sea-scape, but nothing happened. He waited, scanning as time flowed by, but the view before him remained undisturbed by wake or ripple.

The unmistakable sound of Reegan dragging his twisted leg through the grass in a furious effort to catch up reached him, but Crowlin largely ignored it as he studied the glistening water. "Where is it?" Reegan rasped when he neared.

He passed his gaze over the horizon in a long, slow sweep. "Gone," he said.

"What do we do now?" Reegan asked, himself looking at the water. Crowlin turned his head, a thoughtful expression working onto his thin lips.

"We ride after them," he said.

"Where did they go?"

Crowlin slid the forgotten blade back into its housing and strode away from the water. "North. Over the sea," he replied.

Reegan cast one last glance at the sparkling water then began limping after him.

Chapter 72

Disappointing Findings

*S*he was going to cry; she felt the tears welling, blotting out the details of the building, fuzzing the flickering torches into globes of hairy light. Maybe that, or scream, she didn't know which. Quickly, she scrubbed the heel of her hand across the hollows of her eyes and looked at the face that hung over the wall, staring down at them like a miniature version of the moon. "Can you make an exception?"

"No," the guard yelled down. "The gates do not open until sunrise."

"But this is very important." Maelyrin yelled back.

"So is keeping the gates closed until sunrise," the guard said. "Come back then!"

"Come," Kiyo rumbled softly. "Let us retreat and find a place to camp." While talking, he surveyed the multitudes of white tents glowing in the moonlight. The tent city looked like some contorted landscape in winter blankets.

"But we are so close," she insisted. "He is in there. I know it."

"That may be so," Kiyo said. "But we will not be sure until morning. Shouting at an oak will not get you an acorn."

The knot of frustration that hunched in her chest vibrated and swelled, began to rupture, sweeping through her body in quaking waves. Words came to her mind so fast she couldn't keep up with them, much less form them on her tongue. She was gripping the pommel of her saddle, the reins coiled around her hands so tightly that the leather was biting into her skin and her joints hurt. In a momentary flash of clarity, she thought about reaching for an arrow. If you couldn't get an acorn by shouting at the tree, then maybe she could shoot one right through that moon face looking down on them with smug certainty.

Her mouth tight over gritted teeth, she stabbed a glance up at the guard only to find he was no longer there. A shriek crawled up her throat.

And then, all at once, her body slumped as if she just took a drought of a sleep potion or got clubbed over the head. Her ire bled off into the night leaving behind tired annoyance. She reined the horse around and nudged him into a walk. Several refugees peered at her from between tent flaps and beneath lean-tos, no doubt awakened by her exchange with the gate guard. "Alright," she said. "We will wait until morning. I've waited this long. I suppose a few more hours won't hurt."

Chapter 73

Travel Plans

"*You* can't keep doing this to yourself," Marc said as he dragged Alexandra's still slack body through the rolling surf and back onto the wet firmness of the shore. She was awake and able to speak, but waited until they were sitting on the drier sand further up the beach.

"Thank you," she said, her voice gravelly. "I'm a little surprised it's you, though."

"It was still a struggle, but I had plenty of time to cajole and coax my body into movement," Marc said around his attempts to recover his breath. His words were an understatement. A vast understatement to describe something more like an epic battle, but he refused to admit it. It would do her no good to describe each and every measure he took to fool himself into believing he was doing something other than helping her. "Still, you must not be so hard on yourself." Marc said it expecting a curt rebuttal. He was not disappointed.

"You worry about your own hide," she snapped. "And I'll worry about mine."

"Up until a couple of days ago, that's all I could worry about," he returned. "And since you are the only one of us that knows what we are doing, it stands to reason that your stubbornness should not be so . . . . stubborn."

"Yes, well . . . I'll consider that," she said. Alex looked at him and shot him a false smile. "Where are we? Where's Sandoren and Del?"

"Sitting on a beach on the north shore of the sea we crossed," he said. "Your Guardian and the boy are trying to figure out a more substantial answer to that."

It was midmorning. The sun shining down on them was cheery and offered just enough heat to keep them from suffering, though shivers ran through both of them at irregular intervals. They reached the coastline just after dawn, and Marc waited until it was a little higher before trying to get Alexandra into the surf so the cleansing water could work on her drained body. Again. "How long since . . . . How long have I been out?" she said. The back of her wrist was pressed against her forehead, but it didn't completely hide the death of the trees from surfacing across her face. A sardonic smile touched his mouth. She had nearly died, too, but it was the trees she worried about.

"Only a few hours," he said. "We haven't lost much time."

Relief flowed over the memory, burying it, then she let her head hang backward over the gulf created by the supporting elbows that held her in a semi-reclining position. Her wet, tangled hair fell against the loose sand. Sunlight bathed her face and the length of her exposed neck, and she closed her eyes, tasting it with her skin, still pale but slowly coloring. He was suddenly very aware of the way her wet clothing clung to her stretched out body and transferred the view of flesh through the now translucent material and prompted him to retrieve their dry and warm cloaks. While they were toweling the wetness from them with the heavier cloth, she hummed absently.

"Did you happen to see any type of berry bushes around?" she asked suddenly.

"Why," Marc answered. "You hungry?"

"Yes, but not for berries."

He shook his head. "No. I was a little preoccupied."

"That's alright. I'll look around in a bit." Alexandra clasped the cloak around her neck and let it hang while she freed her hair of its grasp and shook out the sand. She made her way to their equipment, which lay in a pile near the tree line, fetched out her brush from her saddlebags, and began combing her hair as she gazed up and down the infinite seeming beach. An expression both thoughtful and bothered lay on her face.

Marc watched her for a few minutes, drinking in her movements and the way the sunlight bathed her face, walked up to sit beneath a tree. On the way, he stopped at the pile, fumbled through a pouch, and came away with some oat clusters that he procured from the knight's safe house and took them to the grazing horses, Whitesteel and Clover. Both of them snuffled and whickered at his approach. Keeping a lump for himself, he gave each one of the others while he patted and spoke softly to them. Whitesteel suffered only moments before he began nudging and sniffing at Marc, looking for more. Clover was, by far, more agreeable and less greedy. When he had the notion to look up and find the strolling Alexandra, Marc found her gazing back at him, still wearing that thoughtful expression. Her hair was more or less dry, and she was tying it back with a leather cord.

"Something wrong?" he asked. The question seemed to surprise her from her musing, and her eyes regained clarity.

"N-no," she said. "I was just. . . . Do you think the ground ahead of us is too dangerous for night travel?"

"I don't know," he said, crooking Clover's head in his arm so he could scratch behind her ear while leaning against her cheek in something of a hug. Her earthy scent coiled in his nose. "The land between here and Calif is relatively flat, but that doesn't mean it's not riddled with chuck holes and deadfalls, if that's what you mean. Why do you ask?"

"I want to give the horses something that will make them . . . tireless . . . for a while. So we can get to Calif."

"That's what you want the berries for, isn't it?" Marc asked. She nodded. "And you would risk that?"

The shadow of the previous night moved across her eyes like storm clouds, and she had to shift them to something more neutral than his hard gaze. His chest. "I don't want to risk them, but we have little choice. We have to get to Calif as quickly as possible," she said. "What I have in mind won't have terrible side effects if we let them rest once we get there. Let them balance it out. But I'm more worried about more mundane problems."

He started to protest, thought better of it, instead let out a huff through his nose. "It would be optimal to find a road to travel on, but the light from the moon should give us enough view as long as we don't try to run them during the night. It will still be dangerous."

A ghostly smile drifted past her lips. "What hasn't been?" she said. "At least we seem to have left behind the Eldritch."

"Yeah, maybe," he said, gave Clover a last pat and let her head go so she could munch at the grass. "But I think you should give it more consideration."

"What do you think I'm doing?" she spit.

"Between your morose Guardian and your lunatic actions, I haven't figured that out quite yet!" he returned.

Alexandra's face clenched, and her hands balled into fists that were pressed into her thighs. She became flushed, the red rising into her cheeks so quickly that he feared she might pass out. Marc waited for the coming eruption, prepared to meet it head on with all the same arguments he used on Gyssel when she was being stubborn. Regardless of its ineffectiveness. Instead, she ground her teeth at him and spun away to stomp down the beach, hugging herself tightly. He blew out the breath he had been holding and turned towards Whitesteel and said, "Get ready for a long ride, my friend."

Whitesteel laid his ears back and snorted.

Alexandra was gone for the better part of an hour and when she returned, she wore an expression that was only partly mollified. The anger was still there, but carefully cordoned off by studied neutrality. Her cloak was twisted and held up by the bottom in front of her like a sack. He chuckled and took a bite from the jerky he dug out of his pack.

With one hand, she unclasped the cloak and laid the bundle beneath a tree a few feet away from where he sat with their supplies. She was arranging it when she suddenly stiffened. "I don't like making decisions like this, but I don't see any alternative, do you?"

"Not any that will get us to Calif any faster," he said.

"Then why are you giving me so much guff?"

"Because I need to know that you aren't losing yourself to obsession."

"And that means what?"

"It means that you've pushed yourself too close to the line in pursuit of this goal and you know it. Several days ago, it was your Guardian's self-control that was putting everyone in danger. Now it's you."

She whirled on him. "I don't need any lectures about what kind of dangers we face."

"You do as long as I'm with you and a part of this madness!"

She sputtered, her face screwing up in red anger again. "How dare you?" she finally hissed out. "I am an Earthmother of the highest order with a Lineage that extends into the mists of time immemorial. I am trying to stop something that will eventually rip this world apart! How dare you speak to me like this?"

"Am I supposed to be intimidated by this little outburst of elitism?" Marc said. "Or have you forgotten that *I* extend into the mists of time immemorial?" He stood up, threw the bit of jerky he had left to the ground. "You worked hard to get me here. Don't shirk away now that the bill is coming due."

"Am I interrupting something?" Sandoren's voice startled them both. That neutral look swept over Alexandra's face as quickly as it had gone, and Marc cleared his throat loudly.

"No," She said. "We were discussing the rest of the journey to Calif."

"Really," Sandoren said, stepping nearer, his hand resting easily on the hilt of his sword. Del was walking just behind him, staring down at the ground, and bumped into the ffolk's back when he stopped. The man's face pinched up in irritation for a moment. "By the way all the animals are fleeing, I thought maybe there was a fire."

"Do you know where we are or don't you?" Alexandra asked.

"We're on the north beach of the sea," he said. Marc smirked.

"Thanks, genius," she barked. "Why don't you two men go find a bear to wrestle or something while I prepare these berries?"

"It'd probably be easier than this," Marc mumbled. It was Sandoren's turn to smirk, though it lacked substance, and Alexandra sniffed loudly. Del suddenly let out a burst of laughter that caught all of them off guard and before they knew it, Alexandra was smiling, though somewhat wanly.

"Just leave me be for a while," she said softly. "I'll be finished within the hour."

"Sure, okay," Marc said, his former anger dispersed, the void it left unable to re-inflate. When they turned away from each other, he found Sandoren walking next to him, Del closely in tow.

"What is she doing?" he asked quietly.

"Dumping Earthpower into them so we can ride nonstop to Calif," Marc answered. Sandoren frowned and, Marc could tell, mentally messaged his backside. A second later, he uttered a curse.

"Guess I'll get some sleep while I still can," he said and peeled away from them. Del continued to follow Marc as he walked down the beach.

He found an outcropping of rock that was large enough to lounge on and sat down. Del plopped down next to him and arranged himself in reflection of Marc's posture. Almost immediately, tiny fiddler crabs popped out of nearby holes and scuttled over to the rocks, encircling them in a dancing mob. Marc pulled his legs up, placed one on another rock, away from the small creatures, and hooked his other leg over it. Del, experiencing a seldom seen alertness, copied the gesture.

Marc smiled, crossed his arms. Del crossed his. Marc placed his hands in his lap. Del did so as well. Marc made a few more gestures and watched Del mimic them, then pulled the honeyed oat lump from his pouch and handed it to the boy.

"Thank you," Del said and popped it in his mouth, a slow smile spreading over his moonish face as the substance dissolved in a sweet explosion.

"You're welcome," Marc said.

"You're welcome," Del piped. Marc raised an eyebrow and chuckled. Again, he was copied. Marc tousled his hair. Del tousled his. They played the game for several minutes until Del suddenly stopped and stared out over the water. Marc expected his face to go slack and lifeless as usual, but it took on a shrewd, thoughtful one instead.

"What's wrong, Del?" Marc asked, not really expecting anything.

Without pulling his eyes from the horizon, Del said, "It comes." Then, within a span of a heartbeat, his face went flat and his eyes clouded. A thin line of drool fell from his opening mouth. Marc shook his head. "What happened to you, kid?" He gave Del's hair a last, tender tousle, and lost himself in the waves that rolled against the shore farther down the beach.

While the sun crawled overhead, Marc occasionally pulled his gaze away to check the missing boy. When he found Del still staring numbly out at the water, he passed his eyes over the tiny crabs scrabbling at the bottom of the rocks like children vying for attention from a busy parent. Or like worshippers seeing their god suddenly in the flesh.

Once enough time had passed by them, Marc carefully eased himself off the rocks so as not to step on any of the jostling creatures. He gently tapped Del's meaty arm, leaning over just short of being unbalanced, and had to do so several times until the boy's ponderous gaze swung in his general direction. "Come, Del," he said and watched the fog in his eyes part just enough for a spark of understanding to reach beyond them into his mind. He smiled and turned and dropped his feet to the sand.

Marc hid a wince, waiting to hear the characteristic crunch of the hard-shelled bodies beneath him, but the crabs scuttled aside so that Del's feet only crunched into sand. Marc watched in fascination as the little beach-bugs drifted back into their homes once Del began moving away from them.

When they returned, Alexandra was feeding the horses a handful of berries, a subdued but pained expression marring her simple beauty. She was about to give Whitesteel a portion, when he called out, "That's not necessary." Her eyes flashed as she looked at him, course words riding her lips, and he had to hold up a hand. "He doesn't need it."

Her anger turned to perplexity. "Are you telling me he doesn't get tired?"

"Yes, he gets tired, as do I," he said. "But it'll take more than the few days it'll take us to get there."

She looked as if she didn't quite believe him, but put the remaining handful into a pouch already filled with them, and proceeded to tighten the cinch straps around Clover and Day. Sandoren still lay beneath a nearby tree, eyes closed and arms tucked behind his head. The anger that he carried around him like a banner was absent, and it gave him totally different look. Peaceful. It brought out the natural beauty and grace his kind were noted for instead of the tense, straining expression he normally wore.

Marc swung himself up onto Whitesteel's back, watched Alexandra as she climbed into her saddle. "Have you ever done this before?" he asked suddenly.

"What, exactly?" she asked, her eyes closing to slits.

"Ridden nonstop for several days?"

"Uh. . . no? Why?"

Marc smiled and clucked at Whitesteel. Never suffering idleness well, the great white horse started beneath him with barely controlled energy. Marc walked him down to the water's lapping edge while Alexandra's, "What? Why are you smiling?" followed him. When an answer wasn't forthcoming, she turned her attention to the napping ffolk, prodding him with her voice. He answered her with a tired groan, but was up and on Veraddin quickly enough. Del climbed up on Day like a pro.

The sun was dipping toward the western horizon when they left, and the glittering water was far, far behind them, cloaked now in darkness and silvery moonlight, before they did make a quick stop for brief repast of jerked beef. After taking care of other of Nature's needs, they were back on their horses and moving through the moon swept plains at a trot.

Chapter 74

Almost

"*My* lady?" It whispered through the shock that numbed out her senses. The young man held out the parchment, unrolled and crimped to keep it from falling in on itself. It was like a dead leaf, a squared off piece of whiteness that caught the moving air and struggled against the grip that held it. It crackled, not loudly, but it filled her ears, blotting out all the other sounds that railed back from the street, including the young man's voice which seemed to slow down so far that it became a slow rolling thunder. "My lady?"

"What," Maelyrin said. "What did you say?"

"My Lord Pendragon and his party left this past eve," the young man said, holding out the parchment which bore the crest of Lord Baland. His eyes told her that he was concerned for her, her sanity most likely, as his own eyes were squinting up from the bottom. Yet it did not pass into her brain, staying only where it was safe. Not that it was able to be considered. Her mind was reeling in terrible frustration. *He's saying he's gone. That Marc's gone. How can this be? He was here. He still has to be.*

"W-where did he go?"

"I'm not quite sure, my lady," he said. "They left rather suddenly." He still held that crackling paper, and she suddenly felt the urge to rip it out of his hands, tear it into shreds and throw the pieces of it into his idiotic face. She looked back at

Kiyo and hated his impassive look. Hated that she did nothing last night to get them into the city. If she were here last night, they would have met him. Only a scant few hours and a single guard had thwarted her. No bandits or monsters or bad weather. Only a single ovoid face peering over a locked gate back lit by pale moonlight. She wanted to scream until her voice gave out.

Behind her, the city went about its business. Hand-drawn and horse drawn wagons full of goods rumbled on the walks amidst lacquered carriages pulled by teams of four and even six horses and hand carried limousines. Mounted soldiers clopped among throngs of pedestrians. Women wearing simple clothes all the way to fine silk, high necked dresses, walked next to men in similar finery all the way down to worn leathers and burlap. Artisans, merchants, nobles, and laborers mixing in the transitory veins and arteries that connected their respective, exclusive, communities.

Yelling, hawking, talking, jingling, creaking, clopping, clacking, clucking—all a swirl of sound that mixed into a dull drone over and above the singular sources. The heavy odor of horse and beast, the acrid smell of smoke, the delicious scent of cooking food, the rotten fish and salt stench of the harbor, and even the dry, dusty whiff of the old wood and brick of the buildings and docks and ships drifted among the movement and sound of the living city of Hestaff, knocking softly on the shield of frustrated anger that surrounded Maelyrin.

If she wasn't so focused on her internal conflict, she would be amazed and wondered at the sights going on behind her, even though the whole of Hestaff was relatively small to some of the other cities across the land she secretly wanted to see. But her mind was barely in a state just for her to answer the young man that had delivered the message she least wanted to hear. "W-where did they go?" she finally asked.

He was looking over her shoulder in a blatant stare at Kiyomori, his eyes wide and his mouth drawn in a thin line with a quirk at the corner, as if his tongue wanted to stick out that side. He didn't take his gaze away, as he said, "We do not know, my lady, but they abandoned their plans to go by arranged ship." His brows drew together for a moment, a thought flashing by his twin walnut windows. "Please, remain here while I consult on this matter," he said. He waited for a stumped nod and disappeared inside.

With non-seeing eyes, she let her gaze roam over the porch of the structure, of the men sitting there watching Kiyo with more than a passing interest, and let it wander out over the yard and the nearby side street. The people moving there were just blurs of color and noise. Like her mind.

Somewhere in the foggy mass, she struggled to quell the hopeless feelings that locked up her ability to think. She sucked in a deep breath and blew it out like Kiyo had showed her in the down times during their travels. Some of the anger went with it, the muscles at the back of her neck began to loosen. Another breath, more clearing. She concentrated on it, on the air moving through her nose and into her lungs.

When the young man returned, she had obtained some measure of functioning. Enough to see the people and wagons crossing her vision. Not enough, however, to be moved by it. "Can you tell me which ship they were going out on?" she asked.

"I can do better than that," he said, holding out another of the small scroll tubes. "This is a request to book passage on the ship Lord Pendragon was to take. Present this to the offices of Blason Shipping. They will see to it that you reach, at least, the destination he arranged for."

She took it. "Why are you doing this?" she suddenly asked. Where the flicker of suspicion came from, she didn't know. He blinked a few times.

"Lord Pendragon is a friend," he said. "We try to assist him in any way we possibly can."

Lord Pendragon? "Thank you," she said, was about to tuck the scroll down in her belt when a thought struck her. "Uh. . . How do I find this . . . Blason Shipping place?"

"First time in Hestaff?"

A shadow of a smile creased her lips. "First time anywhere."

"In that case," he said. "I shall be happy to escort you to the shipyards."

Chapter 75

Homecomings and Old Friends

*I*t took them a little more than two weeks to make the journey from the shore of the sea to the lands surrounding the City of Towers. Calif. Stopping only to eat, stretch and water the horses. Sleep came with the steady plod of horses' hooves in shifts so they didn't lose their bearings or each other. While Alexandra was determined to run the whole way, it didn't turn out like that, the practicality of the situation seeping into her as quickly as the constant pounding trot wore on her muscles. Still, they made good time, especially when they intersected the flat expanse of the old highway and altered their course only enough the follow the well-traveled ribbon.

Luckily, as they pushed north, the weather stayed mild even though the season was supposed to be advancing into late autumn. The worst bothersome condition came only from a stiff wind that crept up from the direction they were headed and struggled against them for two days straight before giving in and disappearing. The group mostly bypassed the villages and towns that littered the road, becoming more and more numerous the farther they went, and stopped only when they needed to buy supplies or, once, to get a shoe replaced on Day after he threw one. Many times, they came across abandoned communities, one of the silent testimonies that the Dark Night had wreaked its havoc. Some of them were simply ravaged by time, but others bespoke more tragic or violent ends. Fire.

Plague. Redolent death lurked in these places and those traveling the roads with them observed silence while passing by. And Marc didn't necessarily think it was out of any sense of respect. It was more like suspicion. Or superstition. And even he found it slightly disconcerting when they fell under the watchful gaze of the many crows and vultures that rested on roof-peaks and tree limbs.

Just past Port Morgain, Marc showed them the remnants of an even more ancient roadway than the one that they were on. Instead of heading east, taking them to Balinoch, this one cut north through the heavy forestland and ran parallel to the coast and shaved several more days off their trip, not to mention that it might keep them from running into the armies of King Flandric. It would also take them to the small valley in which he built one of his many cabins. Although the ages old cobbles were mostly swallowed by the earth or long carted off for some house or pig sty foundation, it still offered a wide swath of open grassland that was little traveled.

It wasn't without a small amount of nostalgia that Marc looked down on the building once they finally entered the softly flowing valley. But it passed quickly, blending with thousands of other similar sights from the long chain of his past. It more brought about in him a pitched anxiousness that seemed completely opposite to the ragged exhaustion that infused his body, but was simply the strong urge to lay down and sleep for a few years.

Though Whitesteel was far from total exhaustion, he, too, had lost the pep that normally coursed through his veins. He wouldn't put up too much of a fuss if he were stabled. Of course, here, there was no stable, only wide, open grassland.

Marc was so lost in looking forward to sleeping in his bed that he didn't notice the wagon sitting out in front of it until Sandoren pointed it out. The door gaped open like a mouth. His sleepiness was suddenly pushed aside as was the thong holding his sword in its scabbard. Calmly, they moved down the slope toward the stone house.

Marc brushed a glance over the wagon and noted some casks of dried goods and let a small smile work onto his face. *Of course, it's only Marrillon.* After telling Alexandra and Sandoren, he slid from Whitesteel and crept to the door. Marrillon was a thief of the utmost ability and normally silent as the grave, but the rattle and clap of movement followed by muttered curses told him he was far out of his element. Idly, he wondered if Varn were with him.

Marc slipped into the dim interior. This house was newer and larger than the one near the grave site but no less familiar. It took him only a second to learn where the sounds were coming from and quietly moved toward the kitchen, unable to keep a grin from his face. He looked into the room and saw the man sliding some similar casks across one of the large counters that circled the room. His face bore the concentrated look of a man that would rather be doing something else. Anything else than moving lumps of heavy food stuffs into a little used house well outside the city walls.

Marc leaned softly against the door frame and waited while the ffolk moved and lifted and shifted the stores. When he finished and was just about to turn completely toward him, Marc, smiling broadly, said, "Getting along well?"

Marrillon leapt back, his fine boned face turning into a snarl, his violet eyes flashing. The fan of his long, silver hair tipped black obscured it only for a moment. The two short swords he kept strapped on his thighs in shortened scabbards appeared in his hands as if they had jumped there themselves.

Though playing with fire, Marc bellowed with laughter and remained in the vulnerable position against the door jamb. A storm of emotion flowed over Marrillon's face that finally ended with a smile and a slowly relaxed posture. With a showman's flare, the short swords returned to their housings. "You really shouldn't creep up on a person like that," he said.

"Are you admitting a lapse in attentiveness?" Marc asked.

"No," he said. "I knew you were there the whole time."

"Uh-huh," Marc said. "You look well, at any rate." He was lying. The man that stood before him looked as if life chewed him up and spit him out because of a bad taste. His skin was drawn and folded over the bones of his face like paper thin leather. His eyes, sunken within their sockets, were a disturbing blend of red seeping into the violet and the left one picked up a slight twitch in the outer corner; the pupils overly large in the colored irises. His hands seemed almost skeletal.

"Yeah," he said. "So do you." Marrillon held out a bony hand, which Marc took. At least his strength appeared steady and firm. Marc drew him into a heartfelt, slap on the back hug. "I'm surprised to see you so soon," he said, stepping away. "Sharla's message indicated you wouldn't be around for another cycle."

"We made better time than we thought," Marc said.

"We?" he asked. Another twitch flitted along his eye.

"Come," Marc said. "I shall introduce you."

He licked his lips. Marc narrowed his eyes. It seemed Marrillon's physical features weren't the only thing ravaged. The sudden flash of paranoia in his expression startled Marc deep in his breast. *He's . . . . changed,* Sharla had said. Yes, apparently more than he had considered. "How is Varn?" he asked as he led him out of the kitchen.

"He is well," Marrillon said. "Though he is not as active as he used to be."

"Is he ill?" Marc said.

"Just getting old," came the answer. "Present company excluded, humans tend to do that fairly quickly. It's been awhile since you were around."

"So I've been told."

Marrillon glanced up at Marc, that suspicion flitting over his face again. "You should come by," he went on once the episode was over. "He would be happy to *see* you."

Marc chuckled at Marrillon's choice of the word. Since Varn was blind. It meant little in practice though. The ffolk's longtime partner was anything but impaired by the loss of his physical sight. In fact, Marc often thought that his incredible skills would have been lessened had he had the use of his eyes.

Marrillon stopped just outside the door, shielding his face with one hand and, Marc noted, allowing his other to hover very close to the hilt of one of his swords. Sandoren's face pinched in disgust and outright hatred. Alexandra, always the cordial one, flashed him a wan smile. Del was occupied by a swarm of flying insects. The three of them still sat astride their horses.

"Marrillon del 'Abon. . . . This is Alexandra Moonglow, Sandoren, and Del," Marc said holding an arm out to his companions.

"Greetings," Marrillon said, a little too quickly, as he began to lower the sun blocking hand. The one near the weapon stayed where it was. His eyes flicked from one to the other, lingering a few moments on Alexandra, a glimmer of something moving behind his eyes. Interest, maybe, or suspicion. It was gone too fast for him to tell and then his eyes moved over to Sandoren. They stared at each other like two predators considering the same territory for several moments. Marrillon's gaze, full of the Traelynn arrogance, despite the man's more nefarious choice of careers, battled with the Faellyn's xenophobic one.

Marrillon broke off first with a diffidence that made Sandoren scowl. Marc stood passively aside, watching the interchange though he had an urge to cuff the both of them. Instead, he said, "Let me help you with the rest of these bundles," and grabbed a cask off the back of the waiting wagon, biting back the urge to groan as his aching muscles protested. Marrillon grunted and pulled off a burlap bag, the beans within clicking audibly.

Alexandra slid from her horse with deliberate care and stood stiffly next to Clover. Marc chuckled, not loudly, but enough to draw a quick look from her and a flash of anger that just as readily turned to amusement. She sniffed loudly, then with some pomp, straightened her clothes and walked, straight legged and slow, into the house, Del trailing after with a half blank stare.

Sandoren, too, was moving slowly, but wore it better than Alexandra. He gathered the three horses and began leading them around toward the back where a smaller feed house stood next to a well. Whitesteel simply moved off a ways and grazed.

The wagon was emptied fairly quickly with the two of them, even through a flurry of small talk questions finding out how each other was doing and the not so truthful answers given glibly past smiles and good natured claps on backs and shoulders. Still, as always, it was a warm pleasure for Marc to see people he could call friends. Friends that hadn't yet beaten him to the afterlife and could re-instill the bond of once familiarity they had shared in the years past. A solidifying of a history that, at times, seemed elusive and ghostlike.

Several times, he found him close to asking after Marrillon's health, but something stopped him, as if doing so, he might damage the frail rebuilding they were involved in. So, he kept his mouth shut when it wanted to spit out something about the way his skin pulled tight against his bones or the way his lavender eyes flicked from one thing to the next without really seeing anything or that twitch. The Marrillon he knew was not this Marrillon. Even the five points on his face, the places where he was touched so long ago by the hand of Terran'non, the Courier of Death, stood out where they didn't before, like small puckered scars.

It seemed quite fast when Marrillon was driving the draft horse forward with unpracticed gracelessness, but more than two hours had crawled by. When Marc returned inside, he found Sandoren asleep on the single couch that faced the doorway. Del was sitting on the floor quietly studying a number of black, clicking beetles gathering around him.

His body reminded him how tired he was, the ache groaning deep in his muscles now that there was nothing to keep his mind from noticing it, and the fog of exhaustion that swept up through him came so fast that he was finding it hard to keep his feet on suddenly unstable earth. He made his way through the house and stepped into his bedroom.

Alexandra lay curled up on the bed, a quilt from the wooden chest at its foot covering all but a wash of raven hair on a pillow. On a nearby chair, carelessly draped, was her travel cloak, pack, and, on the floor, her boots.

He smiled, then wobbled back out and went outside. Sluggishly, he dragged his saddle from its place on the railing and flopped it into the shade of the nearest tree and plopped down under its reaching branches. Sleep came quickly.

And it fled quickly. The shaking bringing him up out of his torpor to look into the emerald green of Alexandra's eyes while trailing prickles worked through him. "What's wrong?" Marc said. The daylight was fading into dusk, and it took him a few moments to remember where he was.

"Nothing," she said softly. "I'm going to the Grove now. Most likely I'll be gone all night."

He blinked while her words sunk in and he started to sit up. A touch of tingling velvet kept him from doing so. "Don't get up," she said. Her restraining hand lingered on his shoulder.

"Don't you want someone to go with you?"

"No," she said. "I shan't need any company."

"Alright," he said, laying back against the saddle with nonchalance. "If that's the way you want it."

Alexandra rolled her eyes and smiled broadly. "I'll return by morning," she said.

Marc grunted, feigning sleep, but watching her through slitted eyelids as she walked away.

Chapter 76

Urgent Messages and Painful Bonds

*T*he Grove was a little more than three hour's travel on foot north of one of Marc's many homesteads. It could have been quicker but Alexandra could not bring herself to Treewalk again. She supposed that she could have used the ground in much the same way, now that she was alone, but it had never been a strong skill. Mysodia, her sister Earthmother, always had more of an affinity with that form and she guessed it would only save a small amount of time. Besides, sometimes, using her own legs, especially after the lunatic ride from Hestaff, yielded unexpected benefits. Not the least of which was the working of her muscles; slowly leeching the ache and stiffness out that was unaffected by her use of her healing Power.

The median between day and night seemed to last forever, a calm of preternatural quiet as the sky went from burnished brass to deep violet, the icy crystals of stars as they winked into existence, the creatures of daylight as they settled in for the coming night and those of the darkness that were not fully awake yet. The stillness of the cool air held just the right amount of sweet scents of the surrounding forest. She could taste the coming winter.

The walk and the silence also seduced her mind into quiet, caressing away the worry, anxiousness, uncertainty, and fear that permeated her so subtly that she realized it only after it was buried under a fluffy comforter. For the first time in a long while, she was able to appreciate the wonderful solitude without the heaviness of her burden. She wasn't thinking of the Wound, or Del, or Marc, or Sandoren. She wasn't thinking of the Grove in any context other than that was where she was headed. There was no tiredness. There was no straining.

There was only the silence of dusk.

When she arrived at the Grove, the surrounding trees dropped their branches around her, touching her lightly with their ends.

So you have come.

Yes.

It is good that you hastened our call . . . . Our time here will soon lapse.

Call? It took her a moment to understand what that meant. Of course. The nearly overpowering obsession to get here, even by jeopardizing her life and the lives of her companions. And others. The dead trees suddenly flashed up in her mind's eye. *You are in danger?*

Do not mourn over those that gave themselves to this. Sacrifice is often necessary.

I killed them.

No. The danger was understood. The Wound spills its corruption into our Realm, taking the Blood of the Earth with it. Our progeny died willingly so that the precious cargo could be brought.

Are you in danger?

Come closer, that we may tell you of the path you must take.

The dawn was just lighting the eastern horizon as she made her way back along the trail she walked fully twelve hours prior. A chill had settled into the land overnight but she hardly felt its biting touch on her skin. Nor did the puffs of mist billowing out from her lips receive attention. So intent on what had been told her that she didn't see the shadowy figures crouching around a dark outcropping of rocks near where she exited the ancient Grove. She didn't feel their eyes upon her, and once well past, did not notice them slip from their positions and steal into the trees, headed for the city which cast a pale glow into the sky not far to the west while guardedly watching her. Alexandra only felt the passing danger as an afterthought that tickled the back of her neck. But it was well into sunrise when she did so, pausing to cast a hazy glance behind.

It was a stream winding through a meadow that finally split the fuzz in her mind enough to bring forth the full realization of the burden she was being asked to bear. Alexandra sat on the bank and watched the glimmering water while the shock worked its way through her body. There were no tears or wracking breaths. Only a buzzing numbness as the trickling water flowed by below her. It took the better part of an hour before she could erect walls strong enough for her to get up and resume walking.

She did not stop again until she was looking down into the hollow where Marc's house stood, and then, screened off from view by the tree line, watched the mundane activities going on there with a distant confusion. Sandoren was throwing out flakes of pressed hay to the waiting, excited horses, thin wisps of it trailing momentarily behind each portion. The bare whisper of morning breeze brought to her nose the sweet smell of it. Marc reclined on a chair beneath the overhanging porch, legs propped up on the railing, arms tucked behind his neck. Del sat nearby studying the ground, no doubt at a gathering of bugs.

The scene translated into something she never experienced, only saw in other people's lives as her travels brought her in contact with them, and it struck her as something odd. Because they were not what they seemed just then. They were dangerous, powerful persons. Anything but the sudden flash of family that posed itself. This place was not a farm or a ranch, but simply a weigh station before they plunged back into the unknown, probably to court death a hundred times over.

Yet, there they were, portraying the world of the normal that she never knew. Marc the wise father, Sandoren the rebellious youth, Del the introspective child. No worries or cares, only the day to day chores which, while a tough, hard business, guaranteed a deep sense of comfort and security. There was a pristineness to it that warmed her; a private slice of things that could have been.

Once.

And when the moment passed, it was as if it were lost forever. It was as if, just then, she had had a choice between a safe and secure world and the life chosen for her so long ago and that by dawdling, watching, the chance moved on.

And once her cognizance returned and the burden she carried again settled itself on her shoulders, she looked down to see only Marc and Del within the early morning light. A couple of minutes must have moved by as Sandoren finished feeding the horses and disappeared inside the house, but he could have been a ghost for all the notice she took of it. Even though she had been staring at the scene the whole time.

She sighed, saw the cloud of vapor vanish quickly in the warming air and headed down toward the house. A constant battle raged to keep the knot of anxiety nestling in her guts from growing out of control. *How am I going to tell them? How?*

"Good morning," Marc said, only one eye opening to greet her. When he got a good look at her, his feet came down from the railing and he sat up. "Are you alright?"

"I must speak with you," she said, leaning on a post. Her voice was hollow and far away; her face without emotion, though the emerald of her eyes fairly blazed with the light of turmoil.

"You are," he quipped, knowing as soon as he said it that it was an impropriety. Alexandra's face suddenly pinched in anger.

"This is important!" she snapped. Marc was already holding up his hands in supplication, an apology on his lips. Her anger washed back into an almost fearful look, and, for a moment, her hands came up to fold over her mouth. For one tiny moment she shivered and thought a sob was about to break from her throat, but instead, she removed her hands from in front of her face and said with a voice hard and steady, "I need you to take me to the Catacombs of Mordaanimer."

"What? The Catacombs? Of Mordaanimer, the Dragon?" Marc said, coming to his feet. "Are you insane?"

"I might be," she said. "But that is where I must go. Only through the Catacombs can I complete the task laid out for me. It holds the key that I need to close the Wound that is destroying our world."

Marc sat down slowly, the color all but drained from his face. "And I thought you were going to ask for something difficult," he said, staring out into the field that surrounded them.

"I would have thought someone who has lived as long as you would not be perturbed with facing death." She said it with a feeble smile and a small voice.

"Death is not the problem," he said. "It's all the suffering that will come before it that I'm concerned about. That is not something I relish."

"There's more," she stuttered.

"Of course there is," Marc answered, blowing out a loud breath. Silence followed, a long and uncomfortable one.

When their eyes met, she said, "I-I need to ask you something. . . . Something that is intrinsic to my quest . . . Something I have no right to."

"And that would be?"

Another minute drew out too terribly long. She was vaguely aware of a shadow in the doorway. Sandoren. Though Alexandra never looked at him. Instead, her fiercely blazing eyes cooled into windows to elsewhere for that small eternity. "The Forever one is the key," she said softly, an echo of some other voice.

"Alexandra. What is it?" Marc asked, suspicion rising into the back of his throat.

The sound of her name brought her back, if slowly, nearly uncomprehendingly. "I need . . . . Will you. . . . There must be a Spirit Bond between us."

"What?" Both Marc and Sandoren said. While Marc's was heavy with disbelief, Sandoren's carried a strong note of betrayal. Alexandra's eyes moistened with panic, and she stopped breathing.

"Spirit Bond," she finally croaked out.

Sandoren could only repeat his interrogative, but it was Marc that hissed out, "Absolutely not!"

"Marc," Alexandra said quickly.

"No!" he retorted. "I will not!"

"Please."

"How can you . . . . Do you know what you are asking?"

She nodded.

"No you don't!" Marc was nearly yelling, his voice going course. He stomped off the porch and down into the grass, staring up into the blue heavens as if it were a dream he was about to wake from.

"I know what I ask—"

"No, you don't!"

"Please. Listen to—"

"No!" Marc looked at her, fury lining his face like cracks in stone. "I will not do it! You have no idea what you are asking of me. No!" Before any other words could be uttered by her or the stunned into silence Sandoren, Marc hissed out a breath and strode away from them, making his way for the tree line.

He was sick and angry, afraid and stunned all at the same time, a cloud of heat suffused his entire being. The house had passed from view, blocked by the hill and trees, when he consciously picked up on the soft foot falls moving not far behind him and whirled, terse words coming to lips pressed firmly together over grinding teeth.

He stopped and stared, his mind slow to translate that it was Sandoren standing only a few feet from him and not Alexandra. Though Sandoren, too, wore an expression filled with anger, there was a softness smoothing the edges away. Deep wonderment clouded his amber eyes. "What do you want?" Marc snapped.

"You must reconsider," he said. His voice was steady.

"Have you taken a fever of the brain as well?" Marc said. "No. I will not."

"There has to be a reason," Sandoren said through a clenched jaw.

"None good enough," Marc spat. "Now leave me." He turned and began walking again.

"Listen to her!"

Marc stopped short, spun on his heel and was standing in front of the ffolk before another breath could be taken. He grabbed the man's tunic with both hands and jerked him within an eye width of his twisted face. "You love her so much," Marc hissed. "You Bond with her."

Sandoren heaved, pushed Marc away even though the human weighed nearly half again as he. "She doesn't love me," he said. Pain bled underneath his angry countenance like a bruise. Marc was about to shove back when the insinuation slapped him.

"What?" he said.

Sandoren shook his head once, violently, and swung, clubbing Marc on the chin. His head snapped back with a pop, while balls of lightning exploded throughout his vision. Sandoren's voice took on an ephemeral sound. "You're as blind as you are stupid," echoed through his mind like an undulating wave. Unreal yet full of power. When Marc was capable of seeing the world around him rightly, Sandoren was striding away, flicking the hand that pounded him.

Marc watched him go as he slid to the grass, slowly messaging his chin though he was too numbed to really feel the pain throbbing there. Sandoren's words and their meaning batted against the inside of his head like a moth against glass trying to get at a flame. He knelt for several minutes silently willing strength back into his limbs.

Alexandra was sitting in the chair he had vacated, staring off into nothing, once he made his way back to the house. He, in turn, took to leaning against the post she had used. "Tell me why," he said softly.

She looked up at him, scouring his face with the dulled out green of her eyes. "I don't know why. Only that the Living Trees said it would be necessary. They said 'The Keystone of Fate is the Foreverman. Bind him to you that you may keep the path ahead'. Will you do it?"

Seconds passed. Marc crossed his arms over his broad chest and huffed. "An Earthmother tried to Bind me once."

"What? When?"

"Ages ago," he said. "She was foolish, but so was I. I allowed her to do it."

"And?" Alexandra's prompt was sallow, but he could just see the curiosity there, not quite hidden.

"She died," he said slowly, emphatically. "It was a horrible, agonizing passing. She suffered and I suffered" She blinked at him but said nothing. He spread his hands. "I cannot be Bonded that way."

"If the Trees say it can be so, then it can be so."

"And you would risk it on their say so." It was not a question. And there was no hesitation in her answering nod. Marc could only huff out another breath and try to relax into the wood of the post he leaned against. Defeat was creeping into his voice, but he could not give in. "Have you ever been Spirit Bonded?"

She shook her head.

"Do you know how intimately terrible it can be?" he asked. "Do you know what passes between the Bond?"

"Yes," she stammered. "Yes, I am versed on it."

"I know you can pull it from your instruction so long ago," Marc pressed. "But you do you really know?"

"No."

"I will know every wish, every desire, every secret. I will know every pain of every scar on your body. I will know what you like, what you hate. I will *know* you like no other can."

"Yes," she said.

"But you will know me, as well. You will experience all the suffering I have suffered in all the generations I have existed and you will *feel* it in that single moment when the Bond opens. You will experience every horror I have witnessed in my cursed life. Every revulsion. Every tragedy. In that single moment. That is what killed Brysell. That is what nearly took me in a blazing torment. And that is what you are asking of me."

"I know it," she said.

"And you still want it?"

"It's not about 'want'," she said. "It's about need. It has to be done."

Marc grunted and spun himself around the post, the urge to flee up the hill again pressing into the pit of his stomach. "Marc." He resisted the pull her voice had in it, but failed.

"Yes?"

"I would not ask this of you if I didn't believe it was necessary. I wouldn't ask this of you if I had not argued this against the burden laid at my feet. . . . I would not ask this if I . . . didn't want it."

Marc staggered. Like the time before, when she levered him into coming on this fool's errand, his shoulders slumped. "Alright," he said. "Alright. But you must know that I do this under protest."

"I. . . understand," she said.

"When . . . . When does this have to be done?"

"Now," she said. Marc dropped a curse into his hand.

"What about Del?" he asked. Marc was groping for time and he knew it, though he also knew there was no getting it.

"What about him?"

"What if something goes wrong?"

Alexandra considered briefly. "Nothing will," she stated. She stood slowly and extended a hand. "Please," she said. Marc looked at the hand as if it were covered in blood and gore; looked at it as if it held his very life in it. Which, in a way, it did. And though he knew all the dangers, indeed, could feel the old agony bubbling up from the swamp of his memory, he realized he was anxious too. His body was flushing with heat, even as he stood looking at her.

Suddenly, he sensed her discomfort, her rising embarrassment, and took hold of her hand. The familiar tingle started immediately from the touch and jolted through him, increasing the reaction of his blood. And before he realized what he was doing, Marc pulled her into his embrace and kissed her.

Alexandra went rigid when his lips met hers. But it quickly melted away, taking with it her embarrassment, and she began to return the kiss with an awkward reluctance born out of innocence. The current that went through him tripled in intensity, becoming nearly unbearable as it worked its way just under his flesh. The longer it raged the more he reacted. Yet Alexandra relaxed deeper. Finally, he could stand it no longer, so sweet its taste, like honey, and so soft its touch, like silk, that he had to pull away. Alexandra did not resist, sensing the need to break the connection.

She stood back at arm's length, her eyes resting languidly on his. Her cheeks were flushed, and it radiated out from her in waves of confidence and need, surrounding her in a charged envelope that fairly crackled. No doubts or fears existed there. However, it was Marc that began to twinge with a pale fright. It raised the hairs on his arms. The danger that had been washed over by the ecstasy of the kiss began rising like the sun within him.

Sensing his reluctance, possibly even the why, she stepped forward and placed a finger across his lips. "Don't," she whispered. Arcs of lightning flew through him, carrying her words into the depths of his being and pushing aside his growing fears. A quake moved through him.

He followed her inside, and when the door closed, casting them in a dusty dimness, it also closed him in dread. Alexandra turned almost immediately and looked at him piercingly. Her breath was coming in long controlled rhythms and though she appeared relaxed on the whole, her face was still showing a weighty tightness around her eyes. "Ready," she said softly. Her voice was tremulous.

"No," Marc said, smiling. "But that hasn't stopped you before."

It brought a smile to her that was, if not brightly filled, certainly genuine, but she said nothing. Instead, she placed her hands on his chest and leaned on him ever so slightly. Marc flinched, held a breath in pinching ribs as the shockwaves radiated out from the press of her hands. Alexandra drew in a deep breath and closed her eyes.

The warmth was almost instantaneous, flowing from the point of her hands and through his body in a rush, outward, into the room, enveloping them both in its cocoon. It filled his ears like wind, taking away all other ambient sounds and displacing them, gently swarming into his nose and whiffing away the dusty scent of his long unused home and the slight, flowery scent of Alexandra. From within him, he heard a dull thrumming, felt it reverberating inside him. His heart. It became audible in the warm pocket, a thud-thud that pushed against the warmth in his ears. Following it, a fainter sound, like an echo but faster, shorter. One that matched a pulsing from Alexandra's palms. Slowly, the thump of his heart and the beat of Alexandra's moved into one another, hers slowing, his speeding up, until they became one. And all at once, the thrumming matched the pulsing matched the reverberating.

Tingles rippled through him and into her. He could see the prickle along the bare skin of her arms. His body felt slogged but enervated all at once, a deep relaxation that made his very bones feel jellied. He began swaying to the heartbeat. Rhythmically, softly, not the least bit jerkily. A smooth rocking back and forth completely in tune with Alexandra.

The undulating comfort slid over his eyelids, making them heavy, and his head started to bob. But just when he thought he was about to fall asleep, his gaze fell upon Alex's and locked there, inextricably caught. Her eyes were depthless, infinite, and blazing with a cool green fire that filled the entire exposed surface.

The sensation of falling slammed through Marc, almost as if a hole had suddenly appeared beneath his feet and he was dropping away from himself. He had vague recollections of the time before, when that long ago Earthmother tried this, but it was not important now. In fact, nothing but Alexandra's eyes mattered. Nothing but the falling mattered.

Because the falling brought him closer to her. Not physically, but something greater than that. A coldness washed over him, making him shiver, freezing his thoughts, though it was the refreshing sort of briskness gotten from stepping into a breeze after too long a time spent in a stuffy room. After the initial rush, a whisper of a thought bubbled through him.

Souls.

Their souls were joining, melding together. The falling stopped and with it the numbness of his mind. However, the clarity that remained was anything but normal. There was no extraneous thoughts, no musings backed by the more primitive of his urges. Hunger, pain, the drive to procreate, all emotion was gone save for swirling warmth and chill and a pure clearness of mind. It was through this clearness that he was able to understand what was happening.

There was a steady compressing as their spirits juxtaposed themselves, a pressure building behind some dam of flimsy material that would only hold so much before bursting. And it was going to burst. Soon. He could feel it already, coming slowly, inexorably as the pulsing chill, the throbbing warmth started to smooth out and come together as their heartbeats had.

Though he had lost much of the sense of his body, he knew he was grimacing, knew that his muscles were tensing in sporadic waves. Though he could only really see the green of Alexandra's eyes, he could sense the same happening in her body.

The pressure became unbearable, reaching almost a sweet pain.

At the same time, they sucked in a breath.

The bubbles of their pressing souls suddenly conjoined in one quick flash of freezing heat, becoming one. . . .

. . . . a hurricane roared through him, sweeping him up in a sudden blackness full of silent noises and raging feelings. The chill became biting and the warmth became searing. Before his eyes, images blurred into streams of color and motion, whizzing by from the force of gales nonexistent. They spun and whirled, flashed and darkened. All in the span of a thunderous heartbeat.

After another of the roaring swirling gusts slowed, and his mind came back to him enough to begin to see them. Images of Alexandra, the ghosts of her past steeped with feeling and emotion, giving off its aroma like freshly baked bread. Her memories. Her thoughts. Her being. All of it flowed into him, channeled now by his exerting mind and filling him slowly as honey fills a cup.

Further they slowed, disseminating into singular, understandable bits. He could feel the pain of the trees' deaths as sharply as a pinprick even as he witnessed it through her eyes. Following it closely was her guilt, still clinging to its rafters and casements like cobwebs. The long ago rush of the first time she was able to draw Power from the Earth was like a thousand mint leaves falling on his tongue and like biting full into a lemon. The love she felt for Sandoren was the warm comfort of an old blanket.

The love she felt for him, an inferno of confusion.

Each memory passed through him, the flood slowing further and further as they went by now that the dam that was their individual spirits was broken. Once it became a trickle, Marc's awareness of his surroundings began to reassert itself. Reality became caught up in the fading interchange and, for moments, he could not tell the difference, but it was there all the same.

It was Alexandra's ragged screaming that brought him back completely.

Marc's eyes were watering profusely and fuzzed out his sight, making her face look like a blossom of blurred light, but he could not yet pull his hands up from his still rigid body to wipe them. So, all he could do was stare at her form while her crying filled the air around them.

It was him that was flooding through her that made her scream. His vessel, so much larger than hers, backed by so many centuries of existence, poured in the torment as an ocean instead of the mere stream of her consciousness. Her pain shocked through him, still yet a dull throbbing awakening his tired nerves, but growing and would soon fill him with liquid agony, driving him up into the heights of unawareness. As the echo of the new Bond strengthened, her pain, driven into him, would yet bounce back into her, and so forth, until her body shut down completely from the pain. He knew he himself probably would walk away, but not before he experienced her own death, repeated tenfold through the fledgling connection she had so hoped for.

Like Brysell, the one before, Alexandra was caught off guard by the torrent rampaging through her, and he could feel that part of her conscious mind struggling to find purchase somewhere, anywhere that she could halt the flowing torment and ride the wave. But it was feeble at best against the terrible strength of his past and the curse which held him in his state of immortality. She scrabbled frantically, but it was not enough. The fingers of her sanity held no chance of finding a hold. And she was tiring. Not only could he sense it in the flood of sensation flowing back to him, but could also hear it in her fading, tightening screams. The thrumming single heartbeat, now more of a distant tone, started tugging in erratic jerks and flops.

But Marc could do nothing. Only watch and feel and wait as she slowly drowned in his memories. Though he knew her love for him, though his feelings burned fiercely just the same, it was his curse that rose up and clapped shackles on them, her as well as he. Like so many times before, he stood rigid, unable to act but forced to observe with the clarity of the insane as his very soul tore and rent Alexandra's.

Mentally, he turned away, struggling with every ounce of will he possessed to accept the pain that was filling him in lapping wavelets. Waited for it to consume him as it was only right of him to do so for letting her do this thing. Wanting the punishment as fertilizer for his guilt.

It itched and burned like an open sore, was fueled by her cries. And, like so many times before, he scratched at it, widening it as he sought to quell the prickling, driving deep his knife of guilt until his very nerves were laid bare, raw and blazing, to take in the agony. Mentally, he yelled in frustration, knowing that no matter the suffering, the circle would not be complete. No matter how much he wanted it, Death would only tease him as it came for Alexandra, and he would waken at some time in the future, next to her inert body, to a new crop of anguish ready to be harvested.

Circle.

The thought struck him even as his physical self began to growl. And it was then that he remembered the riddle posed to him through Alexandra's actions previously. Concentrating on his own pain made it possible for his body to unlock. Once it did, he acted, coiling his flagging muscles into jerking movements.

Marc grabbed Alexandra by the shoulders, feeling his fumbling grip as a lightning strike flashing through the Bond, yanked her close and slammed his mouth over hers.

The massive discharge of his touch brought a strangled gasp from her, but it immediately lessened the uncontrolled freshet that raged in them, channeled it into a stream that allowed her to get the tiniest grip against the force of his past. The Bond shuddered and Alex's strength surged. She renewed her struggle at the same time surrendering to Marc's kiss.

Minutes slid by on snail trails, each one bringing the lessening of the terrible pain that engulfed them and strengthening the new Bond. The passion that they felt for each other, held strong by the kiss, kept the now fading rush channeled safely inside boundaries she was able to manage. And as the transfer wound down, so did the anxiousness of the kiss.

But it did not stop, only became deeper. Even as their heartbeats began to separate into their respective rhythms. Their bodies were left empty of strength once the Bonding process finally wound down completely.

Finally, she stepped away, still holding onto Marc's arms to steady her swaying and said, breathlessly, "What did you do?"

"I completed the circle," he said.

"Thank you," she said and fell back into his embrace. Several seconds went by before she said, "I almost died."

"Shh! It's not important now," Marc said. Though the Bond was now complete, there was only the barest hint of its existence, placed into the background of his exhaustion. Unconsciousness was stealing over them both like the sunset.

"But it is important," she said against the plain of his chest. "You warned me, but I didn't listen."

"You, yourself said you had no choice," Marc answered. She pulled away only enough to look up at him.

"Marc," she said. "You have been warning us about things ever since we met and we, both Sandoren and me, have argued or ignored your advice almost without fail. Our pride has gotten us into more trouble on this trip."

"Stop it," he said. "It hasn't been that bad."

"Yes, it has. It is very difficult for me to admit that you make me feel like a child in this world. And I believe Sandoren feels the same. I should have listened to your objections. I should have given you time to think about it. I should not have pushed—"

Marc's fingers on her lips quieted her. "It's not important now. It's done and both of us came through it."

"But—"

"It would not have happened had I not wanted it on some level. . . Wanted you on some level." He felt a surge of feeling flow into him, matching a surge that rose in him as he said it. It, at first, caught him off guard. "It is going to change everything between you and your Guardian," he said, not knowing why.

Her face pinched in concern, and she looked at the front door. Through the Bond, a sallowness flowed, solidifying it more than just the look. "Everything changed the moment I started this damnable journey."

"He loves you,"

"I know he does," she said, then looked back into his eyes. "But let's not discuss it now. All of my strength is gone and so is yours. We must rest."

Marc nodded. "Yes, I suppose we should." He took a step, at the same time letting go of one of her arms so he could pull her to his side, and stumbled. Alex laughed, weakly. "I guess I need it more than I thought," he said.

Supporting each other, however weakly, they moved into the bedroom and fell upon the large bed dominating the room. Clouds of dust exploded up from the linens, and they coughed amid tired giggles until it settled. "Thank you," Alex whispered, then gave him a soft lingering kiss. Both of them were asleep, soundly, before Marc could reply.

Chapter 77

The Consequences of Choice

"*My*, my. Isn't this cozy." The voice reached down into the waters of sleep, grabbed Marc around the throat and lifted him from the oblivion into a deep fog of grogginess. His arm snaked out to find the handle of his sword but found nothing. Like a lightning bolt running through his body, his eyes snapped open, and he thrust himself up from the blankets Alex and he were nested in.

Several shadows hovered in the doorway, but he couldn't quite make them out. Alex moaned next to him. "Collar the witch before she can call on her magic!" the shadow in the center said. His voice was rough and overly loud. A voice that enjoyed the mantle of command but without the strength to back it.

One of the nearer unknowns moved closer, holding out his arms. In his hands, he grasped two half circlets made of some metallic substance Marc didn't recognize. They seemed to be joined in the middle, but not by a hinge. The shadow was shoving it towards Alex's neck. Marc tried to react, tried to knock aside the man's hand, tried to do anything to keep him away from his slowly wakening Bondmate, but his body was frozen rigid.

Little did it matter, however, for another man was close to him and planted a boot into his chest and drove him back into the bed when he flinched. His head thudded against the headboard and sent flashes of light through his vision. Over the buzz that suddenly rose in his ears, he heard Alex cry out in surprise and fright.

Now that Marc was being personally brought into the scuffle, his curse unshackled his body, and he swept his arm up underneath his assailant's leg, surprising the man. He spun away, his heel ripping into Marc's shirt and scraping his chest. Flailing for nonexistent hand holds, the man twisted down to the floor amid a yell. Marc's eyes were clear enough for him to see the man was wearing a gray uniform. Though he had never seen the insignias, he could guess whom they represented. The question of how the Imperials found them, though, still missed him.

"Marc?" Alex cried at almost the same moment as the order giver bellowed. Her attacker was dragging her up from the bed by the metal-like ring that now encircled her neck, his face a grimace against her struggling. Marc tried to get up again, but the softness of the bed began working contrary to his efforts, as if he was suddenly in a bog, and, coupled with the terrible heaviness in his body from the Bonding, he floundered instead of escaped the coiled blankets.

Another Imperial quickly appeared over him and there was a flash of light on steel.

Alex screamed, "NO!"

Liquid agony slid through Marc's belly as the Imperial grunted through the lunge. Marc went stiff and a gurgling growl fell from his lips. Hands flew to the blade that impaled him to the bed, slicing his palms against razor edges, sending arrows of pain radiating out from the deeper torment in his guts, but his strength was gone, seeping out into the blankets with his blood, and he could do nothing to stop the Imperial from his thrust. His eyes were stapled to the man above him, on eyes that were terribly young and terribly frightened. But as the moments passed, his gaze began to ooze down the Imperial's face. Before Marc fell back to the mattress, before the rigor of his body loosened from the transfixing blade, he saw that the sword was his.

Alex screamed again, this time in pain, and tried to double over in her attacker's grasp, but was only able to bring her legs up which allowed her to get dragged toward the door much more quickly.

"Get her out of here," the Imperial in charge barked. The motion and sounds around Marc began coming to him through molasses, and it seemed that it took more than an hour for Alex to be wrestled from the room, even with the addition of two more Imperials. Someone asked about the boy, and the terse reply from the leader was, "Kill him."

Again Marc struggled against his pinion, tried to speak, but only a gurgle and a wash of hot liquid poured out onto his chin. The sound drew the Imperial's attention, and he turned away from his men to step closer to the bed and look down on him.

He smiled. A thin wormy movement that cracked the planes of his lower face, but not beyond. Nowhere close to his cold brown eyes. "Some Guardian you are," he said, studying Marc's pallid face as if the prospect of watching him die was exciting. "Know that the witch will not receive the mercy you have." He frowned suddenly, and then, without preamble, leaned over and dropped a glob of spittle onto Marc's forehead. It burned where it struck and drooled over his skin. "A gift from the Empire," he said and turned toward the door while Marc fought the creeping darkness coming on him. At the threshold, the Imperial paused and half looked back at him, another grin etched into the bottom of his face. "I'd give you warning to watch out who you associate with, but then, it really won't help you," he said and sauntered from the bedroom. From beyond the door, he could hear Alex crying out and, barely, felt her pain and anger washing through the Bond.

Marc pushed once more against the sword hilt but could not muster any strength. It seemed that a ghost's hands were working on the weapon, so pale his flesh was and so little they could accomplish. Finally, they fell to the mattress with a dull splatter that Marc could only pick up through the sucking sounds his mouth was making. There was a final gasp that caught deep in his flaming chest and stayed there, growing rancid while a veil of darkness drew across his vision. His heart echoed in an empty breast, a slowing thud that pushed a fading warmth out of his back with each sallow beat and allowed an ethereal chill to settle in him.

Death stole over him while he was trying to remember why it was getting dark. . . .

Chapter 78

The Bitterness of Rejection

$\mathcal{S}$andoren ran Veraddin without thought or direction, letting the cool wind rush against squinting eyes and upturned face. Cold trails of dried breeze tears streaked his cheeks.

When he saw Alex and Marc going into the house he was suddenly taken by a terrible anger that demanded he get away, even though it was he that told Marc to go back. That whatever reason Alex wanted to Bond him must be a good one or she would not have suggested it. But seeing them, thinking that they were actually going to go through with it, gave him reason to think otherwise. With the force of a blow, he remembered all the looks and stares she cast in Marc's direction during their travels.

Now, his anger had been replaced by a morose numbness.

Veraddin's snorting and huffing brought him to the present long enough to realize the beast was getting overextended, so he reined him in, let him walk as he may. The horse took him through the trees in a slow meandering course while he looked for tufts of grass to munch. Limbs slapped Sandoren in the face but he hardly noticed.

On some level, Sandoren knew he was acting irrationally. He knew Alex didn't feel for him the way she felt for the human. Never had. And he wondered if what he was feeling was real or something that had blown out of control. Up until Marc Pendragon came into their world, his relationship with Alex was more on a level of close family than anything else. Brother to sister. But since, he could no longer accept that relation to her. He wanted something else. Something that he wasn't quite sure of.

Or did he?

The utter confusion that coursed through him built walls to his thinking mind. Every time he thought he had an answer, or was about to come to some sort of acceptance, he ran into the cold bricks of quandary and found himself turned away, led deeper and deeper into a labyrinth of half answered questions and festering emotion. A maze he was afraid he would not be able to find his way out of.

And fear. There was that.

"Coward," he mumbled, swallowing hard the metallic bitterness in the back of his throat. As Veraddin grazed, he drifted in and out of his reverie, unconscious of the sun's movement above him. As it drifted down towards the western horizon, Sandoren was finally able to seize on the sanity lurking within his mind and pull himself from the maze he locked himself into.

His feelings for Alex were strong. There was no denying that. That she had strong feelings for Marc Pendragon was fact as well. Regardless of that, he decided her reasons for Bonding the man was based on a need stronger than her feelings. It had to be. She was ever adamant about doing it. And though the human changed things, brought out feelings in her that he didn't think she realized, he couldn't see that it would sway her to change her decision. He forced himself to accept that things would never be the same. His relationship with Alexandra was no longer exclusive and, in that, his silent hopes became quenched as a morning fire.

His decision did nothing, however, to fill in the throbbing emptiness within his heart. It just made it possible to box it away behind walls of stone. For a time anyway.

Now, with dusk coming rapidly, and not sure how far he was from the cabin, he set his mind to getting back. Veraddin was reluctant to give up on his free head and jerked on his reins at each gentle tug Sandoren gave them. He was about to apply a firmer hand when a sharp twang lifted above the natural sounds of the woods.

Instinctively, he dropped closer to Veraddin's body, ducking just fast enough that the whistling arrow sped over his back and lodged into a nearby tree with a resounding crack. He freed his sword from its scabbard and slid off the opposite side of the horse and stepped behind the tree, pulling Veraddin with him. The beast, sensing the danger, gave up his munching and complied.

The arrow, still vibrating within the trunk of the tree, was black with red fletching, but he could not follow its path back to the bow that shot it. He dropped to a knee and scanned the forest, waited for the mysterious assailant to reveal himself. Spears of fading sunlight slanted through the canopy illuminating the bugs that filled the air with their humming. Seconds slipped by to their music.

Sandoren sank into the emptiness of his combat mind, all his previous thoughts and hurts pushed far away from him. He took in a slow breath through his nose. Skulking under the smell of loam, he could just make out the tangy odor of musky sweat and leather but could not decipher a direction in which it lingered. It seemed to be all around him as if whoever exuded it passed through the area several times just before Veraddin carried him here.

He bounced his gaze around a final time, sprang onto Veraddin's back, surprising the horse into a flinch. Quickly, he pulled the beast around to face the direction they had come and began nudging his flanks with his feet while keeping his head low and scanning the surroundings.

Movement within some hedges yards away grabbed his attention, and he let out a sharp shout as another arrow launched out from behind it. Veraddin lurched forward, bringing him out of the shaft's path, simultaneously breaking his fragile gaze with the form that released it. There was only a shadow in his mind's eye left of the figure.

Veraddin surged onto a trail chosen only by him, though Sandoren could feel the horse's weakness leap up almost immediately too. It would not be long before the steed faltered, but he hoped that it waited until they were out of bow range. They shot through the trees, weaving as they needed, while the twang and zip of arrows followed them, lodging into trunks and skittering off branches. Several times, bits of bark flew into Sandoren's eyes.

Suddenly, they broke out into a glade, and Veraddin heaved forward at a full gallop, putting all important distance between them and the bowmen. But Sandoren had to rein him in when several figures broke the tree line before them, running toward them with swords and yells high. Muted black armor caught the light and defeated it, giving the marauders a splotched appearance, like dark lichen on the lee side of rocks. Feathers adorned them in bunches at the joints of their arms and legs, dark and glistening.

"Skor," Sandoren said, nearly laughing. "No wonder they can't shoot straight." He cast a look back and saw the Skoran archers advancing on the perimeter. "Vishet!" he cursed, turned Veraddin away from the advancing Skor and kicked him into an easterly direction. The horse was slow to move, however, and he was still huffing from the short run through the woods. It took a few moments before he was able to work up to a gallop.

Sandoren cursed again when another Skor warrior rushed out from the trees and, sweeping his gaze forward, saw many more figures moving in there, under the cover of the wood. Because Veraddin was already beginning to break, he did not stop him again. Instead, he spurred him on, directly for the creature. Seeing his prey bearing down on him, the Skor let out a howl and raised his sword, a blocky weapon meant to rend flesh rather than just cut it.

Veraddin struggled to turn away from the warrior, but Sandoren held him until the last possible moment, letting him veer away just as he came within reach of the sweep of his own sword. Fortunately, the Skor misjudged him and started his swing too late. Sandoren's arced beneath his and bit deeply into armor and flesh. The force of the blow sent the creature howling away from him, the large weapon flinging out to the forest floor.

Around him, shouts broke out like a cacophony from a murder of crows. Arrows sang in the air. Veraddin was snorting with each breath and his chest was heaving erratically, but Sandoren slapped his flank with the flat of his blood wet blade, urging him forward faster still. The beast tried. Sandoren felt the burst of speed, but it was quickly gone, and his steed was again groping for energy.

More Skor closed in, swinging their great swords. Sandoren's flashed back, his steel ringing clear against the heavy metal born against him. Things were rapidly becoming frantic, but, as yet, Sandoren was not fazed much. The experience with the Chyldren of Khemosh still rested large in his breast, and, in no way, did the warriors about him begin to even become a whisper of that fell night not long ago. He almost struck them down with impunity, both with his sword and Veraddin's haunches. Howls of pain and anger filled his ears.

Veraddin stumbled.

Sandoren lost his rhythm, for only the tiniest moment, and he came away with a gash on his thigh that burned more brightly than deep, but it brought the world out of focus as the lance of pain slid up his body. He grunted, scanned quickly the battlefield and found a gap through which he forced his fading steed, through nearly his will alone. An arrow thudded into the cantle of his saddle, lodged there with the tip punched through the material and scratching at his back.

Speaking words of comfort to Veraddin seemed to help keep him going, and they started to outdistance the war party, and, fortunately, there did not seem to be anymore ahead of him. What they were doing in battle dress this close to a major city, he didn't know. Nor did he care much; however, for some reason, the thought refused to leave him. It pecked at him while he urged Veraddin to keep on his feet.

Sandoren kept a survey of the woods behind them as they ran. Though the Skor were giving chase and were known for a high level of endurance, they seemed to be falling further and further behind, as if they were not as committed as they seemed. Of course, he felled many of them, wounded more, but neither were they bothered with loss.

When Veraddin stumbled again, jolting him in the saddle and drawing an icy sting down his lower back, he could hear some of their calls echoing among the trees, but could no longer see them. Sandoren peered up into the canopy, taking in the late light while Veraddin shuffled along. He needed to get back to the cabin to warn the others about the Skoran war party, but there was no way Veraddin was going to make the journey. Not this night.

They lurched along through the forest, moving slowly down a soft incline that soon faded into a glen through which a crystal stream burbled a southern route. They halted. Veraddin was chuffing, his head held low, his sides billowing out convulsively, and it brought another curse to Sandoren's lips.

He stared behind them for several beats of his heart, expecting the Skoran bunch to come trotting down the incline, but they didn't. The only sounds that reached him, now, aside from his horse's coughing, were the quiet music of the forest. Reluctantly and with many glances backwards, he slid from the saddle, scraping himself again on the peeking arrow tip and sucking in a sharp breath when he landed on his wounded leg. He stabbed his sword into the ground and, with a growl, ripped the black missile from the cantle and cast it into the trees, then turned back to Veraddin, using a gentle hand to get the beast to raise his head.

Veraddin nickered softly and blinked half lidded lashes over tired eyes. His mouth hung open, the lips and creases rimmed by pink foam. Softly, Sandoren unstrapped the cinch that held the bit in Veraddin's mouth and took it from his slackened lips, careful even not to let it clack against the horse's teeth. Then, with cool words against his soft ear, Sandoren led him to the stream and coaxed his head down. Veraddin's snuffling was weak, but once he caught the whiff of the water, he dipped down and began to drink, loud sucking sounds coming up around a mouth that wasn't quite working.

Sandoren gave him a pat and left him to his drink, taking his sword from its sheath of dirt and cleaning off the clinging soil and drying Skoran blood with a handful of pine needles. Then, after he slid the blade back in its scabbard, he moved along their back trail for several yards to make sure they weren't being followed; walked back once he was reasonably sure they weren't. Veraddin had moved from the water and was clipping grass at the edge of the stream. The slow munching he was doing reminded him that he hadn't eaten, so he pulled some dried meat from his saddle bags and snapped off a bite. He considered taking the saddle from Veraddin's back, then decided against it. Just in case the Skor showed up again. Instead, he loosened the cinch strap enough that his chest wasn't so clamped then found himself a soft tuft of grass to sit on and tend to the gash in his leg.

Once it was bandaged with strips of his cloak and he had finished his meager meal, Sandoren gathered Veraddin and gently led him into the stream. The water was crisp and, though his boots were waterproofed, it chilled his feet, but it wasn't very deep, only rising up around his calves. It would serve his purpose, however, and he moved down the stream as it made its way southward. Veraddin came hesitantly and stopped many times, refusing to move again until several minutes of quiet coaxing came from Sandoren lips.

The night was full on them by the time Sandoren decided they had gone far enough and stepped back onto dry earth. Without much thought, he unlimbered the horse of his saddle and harness and rubbed the animal down with dry pine needles before letting him loose to graze and drink on his own. Then, he saw to himself, rummaging out another bit of meat and unrolling his blanket. His feet were numb from the cold of the water and he wanted to start a fire to warm them by, though didn't. Neither did he take off his boots, by necessity and to keep them from the possibility of shrinking, and settled in for a long, miserable night.

He was staring up through the limbs of the tall pines at the fullness of the moon that hung forever above, pondering the question of the Skor and what they were about. After a while, his mind moved to other, less complex topics, only passing over his grief about Alexandra, until his thoughts became smooth and quiet. He began to drift off into a light sleep, considered fighting then accepted it, too tired to worry about Skor hunters. Besides, he would be able to smell them long before they could overtake him, though he was quite sure they had greater interest in something else.

Just before the sun crawled up over the eastern horizon, Sandoren awoke to a shivering body and biting numb feet. Vapor plumed out from his mouth into the ethereal morning cast with pale moonlight and the diffuse light of the coming day. Near him a shadow shifted and whickered.

He stood with aching slowness, cursing himself for not taking his boots off and doubly cursing himself for not starting a fire. Even a small one. Just enough to chase the chill back into the darkness where it belonged. Skor be damned. When he was finished griping about that, he stomped his feet on the cold ground to help warm his blood and send the prickles of numbness from him.

Once his blankets and saddle were affixed to Veraddin, he stood for many long minutes with his hands tucked between the horse's warm coat and the saddle while his body quaked in frequent spasms. They were the kind of chills he fancied came at the fingertips of Death when that last embrace was only heartbeats away. An uncontrollable trembling in the bones.

When some of the horse's body heat made its way into his muscles, Sandoren pushed his thoughts to travel, looped the reins around the horse's neck and gently tugged on them. He came easily, giving Sandoren a nudge with his nose and nickering. Together, they walked along the bank of the stream in its southerly route, stopping every now and then for a drink of the icy liquid and to allow Veraddin to clip some of the lush grass at its bank.

The sharp edge of cold was dulled once the sun was high enough to shine down on them through the treetops, but not completely. The chill remained under the boughs like an invisible fog. However, from the smooth working of his muscles coupled with the warmth of the horse next to him, a sheen of sweat soon filmed his skin.

Sandoren purposely kept the pace leisurely for the better part of the morning, giving Veraddin as much unhindered time as he thought prudent. The animal still looked ragged and his movements were somewhat stiff, but the hard breathing had gone. It was his hope that yesterday's encounter hadn't pushed the beast too far over, but suspected otherwise. His only recourse now was to find out if Alex could do something for him when they got back, which he was certain she would be able to.

So, as the sun neared its daily meeting with the pale ghost of the moon above, he finally tightened the girth strap of his saddle and swung himself up into it, bearing only a slight wince from the sting in his thigh. He allowed Veraddin to move into a light trot with little urging and guided him only with knee pressure instead of putting the gum cutting bit back into his healing mouth.

They traveled that way, with several stops and walks, as the day wore on towards its death. It wasn't until late afternoon that they neared the cabin, or rather, the surrounding area. At least, the overall scope of the land began to take on more familiarity. Sandoren's realization that they had gone much further abroad yesterday than he first thought brought another round of cursing to his mind, and the Skor must have driven him further. Veraddin's condition only made the travel slower.

When he topped the low rise that approached the cabin from the north, he reined in the horse with an over-quick jerk to the straps around his neck. Something was wrong. Spider webs fell onto the back of his neck, making him rigid and quickening his hand to the hilt of his sword. The blade slid free with ominous portent.

Below, the cabin stood just as he left it yesterday, only there was a silence there that he more felt than heard, and there was the odd look of abandonment about it. A sense of aloneness that nagged at the base of his skull. A dry bitterness suddenly salted the back of his throat and turned to molten iron that filled his gut when he swallowed.

Sandoren could see none of the horses. Not even the magnificent white stallion that Marc Pendragon called friend. No smoke curled from the chimney, and, though the door stood open, it was only slightly so, a warning rather than an invitation to pass beneath the frame that held it. The glint of metal in the sunlight caught his eye. Near the edge of the porch lay something. A bundled heap that could be simply sacks of the grain they lugged off the wagon, but, in his mind, it was more sinister, and it put ice chips into his blood stream.

Because he knew it was a body.

His warrior mind took over, and he scanned the area about him with all of his senses, seeking any unseen enemy with eyes, ears, and taste, but found nothing. Suddenly, he kicked Veraddin in the flanks, startling the horse into a canter that he directed down the rise, his only thought centered on the one person he was sworn to protect.

Alexandra.

Sandoren was off Veraddin and running the rest of the distance before the horse was at a standstill and slid to a kneeling halt next to the body that lay near the porch. For a single moment, confusion washed through him.

It was Marc that lay there on the grass, his clothes turned a dark russet from dried blood. His own sword driven through the thick strong gut and keeping him from lying neatly on his back. A bloodless face bore a look of shock and pain that was more than the physical hurt he must have suffered. Little blood stained the ground around and underneath him, and his body was skewed by the exiting sword tip such that he was partly on his side. Though trepidation was a festering boil about to rupture within him, Sandoren thought that Marc was placed here rather than killed here.

As an afterthought, Sandoren reached out and placed his fingers on the underside of the human's jawline and felt for a life beat. There was none. His hand went to Marc's half lidded eyes and closed them to the darkness in which they belonged.

Then he stood quickly and surveyed the ground. Some of the turf opposite him was torn and the grass immediately in front of the cabin door was pressed down by many feet. He could see a trail of shine running off in the direction that he had come. A trail of flattened and scarred grass caused by horses.

Finally, his eyes rested on the vertical shadow that was the door, and his mouth went dry and aching, and it seemed his feet sunk down into the ground as if he stood in a bog rather than solid turf, because he could not will himself forward to look inside. The willful part of his mind, the critical part, began railing at him for his cowardice, but it was small and still easily ignored. He did not want to move, to open the door fully and look upon the horror that he knew must await him as there was no sign of Alexandra or Del out here.

But, slowly, he did so, creeping forward on leaden feet until the shadow of the roof fell on him and threw him into a chill. There he stopped again and waited for reality to change back to what it had been yesterday. Sweat dribbled down his cheeks and forehead like glacial flows, and no sound touched his ears save for a whisper of breeze and the shrill, far off cry of a bird. Another long round of endless heartbeats passed before he finally held up a hand to the door and found that a quiver had settled into it. Something that he had never experienced and stared at it as if it were some rare flower. Out of necessity, just to see the shaking stop, he willed his hand to touch the door, but it was at that moment that he heard something that tightened the skin over his bones, freezing him solid.

A sound came from inside. A sound of something heavy walking along ill-fitting floor boards, only it halted just as quickly. A single step of that something not wanting to be heard but betrayed by its own movement.

Sandoren took a deep breath, put the tip of his sword against the wood and pushed. The door creaked open slowly, spilling light into the living-room floor in an angled bar that washed up against something black and glistening. A wave of tingles stood the hairs on his body up.

Baleful eyes flashed against the back of his before he was struck in the chest by the shadow and sent reeling backward. A blur shot by him out into the sunlight. Anger boiled in Sandoren, and he spun around to take in the interloper, his mind's eye thinking that it was yet another Skor.

But it was not. Sandoren's throat cramped and his legs began to jelly and it felt like his eyes were about to fly from their sockets the pressure was so great behind them when the illusion was dispelled.

It was the thing from the glade in the ffolk village. All teeth and fell looks.

And pain.

Sandoren moved, slashing out with the cold steel in his hand, but it was like moving through syrup, his body was so sodden with fear. The blade glittered in the brilliance of the afternoon light, silvery in its killing intensity. Its arc was true and his distance from the creature perfect.

The Eldritch seemed to be smiling the way it held its feral mouth, and then it moved, hideously quick, caught the sword edge in its overlarge hands and jerked. Fingers snapped as the pommel wracked against them and Sandoren let out a hiss. His sword flew from his broken grasp, twirled and tumbled away in flashing despair, struck a nearby tree and shattered.

Time turned thick as the pieces fell to the grassy floor in silvery hail. It appeared that the creature wanted him to watch his last hope get dashed as it simply stood, grinning its needle grin, while he watched it. But once the shards were resting in the grass, the Eldritch moved again and pain exploded in his face. His head twisted violently to the side, and his body followed.

Thoughts whirled among feelings, disjointed things knocked loose by a blow that he instinctually knew was restrained and clouds formed along the rims of his vision. He caught himself before his legs went out from under him and stumbled away. As he did so, thin trails ripped down his back, claws tearing into cloth and skin, then, something harder than marble slammed into him, lifted him from his feebly dancing feet and threw him to the grass. His breath fled in an explosion, grass and dirt replacing it in his mouth, a choking grit and stink of loam.

He was lying on his belly, trying to force the bellows of his lungs to start moving again, gasping in strained reflexes, when he felt the Eldritch's hand on his shoulder. It was light, gentle, as Alex's touch was, but he was quickly whipped away from that thought. The world blurred with a loud pop and liquid agony that spread from his shoulder. When his vision cleared of the red cloud that stormed across it, the clear blue of the sky faced him, and a little off to the side, the ephemeral moon stared down.

From the direction of his chin, the creature lurched into view. It perused him with lamp-like eyes that glowed a sickly yellow even in the daylight, doing so for many long moments as Sandoren struggled to breathe, to hold back a scream. Its thin lips pulled away from glittering teeth a few times, and it snuffled at him. Then, it let out a mewl from deep within its dark throat that rattled the bones of his spine and jangled his nerves.

Sandoren's head was shaking from side to side though he could not pull his eyes away, and something was trying to come out of his own throat, a cry, a gurgle, he didn't know, but he resolved he would not beg or whimper, so clamped down hard on his tongue. A wash of copper slid into his mouth, and the sudden, sweet pain cleared away the fog that was impending on his mind.

It mewled again while looking at him, worming its gaze deep into his spirit while the Abyss was revealed to him in turn. Within, he saw the beginning and ending of eternity, the blackest light and the brightest darkness, of things that no mortal eye should ever have to gaze upon. He thought he might have screamed as his sanity began to rend, but the vision pulled away, and he was looking up only into the face of the Eldritch.

His doom.

Sandoren whispered a goodbye to Alexandra as it raised a long arm and forced his eyes to remain open as it drove down, sending dagger-tipped fingers through the flesh of his chest, bursting bones as they drove into him.

He spiraled up out of the darkness sometime later and found he was leaning against a tree, a vague memory of dragging himself through the grass to this point hanging on the periphery of his waking mind. Icy fire burned in him, but, thankfully, it was as if his being could not handle the torment inflicted upon it so it simply stopped dealing with it and infused his body with a distant numbness. The only time he drew near to the inferno was when he moved too much and breathed too deeply. Otherwise it was as an itch on the bottom of a foot, an annoyance that would not leave.

The Eldritch ravaged him and he was dying. There was no doubt. He could feel his life slipping slowly through the wounds. But why it did not finish the job, he didn't know. It simply stopped, mewled, and then it was gone, leaving him in an ethereal blackness.

Now he sat, breathing shallowly through his mouth while the grave crept into him, staring out over the moon swept glade at his dead companion. Marc Pendragon journeyed ahead of him even now, but he could find no fault in the man. Indeed, all his former anger seemed unnecessary, and the realization brought forth a welling respect for the human. It was too bad that neither of them would get to know that now.

A flickering within the shadows of the house tickled his attention, and he swung his eyesight in the direction, but could see nothing. An image formed by his own fading mind, he decided. Sandoren tried to chuckle, coughed instead. Hot blood burbled out onto his chin. At least, the chill that wracked his body earlier in the morning was not present now. He leaned his head against the bark of the tree and looked off into the night. There it was again. Another flicker. This time, with his eyes peering off to the left a little, a figure appeared, draped in darkness and began walking out toward him. At first, it was difficult for him to focus on, but as it neared, it seemed to solidify.

"I was wondering if I'd meet you," Sandoren gurgled through a ragged throat. More hot liquid spilled from his mouth and washed across his chin, dripped onto his chest.

It was Terran'non, the Courier of Death, come to take his Spirit into the Next Realm.

"Will you not speak, even to the dying?" His words were ponderous and slow, coming through chokes and coughs that sent a fine mist of blood out into the cool evening air.

The figure did not speak, nor even acknowledge that it had even heard him. It simply drew closer and squatted across from Sandoren. He could see now that the Courier wore a dark corselet and long overcoat rather than the billowing cloak that he had, at first, saw. It creaked like new leathers when first worn. A pallid, empty face perused him, seeming to float above the dark material like it was incorporeal, and it bore the likeness of a human, strong planes and structure, which gave him a start. He assumed the Courier would have more fine boned qualities, like his.

But it was its eyes that finally grabbed his attention and pushed everything away from it. Unlike the Eldritch's lamps into eternity, the Courier's were windows into nothing. Absolute and utterly. If anything showed him the way to death, it was Terran'non's gaze.

A shiver rolled up through his body. It was not something born of fear or loathing, but a more deep seated precursor to the coming darkness. It was the shiver of his soul trying to escape from his mortal vessel. And it separated his filming mind from his numb, throbbing flesh.

He tried to challenge the Courier, tried to force it to act instead of just staring at him impassively while he choked off his last few breaths, but found he could no longer form words on his cooling lips. All that would come from his throat was a bubbling groan. He had better luck moving his hand, only a flick.

Finally, Terran'non stood, stepped next to him and knelt again. A cold wave of something moved over Sandoren, something colder than death, and he suddenly wanted to get away from the creature, and mentally cried out in frustration that he couldn't. Though he wasn't sure, he thought he smelled old fungus and arid dirt coming off the Courier.

The sky seemed to rush down on him all at once and blur at the same time, and he steeled himself, thinking that his spirit finally loosened enough to fly away while he was still watching. He expected he would move right through the tree limbs and into the welkin above, but that did not happen. Instead, he started floating along the ground. As he did so, the view he had of the surroundings bounced and gyrated so much that a black rind began forming around the edges.

When he realized that Terran'non, the Courier of Death, was physically carrying him, the darkness stole over his vision completely.

Chapter 79

Waking in Darkness

The last thing Alex had felt was the burning agony of the sword entering Marc's body and the lingering pain before he died. The first thing she felt upon waking had been the same, and it continued to haunt her, bringing terrible wrenching sobs when she least expected, though in the darkness of her cell, she hardly felt compelled to fight it. She simply sat, knees drawn up to her chest, leaning against cold stone, and waited for her own death to come. Wanted it to come.

Every now and again, as if of their own accord, her hands went to her neck and felt the smooth, cool metal encircling it, looking for clasps or seams. But there was none. Only a complete, single circlet that lay tight enough against her skin that it was uncomfortable, but loose enough not to chaff. Her fingertips were sore from picking at it, and several places around her neck stung where her nails had slipped from the collar and scraped away the top layer of flesh. After several moments of checking, her hands inevitably flopped down to her knees.

What it was, she did not know. What it did was a nightmare in itself, and coupled with the terrible pain of Marc's death, the rip of the Bond, the collar bound her up in such hopelessness that even moving around was too much of an effort, though her joints and muscles had long passed the stages of ache and moved into near numbness. She could not touch the

Earthpower. Though the Blood still pounded within her, there was a shield between it and the vessel she made of herself; a hairsbreadth, it seemed, but a gulf of infinite distance nonetheless.

The despair she suffered made the tiny, dark cell almost an afterthought to her otherwise clogged, aching mind, and however much her eyes dragged over the shadowed, featureless, stone and unfurnished space, nothing penetrated any further than that. Even the two bowls of food that sat near the thin door, untouched and cold, did nothing to stir the pit of her stomach.

Only an infinitesimal knot of rage deep beneath the layers of her sorrow kept her heart beating, her blood pumping. Only a tiny hope of revenge kept her from smothering the flame completely and letting death steal over her. With the Bond ripped and Marc dead, following him would be easy. For any who lost a Bondmate, the period immediately afterward was the most dangerous and few of her sisters ever survived before her soul began to heal. But, from that spark of white hate, Alex made the decision to endure, at least for a while. At least until the words spoken by her captor came to pass.

When she had been cast into this dark place, the sneering man told her the Emperor would question her personally. Why he was in Calif, she didn't care. She only knew that when that visit came, she would release that knot of fury upon him, even if she only had her fingernails to scratch out his eyes. In the darkness, devoid of any eyes but hers to see, Alex smiled grimly.

Chapter 80

Awakenings and Hopelessness

*H*e was drifting in darkness. Thick. Enveloping. Peaceful. A womb of comfort that he intimately knew many times over. Indeed, nearby, he could see the Doorway in which he had, heretofore, been unable to pass beyond. A shifting whiteness that often took the shape of a normal rectangular portal, an earthly portal, when he drew . . . nearer . . . to it. Now, it was a shapeless hole in the blackness through which soft, pristine light shined.

However, this time was different than all the previous times in this place. There was consciousness here. He knew his name was Aeric, though he called himself Marc and even had vague memories of his life beyond the darkness. A flash of steel, sweet agony, the laughter of a killer. Also, there was something else. A connecting line between his awareness and one elsewhere. An umbilical of some kind that he suspected was the reason he was able to look around him with sober knowledge.

And though he could see the Doorway, he knew he could drift no closer than he was now, that the thread that held him kept him where he was and aware. It did not keep him from trying. He willed himself closer, or it closer to him, but there was no change. He tried equally ineffective forces of his wishes in other ways, then, frustrated, gave up when he remained exactly where he was.

So, he resigned himself to floating in eternal timelessness, halfway between the pain of life and the promise of oblivion. At length, there was a tug at the line, as if he were fishing and something was nibbling at his bait deep below the surface of a depthless lake. It seemed to shake something loose that was previously unknown to him.

He tugged back. And found himself somewhere closer to the place of life. A tiresome place, or time, that he wished to inhabit no longer. Only that was the way he was destined to go. The only way he could go, lest he settle for remaining within this great in-between. Yet he tarried, unwilling to give up the limbo in which he floated as it was preferable to where he was supposed to be.

Again the line tugged and jiggled, more violently than before and seemed to pull him from his place. He resisted, but found himself curious as well. The pull of oblivion was lessened, and its hold over his being faltered. Marc knew what the cord holding him was, knew he knew, but could not make himself look at it. Would not, for doing so, no matter how curious a part of him was, was liable to yank him further to the land of light once more.

You must go. Now is not the time.

It was a voice at once recognizable and unknown, hallowed and terrible. There was a flash of memory. An old man from some other place and time. And then silence. He floated in limbo between oblivion and pain.

You must go. Now is not the time.

He shifted, hearing the voice again for the first time and cast about for its source. There was none.

Time?

Eternity is not yet your destiny, Aeric Pendragon. You must return.

I want to stay. I don't want to go back. Marc was no child, but in the presence of the words, he felt like nothing less. *I've been there so long. I'm tired.*

Your time has not yet come. Go back.

I'm tired.

Soon. Soon you will come into this embrace, but not yet. You are the Lynchpin and must return. Too much rests with you.

What does that mean? Silence. No answer was forthcoming. *What does that mean? I don't want to go back! What does that mean?*

It seemed that he yelled into the abyss for eons, but nothing came back. No answer, nor even an echo of his own frustration. There was nothing, now, for him to do. He could go back, or he could stay. He could not go forward. His decision was not difficult, or lengthy. He would stay.

The line connecting him to the place of life jerked, and this time a translation came through to him. One of pain. Not his. Not the pain he associated with living. But something else. Something that his memory scratched at as if it could unearth the answer. It came from far away, over the . . . length. . . of the umbilical that bound him to this purgatory.

Something. . . . Alex . . . . Alexandra. She was holding him in this place. She was at the other end of the cord.

The memory flashed past, leaving behind only enough residue that he couldn't go completely back into his contemplation of oblivion. Only the tugging did not stop. It kept coming, kept shaking him until he was forced to pay attention to the connection. There was a thrumming that reached him during the brief pauses, and with some effort, Marc realized that it was a lifebeat.

Curiosity welled again, dragging his wonder back along the line to its terminus so far away. He had the impression that he knew where it led, and that he had just grasped the identity of the form whose heart echoed through it. The awareness would not come, however. Only by following the line back to its other end would he find out.

Doing so, though, was terrible in its effort and resisted every attempt. Staying was overwhelming him. The peace and tranquility were greater bonds than any formed of steel or iron, and it pushed aside his curiosity and consciousness with abandon.

Marc concentrated on what he was trying to accomplish, looking far deep into his being for answers he knew were there. None came and a desperation began welling up from somewhere, a widening crevasse that threatened to swallow him. And, finally, he came upon a part of his being that was shackled just as he was. A portion that desired to feel sunlight on skin, food in a mouth, smells in nostrils. He grabbed for it, latched onto it with a power borne of his desperation and used it by freeing it and letting it do what it naturally did. Immediately, it pulled itself along the umbilical, back towards the life that waited, and all he needed to do was hold on to it. Clasp it close to his ephemeral consciousness.

When the pressure began building, he let go, out of reflex, wanting to drift back down into the depths of the abyss, but still he moved toward the destination he dreaded. Back to life. Back to pain. And, now, there was no stopping. He went, helpless, the pressure becoming greater and greater, the darkness starting to lighten into a dull redness and a distant roaring coming to his ethereal hearing. Memory began flashing like lightning in a thundercloud, there, but occluded by the billowing mass around it.

Though he knew what was coming, he was still unprepared for the great wracking breath that filled the body his being suddenly lodged into. A conflagration erupted within, wrapped around a steel shaft of agony. A great gasp burst from him and spears of light imbedded deep into his eyes, blinding in its intensity. Marc tried to roll but found he couldn't, and, what's more, the movement caused clean pain to wash through. He was aware of his mouth hissing out a moan.

His hands went to the impaling blade and fumbled there, coming away with slices from the keen edges and more hisses as bolts went through his body. Just lifting his head to look at the blood stained sword hurt, though it was more of a deep wounding when he realized that the steel weapon was his own. He stared, his eyes roving over the metal for several minutes while the sun rose higher in the morning air. Afterward, he let his head flop back to the grass and waited for the roaring of his body to lessen. It was a while before he placed his palms against the cold, exposed flats of the blade, gritted his teeth and pushed.

An echo of his yell came back to deaf ears, and his body jerked, but he willed his hands to stay pressed against the steel. Hot blood spurted as the blade moved, washing his hands in liquid. The metal pulled at his insides like the tenfold feeling of thread through flesh, sending waves of white heat slamming into every part of his being. His vision faded, dark clouds closing in from the edges, and what little strength he had began to flee.

Marc yelled again, this time in anger as a fury at his failing body rose up in him, making his muscles react, forcing a surge of vigor into his quaking arms. The blade inched from him in slick agony, yanked at his guts with nauseous tenacity. Copper flooded the back of a throat raw from yelling. With a last agonized holler, the blade came free ahead of a gout of blood and was tossed down into the grass next to him. Pain raged, firing every nerve ending throughout his consciousness, and with a final groan, Marc rolled over and slid into a stupor.

The sun had gone when he awoke again, but he didn't know for how long. Replacing the pain was an insistent itch that centered around his wound. He needed little investigation to know that the hole had closed and was healing over with the rapidity that somehow came with his curse. Still, his body was steeped with lead, and moving his head to look around took such a great effort that his breathing came hard and fast, and it was with little striving that he closed his eyes and fell quickly back into sleep.

Marc again woke up, this time to the slate ambiguous gray of an overcast sky. He was sheened with moisture, and his clothing stuck wetly to him. His fingers and toes ached from chill. The terrible itching in his belly was gone, but there was still a dull throb deep inside that growled with warning when he sat up. He fingered the soft, new skin for a few moments then stared at puckered fingertips that came away painted with old blood from the torn material that was once his shirt.

Normally, his memory was wiped upon wakening from such a wound, but, although he found his thoughts muddy and disjointed, his past was laid out in near totality, his identity was sound, and his personal torment was formidable. There were no false perceptions or hopes. He was who he was. Now, he needed to figure out how he had come to be here, alone, wounded as he was, and what to do about it.

Slowly, he stood, a stooped figure in the mistiness, and looked about him with the bleary, stunned look of someone coming off a four day holiday. The grass was scuffed and torn in places and pressed in others, not yet regaining its normal resiliency. He tottered over to the nearest rip in the grass, knelt, inspected it, then stood and looked toward the house. A line of hoof prints arced away from the building, next to it, a large area of ragged, pressed grass attached to a singular drag mark that wormed its way to the sheltering arms of a nearby tree. To this ragged area, he moved and again knelt to repeat the process and was taken immediately by the dark liquid shining on the blades. It confirmed his suspicion when it stained his pinky red.

"Del," he said through a thick throat and began throwing his eyes along the drag marks and around the glade, looking for the boy. He saw nothing of him, however, so he headed for the tree to which the press marks headed, changing course when he caught a quiet glint of metal beneath another tree. The broken pieces scattered among the grass caused an angry curse to form on tightly held lips.

Marc turned away from Sandoren's shattered blade. Silence lay heavy on the meadow, held there by the muffling gray air above and it infuriated him. Indeed, he nearly screamed out his fury, wanting something to shatter the indifferent quiet, but thought better of it. Perhaps the silence was better. A graveside testimony to the unknown tragedy that befell his companions.

He returned to the house, leaving his bloodied sword lying in the wet grass out of contempt, and stood looking over the ruin that had become of the inside. The stores so carefully piled earlier, now lay strewn across the floor and furniture amid bits and chunks of the containers that they had come in. The bedroom was worse, permeated with the stench of decay coming from the blood choked bundle of blankets and linens. The bed frame was sundered and the mattress ripped. Feathers lay over the room like new fallen snow. Clouds of black flies droned lazily over the old blood.

Standing there, he recalled the last words he heard from the worm faced Imperial and wondered at them, rolled them over in his muddled mind while a sickened knot formed in his belly separate from the throb of his wound. His mind clicked down into a slot and Sandoren bubbled up. But why would Sandoren betray them? Him, he could imagine as a certainty, but the ffolk would never sell out Alexandra, no matter how angry he grew with her.

But, then, Sandoren's sword was laying, shattered, in the grass not far from his own. And the Imperial seemed to think that he was Alex's Guardian and not the ffolk. So it couldn't have been Sandoren that betrayed them.

Del strayed through his scrutinizing mind but he pushed that aside as an impossibility. That was everyone in their little group. He ruled out Sharla nearly as quickly as he ruled out Del. The woman could be many things if her ire was raised but disloyal was not one of them. And he didn't think she was angry with . . . . *he's not the same anymore, I don't think you can trust him.* . . . Sharla's voice was so strong, he almost turned his head, expected to see her standing in the doorway with an 'I-told-you-so' smirk riding her pert lips.

Marrillon.

They were betrayed by Marrillon, his friend of old.

Marc lashed out and struck a shelf, splintering it amid a yell of fury. And for good measure, he picked up a length of the wood and cast it into the wall. After the overall silence crept back into the room, he forced himself to calm and set about getting some provisions together, lighting a lamp to push back the shadows that were encouraged by the grayness outside. Only minutes later, he stepped outside clothed in clean dry clothes. He packed some dried meat and wrapped cheese into his saddle bags then stepped out from under the porch and gave a long, piercing whistle into the mist. Though it dissipated quickly, it found what it sought. An answering whinny came back to him.

While he waited for Whitesteel, he gathered his sword and cleaned it with a scrap of burlap and slid it into its scabbard. He propped it against the railing, staring out at the spot he woke up, and suddenly wondered how he got out there. And why he was moved. His only conclusion was that maybe Sandoren moved him out there to bury him before being waylaid. Deciding it really didn't matter, he turned back into the house and tossed the burlap rag onto the pile of broken casks and crates.

Outside, the great horse pounded up. Marc stared around the dim emptiness of his house while a heavy pall settled down on him. He silently cursed himself many more times for his lapse, stopping only when Whitesteel snorted and pawed at the ground. Then, he placed his feelings into a cell in his heart, closed the door and went back outside. Before picking up his gear, he casually picked up the lamp from its table next to the door and tossed it on top of the pile of broken wood. The pungent oil splashed out and, with a whoosh, caught immediately.

Whitesteel stood nearby, and though he looked well, long streaks of maroon lined his flanks. Marc studied them for only a moment then headed out from under the porch toward him. "Fell into some badness, too, did you?" he said. The horse gave him a nod and a snort and suffered enough stillness while Marc strapped the saddle onto him.

They came across Veraddin's torn body not far from the already smoking cabin. It had been abused by something other than a sword stroke and it brought only a modicum of surprise into Marc's being. But he didn't mull over it long. Again, he didn't see how it really mattered now. Whether Del and Sandoren were dead, he had no way of knowing, other than the bloody grass and broken sword. But he was sure of one thing. They were gone, Alex, at least, alive and not far. And he knew who was responsible. His curse gave no inkling that it would thwart what his plans were just then.

After giving Veraddin another once over, he angled Whitesteel toward Calif and nudged him into a canter.

Chapter 81

Flying Home to a Visitor

*W*ending his way down Meadow Lane, Marrillon, master thief, did not measure the length of the vanished daylight, nor the apparent disappearance of the two strumpets that had seemed, only moments ago, to be clinging to his arms and whispering naughty verses into his ears. He barely had enough concentration to keep his feet moving in a straight line, though, in reality, he wheeled and veered like a rudderless ship in a storm down the pavement.

Reflexively, his hand drew into his cloak to a pocket that held the only important thing to him. And when he felt the soft, giving pouch, felt its reality, another geyser of need for what was in it rushed up into his swirling head, around his eyes and down his spine. There was guilt there, too, but he ignored it. He knew, even though he was still in a stupor, that the floating feeling would be gone by the time he made it home. And that was the time when he could go soaring again. Then there would be no guilt for . . . . nothing. There would be no guilt at all. All he had to do was struggle to keep from dipping into the pouch. What it held would do nothing for him now, and while he craved it, he had more strength to save it for when it was useful again.

After all, he didn't attain his excellent skills by wasting his efforts. And he would not start now, although he could not pick a lock that was already open.

By the time he turned off Meadow Lane onto Medlin's Run, the cold shivers began deep inside his head. His teeth chattered, but he weathered it, steeling himself for the flames that would come next as one who had no other desires but to get past it so he could fly some more.

He was still sweating profusely when he began traveling the Noname streets and alleys that abutted up against the warehouse district and the Lakedocks. But the worst was over and Marrillon's steps became more even and stable. His mind was clearing. As he was approaching the small house he shared with his aging partner in crime, Varn, a thickness of sorrow filled him. And though his mind would not let him understand the guilt, he knew he had returned to his home, his body, and that he was, for better or worse, Marrillon, master thief.

He stopped before the front step of his door and looked up into the night sky, noting blandly the puff of mist that came from his breath. The stars were like jewels up there, too far to pluck from their velvet backdrop, tempting some feeling from his heart that he tried to ignore but couldn't. "Why?" he asked softly at them.

After a moment, he dropped his gaze and let it stab at the darkness around him, searching for what he didn't know, but felt. A lingering presence that followed him with hateful glances and silent calls wherever he went. He almost called back for it to show itself, but he didn't. There was nothing there. Just like there was nothing there the last time. Or the time before that. Though he wasn't so sure that whatever it was would not be there the next time he was compelled to search the shadows. The ones who introduced him to soaring mentioned something about the followers, but he put about as much stock on that as he did a stable boy carrying a purse full of rubies and emeralds.

Marrillon spent a few more minutes feeling the crispness of the night air, then screwed his face up into a semblance of happiness and pushed through the door. "It's getting chilly out there Varn," he said as he entered the house.

His longtime partner sat across from him, facing the door, his sight staff cradled in thinning arms, while his milky orbs stared at him. A single lamp burned on the table next to him, casting warm yellow light onto his frail looking, robed frame. "I do believe winter is finally going to show itself . . . ." Varn was stiff, too stiff. Though the balding man was a model of graceful posture, he always seemed relaxed. But now, it was as if a steel rod had taken the place of his spine and iron was now in his grip. Even the skin of his face, normally peaceful, seemed tight, giving him a skull-like appearance that went all the way back into his graying braid. "What's wron—"

The door thumped and shuddered closed, slamming into its frame so loudly that he jumped. At first he thought maybe he hadn't fully recovered from his entertainment. Then, his mind wildly jumped to the following presence he always felt now. But when he had the presence of mind to look beside the door, at the figure sitting there, the hands that suddenly held his short swords went limp, and the weapons clanged to the wooden planks under his feet. No amount of Dust would keep down the rush of fear and guilt that tore through him now.

"Miss me?" Marc asked, steely eyes pinning Marrillon's with deadly intent. He was leaning a chair against the wall, his feet propped up on another chair, but when Marrillon twitched, the big man was up, quick as an adder striking, and the razor edge of his great sword, Anduin, rested against the flesh of his neck. "I thought I'd come over for a little chat. Whadya say. . . old friend?" Marc's voice was acid.

"B-b-but . . . Y-you're . . . ."

"Dead?" Marc hissed. "Not quite. But how would you know that, Mar?"

"I didn't. . . . It wasn't . . ." As he clamored for some kind of words, Marrillon's hand moved to his belt knife. There was a flash of silver and fire erupted in his wrist. He grabbed it with the other hand and tried to move away, but the blade that had slapped him away from his knife returned quickly to his neck, this time drawing a thin line stingingly on his skin. "Now,

now, Mar. Let's not get hasty," Marc said. The rest of his body seemed to have stood still the entire time. "I wouldn't forego the chance to hear you out before I gut you." He kicked at the chair he had his feet propped up on, sending it scrambling in Marrillon's direction. "Take a seat," Marc ordered, and, as Marrillon slowly complied, he sank down into his. The blade never wavered from his neck.

Marrillon cast a glance at Varn, wishing for some miracle to come through a window and cure his sightless eyes enough so that the man could see his expression and help. However, he suspected Varn knew exactly what was happening but simply was not involving himself. It was difficult to get anything past the eyes the man seemed to have deep within his mind. Why he did nothing but sit there, Marrillon didn't know, but it sent cold bolts of confusion ricocheting through him. "Varn?" he said.

"It seems our good friend, Marc Pendragon, is slightly peeved about something that you did," Varn said. "Perhaps you should direct your questions at him."

A sweep of anger tried to cut through him, but his aching fear shrugged it aside.

"Now," Marc said, pinning him with his eyes again. "Where is she?"

"W-where's who?" Before the words had completely exited his mouth, pain splashed across Marrillon's cheeks as the flat of Marc's sword slapped it.

"Where is she?"

"The Council Manor," Marrillon said, seeing his doom within the diamond hard eyes. "I didn't know . . . . They said they only wanted to speak to her . . . They had me. . . ."

"What about the others?"

"Others?"

"The boy. What about the boy? And the Guardian?"

"I don't—" Another stinging slap hit him, bringing tears to his eyes. "I don't know," he yelled. "The Guardian wasn't there. The boy went with us, but I slipped away once inside the city gates."

"Once you got paid." Marc's statement left no room for him to argue, so he only nodded. Marc's face pinched and his eyes narrowed. Marrillon was sure the man's control had slipped, but it quickly smoothed back into the calm rage that had been there previously. "Why, Mar?" he said. His voice was soft but full of venom. "Why did you betray us?"

Marrillon's resistance crumbled before the terrible guilt that welled up inside, but still he fought to hide the sudden shame. "I thought they were going to talk. I didn't know they were bent on . . . . I didn't know."

"Why?" Marc hissed.

"Dust," came a soft answer from across the room. Varn still sat, steel straight, but passive. Marrillon grimaced and clenched his teeth.

"What?" Marc asked, looking at the man from the corner of his eyes.

"Shutup, Varn," Marrillon said through gritted teeth. His hands reflexively went into fists and back.

"Look in his cloak pocket," Varn said.

Marc's blade cut through Marrillon's unnatural anger as it cut into his flesh again and brought him back to a place where he could exert his will and smooth over his own features into a sickly grin. "He doesn't know what he is talking about," he said. "Varn is getting a little mindless in his old age. I have noth—"

"Hand it over!"

"Hand what—" This time the blow to his face with the flat sent flashes of light back behind his eyes.

"Give it up, Mar," Marc said. Again, the hardness of the man's eyes foretold Marrillon's imminent death, but this time, he locked gazes with Marc, while he battled his surviving will against the preservation instinct of his denial. Minutes past while hearts thudded in chests, Marc's stare became heavier and heavier, until, feebly, Marrillon reached into the pocket and brought forth the most precious pouch and tossed it to Marc.

The man lifted the soft leather bag and sniffed at it once, wrinkling his nose at the burnt metallic smell that steeped the pouch. "For this," he said, holding it up toward him. "For this trash, you betrayed us. Betrayed me?"

"You don't understand . . . . I didn't . . . . You don't," Marrillon tried to get the pleading tone out of his voice, but it would not go.

"You are going to take me to her, Marrillon del Abon," Marc said. "Or even Terran'non's touch upon your brow is going to hold nothing against what I will do to you. Understand?"

"Yes," he said, nodding as well into his hood. "Please," he added, ashamed at his weakness. "Please, can I have that back."

"This?" Marc said, taking his eyes from the ffolk for a moment to look at the pouch. "Not until you take me to her. And the boy, if he is in the Manor."

Marrillon flinched toward him, his hands turning into claws. "No, you must—" He caught himself and forced his body back against the chair, but not before Anduin cut another slice into his shoulder. The fiery pain gave him enough strength to resist the pull of the Dust, but he could feel it begin to re-exert itself before even the first drops of new blood made it down to his chest. "Yes," he hissed past the stinging. "I will take you."

Varn was listening to the interchange, but suddenly tilted his head and murmured. "What is that?"

Before anyone else could speak, the roar of an explosion reached them through the window.

Chapter 82

Under the City

"Somebody's been here," Marrillon said, his voice quavering slightly. He brushed at the ground with one hand while, in the other, he held a tiny ball of crystal that gave off a tiny, diffuse light.

Marc considered the tunnel that they came through, part of an extensive web of sewers beneath the city of Calif. The confusion and chaos caused by the explosion above them would probably prove to be helpful, but he didn't want to count on it.

"Doesn't matter," Marc answered, peering up at the rubble and crack they stood before. The trickle of water did much to soak up his voice, but Marrillon's pathetic tones rose and fell too much. He wanted the ffolk to stop talking.

Standing as if his bones ached, he cast several glances around and behind them before lifting a hand toward the pile. "That way," Marrillon said.

Marc pushed by him and set foot on the nearest stones, testing their solidity almost absently before levering his full weight on them. He stopped, listened, and felt around, while Marrillon shifted from foot to foot. It distracted him somewhat, and he had to hold down the anger-backed comment he was about to make. Marc could not remember the thief ever being so fidgety, even under the most stressful of situations. The ffolk was cat confident and grave silent, usually. But then, he knew the power Dust could hold over even the most strong willed person. For him to be using the substance, even a little, was most assuredly a sign that his will had faltered for some time. Marrillon told him that he encountered Death's Courier once, and that it touched him, but that was long ago. Surely he couldn't have been using Dust so long. He would have been dead by now if he had.

Whatever happened to his old friend was of no concern to him now, however, and, angrily, he thrust aside the curious pity that was itching the edges of his mind. Marrillon's plight was his own, as finding Alex and somehow rescuing her from this place, was his. As if in answer to his thoughts, he felt his soul being tugged at through the now elusive bond, like a fish nibbling at the bait. It was further up than the stone ceilings above them and deeper inside. Marc gave Marrillon one last cautious look before he climbed up into the dark room of the Council Manor's dungeons through the broken hole above a long nonfunctioning sewer tunnel. Behind him, Marrillon struggled up the pile, knocking smaller stones loose and grating hands and feet on the dusty surfaces. Within the emptiness beyond, the sound he made seemed like thunder. Marc peered out of the tiny room, waiting for the inevitable appearance of a guard. When the ffolk was standing next to him, huffing, Marc whispered, "You know that stuff is going to kill you." He received a sharp look, but even in the wan luminescence given off by the ball, he saw a deeply embedded fear in his eyes. After a heartbeat or two, Marrillon shook his head.

"Yeah, well, that's my problem isn't it?" he said. His voice was sullen, but at least modulated enough that it didn't shake. Marc reached into his tunic and grabbed the pouch containing Marrillon's spirit and pulled it out. He was instantly aware that Marrillon knew what he held; the man suddenly became so tense that Marc thought he would creak like old wood if he moved.

"You can go now," he said simply.

Several seconds drew out. He could sense Marrillon's struggle, but finally, the ffolk blew out a breath, and said, "I can help you find her."

"No, you can't," Marc shot back. "You can barely walk much less do it silently. Go back to your . . . life, Marrillon. At least the rioting outside will cover your trail. I no longer need your help."

"But . . . How will you find her?" Marrillon said. The incredulous tone of his voice caused it to rise in pitch, which, in turn, pinched Marc's skin between his shoulder blades. While his voice would have been swallowed in the din above them in the city proper, down here, deep under the huge Council Manor, it seemed louder than the explosion and resulting chaos.

"Doesn't matter," he hissed. "You've done enough. Now go."

Despite Marrillon's earlier reluctance to remain separated from his Dust, his eyes blazed with anger and stubbornness sunk into the skin of his haggard face. "No," he said, so loud that an echo flipped back at them through the doorway. "I will—"

Marc caught him on the side of the jaw with a solid blow. Marrillon's head jerked back and to the side, surprise rocketing through his features. His body followed in a tight swirl that sank to the ground, where he lay motionless, in a heap. The tiny globe, apparently robbed of concentration, went out, casting them in blackness. "I told you to go," Marc said, tossing the pouch of Dust onto the man's chest. Then, he slid his sword from its scabbard and moved cautiously out into the corridor, going slowly while using his empty hand as a guide along the rough stone.

Chapter 83

Feeling Ahead in the Dark

*M*arc moved slowly through the dungeon corridor, more by feel than sight. Time seemed at a standstill, so he didn't quite know how long he had been moving when the unmistakable sound of disembodied yelling reverberated around him in an ephemeral cloud, coming from somewhere ahead and bouncing along the massive stones away behind. He stopped and listened, his grip on his sword tightening in response. It was indeed the sounds of battle, but it was still distant enough that the maze of halls before him distorted it into something more alien. He concentrated on the feeble tugging inside him.

Alex was somewhere in that direction as well.

Ignoring the fighting noise, he moved forward again, or tried to. His body didn't respond to the mental command to go forward and, for several seconds, he ground his teeth while trying to take a single step. All at once, he stopped and turned around. His body relaxed completely, and he took two steps back the way he had come. It was as if he were fighting to move up a strong flowing river current and suddenly turned around and let the flow carry him. But that was not the way to go.

Alex was in the opposite direction he now faced, and she needed him. So much so that his guts were twisting inside his belly and his mind was focused on that one thing.

Marc took a breath and released it slowly into the stale air of the dungeon corridor. With it, he forced his need to rescue anybody out. Then he took another, and another, until his mind was clear and he could imbue his thoughts with other details. Like his interest in exploring this forsaken dungeon. Strange details, yes, but neutral. It allowed him to turn back and begin moving again. It helped considerably when he refocused on the sounds of battle ahead. Blocking out all other things except that, he was able to move faster, instinctively taking turns as he came to them, even though he could only see vague impressions of greater darkness beyond his guiding fingers.

As time meant very little to him, he was not surprised to find, at length, a lightening of the air ahead of him, one in which the fuzzy outlines of passage borders and door frames slowly revealed themselves. He picked up his pace again, unhindered now that he could see better. The light became brighter quickly as he passed through a four direction room and turned left. At the end of that tunnel, where it met another, bright white light slashed across the opening and the sounds of battle tripled. Not worried about being discovered, he trotted to the end of the hall and peered around the corner.

Two men wearing red uniforms stood within another of the intersecting guard rooms with their backs to Marc's hallway. Every now and again, one of them raised an arm and pointed in the direction they faced and small red spears of light flit from their fingertips and lanced away from them. Beyond them, within the tight confines of the corridor, several other men crowded, these wearing armor, red fading to black. There was a greenish flashing light from the far end of the hall, but he could not see what was causing it. That was where the yelling was coming from, and he decided it was probably another Warmage, like the two standing nearest him, using his magical skills to ward off the red darts and sword thrusts of the armored men.

Marc considered his next move for several beats of his heart as he viewed the battle. Alexandra was somewhere beyond the occupied hall, but he pushed it aside as quickly as he realized it. Then, a grim smile worked onto his face. Some of his frustration was about to come out through the end of his own sword. As soon as he figured out who was fighting whom. He hoped that some Imperial dogs were holding out at the other end of the corridor.

Without another thought, he stepped from the hall and strode towards the two men with their backs to him. One of them was nearer than the other, standing about midway from the exit while the second was up next to the corner that formed the opening. To his right, another of the steep stairwells rose into the stone. As he walked closer to the first man, he hissed at him to get his attention, without, he hoped scaring the man into blasting him with some form of magic.

The man tensed for a moment then turned to face Marc, a slow grin pulling at wide lips. Marc almost stumbled, and a remembrance of pain shot through him, coming up from his stomach. The man's face turned to utter surprise as Marc's sword buried itself in his chest, just beneath the Imperial insignia that emblazoned the uniform above his heart. Marc watched the coat of arms unceasingly as he yanked out his blade and the young Warmage slid to his death upon the cold stone.

The second Warmage never knew doom had claimed him. When his head stopped its roll against the wall, it still bore a look of distinct concentration.

Marc's lips peeled back from his teeth, a smile more feral than anything else, once he confirmed that the second man bore the sign of the Emperor on his chest. As if he were threshing wheat, he headed into the hallway, raining death on the Imperials in their dual colored armor.

Whoever was holding them off at the end of the hallway was lucky in that he seemed to be in a natural choke point, so many of the Imperials pushing forward were simply waiting. Once he had struck down the two soldiers in the rear, the next realized they were under attack and turned towards him after yelling out in surprise.

Above them, somewhere deep in the formidable Council Manor above, the tolling of bells began ringing. Marc was fairly certain this ruckus down here would have little to do with that and surmised that the city must be under attack, considering the explosion earlier. And it wasn't the Imperials attacking the city, which seemed fairly odd since at some point the power greedy Emperor would have cast his looks east at Calif. Most likely, it was Flandric, though Marc would have thought he would have attacked the Span rather than the city proper. What he knew of that family line suggested that their adherence to old codes and honor would take precedence. Desperate times, it seemed, changed that.

Worrying about it now was moot, however. The Imperials were down in the dungeon, with him, and more importantly, with Alex. The hallway constricted him somewhat, but worked against his foes even more, destroying any maneuverability they may have had in open ground. With a grim smile, he slid under their clumsy attacks and dispatched them easily, moving through their ground into the next ranking.

Marc continued moving smoothly through the double ranks of Imperial soldiers like fluid death, blade sliding easily into and out of the vulnerable parts of their armor. When the second of two remaining soldiers slid from his blade, he regarded the last as he fell from a slashing bar of light wielded by what he would otherwise say was a farmer.

He was dressed plainly in soft colored woolens and had the sun worn face of one long under its umbrella; thin and wiry in body, and older of face. Only he hadn't moved like a farmer, stiff and clumsy. Not only the fact that he was alone at this end of the corridor stood testament to that, but he had watched how quick and sure his movements were.

And his weapon. A green blade made of light. It brought back fables of his own childhood of a time long gone. The man held it up in a standard guard while studying him. For a moment, their eyes locked on each other's. He lowered his sword toward the ground in a low guard while they regarded each other.

"Thank you," the farmer warrior suddenly said, standing back out of his fighting stance into a more relaxed one. "Good thing you came along, sure, othernway I mightn't be standing here right now." The green lightsword suddenly winked out, leaving them standing in fading light from the Warmages casting. He held out a hand. "The name's Hal," he said. Marc looked at him a moment longer, then stepped forward and took the hand. "Marc Pendragon." The hallway cornered where Hal made his stand, the tugging Bond pulling his gaze that direction.

"I'm here rescuing some people," Hal said. "Would you be willing to lend a hand?"

"People?" Marc asked, swinging his gaze back to the farmer, then beyond him to the door behind him, which stood open a crack. Within the blackness, he could see movement. "Who?"

Before he could answer, Marc followed it with, "Is there a woman with them? One wearing a metal collar?" Hal's face pinched a bit in confusion as he looked back down the side hallway. "Never mind," Marc answered himself. Of course there wasn't. The Bond was still tugging at him from a distance.

Hal looked at him for a few moments before casting his gaze back up the corridor where the battle took place and cocked his head as if hearing the distant bells from overhead.

"Alarms," Marc commented, turned from the strange fable-like warrior and moved down the side hallway.

"Wait," he said a second later. "Where are you going? Can't you help?"

"I already did," Marc said, striding away. "Good luck to you." He could feel the man's stare follow him into darkness.

Chapter 84

A View From Outside

$\mathscr{B}$alphor wiped his soaked forehead with a now soiled handkerchief. Immediately, beads of sweat reformed on the wide pate. He huffed for maybe the thousandth time and wiped at it again. Below him, on the street, more people were streaming towards the Manor grounds, some of them with taken up arms, some with panic stricken faces. Even from his vantage point on the third floor of this inn, he could no longer make out the soldiers fighting at the front gates, though the screams of the dying still rang high in his ears.

Of all the nights. Calif, most of her army gone to the Span to meet the marching Flandric, was ripe for the Resistance to get into the dungeons and rescue their leaders. Who knew there would be an invasion from the east. While staging their minor uprising, word came that an army of Skor had launched a surprise attack at the Far Gate. Skor! How in blazes that happened, he didn't know. In fact, no one really knew until that wizard's tower went up in a plume of fire. Then everything went to Perdition.

"What in blazes are you doing, Balphor," someone said from behind him. His body tried to jump out of his skin, but he managed to hold onto the squeaking scream that attempted to fly from his clenching jaw. Barely. He turned and a flood of relief partially doused the raging excited fear that filled him.

"Sharla," he stammered. "It's so good to see you. Everything has turned to disaster." The woman wore a fierce look on her face that more than matched that of her flaming hair and was a stark contrast to the revealing skirt and blouse she wore, but Balphor was far too preoccupied to really notice her enticing features just then.

"What do you mean?" she nearly yelled. Mentally, that portion of him that was yet untouched by the excitement rolled eyes. She had her dander up; things could only get worse for him.

"Things have gotten out of hand."

"I'll say!" She strode past him and leaned out the window. A spicy, sweet scent wafted off her and curled inside Balphor's thick nose, causing him to miss a breath. "What fool-possible reason would you have to attack the main entrance?"

"I didn't. It was only supposed to be a distraction while the Cadres attempted to get inside through the servants' entrances, but . . ."

"But what?" Sharla continued watching out the window.

"As soon as we started, mobs of other people joined in, right off the street. . . . They . . . uh . . . I guess they panicked when they saw the guards form up to push them back. It's a huge mess. . . . Skor coming from the east, the army gone. . . Most of them down there now are not even our people. . . . At least that is what the runners are telling me. . . . You know I'm not the general type. My function is more about . . . gathering. . . . What in the Creator's name is that?"

Balphor pointed past her though he hadn't needed too. Sharla was already staring at the gigantic shape floating above the buildings. It looked like a ship of some sort, though it had to be three times the size of any ship he ever saw. And wider. But without sails, though it had masts and yardarms. Its railings and trim were like spiders' webs, curls and twists in myriad decorations that gleamed in the firelight like hot metal. It moved . . . gracefully . . . through the air and roiling smoke on a plane with the tallest battlements of the Council Manor. And quickly as well, gliding to a halt not long after he spotted it. Immediately, streams of liquid began pouring from its length. Balphor gulped. What his eyes originally thought was liquid soon showed him it was men. Soldiers. Warriors, almost antlike, flowing onto the battlements in what seemed never ending lines.

"I don't know, but we better do something to get this cockeyed plan of yours back on track," Sharla said, a tone of wonder in her throat.

"W-what?"

She shook her head, sending the coils of hair along her back dancing in undulating waves that momentarily caught Balphor's eyes. "We'll see," she said, then was gone, only a spicy-sweet fragrance and tendrils of pale mist occupying the space she had been standing. Balphor, not ready for it, nearly tumbled out of the window in surprise, catching most of his weight on the sill before doing so. The frame, for its part, creaked alarmingly and a portion of it came loose when he pushed himself back up.

"I hate it when she does that," he muttered, then looked down into the moving throng before the main entrance. Several people seemed to be pushed away from a space of air, yelling crazily. Into this circle a faint puff of smoke, and then, there she was, in all her long, lean splendor.

"Move aside," she yelled, her voice booming over the din like thunder. The magically enhanced order sent those nearest scurrying to the sides, ears buried in hands. Around her, in a line towards the entrance, combatants and panic stricken alike froze as if seized on the back of the neck and threw fear wrought gazes backwards. "Move aside," she yelled again, this time holding her bare arms up in a gesture to clutch the sky above her. An immediate shimmer began within the space between her hands, a distortion of night that was not lost on anyone. As the shimmer built in intensity, outward like a ball, eyes widened and feet shuffled to the side away from Sharla as if they were avoiding a charging bull. The result was a path that opened all the way to the wide steps leading up to the huge entrance.

The soldiers, thinking the crowds were beginning to route, stood back, leaning on knees or against the planes of the walls in order to take a much needed rest. They were blood spattered and soot stained, and for moments did not notice the workings of the wizardess in the midst of the crowd. Once they did, in a wave, they began yelling and jumping to the sides of the terrace that formed the top of the stair.

Sharla made a throwing motion with her arms, and the ball of energy above her shot forward like a dart and slammed into the great planes of molded silver and gold, flattening itself only half a heartbeat before it exploded in a terrible flash of light.

Balphor threw his arms over his eyes and stumbled backward, but was too slow to intercept the brightness that burned his vision. The roaring squeal of ripping metal flew through his window, all but blocking out the screams of people falling over each other, and a gout of hot wind tore at the curtains and moved across his already warm skin, stripping it of sweat.

Chapter 85

Searching the Darkness Inside and Out

*T*he battle rush passed quickly, leaving Marc again resisting the wall that kept him from moving in the direction he wanted to. To Alex. As before, he had to stop and refocus his thoughts away from rescue and assistance to something banal or unimportant. Or selfish. That seemed to work out well, too.

Voices were drifting down the darkened corridor from the guardroom where he had met the man, Hal, though they were no longer in view, and offered him the distraction he needed to continue. He concentrated on the pull of the weak Bond for only enough time to get a feel for its direction, then let his mind slide over to myths and legends he had been reared on, before he was a grown man.

The man with the light blade had jolted him, and from the silt of his mind, one myth in particular was revealed briefly amid swirling sand. However, it settled quickly and covered the memory back over, which he now dug for.

It was something about men long, long before his time, called Jon, or Jun, or something. He seemed to recall his mother saying something about swords of fire. Or maybe it was his father. It mattered little. So did the memory, though in all his many lives in this world, among all the strange and wondrous things and events he had been witness to, this was something new. A shaft of green light that hewed like a sword. Of course, he remembered seeing 'swords of fire' before, but nothing so simple, so elegant. So *clean* as the weapon that man wielded.

"Interesting," he whispered. In the hall, it sounded harsh, but he remained unconcerned. He simply tumbled the thought around in his head, wondering where the weapon came from, where the man got it, if there were others, and so forth, all the while, allowing his body to be drawn by that tiny, ethereal pull. The sound of the voices soon disappeared, and he was only left with the dull mumble of the Manor alarm bells clanging away far above him.

Marc knew he was close, he could feel it, but the direction sense that seemed to go with it whiffed away like a dandelion seed. One minute he was working his way slowly down a corridor following the tugging sensation, and the next it was just gone. The tugging, that is. Not the overall sense. It felt as if she were all around him now, a cloud into which he just walked and now stood without direction.

Doors lined the corridor in both directions, darkened blobs against a slightly less dark background. Above, the sound of the alarm bells continued, muted so by the stone that his heartbeat was louder. It was stuffy and a stale sweat greased his skin, mixing with the ages of must and dust that lay beneath the Calif seat of government. He could only stand and flick his gaze around the blackness.

Where was she? Alex had to be around here somewhere. But where?

Marc thought to call out her name, but once his mind was filled with calling her, his throat tightened and wouldn't speak. As an afterthought, it probably wasn't a good idea to make known his presence, though there was no one around but him that he knew of. Still, he tried, fighting the curse. All that came was a wheezy grunt.

He huffed and turned his mind to something else, thinking of blue skies and green vistas until he could not only see them in his mind, but feel a breeze on his face. Then, without thought, he moved to the nearest door and peered into the stygian darkness beyond the tiny window. The haunt of mold and old stone breathed back in his face. He could sense a nothingness there in the tiny room. Marc moved to the next and strained his eyes into that one.

Nothing.

The next was the same. He stopped and stared down the line as far as he could, then back the direction he came. His eyes roved down the other side of the hall. There were at least twenty doors that appeared in his glance, and many more that went past it. Alex could be behind any of them, unconscious or worse. He moved to the next. Nothing. And the next. Nothing. And the next.

What was that? He turned around and stared hard at the door he just passed. The sensation still hung about him like a shroud so gave no help.

Nothing. He was making himself hear things out of desperation brought on by the disappearance of something he depended on. Or neutralization of. He had the sudden inclination to turn around and go back. To get out of the castle, to leave Alex to her fate. It was a slicing wound, old and unhealed. He was foolish to think that he could change the way his curse worked now, after so many times before. After so many people destroyed while he stood by and did nothing.

Anine.

What made him think that he could possibly be helpful now?

Marc stood by the door for many beats of a guilt ridden heart, staring into the blackness surrounding him waiting for the strength of his curse-induced thoughts to wane. He stepped away from the door, thought of cool breezes in a sun swept glade, and took a step.

A subtle shifting, grit under foot muted by the thickness of wood, sounded from the room. *Yes! It was real. Someone was behind the door.*

Alexandra.

With his mind suddenly filled with her being, his body went painfully rigid.

"Alex," Marc said through spasming lips. "Is that you?" He urged his body to move, but it wouldn't. His voice sounded scratchy and far away, as if he whispered it, but he again heard the shuffle of someone, or something, behind the door. "Alex?"

A low moan issued in answer, but was ambiguous in tone. There was someone behind the door, but it could be anyone. Marc hitched onto that thought and allowed his natural curiosity to bubble up. A moment later, he was able to move to the window in the door, albeit slowly, like he was in a vat of molasses.

Inside was blackness, utter blackness, and the rank odor of long sitting moisture. He could see nothing; tapped the pommel of his sword to the door once. The thud resounded up and down the hallway, but it fled quickly enough that he heard movement from behind the heavy wooden obstruction. The sound came from below, near the floor. "Alex?" he croaked again. But nothing answered.

Marc tried the handle, not surprised to find the door locked, and stepped back. Thinking that sword of fire might come in handy right about now, he knelt and inspected the lock housing with his free hand. The door had a manual lock that didn't require a key. A moment later, the spring bolt clacked back, making a sharp sound in the hall that pinched his ear drums, as he threw the release lever. His luck seemed to be holding. Smiling, he stood and placed his hand on the handle.

"Marc?" a dull thick voice said from behind the door. Marc froze, his jaw clenching so badly that his teeth squealed. His hand became a claw around the iron handle while his mind went back to the night Anine died.

His reaching arm was a painful rictus that would not move no matter how much he willed it. Though thick and low, the voice that drifted through the window out into the hall was Alexandra's. She was behind the door, and Marc could not open it, or speak. His battle with his curse sprung up so powerfully that he almost felt he couldn't breathe. His chest heaved with effort, but very little air seemed to be getting into his rigid body. Within moments, he was growling through clenched jaws and water was tumbling from the corners of his eyes. All his thoughts were on one purpose. Reaching Alex. And he was determined to explode rather than fail at this.

Minutes passed by as he struggled. A dull inner thunder replaced the stale sounds of the dungeon falling back against his onslaught of grunting. Heat rolled off his body in waves and a whirling sensation began slowly behind his eyes. His efforts were going nowhere, instead turning back on itself and striking out against his own self like a dying snake. Clouds were beginning to form around his vision, gray clouds filled with pulsating lightning.

"Back off," Alex's disembodied voice seeped into his consciousness. "Back away." It was like listening to a faraway echo, but like a tensed spring, once he heeded the command, his body rocketed backward to slam into the opposite wall, where he leaned heavily as blasts of air exploded from his lungs like the huge bellows of a blacksmith's forge.

In the dimness, he saw a dark vertical line appear before him and widen. It took him more than a couple of raging heartbeats to understand that the door was now open, pushed by Alex, who lay crumpled at its foot like an ephemeral spirit. He watched breathlessly as a pale arm lifted towards him.

"Take my hand," Alex said, her voice a weak rasp.

Marc hesitated only a moment before crossing the hall and grabbing her hand in his. As he did so, Alex lifted herself from the floor as much as she could, so that when his hand found hers she was high up on her knees. As soon as she grasped him, she threw herself backward, rocking onto her feet. A groan fell from her lips, but her maneuver forced Marc to tighten his muscles and lean back as her weight, light as it was, threatened to drag him face forward onto the cold stone. Alex came up like a drunken swan taking flight and fell into Marc's chest, where she leaned, breathing heavily. "Thank you," she whispered finally.

Shame flooded through Marc, but he pushed it aside, labeling it another fell side effect of his curse that needed to change. "Thank you," he echoed. A fierce shiver moved through her sagging body. "Alex, what happened? What did they do to you?" Though she was leaning on him, Marc still could not feel her through the bond as he had been able to previously. The sensation was still spread out like a fog.

"Nothing," she coughed. "They just . . . dumped me in here . . . and left me. . . I thought you were . . . dead."

A sad smile worked onto his face, and he drew his arms tightly around her quivering form, not because she needed warmth, but because it felt good to have her in his arms. "A temporary setback," he said. "You should have realized that when I woke up."

"I can't feel . . . the Bond . . . The collar," she said.

Her hand shakily guided his up to her neck where he felt the chilled ring of metal around her neck. "What is this?"

"Don't know . . . but keeps me from . . . touching,"

"Don't over extend yourself," Marc interrupted. "We've got to figure a way out of here."

"Where's Sandy?"

Marc sighed and his heart lurched. "Sandoren is dead," he said, not knowing how else to say it.

Alex shuddered again, but this time not from the chill or weakness that permeated her. When she spoke again, her voice trembled with anguish, "Del?"

"I don't know," he said. "Gone."

"We have to find him," she rasped.

"How?"

"I don't know," she yelled. Feeble though it was, it still thundered up and down the halls, causing Marc's neck muscles to stiffen. She had pushed herself away from him to glare up at his face, to show her resolve, but now that the flash of energy had passed, she slumped into him again.

"Okay, alright, but first we have to get out of here," Marc said. Moments later, before his mind could react, he bent over and swept Alexandra up into his arms, bearing her light frame with ease. She stiffened and grunted out in surprise.

"How," she squeaked.

Gritting his teeth, he said, "I'm thinking of you as a sack of potatoes."

Marc thought he saw a wan smile crawl across her pallid face, but in the dimness was not sure. Immediately, the walls he had erected around his curse to get away with this design began cracking so he wrenched his gaze away and closed his eyes, allowing himself to feel only her weight in his arms as it was and not attaching any importance to it. He forced himself to see her as just as he said she was. A sack of potatoes. Nothing that needed assistance from him. Nothing that needed his help. Only a slight burden that he had to carry in order to get himself out of this stinking dungeon.

Though a tenuous ploy, it worked. He placed one foot in front of the other, moved quickly back down the passage way he had come while trying to ignore Alex's breath against his neck and her faint flowery scent, unconquered completely by the foulness of her capture, which curled into his nostrils. The first stairwell leading upward he came to, he started up.

Chapter 86

Chaos and Death

*7*he Council Manor was swarming with chaos. Combatants raged against each other in small groups while staff members and other citizens ran in panic for cover or escape. It served as a screen to Marc's movements, not that he thought about it much. But, more importantly, it gave him something to concentrate on while trying to carry Alexandra. Twice already he had stopped, a trembling statue, unable to move because his thoughts glared down on the actual part he was playing. And both times, it had taken an extreme act of will to move the attention of his curse away from his true purpose. Now he had other concerns. It helped, but didn't get him moving any faster.

Each step was still like walking in a bog. A heavy sweat trickled down his skin and his flesh felt hot, as if he had been running all day. Cramps in his muscles served as minor distractions as well. Luckily, they were close to the Grand Hall and soon would be outside and headed to the Inn where Whitesteel was stabled. Soon, they would be out of Calif and away from all this mess. Until then, one step at a bloody time.

By the time they made it to the Grand Hall, only a remnant of battle could be seen. Small knots of fighting amid a sea of slain and wounded. The once mirrored marble surface of the floor was now shining red, and the stench of spilled blood hung in the stifling air and even coated his throat with a metallic taste.

Above them, they could hear more battling, and he paused a moment to take a look around. Surprisingly, three floors up and behind him, was the man he met down in the dungeon halls, Hal he said his name was. He and another were fighting more of the red and black armored men. The other, a slimmer man, a ffolk it looked like, but with white hair and obsidian skin, also used a fire sword, but his was a light purplish color. A momentary crease in his brow was the only recognition that flashed through his brain. *Owl.* A third man, dressed in black and gray leathers wove around behind the group, bearing a blue fire sword, though this one seemed not to be with Hal and the ffolk. A fourth stood off to the side, watching the fight. He was a giant, completely in black, and his calm force of will rolled off of him like the surf. Marc could feel his presence all the way down where he stood. That one had to be the one called the Devastator.

He watched them for a few seconds, the weapons in their hands and the smooth ways in which they moved prodding at some long buried memory. Alex mumbled something into his chest and broke his attention. Steeling himself against his curse, he turned and slogged toward the hole where the doors once hung, the heavy planes, now twisted and ripped and laying off to the side.

Outside, the noise and fighting was worse. Against the heat and back glow of the burning city people ran and died, fought and killed. A large group of city guardsmen were locked in mortal combat with streams of dark armored Skor coming from the east. Rioters threw rocks and shot arrows indiscriminately among them all while other people ran from the Manor or to the Manor. Some were helping the guards, others were trying to put out fires or tried to drag out the wounded or dead from the fray. Several Servants of the Light were proselytizing their views even while falling under the rain of missiles. Smoke curled and trailed along the streets, and hot ash floated down from higher up, touching off more fires where they settled. The coming morning was scorched with soot and flames. Screams sang counterpoint to the ring of metal and the roar of the fires.

Marc moved off the stair leading up into the Manor and began sidling along the wall to avoid the nearer groups of combatants. What went on inside, held out here; hardly anyone glanced in their direction. With a little more luck, the two of them would be able to slip around the courtyard and leave the bulk of the terrible storm behind them.

Of course, Luck was rarely kind to him.

He stopped and stared. Across the courtyard, amongst a large group of battling guardsmen, rioters, and Skor, were five mounted figures in dark robes, all of them hacking at whoever was closest with wicked thin blades. On occasion, a sickly blue flame belched out from an outstretched hand and encapsulated a victim in a blob of oily blue death. Their horses, ugly, mistreated things not more than leather-covered skeletons, screamed in fury.

Marc's insides, at once, turned to ice and flame as both hatred and fear rose up in a swirling tornado that twisted into his guts. Faces, names, washed through his brain only to get caught in the tempest within him, fanning it, feeding it with memories of vile tragic loss, a flood jetting through the broken dam of his residual amnesia. Anine, the most recent. Each one a cruel, tormented death at the hands of these creatures and the thing they called Master. The Black Skull. An unholy nemesis as old as he was. Each one a reminder of his impotence as he stood by and watched. Each one a cold slap with a hooked whip that tore into the deepest recesses of his soul. The ripping cyclone grew, then plummeted, then grew again. A gale force of guilt whipped at it, chewed at its trailing edges, while a blizzard of anger worked at the base of a spine steel stiff with ice.

When he heard Alex's muffled question, he realized he was trembling, not from the efforts of moving, but from the storm inside. The sweat that coated him was clammy in the overheated morning air, and he could smell his own hate rising from his flesh. He noticed, from beneath his shirt, the amulet glowing almost whitely against the fabric and knew, then, that it did that when they were near.

Slowly, he knelt and placed Alex on the ground, her back against the solid foundations of the Manor proper then slid the ancient sword of his lineage from its scabbard. The singing of the metal as it left its home was the clear crispness of a winter morning to his mind. The tone seemed to travel the distance between him and the riders, slicing through the sounds of death around them as if it wasn't there. At the same moment, five sets of evil steeped eyes lifted from their cruel tasks and glared in his direction. While the vortex raged in his heart and guts, his mind began to empty of all except one thought and he smiled.

Chapter 87

Hubris and Revenge

*T*he death, the killing, the chaos was scrumptious. Each blow of his sword, each cast of soul-devouring fire gave Crowlin just a little more life, a little more freedom. And now, his quarry was here. The single goal that was burning in him was standing before him over the span of the death field and was waiting. Seemed to know who he was.

Pendragon.

What a gift! After he destroyed the man, they would feast like it was their last.

The fact that it actually may be, at least his last, did not escape him. Crowlin knew his act of defiance would be punished. The target of that revolt, Pendragon, once killed was sure to bring the worst torture imaginable.

Crowlin smiled anyway.

The scent of death, blood, and departing souls was thick in the smoky air and clogged his mind with a heady euphoria. He, Crowlin, the Threadbreaker, did not care what punishment he received. Not now. Now, there was only one thing to do.

Kill Pendragon.

He dismounted slowly, breathing in the fetid, feral air. Though he didn't look, he sensed the others doing the same. "He's mine," Crowlin hissed. "You take the Earthwitch!"

Muttered acceptance filtered through his spinning mind as they stepped toward their prey. The human merely stood, frozen to the spot as usual, unable to do anything. His face was a twisted mask of fear. Behind him, the woman pushed herself into a leaning stand against the heavy stone outcropping of the building.

The group prowled into a half circle that encompassed Pendragon and the woman, pinning them against the wall. When they were close enough for Pendragon to hear his voice over the tumult, Crowlin said, "Burn her! Let him watch another die before he does!"

Reegan, next to him, hissed and threw out a hand. Blue Soulfire arced out from it toward the woman. Pendragon screamed. Pleasure at his agony suffused Crowlin, but he had to fight to keep his eyes on him instead of watching the woman's death as the fire engulfed her and burned her flesh from its bones and devoured her essence.

The stream struck her squarely in the chest and burst around her. The pull of the sight was so great that Crowlin allowed his eyes to skip over Pendragon's shoulder to take it in. He sought no solace for failing to reign in his desire. He could still see the man's form at the side, and his impotent screams would surely make up for not truly seeing the pain that would contort his face.

However, something was wrong. The woman did not scream the frenzied scream of torture common to that favored attack. In fact, the bluish fire surrounded her only momentarily before drawing away from her, as if a great wind took it. It caused Crowlin to pause as confusion settled into his gait.

Pendragon yelled again, then moved suddenly, quickly, his sword swinging in the filthy light. *No! It can't be!* Crowlin's mind, shocked by the sight, fought to find explanation, though nothing came, even as Reegan fell beneath the violent cut of the man's blade. There was only a pinching coldness engulfing his thoughts. *How could this be?*

The others had no such effects staying their hands. Meerdon, Teraard, and Gorn immediately swarmed toward the human, their own blades hissing in the air. Steel rang in the morning air.

Meerdon's sword shattered, throwing glittering arcs around them. A flash of silver from Pendragon's blade sent him reeling backward, his hands clutching at his throat, trying to hold in the gurgling sounds that came from it.

Smoothly, the man moved to Gorn, bringing his sword up under the other's guard and slicing it along his chest. Gorn cried out, a wild cry that sent shivers of clarity through Crowlin's mind.

This man was not helpless! This man was more dangerous than he could have imagined! *How could this be?* Pendragon was supposed to be held at complete bay by the curse hanging over him. It had always been that way, since the beginning, for untold ages past. Pendragon was cursed! *So this is to be my punishment!*

Crowlin wailed in fury. All other thoughts went out of his head and he rushed the man.

Gorn, badly wounded but not down, stumbled backward, while Teraard came at Pendragon from the opposite side. Unable to move his sword into position to defend, Pendragon drove a thrusting kick into Teraard's face that heaved him into the air and backward. His landing on the pavement was loud, even in the riot around them.

Crowlin swung, wanting to cleave the man's head in two, but it met midway with resistance that stopped it with a terrible clang and sent vibrations painfully down into his hands. Pendragon's sword moved from the block quickly, cleanly, and sliced into Gorn again. He screamed as the steel bit him, and it seemed that a flash of light erupted around the contact point. Gorn's arm flopped down into his robes, followed by the rest of his body. Teraard, for his part, was up and lunging back into the fray.

Immediately, Pendragon's sword flashed back, impossibly fast, met his blade again, nearly forcing it from his singing hands, sailed right through to catch Teraard's unwieldy attack. Crowlin's mind was a puddle in a hailstorm. Thoughts brought on by shock and fear blasted through it. *This cannot be happening! This is impossible! This was a mistake!* But fury at this impudence kept him swinging. Kept his body moving in the ways of a killer.

Pendragon's sword flashed again and liquid agony raced up and down his side. Bursts of light went off in front of his eyes, and he heard his mouth yelling hoarsely. When his vision cleared, he found his arms clutching his belly, trying in vain to hold in the substance that coursed through his body that was once blood. He was stumbling backward, away from the terrifying man and his biting weapon. His own sword, coated in gore lay near Pendragon's feet, an echo of its fall still in his burning mind.

Teraard met the evil man's blade, sheathing it with his body. Another cry ripped the morning air. Whether it was his or Teraard's, Crowlin wasn't sure. Pendragon turned his terrible gaze back on him.

Must escape! his mind screamed. *Flee! Flee! This was not supposed to happen!*

Pendragon's mouth was moving. Seconds later, his voice thundered into his ears. "Tell your master I'm coming for him," it said, but Crowlin was too busy trying to drag his agony torn body back onto his nearly dead mount to receive the full impact of it. "Must escape! Must feed!" he found himself whispering over and over, a charm to keep him alive. He could come back for the others once he had healed himself. He could restore them all once he was safe and Pendragon gone.

The animal was screaming beneath his fumbling attempts to mount, and he cuffed it sharply on the head several times and jerked the reins harshly while his panicked body continued to climb. Crowlin was oblivious that Pendragon was standing still, watching him. Even had he seen him, Crowlin would not have understood that the man was not coming to finish him off.

Had that notion occurred to him, Crowlin might have changed his plans and rushed him, forcing him to kill him. At least he would have avoided a worse fate. But that was not to be. Crowlin was in a desperate fight for survival, and once the beast was under him, he flailed its haunches with his heels even as he yanked back on the reins, causing the creature to dance beneath his burning body. Finally, he whipped the horse into a headlong run into the streets, caring not where he was going as long as there was growing distance between him and the terrible, hated Pendragon.

Chapter 88

Directions and Plans

*M*arc watched the robed creature only until its dying mount began stumbling away from him, then turned back to Alex. She had fallen back against the stone wall and slid down to the ground, but her eyes were open and alert. In her hands, she held the crumbling remains of some type of metal. Thin strips, it seemed, that had once curved into a circular shape. He didn't realize it was the remains of the odd collar she had been shackled with when he found her until he felt the tremendous rush of feelings flowing unchecked through the Bond.

"Are you alright," he asked anyway. Out of reflex. Immediately, his body went rigid and he forced his attention to the death around him.

"Yes," she said, haltingly and in a voice tinged with wonder. "I think I am okay."

"Good. We best be getting out of here before something else happens."

Alex stood, still a little shaky, and managed a worn smile. "Agreed. We have to find Del."

"Are you sure—" Marc started.

"Yes. He's alive," Alex said. "I can feel it, now that this damnable collar is off. But I can't tell where he is like I could when I first found him."

"Well, I know where we can begin our search," Marc said, his jaw tightening. "My *friend* from the cabin was with them when they came."

Alex stared a moment. "Your friend? The Greyffolk? He betrayed us?"

"He betrayed you," Marc said. "For the bounty."

"Then why would he help us now?"

"He doesn't really have a choice in the matter," Marc said, looking at Anduin meaningfully before sliding it back into its scabbard. "That is, if he's awake from our last encounter."

Alex only arched an eyebrow.

"Come," Marc continued. "Once we visit Marrillon, we'll pick up Whitesteel and a horse for you. We'll have Del back before the day is out. Then, we'll get out of Calif."

"Marc," Alex's eyes were lucid, the rush through the Bond intense, already telling him what she was saying. "Thank you for coming for me."

Marc smiled. "Thank you for showing me how." He held out his hand, waited for Alex to take it. The Bond between them didn't lessen the tingle that he felt at her touch. "Come," he said.

Chapter 89

The Ravages of War

*A*gain, Maelyrin was surrounded by the terrible deeds wreaked by the races outside her former world. Again, she was faced with its horrific visions of death and destruction, another buttress to her growing belief that the world was doomed to acts of violence that threatened to burn its entirety.

But, she realized, she was slowly getting hardened to it, too. And that revelation was still under a preponderance of ambivalence. Somewhere, deep inside her, in the attack of her innocence maybe, she suspected that growing accustomed to death was, itself, a greater death.

She yanked an arrow from her quiver, nocked and drew, then sent the shaft into a Skoran warrior running at them. Pain flashed through her as the creature fell and prompted her to glance back toward the harbor. She again cursed herself for not arguing Kiyo down from his decision to come ashore once it became abundantly clear that the city of Calif was under siege. After getting over the awful sickness brought on by the rolling of the ship, she found she enjoyed sailing. Staying aboard the Lady Rain would not have been a terrible thing.

But Kiyo had insisted. And there had been an intensity to him that she almost overlooked as being cooped up on the ship for the time they were aboard, that kept her from resisting.

Now, he was a frightful killing machine next to her, his sword a silver gleam in the smoky morning light that took down any that came against them. Especially, it seemed, the black armored Skor. And his path of slaying was taking them closer and closer to where the fires burned and battle was most concentrated. The place of screams. Every now and then, colored balls and streaks arced and sailed through the air. Magical energies and explosions that rocked the very ground on which they tramped.

Another Skor moved against them and was met with another arrow.

"I only have two arrows left," she yelled up at the giant after she looked to the quiver at her hip.

Kiyo didn't hear her. Or didn't acknowledge that he heard her. In fact, only a moment later, he dashed forward, leaving her gaping at his back for a heartbeat.

Maelyrin ran to catch up to him then stopped suddenly, her mouth dropping open. They were on the edge of a small plaza crowded on each side by unwieldy looking buildings that rose high into the air like large, squat trees. Across from them, men were fighting, screaming as they died. Dealing out their deaths was another Turgatha 'mal. Another giant that, at first glance, she mistook as Kiyo, thinking he somehow split himself in two so he could dole out more damage. But a moment after, her Sight caught up and she reeled back with disgust. This one was a thing steeped with blackness and hate. This one was completely filled with the essence of the stories she grew up with about the Turgatha 'mal.

Kiyo stopped midway through the plaza and bellowed. "Jegrutak!"

The other giant finished off his last combatant with an indifferent slice of a blade similar to Kiyo's and looked their way. It smiled, its obsidian eyes sparkling in the soot stained light and began approaching Kiyo.

The creature, Jegrutak, said something in a guttural, chopped language that hurt her ears. Kiyo answered using the same and gestured with his sword. Jegrutak bowed slightly and came forward again. Within a breath, the plaza was ringing with the clarion tones of the giant's swords as they moved against each other. To Maelyrin, it seemed like two ribbons of silver dancing with each other, as terrible as it was beautiful. Both giants were wells of emptiness and calm, though she thought she could detect a hint of grime coating the being of Jegrutak.

Fascinated, Maelyrin stared at the death dance, no clear definition as to what she was watching, but enthralled nonetheless. They were like mirror images of each other, moving like water through the plaza, each one singing the others' fate with each ring of sword on sword. Several times, she confused one for the other. Only her Sight was able to keep the two as separate entities rather than the blurring, interchanging echoes of one another.

Presently, the singular spectacle of the two combatants was lessened when a running battle spilled into the plaza. Many men and Skor stabbing and slicing, yelling and dying began flooding into the area from the direction of a huge building that stood starkly against the boiling backdrop of the burning city. Like a wave on the sea, the crowd rolled through the plaza and crashed against the two giants, disrupting and pushing them apart. Men and Skor began falling left and right, as desperation-filled mania attempted to pull the Turgatha 'Mal into their chaotic storm. Their attacks, crude and brutish, were instantly met with surgical precision.

The tide was sweeping the plaza off to her left, toward another street exiting it, keeping her out of immediate danger, but Maelyrin nocked an arrow just as a precaution. When she looked back, she was surprised to see Kiyo wading back in her direction, his presence exacting so much respect and fear from the unruly crowd that all the combatants gave him a wide berth. Her gaze flicked over the throng, a wild notion coming to her that gripped her heart tightly. The other giant was gone. She had to use her *Sight* to make sure the one nearing her was indeed Kiyo. Just before she was about to yell her question to her giant companion she looked past him then drew her bow.

Slinking behind the fading crowd was something that grabbed her mind in a furious grip, pushed all other thoughts aside and turned her insides into heavy sludge. A *Laekthymin.* A twisted perversion of her own race. Cursed with flesh the color of obsidian glass and hair as white as down, the *Laekthymin* meant doom for her entire people. They were eradicated wherever they turned up. Surely, this whole terrible destruction lay at the feet of the thing crossing the plaza.

Maelyrin sighted her arrow, consumed with loathing, using it to guide the missile, and let loose, only vaguely aware that Kiyo was turning to look at what had pulled her attention into so hateful a grip. The arrow sped true, the twang of her bowstring slapping against her forearm with solid force. The sting felt good.

The *Laekthymin* was oblivious to its coming doom, and appeared to be wounded as well, as it gripped at its side and walked slumped. Despite her disgust with death, Maelyrin smiled a smile born of generations of systematic hatred. The arrow was going to take him in the throat.

At the last second, though, sensing the danger to it, the *Laekthymin* spun towards the missile. A flash of lavender light burst from its hand and intercepted it, knocked it aside with superior speed, then, its horrid gaze fell on them and it started forward, holding out the shaft of light before it like a sword.

Maelyrin thought she heard Kiyo say, "Jynn'd," but he moved towards the creature, a graceful deadly predator against a mangy jackal. She fumbled at her side for her last arrow, finally having to look down to grab it. She found her hand shaking so badly that she had to will it to wrap around the shaft without crushing the fletching. Kiyo again was speaking to it, but his voice was muffled by the ambient noise.

Regretfully, she released the arrow, her quaking body now no good for the bow, and looked up at the creature and Kiyo, just as the *Laekthymin* mewled out a cry and struck at the giant with the lavender shaft of light.

Kiyo parried it easily. The *Laekthymin's* face contorted into a mask of fury and it coughed out a curse about magic swords and swung again. Kiyo caught the light shaft and spun it away. The *Laekthymin* screamed in fury and began attacking in earnest. While it was terribly fast, the *Laekthymin's* strikes were crude and overreached. Kiyo, that well of nothingness undisturbed, blocked each slash and thrust easily, each time sending a ripple of furor over the thing's face and eliciting a string of curses or incomprehensible yells. It was tired, she could tell by its jerky movements, and was, indeed, wounded, favoring its left side and trying to compensate for the pain it must be causing.

Soon, the *Laekthymin* was sure to exhaust itself completely and make a terrible mistake that would allow Kiyo's blade to slide in and send the creature to the dark place it belonged. She was rather surprised that the giant hadn't already killed it. The *Laekthymin's* fighting ability was nothing compared to the skills of his former opponent, Jegrutak, but yet, he still simply parried each clumsy blow.

Maelyrin's loathing began to transform into anger and she again thought of using her last arrow, but her body was still shivering from the effects of seeing such a terrible abomination. She might hit Kiyo, even if she were able to sight the bow. No, she wouldn't. Kiyo would handle the thing. She just wished he would hurry up and kill it. Several times, Maelyrin found herself cursing under her breath as the battle seemed to drag on and on.

Finally though, Kiyo appeared to tire of the thing's ungainly attacks and stepped away, breaking the confrontation. Maelyrin stared, her body rigid with hate. *What was he doing? Kill it!* she willed. The *Laekthymin* issued a terrible scream of fury that echoed her own distraught impatience and shock and closed with Kiyo again. The giant parried. Maelyrin thought he was going to acquiesce and calmly defend himself again, so was partially surprised when he blocked another slash then lashed out with his hand and struck the creature on the side of his head with the back of his massive fist.

Immediately, the *Laekthymin's* eyes rolled up into its head and it crumpled to the ground. The lavender light flashed out of existence, and when the thing crashed to the pavement, something like a sword hilt clattered away from its loosened grasp. Kiyo spun his sword in a fanning gesture then sheathed it with such fluidity that Maelyrin hardly realized he had done so until he was kneeling by the creature. The giant reached down and felt for the thing's life beat.

"Aren't you going to kill it?" Maelyrin stammered, not quite able to will her body to move any closer to the abomination. Kiyo looked up at her, his face serene, eyes calm, and said, "No."

"W-what? What?" she said, clenching her jaw. "You must. You have to. It's . . . It has to . . ."

"Has to what?"

"Has to be destroyed!"

"Why?"

"Because . . . because it's detestable . . . It is . . . . It just has to be!"

"No, it doesn't. And it isn't" Kiyo reached out his other hand and picked up the sword hilt, examined it a moment and slid it into his belt. Then, he placed his arms underneath the creature and lifted him.

"W-w-what are you doing?" She was nearing histrionics but didn't care. An entire portion of her past was being kicked around like a toadstool. "You can't . . . You mustn't!"

"I will and I am." It struck her, lightly, that he was angry and though her *Sight* was useless in her state of mind, she realized it was directed at her. Confusion bubbled up into her carefully walled pool of disgust and hatred.

"W-where are you going?" Kiyo was striding past her, headed back in the direction he had come.

"To get this man out of harm's way," he answered.

"That's not a man," she yelled. "That's a thing that must be destroyed! Hey, stop."

Kiyo did stop and turned to face her, his presence filling her view. Just then, the fear she had upon meeting him welled up inside of her and choked off the biting words she was about to let forth. "Your sudden change of heart is disappointing," he said. It was a slap that stung more than a physical blow would have. "This man is in need of rest and healing. I am going to help him. Come or stay as you please."

"But . . . but . . . But it tried to kill you . . . ."

"Yes. *He* did try to kill me, but look around you and learn the folly of that argument." Kiyo turned and began walking away, leaving Maelyrin sputtering. As if he had used that compelling voice on her, she looked around and saw the terrible reality around her as if for the first time. People lay scattered throughout the plaza and side streets, human, ffolk, and Skor alike, some of them still alive and wailing out their torment to any who would listen. Most of them were unmoving, however. Blood and gore spattered walls and pooled in the cobbles of the street, its reek a sobering presence in the acrid filled air.

Maelyrin's stomach lurched and her head began to spin lazily. Quickly, too quickly, she cast her gaze at Kiyo's receding back, swooning from the effort. The *Laekthymin's* legs bounced with his gliding movements, and the loathing she felt for it tried to reassert itself, but fear of being stranded in this place of death remained a presence too powerful to pull down. Not knowing what else to do, cursing as she did so, Maelyrin began stumbling after Kiyo.

Rest For Those Who Can

𝓕ar above Calif and the chaos it had become, circling down in a slow wide glide, the owl dropped from the heavens, eyes searching the Man-city below it as the morning sun lifted itself above the far horizon. Foul multicolored smoke billowed up heavily from the eastern side of the city and was caught by the dawn's breeze and dragged northwesterly away from the many fires that burned there. Though still high enough above the conflagration that its vision remained unimpaired, there was, nevertheless, an acrid odor to the air that stung the owl's sense of smell.

But it was the tang of death and blood riding the currents that threatened to distract the bird from its purpose, its predatory instincts rising up so powerfully that the voice of the Source seemed at times to fall to a whisper, barely heard. Only the insistence of the still small voice kept the owl searching as it winged ever closer to the tumult. Already the skies above the city were darkening with its carrion-eating brethren, crows and vultures drawn by the smell, circling in great raucous clouds, causing the owl to dodge and weave in its circuitous route.

Back and forth the owl flew, searching the bedlam below. Men and women running and screaming, knots of fighting in the maze of streets, the clashes and sounds further disrupted the owl's senses as it tried to follow the directions so counter to its instincts. The need to hunt, the need to panic. But the Source continued to forestall any action contrary to its purpose, directing the owl's flight and eyes with its continued pressure.

Had the owl been capable of sighing, it would have done so in relief when, finally, it found all that was sought, but instead, instantly pumped its wings to gain altitude and angled its flight in the shortest direction to the forest outside the walls of the Man-city. Once free of the cacophony, it found a suitable tree and came to a less than graceful rest upon a low hanging branch, where it sat, waiting for its rapidly beating heart to slow.

"Do not fear, small one," a man's voice said from below it, soft, gentle, but also commanding. "You are protected."

The owl looked down at the robed figure that had not been there a moment ago. "Please don't have me do that anymore," it said, its voice filled with both the tremor of fear and reverence.

The figure did not look up, his hooded head continuing to gaze in the direction of the City of Towers. Even here, the owl could smell the carnage of the battle and the stink of the fires. Several moments passed before his voice lifted again. "Be well, little one, the tasks set before us serve a greater purpose."

"Yes, my Lord, but it frightens me much," the owl replied. Any sarcasm that was presented to others was completely gone from its tones.

"I know it does, little one, but it still must be done," he said, lifting a hand to his chin. Another pause, before, "Did you find them?"

"Yes, my Lord. The one Chosen is in the company of the teacher. The Ever-one and Mal' Andel are nearby. The Healer is not with them but is also not far."

The only response was a slight nod. "Then, it is well."

"But what of them?"

"Assuredly, all of them are where they are supposed to be."

"Then it is almost over?" the owl asked, hope filling its voice. The man looked up then at the bird, his eyes startlingly clear, of all colors yet of none, but with a sadness that touched the owl in a way that frightened it.

"It is only begun, small one," he said. "It is only begun."

For what seemed a lifetime, the owl gazed at the man and he back at the owl, until finally he broke the contact and looked back at the city. "Rest now, faithful one," he said into the rising sun.

The owl was asleep before the man faded away.

www.ingramcontent.com/pod-product-compliance
Lightning Source LLC
Chambersburg PA
CBHW051926020726
47501CB00001B/4